WAR

The Finest in Fantasy from
MICHELLE WEST

The House War:
THE HIDDEN CITY (Book One)
CITY OF NIGHT (Book Two)
HOUSE NAME (Book Three)
SKIRMISH (Book Four)
BATTLE (Book Five)
ORACLE (Book Six)
FIRSTBORN (Book Seven)
WAR (Book Eight)

The Sun Sword:
THE BROKEN CROWN (Book One)
THE UNCROWNED KING (Book Two)
THE SHINING COURT (Book Three)
SEA OF SORROWS (Book Four)
THE RIVEN SHIELD (Book Five)
THE SUN SWORD (Book Six)

The Sacred Hunt:
HUNTER'S OATH (Book One)
HUNTER'S DEATH (Book Two)

WAR

A *House War* Novel

MICHELLE WEST

DAW BOOKS, INC.
DONALD A. WOLLHEIM, FOUNDER
1745 Broadway, New York, NY 10019
ELIZABETH R. WOLLHEIM
SHEILA E. GILBERT
PUBLISHERS
www.dawbooks.com

For Thomas, the heart of my household

And Terry, the heart of my books

Acknowledgments

I have a large, extended household. There is no single person at the helm, but Thomas is the glue that holds it all together when things get tough. When I am mired in deadline stress and horrible anxiety, to the point that things like, oh, eating seem entirely irrelevant to life, there is nonetheless food on the table at roughly dinner time. It's a blessing.

My mother has continued to be a godsend. She is constant as clockwork, to the benefit of my sons, their godfather, and their godfather's family—all of whom join us twice a week for two of the aforementioned meals. Also: Kristen Chew answers my infrequent queries about grammar and usage of things like punctuation.

Terry Pearson not only read this in its initial draft, but in every successive draft that followed, including the one you have in your hands. I am constantly reminded of how, over the years, he has become a necessary part of the writing process—not so much the words on the page/screen, but . . . the joy with which he reads them. When I am terrified that nothing works, his becomes the voice of reason.

Joshua Starr answered all of my emails practically the minute I sent them and carved out extra time for me with the copy-edits of *War*. He didn't even complain when I fell sick, and lost much of that time in the process.

Sheila Gilbert is an island in the ocean of publishing.

And thank you to the readers who, throughout the long period of writing this book—and all the rest—encouraged me by telling me, time and again, that they would wait, and could wait, until the book was done.

WAR

Prologue

"**T**HE MAN IS AT the service entrance. Again. Shall I send him away?"

Muriel A'Scavonne rose from her writing desk. Her hand was almost cramping; she'd been at her letters all morning, in a state of banked panic. It was not the panic caused by consideration of the recipient of this particular letter, although Healer Levec could be an unpleasant, suspicious man on the best of days.

"No. Please have him escorted to the parlor."

"And shall I make certain the young mistress is not informed of his presence?"

That was the question, wasn't it? Muriel was certain that the old, scarred man was not good for her daughter; certainly her daughter's manners disintegrated completely when she faced him. But it was more than that.

"Yes." This was, in some fashion, a test. Not of her servants, whom she trusted, and not of her daughter, whom she understood well, but of the very strange, inexplicable interaction between Stacia and the old soldier.

"Shall I send for the guards?"

"No. Perhaps you might send a page. Barryl, if he's free." Barryl was a handful of years older than Stacia; although he was a servant, he was also one of the few people to whom Stacia looked for social cues. He did not mother her—he couldn't; she had a mother. But Stacia had not been blessed with siblings, and Barryl was as close, social strata aside, as she could come to having one. It was Muriel's hope that Barryl would, with decades of experience, become steward of Stacia's home in some distant future.

The future, Muriel thought bleakly, that might never arrive.

She rose, straightened her skirts, and headed toward the parlor.

*   *   *

Stacia was not the first to be struck with the sleeping sickness; nor was she the first to be ensconced in the Houses of Healing—and that had been a terrifying, bitter blow to her mother and father, the latter of whom refused to discuss it at all with his wife. But he refused to discuss anything of import, or anything emotional, and Muriel could not deny that she had been emotional.

When Healer Levec had announced that the victims laid low by that illness had fully recovered, she had been ebullient in her quiet joy. She had come to the Houses of Healing in her carriage with clothing appropriate for her daughter and had discovered that there were very few suitable rooms in which to change. They had managed. Her daughter had lost weight—all of the sleepers had—but she had become her old self, and Muriel fully intended to spoil her rotten, at least where food was concerned, until that weight returned.

She had been happy to put the fear of that sickness as far behind them both as she could. She did not speak of it. She did not ask questions. She did not allow questions to be asked by anyone. Her husband approved of this, of course; it was, to him, a sign of necessary maturity in a wife of her stature. Which, she thought, with a trace of bitterness, was a wife of *his* stature, or rather, the stature that he desired.

But in the past week, Stacia had begun to fall asleep without warning, often in the middle of the day. The first time, she had been mounted for the riding lessons she loved and demanded. Those lessons had been canceled for the foreseeable future. So, too, hope, although she tried, the first time, to keep it bright and untarnished.

She had been sleeping for days when Muriel began to write to Healer Levec.

And the old man—Colm Sanders, she thought, although she had heard his name only once—had appeared at the service entrance of the manse, with no business that would generally allow him entry. No business but Stacia.

He was weathered, sun-dark, lines etched into the parts of his face that weren't scarred; his hands were the callused, hard hands of a laborer. His hair was gray, with more white now than dark, although both persisted. His eyes were brown. He carried himself as a man who was accustomed to a certain kind of authority; she thought him a primus, or a former primus, of the Kings' armies. He had no business at all with her daughter.

But he, too, had been felled by the sleeping sickness. He, too, had lain abed in the Houses of Healing. And he, too, had awakened on that final day in which Levec had proclaimed the sleepers cured.

The only thing that connected her child with a man she would never otherwise have met was disaster. Had he not known—had he not come to her with a warning—Stacia might have been out on that horse. If a fall would not kill her, it would have injured her, and he had prevented that.

He had come that day to tell her that Stacia would sleep. He could not be certain when, but he wanted to give her mother enough warning that Stacia would not be engaged in activities that would actively harm her if she lost consciousness.

And had she believed him when he first started to speak, her daughter would not have been on the horse's back at all. As it was, the old man had caught her, racing to the stables and the corral at breakneck speed the moment he had discovered that that was where she was. The moment Muriel herself had, in growing panic, let it slip.

He had caught her. He had stopped her from hitting the ground. He had carried her to her room, a place he had no right to approach. And he had, at Muriel's stiff, frightened direction, laid her in her bed and retreated.

This afternoon, Stacia had woken. She was, she said, hungry, and the kitchen went instantly to work. But the waking itself, while a great comfort to Muriel, could no longer dim her fears; her daughter had slept for far too long, and it was a familiar, dreaded sleep: she would not wake, no matter what was done.

Even her presence at the table, when it came, was duller, dimmer; her usual effervescent cheer and almost puckish demands were absent. She had looked across the dining table, to her mother, and said, "What do you do to make someone happy again?"

"It would depend on why they are sad. And it would depend, as well, on how you know. If you know because you are listening to gossip, you should do nothing. They have not shared their sadness with you. It is theirs, not yours, until they do."

"What if I know, but I *didn't* listen to gossip?" Stacia demanded, with a little more of her regular fire.

"Then it would depend on why they are sad," Muriel answered. A place had been set for her, although she had already eaten. She did not touch the food.

"She had to abandon someone she loved. He's like a brother. He's as important as Barryl."

Stacia was, at heart, a kind child. She could be; she did not have the hard choices that life sometimes forced upon others. That she would, in future, Muriel had no doubt—but she desperately wanted to protect her child from having to make any of them.

"Sometimes," Muriel said, after a longer pause, "there's nothing you can do to make someone happy. What you are describing is grief. If a mother lost her child," she added, reaching for the nearest, the truest, of her many examples, "she would be devastated. There would be nothing you could do that would make her happy again. There are some sadnesses that are, at their very heart, part of life."

"But—then she'll *never* be happy again."

"She will, Stacia. But not immediately, and never in the same way that she was before the loss. Think, though: the grief comes because the love existed. Without that love, she would feel nothing because it would mean nothing." Muriel swallowed. "I think grief is natural, and I think—I think, even grieving, that grief is better than not loving at all."

Stacia, at that precocious age, nodded, but she was not satisfied with the answer. She was, and had always been, a child who would stick her own hand into the fire to see if it burned because fire burning *other people* did not serve as an adequate lesson.

Colm Sanders bowed to her when he entered the room. It was a precise, almost regimental bow that lacked subtlety or finesse.

"Stacia is awake," Muriel said.

He nodded as if this was not news to him.

"She asked me a very strange question shortly after she woke."

He nodded again, but this nod was more wary.

"She wanted to know what she might do to make someone happy again."

Muriel felt the chill of winter on this summer day when Colm Sanders closed his eyes. She saw a twitch of muscle at the right side of his jaw.

"You know why she asked."

He opened his eyes but did not speak.

"Tell me. I am her mother, I have the right to know. Is that not why you came?" Her hands had balled into inappropriate fists; she unclenched them with difficulty.

The man opened his mouth, but the answer he might have offered did not come.

Instead, Stacia did, careening into the parlor, her skirts flapping at the width of her stride. The fists Muriel had denied herself, Stacia adopted.

"Why are you here?" she demanded. "You're scaring my mother!"

"Stacia," Muriel said.

"He *is*! What do you want?"

"I wished to speak with your mother. I have spoken with her. I will take my leave."

"Oh no, you don't!" She stepped forward and caught his arm, to Muriel's distress.

But if the man looked dangerous, his glare, when transferred to her daughter, was not frightening. "You listen to your mother. Now."

"She's not talking. You are."

Barryl unobtrusively entered the parlor, saw what was taking place, and visibly winced. If he was older than Stacia, he was not yet fully adult.

The old man's glare intensified. But so did her daughter's. Muriel felt a moment of pride, although for the most part, she was embarrassed.

"I came," the old man finally said, "to see if you were awake."

Stacia did not deflate. "Of course I'm awake. You wanted to know if I remembered the dream."

He nodded.

"Well, *I do*. And you do, obviously." Although she continued to grip his sleeve, her free hand was no longer a fist. "Do the others?"

"No one was dreaming for as long as you were. Not even me."

"You cheated."

His brows rose.

"You woke yourself up."

"You didn't try."

To Muriel's surprise, Stacy looked at her feet. ". . . You wouldn't talk to him."

Him?

"And he's going to be alone now."

"He won't, Stacy. He'll have the—" He stopped.

"It doesn't understand people," Stacia insisted, oblivious to the presence of her mother. "It doesn't understand us." And Stacia, of course, felt she did. As if all people were the same, everywhere, as if being a person was a universal truth.

Muriel could not remember being so young, and maybe that was the kindness of memory. She doubted it.

The old man exhaled, and to Muriel's surprise, he patted Stacia on the head. And her daughter, who famously disliked being touched by strangers, seemed to draw strength from this. Something was happening. Something that she had no part in. And her daughter was *a child*.

"Stacia," she said, with an emphasis on the last syllable, "I'd like you to go with Barryl now. I haven't finished speaking with Mr. Sanders."

Stacia was mutinous. "Why do you want me to leave? He can't have anything to say to you that I don't already know—and better."

"Stacia."

Barryl interceded. Muriel didn't hear what he said, but she wasn't paying attention; Barryl led Stacia—or perhaps, regrettably, dragged her—out of the parlor. She turned to her visitor. "Please," she said, "be seated."

"I'm not dressed for your fancy chairs," he replied, placing both of his hands behind his back. As if he were a soldier, and not a guest.

"You know something of my daughter's illness."

"I suffer from it myself." He obeyed a request that was not a request and took his place in a chair. It was farthest from the chair she occupied.

"I believe I saw you when I visited Stacia at the Houses of Healing. You were present on the final day, when I was told I could finally bring her—bring her home."

He nodded. She remembered: no one had come for him. She had asked Healer Levec—boldly—if perhaps they might take those without family to collect them to their homes; he had winced.

"Why did you come?"

"I was asked, specifically, to keep an eye out on Stacy. Stacia."

"By who?"

"By a friend of both hers and mine."

"This is not a person she knows when awake, is it?"

Silence. A beat. Colm Sanders was measuring her. Fair enough; she had been measuring herself—and her worth as a mother—for months. Years. It had been far, far worse when her daughter had succumbed to the illness. There had been so many questions about what she could have done differently, what she'd done *wrong.*

And when her daughter had been pronounced cured, those questions, the weight of that doubt, had vanished. It was almost like being happy. But the shadow of that illness had clouded her every evening, when Stacia was at last asleep.

Would she wake? Would she wake tomorrow?

"It's not over yet."

"Not yet, no."

"What is happening?"

"When we sleep, we dream."

"We? You and Stacia?"

"Stacia and I, yes. But there are others as well. When we dream, we occasionally dream the same dream. There, we interact—as we interacted once before, in dream—with each other. The surroundings are not the same, and the dreams are often nonsensical, as dreams are.

"Recently, that has been in the evenings, where such an event occurs naturally to all concerned. But in the past week Stacia has been dreaming far more constantly, far more consistently."

"And you?"

"I have been dreaming with her."

"She said you could wake yourself up."

The hint of a dark smile touched his lips. "I was a soldier. We were often on watch; food was sparse at times, and the days and duties were not diminished for food's lack. We learned to sleep standing up. We learned to sleep whenever we could. And we learned to wake instantly when the situation demanded it, no matter how exhausted, how sleep bound, we were. I can wake myself, yes. It's my sleep that's often broken. Or it was."

"And Stacia could do this as well."

"Dreams are real for her. And sometimes she considers waking an act of abandonment. She has not tried to wake."

"You believe she could?"

He exhaled. "Yes. But I am also tasked with waking her if she won't, and if I am not likewise asleep."

"We couldn't. We couldn't wake her."

"She will wake for me."

"Why?"

"Because she will assume that she hears me while she dreams, and she will turn in the direction of a voice she can hear in both places. I can wake her."

Muriel swallowed. "Do you live far from here?"

"I live in the twenty-fourth holding. It is not close, but it is certainly a shorter distance than many I've marched."

"And if a room were prepared for you in the servants' quarters, would you consent to remain here?" She spoke before she'd had time to think, but did not withdraw, or attempt to withdraw, the offer. If he could do what she could not do—what her husband and Barryl could not do—she wanted him *here*. At hand. Where he could wake Stacia.

Where he could wake Stacia, and Muriel could believe that she had some small control, some small cure, for her own fear.

He was silent for a long beat. "When I sleep," he finally said, "I am not easily woken."

"Except by yourself?"

He nodded. "If you want me here because I can wake Stacy—Stacia, I can't guarantee that I'll be useful to you."

"And you can't wake her while you're sleeping."

"Not Stacia, no. She's—" he appeared to be searching for words.

"Headstrong? Willful? Stubborn?"

At that, his face cracked the hint of a smile. "I see you do know your daughter."

And hers cracked a smile in response.

"You can wake the others when they're dreaming?"

"Not always, no. But when we don't dream the same dream, it doesn't matter. Sleep is necessary for everyone; we're no exception. But the dreamers have to be willing to wake, and as I said—"

"Stacia isn't."

He bowed his head, his gaze hitting his hands, which rested in his lap. "I'm not used to young girls. Or young boys, if it comes to that. I'm used to young men and women, and I'm used to giving orders that they have to obey. Stacia's not a soldier. She's not a green centrus."

Muriel rose. She walked to the parlor windows; the curtains had been drawn, and sun filtered in through the glass. They were large windows. Expensive windows. Everything in the room was; how else could one impress important guests?

"Attitude like hers wouldn't get her far in the army."

"No. We hadn't intended she be a soldier."

"Because the army's for poor grunts like me?"

Muriel exhaled. She did not turn to face him. "Partly for that reason, yes. But we've just had the army return from the war in the South—not the first war and, likely, not the last. What I want for my daughter is not the life of a soldier. The privation. The lack of sleep. The lack of food. All of those, I could accept, but not happily.

"No, it's the killing. It's the loss. It's seeing your friends—your comrades, if you prefer—"

"Friends works."

"Friends, then—it's seeing them die. It's the killing," she continued. "Because you kill, or you are killed. It's the taking of a life. And I'd want her to learn, and learn quickly, because I'd rather she kill than be killed. But I'm not sure she could come home from that unscarred. You've seen it. You've survived it. Would you want that for your own children?"

"I don't want it for anyone's children."

She felt a twinge of guilt, but not nearly enough to swamp worry, fear. No, she didn't want that for *any* child. "What is happening in the dreaming? What little Stacy is willing to tell me is confusing at best. I can't tell if her words are the words of a dreaming child or a daydreaming child." Her face was turned toward the window, as if she were a plant in need of sunlight.

It was a long while before he answered. This was a man she couldn't force words from.

"You are aware of the events on the day of the victory parade?"

She froze. Sunlight lost warmth. She turned toward him, her back to the window, her shoulders curving inward as if to ward off physical blows. He was watching her. Waiting. She nodded. *What does this have to do with my daughter?* The words would not come.

"That was a skirmish. If we won, we won because of one woman and, even then, only because she chose to take the fight to her own turf."

Muriel had not heard this.

"War will come. Not a skirmish, but a battle—and it will come here. To Averalaan. Even to the Isle. I don't know if you were there. I don't know if you saw the demon. I've seen the demon." He exhaled. "So has Stacy."

She didn't even correct his use of the diminutive. She was frozen; the only things she could see in this room were Colm Sanders and the shroud of her own fear. She managed to keep control of her expression.

After a moment, he nodded. "That demon will come here again. But he won't come alone. And in the end, it is not that demon that threatens us. He is almost irrelevant. You've perhaps heard the phrase: *When the Sleepers wake?*"

She nodded, almost confused.

"The Sleepers are waking. It's why the sleeping sickness could exist in the first place. The Terafin intervened, and we woke. But she can't prevent the Sleepers from waking. The gods can't. The Kings can't."

"But they rode—they rode with Moorelas—"

"Yes. And they failed. They betrayed him. This was their punishment. They don't like mortals, much. They certainly won't like us. And we'll be here, in great number, in lands they might consider in need of cleansing. These are the lands which their ancient enemies ruled."

"How do you know this?"

"I sleep. I dream."

"Stacia—"

"Sleeps. Dreams. Do you understand?"

She shook her head. What Colm Sanders might have said next was lost to the furious entrance of her child. Her Stacia. At any other time, she might have been horrified at what Stacia did next—she stormed toward Muriel's visitor and kicked his shin.

"You're making my mother cry!"

"She is not crying," the old man said, unperturbed by Stacia's display.

Stacia wheeled toward her mother, who was not, as Colm Sanders had said, crying. Proved wrong, Stacia did not admit defeat. She did not, however, choose to kick him again. A movement caught Muriel's attention; Barryl was in the doorway, almost frozen there by Stacia's behavior. Ah, no, Muriel thought. Frozen by fear of his mistress' reaction to that behavior.

"You're scaring her."

"Yes, because she's no fool." His tone implied that Stacia could learn something from her mother. "And it's not me that's scaring her, it's you."

She did turn toward her mother then.

Muriel had never encouraged public displays of affection; she had been taught just how unseemly they were. But she opened her arms, wordless, and when Stacia met her gaze, she ran across the room and wrapped her own arms around her mother's waist.

"Don't be scared," she said, her voice muffled, the small vibrations of moving mouth against body a comfort. "Don't be. She'll save you."

"It's not myself that I worry for."

Stacia said nothing, only tightened her hold on her mother. After a moment, her muffled voice could be heard—but just barely. "I don't want anything bad to happen to you."

"I don't care—"

"Your mother would die for you," Colm Sanders said. "She would die to save you."

Stacia pulled back and turned to look at the soldier. "I don't *want* her to die. I don't want her to die to save *me*."

"And you think she'd want you to die to save her?"

"If she knows—if she knows that she'd die to save me, then she *knows how I feel*!"

"And you know how she feels, because you don't want that."

"But she *can't*. She can't do it anyway."

Muriel put a hand on Stacia's shoulder; her daughter wheeled. She was flushed, angry, defiant—and beneath that, beneath all of that, afraid. "I would like Mr. Sanders to stay with us."

"What, here?"

"In the manor."

"Why?"

"Because whatever it is you're facing, he's facing as well. And I would like—in some small way—to help."

"He doesn't need help. He gets really mad if you even try."

"Would it be acceptable," her mother continued, as if Stacia had not spoken, "to you? I won't offer if you don't want him here." She had, of course, already offered.

Stacia frowned. "Can he bring his swords?"

"Pardon?"

"Well, he knows how to fight."

"Stacia, we have guards."

"They won't be as good as him. Besides—he sleeps almost as much as I do."

"Is that true, Mr. Sanders?"

"Yes."

Muriel inhaled. Exhaled. Loosened the white-knuckled hand on her daughter's shoulder. "Do you sleep as much as Stacia because my daughter refuses to wake up?"

Silence. In it, she could hear Stacia's displeasure, although her daughter was well-mannered enough—barely—not to put it into words.

The visitor watched her daughter. Whatever he saw in her face made him smile. "Yes. I'm a suspicious, cynical old man. Your daughter is none of those things."

"But he doesn't *need* to live here to do that! And I'm not a baby!"

No. No, she wasn't. *You will always be my baby.*

"If you're not, you might consider acting like the adult your mother clearly is," the soldier snapped.

Stacia shrieked. So much for well-mannered. Or any manners, really. But the soldier was not a lady of the manor, worried for her daughter and aware of her station; he was, however, clearly familiar with Stacia. Stacia wrenched herself free from her mother and once again marched toward the visitor.

"Fine! You can stay—but it's *my* house, and you have to listen *to me*!" Before Mr. Sanders could reply, her daughter stormed out of the parlor and into Barryl.

"She's a handful," Mr. Sanders said, when both Stacia and Barryl were out of earshot. "But she believes in heroes. In stories. She's got a big heart. I'm not sure this is a good idea," he added, as he pushed himself out of his chair.

"You do sleep because she's sleeping." This time, there was no question in the words.

"I find your daughter frustrating. Very frustrating," he replied. "But for all that she's a handful, she's precious. She reminds bitter old men like me of the reason we fight. I have to go home to get my things." He hesitated. "She'll be upset if there are no swords."

"Bring the swords, by all means. You can't use them when you're sleeping, and—given everything—it will be one less thing that upsets her."

She wanted to ask him many things, then—but she was afraid of the answers. Later, she would. Later she might tell him just how much she was forced to trust him, against all reason, all experience.

And later, she would find that bitter trust her only comfort.

Chapter One

6th day of Lattan, 428 A.A.
Terafin Manse, Averalaan Aramarelas

JEWEL MARKESS ATERAFIN WOKE to familiar walls in the morning. She did not appreciate the room in the West Wing her ascension had forced her to vacate because she could barely breathe. Shadow was lying across her chest. Finch was awake and glaring at the great cat, who appeared to be sleeping.

He wasn't. Jewel attempted to push him off. In the halls beyond her closed door, she could hear movement, discussion, minor commotion; nothing in the tone—the words being too muffled to catch—implied disaster. Or at least not the disaster she had been facing recently. She glanced at Finch.

"Permits," Finch said, grimacing. "It's almost the start of the King's Challenge." Her hair, which had always been straight, wasn't the mass of tangle and snarls that Jewel's was. "Don't you dare feel guilty."

"I hate the paperwork of the festival season."

"Of course you do; you're reasonable. It's better than an angry House Council session."

Jewel grimaced again.

Finch held up one hand. "I'd take both for the rest of my natural life if we could dispense with evil gods, demons, and immortals who consider us vermin. I can't do anything about them. You can." Unspoken, but clear in her expression and her tone, was the wish that she could—because then she could help.

What Finch didn't say out loud, Jewel couldn't respond to, not in words. She rose.

"Do you want me to call—"

"No. I'm not technically here yet, and I don't think I'm going to be interacting with people as The Terafin." Jewel exhaled. "We need to go back to the castle."

Finch nodded.

". . . if, in fact, it still exists *as* a castle."

Jewel dressed as a traveling merchant, in slightly cleaner variants of the clothing she'd arrived wearing. She woke Adam; although he was better rested, he was still tired. "You can stay with Ariel for the day," she told him. "We're just going to look at my new rooms."

"He will go," Shadow said, before Adam could reply. "We will *all* go." Pausing, he glanced at Finch and Teller. "All the *important* people. You can stay *here*."

"Shianne needs rest," Adam told the cat. "And Lord Celleriant must teach his people the Matriarch's laws."

Shadow hissed. He then told Adam just how stupid he thought Adam was. Or, rather, described the new lows to which Adam had sunk.

Unimportant people were comprised of those who had remained in the Terafin manse while Jewel had stepped onto the path created by the Oracle. Jewel, however, made it clear to Shadow that they were important to *her*. While she knew better than to be irritated by the cats, it was early morning, and she was still emotionally unbalanced. And as she had no intention of leaving immediately, they deserved—and would get—rest.

Shadow was not pleased. Loudly.

Finch and Teller, as regent and right-kin, had a functional need and right to know. Jester wanted, in his own words, to sleep through it and wake up after all the fuss had been dealt with, although he was up and dressed and restless. Jewel thought it likely that what he wanted to avoid was the current argument that Finch had started while dressing for the day and had continued as they spilled into the halls.

"I'm saying I'll stay *with* her. I'm not asking you to risk anyone else—"

"And I'm saying it's not safe for you to stay in whatever the hells my rooms might end up being if I sleep with indigestion."

"You want her. She's going to be our den-kin, same as Duster. But she can't be den-kin if we're not with her. I'm not telling you that we *all* have to move— but I'll move. I can handle it."

"Finch—it's *not safe* in the wilderness. That's why the House Mage is on permanent contract—he can survive it. The rest of us can't."

"It'll *be* safe if I'm with Calliastra."

And that's what it came down to, wasn't it? Would it be safe? The wilderness and the creatures it produced weren't the only threats the den had faced. They weren't the biggest threats, by far. Finch had always been safe with Duster. Finch and Lander. But Calliastra didn't have Duster's history with them.

"You wouldn't have tried to keep her," Finch continued, voice softening. It was a trick that she had learned from somewhere—but where, Jewel wasn't quite certain. Everything about her tone implied that she was relenting, sur-rendering. The words themselves, however, showed that she hadn't budged. "If you didn't know it was safe for the rest of us. If something happens, she'll be here, and I don't think random demons are going to get past her."

"That is true," Calliastra said, appearing not far away from the discussion, as if she was stepping out of shadows cast by magelights. She looked down a perfect nose at Finch. "But I have no reason to protect you."

Finch glanced at the darknessborn woman. "No. Neither did Duster." She turned more fully to face Calliastra. "Duster was the toughest of us; she was the most dangerous. None of us could give her orders, and none of us tried. She'd listen to Jay."

"Jay is a bird, in Weston?"

Jewel exhaled. "And Jewel is a cut, polished rock. I preferred the bird."

"Could you not perhaps have chosen an entirely different name?"

"Not and forced my parents to use it, no. Jay was the diminutive as far as my Oma was concerned, and the rest of the family fell in line." *Na'jay*. A child's name. A name she had never called herself, but a name it had always been a comfort to hear. Anyone who had used it was gone. Jay was the closest she could come. She did not feel up to explaining this to Calliastra. Not now, and maybe not ever.

She might have returned to the forest immediately had it not been for Calliastra—but Calliastra could not stay in the West Wing. If she was to be at home in the Terafin manse, it was here, beyond the doors that still separated The Terafin's personal chambers from the interior of the manse. Wherever that here had currently become.

The mist-laden stretch of path remained unchanged from the previous day; the waterfall was also present. The skies remained blue, not the amethyst they had been when the forest had been a library, with trees that had bookcases and shelves instead of branches.

Those books were probably on the inside of the castle Jewel had not yet examined; Ellerson's arrival—and the brief, sharp hope that Carver was with him—had interrupted the apprehensive examination of what was, in theory, Jewel's new home. Teller's concern, on that first trek, had been the library and its many books.

Judging from his expression, it was still his concern, but he said nothing while Finch and Jewel continued their discussion. They spoke more quietly because Calliastra had joined them, and it was difficult to treat Calliastra as a third person, if not downright suicidal. He did say something when Snow stepped on his foot, but Jewel thought, judging tone as the words were too soft to catch, that he was apologizing to the white cat for his obvious neglect.

Shadow was bored. Snow was less bored with Teller's attention. Night was, for the moment, absent, but not in trouble—had he been, Snow, envious of the lack of boredom, would have been with him.

The contents of the Terafin library were not what they had been before Jay had become Terafin. Teller knew that it was larger, the books older, some of the contents forbidden by magisterial law. The volumes contained in Amarais Handernesse ATerafin's library still existed, but they shared space with volumes that might once have been part of an earlier Terafin's library—in the time of the Blood Barons, when demons had been considered the only reliable guards.

This castle reminded Teller of that ancient history.

Snow snorted. "It is not *ancient*," he told Teller. He rarely called Teller stupid.

"What do you see," Teller asked, "when you look at the fountain?" The fountain was the first thing that could be seen when the gates opened. Although all eyes were upon it, they did not see the same thing; the differences could be dramatic.

Snow glanced at Shadow. Both of the cats disliked water on principle. They had therefore avoided the fountain which now seemed the centerpiece of this new building's front causeway.

"We *don't*," Shadow replied. "There is nothing to *see*." The sibilant turned the last word into an extended hiss.

Calliastra said, "It is clearly not only the mortals who are obtuse." Which caused predictable outrage. The outrage seemed to dim the importance of the fountain to Calliastra, and she turned toward Jay as they all turned toward her, sooner or later.

Quietly, Jay said, "Library."

Teller was happy to go. He was happy because he could see Jay's face in that fountain—made strange, made majestic, made hard and cold as stone. Not even in anger—and she had had a temper, especially in her youth—had she appeared thus. No, only The Terafin had, and when she had, it was always bad.

Jay was The Terafin now.

Jay had never wanted to be The Terafin. She had respected, even revered, Amarais Handernesse ATerafin enough that she had promised to take up the mantle so that her predecessor might know a moment of peace. She kept her promises. She always had.

She headed up the stairs, stopping at the grand, closed doors of her castle. The doors did not magically open. Carver did not—as Ellerson had the day before—open them from the inside, either. Ellerson's report made that a daydream, but it was a daydream with roots in pain and hope. Hard to shake, ever.

Avandar moved to join the Chosen at the height of the stairs, and they stepped back, a human wall between door and Terafin. Her domicis spoke; he gestured. The door did not open for him. Jay's impatience was felt; she had expected neither the Chosen nor the domicis to succeed.

She disliked the necessity of waiting until they had tried, but accepted it, her expression pinched, until Avandar also surrendered. It took the domicis much longer than it had the Chosen, and Teller wasn't entirely certain this wasn't deliberate. Avandar would give his life to protect Jay—but Teller suspected the cats would, as well, if it came to that. It didn't mean the cats were more tractable or obedient.

Jay stepped up to examine the door. After a brief pause and a quiet curse, she thumped it with the side of her fist. "It's just like me," she said, "to somehow create a castle I can't even enter."

Teller watched the doors. He watched Jay. The sound of water falling did not draw his gaze to the fountain; there, the statue was cold and hard; it seemed to know nothing of struggle. Jay in life was not that person, had never been that person.

She'd made this castle. She'd made it without knowledge, without intent. It had come to her the way the forest had come to her—and every creature in that forest had come as well, liege to her Lord. But here, she was like any other member of their den; she was frustrated and stymied by the wilderness.

The wilderness, he thought, that was within her, part of her, inseparable from the woman she had, over half her life, become.

"You are not *listening*," Shadow brought his left front paw down, narrowly missing Jay's foot. He didn't miss the flat of the stairs, though; they cracked, the fissure spreading slowly as if it were liquid.

Jay glared at him.

"*Why* are you so *stupid*? Can't you *hear* it, *stupid* girl?"

Snow hissed laughter, which didn't help Shadow's mood any.

"It is speaking your *name*. Anssssssswer it, or we will die of *boredom*!"

"It is *hers*," Snow told his brother. "We will die of boredom *anyway*."

Shadow had no response to this. He took an ill-tempered swipe at Jay's leg.

Jay, however, straightened her shoulders, lifting her chin. Her lashes became a dark fan as she closed her eyes, brown to the auburn of her hair. She lifted her hands to shoulder height, turning her palms toward sunlight. Her expression was calm. No, not calm exactly. Absent fear, frustration, worry. Blank.

She looked like the statue that he would not look at, but rendered in flesh, not stone.

Without thought, without intent, he ran up the stairs toward her, pushing through the Chosen who allowed him to pass unhindered. He caught Jay by the shoulder—the right shoulder.

Finch joined him, her hand across the left.

"Jay," Teller said. "Jay. Jay, you're with us. You're with us. We're here." As if it needed to be said.

Jay blinked rapidly as the doors began to open. She didn't look toward the hallway that lay beyond the doors. She turned to look at Teller, and then at Finch, exhaling as she did. She shook her head, as if to clear it, and then pushed stray curls out of her eyes.

She signed. *Thanks.*

Shadow pushed his way past them and into what appeared to be a great hall. "*Boring*," he said, over his shoulder.

"I *told* you." Snow entered next; Jay dropped a hand to the white cat's head, stalling him for long enough that Shadow's tail was not a target of easy opportunity before she lifted it. Snow then followed his brother into the great hall, of which he disapproved. Loudly.

"Is that wise?" Finch asked, when they were out of earshot.

"Probably, given what occasionally made its way into the previous iteration of the library. It's going to be hard for things to drop from the sky—" She stopped. It wasn't the creatures from the sky that had taken Carver.

The Chosen followed the cats, and Avandar followed the Chosen. The hall didn't swallow them.

"Are you worried?" Calliastra asked.

"She is *always* worried," the previously absent Night replied.

"I didn't ask you. I can't imagine wanting your opinion."

Jay dropped a hand to the top of the black cat's head.

"Why *me*?" Night asked. "*She* started it!"

"Sometimes I require you to be the better man."

"Men are *stupid*!" Night stormed into the main hall, cursing and spitting.

They walked in silence. This hall was older than the Terafin manse, at least in architectural style; it was both grander and colder. The predominant colors were gray, with hints of Terafin blue that added no visual warmth. Weapons lined the walls, and only as they passed beneath the arch in the distance did that change.

The Terafin library no longer rested on shelves that had sprouted from the trunks of standing trees. The unreality of that transformed library had given way to a less fanciful, impossible space: the shelves were of hardwood, the floors, rug-covered stone. The rugs were blue. There were windows that allowed natural light to enter the room on all sides; the windows were tall, the glass clear.

The ceilings were equal in height to the ceilings in the great hall, but this was because there appeared to be three levels of shelving, which hugged the walls that were not possessed of windows. Or perhaps four levels. Ladders rested against rails. Teller had twice visited the royal libraries. He had once visited the great library in the Order of Knowledge, the personal collections being entirely off-limits if one did not have access to the collector. A cursory glance strongly implied that neither would be the equal of this one.

A cursory glance was all he had time for; he did not imagine that many would be allowed to make a more thorough comparison. The Terafin no longer knew for certain the contents of her library, and in the reformation of the prior collection, volumes that could not be possessed legally had been found, lying closed on a library table.

Teller did lift a random book or two within easy reach, more to check for dampness or damage than for the contents. Books, however, were always difficult objects; the second caught and held his attention.

He was surprised to see Calliastra's shadow darken the page and did not wonder, as he lifted his head, that he knew it for hers; there was, about her, a darkness that spoke of danger, of desire. It reminded him of Kiriel, but Kiriel's darkness had been death. Just death.

He wondered, not for the first time, what Kiriel was doing. Kiriel had come to the den with Jay, just as Calliastra had, but Kiriel had not remained. He wondered what Calliastra would make of Kiriel, or perhaps what Kiriel would make of Calliastra, but knew better than to ask.

Snow, however, said, "What are you *looking* at?" and bumped the underside of the book with his head. Teller was accustomed to tightening his grip—on anything—when the cats were underfoot; the book did not fall. He would have been upset had it, because it was old, the pages brittle, the colors of the illustrations—a separate, painted page—faded and slightly uneven.

"Where," Calliastra said softly, "did you find this book?"

Teller waved at the shelf at which he'd stopped although he did not take his eyes from the illustration. In the scant time between opening the book and looking at the page, the colors had deepened. He wasn't certain what he was looking at. He had thought it a dawn or a sunset at first, because the colors that remained on the page had suggested one or the other.

As he watched, the colors resolved themselves, hardening into something that looked much more like fire than a distant start or end of day. The edges of what might have been sun were orange, red; the blue that surrounded the whole was indeed sky.

"Do you recognize what this is?" Teller asked. "Snow?"

Snow hissed. It was not the laughter hiss. Shadow snickered. No one who might be able to answer the question answered it now. Calliastra said, "Let me see the book."

Teller passed it to her. He was not surprised to see the book change physical shape as it came into contact with her hands; it grew larger, the covers darker, the words pressed into the binding clearer. The book in the godchild's hands would no longer fit the shelf from which it had been taken.

Relieved of his precious burden, he turned to Jay; Jay's eyes were wide, shadowed, as she looked past Calliastra to the open page. Teller could no longer see it.

"Do you recognize it?" Teller asked Calliastra.

"Yes." The word was flat. It did not invite further questions; it slammed the door on them. She did, however, turn the page, something Teller could not have done. "The book is a bestiary." She closed it firmly, setting it flat on a table. Until that moment, Teller had not seen the table, but he had become accustomed to the warped rules of the reality of Jay's personal space, and he recognized the table. It had existed in the previous Terafin's library. It had existed in the remade forest of shelves and books.

It existed here.

The chairs that surrounded it were also familiar. He was surprised at how much he wanted, or needed, the familiar in this grand space. Perhaps Jay was no different. She sat gracelessly in one of those chairs, as if the strength to walk had deserted her. To Teller's surprise, Avandar bowed to Jewel, turned to nod at the Chosen, and followed.

Jay's collapse into the chair was not, as Teller had first thought, an accident of exhaustion. She had taken a seat in front of a small stack of books. Teller did not have perfect recall, but this table and those books seemed almost unchanged, as if the whole of the landscape revolved around them. Ellerson had said, however, that The Terafin's clothing and personal effects were within the castle, so perhaps that was simple fancy, a desire to make some sense where almost none was available.

The roar that broke Jay's moment of rest was familiar to the den. Jay pushed herself out of her chair; Calliastra was already halfway across the library, pushing herself between the Chosen who had also moved into loose formation.

Finch looked at Teller, who shrugged and made to follow.

There was a bear in the hall.

It was brown, it was huge, and its mouth seemed to be composed of fangs that shouldn't have fit in its hairy, unfriendly face. The cats were discomposed; their fur had risen, and their wings were stiff and high. Shadow was tensed to leap; Snow was just tense. Night had not rushed to join his brothers, which allowed Jewel to relax. Marginally.

Jewel could not push her way past the Chosen and didn't try. She drew breath. "*Snow. Shadow.*"

Cat words had given way to guttural growls; neither bothered to look in her direction.

"He is Ellerson's guest."

The white cat began to sputter, but his fur fell.

Calliastra, not being Terafin, pushed her way between Torvan and Marave, and to their credit, they let her go. They would not have let Jewel through unless Jewel had ordered them to do so. Ruling, she thought, was complicated, unwieldy, and inconvenient.

"What are *you* doing *here?*" Calliastra demanded.

The bear turned instantly at the sound of her voice, but almost everyone in the hall did, even Shadow, whose fur was still high. Snow, however, affected nonchalance and strolled across the library floor, nose in the air, until he reached Jewel's side. Jewel dropped a hand to his head without a second thought, or perhaps even a first one. She was staring at the bear. And at the godchild.

"What are *you* doing here?" the bear countered.

"I was *invited*."

"I was invited."

"I was invited by the Lord of these lands."

The bear did not condescend to reply. From this, Jewel understood instantly that he had extended his own invitation, and Ellerson had agreed. She was not offended; Ellerson was like kin, and this was his home. The bear could not be more trouble than the cats.

Snow hissed.

"Did I say that out loud?" she asked, shifting her hand to scratch gently behind his ears.

"We could be *much* more trouble."

"It wasn't a challenge, Snow. Shadow, come here."

Shadow ignored her. He ignored Calliastra. He ignored everything but the bear. "Where is *he*?"

"He is sleeping," the bear growled, his voice softening, the rumble that underscored his syllables fading. He began to shrink until he was no bigger than a dog of intermediate size and parentage, although his shape changed; his body became rounder, his ears more pointed, his tail bushy; his eyes were ringed with dark fur and his snout was pointed, a bit like a fox's. "But he was almost awake."

Shadow hissed. There was no amusement in it.

"Did they wake him?"

"Almost. Almost, but the boy quiets the earth now."

The creature turned toward her, seeing past the Chosen, Calliastra, and Shadow. Seeing, Jewel thought, past walls and rooms, past anything else that formed the heart of The Terafin's current chambers. The creature ambled toward her.

"Let him pass," she said.

Torvan stiffened, but Marave immediately turned to the side; she did not sheathe her weapon. It was the weapon that caught the creature's attention, causing fur to change the shape of his face as his large eyes rounded. He did not, however, talk to Marave, the Chosen being mere guards.

"They are dreaming here. Here, where the mortals dwell."

Calliastra's frown was edged enough to cut. "And you know this how?"

"Are you not Calliastra?" the creature countered. "Can you not *hear* them beneath your feet?"

"I hear nothing over your screeching, irritating voice." As Shadow hissed laughter, she added, "Or yours." To Jewel, she finished. "What will you do with him?" The tone in her question made it clear what her own preferences were.

"I'll send him to the forest," Jewel replied. "I think he must be kin to the eldest there."

"Oh?"

"The trees in my lands are awake. They take different forms when they choose to speak with us at all, but one is a golden fox."

"Golden?" the creature said, tilting his head.

"It's the color of his fur. However, while you are in my domain, you will cause no harm without my permission. You will not torment the mortals you happen across, and you will not cause more damage to my abode."

The creature seemed seriously offended at the latter, and Jewel had to struggle not to think of him as a cat. Well, as one of her cats.

"You should let us *eat* him," Snow suggested.

"Try."

"Snow, please."

Snow hissed, and not with amusement. "What is *his* name, hmmm?"

The Terafin, the Lord of the lands, the Sen of a nonexistent city, exhaled. "My manners are not what they should be. I am Jewel Markess ATerafin. This is Finch, this is Teller, this is Adam. Calliastra and my cats, you apparently know."

"And the others?"

"The captain of my oathguard, and one of my Chosen." She finished and waited. After a longer pause, she said, "And you must be Anakton."

Calliastra was the first to respond. She laughed. It was not particularly kind; she reminded Jewel viscerally of Duster. She was the only person to laugh. The name meant nothing to Jewel; it clearly meant nothing to Finch, Adam, or Teller, either. But she felt, rather than saw, the stiffening of her personal domicis, and when she glanced to the side and back, she saw that his expression was rigidly neutral.

"Why is that funny?" the creature now demanded of the godchild.

"You are, currently, a large, silver-furred weasel."

He instantly bristled. To Jewel's eye, he did not resemble a weasel. He resembled a badly put together fox, with odd feet. On first sight, however, he had been a bear. Jewel, who tended to use the names she was given, had named her cats in order to lessen their bickering. Had she been asked to name the creature, she might have called him Silver, for just as good a reason.

"It is like your clothing—which is deplorable, by the way. I might be a large, dirt-brown bear. I might be a midnight steed, with wolflike fangs. I might be many things." One of which was angry. "I might even choose to look like *you*."

"You could not."

"Might I remind you about my rules regarding destruction? You are, at the moment, a guest here. Guests can be asked to leave."

"Can they?"

"Or made to leave, if it comes to that."

"She is Sen," Calliastra said. She had settled on bored rather than annoyed or angry, and her voice was almost a drawl.

"She is not. Not yet. But the castle speaks her name." He glared at Shadow but spoke to Jewel. "Have I permission to enter your wilderness?"

Jewel nodded.

To Calliastra, Jewel said, "Come. Let's find you a room. There are probably a lot of them. I'd warn you that closets are dangerous, but I don't actually think they are for you."

"You don't look happy," Jester said, leaning against a tree and examining his fingernails for inappropriate dirt.

"You don't look awake."

"And you have eyes in the back of your head now?"

"They're not really required," Birgide replied, but she did turn, the hint of a smile at play across her otherwise severe face. "You have no idea how angry Duvari would be with me."

"Because of the new guests?"

"No. Because although it is impossible for me to be unaware when you approach me, I am willing to expose my back to you."

"Ah. I thought you were just being condescending." He grinned, and the slight smile deepened into something that resembled genuine amusement. It helped, because her eyes were blood-red. He came to stand by her side. "Am I interrupting anything?"

"Yes."

"Am I interrupting anything important?"

"It is a small wonder to me that The Terafin has not strangled you."

"And not simply removed the House Name?"

"She would strangle you first."

"True. She's been busy. You're not happy about our guests."

"The elders are not entirely happy about the guests. The majority are Lord Celleriant's people, yes?"

Jester hesitated; Birgide marked it.

"Celleriant," he finally said, "is like the Chosen, but with less humor. He's not one of us, but he is The Terafin's. He would die defending her."

"Not happily."

"Probably not. But they wouldn't."

"Have you spoken with them?"

Jester shook his head. "You're watching Shianne."

"Yes."

"You think she's dangerous?"

"Or possibly in danger. If the influx of Lord Celleriant's people has unsettled the forest, it is her presence that has truly alarmed it. I think it not impossible that were she here as anything but The Terafin's personal guest, the elders would try to kill her."

"That . . . would not be good."

"No," Birgide agreed. "But I confess I did not expect the animosity. To my eyes," eyes that had been altered by the forest itself, "she is a pregnant, mortal woman. What they see, I do not, and cannot, see. But you did not come here to discuss my discomfort."

"Actually, I did. I wanted your impression of the Arianni—that's what they're called by the lesser races, apparently."

"You wanted, or Haval wanted?"

He grinned again. Birgide was suspicious by nature, which meant there was no fear, no condescension, in that suspicion. "Both, actually. And if I'm being honest—"

"Don't put yourself out on my behalf."

"—Haval is occupied by Jarven. If the forest considers Shianne the threat, Haval is more concerned with Jarven." Jester shrugged. "Jay's not happy about Jarven."

"No; she doesn't trust him. It gives us all hope."

And at that, he laughed. "I also wanted to hear what you thought about the other significant guest."

"Which one?"

"Calliastra," he said, but he said it uneasily. Too much was changing, too quickly. He was not Warden, as Birgide was, but he could almost feel the tension in the forest as a pressure, a growing weight.

"The elders do not seem to be concerned about Calliastra, one way or the other. They do not believe she poses—or can pose—a threat to The Terafin."

"Never say that where Calliastra can hear you."

"Oh?"

"Trust me on this."

"Do you wish to speak with the guests?"

"I had hoped to discreetly observe them, but I found you first."

"The forest is being defensive," she replied. "I am Warden; the forest cannot protect me if I am to fulfill my duties. But you are important to The Terafin in a way that I am not." She said this without apparent unhappiness; it was observation, nothing more. "It is possible Haval could reach them; I do not think anyone who is otherwise not accompanied by The Terafin herself will."

Jester exhaled.

"That was what you wanted to know, wasn't it?"

"It was."

Birgide paused as if listening to something inaudible to Jester's ears. "It wasn't the only thing."

"No. I'd say you're wasted here, but actually, I don't think you are. Where is the House Mage?"

Her frown deepened. "I do not interfere with the House Mage; his duties and mine overlap, but we perform them independently."

"Can you find him?"

"Can the Chosen not summon him?"

"I wasn't sent to ask the Chosen; I was asked to ask you."

"Because Haval is occupied."

"Yes. Personally, I would leap at any task or chore that got me away from Jarven. Haval, however, thought to send me."

Birgide was silent. "He thought it necessary?" she said at last.

Jester nodded, uneasily aware that he could have asked this question two weeks ago and she would have answered without hesitation. Possibly without thought. "What's happening with Meralonne? I thought he might be with the Arianni or with Shianne."

"There will come a time when Meralonne is no longer welcome in the forest, in Terafin, or perhaps even within the city itself. The elders discuss him frequently, but only when they are near the tree of fire—and they are not particularly fond of that tree, although it doesn't burn them."

"When?" Jester asked.

"I'm not certain. I've asked the elders. I've asked the trees. They are not afraid of Meralonne; when they speak of him, they do not speak of betrayal. They are worried for Terafin, but they are not worried for the woman who rules the House. I would say they are almost . . . excited."

"Is Meralonne with Celleriant's people?"

"No."

"Then where, Birgide?"

"I am uncertain; he is not in one place." Silence. "I believe, however, you will find him in the heart of The Terafin's personal space."

"You believe."

Her silence was the silence of thought, of deliberation, as if she were picking a path made of words in a landscape that was only barely stable enough to support their weight. "Would you trust yourself with The Terafin's power?"

This was not what he'd expected. "Hells, no."

Birgide seemed slightly surprised.

"I've got a much fouler temper, and I don't give a rat's ass about anyone but us. No one cared about us except us when we had no money and no position. I'd trust her with power because she *did* see us. We'd've died, without her. She rescued me from a brothel—but she didn't come *for* me. She came for someone else, and she didn't want to leave any of us behind." He shrugged, uncomfortable and irritated. "I'd trust her with power because when she had power—and it was nothing compared to what we have now—she pulled us up with her.

"Me? I'd let most of the city burn."

Birgide bowed her head again. "What she has to be, she isn't. The choice is hers, but she hasn't evaluated it, won't face it, won't look at it. She will," Birgide added. "But Haval is very concerned."

"You've discussed this with Haval?"

"It wasn't necessary. Inasmuch as a man of Haval's nature can, he views The Terafin as a daughter. Were it not for his wife's obvious affection for The Terafin, I am not certain he would have. He is far more like Jarven or Duvari than any of you."

"Except for the wife part."

"Except for Hannerle, yes. It is a huge exception. It is a defining exception. But absent his wife, he would be as terrifying as Jarven or Duvari, and as scrupulous."

"And he thinks that I have the potential to be Jarven or Duvari?"

"No."

"He just believes I'm callous enough to be a close second."

"He believes you well-situated and observant enough; he does not believe your sense of self-worth is derived from social scruples. He will use you, yes, because you consent to be used; his focus is turned toward Jewel and her survival, as is yours. The survival of the rest of the city is, I feel, ancillary to his concerns—or would be, if the city were not where his wife lives. And you have once again broken my attempt at analogy.

"Your Jewel, your Terafin, is not what she must become if you are all to survive. But if she becomes what she must become—and no, I don't know what that is; the trees speak of it in a hush, and the cats themselves mutter—she will not *be* your Jewel. Can you accept that?"

"Can she do what must be done if she doesn't become something other or different?"

"I do not know."

And that, Jester thought, was a half-truth. "Is Haval in the forest?"

"He has returned, albeit briefly, to the manse."

"Then why don't I speak to Haval? It's not like I care what he thinks of me." He had taken less than a step when Birgide's voice caught him, almost as if it were a snare.

"And you care what I think?"

Jester did not look back. He did, however, answer. "You're not den."

She accepted that. That was the thing about Birgide: she accepted everything. As if people were distant mountains, arboreal trees, raging oceans: things she could witness but could neither control nor own. And perhaps because she did, he spoke again, his back toward her because he *could* turn his back to her without fear.

"You're not den, but you could have been."

Haval was, as Birgide had said, in the manse. Given that he was in the act of what might pass for cleaning or tidying in a room that was covered in the detritus of his tailoring work, she was less correct about the "briefly" part.

He did not seem surprised to see Jester. Jester stood in the open door's frame, as if daring Haval to leave until he moved. He was aware that were Haval determined, there would be no contest, even given the disparity in their ages.

"If you are determined to remain there, you might at least offer to help."

"My offer to help involves creating one large pile—preferably in a fireplace—and setting it alight. I believe you raised objections to that."

"Some of the materials would not burn, and the attempt might cause you difficulty. While I personally would have no qualms with this—playing with fire often has consequences, and if you survived, you would learn—Jewel would be upset. Why are you here?"

"I don't like Jarven, I dislike what I see between the two of you, and I would consider war a boon if it divested the House of Jarven."

"I believe that Jarven is fond of you."

"Jarven could adore me, and it wouldn't stop him from slitting my throat if I happened to be inconveniently in the way."

"No. But prior to that, he would at least be amusing company. You'd prefer Haerrad?"

"That's low."

Haval smiled. "Did you come to ask about Jarven? If so, I am not inclined to answer."

"Not really. I'm grateful that Jarven is your problem. I would love it if he became solely your problem, and he ceased to be any part of Finch's."

"He has saved her life at least three times in the past year. I believe she is only aware of one. Be careful what you wish for." He exhaled. "There is a reason that I have never advised his removal. Loss of Finch would cause far more damage than Jarven's presence. Even were Jarven to attempt to assassinate Jewel—and I hold that as an outside possibility, but a possibility nonetheless—it would not cause the damage that Finch's death would."

"That's not why you keep him."

"No. I keep him or, rather, have ignored his presence, because the cost of doing otherwise would be too high. The magical fortifications that have prevented Finch's death would, of course, prevent Jarven's; to circumvent his protections, one would have to be able to predict them. And even then, the only guarantee is that Jarven would then become an enemy and would remain so unless a greater advantage convinced him to disregard the unfortunate past."

"And now?"

Haval shook his head. "I have discussed Jarven as much as I am willing to, with you."

"And with Jay?"

"She will not ask."

Jester considered this briefly. It was true. Without external prompting, she wouldn't. She didn't like Jarven, and never had, because she couldn't trust him. But she also understood that, in some fashion, he was Finch's. "I came to talk about The Terafin."

This caught Haval's attention. "The Terafin, then? Not Jay?"

Jester ignored this. "What will happen to her?"

"I am not entirely certain."

"What do you think will happen?"

Haval stopped his packing. He turned to face Jester fully, his face expressionless, his eyes unblinking. His arms dropped to his sides; he might have been a maker-born statue—something that suggested life without containing it.

"You have, no doubt, heard the stories. You have observed Jewel with her domicis, with Lord Celleriant. You have seen the cats. None of these things are what we would have once considered normal. You have seen demons, Jester; you have seen gods. You have seen someone who seems to walk through time, as if time were a path that could be followed. Have you attempted to understand what once happened when the gods were free to walk the mortal realm?

"Do you understand that, when they did walk, there was no mortal realm?"

Jester nodded.

"Jewel does. She, like you, is mortal. And she, unlike you—unlike me—is talent-born. That has always been the truth by which she has lived. But if you have listened to the reports of the House Mage—or, rather, if you have bothered to read them when provided the opportunity—you would understand that it is not all of the truth. It is a simple window, a narrow view of only a portion of the greater whole.

"The mage-born find their magics more powerful than they have ever been. So, too, the healer-born. The world that we have known as the only world is shifting and changing; things have been broken that have existed for the entirety of our lives.

"Not even in the days of the Blood Barons did such a shift occur. You have seen demons and you have heard the whispered name of the Lord of the Hells. You have even understood, in some fashion, that the Lord of the Hells is a god, and that he is here. Here, in the same world, the same reality, as Jewel. Do you honestly think that we are the equal of a god? The gods once shaped whole continents on a whim and destroyed them in the same fashion; they did not privilege or prize life or their creations, and they certainly did not grant them autonomy.

"And yet, we have some rudimentary autonomy. And man, as a species, survived. Does it not strike you as all but impossible?"

Jester understood a rhetorical question when he heard one.

"Have you noticed that the immortals grant Jewel respect that they do not offer to anyone else? They call her Sen."

Silence.

"You were present when we went to find Jewel in what, to her, was a dream. You went to the twenty-fifth holding."

"Enough, Haval."

"No, it is not. Because if no one else is willing to see the truth of this, we will be caught in the dreams of Jewel Markess, made, remade, or vanished without any conscious thought on her part. She would not willingly do so. But what we dream is not what we live, and the choices we make in dreams are often counter to everything we believe we stand for." He frowned. "Surely this cannot come as a surprise to you, if you have invested any thought in it at all."

Lazy, remember? Jester started to speak the words, but they would not leave his mouth. Had he thought? No, but it was worse than that. He had avoided all such thought. The den trusted Jay. Had always trusted her. She had given them no reason, ever, to do otherwise. But Teller—Teller had been thinking. And Finch, in all probability.

"I have searched," Haval continued. "I have had others search. The people who lived in that apartment at the time that Jewel returned there in her dreaming no longer exist. They have never existed. There are gaps that imply that existence, but even those are closing."

Jester didn't give a damn about anyone who wasn't den. Jester didn't think twice about people who had mysteriously vanished from the twenty-fifth holding. What Jester thought—the only thing he'd thought—was that if the dream were *stronger*, they could have pulled Lefty, Fisher, Lander, and—yes— even Duster, out of that apartment and into the world, where they would be alive again.

And then he had stopped thinking, because it was painful, and it led to places that were unprofitable.

"You do not care."

"No."

"You would let the city burn as long as your den survived."

Jester shrugged.

"Can you say the same of Jewel? No, that is unfair. You might lie, and you are not particularly accomplished at it. Far better, however, than your Lord. She is not what you are. Were she, none of you would be at her side. Because she is who she is, your den has become what it is. In my opinion, Arann would be almost unchanged; perhaps Teller. But the rest of you have always been more flexible. It is why Finch can work with, and even admire, a man she does not trust.

"Jewel felt no ill-will for the people who vanished. She simply did not think about them at all. How much does one think about the setting of one's dreams—or nightmares? But, in waking, she will be burdened with guilt and self-loathing, and that will quite probably destroy us.

"I am not unlike you. I care for few, but that care is absolute and unshifting. Jewel is, in the opinion of the denizens of the wilderness, our only hope. And Averalaan will be her seat."

"That hasn't answered my question."

"You are not stupid. You are no longer young, except in the relative sense. I have answered your question in as much detail as I now possess. Let me be clearer. She will become what she must become; she became Terafin against her personal preference. But our ability to survive it does not depend entirely on Jewel. It depends on you. It depends on the rest of the den. It depends, in some small fashion, on men like me.

"And men like Jarven. There are things we cannot ask of her that must, regardless, be asked of someone."

"Anything done in her name, or done for her sake, she considers her responsibility. Anything. It's why she's never asked me to do what you might ask in future. If people are to become simple tools, they have no will of their own, no direction, no innate morality. And if they become her tools, she's the one to blame for the work they do, not them."

"Ah. Then tell me, Jester, why did she keep Duster?"

Chapter Two

6th of Lattan, 428 A.A.
Terafin Manse, Averalaan Aramarelas

JEWEL WAS NOT AN architect; nor was she a carpenter or a stonemason. She did not design spaces in which people were expected to live and work. She could not, therefore, tell whether the inside of this castle was larger than the outside had implied and spared the question no thought.

Avandar and the Chosen relaxed marginally once Anakton had ambled out the front doors—doors that remained open while Jewel was in residence. But their lack of familiarity with the environs of The Terafin's new personal chambers put everyone on edge. The presence of Anakton had not helped. But if this castle had appeared overnight, it seemed to conform more precisely to what might otherwise be expected of an unknown building, the single exception being the library.

The castle contained many rooms; those rooms were empty, but they contained the beds, chairs and desks that might be offered to guests of note; the floors were wooden, covered by long carpet runners; the windows were tall, wide, and let in normal sunlight.

Jewel recognized the rooms in which she was intended to sleep, to dress, to prepare for the day that awaited her, in part because the doors were carved with the insignia of The Terafin. She could not fail to recognize it, although she no longer wore The Terafin's ring. But these rooms were behind doors at the end of the longest of halls, and when she opened them, she faced a shorter hall, with doors that were likewise carved. At the end of this shorter hall were more modest doors, also engraved with The Terafin's seal made large.

Calliastra approached one of the doors—the first on the right. "I see. You were expecting me."

"Seer-born," Jewel replied. There was no room for Finch. No room for Teller, or any of the rest of her den. There was one door that bore a crest that tugged at memory; she couldn't immediately discern who owned it or where she'd seen it before.

"Will you stay here?" she asked Calliastra.

"Let us see what the seer-born believe would be home to one such as I." The door opened before Calliastra could touch it. The room was darkened, shadowed; Jewel couldn't see what it contained.

Calliastra, however, didn't have the same problem. She entered and glanced, once, over her shoulder. At Jewel. Jewel entered in her wake. The door did not magically shut behind her as she passed through the frame; the room did not magically brighten.

She stumbled her way across a floor that was wider than the rooms the West Wing contained, until she hit wall. Or rather, curtain. She then fumbled her way to the curtain's end, reaching for the rope that would allow her to gather that curtain, to bind it in place. As she did, light entered the room. Apprehensive, she looked at the room that she had somehow built for this child of two gods.

Calliastra, however, did not appear to be doing the same. She stood frozen in what was, in the end, a large bedchamber; the room was well-furnished. Near the ceiling—which was high and rounded—something floated in the air. It reminded Jewel of the dangling things put over baby cots, something to catch an infant's attention when they were old enough to see it.

But this was not something that would *fit* over the cot of a small child; it was large. Stars glittered; an oversize moon hung beneath something that could have been a cow, although it appeared to possess wings. Black and white implied ebony, ivory, but there were flashes of light that might have been the reflections cut gems cast.

This was not a room that Jewel would have consciously offered the child of the Lord of the Hells. It wasn't a room she would have offered anyone who wasn't a child, and she froze, just as Calliastra remained frozen, but for entirely different reasons. She could imagine just how enraged Duster would have been, and flinched.

Duster would have stormed out in an unreachable fury, probably for at least a day.

Calliastra was not Duster. She was white; all color seemed to have fled her face, her frozen expression; she looked a thing of alabaster or ice. But she lifted her face slowly, slowly, until she was looking at a child's night sky made of black, of white.

On the other side of the door, Finch was looking as wary as Jewel now felt. But Calliastra did not attempt to destroy the room; nor did she turn to shout—or scream—at the rest of the den.

For another long beat she did not seem to be aware that anyone else existed, and then she lowered her face and met Jewel's gaze, searching for something. When she found it—or perhaps when she didn't find it—she relaxed. "Yes," she said, voice softer than she had intended. "Yes, I'll stay here."

She did not leave the room to accompany the rest of the den when Jewel at last dared her own chambers.

Her rooms, however, were unremarkable. They were the rooms, on the interior, that The Terafin had always occupied. The ceiling was no longer a network of branches—or roots—but the lack allowed her to see a familiar trapdoor which, no doubt, led to a roof on which she could stand and think. Her clothing had been preserved in one long closet. She flinched as she opened the door. Her boots and shoes were there as well. In the dresser, the jewelry that The Terafin required was placed on several nested trays; her combs, pins, and brushes were also there.

The bed hadn't changed, but a smaller bed had been made and readied by the wall nearest the window.

Finch and Teller exchanged a glance, their fingers dancing briefly before their hands once again fell to their sides. It was Teller who asked, "Is the old apartment still here?"

Avandar glanced at the captain of the Chosen.

Torvan nodded. "The war room appears to be below, on the first floor; it is now adjacent to the armory." He hesitated, and then said, "Your previous rooms did not possess an armory."

"My previous rooms weren't a castle. Is the armory empty?" Jewel's question was quiet, but sharp.

"No, Terafin."

Shadow sniffed. He padded across the room and leaped up on the bed, where he then lay down, folding his wings. He was, of course, in the exact center of the mattress.

"It's been a long day," she heard herself say, as she glared at the cat. "And I'm about ready to fall over."

6th of Lattan, 428 A.A.
Terafin Manse, Averalaan Aramarelas

Jewel woke to darkness and the glowing golden eyes of a large, gray cat. His paws were resting against her chest with enough weight it was difficult to draw breath.

At the far wall of the very large bedroom, Avandar leaned against a wall; he was on two feet, his arms folded, his head bent. There was no magelight in this room, but a lamp flickered on a table too far out of reach to be hazardous should Jewel move while asleep.

Finch was sleeping.

"Shadow."

He hissed. There was no amusement in it.

"Your feet."

The removal of large paws withdrew warmth; she felt the air as cool, even chilly, in their absence. Avandar immediately detached himself from the wall and bent to retrieve clothing.

"What time is it?"

"I am uncertain."

Jewel rose in the scant light and began to dress, which involved more exposure to chill air. She turned to Shadow. "Is Calliastra in her rooms?"

"Who *cares*?"

"I do, obviously, or I wouldn't have asked."

"Why does *he* get the *easy* question?"

"Because he's not as smart as you are."

This time Shadow's hiss contained laughter. "She is with the *other* one."

Sleep had clearly not deserted her, but Jewel eventually asked, "Shianne?"

"*Yessss.*"

"And everyone else?"

"Night is with *them*. They don't *like* him."

"He's not to kill any of them unless they try to kill him first."

"Yes, yes, yes."

"Avandar?"

"Calliastra was disinclined to sleep and even less inclined to wait while you did."

"How did she get to the others?"

"She did not prowl through the manor, if that is your concern."

It wasn't. Jewel was not certain how to reach her forests from her castle.

The clothing that Avandar had chosen for the very early morning was practical, but it was not clothing meant for the road; the weave of the cloth was too fine and too delicate, the skirts too fussy.

She remembered very little of what had occurred in the hour before she finally succumbed to exhaustion. The only thing that remained firmly fixed in her mind was the fact that Teller had agreed to plead with Barston to arrange an appointment with Gilafas ADelios. He seemed highly doubtful that she would get the appointment she desired.

Jewel, however, was not.

She dressed as quickly as she could in the dim light; Finch was still asleep, and she didn't want to wake her. Let her put down the burden of regency for a day or two, if even that long.

Jewel had set out on a journey, on a quest of sorts, and the path she followed had led her home. But the path itself was not yet finished, the quest not yet completed. She might vanish—as Evayne, the only other living seer she had ever met—often did as a matter of course.

When she was dressed, she ruined the ensemble by attaching a pack to her waist that was neither subtle nor suitable for anything but travel. Avandar did not insist on carrying it for her. He knew what it contained. And he knew, as Jewel knew, that the road she now walked could appear or disappear with little warning; that the landscape could separate her from her domicis without any desire or will on her part.

Only when she was prepared did she ask him why he had allowed Shadow to wake her.

"He did not ask permission," Avandar replied.

Jewel exhaled. "Shadow."

"It is Illaraphaniel. He has come. He is *waiting*."

The castle had not changed shape overnight. The halls remained the same, although there were now lamps along the walls. She did not see Ellerson, but did not expect to see him; he was not hers. He would be here when Finch woke, and then he would return to the West Wing. She did not resent him for failing to bring Carver back. How could she? Had she not, herself, made that same decision?

She closed her eyes, inhaled, exhaled, and straightened her shoulders. "Where is he?"

"If, by 'he,' you mean the House Mage, he is at the gates."

"At the gates?" She was almost appalled.

"He could not enter."

"I gave him blanket permission to enter these rooms."

"Yes, Terafin."

She let that sink in as she walked, and her steps grew heavier, more cumbersome, with the thoughts that now accompanied them. She thought she might add a visit to the Order of Knowledge to her schedule. She wanted to speak with Sigurne Mellifas.

Meralonne was, as Avandar had said, at the gates. She saw him the moment she left the great hall and reached the height of the stone stairs that led up to the doors from the outside. She had almost expected him to be surrounded by the wild wind, as was his wont when he fought; he was not. His feet were on the ground, but his attention was riveted to the fountain, as if by a blacksmith.

What he saw, she thought, was what Calliastra had seen—or if not the same, at least as grand, as lofty in height. And what she saw?

A song. A ridiculous, political song, written by The Wayelyn.

She lowered her chin, squaring her shoulders to brace herself, as if this meeting were hard, physical labor. It was not, of course. The Terafin was not required to do that physical labor, and if she tried, she upset the Household Staff. Or worse, their terrifying master.

Meralonne became aware of her slowly; his gaze fell from the heights to the level of the merely mortal, and when it did, their eyes met. He tendered her a fluid, graceful bow, and he held that effortless supplication for too long. When he rose, his eyes were silver light, his hair a curtain of pale white that seemed all of Winter.

He did not step into the courtyard. Instead, he waited, forcing her to descend if she wished to speak to him without shouting.

"Speak," Shadow said, having nudged Avandar out of the way to occupy his preferred position by her side. "Shouting *here* is bad."

"Will you not enter?" Jewel asked, although she did begin to move.

"No, Terafin. It is no longer safe to do so."

"For you, or for me?"

One brow rose. He carried no sword, but also no pipe.

"Do you have a report for me?" she asked, as she approached, the gurgle of falling water a constant sound that underlay all her words without overwhelming them.

"None that will give you information you do not already possess. You have brought the Winter people."

Jewel inclined her head. "We walked the tangle."

Both of his brows rose then.

"And I met the Winter King. They served him. You would know this if you spoke with them."

He inclined his head. "Winter was new, when they walked it. They would know me, Terafin, and they would not. It is too dangerous to remain among them." He shook his head, as if to clear it, and reached for something.

"Pipe," Jewel said, almost as if compelling him, her breath held after the release of the single word. But he did withdraw his pipe, and as he set about lining the bowl with dry leaves, she felt herself relax.

"Where," he asked as he worked, "did you get the ring you now wear?"

She blinked. The ring had become almost part of her hand, she had become so accustomed to its light—but that should be wrong; she had worn it for so little time. She lifted the hand, placing it between them. "What do you see when you look at it?"

"I see the White Lady's name," he replied. His eyes seemed to catch the subtle radiance of the metallic band and absorb it; they grew in brilliance, gray passing into silver and beyond. "But no, that is not all I see. It is not a ring of binding, and it is not a ring of promise. Those, she gave when she chose to honor those who were not her own kin. It is of her, in a way that no other such rings are, or were.

"You are Sen, but even so, I would say the creation of such a thing is beyond you. If the elders believe that the Sen had no limitations, they are wrong. You could dream of the White Lady, but you could not—ever—create her."

"I didn't create it."

"No. Who did?"

"Gilafas," she replied. When Meralonne did not speak, she added, "He took the strands of the Winter Queen's hair."

His eyes shifted, his brows rose. "You *gave* him those?"

"No." She hesitated. "And yes. I wanted—" She swallowed air awkwardly, and in a rush. "I think I wanted him to create something which would keep her gift safe."

"None would dare to take what the White Lady offered you."

She hadn't exactly offered it, but Jewel did not correct him. "None of your people would, no. But the world is not only Ariane's. Nor was it ever. Three strands of hair, Meralonne. Three delicate strands. Nothing, now, will take them." And speaking it, she knew the words for truth.

"That is not all he took."

She did not speak of the pendant. "The hair, the leaves of my forest."

His eyes widened again, and he spoke a word that Jewel did not quite hear, could not quite retain. The pipe listed in a hand that appeared to be suddenly nerveless.

"If you asked my advice, I would tell you to remove it and hide it. Were you any other person, such an attempt would fail, but you are Sen; there are places where you might hide that light that would protect it from discovery."

She shook her head.

"Do you understand what it is?"

"No. And you know this."

His smile was slender, sharp. It was also breathtaking. She realized then that she had never seen joy shadow his face before. But it was here, in the light of his eyes, in the lift of his lips, in the perfect lines of his unfettered smile. She thought he might have looked like this in a youth so distant even the gods had been young. "Yes, Terafin. I will ask no more. But even my brethren would think twice about fighting you should they see that ring."

"If you would counsel me to hide it—"

"My brethren are not the only enemies you will face. Your Ellerson has returned."

She nodded.

"Do you understand what it is he now wears? It is a lesser work, but a work nonetheless."

"What he wears?" She tried to think back to what Ellerson had been wearing, but the familiar suit imposed itself over true recall.

"I will assume that that is a no." He spoke with the familiar condescension that his graceful, fluid bow had almost obliterated. She had no desire to examine why this made her more comfortable. "I recognize it. The wilderness will see it, and they will not reach the same understanding unless they understand mortals and mortality." He blew lazy smoke circles in the air, misshapen but complete; they drifted above his head, untouched by the breeze that altered the fall of his hair.

"The time is coming," he said softly. "Ask Sigurne what she wears. Ask her why."

Jewel said, "I'm not ready yet."

"No, Terafin. No more am I. But time turns, regardless. For you, time is death. Near or far, it is death. I cannot enter your abode now. I believe that soon, I will not be able to enter your forests."

"But you have my permission to do so."

"No, Terafin. What I will be when I wake is not what you have given permission to, and if you are foolish enough, or cowardly enough, to look away from that truth, you know it on some level. Your forest knows. Your servants—the immortals, who turn by the seasons that have governed my long existence, with one brief sojourn—also know. They bear me no enmity yet, although one of the eldest thinks he might save you all grief by orchestrating my early demise." He smiled at the outrage of her expression.

"Why did you come?"

"To tender my farewell. I will no longer be able to serve as the Terafin House Mage."

"You will return to the Order of Knowledge?"

"No, Terafin. Nor will I accompany you on the journey you must undertake. But I am comforted, nonetheless. You will have with you men who, if not singly the equal of me, will nonetheless serve in my stead. They are the White Lady's, and they will understand the import of your mission. They will understand it far, far better than you."

"And Shianne?"

"I will speak with Shianne before the ways are fully closed. She is my only regret."

"You will not harm her."

"Even were that my intent—and I admit to you, whose sight is deep when turned, that I have considered it long and hard—I cannot. She is not without power; she is merely, now, without time. I could kill her; I could not do so here. She understands that, as well as I. And where there is no hope of success, I am no longer a youth; I will not throw myself against that wall until I am bruised and bloody." He stopped speaking then, and lifted his head, turning it slightly toward the grassland and path that led to this place. "Can you not hear them, Terafin?"

And the worst thing was, she could.

Horns.

They were like voices, like raised voices; they had tone and texture that implied not music, but speech. There existed a mournful dissonance as those notes played out. After a moment, she could separate them; there was not one horn, but three.

"They don't call you," she said, almost without thought.

"No, Terafin. They have been sent on wayward paths by the wilderness, both High and Low, but in the end, they cannot be kept from their masters. Not now."

"You did not sleep."

"I did not fail." He paused, and then added, "Nor did I succeed. And sleep, I think, would have been a kindness. But if I did not sleep, I am not awake. It is coming." He glanced again in the direction of those horns.

"Will you recognize us at all?" Jewel finally asked, as the notes softened into stillness and muted wind.

"If you cannot answer that, Sen, I cannot. I will know Sigurne. And I believe, in the end, I will know you—but you, too, are waking. Or perhaps you ask me the question you will not ask yourself. I am a danger to your kind, to your kin, but not the danger I will become. You are the same. Perhaps we will both find answers that are, in the end, pleasing to us."

"You were never what I was."

"No, Terafin. But I have lived centuries now as if I were. My kin change slowly, when we can be moved to change at all; I do not believe I would have changed had the world not shifted beneath my feet. Change is not a boon to the immortal; it is like death. It is as final, in some fashion, but far less convenient." He then gently upended the ash from his pipe, and the wind swept it away before it made contact with stone, as if he intended to leave no trace of his passing in his wake.

He handed the pipe to her. "Take it, in the hope that you might return it to me, and I might smoke and converse in future; there is and has been no need for pipe among my own. Lord Celleriant dislikes it intensely," he added, with a trace of petty amusement.

"He hates *everything*," Shadow said, speaking for the first time. Jewel had almost forgotten he existed.

"He is the youngest, and the last," Meralonne replied, speaking as he often did when confronted with a talking cat. "Eldest, I do not understand your duties here. But Celleriant was given in service to The Terafin for a reason."

"She was annoyed at his failure," Jewel said.

"Is that how you truly see it?" He bowed. "Were it in my hands, I would fight the war at the side of your Chosen, both mortal and immortal. It is not."

Jewel cleared her throat. "They served the Winter King."

"Yes."

"He is dead."

"Yes. And so their service to you is compromised, incomplete. But if they understand what it is you carry, and why, they will be utterly and completely yours until the moment you relieve yourself of that burden. Nothing will deter them. Not the Sleepers, and in the end, not even I. But they will not mindlessly obey."

She looked at him, held his gaze. "I don't understand the firstborn concept of children," she finally said. "But mindless obedience was never, ever your strength."

At that, he smiled. "I remember my lost more clearly than you remember yours, but we are both haunted, and by our own will."

"Will you—will you stand beside them when they wake?"

"I do not know. But I will not lie to you now, so close to the end of things. I desire it. I desire it as greatly as the old and feeble among you desire their youth. Perhaps, as is true of your kind, that youth is gone; it is a dream because the desire cannot encompass truth or reality. I wish to see them again. I wish to hear their voices." He turned.

The song of horns began anew.

Shadow growled.

Meralonne bowed again, then turned and walked—walked—away.

Jewel did not follow; instead, she turned back to the castle and her own sleeping kin. Avandar had not approached the House Mage or the former House Mage. Nor did he approach Jewel; he waited until she had once again mounted the steps.

He remained silent as she found her room and remained silent as she returned to it.

"I don't think the clothing is appropriate," she finally said.

"We will travel?"

She nodded, her hands numb.

"Fabril's reach."

She nodded again. "I don't know where we'll end up. They'll probably turn us away at the door—or at least ask us to use the servants' entrance—if we prepare for any outcome. But I'd rather be turned away up front than freeze to death."

He did not ask any further questions.

But the Winter King said, *I will be there.*

Finch was not quite awake. Jewel watched her move slowly out of sleep and remembered, clearly, Rath's apartment, and their first room there. Teller had stayed with the girls. So had Duster. So many shadows, in this darkness, cast by things that were not actually in the room.

Finch woke. She smiled, rubbing her eyes, and looking much younger than she did when she armored herself in the daily clothing she wore to the Merchant Authority. It made Jewel feel young again, and here, youth was not an advantage. Or perhaps it was just the growing uncertainty she felt. None of her training and none of her experience had prepared her for what she was facing.

Not none, Avandar said. He glanced about the room for Ellerson, but the domicis failed to appear, and he then gathered the various items of clothing that Finch had removed from her own rooms and laid them out for her.

She dressed slowly, looking around the oddly lit room until she saw Shadow. Prowling winged cats seem to be a comfort to her, which was fair; they were, in the end, a comfort to Jewel.

You have met the Winter Queen. You have bested her. You have seen gods, you have seen the firstborn, you have walked both the Stone and Green Deepings. You have fought the Wardens of Dream and Nightmare. You have faced a Duke of the Hells, and you have forced him to retreat. You have commanded the wild earth, water, and air, denying them free rein in the lands you have claimed. You have faced the Oracle and walked the Oracle's path. If there is experience to prepare you for what we all face, what form do you think it would take, if not the life you have lived?

She had no reply to offer.

"Will you speak with Barston?" Finch asked, when she had finished dressing.

"No. I can't face Barston this early in the morning. Unless it's a choice between Barston and the Master of the Household Staff."

Finch laughed.

"I'd personally rather face demons."

Finch's laughter trailed into a gentle smile. "If not Barston, do you intend to address the House Council at all?"

Jewel was silent for a beat. "I'm grateful," she finally said, "that you're my regent."

"Which means no."

"I'll take Barston."

"I'd take the Master of the Household Staff, myself. She is splendidly intimidating. I've watched her at work, and I did consider attempting to mimic her, but I don't possess the force of personality she does." She paused and added, "Do we have umbrellas and rainwear?"

"Yes," a familiar voice said. "It took some searching to find." Ellerson nodded to Avandar and stepped in. "I am not certain how easy it will be to attend to both you and the rest of the den, but I shall make the attempt in future."

If the Chosen were surprised when Finch, Jewel, and Avandar emerged from the staid doors to The Terafin's chambers somewhat damp, they kept it to themselves, as they always did.

The servants were less circumspect, but everyone expected that. None of them spoke directly to The Terafin, but the way they stilled, and the way they turned to each other almost before she had passed them, was noticeable. Jewel didn't mind this. The Master of the Household Staff would have had a hissy fit to make the cats envious in comparison, and that thought was amusing. But the servants reminded her of Carver, because Carver had always been their necessary entry into the Household Staff.

Barston rose immediately when The Terafin entered the right-kin's office. The outer office was almost empty; there was a man in a reasonably tailored suit who rose as well. They offered Jewel their perfect, silent bows, and she nodded them back to their chairs, clenching her ring hand as she did.

She had left the Terafin ring in the keeping of the Oracle, and it had not magically returned to her. This was the first time she had missed it.

Barston returned to his seat. He immediately reached for one of the several books that stood on his desk, spine toward him so that contents were not instantly understood by observers, and opened it.

Jewel, however, said, "I expect that my schedule is currently empty."

He lifted his eyes, achieving the baleful expression that was not, quite, a glare. "It is currently open, yes."

She lifted a ringless hand. "I require an immediate meeting with Sigurne Mellifas. Location is of little consequence; I am willing to travel. I am not, however, finished the responsibilities I have undertaken. I have returned to retrieve necessary items, not to stay. Not yet."

"And when will you be back to stay?" From Barston, this was almost a shout. It was, however, better than she possibly deserved as ruler of the House.

"I am, as of yet, uncertain. Time does not pass in the same way in all the lands I have walked since leaving. It might—with luck—be tomorrow. It might be an hour from now. And it might be months. Before I leave, however, I must speak with the Guildmaster of the Order of Knowledge."

Barston's nod was clipped. Had he dispensed with the nod, it wouldn't have mattered; she had given him the equivalent of an order, and he would obey.

Jewel sent Ellerson to the West Wing with Finch. She did not choose to accompany them. She wanted to speak with Haval, and she needed to speak with Sigurne. The former was not in the wing; she did not know where the latter was currently situated.

But even thinking that, she felt uneasy, because she was suddenly certain that Sigurne Mellifas stood at the height of the Order's Tower, not in her room, and not in the very inconvenient chambers that adjoined them, but back from the crenellations, where the open wind might reach her upturned face.

She was not alone.

And perhaps that was why Jewel knew where she was, of a sudden. She *knew*.

Meralonne bowed. She thought, in this odd vision, that he bowed to Sigurne, as he had come to bow to her: in leave-taking. But Sigurne Mellifas, her age unfeigned, turned away from him, turned to look at the object of that greeting.

Jewel's gaze met hers.

Sigurne's brows did not even rise, but the lines of her face changed the shape of her expression. There was sorrow in it, and fear, but there was also resignation and a weariness that was so sudden and so complete, Jewel wondered if it would ever leave her face.

"I need to speak with you," The Terafin said, to the guildmaster.

Sigurne nodded.

"I will come to you," Jewel then said, giving weight to the difference in age and mobility, as she had been raised to do.

But Meralonne said, "No, Sigurne. Meet The Terafin at her seat of power. You will be required, in the end, to do so; begin as you must continue." And he, too, looked across the small expanse of sky underlined by the existence of this tower, and his gaze was, for a moment, kin to Sigurne's.

"Terafin?" Barston's tone was pinched, which suited his expression.

Jewel swallowed. "Belay that," she told him. "The Guildmaster of the Order of Knowledge will come here."

"When?"

"This afternoon." She nodded and turned before Barston could ask any further questions. Her back turned toward him, she said, "After our meeting, I will attend the Guildmaster of the Order of Makers." She swept from the room, glancing only once at Teller's closed doors.

No one spoke as she walked the length of the public gallery which led away from the right-kin's rooms. Those offices were meant for the men and women considered worthy of The Terafin's personal time, and in general, that meant, or had meant, they were monied, powerful.

The offices in which she did her own work were far less grand, and it was for that reason that no meeting of import occurred there. If the office was used at all, it was used for House business.

She was losing all sense of what House business was, and knew it. She had promised Amarais that she would take—and hold—the reins of power when Amarais was no longer there to do it; that she would preserve what The Terafin had built. But her gaze swept out, and out again: to the spires, to the peaks of *Avantari*, and beyond them all, to the bay, to the hundred holdings, to the statue of Moorelas, the mortal chosen to accompany the four princes of the Winter Court in their ride into Allasakar's shadow.

She could see the *Ellariannatte* that graced the Common, could see the outline of the Merchant Authority, and in the same line, the new Merchants' guildhall. None of these things were Terafin.

She was not surprised to find herself in the forest that hid behind the manse; she had walked and was walking. Shadow was by her side, and the Chosen walked ahead; Avandar had surrendered his position to the gray cat with a modicum of annoyance but no real anger. The silver leaves above her moved, adding a metallic tinkle to the breeze at play above her head.

She could hear the movements of the forest's denizens, and as she walked, could hear their voices. She was not surprised when the trees themselves briefly exposed their hearts, and two people stepped out from the illusory space in the bark. Their skin was golden, and they were of a height, slender, tall, with hair that seemed at times to be bark brown, and at times to be vine and leaf.

"Jewel," one said. "The Councillor bid us greet you, and so we have."

"Have you come to lead me to him?"

"Ah, no. You do not require an escort; you cannot be lost in this forest. Nor can we be hidden. The Councillor has played such games of hide-and-seek— that is what you call it among your kin?"

Jewel nodded.

"But there is no way to hide from you here, and in truth, if there was, the one hidden would feel little triumph, for he must remain apart." The woman, silent until this point, now offered Jewel an arm.

Jewel took that arm, not up to the task of explaining that certain manners were best left to the patricians on the other side of the forest. If Haval had taught them this, she would have words with him. But if he had, he had not taught them to clothe themselves as if they were of that patriciate; the vines and leaves that were hair were also, in some fashion, clothing, but clothing seemed irrelevant to her now.

Haval was not, as she had expected him to be, by the tree of fire. Nor was he alone. She recognized the golden fox that now sat in Haval's arms; it was the fox who spoke, and Haval who listened. Or so it appeared. Haval's face was absent expression until he turned to her. He set the fox on the ground—which was clearly not the fox's desire—and tendered Jewel a perfect bow, its fluidity undiminished by Haval's apparent age.

There were many things she could have said. "Rise," however, was the first word out of her mouth. He obeyed, his expression carefully guarded.

Shadow glanced at the fox in a speculative way. Jewel dropped a hand to the top of his head. "Not now," she said.

"But not *never*?" Shadow asked, with genuine curiosity.

She ignored the question. To Haval, she said, "The House Mage has resigned."

Haval nodded. He did not ask her what had occurred in her absence and did not offer her anything that might be remotely construed as welcome or comfort. And why, she thought, would she desire the latter?

"We believe we are now capable of defending your lands in his stead."

"Did you send Jarven?"

"No, Terafin."

"Did he bring you any remotely useful information?"

"Almost certainly. How it is to be used, however, is not yet clear." Haval smiled then; it was a cool smile. Distant.

"How is Hannerle?"

The smile deepened. "Were any other to ask that question at this time, it would be a very subtle threat."

"I'm not stupid enough—I will *never* be stupid enough—to threaten your wife."

"No, Terafin. Only stupid enough to feel strong affection for her. It is a stupidity I share. She is, as you discern, unhappy with me. Were it not for your existence, were it not for Teller and Finch, she would have ejected me from our store, our home, and her life."

Jewel winced.

"She does not believe that you can handle what now happens on your own. She believes that I am necessary."

"And you aren't above using that belief against her."

"I happen, at the moment, to believe as she does. It is why she believes it. I made one promise to her, decades past: I would not lie to her. I have not. Where I cannot speak truth, I do not speak. She dislikes silence," he added.

But Jewel remembered. To the fox she said, "Have you ever visited the tangle?"

Brows twitched so suddenly Jewel thought the fox was sneezing—but without the sound. "The tangle," he said, when he spoke, "is not here."

"The tangle is everywhere, if I understand what Corallonne was saying."

"You met her?"

"Yes. Calliastra is not the only firstborn we encountered on the way."

"You should not have brought her here. She is not a danger to us—not a danger to your trees or the ancients who have but recently stirred. But she is a danger to you and your kin."

"She is a danger—when she chooses to be—to *anyone*. It is not only my kind that have perished at her hands."

The fox blinked. Haval did not.

"She has told you this?" the fox asked.

"How else would I know it?"

The fox opened his mouth, but Haval knelt to retrieve him from the forest floor, and the words that he might have spoken did not follow. Instead he said, "They are waking . . . soon."

"I heard the horns," Jewel replied. "The horns of the heralds. I heard them while I stood in my own courtyard, in my own home." Her hands were shaking; they had become fists while she had been speaking, as if they did not quite belong to her.

"Yes. Should you desire to preserve your city, what must you do?"

"Find Ariane. She is the only person to whom they might listen."

"If her own kin cannot find her, how will you?"

Jewel said, "Her own kin weren't seer-born. Her own kin weren't maker-born. Her own kin," she added, after one long exhale that seemed to empty her body of breath, "weren't Sen."

"Even so," Haval said, inclining his chin. "You wished to speak with me."

"To seek your counsel," Jewel replied, her words heavy with irony.

His smile acknowledged it. "Jarven was not attacked by demons."

"The claws—"

"They were, if he is to be believed, caused by a great, gray wolf. Or two. They were not," he added, "wolves in any sense of the word that is currently fashionable. They were, however, mounts."

"Mounts."

"Yes, Terafin. They were ridden by the Arianni in the lands outside of your own. But it is, in the end, into these lands they must travel."

"They don't have my permission."

"No. I admit that I found that slightly confusing, given the emphasis on such permission—but permission grants only safe passage, not passage. Where the wilderness is concerned, the greater power is always in the figurative right."

Silence for a long, stretched beat. "He met the heralds."

"That is my belief."

"Did he injure them?"

"Yes, but not fatally."

The fox's whiskers twitched.

"You sent him," Jewel said, turning her attention to him as he so obviously desired.

"I did. But not against his will. If I am his master—and in some fashion I am—it is a dubious claim. In the end, he will do what he wishes. He has a freedom of movement that I do not outside of your own domain. And, Jewel, it is clear to all who dwell here that you do not desire the Sleepers to wake.

"But were you not the Lord of these lands, they would already be awake."

The fox nodded. "What you must do, Terafin, you must do soon."

I don't know *what I must do*. She wanted to scream the words. Her life to this point had taught her the weight of responsibility—and the cost of failing it. It had taught her that some responsibilities could not be completely shouldered; they were not like the pack she wore strapped to her waist. They could not be carried in the same way.

She exhaled again. "My rooms have changed."

Haval nodded, as if this information was not new to him.

"Has anyone else tried to kill Finch in my absence?"

"Or Teller?"

She stiffened.

"No, Terafin. Finch is both more and less protected than she was before Jarven became distracted. Teller, however, is safe. If Haerrad once broke his limbs as a warning to you, he has come full circle. Teller is right-kin."

"And Rymark?"

"Rymark is not, sadly, within your lands at the moment. As you would know if you paused to consider it. I do not believe he is dead."

"How long do I have?" she asked, yearning now for the warmth of the sole tree she had planted from the fire of her enemies. The forest answered. The tree appeared.

But no, she thought, it was not the same tree. It was a different tree, and she had called it into being with the desperation of the unspoken desire. She was afraid now.

Haval sensed it; he must have. He pinched the bridge of his nose, and the gesture—which indicated frustration or annoyance, and always had—was a comfort. As much of a comfort as the whining squabbles of her cats when they were bored.

"Not long. Not long at all. The forest was relieved when you arrived."

"You weren't."

"No. I am seldom given to feelings of relief; they are lies that we tell ourselves in order to function with a modicum of normalcy. You have not yet finished whatever quest you have undertaken; that your path brought you here is, if not coincidence, then luck. What can be done to prepare your lands for invasion has been done, and the city will stand in your absence.

"But it is my belief that it will not stand for long. I have nothing of value to report to you, and very little advice to offer."

"And the advice?"

"Keep Shadow by your side."

She heard, or thought she heard, Snow's outraged hiss.

"And keep moving. Do not tarry here. This is the heart of your personal fiefdom; it is your strength. If it cannot stand on its own in your brief absence, nothing will survive."

She nodded. "Tell my guests to ready themselves for our departure. I must speak with Sigurne before I return."

Sigurne arrived so quickly she must have left for the Terafin manse the moment Meralonne had stopped speaking. Jewel suspected that she had used magic as a means of transport. The absence of Matteos Corvel cemented this suspicion.

Jewel had been undecided about the venue for their meeting; the river with its waterfall made traversing the distance between the doors and the castle itself a damp, chilly prospect, and Sigurne was not young. She was saved from having to make the decision by the guildmaster's hasty arrival.

The guildmaster's smile was complicated. She had been ushered into the right-kin's outer office as a matter of protocol, but the page seemed surprised to see Jewel there.

"Terafin," Sigurne said. She offered Jewel a bow that was far less fluid or graceful than the bows that she'd otherwise witnessed recently. Jewel almost told her not to bother, the gesture seemed so superfluous. But Barston was already annoyed with her, if not actually angry, and she wasn't willing to add to the burden by bypassing protocols he would consider the bare necessities.

"Sigurne."

The guildmaster rose. If she was surprised by the use of her name, she kept it to herself. Or perhaps she was weary enough that it simply didn't matter. Jewel offered her an arm, and Sigurne took it, allowing Jewel to bear, for a moment, a larger part of her weight.

"I apologize for my appearance," the guildmaster said. "The wind is not kind to mortal hair or clothing. You look peaked, Terafin."

Jewel almost laughed at the pinched expression. It was not an expression well suited to the woman who oversaw the Order of Knowledge. Jewel lifted a hand to cover her mouth—something she had trained herself not to do when dealing with the powerful.

Sigurne's face froze. She did not speak again for one long minute, and Jewel saw strands of orange-and-blue light surround her, as if they were forming a veil over her eyes, her face. "He is wrong," she finally said.

Jewel blinked. "Wrong?" She shook herself then. "My apologies, Guildmaster. I have only barely returned to the manse, and I cannot stay. Will you keep me company while I prepare?"

Barston's jaw made a sound—Jewel would have sworn it—as it fell open.

"I would be honored, Terafin," Sigurne replied. "It is seldom that I keep company in circumstances the powerful consider so casual."

"Let me apologize in advance for the state of my personal rooms."

"They have changed?"

"Markedly, I'm sorry to say."

Jewel was forewarned enough that umbrellas and oilskins were procured for the guildmaster before she walked through the doors that had once led to a library. Sigurne accepted the need for both without comment; her eyes were bright in the worn, weary map of her face.

Jewel noted that Sigurne now wore a ring that was similar in size and shape to the ring Ellerson wore. It was similar in some ways to the ring she herself wore, but she would never have mistaken them were they laid side by side.

"Meralonne told you that he had resigned?"

"Yes. He . . . did not feel that a House Mage was relevant to Terafin for the foreseeable future. I will add," she said, her voice dry as kindling, "that rumor of his resignation has spread throughout the Order like brush fire. I have had dozens of requests—some wheedling and some demanding—to be recommended as his replacement."

"Are they aware that he was working for free?"

"Oh, indeed. And three of the men in question have offered to pay you, if that is what is required to be accepted."

"I do not envy you your position."

"No. But it is fair; I do not envy you yours. I will assume that you did not consider the full effects of proximity to waterfalls."

"No."

"I have seen so few of them, myself. I find this both striking and uncomfortable."

"It might be better if it were warmer." Jewel exhaled. "How long do I have?" It was not the question she'd meant to ask; it was not the location at which she'd meant to ask it.

She was tired. No, it was more than that; she was afraid. She considered fear to be wisdom, in this case. The Lord of the Hells was in the world, and if he weren't, the Sleepers—almost gods in their own right—were waking beneath the thin surface of earth over which the whole of Averalaan had been built in the shadows of history.

The city housed everyone she cared about. Some, she could save. She was certain that her den—those who remained within the manse or the forests that whispered her name—would survive.

But Farmer Hanson would not. Helen, in her stalls of mismatched cloth and clothing, would not. Taverson and his family would not. Not unless the Sleepers could either be controlled or reasoned with. The man who knew them best gave no chance at all for the latter, and really only one for the former.

"Not long now. Where you travel, where you must travel, time flows differently. Tell me, can you hear the heralds?"

Jewel nodded.

"I could not, until I donned this ring. I hear their horns now at all hours, and they are growing louder. Closer. It is, to me, a small miracle that they have not already arrived."

"Does he think that you'll survive?"

"At this point it is his only concern. Kings, demons, duties—they are becoming irrelevant. He knows this, and he fights against it—but, Terafin, it is my opinion that he is fighting his very nature. There is, in him, a light that has begun to burn." She did not mention Meralonne by name.

Nor did Jewel. Her Chosen preceded her; her domicis walked behind. Shadow, however, had grown unnaturally silent. Jewel was as alone as she was likely to get when she was on her own ground; she had as much privacy as she could expect to have.

Shadow, mindful of her dignity, said nothing. That should have been a clue.

"You are quiet," Sigurne said, the final syllable tailing up slightly. It was an invitation, or as much of an invitation as she could make when speaking with The Terafin.

And it was not as The Terafin that Jewel wished to speak. It had been more than two decades since she had heard her Oma's voice in the flesh; more than two decades since the whole of her life had been built in and around that old woman's harsh dictate.

It had been, therefore, more than a decade since she had felt safe.

Safety is illusion, two voices said, with the requisite amount of disapproval.

I know, she told them, staring at Sigurne's hands. Staring at her own. It was better than lifting her face to meet the older woman's eyes. *I know.* But if it was illusion, if it was phantasm, it was nonetheless the illusion to which she'd dedicated her life. And she wasn't the only one; the den had done the same.

They'd seen her through the holdings, when starvation was the biggest threat they faced—that or freezing to death in the winter. They'd stayed by her side when the threats expanded to include demons, magic, death. Even death. They'd come with her to Terafin, and in her early years she had believed that with the Terafin name behind them, they'd be safe.

And they'd been safe, given demons and magic and gods.

But they'd been safe because they'd stood—all of them, Jewel included—in the shadows cast by Amarais Handernesse ATerafin. Jewel was not, and could never become, Amarais. She felt the lack keenly, as she stood in the mist raised by roaring, falling water.

"Jewel."

She lifted her head. What she saw in Sigurne's face almost made her lower it again. She was not a child. She had not been a child for years. But Sigurne reached out—slowly, deliberately, her hands losing the orange-and-blue glow that was so familiar it was almost like gloves—and touched her right cheek.

"You are not like I was in my youth. But had you been raised among my kin, I think you would have been. I have no children. I will not embarrass you by pretending that I think of you as my own—I confess that the intricate dance between parent and child when one has multiple responsibilities has often confused me.

"Had I a daughter, had you been that daughter, I am not sure what I would now do. But I believe I would do everything in my power to spare her the future that is coming, regardless of what we now choose to do. In the darkest of my moments, I see so little hope I do not feel that I can give advice. Is it my advice you seek?"

Jewel shook her head. She knew that Sigurne had no advice to give. What she wanted, for just this moment, was to give over the responsibility of choice to someone she trusted—someone powerful, someone wise, someone steadfast. Sigurne Mellifas was all of those things.

As if she had spoken the words she would never speak aloud as The Terafin, Sigurne's smile softened. "Were it in my power, Terafin, I would do what you must do. It is not."

"I don't *know* what I have to do."

"No. No more do the gods or the wise, and it has been discussed in admittedly very closed circles. To me, you are young. Not a child, but young. We fear that the fate of the world rests upon your shoulders, and you lack the experience and the wisdom to make the correct choices. But child, we do not truly understand what those choices might be; we cannot see them.

"Why did you wish to speak with me?"

"To ask you what I asked." Jewel swallowed. "And to ask you what that ring means."

"Ah. And I can answer neither question. No, it is not that what you have asked is impolitic or prying; it is not; I simply lack knowledge. The ring you wear and the ring I wear are not the same. Tell me, Terafin, what do you hear?"

"Besides horns?"

"Yes."

"Water. Wind. Birdsong." Jewel closed her eyes. ". . . My name."

"That is all?"

Was it? She listened; the horns made it hard. "That's all."

"Then we have more time than Meralonne now fears." Sigurne inhaled, and gained inches in height, although her shoulders and back were still bent. "Come. I am as prone to curiosity as any other member of the Order of Knowledge. Let me see what you have made of your personal chambers."

Sigurne did not seem overly concerned—or impressed—by the castle. If she was curious, she kept her questions to herself, or perhaps she understood that Jewel couldn't answer them. But when they entered the courtyard, she froze beneath the housing of the gate, her eyes drawn to, riveted on, the fountain.

"You did not create this," she said, her voice so thin it was barely audible.

"No."

"Fabril did."

"That wasn't a question."

"No, Terafin. No, Jewel, it was not." The orange weave around the magi intensified, but the blue did as well. "May I?"

She did not wait for permission, but permission wasn't necessary. What Calliastra had seen, what Meralonne himself had seen, she did not—but Jewel didn't ask. Instead, she kept pace with the guildmaster as the guildmaster stepped toward the rim of what—to Jewel's eye—was the stone into which the water fell from on high.

She stepped through it, as if it were simple illusion; the orange light wavered, buckling as if at a blow.

Avandar.

Jewel.

What do you see? When you look at the fountain, what do you see?

His silence was marked, long; Jewel watched Sigurne as she traversed the edge of the structure seen by the guildmaster. She thought Avandar would not answer, and was surprised when he said, *There is a reason that your personal space now includes a waterfall.*

"What is an Artisan?" Jewel asked.

Sigurne froze and then slowly turned, as if avoiding something physical that Jewel herself couldn't see. She could see water; she could see that Sigurne was standing in it, and could see, as well, that the guildmaster wasn't any wetter for the experience.

"That is a question that has occupied many of the Order's researchers since the Order was founded. And no, Terafin, I have no answer. Or rather, I have too many, and I am certain of the validity of none of them."

"But this fountain was created by an Artisan."

"Some say it was created by *the* Artisan. And some say Fabril was not mortal; that he was not, in any true sense, maker-born. Fabril was many things to many people; he was rumored to exist at the dawn of time, under other names. If he created this monument, I can almost believe it."

"He created it," Jewel said.

"I see. Will you walk its path?"

"Path?"

Sigurne was silent for another beat.

"We don't see the same things when we look at this fountain," Jewel said, when the guildmaster did not immediately speak. "What the firstborn see, what the Arianni see, what other mortals see—all appear to be different. To me, you are standing in the middle of a stone pool into which water falls from the hands—and the eyes—of a large, alabaster statue. But you are not wet; the water that I see—and Sigurne, I can touch it—does not affect you. If you see a path here, or a path from the fountain, it's a path that is open to you."

The guildmaster bowed her head a moment, her chin dipping, her lowered face shrouded by shadows cast by the statue that Jewel had, for the first time, described in words, even if the words were scant. Sigurne left the fountain, left the water, and came to stand once again by Jewel's side.

"It is not," she said quietly, "a path that is open to me. A man you once knew specialized in relics that contained written or carved Old Weston, possibly Ancient Weston. Did he teach you much of it?"

Jewel blinked. "Are you talking about Rath? Ararath Handernesse?"

"Indeed."

The name echoed in the stillness. The fall of water, both within and beyond the castle's walls, did nothing to diminish the syllables. The import of the name seemed to diminish all other questions.

She could hear it; it seemed to break free of Sigurne's voice, and the echoes, like the resonant tail end of specific bells, were louder, larger, clearer.

"Jewel?"

"He taught me to recognize it so that I'd know what was valuable. To sell," she added, turning in the direction of the single word, the single name.

"Very well. The path I see leads to a . . . door. The door is engraved with runes I recognize as Old Weston; the work seems new, but it is maker-made; it might be millennia old."

"And the words?"

"I do not recognize them. I can repair to the Order and set my experts to translate. . ."

"You don't think it will help."

"I think the words that you cannot see are words that are nonetheless meant for you."

Jewel whispered a name. Once. Twice. A third time.

And the waters of the fountain parted, the hem of stone robes shifting as noiselessly as if they were of the lightest, finest silk.

Chapter Three

"**C**OUNCILLOR."

Haval lifted a hand but made no further motion; he demanded silence in all its forms. Had he not, Jester might not have heard Jay's voice. His own hands froze as what she was saying penetrated a stillness that allowed for no other noise.

The syllables died into stillness; the forest held its breath until forced—as Jester was forced, if he wished to retain consciousness—to exhale.

Then, motion returned.

The first thing to move was short and golden-furred. He walked around Haval's feet and came to stand before Jester, his nose raised in a lofty way that reminded Jester very much of the worst of the patriciate. He understood the demand inherent in the posture and folded his arms.

Haval, however, bent to one knee to offer the fox the seat he demanded; he rose, and the fox, held in his arms, rose with him.

"We do not know this *Ararath*," the fox said. "What is it?"

"Who," Jester said tersely.

No immortals appreciated being corrected. To Haval, the fox said, "Who is it?"

"A mortal of our acquaintance," Haval replied, his voice smooth and uninflected.

A fox face was not shaped for frowning; the elder had to settle for baring his teeth instead.

"He is dead."

The fox snorted. "Of course he is. But she is not mourning."

"No?"

"I am of her lands, Councillor, in a way that you are not. I know mourning when it is felt. Why does she speak his name so loudly? Why does she speak it so clearly?"

"They are very good questions," Haval replied. "And as is often the case with very good questions, there are no simple answers. But it is the question I have been asking myself. I believe I am wanted. I must set you down; I will have to return to The Terafin's side."

"And you will take *them* with you?"

Haval did not turn. Jester, however, did.

The Wild Hunt had gathered. The fact that their gathering had been silent was irrelevant; they stood upon a path that had widened to accommodate them. They were armed, armored, their platinum hair a spill down their glinting backs. They did not ride.

"Ah, no," Haval replied. He turned toward the Arianni, as if inspecting them. "Where," he finally asked, "is Lord Celleriant?"

"He has gone ahead," one of the Arianni answered. "So, too, Shianne and the firstborn."

"And Kallandras?"

"With Lord Celleriant."

"Very well. Your numbers are too great to take through the manor; your presence would cause alarm. We will have to approach The Terafin along a different path."

This was news to Jester.

"Will you go to The Terafin?"

"Yes. But I'd like to see this different path with my own eyes."

Haval did not argue. Instead, he turned to the right, which appeared to be composed of standing trees, and nodded.

Birgide Viranyi stepped from between the trunks. Or rather, she took a step forward, as if she had been standing in plain sight the entire time.

"You are Warden. The decision is yours."

"Jester ATerafin has the run of The Terafin's lands. All of them."

"Apologies; I was perhaps unclear in an attempt to be concise." Jester recognized the sarcasm that indicated a special type of Haval annoyance.

Birgide, however, was not Haval's subordinate. "I agree that the movement of the Wild Hunt through the manse is too risky. I am not entirely certain—" She stopped. To Jester, she said, "The Terafin's rooms are not what they were."

"No," Jester agreed. He was not surprised that Birgide knew this, although he was certain she had not been invited to view them herself.

"They are here," Birgide continued, when she failed to see any hint of comprehension or enlightenment across Jester's feature.

"You said they were always connected to the forest."

"Connected, yes. I could reach her rooms from any path in the forest. But the bridge between forest and her rooms had to be . . . built. The whole of those rooms overlooked domains of which she was not Lord. Now, they do not."

"And you have reservations?"

"Yes. I understand that the changes she makes are made subconsciously, but her state of mind is of grave concern to the Kings."

"To Duvari, you mean," Jester could not prevent himself from saying.

Birgide, however, didn't blink. "Strategically, a window into multiple lands might be desirable."

"To you."

"To us, Jester. To everyone who is not Jewel Markess ATerafin."

"She is Lord," the fox countered. "And it has not always been wise to allow other lands to trespass into ours. If she has made this change, it is for a reason."

Birgide inclined her head. "But it is not a reason she herself understands, and she has given stewardship of these lands to one of the merely mortal."

"Meaning you do not understand it."

Birgide did not answer.

Jester said, "I'll go through the house with Birgide."

"It is not—" Birgide began. Jester grabbed her by the arm and dragged her off, and after a very tiny resistance, she allowed this.

"You do understand," Jester said, trying to sidestep the mountainous bank of normal flowers that had appeared almost beneath his feet. "Birgide, it's me. I'm generally quiet and famously lazy, but I will hound you to death if you do not answer me."

"That is a poorly thought out threat."

"It is. I'll have cats hound you instead."

"Do *what?*"

Jester cursed.

"She isn't home yet," Birgide said quietly, giving Night the side-eye although she spoke to Jester. The cats acknowledged that she was Warden—whatever that mystical position meant to the wild—but accorded her the same respect they generally accorded The Terafin: none at all. "She means to make her home as safe as possible in her absence."

"She was absent before she built a castle in the middle of nowhere."

"Yes. She was. But the House Mage was here, and he was, for the moment, on our side."

"And now?"

"He will not be."

"Here, or on our side?"

"Here," Birgide said. "The latter, I do not know. But the forest elders fear that he will be one among the horde of enemies we will face. And we will face them soon. Can you not hear the horns?"

"No. The cats make too much noise."

Night stepped on his foot. As Jester cursed him, Night said, "*Now* who's making *noise?*" To Birgide, he said, "He can't *hear* them. He is *stupid.*"

"Stupid and deaf are not the same thing," Jester protested. He turned to Birgide and paused; she was smiling. He seldom saw her smile, but there was affection in it, and he was almost shocked to realize that she liked the cats. Or at least this one.

"He is *leaving*," Night continued, talking down his nose at Jester, which should have been awkward given the disparity in the heights of their noses. "He is *waking*. She *cannot* stay. She cannot leave him here. But if he is awake, he will be able to *enter*. There is nowhere he cannot walk."

"There is," Birgide said softly. "And as is often the case, it is the only place he desires to walk. She will walk there," she added.

"Who will?"

Night stepped on Jester's foot, even harder. "She won't take *you.*"

"No. She knows I'm useless."

Night nodded. Birgide, however, frowned.

"Please don't start," Jester said, waving a hand in front of her expression.

"She does not consider you useless. She does not consider any of her den useless."

Jester, uncomfortable, retrieved his foot from under Night's paw, which took effort.

"Your strengths are best utilized in the manse and in the city itself, where people live. And yes, she wishes you all to be safe—but she is not a child, ATerafin. She understands that safety is a gamble, an illusion. She would not, and has never, considered you a burden."

"She does. She doesn't call it that, but she does. If not for us, most of her fear would vanish. She's always wanted to keep us alive; she wanted us to be ATerafin because we were all too ignorant to imagine that people who had the name wouldn't be safe. Even her."

"You are wrong."

"I think I know her pretty well."

"I think you care about the den, and only the den—and you imagine that she's the same."

"I don't."

"Stop *squabbling*," Night said, snorting in disgust.

"That's rich, coming from you."

"I didn't *start* it."

Jester snorted back.

Birgide, however, was not fooled. "The Terafin almost died because a stranger's child was held hostage by a demon. She knew—who better to know it—that attempting to save that child was death. And she made the attempt anyway."

Jester didn't ask her how she knew because, in the moment, he didn't care.

"The whole of the city is composed of the children of strangers. They are not den. They have never met her, and given her lofty status, they likely never will. But she still sneaks out—or did, before she assumed the title—to visit the Common; she has friends there. Her den is her kin, her family. But her concerns for those outside that family are not yours.

"You were enraged when you thought Vareena had been abused by a member of the House. I do not believe you could turn your back on the rest of the world as easily as you believe you could. I could," she continued. "Duvari could. And your Haval?"

"He is *not* my Haval."

"He could."

"Not if his wife has anything to say about it."

Birgide smiled again. "I have yet to be formally introduced to his wife, and I doubt it will ever happen."

"You failed to list Jarven."

"I don't believe you enjoy it when I belabor the obvious."

That did make him smile. He was uneasy, however. "Hannerle isn't like her husband. She's louder, for one, and she's genuine. What she says, she believes. She might be wrong," he added, "but never deliberately. And she hates what Haval is now doing."

"Yet he does it."

"He does it because she hates what walking away would do to the rest of us more. She truly believes that Haval can somehow protect us—well, Teller and Finch. And she's inordinately fond of Finch. If she weren't, Haval wouldn't be here."

"You are so sure?"

Jester nodded. "Around his wife, he's a different man. No one—no one who wants to survive—would threaten his wife. I wouldn't, even if I had the Kings' own armies to back me up."

"And that is the only reason?"

Jester grimaced. "Hannerle is loud and bossy. And she nags. She is not my idea of restful companionship. Finch was genuinely sad when Hannerle left the West Wing. I think Jay was as well. But Haval *is* different with her. If he has a weakness, it's his wife. I don't know what Haval used to do before he met her, or married her, or became a clothier. But by this point, I can make an educated guess."

"And by this point you know enough that you would never do so publicly?"

"Got it in one. I don't like him," he added. "But I can't stand Jarven, and Haval is a small shield that can be placed between Jarven and the rest of the den."

"Is that how you see it?"

"I've got nothing against lying, as you well know, but I don't see the point in lying to you. Yes."

"One day, I'll tell you what little I know of his history."

"When he's dead?"

"It will be safer then, yes." She spoke so gravely, Jester almost missed the humor in the words, but it was there in the glint of her unnaturally colored eyes. Those eyes at the moment could pass for brown in poor light, but the galleries of the Terafin manse were not poorly lit.

"You tried," Birgide said, "to save me. I don't believe you're heartless. I do believe you wish you were. But believe it or not, Jester, it is you—and your chosen kin—who will define the shape of the city."

Jester snorted. "If it were up to me, she wouldn't be living in a castle."

"Funny."

He rolled his eyes. "I only like to be funny when it's a deliberate choice. What's funny?"

"Of all the den, I think you would be happiest in a castle. It's a fortification, and it's meant to repel invaders and discourage visitors."

After a long pause, Jester said, "Tell me about Meralonne."

And as they walked, she did. For a time after she had finished, Jester had nothing to say.

"Did you know Ararath?" Birgide asked.

"I lived with him for a couple of years."

This seemed to surprise her.

"Jay was living with Rath when we first met. It was Rath who found us, indirectly, when she decided to come searching. She meant to save Duster," he added. "The rest of us were afterthoughts."

"That's harsh."

Jester shrugged. "So's life. The manor at which we were held captive, and from which our services were sold, burned to the ground. Everyone alive, she rescued from the fire. When she realized we had nowhere to go, she took us in." He grimaced. "I really don't want to be talking about this."

"No. I apologize. But I hear his name almost as strongly as I hear hers. The forest is afraid," she added. "The Terafin will not stay, but none of the elders are certain how she intends to reach the Hidden Court of the Winter Queen. Even her own kin can no longer find it—and they have tried. I am not certain it was wise to bring them all here. They are not hers, and do not serve her; they serve only their queen.

"But the name is causing eddies. Haval recognizes it."

"He would. Jay would never have met him if it weren't for Old Rath." He paused, and then added, "Hectore would recognize it, as well."

They had reached the doors to The Terafin's inner chambers. The Chosen stopped them both, but it was entirely cursory; they could not keep these doors barred if Birgide chose to enter, and they both knew it. Birgide, however, bowed.

"Jester wishes to speak with The Terafin before her departure and has been summoned to do so." As far as Jester knew, this was a lie. But Birgide heard what the forest heard.

"And you came with him?"

"I intended to approach her rooms from the outside," Birgide replied. "But it is not a road that Jester can easily walk, and it would have delayed my ability to make my own report. The others," she added, "will take the longer route; there are some among them who would not be welcome in the manse but are accepted in the forest."

The Chosen nodded, as if the information was not news to them. Then again, when in this position, they could be set on fire and react the same way.

Birgide reached out to touch the door; it opened before her hand made contact with the wooden paneling that comprised it. Not for the Warden the regular handles.

He had been prepared for waterfalls, water, and a wet trek to a castle.

"Does this look like a waterfall to you?" Jester was standing at the gates of what he assumed was the castle Teller had described. The gates were open.

Through them, he could see Sigurne Mellifas—or so he assumed, given the color and the fall of her robes—and Jay. Torvan and Marave were to either side of her, stiff as boards; Avandar, however, was a step back. As was the gray, winged cat.

Night sauntered over to Shadow and stepped on his tail. Or tried.

"Why did you bring *him?*" The gray cat demanded.

"He followed me," Jester replied, before Night could. The black cat hissed in outrage, but before he could shred any part of Jester, Jay turned.

Her face was ashen. Her hands were fists. Her eyes were reddened, not with figurative rage, but tears held back. She swallowed.

He lifted his hands. *They're coming.*

"They can't, not yet. I have to speak with Gilafas."

"Unless you've got some convenient way to tell them to stay put, they're coming. I don't know how," he added. "Birgide probably has some idea."

Birgide, however, was staring at the fountain itself. Or at a statue that might once have been a fountain. Only a trickle of water remained in its basin. Her eyes, however, were now almost crimson in her otherwise pale face. Her hands were fists.

"They will come," Birgide finally said, as Jester thought to remove himself from the physical line of conversation. "They, too, hear the horns. The Sleepers are stirring."

Jay opened her mouth, but no words came, and after a pause in which she clearly struggled, she closed it again. She turned to Sigurne, and to Jester's surprise, Sigurne opened her arms and enfolded The Terafin in a hug. He wanted to call it maternal, but he had no experience with that.

"Can you see the road?" Jewel asked, from the region of Sigurne's shoulder.

And Birgide said, "Yes."

Jester could not see the road.

"That is because you are *stupid,*" Shadow told him. He had ambled over to where Jester stood. "Why are you *standing* there?"

"I'm stupid," Jester replied, not much caring about his dignity when it came to the cats.

Night hissed.

"Where's Snow?"

The black cat shrugged. "Who cares where *he* is?"

"We do," Jester replied. "Shadow, are you going with her?" Because he understood and accepted that Jay was leaving. She was leaving, and she had not said her good-byes to any of the den; Finch was at the Merchant Authority,

Teller in the right-kin's office, Arann with the Chosen. Angel and his friend were in the West Wing, not here; Jester realized that she might leave without Angel, and something in him rebelled.

He didn't want to interrupt Jay; not when she was all but clinging to Sigurne Mellifas. But Angel was the only part of them she was willing to take with her, and he wanted Angel here.

He turned to the gray cat. Shadow was watching him with speculative eyes. "Go get Angel."

The cat's eyes narrowed. "Why don't *you* get him?"

"I won't get there in time."

Night yawned. Loudly.

"What if she doesn't *want* him to follow?"

"Doesn't matter what she wants. She promised. And I know what he'll be like to live with if she leaves him here. I'm not going through that again."

"Oh?"

"Carver kept him in line. And Carver's—" He held breath, exhaled. "Carver's not here. I'm not his equal. Never was. Go get him, Shadow."

If cats could smile, Shadow did. "You are not *very* stupid," he said.

"He *isssss*."

"Where is Snow?"

"Why do *you* care?" Night demanded.

"Because she's only going to take Shadow," Jester finally replied. "Last time, she took you all. She didn't want to take the risk of leaving you behind. But this time, she'll only take Shadow—and actually, I'm not even certain about that."

Shadow's voice was a low-throated growl. "She *will*."

"What will they do when she's gone?"

"Do I *look* like *them*?"

"Yes."

Night hissed laughter. "He *is* very *stupid*." He twined a tail around Jester's left leg. "Maybe we will *eat* you."

Birgide snorted. "They will do what Meralonne did when he could trust himself enough to serve. Like the House Mage, when they fight, they're less difficult."

"They create difficulty," Jester replied, thinking of the bills that had landed on Teller's desk, the sums a staggering accusation of malfeasance.

"When they're bored, yes. I seldom hear them complain about boredom when they fight. Jarven was injured on our borders," she added, as if this would tip the scale that Jester appeared to be carrying.

"Jarven's not a match for the House Mage in outright battle."

Birgide said nothing. It was often her way of disagreeing when the discussion itself would yield little of practical use to her. "The cats will become Meralonne."

"We will be *better* than *him*," Night said, growing inches as he raised his head. He looked either regal or pretentious. Probably both.

Shadow evaporated. There was no other word for what happened to him as Night preened. Birgide didn't seem concerned, and Jay hadn't noticed, so Jester decided not to worry. He waited, his hands behind his back, until Sigurne released Jay.

Jay turned to him, her eyes sliding away from his.

And Jester exhaled. "I didn't blame you for Duster's death."

Her confusion was instant, genuine.

"I didn't blame you for Lefty, Lander, or Fisher."

Confusion receded. So, apparently, did breathing. He hated to have to say any of this; he was good with words precisely because he refused to give them any real meaning. He could talk for hours about nothing and be witty and entertaining. This kind of talk? It wasn't in him, not for long. And Birgide had already used up half of his annual allowance.

"I do not blame you for Carver. I don't blame you for not bringing him home. If what Ellerson told us is true, he chose." When she didn't respond, he continued. He accepted that he had to say this because he was the only one who had made clear that the rest of the world could burn in Carver's place if she brought Carver back.

And he had meant it, but Birgide had unsettled him.

"You left something with him you shouldn't have left. I personally love you for it. You know how I feel."

She did meet his eyes then, her own still tinged red with weeping for an entirely different man's loss.

"But I also know how Carver feels. He *chose*, Jay. It wasn't your fault the gods chose to bury the ancient princes beneath Averalaan. It isn't your fault that they're waking. Everything we're suffering now comes down to those two things. Carver isn't like me. He loves the servants. He loves the back halls. He loves the den. He's friendly in a way I'm not, and never want to be. People like him because he's Carver. Hells, I like him because he's Carver.

"If you did what *I* wanted, you'd have to go over his head. You'd have to ignore that he's Carver; you'd have to trample all over any choice he might make."

"He did it for us." Her first words.

"And? So did Duster. Doesn't make it any less their choice." He shoved his hands into his pockets. "I don't feel guilty. I know what happened isn't on me. Storms in harbor aren't on me, either. But you? You feel guilty.

"The fact that you *can* feel guilty, that part of you wants to protect us, is what we love. It's where we feel safe. Terafin is only home because you're here. You're The Terafin. And you didn't even want that. But guilt is double-edged. If you start to feel guilty about everything bad that happens, if you start to think it's all your responsibility, all the time, we're useless. We're impediments. We're the thing that makes your life difficult.

"I thought you'd learned that lesson, way back. Before we took the name. But maybe Shadow's right."

"I am *always* right," Shadow said. "About *what?*"

"Me being stupid," Jay said.

"Oh, *that*." To Jester, the gray cat said, "He's coming."

"And Adam?"

Jay said, "He's staying."

Jester withdrew his hands from his pocket and signed.

Jay signed back, this time. *I want him here.*

He can help.

Not where we're going.

Anywhere.

She shook her head. "Adam is staying. I expect you two," she added, to Night and the absent Snow, "will keep him safe. Do you understand that? My part of this whole war is mine to shoulder—but he has a role to play, and that's his. I'm leaving him here, and I expect he will be whole, healthy, and uninjured when I come back." She then returned to Jester. "I'd like to leave Angel as well."

"No dice."

"If—and it's an if—we make it to the Hidden Court, he might be at risk."

"It's not me you have to convince," Jester said, raising both of his hands. "It's Angel. And frankly, what you just said wouldn't convince me, so you're going to have to work harder. Jay, it's his choice. We were kids when you found us. You were a kid yourself.

"We're not kids now. Finch is regent of arguably the most powerful of The Ten. Teller is right-kin. Arann is Chosen. Daine is needed in the healerie. I'm useless, but I've made my peace with that. We're your mortal face. We're not talking trees or foxes or cats. We talk to the people in Averalaan, and we react to them. If they play games—and they do and will—we're there to block them. If we die, we die. But we'd've died if you'd never met us. All of us except maybe Arann and Daine. Don't turn us into a burden."

"Terafin," Birgide said quietly.

Jewel looked past the Warden, through the open castle gates. She then signed again. She looked as if she would hug Jester, and he stiffened; he could endure hugs from den-kin but had never enjoyed them and probably never would.

Remembering this, she stopped, her lips quirked in a familiar, rueful grin. She pushed her hair out of her eyes. "I wasn't always like this."

"No. Before, we were all helpless, and therefore we were all equal. You needed us then."

"I need you now," was the fervent reply. "I need you to remind me. I need you to say what you just said. I don't have to *be* a god. I just have to be myself."

Shadow grimaced and yowled. "Boring. Boring, boring, *boring.*"

"Tell Finch and Teller—"

"No, please, don't make me deliver sentimental messages. Unless you want to take the time to write them, in which case, feel free."

She laughed. He would remember that later. She laughed.

He did open his arms then, a bit stiffly. He did offer the hug that she was certain would be an imposition. It was awkward, but he hadn't lied to her; he was not comfortable with obvious sentiment. In that, he was more like Duster than any of the rest of the den.

And she accepted it, the gesture grander to her than any of the obvious trappings of wealth or power. Her grip was gentle, even tentative, and he felt two things: her trembling, and the sudden difference in their size. Jester was not tall, would never be tall—but he was taller than Jay. Taller, broader. If he had ever paused to think, it would make sense, but he had never paused to think of it, not this way. And so he was confronted with the unwelcome sense that she was small, that she was slight, possibly too slight for the weight she had willingly shouldered.

And then she pulled back. Her smile was fragile, but it was there, and it was entirely hers; he had seen that smile at twelve years of age, and at every age that followed. She pushed her hair out of her eyes, and that, too, was familiar. Only when her hair was utterly and completely pressed flat and confined did it stay where it was put.

She did not leave, not immediately. She stayed in the courtyard, Sigurne by her side, until the Arianni arrived. They came on foot, and they offered her the obeisance due a lord in Weston lands; she accepted it without comment, as if it were her due. Calliastra came with Shianne and Celleriant, and behind them, silent and graceful, Kallandras of Senniel College.

She waited, still, until Angel arrived, wetter than the Arianni—of course he was—but ready for the road. Beside Angel came Terrick, and beside them, Snow. Last came the great white stag. He approached her, passing through the ranks of the Arianni to do so, and when he knelt to the ground, bending supple legs, she nodded and mounted his back.

True to her commands, there was no Adam. Jester didn't like it, but he understood why she wanted to leave him behind. He was young, and he was kind. As a healer, he had not been raised to war. Ah, but he hadn't been raised a healer. And he knew the effects of war, and the cost to those who did not have the power to flee or to fight. Adam had seen as much death and destruction as Jester, in half the time.

Jay looked down at Snow and Night. "I'm leaving my home in your hands," she said. "I'm certain you can do a *much* better job than Meralonne at defending it."

"Of *course* we can," Night said.

"Everything of import is here. Everything. Guard it well."

No one asked where she was going. But Celleriant drew close—as close as Avandar—and she allowed it. Seeing her this way, it was hard to imagine that she had been a petty thief in the hundred holdings. It was hard to imagine that she belonged to a den—any den, anywhere.

Last, very last, came Haval, the man the forest denizens called Councillor.

"Listen to Finch and Teller," she said, her voice drifting into something less grand, less mythical. "The forest trusts you because I trust you—but listen to them. There are prices that I cannot pay and survive, and they understand them well. Listen," she continued, "to Jester."

"For my sake," Jester said, lifting a hand, "I'd like you to withdraw the last one."

Her smile was her own. "I bet you would. I'm doing everything I can—even the things I don't know I'll have to do until they're right in front of my face. But I need—" She stopped. "You know what we were. Keep as much of the good parts alive as you can."

"I will have you know," Haval said, "that my wife has issued the same orders—and in far less friendly language." He bowed to her then. He bowed as if she were the Kings. "Return to us, Terafin."

The road that Jester couldn't see was obviously there because Jay began to walk it; the waters of the fountain swallowed her. None of the men and women gathered here were as blind as Jester now was: they followed in her wake, disappearing from view.

Birgide waited until the last of the travelers had vanished and then turned to him, an odd half-smile across her lips. "That was well done, ATerafin."

"And my reward is a stodgy title?"

"Your name, but if you prefer, Jester." She grimaced. "That can't be the name you were born with."

"Probably not. It's the name I prefer. What was well done, by the way? I don't hear a lot of praise, so if you could be more explicit, I'd appreciate it." He grinned.

She didn't. "We should leave. You'll need to speak with Teller, and possibly Finch." To Sigurne, who had remained behind in the wake of the company, she bowed. It was a low bow. She did not—as Jay would have done—offer the guildmaster her arm.

Jester, sighing inwardly, stepped in with his, which the guildmaster accepted without comment. She was still gazing at the fountain.

"Do you know where they're going?"

"For the first leg of their journey? Yes."

"Will you share without demanding an arm or leg in return for the information?"

Sigurne frowned. "Because you are hers, yes. They are going to Fabril's reach."

"With an army?" Jester's shock was only partly feigned.

"Fabril's reach is an uncharted wilderness that is, in the opinion of our experts, the equal of your Terafin's forest. If that army intends harm there, they will be sundered from the Lord they have chosen to ally themselves with. She will, however, continue."

Birgide said, "Fabril made this fountain."

"That is our belief, yes."

"Could he know what would happen here?"

"I have never understood Artisans. I would say yes, but he was not seerborn. Perhaps he understood that in the heart of the wilderness, some way must exist that could reach the heart of his own domain. The fountain did not appear until Jewel declared herself. Fabril was, by all accounts, mortal. And his time is centuries past."

But Jester, thinking of the Terafin spirit, said nothing.

He was afraid of only one thing: Ararath Handerness. Old Rath. Nothing appeared to happen in these forests by accident, and nothing by coincidence, and she had spoken Rath's name so clearly that all of the forest had heard it. Even Jester, who was an outsider there.

Chapter Four

JEWEL FOLLOWED THE ROAD that Sigurne had opened. She knew that were she to put it that way to the magi, the old woman would demur, and might even do so in the honest belief that her denial was true. But she *knew* that the road would not have opened were it not for Sigurne Mellifas' presence.

The Winter King was silent. His hooves were silent as well; he didn't appear to be touching the road at all.

You said you could walk any road that the Winter Queen has walked.

Yes.

So . . . she walked here?

She has had cause to enter your city, your Empire, before. But yes. I recognize the feel of this path, and the air tastes familiar.

It tasted like winter to Jewel. The air was cold enough that mist rose from the collective breaths of the people who had joined her.

Are these my lands? she asked the Winter King.

No, Jewel. Can you not hear the name of their Lord?

No. But I can't hear my own name in my lands, either. What you hear, what the elders hear, what the cats hear, I don't. I'm mortal.

These are Fabril's lands. This is part of Fabril's reach. Tell me, did you know that you could walk from your lands to his?

No. And yet, she had taken the path. She had known that she must.

The Wild Hunt was as silent as the Winter King, and their silence was charged, like clouds in the full thrall of thunderstorm, waiting to shed lightning. Jewel glanced at them briefly, and then turned her eyes to the road. It was composed of almost pristine stone block, as if it had been built very recently, but never traveled. There were stone roads in the city, but they chipped, they cracked, they became homes to persistent, stubborn weeds; this was like the ideal of those roads.

They had been built in a land without people, without carriages, without wagons. Those creatures that might exist to either side of its parallel borders didn't require roads. As a shadow crossed above them all, she thought some didn't require feet; she looked up.

The sky was a shade of winter blue, and indeed, beyond the road the landscape seemed to solidify. Snow. Snow, she thought, and trees that were unlike the trees in her own forest. They seemed things of bark and ice and silence.

But snow did not touch this road.

What do you know of Fabril? she asked her domicis.

Very little that is objective. I know the stories. I did not live in these lands when Fabril lived, and by all accounts, he was mortal. But he was considered a maker without parallel.

Is this his work?

That, Terafin, I could not tell you. We guess, when we view astonishing work, that it was maker-made. The Artisans, however? No. Things crafted by gods might be considered Artisan-made by those who did not see the gods at work.

Could you tell the difference?

Silence again.

You saw the gods at work. Tell me, do you think this was crafted by a mortal?

It has never been wise to interfere in the games of gods, he replied. He said, and would say, no more, but his answer was answer enough.

Tor Amanion. Winter King.

I have not walked this road before. But the White Lady has, at least once. More than that, I cannot say. He glanced at the Winter Host, gleaming as they were in their silent, focused march.

Cannot or will not?

A glimmer of amusement reached her. *Cannot, Jewel. This road has never been walked by the Wild Hunt assembled here, but they recognize the heart of Winter when they see it. Watch Shianne.*

She did. It was easy to watch Shianne once one started, and much, much harder to look away. They had seen snow in the lands in which they had first met. A lot of snow. More snow in aggregate than Jewel had probably seen in her life. But that snow and this snow were clearly different to Shianne; to Jewel, it was almost indistinguishable.

Shadow hissed laughter. He walked alongside the Winter King, his head far enough below Jewel that she couldn't easily clamp a hand between his ears. She could probably fit a foot there, but the results of that were unpredictable, at best. She settled for a glare, which caused his hissing to increase in volume.

The cats were not natural liars. They lied the way young children did: obviously and badly. The great gray cat was genuinely amused. But there was a different quality to the amusement. Although he was aware of Jewel, he was also watching Shianne.

Her eyes were round with wonder, her cheeks faintly rosy, her lips parted as if to speak, although no words escaped. She turned to the Wild Hunt, and then away, remembering at the last that she was no longer one of them.

But Celleriant said, "You have not seen Winter before."

I don't understand what the difference is, Jewel said to the Winter King. *We've seen so much snow in the wilderness.*

Winter—your winter—is not the Winter of the hidden world.

But—but the Oracle's winter—

No, Jewel. This, this is: it is the first snow, the first, fallen snow. It is the start of the White Lady's choice.

Silence.

"Celleriant."

"Lord."

"Tell me, is this the first snow of the hidden world?" Her breath came out in a wreath of mist.

"Do you not feel it, Lord? We are all, for a moment, young again, and the world, at its dawn."

She shook her head, and he looked at her with something that might have been pity.

"I see it only through you. Through you, the Wild Hunt, and Shianne."

"The world holds its breath here. The hush is the hush of anticipation. This is the first Winter—and here, the horns cannot reach. Have you not noticed the silence?"

"No," she said truthfully. "Is that a castle?"

The road was not entirely straight, and if snow did not touch it, branches grew above it; she could not be certain what she glimpsed in the distance through the bare, overhanging branches was. Angel's sight was better, and he answered in Rendish, flushing as he realized his mistake.

Jewel asked the question again in Torra to tease her den-kin, and when he grimaced she realized it had been a while since she'd seen that expression. It was rueful, amused, chagrined. It was home. She couldn't remember, for a moment, why she'd wanted to leave him behind.

"Yes," he replied, in distinct Weston. "It's a castle."

"Like mine?"

"I only saw yours from the gates. And Shadow was walking on my feet, so I wasn't paying as much attention as I could."

Shadow muttered something that had a lot of *stupid* in it.

"But?"

"But I'd almost say we've been walking backward if it weren't for all the snow."

Jewel nodded. She felt obscurely better; the castle that she thought she could see looked like it was twin to the one that had awaited her upon her return—and, clearly, that wasn't because it was her own desire.

That should not be a comfort to you. Avandar's inner voice was sharp, but it was not chilly. He was annoyed.

It's a comfort that a castle wasn't entirely my own idea. It's a comfort that there's no part of my sleeping mind that wants to be locked a mile or more away from my den and the rest of my home. She exhaled. *It's a comfort because Fabril had something to do with it, and Fabril made the weapons that the Kings wield. If they trust his work, I feel like I can.*

This did nothing to mollify her domicis. Avandar was probably right. But she was surrounded by the Arianni. She could not imagine an enemy action that could destroy them all—and Shadow, and Avandar, and Kallandras who survived anything. In a strange way, she had never been safer than she was now.

And she would never be safer again.

The thought came, and the cold came with it, and she understood that this certainty was her gift speaking. She accepted it; she couldn't change it, couldn't argue with it. But she also thought: if it can't be changed, if it's true, why can't I relax for another mile or two? Why can't I look at the world and see it as beautiful?

It was.

Angel was here. Shadow. Avandar. And Shianne was painfully, breathtakingly beautiful because she could not entirely contain her delight; it burst through the chilly perfection of her neutral expression and made her eyes seem incandescent. Jewel could well imagine throwing the entirety of her life away if she could cause that smile, that wonder, to bloom again under her own power.

But how much more, she thought, would she throw away to see that expression on Calliastra's face? She turned; the daughter of darkness walked ahead of

Angel and Terrick, as far from the Wild Hunt as she could. What she thought of this Winter, what she thought of this road, what she thought of Shianne, she kept to herself; she walked gracefully, lightly, as befit a child of gods—but she did not turn to look back at Jewel, not once, and the shadow of black wings seemed to be struggling to emerge from a faint, dark smudge of shadow.

The castle, like Jewel's castle, appeared almost unoccupied. Calliastra stopped at the gates, which were closed; Jewel nudged the Winter King forward, although it was unnecessary. There was some juggling for position as Terrick examined the area around what should have been a gatehouse, barking Rendish orders to Angel, which were obeyed with alacrity.

They had to stop their inspection and move back as the gates opened, parting more like curtains than the wood and iron they appeared to be. The road they had followed continued past those gates to the main building, but between the familiar line of recessed arches at the height of a gentle slope of stairs and those gates was a fountain.

Were it not winter in the world beyond the castle grounds, Jewel might have thought she'd led her party in a circle. She could see alabaster, a figure that had walked out of The Wayelyn's song; it was larger than life, as befit a bardic lay.

"No matter where or how you look," a familiar voice said, "you will not find a different answer." Master Gilafas ADelios was waiting beside the fountain. Were it not for his voice, she might not have recognized him; he was dressed as a traveling merchant might dress, and not the ruler of the most powerful guild in the Empire.

"Where is my butterfly?"

Jewel was by now accustomed to the guildmaster. She did not take offense at the question that preceded the unusual greeting; indeed, she expected no usual greeting. "With the bard. He is coming," she added.

He frowned. "You bring a bard with you?"

"He has traveled with me since the beginning of my journey; I expect he will see it to the end. No mission he has been given has managed to kill him. Rumor has it that he has often been the only man standing at the end of the most difficult of his tasks."

"And you gave him my butterfly?" He seemed agitated.

"No. The butterfly chose to shelter with him. And before you ask, I don't know why."

"I will see this bard."

"Yes. Shortly." She looked at his clothing.

"I have something for you."

She wanted to tell him that he had given her more than enough, but there was as yet little gratitude in her. So she chose to wait. She was surprised when Calliastra approached the guildmaster and, judging by his expression, so was he.

The darknessborn daughter, however, did not speak or demand an introduction, not directly. "This is your Artisan?" she said to Jewel.

"He is not, as I said before, mine. But he is the Artisan I mentioned, yes."

Her dark eyes narrowed. "You are prepared for travel," she said, this time addressing Gilafas directly.

He frowned at her but did not turn away; his expression was almost troubled. "I am prepared for travel yes, and in the cold. It was cold, the last time I ventured into these lands, and I do not think them markedly changed."

"Are you aware of the possible dangers you will face?"

His expression stiffened then, the lines almost becoming cracks in the rigidity of his face.

Jewel dismounted, the motion light and almost graceful. She came to stand beside Calliastra, placing a hand on the godchild's shoulder. "This is Calliastra," she said, before Gilafas could speak. "And this is Master Gilafas ADelios, of the makers. He is the head of the Guild of Makers."

"I cannot imagine," the guildmaster said, "that any danger I might face on the road would be a greater threat than you."

Calliastra stiffened, and Jewel cursed inwardly, but this at least would be unlikely to wound Calliastra's pride. Before she could reply, Shadow stepped on the godchild's foot. The cats habitually stepped on people's feet; it was their petty way of sulking or pulling invisible rank. They seldom—if ever—tried this with Calliastra.

"*We* are more *dangerous* than *she* is," Shadow said, tailing swishing as he spoke.

Calliastra turned her glare on the gray cat, folding her arms as she did. "You are not more dangerous to mortals."

"We *eat* them!"

"Oh?"

Angel signed something, briefly and quickly; Jewel grimaced but kept her hands by her sides.

"Calliastra is concerned for your safety," she told Gilafas, squeezing the words beneath the clipped sentences of growing argument between winged cat and goddess. "She values the maker-born highly—far more highly than the simple seer-born or any of the other talent-born. She feels it is too dangerous for you to travel with us."

"It is too dangerous for you to leave me behind," he countered, fully behind his own eyes now, the odd and almost compelling feyness banished by her words. His smile was chilly. "I am not a child and, as you have said, not a possession. There is only one thing I desire of my life before its end, and you are the only possible avenue to achieve it. You will take me with you, Terafin." It was not a request.

"Yes," she said. "I promised. I have no intention of leaving you behind if this is what you truly wish."

His expression softened slightly. "You are young. But so was she. Have I told you of my apprentice? I lost her to the Wild Hunt and the Winter Queen. But before that I almost lost her to the halls and the rooms and the dungeons; she wandered much farther in Fabril's reach than any before her who were also known to survive." As he spoke, his voice softened as well. "She was an Artisan. She was an Artisan matched only by Fabril—and in my opinion, that might be generous to Fabril.

"I have never seen a man or woman so driven to *create*. She could forget to speak, forget to eat, forget to stop; she worked her hands bloody on several occasions. The pages and the servants that could navigate Fabril's reach— maker-born, all—had one task by the end of her time here: to find her, to follow her, to feed her, and if these could not be done, to find me so that I might do them.

"I was guildmaster, yes—but she was the heart of the guild. I did not see it at first, but I see it every day in her absence. The butterflies are hers. They fill my chambers with the echo of her voice. They have come to me consistently, in ones and twos. Sometimes there are tiny, glass birds. All of their voices are hers.

"She is alive, Terafin. She is alive, and I mean to find her."

"If she can make those butterflies, she might be happy."

"Ah. I am a selfish, selfish man—and I am not happy." He bowed to her then, as if finally remembering that she was The Terafin, ruler herself of one of the most powerful Houses in the Empire. He glanced at the gathered Arianni, who were still entering the courtyard, and frowned.

Then he looked at Avandar, deigning to see a servant for the first time, and he held out a carefully padded rectangle. "Take this, please, and guard it with your life."

Angel choked.

Avandar, however, bowed and retrieved the package from the guildmaster's hands, silent and graceful, as if he were truly a servant, and not the immortal known as the Warlord.

"I have a few things I brought with me," Gilafas continued. "They will, I hope, ease our passage. The road that you have followed does not continue indefinitely, and where we walk, there will be no roads."

"Will it be Winter everywhere?"

"It is only Winter here," Gilafas replied. He walked away before Jewel could ask him how he knew, but in truth she wasn't certain she would have. She had *known* so many things in her life, and in her childhood, being asked how had almost been torture, because she'd had no answers she could give that would have made sense to her parents. Her Oma, however, had believed her. Believed her and forbid her to speak of her certainties, to attempt to use them.

Only after the old woman had died had she begun to push the boundaries of those early demands. Finch was alive. Teller was alive. The gift itself became something more than a curse or a shameful secret because of them. And because it was more, it had become a precious burden. She would carry it until she could carry nothing at all, not even memories.

"We should leave," he said, clearly expecting to be obeyed. She understood that, too. He was a man of such wealth, such consequence, that he didn't have to fit in; people moved to make way when he walked, and people practically abased themselves in his presence.

"Yes," she agreed. She turned to give the order to the man who seemed to be the spokesman for the Arianni present, saving only Celleriant and Shianne.

"But I want to speak with your bard."

"He is not *my* bard, but he is my companion, and I am certain he would be pleased to speak with you." And if he wasn't, he was Senniel trained; he could affect delight and interest without feeling either.

Master Gilafas had prepared for a journey of perhaps two weeks, judging from the pack upon his shoulders. He carried it as if he were a much younger man, and only when he set it down for the first time did Jewel understand why; it weighed almost nothing. It was thick and sturdy and well-made, of course—but the leather itself seemed to weigh less than the sheerest and finest of silks. The contents of the bag likewise appeared to weigh nothing while nested in the bag.

The bag, however, contained far more than the normal packs that Jewel otherwise carried. Whatever Gilafas pulled out of that bag was unwrinkled, as if gravity and weight within the pack's interior were held in abeyance. And, judging by some of the food, time as well.

"Fabril made this," Gilafas said conversationally. "It is seldom used, and when it is, it is used only by the guildmaster." The last was said modestly and factually, as if he were explaining the function of an umbrella or an oilskin. He drew a cloak out of the bag and handed it to Jewel. "This, however, was made by my apprentice. Wear it," he added. "I believe it was intended for you."

"I've never met your apprentice."

"No, of course not," he replied, with evident confusion.

"I believe," Kallandras interjected, "that The Terafin feels it could not have been made specifically for her in that case."

This seemed to make no more sense to the guildmaster than Jewel's comment, and as a man of power, he was accustomed to ignoring nonsensical words from his subordinates or inferiors, his tolerance implying that such ignorance was bewilderingly constant. Jewel almost laughed. But he *was* a man of power, and she knew better.

The Wild Hunt gathered around him in brief periods of activity, examining—discreetly—the cloak, the pack, and even the food.

Kallandras, however, put Gilafas immediately at ease. Or perhaps it was the butterfly, which nestled on the bard's shoulder. Only when he approached Gilafas did it rise; it flew to the guildmaster's face, fluttered around in a dance of gentle light, and then returned once again to Kallandras. During this time, the guildmaster forgot whatever it was he had been doing—eating, in this case—to stare at it with something like heartbreak and longing.

But he did not ask the bard to return it. And perhaps it was, in part, the presence of the butterfly on the bard's shoulders that made the guildmaster comfortable. The Arianni found the butterfly disturbing but were similarly awestruck when it wove light across the air, leaving only its after-impression as proof that it had happened at all.

They reached the end of the road by the middle of what Jewel assumed was the day. The road ended at a cliff, as if some force of nature had seen the road, found it displeasing, and sheared away the land beneath it in one abrupt gesture of displeasure.

To this point, the snow had avoided the road, and when they stopped, they made an odd, elongated camp upon the pristine stone itself.

Angel signed; Jewel shrugged. But the shrug would not carry her far, and she knew it. Almost as one, people looked to her for instructions or commands, as if her life to this point had taught her how to traverse the empty air.

"Can you see what's on the other side?" she asked her den-kin.

Angel frowned.

"Is there road?"

"I . . . don't think so."

"Snow? It looks white to me."

He hesitated, and then turned to say something in Rendish. Terrick batted the back of his head with gruff good humor. Sensitive to Jewel, however, he said, "My eyes are not what the boy's are, either."

Angel, in his thirties, was no boy, but Jewel did not correct the Northerner. "He has faith in you," she said instead.

"Aye, and it's no blessing to have impossible faith laid on a man as a burden."

She did smile then.

Jewel.

I can't fly.

No. You cannot. Avandar turned to look at Kallandras. The bard had not moved until that moment, but rose—literally rose, his feet leaving stone, his body leaving Lord Celleriant's side—and headed toward Jewel. She wondered, then, if there was anything he did not notice, anything about which he was not almost preternaturally aware.

"Terafin," he said, coming to ground where he could then offer her the most correct of bows.

"We are not in the Terafin manse; we are not in Averalaan." He did not move, and she surrendered. "Rise."

"You wish me to ask the wind to bear us across this divide." The last syllable canted up, as if it were a question.

"It is unnecessary," Shianne said, before Jewel could answer, although she was well away from the edge of this unnatural cliff. "You have forgotten those who travel with us. For the hunt, even unmounted, this is not inconvenient. And you yourself can cross on the back of your stag."

"Not everyone is the Wild Hunt." Nor did she want them to be.

"No, Terafin. Order the hunt across, and they will obey. Order them to see your grounded companions across, and they will likewise obey. You are ruler, and you are Sen; you must by this time understand the value of, the necessity of, command." She fell silent, but she was not done.

She lifted her pale arms; she did not wear armor, nor did she wear the winter clothing that girded all other mortals in this place. She wore only the dress that Snow had so reluctantly made for her, and Jewel thought, with a flash of the intuition that had guided her life, that it would be the last dress she wore.

Her hair began to move in winds that did not touch the rest of the company, and her eyes—her oddly silver eyes, so arresting in a mortal face—to glow as well, as if they were either polished silver or steel. The hem of her skirt began to twist in a way that was not consistent with the wind that touched her hair, and although the skirts were nothing like the robes worn by Evayne a'Nolan, Jewel thought of them as she watched.

And in all of this, she was most aware of the fact that Shianne was pregnant, visibly, notably pregnant; that Shadow or the Winter King should have the keeping of her, should carry her across the emptiness. She thought of the emptiness, then, and shouted a single word as if it were the whole of her thought.

"*No!*"

Shianne froze, although the wind still swept across her, and turned her perfect face toward Jewel Markess. Jewel flushed almost scarlet and forced herself to close her mouth on the instant, groveling apology that was her first response.

"No," she said again. "Not you, not the Wild Hunt, and no, not the Master Bard. My apologies. I did not recognize—" She stopped. Did not recognize what, exactly? Air? Cliff? The sudden drop?

The emptiness.

She turned to Avandar; he was waiting, his hands by his sides. But he met and held her gaze, and after a brief pause, he nodded.

"We can't go this way," she said.

The guildmaster frowned. "I believe if the road was built to this point, we were meant to cross it."

"And I believe that if we were meant to cross it, it would not have been so easily destroyed." But even that felt wrong. She turned to the guildmaster, but so did the bard, for the butterfly was singing.

Its song was soft and persistent, but easily missed, at least to start. Kallandras' head was tilted to one side, as if to better catch the nuances of music that Jewel could only barely hear, although she was closest to him, saving only the Winter King. She leaned forward and leaned again; the song buzzed around the edges of audibility, and she felt almost an ache at the echo of familiarity, as if she had heard and loved this song in the past but could not immediately recall when.

Can you hear it? she finally asked her domicis and the Winter King.

No, Jewel, Avandar answered gravely.

The Winter King was silent for a much longer beat. *I hear what you hear,* he finally said. *And perhaps I hear it only because you hear it. It is not a Winter voice; it is not the song of the White Lady or her kin. What does it mean to you?*

She shook her head. *Nothing. But it feels like it might, should I truly recall it.* She turned, once again, to the divide. The emptiness here was not the emptiness of air, as it had first appeared. It was a thin mist, a translucent fog. It reminded her of dreams, of dreaming.

And dreams shifted and changed constantly and without predictability.

"No," Shadow said, "they do not. Not *here*." He looked up at her with golden eyes. He waited, but he was a cat and did not wait patiently, and while Jewel absorbed his words, he lifted a paw, examined his sheathed claws, and then whacked the Winter King's right forefoot. Had the Winter King been mortal, had he been, in truth, a stag, that blow might have snapped his leg; as it was, the leg buckled.

Jewel slid off the stag's back.

"Are you *ready*?" Shadow demanded, his voice more roar than speech.

She could have said no, since it was the truth, but it didn't matter. She had come to understand that readiness in the wild was a state of mind, because the wilderness, like dreams themselves, was treacherous; it changed constantly. She mounted the great, gray cat's back while her company watched her. She was surprised when Angel said, "Move over."

Shadow hissed, but Angel was not of a mind to care; he wedged himself onto Shadow's back, with much less cooperation for mounting than Jewel had received.

"We don't *need* him," Shadow sniffed, in a much more normal voice.

"*You* don't need him," Jewel countered. Angel sat astride the cat and behind her. She understood that if she were lost here, he would be lost with her, but she smiled; he couldn't see it.

"What do you see?" she asked him. "Your vision has always been better than mine."

"I see clouds," he said.

Jewel didn't.

"I see clouds. When I was a kid, we used to lie in the long grass looking up at them. We'd call shapes," he added. "When the wind blew, the clouds shifted. It was a game."

"What shape would you call here?"

He slid his arms around her, as if to brace either her or himself. "Here? I'd be afraid to call any. Things have a way of answering."

"They do," she agreed. She closed her eyes. "They do." Inhaled, exhaled, and opened them again. She could now see Angel's clouds—she would always think of them as Angel's clouds, thereafter—as wind pushed them around the sky. "Can you see the other side?"

A beat of silence. "Can't you?"

"I can—but it's foggy for me. Not fuzzy, just . . . shrouded."

Another beat. Not what Angel saw, then. But Angel hadn't seen what she had seen when she'd ridden up the trunk of a wild tree to find and, in the end, save Celleriant. She had trusted his vision then because she knew that what she saw was not the whole of what was there.

It had been real. Celleriant had been close to the surrender that was death for the Arianni. But it had not been the only reality in that space. The concept of two coexisting realities was difficult for her. The certainty that she could not trust her own eyes to reveal reality made all of reality suspect, unstable.

But she knew that two people could hear the exact same words and derive different meanings from them. She knew that they could witness an event and their stories afterward made the event itself seem as unstable, as changeable, as Angel's clouds.

This was not the first time she had experienced such a dislocation. The first time—the first time that she was aware of—had been in the Stone Deepings. In the Stone Deepings, she had met the Winter Queen. In the Stone Deepings, she had been given the Winter King and Lord Celleriant, as penalties to each for their failures.

She is Winter, the Winter King said. *And the Winter is harsh.*

What was she like in the Summer, then?

He did not answer.

She had faced Ariane. She did not lie to herself; she could not have destroyed the Winter Queen. Victory was simply barring her path for as long as Scarran lasted, and that, Jewel could do.

And how?

She almost smiled. How, indeed.

"Mortals are *so boring,*" Shadow growled. She could feel the rumble of his words where her thighs had tightened for purchase around his body.

"Yes, we are. Have you considered finding a master who isn't?"

He sputtered in pure outrage. "Master? *You?*" He roared into the wilderness, and Jewel thought she could hear the echoes of similar outrage from the two cats she had left in the Terafin manse. The two failed to emerge, for which she was grateful, as Shadow's outrage was only half-pretend.

She had ridden on cat-back over her city before. Had anyone asked her, in her distant youth, if she loved her city, she would have stared at them as if they were trying to grow an extra head, the question would have seemed so irrelevant. The city simply was. It went on around her no matter what happened in her life; it had continued to move when her mother died, when her Oma had joined her, and when, at the very end, her father had failed to come home from the docks. It had continued its commerce, its noise, its religions, its festivals. The Common had not stopped at all. The city clearly hadn't cared for her—how on earth could she love it?

Half a lifetime later, the answer was different, and it was simple: Yes.

Yes, she loved her city. Her city included Farmer Hanson. Her city included Helen. Her city included Hectore and Sigurne. She considered the den so much a part of her that she couldn't separate them, but they lived with her, and she lived in the city.

Some doubtful part of her said, *You love the city* now *because you're not starving and you're no urchin.* And maybe that was true. Maybe the distance from that poverty and desperation made everything easy enough that she no longer resented it. But if she could ask Helen the same question, Helen would say yes. Helen was not of The Ten, nor would she ever be.

And it didn't matter.

Even when she had lived in the hundred, there were men and women who had tried—as they could—to help. Not all of them, no. But Jewel herself could not reach out a hand to every person she walked by. Building her den had been an act of instinct and need.

Duster.

And maybe a deliberate flouting of some of those instincts. She had stood on the road in the Stone Deepings, had held her ground against the Wild Hunt, because she had always had the city; it had always been part of her. Both the poverty and the wealth, the kind and the cruel, the powerful and the powerless. It was not a living entity, of course, but it was *like* one: it encompassed too many things to be all of only one of them.

There were bridges, in her city.

There were roads.

There were great trees that were easily taller than all but a few of the buildings man had made beneath their branches.

Here, Jewel thought, there should be trees. There should be paths that wound their way around them. There should be leaves—and she had leaves. Leaves of silver, of gold, of diamond. But leaves, as well, of the great trees, so like the ones she had gathered as a child, as if they were flowers or delicate toys. The joy had been in the gathering, not the possession.

There was joy now, in letting them go.

There was no ground beneath her feet; nothing into which the leaves might land and take root. Or so it appeared to Jewel as Shadow flew over the cliff at which Fabril's meticulous road ended. But no leaf—no real leaf—was a seed. No real leaf could take root and emerge, in the blink of an eye, at its full growth, its full majesty. What these leaves needed, they would find anywhere. Anywhere at all.

She did not hold her breath. She did not pray. For a moment, Angel at her back and Shadow beneath her, his voluble complaints far louder than something as simple as wind at a height, she *knew*. Those trees would grow. This land was not hers; she understood that. She couldn't live here, couldn't live in it, and couldn't therefore be *of* it. But the trees and the forest? They could. And they *were* hers.

Ownership of anything that lived and grew was complicated, complex.

She saw the branches spread to cover the emptiness that existed at the cliff's edge; saw the white-fringed green of familiar leaves bud and bloom in the winter air. She heard—what did she hear? Something like song, something that was almost familiar.

A butterfly's voice.

A forest's voice.

"*So boring*," Shadow said, but with less growl in the words.

"Can we land yet?"

Angel's arms tightened.

". . . Or not." To her den-kin, she lifted a hand. *What do you see?*

He couldn't sign back and didn't try; his arms stayed put. But he said, "Trees."

"My trees?"

"They must be. They look like the trees in the Common." He hesitated. "They don't seem to be . . . I mean, I can see their roots. The roots are as long as the trees are tall, but—I think the trees are growing in number."

"I think we could land."

"I think we wait. The roots might interlock to form some kind of a bridge, but, Jay—"

"What?"

"There's nothing beneath it. I mean—I can't see anything. It's not that it's dark—there's nothing there. No water, no distant land—just more sky."

"And if the roots could form a bridge, where does the bridge lead?"

"To the other side. There's no road, on the opposite side," he added. "No buildings I can see. There is a forest, and a break between the ranks of trees." He hesitated again. "Or there *was* a break between them."

"It's gone?"

"Yes. I might have seen it wrong, though." He spoke the words with more hope than conviction.

More hope than conviction. That, she thought, was the truth of her den: there had always been more hope than conviction. Her convictions had guided them, when their options had been at their most dire. But there had been hope, in the life they had led in the hundred holdings. There had been hope before then, with Rath.

There'd been hope on the day the life they had built together in the twenty-fifth had ended, although that hope had been swamped with fear and, later, with the shadow of loss. Grief defined part of their life, but only part. They had looked, as they could, toward the future they could imagine—and that imagination had gained breadth, width, depth, with the passage of time and the gaining of experience.

The cost of failure had grown, just as experience had, and the fear of asking others to pay the price for her bad decisions had grown as well. But here, the trees rooted in what Angel saw as nothing, she felt a lightening of that fear, a lessening of it. She felt an odd, giddy hope at the sight of the branches, crowned, all, with the leaves of her childhood.

She had not been awed by trees of silver or gold or diamond. Those things were the outward expression of wealth—but at heart, her feelings about them had not changed much since the days in the twenty-fifth. You couldn't eat gold or silver or diamond. If you were starving in a strange land, unless you could sell them, you'd still be starving at the end of the long day.

She wasn't certain if the leaves of the *Ellariannatte* could be eaten, either. In that, perhaps, they weren't different. But she felt, staring down at the growing expanse of trees, that she would never starve or freeze in a forest such as this. It didn't matter if the trees couldn't speak. It didn't matter if they couldn't serve, couldn't fight, couldn't be owned.

They were beautiful, to her. And for now, they would be her first step into a wilderness that had not been claimed, and it seemed a *right* first step. If she had to shout her own name into a wilderness that gods had once walked, there was no better way.

"Shadow, take us down."

"*Land.* Don't *land.* Land *now.*"

Jewel almost laughed. "I'm sorry, I was rude."

"You are *alwaysssss* rude."

"Yes, I know. I'm sorry," she said again. "Eldest, could you please take us down?"

He sniffed. "These are *stupid* trees."

Angel's snort was meant for Jewel's ears. "Can you find a flight path down that won't knock the two of us off your back?"

"I don't *care* if *you* fall."

"I care, Shadow," Jewel said.

"*Sssssoooo* what? *You* care about *stupid* things!" He veered sharply to the left and then dropped like a stone. Angel cursed freely, but in Rendish, which was unusual. Jewel didn't curse; she caught the steadying arms that Angel had put around her and grabbed them both. She knew that the Winter King would not have dropped Angel had he consented to carry him at all; the Winter King could be trusted with any burden she placed on his back.

She had no such confidence in Shadow.

Branches cracked as he struck them with his wings; leaves flew as they were sheared from their moorings. Down, which had seemed a long, long way away, approached with alarming speed. But Jewel could not see the nothingness that had so concerned her den-kin. She could see roots; she could see the way they overlapped each other as if struggling for dominance or space. It reminded her of the cats themselves.

It was an odd thought.

"I really hate flying," Angel said, in between the Rendish he squeezed out.

"It hates *you*, *stupid* boy." Shadow replied. But the rest of his spiteful commentary was aimed squarely at the trees that dared—dared!—to grow in his way. Although the trees were not as tightly packed as the bars of fences might have been, Shadow ate air the way wild horses ate ground.

The gray cat roared at the trees as if they were his enemies, and he did claw the bark of at least two as he slid to the side to avoid them. Jewel screamed in a rush of breath that ended with nervous laughter as he once again righted himself. But she had held on to Angel's arms until her knuckles were white and she could no longer feel her own fingers.

Shadow came to a stop, digging claws into the bark of the large root beneath his feet. It was angled, but not steeply, and as Jewel slid from cat to ground—a tangle of roots that would never be flat—she rubbed her hands together. The air was cold. Angel was rubbing his forearms, but reserved most of his glaring for the great, gray cat.

Shadow was hissing at fallen leaves, which he then proceeded to shred with great smugness. Jewel almost laughed, but in Shadow's mind, offending a cat's dignity was the greatest of insults. She managed to turn her widening smile in Angel's direction. Angel found Shadow's tirade far less amusing.

"Shadow, tell the others that it's safe to join us. Please," she added, with hasty self-consciousness that did absolutely nothing to mollify the cat.

He clawed at bits of bark. "Fine. *Fine*. They can come *here*, and they can die of *boredom*, too!" He bunched, gathered, and pushed himself free of whatever gravity held him here, spitting and cursing all the while.

* * *

Jewel sat astride a root and leaned her back into a tree trunk. She couldn't hear the Arianni. She couldn't hear the butterfly's unnerving song. She couldn't even hear Shadow—and she was certain he was hissing and spitting up a storm. Angel was silent, across a small clearing of roots, his back likewise shored up by a huge trunk. He lifted his hands in den-sign, and she lifted hers in response, and they idled away the silence speaking as they had once spoken, in their own crowded apartment in the twenty-fifth. She could see that early den so clearly: Lefty leaning against the wall between the two windows, beside Lander who conversed almost solely in den-sign.

She could see Duster. Fisher.

She could see home.

He must have known, because his den-sign stopped for one long moment. But she shook her head, smiling. Thoughts of the dead didn't trouble her here. They'd been alive. They'd been part of her home. Even the silent, active language of den-sign was proof of that. What point regret that they were no longer here? It would change nothing. They *had* been here. And they had laughed. They'd cried. They'd cursed. They'd *lived*.

Jewel hated death because death was loss.

But if they'd never been alive, never been family to her, she would know and feel no grief. She couldn't imagine a life in which nothing was precious to her—because that was the only life that would be impervious to the grief of loss.

And why was she even thinking this now? She shook her head.

Kallandras came down from the skies. The ring on his thumb—an odd place to wear a ring—was glowing faintly, in strange synchronicity with the butterfly on his shoulder.

"Terafin," he said gravely. "*Ellariannatte*."

"The Kings' trees," she replied, rising. She dusted bits of bark and leaf off her legs. "Do you hear the trees in my forest?"

He nodded, but only after a pause.

"Can you hear them here?"

He did not answer. He met her steady gaze, and in his eyes she saw, for a moment, the gaze of soldiers who had seen battle, had survived it, and had never quite broken free of the fields on which they had lost so many of their comrades. "The Winter people are coming," he said. "Shadow has delayed their departure somewhat."

"Please tell me he wasn't insulting the Wild Hunt."

"I make it a practice not to lie to the powerful."

"You're a bard!"

"Indeed, Terafin." He smiled, which warmed the lines of his face. He was like Haval, she thought. His face, his expression, was the mask that he wore. He might shift or change that mask to suit his own purposes, but did he ever remove it?

"Why are you here? Did Solran send you?"

He winced, which Jewel interpreted as a no.

"I am here because of a vow I made in my youth."

"I don't understand."

"No, Terafin. But it is not a vow made to you, and it is not, in the end, a vow made for you or your sake. You are a single battle in a long war, and only when the war is over will I be free." He bowed then. "And I say too much."

"I did ask."

"Yes. But you are not the first to ask, and I seldom answer that question." His smile shifted, becoming something leaner, sharper. "What will you do with the knowledge?"

"Nothing. No," she added, standing slowly. "I'll do what I was going to do anyway."

"And that?"

"Make use of your power while you're willing to offer it."

He looked as if he would say more, but Shadow's invective became all of the noise in this strange forest. Nor was his voice the only one raised. To her consternation, Jewel heard horns.

For one long moment she was afraid that they were the horns of the heralds, even here—but no. They were the horns of the Wild Hunt.

Angel winced and mouthed a single word. *Shadow.*

Jewel, however, said it out loud. Her Oma could not have done better in her foulest of moods. Hands perched on her hips in uncomfortable fists, she waited.

The great gray cat came down, his wings once again clipping bark and scarring it.

"What did I tell you?" she said, through clenched teeth.

He blinked and failed to meet her eyes.

Kallandras said, "I will go to the Wild Hunt."

"I need Shadow alive," Jewel replied. "I can't sacrifice him to the anger of the Wild Hunt, even if it *is* justified." She had no doubt that it was. She had seen one of the cats unseat—and probably kill—one of the Winter Queen's riders. But he had not been her cat at the time. He had been a thing of stone and magic, a thing of Winter, and the ancient Winter King. What he had done there had had no bearing on her, and it could be argued—probably unsuccessfully—that it had been done in self-defense; the Winter Queen seemed to have no love for the cats.

Now? Shadow was hers. If he was not den, he was part of her home. What he did would reflect on his master.

"I warned you," a familiar voice said. Calliastra came out of the sky as Kallandras had done, her wings folding into shadows and then invisibility as her feet touched ground. Or root.

"Did he kill someone?" Jewel asked, voice both higher and softer.

"It wasn't *me*! *I* didn't do it!"

Calliastra ignored him. "He injured someone. I do not believe he will die."

There was a glint of red on the left side of Shadow's jaw. Jewel wished, for just a moment, that she had brought Adam with her—but the immortals of her acquaintance had always refused healing.

"He is coming *anyway*," Shadow said, still refusing to meet her eyes.

"He can't."

"He *can*."

"I want him in the *manse*, Shadow."

"Where he's safe, yes, yes, *yes*. But *she* is not in the manse."

"Shadow—"

"She is *mortal*, and she is *not mortal*. He will come, or the child might die."

"He's not allowed—"

She heard more horns, and she heard a different growl. Failing to meet her eyes, Shadow nonetheless managed to radiate smugness. She looked at the blood—it was blood—at the corners of his mouth.

Shadow, however, was here. Jewel deflated. "It really wasn't you?"

Shadow looked smug while he bled.

The horns continued. They were joined by cries of anger, of challenge.

"You are *never* to injure another member of the Wild Hunt without my *direct* command. Do you understand?"

Silence.

"I *mean it*, Shadow. I need you here, but I'll do without if you can't follow this single, simple rule."

"They *started* it," he finally hissed.

Jewel glanced above his head to Calliastra. The daughter of darkness offered an elegant shrug. Jewel continued to stare; she lifted her hands in rapid densign before she remembered that Calliastra was not versed in that language.

"You worry far too much," Calliastra said. "They are Arianni, but even so, they are not complete fools. Not even Corallonne would hold you accountable for the damage these creatures do."

Jewel exhaled. "And if they were truly mine?"

"They could not be."

"You've said—"

"Yes. I have. But you could not be that master. You have the power; you lack the will. You will always, I think, lack the will. I taunt the wretched creatures because they cannot harm me."

Shadow, who had not once looked into Jewel's eyes, now swiveled a head in Calliastra's direction. "Can *too*."

"I would like to see you try."

"I wouldn't," Jewel said, in the same flat tone. She folded her arms, glaring at the side of her cat's head. His ears twitched as she exhaled.

"Snow, get down here *right now*."

A white cat landed on the tree roots. On his back was Adam.

Chapter Five

"WHAT *I* WANT TO know is: why are you even here?"

Snow had ditched Adam the moment his claws touched ground. Adam fell off, landed with a thump, and sprawled backward into a tree trunk. His pallor was a shade that only suited corpses.

Since the question could have been aimed at either of the two new arrivals, Snow attempted to escape immediately; he bunched his hind legs to push himself off the ground and back up through the crown of trees.

Calliastra kicked his back legs, a sweep of perfect, elegant motion that spoke of deadly grace. Snow growled, turning, the sky forgotten, and Jewel marched over to him and placed a hand squarely on the top of his head. "Don't. You. Dare."

Snow hissed. So did Shadow. Clearly the simple shift in Jewel's anger was cause for amusement. Jewel glared at the gray cat and the tenor of the hissing reversed. It was like being accompanied by lethal four-year-olds.

"You are supposed to be at home, protecting my forest."

Snow said nothing.

"And you," she said, rounding on Adam, "are supposed to be at home with the rest of the den! What are you doing here? The cats hate it when you even threaten to touch them—how did you convince Snow to let you ride?"

Adam, not one of nature's natural liars, simply looked confused.

"He *begged* me," Snow said promptly. "Whiny, *whiny* begging."

Jewel's eyes could not possibly be narrowed any further if she still wanted to see. "So . . . it was your idea, Snow."

Snow hissed; his belly inched toward the ground. When Shadow hissed, however, he said, "It was *Shadow's* fault. He *made* me. He *told* me I had to bring the boy. *Me.* I had to *carry* him. Don't let him *fall.* Don't *eat* him. Don't make him *bleed.*"

"Jay," Angel said. Having caught her attention, he signed, *doesn't matter. Adam's here now.* When she stared at him, her hands still, he added, *trust,* and pointed at Shadow. At Shadow who had just attempted to eat one of the Arianni.

"*Eat* him?" Shadow yowled in outrage. "*No one* could eat *that*! It's *disgusting*!"

"Jewel." Calliastra put a hand on Jewel's left arm. "While Shadow exaggerates for his own benefit, it is true that the verbal hostilities started within the Wild Hunt."

"Did he die?"

"I don't know. I didn't consider it significant, myself."

Silence.

Calliastra looked through the *Ellariannatte* toward Celleriant, who was approaching at Terrick's side. They exchanged a very distinct look; Jewel felt it was the coda to a conversation she had missed in its entirety.

Celleriant approached, but it was Calliastra who spoke; she had, after all, spent far more time with mortals than the Arianni Lord who nonetheless served Jewel. "You walk in the wilderness now, high or low. The Wild Hunt is a part of the wilderness. I do not know why Lord Celleriant chose to serve you, why he chooses to call you Lord. Perhaps because he has, he has forgone the rules that govern the rest."

"What rules?"

"Rule is perhaps too rigid a word. The Wild Hunt is a power." She paused until Jewel nodded acknowledgment of a statement that didn't seem in need of it. "Your miserable, self-indulgent, noisy cats are, sadly, also a power." The last word was drowned out by the outraged yowling of two of them. She didn't wait for them to stop. Instead, she raised her voice.

She raised her voice, and the trees shook. Leaves fell. The roots themselves trembled beneath the feet of the gathering company. But the words themselves weren't loud. It was a very striking contrast.

"When one power seeks to challenge another power, and the challenge is accepted, there is only one outcome: the weaker falls. It is understood by everyone here. It is understood by your human bard. It is understood by— What is he doing?"

She was frowning at the guildmaster, who progressed toward Jewel at Shianne's side. They were moving very slowly because Gilafas was now crawling on his hands and knees as if he were a toddler.

There was a momentary hush as they watched him; in just such a fashion had he examined the dress Jewel had worn at The Terafin's funeral. But here, he seemed to be examining interlocking roots, as if searching for something he had absentmindedly dropped.

"He's an Artisan," Jewel said quietly. "I've only watched him work once, but if I had to guess, given all other reports, I would say he is looking for material with which to craft."

Calliastra's eyes narrowed slowly as she continued to observe Master Gilafas crawling along the ground. Her lips tightened. "*This*," she said, with obvious disgust, "is how you treat your makers?"

A beat of silence followed the godchild's words, which were almost like a miniature thunderstorm of bewildered rage.

"Yes," Jewel said quietly. "We accept them as they are." Her voice was softer—it would have to be—but the words carried nonetheless. Leaves fell; they touched her forehead and cheeks as they traveled along gravity's unforgiving path.

Calliastra, however, was not cowed. "You should be doing what he is doing. You should be finding him materials with which to craft. He should not be lowering himself in this fashion. No one who saw him now would believe that he was a creator. No one."

"We see him, and we believe it," Jewel replied.

Shadow snorted. "Let him grovel."

"He's not—"

"He *is*. But it is not for you. Or *her*," he added, throwing a sideways glare at Calliastra. "He *makes*. He doesn't know what he seeks until he finds it. Let him *find*." And he turned to look up at the multitude of branches, beyond which Snow was once again in the air. Jewel had not seen him move. Shadow roared.

There was a brief pause, and then Snow roared back, shaking those branches with the full fury of his voice.

Since everyone was occupied with waiting, some more patiently than others, Jewel turned to the gray cat again. "Do not eat, injure, or mock the Arianni." She thought about that, sighed, and said, "Do not eat or injure them."

"Can I *kill* them?"

"What do you think?"

"I think you are *stupid* and *boring*. And he *started* it." He glared at Calliastra, who chuckled.

"I did tell her." The brief warmth of the smile left her face. "Understand the rules of Winter. He felt that he could best the cat. He felt that he could intimidate your Shadow. He took the risk, and he failed. He will not try again."

Thinking of her many acquaintances, Jewel frowned. "Sometimes it's the failure that propels them to try again."

"They are not mortals. Until and unless he is certain of his own power, he will not try again—not unless his Lord commands it. That is our wilderness, in this winter. Shadow has proven his power. And . . ." she stopped.

"And?"

"Shadow did not kill."

"They don't die easily,"

"Not easily, no. But I believe your cat could have killed the Arianni who spoke so. He did not."

"Damn good thing," Jewel said. "I'd've—"

"What? *What* would you have done?" Shadow's tail wrapped itself around her left leg. "What? What? *What?*"

"I'd've been very angry."

He stared at her and then sputtered, because up above the treetops, Snow was laughing. At him.

"There goes Shadow," Angel said quietly, as the gray cat launched himself off the odd ground.

"They've never managed to kill each other," was Jewel's reasonable reply. She glanced over her shoulder. "And I don't think we're moving anywhere until Gilafas is done."

Unlike Calliastra, none of the Arianni seemed to find Gilafas ADelios frustrating; nor did they find the studied disregard that Jewel had called acceptance insulting to him. They seldom glanced in his direction. They spoke softly among themselves from time to time, but their words did not carry; they were watchful, though not overtly suspicious. Nor, she thought, overtly condescending.

Given Celleriant when they had first met, this was surprising.

Jewel had to grab Adam by a shoulder to prevent him from walking into the subtle camp set by the Wild Hunt—one devoid of tents, fire, or the other accoutrements of travel—the moment he understood what Shadow had done. Although she had explained that they were immortal, although he had experience with the hostility of the immortals to healing, he nonetheless wished to examine the injured man.

Shianne was even more firmly against this than Jewel herself, and Adam surprised them both; he argued. It was Shadow, spitting and cursing, who ended that argument. He landed on Angel's foot and turned a glare on Adam that would have shriveled small plants.

Adam, accustomed to the cats, barely noticed.

Adam, the one they'd almost killed once.

Jewel reached out for Shadow's head. He ducked. "They don't *want* your help. They don't *need* it."

Adam met Shadow's gaze and held it. It was the gray cat who looked away. But he looked to Jewel. "I will take him. They can tell *him* to *get lost*."

Shianne lifted a hand; she was closer to Adam than Jewel had been to Shadow, and her arm rested easily on Adam's youthful shoulders. "I will go."

"Not *you*," Shadow said. "Not you."

"He came for my sake."

"Not *yours*." Shadow glared at her very obvious belly. "*His*."

"It is the same, in the end. They will not harm him if I am there."

"They might harm *you*."

Shianne's eyes flashed—literally. Mortal, she might be. But she was not mortal the way Angel was.

No. She is deadly. She is far stronger than any of the magi as they are currently constituted. She is stronger by far than Sigurne.

And Meralonne?

No, Jewel. No one, I fear, will be stronger than Meralonne. He is almost awake. There was a hint of regret in those words. *But she can stand against her lesser brethren should the need arise. She is no longer as they are—but she once was. I believe there are those who remember what she once was.*

Then they—

They are the ones most likely to attempt to harm her.

Jewel did not understand immortals. She didn't understand their concept of family. This thought made the Winter King chuckle. *Do not sentimentalize mortal families. I told you—most of my surviving children attempted to kill me at one time or another. We are not, and were not, as you are. And that is why we were powers. Power, Terafin, is its own family.*

If it was, it was not a family she wanted.

No, he replied softly. *But it is, in the end, the family you must also own. I have never seen a successful amalgamation of absolute power and kin in the sense you use the word. To make the choices you have made, most must abandon the choices that I have made, sooner or later.*

She thought, then, of Ariane, the Winter Queen. Of the Winter Queen's daughters, all of stone, in a long-abandoned hall.

Yes.

Shadow pushed past Avandar with a snarl. "Are you coming, stupid boy?"

"Terafin, is this wise?"

"Gilafas has not yet found what he seeks, and Adam is upset about the blood. If it's not wise, I don't think it's harmful. No," she added softly. "Not you, Shianne."

Shianne's lips tightened, but she accepted what was a command.

"You cannot heal the immortal," Shadow told Adam as they walked over the uneven path made of interlocking roots.

Adam said nothing.

"You play with *time*. That is your gift. Why do you *care* about *him*?" He took a careless swipe at the bark of the nearest trunk—the one Adam was currently steadying his weight against. A branch fell on the gray cat's head. Shadow's eyes became circular; he roared in fury, launching himself, claws extended, at the tree.

Adam grimaced with his whole body, and Gilafas rose instantly.

There was almost a hush as the guildmaster, his knees crinkled but strangely clean, stumbled toward the gray cat. Shadow growled, lowering his head as if to stand his ground. But no; he lowered his head to pick up the offending branch between his jaws, his prominent fangs a splash of white against a familiar and comforting brown.

"You'll just get splinters in your mouth," Adam told the gray cat.

The gray cat however shoved his head toward the guildmaster's open hands, and the moment the branch touched Gilafas' palm, those hands closed so tightly Jewel could see the whiteness of his knuckles from where she stood. He immediately straightened, his shoulders and neck losing their stoop, his eyes clearing. "I will keep this," he said, turning to Jewel, "with your permission, Terafin."

She started to tell him that her permission was not needed, but the words would not leave her mouth. Looking up to the endless canopy of *Ellariannatte*, she said, "I would be honored."

This seemed to somewhat mollify Calliastra, whose fingers began to tap her folded arms with impatience. "If we are done here?"

Jewel smiled. "We are almost done. Adam, go with Shadow."

The gray cat had nothing sarcastic to add; he was too busy spitting out pieces of bark.

Adam knew Lord Celleriant as well as one could know something dangerous and inhuman: at a distance. He understood viscerally that Celleriant served the Matriarch, served Jewel, but more than that? No. He was a winter creature, a desert creature, and like the winter or the sand, he was all encompassing, beautiful, and deadly. Sometimes the deadly could drive away all thoughts of beauty, but the beauty itself remained—untouchable, irreproachable, itself.

Shadow walked unusually close to him, glaring at everything that moved. And at everything that didn't.

"You are *stupid*," the cat said. His voice caught the ears of the Wild Hunt, and they turned to face him, their hands, for the moment, free of weaponry.

"Yes," Adam agreed. "It's often safer that way." He inhaled, glanced down at the cat's head, and added, "Thank you."

Shadow hissed. He rarely laughed at Adam, and this hiss was no exception.

"I would have followed the Matriarch."

"She didn't *want* you." This was said with more smugness.

"No." Adam's voice was grave. "To the Matriarch, I am just another child." As he had been to the Matriarchs of Arkosa, past and present.

This annoyed Shadow, but at least it didn't make his mood any worse. "Why are you here?"

"I am here because Shianne is here." Even saying the name, Adam felt his cheeks redden. "I am here because she is with child."

"So?"

"I mean to deliver the child safely if the delivery is complicated."

Shadow turned to stare at Adam, his eyes gold and unblinking. "Do you *understand* what the child is?"

"A child. A mortal child."

"He is *not*."

"He is. Wait. How do you know it's a boy?"

Shadow growled. A volley of insults followed, but these were the insults with which Adam was most familiar, and he found it comforting in the same way the Matriarch did. Adam accepted the cats' obvious distrust of him; he did not expect to be trusted by anyone but kin.

But the den trusted him; they claimed him as kin although they shared no blood and very little history. The Matriarch accepted him as if he were truly one of her own. She accepted his curse—his gift—in its entirety. She was, had always been, hesitant to command him, and he had found that both surprising and difficult at first. He was accustomed to women who ruled and led; he was accustomed to the way that ruling made them harsher, stiffer. There was no other way; something soft and malleable could not bear the burden of responsibility that had always been placed upon the shoulders of the Matriarchs.

Jewel was not quite a Matriarch. She had the power, and she had the responsibility. She didn't have the steel, the stone, the horrible gravity. Her domicis constantly urged her to be different, to be other than she was, and Adam even understood why. He had spent time with his clan on the edge of the Sea of Sorrows; he had seen the vast deserts, the wasteland of the dominion that had once been a true home to the Voyani.

But she was Matriarch.

To her side, she had gathered the Wild Hunt; she had gathered the walking shadow; she had gathered the cats themselves. She rode a beast of the Wild Hunt. She walked beside a man whose existence was distant legend, distorted and made both tragic and grand. No other Matriarch could do this. Not even Yollana.

Thinking of Yollana, he flinched.

How cold, how hard, how deliberate did one have to be to become a Matriarch worthy of an empire?

"Stupid, *stupid* boy."

"Yes, yes, I understand. I won't always be stupid, though."

"You *will*."

"I won't."

"*You will*." Shadow growled and removed bark from the nearest root. "You will because you are *like* her, and if you were *smart*, you wouldn't be."

"You don't like me."

"I don't like *any* of you." The possibility seemed to offend the gray cat. Then again, breathing offended the gray cat on the wrong day. Or the wrong minute.

"Why are you here, Shadow?"

"Because she will *cry* if you die."

Adam couldn't be certain that the misunderstanding of the question was deliberate. He took a breath.

Shadow flexed very, very prominent claws. Animal claws—normal animals—were surprisingly blunt without the force of weight and momentum behind them. The winged cats, however, were not normal animals. Adam swallowed. Shadow could not kill him easily—he healed himself instinctively—but he could cause an enormous amount of pain while making the attempt.

No. I meant: why are you with the Matriarch at all? He swallowed the question. Although Shadow had walked slowly, they had reached the end of their path. Before him, surrounded by and surrounding the trees that the Matriarch had caused to grow, were the men of the Wild Hunt.

They were like, and unlike, Celleriant. Adam thought Celleriant cold and unapproachable. But somehow, he was part of the Matriarch's clan. These men were not. Their stares were cold, but none of them were turned on Adam; they watched Shadow with a baleful hostility. None drew weapons.

Shadow raised his head; his fur sank until he was sleek, his shoulders rising with a kind of angular grace that spoke—of course it did—of hunting and death. And perhaps the Wild Hunt recognized this as a common element; they did not speak. Neither did Shadow.

Shadow was at his most dangerous when silent.

"I've come to examine the man Shadow injured."

Silence, but it was qualitatively different. One man spoke quietly in a language that Adam did not understand. He waited. Farther back, another spoke, and the silence shifted again.

"You call him . . . Shadow?"

"Shadow. Because he is neither black nor white, and if he wishes, he remains unseen."

More discussion, the fluidity of syllables joining but never overlapping.

"And this . . . Shadow obeys the mortal?"

Adam grimaced. "As much as he obeys anyone."

Shadow growled. Adam remembered the Warden of Dreams and froze, the nightmare returning to him so suddenly and so viscerally that his legs locked, and his breath became shallow.

"We do not obey," the gray cat then said. "Who would dare to command *us?*"

"Do you challenge the Wild Hunt?"

Shadow glanced at the speaker but did not answer. Instead, to Adam, he said, "Go."

Adam moved, his body obeying the single word before his will, his intent, could catch up. Swords were drawn in an instant in perfect synchronicity, as if the Wild Hunt were one man. Adam raised both of his hands, displaying his empty palms. "I mean him no harm," he said, his voice surprisingly steady, given that his arms were shaking. "I wish to make certain that he will survive."

"And the eldest?"

Adam blinked. Ah, they meant Shadow. "None of you have challenged him; none have insulted him. He has no cause to harm any one of you that do not try." Silence. "Shadow?"

"The boy is of value. Harm him, and I will kill you all. I have no other interest in any of you."

Adam's shoulders sagged. "Shadow, I don't think that's the way—" The gray cat flexed his wings, and Adam lost the rest of the sentence.

"You are *stupid*. You understand *nothing*."

"Might I see the injured man?"

More speech, and then one of the Wild Hunt disengaged from the rest. "You may call me Vennaire. Follow. I will lead you." As he spoke, he turned and began to walk. "Where did you meet your Lord?"

"Ah—in the South. In Annagar. A different country."

"Not a country I recognize."

"Do you recognize this one? The one in which the Matriarch's forest has grown?"

"Perhaps. We have been discussing it; it is both familiar and foreign. How long have the eldest served your Lord?"

"They came to her when she planted the forest in her own lands. It's—not the same as this one. There are trees of silver, of gold, of diamond."

The man's brows rose, and his lips turned up in something that might have been a smile had it possessed any warmth. "And how did you come to serve her?"

How? "I owe her my life."

"I see. A debt of honor. Those are burdensome, little mortal; it is why your kind so often fails to carry that weight. You are young for your kind."

"Yes. But I am not considered a child by my people."

"Your people are all children, to us." Silence again; he moved quickly and easily across the snarl of interlocked roots. Adam did not, but he moved regardless, following his guide. Shadow walked to the left of Adam, pausing only to criticize his progress.

"You let him speak poorly of you," Vennaire observed. There was a question in the words.

"He speaks poorly of everyone. It's when he's silent that he's at his most dangerous."

"Truly?"

"Yes."

"Then Calliastra was correct. It has been long since we first encountered the three, and they were not then as they have become. We thought them children of the tangle."

Shadow hissed.

"But they travel with you and they defend you, and perhaps that is enough for those such as you."

"Why did your friend insult Shadow?"

"He was restless. It was folly, but a necessary reminder. Where we go, the wilderness does not acknowledge the White Lady." Vennaire did not seem to be troubled by his companion's injury, nor did he seem troubled by Shadow's presence and the very obvious threat it implied.

"We understand what is at stake," Vennaire continued. "Each and every one of us. Given in service to the Winter King, we are the Winter Queen's. And if a way to reach her still exists, we will carve a path to it, be it in the very depths of the Hells. We will not harm your Lord; we will not rebel against her. She is the only hope we have of finding the only Lord we serve."

"And the injury?"

"I do not understand your kind," Vennaire said, in an equally quiet voice. "The Winter King is mortal, but he was not as you are. He understands, and understood, the rules that abide in the wilderness; he is almost *of* it. We had expected that your Lord would be the same—" He stopped and looked up, exposing the perfect line of a long, elegant throat. "But she is not. No more are you, mortal youth, to come to the heart of our gathering.

"Had he not had the power to withstand the eldest's attack, he should not have raised his voice in challenge. What do you intend to do?"

"Make sure he survives," Adam replied. He glanced, once, at Shadow, whose fur remained sleek, his claws catching bits of bark as he walked. His wings, however, were folded and his head was bent, not in hunting posture, not in search of scent, but in the muttering disgust with which Adam was most familiar.

Shadow had almost killed him. He had almost killed the Matriarch.

But it was Shadow around whom Ariel felt most comfortable. For reasons that were not clear to Adam—that might never become clear to him—Shadow seemed to like the child. She was safe around the gray cat in a way that no one else could be; Adam was certain that had Ariel been in the nightmare land of the Wardens, she would still have been safe from what Shadow had become there.

"He won't *like* it," Shadow said.

"I don't intend to hurt him."

"He won't *like it.*"

"Why?"

"I *told* you. We are not what *you* are."

"You live. You breathe. You bleed. Those wounds can kill you, just as they kill us."

Shadow spit. "You die so *easily.* You break so *easily.* We are not like you."

"Are the Wild Hunt as you are?"

Clearly this was the most outrageous insult the gray cat had ever heard. Adam wondered how something as eternal, as immortal, as the cats could have memories so short. His sense of hurt outrage splashed outward as he explained in great detail why the cats were so superior the comparison could not be made by anyone who had functional eyes. Or ears. Or sense.

Adam glanced at Vennaire; the Arianni hunter did not seem at all pleased with Shadow's sputtering—but he did not draw sword and he did not challenge the cat.

"He's always like this," Adam finally offered.

"Yes. And always was," was the grim reply. "You are what the mortals call healer."

It was not a question, exactly, but Adam nodded to confirm it anyway.

"It has been long since we have allowed one of your kind to approach us."

"Lord Celleriant does not seem fond of us, no."

The smile Vennaire offered was chilly, but so was winter. "No, of course not. Tell me, how did he come to serve your Lord?"

She was not Adam's Lord, but he did not feel that he could deny the word safely. He understood instinctively that this was the business of Matriarchs. Yollana was not his master—she was Havallan—but he would never have denied her that title should someone else have used it, either.

"We met in the Sea of Sorrows," Adam said quietly. "It stands, now, where the Cities of Man once stood."

Silence.

"She found us, and she saved my life. I owe her at least this much."

"What did she save you from?"

He grimaced. "The consequences of my own rashness."

"Ah."

"I was carried to her city, and in her city, I learned—" He stopped. "In her city, I was welcomed into her clan as kin. I could not go home, not immediately. I admire her. She is kin to me. I would die for her." The last words seemed to surprise Shadow, who demonstrated this by stepping, hard, on his foot.

The Arianni Lord, however, took this in stride, as if it were no more than expected. And maybe, to the immortals, it wasn't.

"You do not serve her," Adam said.

"No."

"And you will allow me to examine your kin?"

"If he was not strong enough, death is what he deserves. If you feel that he is worth preserving, and he consents, we will not interfere."

And he consents.

Adam sighed, and nudged Shadow gently with his knee. The gray cat removed his paw from the top of Adam's foot and stalked past him through the trees. Adam had to scramble to catch up.

"Wait, how do you know where we're going?"

"Can you not *smell* it?"

"Smell what?"

"His blood."

"No."

"Can you do *anything* useful?"

In the end, there was no permission to ask. The injured Arianni lay, back wedged between the roots of one tree that seemed larger and more significant than the rest. The blood that Shadow could scent was obvious; it smeared the roots themselves, darkening their natural brown.

He was unconscious, and if Vennaire seemed to be nonchalant about the injuries, others of the Wild Hunt were not; two remained by his side, kneeling as if to check the rise and fall of his chest. They rose as Shadow approached, and one drew his sword.

Shadow sneezed at it, but lifted his wings in warning. One feather clipped the side of Adam's face, drawing blood. And that, Adam thought in disgust, was also a warning. He kicked Shadow's leg.

The Arianni tensed. Shadow, however, did not. "What was *that*? Was that supposed to be a *kick*?" Like, very like, the annoying uncles of Adam's childhood.

"You're in the way," he told the gray cat.

"Make me *move*," the cat replied.

"*Shadow.*" And that was the Matriarch's voice. Adam turned.

Jewel was not there.

The gray cat, however, seemed neither surprised nor greatly displeased. He sniffed. He sniffed loudly. "Fine, *fine*." And moved.

Adam circumnavigated the drawn blade, but the blade didn't move; it was aimed in its entirety at Shadow. Adam himself was momentarily inconsequential.

"Because they are *stupid*," the cat muttered.

Adam had reached the side of the injured, unconscious man. He knelt.

"What are you doing?" the unarmed Arianni asked quietly. There was no menace in his voice, or no more of it than his people's voices naturally contained.

"I wish to make certain he survives. We don't," he added, "play deadly games with the cats."

"You are too *cowardly*."

"Too sensible," Adam said, through slightly clenched teeth. "But we've all seen the cats fight the demons."

"Were the cats injured?"

"Not appreciably, no." He hesitated, his hands hovering above the unconscious man's forehead. He expected the man to wake and push him away; he was, in fact, waiting for just that. But the man did not wake. He knew that Celleriant would reject his aid if he had any choice. And knew, as well, that the clans of his youth, in the distant Dominion of Annagar, feared the healer-born—when they did not indenture them for their own use.

He almost understood it. Almost. But he understood, as well, that this man was alive, and that he might not remain so. The Matriarch had chosen to bring the Winter people home for a reason, and that reason had not changed.

"Well?" Shadow demanded. "Are you going to sit here while he dies? Or while we die of *boredom*?"

Adam took a breath, held it, and lowered his hands.

He had wondered, before this moment, what immortals were. He understood the word: they lived forever. They did not age. The infirmity that came with age, the accumulation of a life's injuries and diseases, did not trouble them. He understood that they were not invulnerable, but he thought of them, had thought of them, as essentially similar. Except that they continued on past the point when mortals couldn't.

This was wrong.

This was wrong in almost every way.

He understood how to knit together the sides of rended flesh; understood how to help the body deal with the loss of blood; he understood the ways in which organs and limbs were damaged. He had to understand this, in order to heal. His understanding was meant for, was of, mortals.

He could hear Shadow hiss laughter.

Touching this man . . . had Adam been blindfolded, he would not have recognized what lay beneath his palms *as* a man. Not even as an approximation of one. None of the healing he had ever done had prepared him for this.

Only one thing might have. He had touched the cold earth, beneath the ancient, endless snow in the unclaimed wilderness that surrounded the Oracle's home. He had almost held the entirety of that earth in his flat palms, while he searched for echoes of it that led to the Matriarch's forest, the Matriarch's home. He could not have done that if he had not understood, viscerally, what *home* meant to her. It was not so far removed from what it meant, and had meant, to Adam, for all that she lived in a Northern mansion, with its stiff doors and cold stone.

That, he thought, was like this.

Yes.

Shadow's voice, shorn of the tonality of a petulant cat, was deep and loud and resonant. Adam could not see the cat; his eyes were closed.

We fear you, mortal child, for a reason.

"I mean no harm," Adam said, surprised by the word fear. It was not something the cats ever readily admitted.

A fire in your mortal forests means no harm. Intent is not everything. Intent is not close to everything. Did the gods mean to destroy lands when they walked upon the earth? No. But destruction followed in their wake when their thoughts were not turned toward preservation. So, too, the storms in your harbors. You are stupid. Stupid. Stupid. It is not what you intend, but what you do.

"I only want to make sure he survives."

The cat was silent. Adam thought he was done. But as he once again turned his thoughts to the injuries that were visually similar to the injuries he understood, the cat spoke again.

Remember that. If you wish it, he will survive. But if you are not very *careful, he will not be what he was. And, boy?* She *will know.*

"Yes—she sent me."

Stupid.

How could he heal what he couldn't perceive? The touch of the healer-born could effect miraculous cures. It could pull people back from the brink of death—from either side. But . . . the dead went to the bridge and crossed it, to stand at last in the Halls of Mandaros.

The mortal dead.

If immortals had been created in such a way that they were never meant to face death, what happened to them? Did they have a bridge of their own, a river to cross, a hall in which they must face the consequences of their life's choices? Did they return to their makers, whoever those makers must be?

Or did they exist as part of the tangle—that place where all steps were treacherous and none led in a predictable direction?

Mortals left their bodies when those bodies died. He had seen the dead; he understood that what they had been remained in some fashion. This man, almost dead, was not, had never been, mortal. It almost seemed, to Adam, that he had never been physical; that his body was not a body at all. Ah, wait, there—

Jewel. The Winter King was not immediately visible, but his voice was sharper, louder than was his wont. She rose immediately, her lap shedding leaves. Angel rose as well, signing.

I don't know, she replied. *Winter King.*

The white stag was by her side almost before the thought had ended. His eyes were too wide; he seemed to be trembling.

What's happened?

You must go to your healer now. You must bring him back.

Back? What do you mean?

The healer-born do not heal immortals.

No. Immortals don't like to be parted from their secrets.

You are foolish as you oft are, but today such folly will be costly. Go. Order him back.

She mounted his back; felt his warmth beneath her legs in the chill air. Before she could utter a command, he was off, leaping across roots as if his hooves didn't condescend to touch them at all.

They didn't. Nor did they touch the upturned faces of the Arianni over which he leaped. A backward glance that was more hair than vision still afforded a glimpse of their expressions, the consternation obvious in the width of their eyes. They raised no cry; they made no attempt to halt the stag's passage.

He knew where Adam was. No words were necessary, no directions given. But he slowed abruptly as he came face-to-face with Shadow. The gray cat's wings were high and wide, his fangs completely exposed; his claws had already damaged the roots upon which he was standing. His voice was so guttural it was hard to distinguish words between the snarling.

But trust Shadow; he could always enunciate the word *stupid.* It was not a description he had applied to the Winter King before. The Winter King had no voice, but even had he, he would not normally have returned the cat's insult; in general, he considered the cats beneath him.

"Shadow! He's not come here to harm Adam!"

And Shadow growled, "He has come to *stop* him."

I have come to save him, the Winter King told Jewel. *What he does now is* not done *in the wild. It is not safe for him. It is not safe for you.*

What is he doing wrong? He's healing the injured.

No, Terafin. No, Jewel. Perhaps that is what he attempts, but no.

Shadow growled. The Winter King pulled back on his haunches, bunching them to leap—but so, too, the great gray cat.

"What *happens* to them when they *die?*" Shadow demanded. "*Where* do they *go?*"

And Jewel knew, *knew,* that the Winter King was right. "Set me down!" she shouted, using voice when it was unnecessary. "Set me down now!"

"*Stupid* girl! If he does not *do this*, how will you *find her*? You will *never* find her!"

The Winter King let Jewel off his back without kneeling or otherwise dropping his guard; how, she didn't ask. She could see Adam's bent back, the line of his curved shoulders, the dip of his neck. She could imagine the shape of dark, closed lashes.

She passed Shadow; he upended her with one slap of a wing. "*Think*, stupid girl. *Think!*"

"I *am!*" she shouted back as she struggled to her feet. "This won't help us— we'll lose him!"

"If we *lose* him, we are in the same *position*! We can't *find* her if the hunter *doesn't die!*"

She turned then, and slapped Shadow's wing to the side; her palm stung. She could not explain her sudden panic to the cat and didn't try; she couldn't explain it to herself. But this was the force of the most visceral of her instincts, and she had learned never to ignore it. She could—she'd proved that—work against it when it was utterly necessary. This was not that time.

She caught Adam's shoulders; they were tense, almost frozen. He didn't move, although she shook him. She shouted his name, her lips close to his ear, her hair in her eyes.

And then she reached down and grasped his hands, her fingers sliding into the spaces between his. His hands were snow-cold, ice-cold; she broke the contact, wrenching them both free of the man's face.

She spared that man a single glance; his face was the color of bleached bone, and his hair, Arianni silver, was dull, matted. She had seen the Arianni fight before. She had seen what happened to demons upon death. She could not remember seeing what happened to the dead of the Wild Hunt.

She thought she might see it now and did not care.

Adam's eyes remained closed. She shouted his name again and then untangled her right hand in order to slap him. But Adam, sunk into a healing trance without anything *to* heal, was beyond her. He did not open his eyes.

She turned to Shadow, growling in her own fashion. "What's happened to him?"

Shadow's growl was lower, louder. He was almost enraged. But his anger was only barely the equal of Jewel's.

"This is not the place for Adam. This is not the place he's meant to be."

"He can do it! If *he* does it, *you* won't have to!"

"I'm The Terafin, Shadow. He's not even ATerafin. He's not of my House, and he's—"

"Do you *think* there will be no *sacrifice?* Do you think you can take that tree to *her* without loss?"

"I won't sacrifice a child—"

"He is *not* a child. And he can do what must be done. Now?" The cat spit. "Now we will have to *start over.*" He glanced once at the body of the fallen man, took a swipe at the Winter King. His fur had risen, and his claws seemed elongated.

Jewel needed the Winter King. She needed the gray cat.

But what she needed of Adam was entirely different, and she was not Matriarch, to simply surrender it to the blight of necessity. "There must be another way."

"Then *find it.*"

Calliastra joined them, falling like winged darkness into the space their anger occupied. She glanced, once, at the fallen man, and once at the healer.

"Boy," she said, her voice soft, her tone sharp and cold, "what are you doing?"

His hands were clenching and unclenching in involuntary fists; his eyes were closed. Arms straining, he seemed to be reaching for the Arianni, with no true sense that they had been forcibly separated.

"He'll die," he finally said.

Jewel drew her right hand back and slapped him once, hard.

He blinked, his long lashes fluttering as awareness of reality finally returned. But he looked down to his hands, curled in white-knuckled, empty fists. "Matriarch," he said, pulling himself away, his eyes seeking—and finding—the bleeding man.

"You can't," Jewel told him, voice flat. "He's dying. And the Arianni don't cross the bridge. Wherever he goes, you can't follow."

Shadow spit and cursed. He even cursed in Torra, which Jewel had never heard him do before. "He *can*, you *stupid, stupid, stupid* girl!" And with that, he was done guarding Adam; he pushed himself, with a growl that shook every tree in sight, off the ground. A scattering of leaves fell in his wake, like an afterthought.

Jewel threw her arms around Adam and tightened them before she could consider what she was doing. But Adam was already straining against them. "He'll die—"

"You can't prevent that now. Adam. *Adam.* Listen to me."

For perhaps the first time, she was grateful that he called her Matriarch because that word had a meaning and resonance that had existed long before he had come into his healer-born power. He froze, forcing everything but his hands—still clenching and grasping at air—to be still.

"Maybe if the injury were less severe." She looked up to branch-laden skies and caught no sight of Snow or Shadow. She knew, however, why Snow was avoiding her. "It won't happen again. But it *has* happened."

He shook his head, and the motion continued for one long breath; he broke free of it, his eyes wide, his lips trembling slightly. He looked much, much younger at that moment than Jewel could ever remember being.

"Where do they go?" he asked her, the wilderness in his voice. "Where do they go when they die?"

She had never asked herself that question, not seriously. She didn't ask it now. "I don't know. But," she drew breath, "not where we go. I know you can heal the dying. You can, according to Levec, heal the newly dead. But he was talking about mortals—"

"They return to their source," Calliastra said quietly.

All sound died. Even the breeze seemed to quiet, as if to listen.

"What do you mean, source?" Jewel finally asked. She was the only one who would. To the side, she could feel the restive, restless energy that was the Winter King.

"They are—*we* are—not born as you are born. We have youth and childhood in a fashion, and it is not dissimilar, but we are not babes in arms, not the way animals are."

"And we're animals."

Calliastra folded her arms and looked down the length of her perfect nose. "You are like the animals in your habits and your impulses, yes. You bear young as animals do. But unlike animals, you speak, you think, you make art—and you make war. Your children are born from your bodies, not your mind, not your spirit; they are flesh of your flesh, but they are not you. What you give them is life. You protect them when they are weak. You teach them to walk. You feed them when they are toothless and insignificant.

"We are not like you. Our youth is a youth of experience—we lack it, when we are first born. But we do not lack awareness, and the experience of our parents is never far from reach."

"You know what your parents know?"

"Not all, because we are not all of either parent. But yes, our birth conveys much of the experience of our parents to us. It conveys, as well, the compulsions that govern their existences. It is why Namann was a failure, who was meant to be a scion of lasting peace.

"It is why I—" She stopped. Jewel thought, given the way she flexed her shadow wings, that she would not continue. She was therefore surprised. "The Arianni are Ariane's children, all. Even Shianne. They are not Ariane; they are echoes of her, shells of her; they resemble her in color, in texture, in focus. What delights Ariane will delight them; what angers her will anger them. What moves her will move them."

"But they have free will."

"Yes, in a manner." This smile was grim and bitter. "I, too, have free will. But, Jewel, if you decided that food was a great evil, you could force yourself not to eat. And you would die. It is thus with us."

"The *Allasiani*—"

"Not here," Calliastra replied. "Never here. Do not mention them by that name. Do not ask the others the question you wish to ask me. It is death." She bowed her raven-haired head. When she lifted it, her eyes were a shade of gray that was almost black. "Yes. My father is compelling. He is beautiful beyond compare. Of the gods in any form, he was the most striking. Those mortals who saw him yearned for him. You think Ariane beautiful." It was not a question.

Jewel nodded anyway.

"She is a candle to his bonfire. No; she is a candle to his sunlight."

"But—"

"Lord of Darkness. Lord of the Hells."

Jewel nodded again.

"When we speak of darkness, we do not speak of night. He takes, but he cannot give, not truly."

"Did he have other children?"

"Only one. Only one that survived."

"What would happen to you if you died?"

"I would end. I would end, and I would return—or so I believe—to my parents. I would not be aware of this, of course; the spirits of dead mortals and the essence of dead immortals are not the same. The awareness of 'I' would be erased, eradicated."

"And the rest of your experience?"

"Perhaps they would know, should they care to look; I am uncertain. My mother was ever busy, and my father was not one of whom one might safely ask questions. But Ariane is like unto me; her parents were different, but she, too, is firstborn. She, however, could do what we could not."

"Oh?"

"She could create, Jewel. She could have children. She could send them out into the wilderness, her scions, her servitors. They are unlike me: they have only one driving force."

But Jewel thought, again, of the *Allasiani*.

"Yes. That is the flaw. Ariane herself is not one simple thing. Her desires are complex and shifting; she can control them all, but they exist, regardless. I have never asked, nor cared to ask, how she first met my father. Nor have I cared to ask what that meeting involved. Now? She hates him. There is no eternity that will exist in which that is not true." She looked down at what was now, Jewel was certain, a corpse.

"Little mortal," she said, reaching out to gently touch Adam's cheek.

He looked up at her—had to look up. She had gained height while speaking, as she sometimes did.

"What you attempted was folly. It was not wisdom. If you seek a dying mortal and you find him—or her—you hold onto them, and you fall back into your own body. They fall back into theirs. That is the nature of mortality.

"It is *not* the nature of immortals. Could you understand the whole of our thoughts, could you contain the whole of our existence, it would nonetheless not be the same. In the worst possible case, you might merge with them, you might be submerged beneath them; you would lose whatever is considered life among your kind. You have a gift. It is a great gift, poorly understood by those upon whom you squander it."

Jewel bridled, but Calliastra had not intended the words as an insult. In just such a fashion might she criticize the edge of a dull blade or the behavior of a pet.

"Do not waste it here. Do not waste it in ignorance. If you intend to truly heal the immortal, you must understand the immortal. Your knowledge of the immortal is superficial at best. It is a weave of stories, half-truths, and awe. Do not approach the wilderness in that fashion, or it will devour you one way or the other." She lowered her hand; there was a thin sheen of perspiration across her forehead, her cheeks. Her lips trembled, and even as she pulled her hands away, Jewel saw the elongation of her fingers, her nails.

"And now, I have had enough of your appalling ignorance and your suicidal arrogance. I am beginning to understand why the cats are so disrespectful." And, so saying, she spread wings—much the same way Shadow had done— and pushed up into the air.

"What were you trying to do?" Jewel asked, when she was gone. She turned back before he answered but walked slowly in order to keep pace with him. Words and syllables were broken by the effort of crossing the uneven terrain made of exposed roots, but the roots were interwoven so tightly, she couldn't see the empty space between—or beneath—them.

"I was trying," Adam replied, sentence fragmented in the same way, "to save him. But she was right. Their bodies look similar to ours, but they're not. They're not the same."

"They're alive?"

His answer took longer; Jewel looked over her shoulder to see the intent concentration on his face. "Yes." A lot of effort for a single syllable.

"Do you feel that, or are you rationalizing?"

Another pause. "I feel it. I think." He reddened, which made him look even younger. "I feel it. But it's not life the way you and I are alive. It's not life the way Shianne or her unborn child are alive."

"And the cats?"

"I haven't tried. If I can be killed before my power heals me, it would be by Shadow."

"Or anyone else who could separate your head from your body?"

"Or anyone else," he agreed, "who would know to do that. But Shadow avoids being in arm's reach of me. I was shocked when Snow came to get me. I was more shocked when he said Shadow told him he had to bring me. I thought—I thought that it might be because of the injured man."

Jewel shook her head. "Shadow's worried about Shianne." In the distance, she could almost hear the outrage in the cat's voice.

"I'm not sure I *can* heal the Winter people. I don't understand what life is—and what it means—to them, and to learn it will take time. But I'm not certain anyone will give me that chance." He was hesitant, Jewel thought.

"I think that's what Shadow's afraid of. That you'll learn. That you'll know." The outraged yowling increased. Jewel had never been certain how much the cats could hear, or how far that hearing extended, but the possibility that Shadow himself was afraid was clearly an insult that could not be borne. At least not quietly. Adam grinned. It was something that Jewel did not want to lose.

Branches cracked as Shadow came down from the heights. Bristling, his eyes were golden slits, his fangs exposed. *"Afraid?"* Splinters shot outward in a spray as he mangled roots. *"Of you?"* He was practically spitting.

On high, the sound of Snow's laughter was clearer than the rustle of moving leaves.

Jewel was surprised when the Arianni appeared from around the trees. She recognized the swords they carried; they also bore shields. Both of these were pointed toward her gray cat. They were slender things of blue light that implied steel—or something older and harder—but she felt at that moment that they would not be enough.

Without thought, guided by instincts more primitive, more certain, she stepped quickly between them and placed a hand on top of Shadow's head. His growling deepened, but he did not take his eyes off the Arianni, almost as if he knew that he could kill them with impunity.

"They are *weak* here," he told Jewel, as if that were a matter of concern.

"They follow me."

"They are not *all* needed." Pause. "We only need *one*."

"Shadow."

"*What?*" Although the word was aimed—like a projectile—at the woman whose hand was on his head, the glance he threw Adam was murderous. But it was different from the usual murderous outrage; he was angry, and the anger was genuine.

"You will be surrounded by stupidity for as long as you live," Jewel told him. "There is no point in taking it personally."

"You are *all stupid*."

"Yes, probably. We weren't born to the wilderness, and we are not of it. You will kill no more of the Wild Hunt. They want what we want."

"They *do not*. They want *her*."

"We want her, Shadow. If we don't reach her in time—" She stopped.

"*Yessss?*" He spit to the side. "They are not trying to *kill me*. They are trying to *save* you."

Silence. Jewel glanced at the Arianni. Celleriant was not among them; clearly, he did not believe that her life was in danger. But Shadow was, surprisingly, correct. She exhaled. "He does not serve me as Lord Celleriant does, but he will not harm me here. He will not harm any of you now." When they failed to move, she said, "Please put up your weapons."

They were slow to obey what was only barely a request; Jewel wasn't certain they would.

Adam said, "Vennaire." Just that. Jewel thought it a foreign word but realized, as one of the Wild Hunt put up his weapon, that it was a name. "The cats will not harm the Matriarch."

"And will they harm you?" the man Adam had named asked.

Adam did not answer.

"You are foolish, but I sense you are not without power in this place," Vennaire continued. He spoke softly in a language Jewel did not understand, and the rest of the swords vanished, if slowly.

Adam hesitated, glancing at Jewel as if for permission. She hesitated as well. But Adam was healer-born, not seer-born; his talent was not hers. She could try to protect him—had tried, by leaving him at home.

But even thinking it, she felt cold, and she understood viscerally something that she had feared for far too long: home was no longer safe.

"Yes," she said quietly, although she didn't know what she was granting him permission to do.

He held out one slender hand toward the man he had named. "I will not harm you," he said quietly. "And I will do nothing to change you."

Vennaire stared at Adam's slender fingers as if they were vipers. He spoke again to his brethren, and this time, the conversation was longer, the syllables sharper. No weapons were drawn, but Jewel was aware of the way words could be used to devastating effect in their stead; she waited, exhaling only when silence once again reigned.

"Mortal child," Vennaire said, "were it not for the predicament of the White Lady, were it not for the threat to the seasons, we would consider your request a threat."

Shadow growled. The growl was not a threat; it was, as far as Jewel could tell, conversational. The Arianni were surprised by his intrusion, but they spoke to him, and he growled back. It was the first time she could recall that she could not understand Shadow's words. When he fell silent, they fell silent, and that silence seemed to spread across the forest like a pall, a shroud.

But Vennaire turned back to Adam, who had slowly lowered his hand. He spoke; Adam frowned. He spoke again, and Adam's frown shifted into one of concentration. Jewel did not understand the Arianni's words—but Adam, it seemed, thought he could, or should. Jewel started to speak; Shadow stepped on her foot, demanding silence without breaking it.

When Adam turned to her, however, he was pale. "Matriarch?"

"I'm sorry," she replied, "but I don't understand what he said."

"It is—it is the Matriarch's tongue."

"Not *this* Matriarch. I didn't understand it. What did he say?"

Adam repeated what she had already heard; it remained incomprehensible. He tried a second time, speaking the syllables with greater volume.

"Adam, I don't understand. Saying it slowly, saying it louder—none of this is going to make me understand. It's not a language I recognize."

He fell silent.

"Where do you know it from?"

And flushed, his shoulders sloping toward the ground, his chin dropping as if it had sprouted weights. "Arkosa," he said quietly. "My mother taught my sister when my sister would mind her."

"And she taught you?"

He cringed, although his mother was dead, his sister absent. "I listened. I eavesdropped."

"Matriarch business," Jewel said.

". . . Yes."

"Arkosan Matriarch business."

"Yes, Matriarch. I am sorry."

"I'm not. I have enough business of my own, I don't need to mind your sister's for her. I am not Arkosan, and I never will be. I consider you kin; you are ATerafin to me for all that you lack the House Name. Nothing you say or do will change that; I owe you my life. If you cannot tell me what he said, I accept that. I ask only that you do not act if you believe you yourself will be in danger. Because, Adam? I've lost enough kin for one life. We haven't known each other long, we share no blood, but it would kill me to lose you."

His smile was uncomplicated; there was a trace of surprise in it, but also joy. "I was told that I might save my own people if I spent time with yours. I thought it meant that I was to learn how to be a ruler."

She said nothing.

Adam once again held out a hand, and this time, Vennaire placed his own hand across it.

Chapter Six

7th of Lattan, 428 A.A.
Terafin Manse, Averalaan Aramarelas

FINCH WOKE TO DARKNESS in a room that should have been silent. She was out of bed and stumbling into awkward clothing before she was fully awake. The clothing her half-asleep self had chosen was meant for the office; the dress had been created by Haval Arwood, a substitute for armor. The cloth out of which he had worked it was dark and heavy; in the light, its sheen added layers of color. It was not light now, but she found her voice, and magelight—the single luxury she had allowed herself when she had set out upon the road to a regency she hoped and prayed would never be necessary—flared to life.

She whispered it to a more bearable glow, and as she lifted the holder, she found herself staring into eyes that reflected that light. They were not, like the visible cloth of her skirts, flat and almost liquid; they were cat eyes. Night, she thought, given how well he blended into the darkness.

Adam and Jay had recovered from their encounter with cats gone wild at the whim of the Warden of Dreams. Finch, standing by Jay's bedside, had not. She could, with little effort, recall the sudden, horrific wounds that had been clawed through her den leader. No; much greater effort was required to push that image out of her mind. She made that effort now. The cats were not cats. Cats did not speak. They didn't fly. And they certainly didn't launch themselves at demons, full of competitive glee.

But they were wild, and they were sensitive in the way predators were. Fear was not her friend here.

Fear, she thought as she shook off the last of sleep, was not her friend anywhere. She had learned that lesson time and time again but could never quite fix it in place enough that she did not need constant reminders.

"Did you wake me?"

He growled. It made the hair on the back of her neck stand instantly to attention. Her hair was the one thing that was still sleep encumbered; while it wasn't as flyaway messy as Jay's come new from the pillow, it was not in a state deemed suitable for either the Merchant Authority or the House Council. Still, when she pushed it back around her ears, it stayed there.

"Night?"

"Get *up*," Night growled.

"I am."

"Wake them. *Wake them.*"

"Who?"

"Are you *deaf?*" he demanded, adding rents to the carpet in her room. She grimaced. Iain had already made clear, with an angry emphasis that was entirely unlike his usual demeanor, that the House funds devoted to repair and restoration were already at their lowest level since he had personally taken office.

"I am not deaf," Finch replied, cloaking herself with dignity. "I am merely mortal."

Night shrieked with frustration; it was not a quiet sound. "Get the *others*. I will wake Teller." He then continued to speak, but many of the syllables were lost to a shrieking kind of growl. If he had hands, he might have been pulling his own hair out. Finch smiled in spite of herself.

It was to be the only smile of that long night.

Finch was not the first person that Night had roused—if it had, indeed, been Night's doing. Haval was standing to one side of her door when she exited her rooms, his arms folded, his shoulders lightly touching the wall. He was dressed, but in clothing that made him seem both foreign and dangerous. This man, her instincts told her, could never be a tailor.

Her experience argued and won—but it was a close fight.

"Regent," he said, the single word brisk.

"Birgide?"

He lifted one brow, and then dipped his chin in approval. "She is awake. She marshals the forest as we speak."

"Haval, what's happening? Night is frantic. And annoyed."

"You cannot hear them?"

Finch closed her eyes. She could now hear footsteps and angry cat; could hear the change of treads as bare feet became booted. "I'm sorry, no. What do you hear?"

"The forest," he replied. "And the horns. The hunters—"

"Jay took them with her."

"Not these ones, alas. I have taken the liberty of speaking with the Chosen; they will require your approval of my suggestion before they act."

"Act on what?" She wondered, for a moment, if she were still sleeping; if this dark-clad stranger with folded arms and a familiar face was a dream that stood on the precipice of nightmare.

"I have asked them to revoke all permissions granted to the House Mage. The former House Mage."

Finch froze.

Seeing her expression, Haval smiled. "Have you seen Jarven?"

"No. I've seen a hissing, angry cat and a very displaced tailor." She squared her shoulders. "I'll go to the Chosen. Can you make sure Teller and Jester are awake?"

"If I am not mistaken, Teller is almost at his door. Jester, on the other hand, will require more effort." His smile was a sliver, something sharp and cold that implied a warmth it did not contain. "Go, Regent."

Torvan and Arrendas were already awake, and given the hour, this was not their shift. Finch was not therefore surprised to see that the rest of the Chosen had been roused. The House Guard did not, as a general rule, live in the manse itself; the Chosen did. The advantage to that could now be seen. Unlike the den, they did not wear their lack of sleep openly; they had shed sleep completely.

Torvan saluted Finch before she had even come to a halt. "Arann sounded the general alarm," he said before she could speak. "What are your orders?"

Jay had only just left this morning, and Finch already missed her. In her darkest hours, she wished—prayed—for just a touch of the gift that had made Jay so instantly valuable to House Terafin. As an urchin, her decisions had affected her den—and that had seemed so large, at the time. Now, they would affect people she could not see, and possibly had not even met.

It mattered, but the fear of that responsibility could not be allowed to take control of her, or she would do nothing. Nothing was not acceptable.

"I've come to request that the permissions granted the House Mage—especially in the interior of the manse—be dismantled."

Torvan nodded crisply enough the gesture was a reply. "The permissions granted explicitly by The Terafin, however, are not in our domain."

Finch had been worried about that, as well. But she trusted Jay. "The Terafin made clear that those permissions would endure while they were relevant, or rather, while he is. I am not magi; I have spent no time in the halls of the Order of Knowledge. I cannot tell you how or why, but I am certain that if he is now considered a threat, these lands will not accept him. Your responsibility— your only responsibility—are the precautions with which the Chosen have been charged."

Arrendas said, "The Warden?"

She understood instantly. "I have been informed that Birgide is marshaling our forces in the forest."

"Regent."

She exhaled. "I will be in the forest, should my presence be required." She glanced down the empty hall. The den woke, or had been woken, but the manse as a whole continued its regular schedule. "I may require an escort when dawn finally breaks."

"You intend to go to the Merchant Authority?"

"It will depend."

"On?"

"Jarven ATerafin."

Torvan shared Jay's opinion of both Jarven and Lucille ATerafin. But he said nothing; instead he saluted.

"I will be safe from almost all forms of attack," she continued. "But the right-kin does not share the same advantages."

"His office is the most secure room in the manse."

"Yes," she agreed. "But I am not certain that he will remain in his office if he has not reached it yet."

Torvan turned immediately and began to arrange a more defensive shift for the right-kin. Finch did not remain to hear the details; it was not her job, nor her responsibility, and there were no two men she trusted more with Teller's life. Or her own, if it came to that.

She made one more stop before she exited the building. She entered Daine's healerie. The large box by the door was so much a part of visiting that she removed her daggers and dropped them into that box without a second thought.

To her surprise, Daine was awake. He sat on the edge of the fountain in the arboretum, his neck bent, his hands crushed against his knees. They were shaking. He looked up when she entered, and she thought that Daine—unlike the rest of the den—had not bothered with even an attempt to sleep. He was younger than any of the den save Adam, but tonight his expression was that of a much older man.

And she remembered why Daine was part of the den, why he was in the healerie, and froze for one long moment.

He knew. He rose, his hands shaking. "I have prepared the healerie," he said quietly.

"Nothing's happened."

"No. Do you honestly believe nothing will?" Before she could answer—and she had begun to gather the strands of a regent's dignity about herself—he said, "Tell me. Tell me that so *I can believe it.*"

She gave up on the regency then, lifting her hands in den-sign. *What do you hear?*

He frowned at the finger movements; she had made them both deliberate and slow. Although Daine had been taught den-sign, he did not use it often. Less, she thought, than Adam—but Adam was the age they had been when they had invented the language.

"Horns," he said. "Horns. Do you remember the last time we heard horns?"

She did.

"The Hunter God." Daine had not experienced that. But Daine, healer-born, had chosen to pull Jay from the banks across the bridge—and Jay most certainly had; he would carry those memories as part of his own until he died. She knew how much of a burden healing was—he was forced, by the act, to carry not one set of fears, but two.

More.

The Terafin—not Jay, but Amarais—had made decisions about who the previous healer tended. She made decisions about who he called back from death, when no other medical aid would be enough to save life. Finch was not certain that, even as acting regent, she could make a similar decision because in the end it was Daine, den-kin, who would bear the cost.

He signed.

"No. I hear nothing. I'm awake because Night woke me. And to be honest, I'm calculating just how much we can afford to piss off the treasurer. Or how much more."

"He damaged something?"

"The carpeting. Again. Night isn't very communicative. How clear are the horns?"

"It's not just the horns," he said, his voice dropping. "When I woke, I went to the window. I opened it."

She waited.

"It was winter, Finch. It was winter, and I could see the shadow of the hunters. They did not ride in a host; they were four."

"Four."

"They seemed almost ghostly to me, but solid. Terrifying." He exhaled.

"The Sleepers."

He said nothing. But he turned toward the room in which all the beds and supplies lay. "I think, if they are not awake yet, they will be soon."

When the Sleepers wake.

She said, "The forest people are gathering. The Chosen are marshaling the House Guard."

"I know."

The moment she set foot on the sculpted garden path, the color of the night sky shifted. It had been dark, if clear; it now took on a tint that implied dawn was on its way. But it wasn't the pink of coming dawn she saw; it was the orange and red of fire.

Finch had always been able to find the heart of Jay's forest, although she entered it seldom. It was not that she felt unwelcome in it; whenever she made her way there, she knew she was safe. But it was not her home. In it, there were trees of silver, of gold, of diamond; in it was a tree of fire that was nonetheless also a tree of wood, with branches and flames for leaf and flower. It was not the Merchant Authority; nor was it the crowded streets of the holdings. It was Jay's, yes—but it was part of Jay that had nothing whatsoever to do with the den.

The den had learned to give each other privacy, when the physical means for it was well beyond them; Finch stayed out of the forest because, in some fashion, she had learned this lesson well. But she understood, as the tree of fire came almost instantly into view, that there were different lessons to be learned. This *was* Jay's, it was part of who she had become, and Finch as regent had to accept it fully.

She was not, however, the first person present; she was almost the last.

Jester was leaning against the trunk of the burning tree; Teller was standing back from it, his arms moving, his elbows jogging slightly as he used his hands to speak. Jester, arms folded, used words instead, because they were easier.

Arann was not here; he was, and would remain, with the Chosen. Finch had accepted that more readily than Jay. Angel was with Jay. Adam was with Jay.

Finch had not been home when Snow had stalked into the West Wing, but she had heard about it—and even if she hadn't, the gouges he'd left in Adam's closed door were testament enough to his mood.

He had not taken Ariel with him. She remained in the West Wing, forlorn and silent. Although the den attempted to speak with her, to interact with her, she was comfortable with Adam and Shadow. Everyone else came a very distant second.

"Finch."

She blinked. Jester had called her name.

"Where's Jarven?"

"I don't know." At Jester's expression, she added, "He has no keepers. Not even Lucille can keep him on schedule if he becomes distracted."

"Fine. Can you tell Haval that?"

"I already did." She grimaced. "Haval knows Jarven better than any of us. There is no way he expects us to have actual information."

"He lives," a familiar voice said, "in hope."

Finch did not gape; nor did Teller or Jester, although both turned in the direction of that voice.

Andrei, servant to Hectore of Araven, stood in the clearing around the tree. The sound of crackling fire grew subtly louder; the movement of chiming leaves stilled. The forest did not like Andrei. Jay did. It was comforting to know that it was Jay's affection that won out. But she could be honest with herself in the silence. Were she Andrei, were the forest to react the way it did when he entered it, she would never have come here at all. She could almost hear the forest's voice, raised in warning and hostility.

Andrei, however, seemed either inured to it or resigned. He bowed to Finch—a full sweeping motion, appropriate for The Terafin herself—and rose, his eyes dark.

"Hectore is not with you?"

"No. Nor is he best pleased to be at home—but his presence is required; it is his grandson's birthday."

"He allowed you to come on your own?"

"You needn't be so surprised, ATerafin. It is not the first time I have chosen to work in isolation."

"Circumstances are different, at least according to the cats."

"Yes. It is my suspicion that Hectore does not fully apprehend this."

"He will," Haval said. He had appeared as if by magic.

"Indeed. But it is my hope that he—and his family—will be safely ensconced behind their walls when he does." His smile was almost rueful.

"Given what the elders in the forest fear, it is scant hope."

"I am not as you are," Andrei replied, stiff with a servant's dignity. "While I stand, Hectore *will* be safe."

"Interesting. The Araven manse is secure?"

"It is."

"You will not, of course, tell me how; I will not ask it. I will ask instead how large an area such protections might be stretched to cover."

Andrei's smile was slender, but genuine. "I am accepted nowhere."

"Nowhere except Araven?"

"Even so."

"And were you to be accepted—"

"It is not a matter of simple discussion, simple argument, mortal persuasion. I am tolerated. This forest tolerates me—but it does not do so gladly, and without The Terafin's immutable will, I would never have found you here. What I can do for Hectore, I am unable to do for the rest of the city."

Haval considered this.

It was Birgide, appearing as suddenly as Haval himself had, who said, "He is right. I believe that Andrei could be persuaded to make the attempt, but it would not, in the end, be successful." She glanced at the Araven servant, but her eyes slid almost instantly to the side. What she could see as Warden of Jay's forest was not what Finch saw.

Haval, however, nodded. "The *Astari*?" he asked, which surprised Finch.

It did not surprise Birgide. Her eyes were bloodred, with a hint of the orange of reflected flame. "Sigurne and the magi have been summoned to *Avantari*; the High Priests—the god-born—have been summoned as well. They intend to meet at Moorelas' statue in the holdings."

"When?"

Birgide closed her disturbing eyes. "Three hours hence, perhaps less."

"You did not ask what they intended."

"I did not feel the information was required. Should you disagree, you might feel free to approach Duvari yourself."

And at that, Jarven ATerafin's loud and dismissive snort could be heard as he, too, joined them in the clearing.

He was smiling broadly, and Finch thought the smile genuine. Everything about his expression was sharp. Where Haval had chosen neutrality as his governing interaction this eve, Jarven had dropped it entirely. She was glad that Lucille was not present; Lucille would be disgusted, and she did not deserve that.

"You are wearing your matron's expression, Finch," Jarven observed.

"I was thinking about Lucille. What have you come to report?"

"Report?"

"I am regent in The Terafin's absence. I assume that you traveled here to give your report."

He laughed. It was loud, bold, compelling. As was he, at the moment—at least to Finch; Jester appeared to be highly unamused. "You assume no such thing."

"You have always understood me," she replied, smiling gently. "But in this, Jarven, you are wrong. I am regent—as you once intended—and I do, indeed, make that assumption."

His smile deepened. "Do you, by chance, understand what I now am?"

"You are Jarven." She folded her arms.

"That is not a good look on you, my dear. You have neither the age nor the size to carry it off to perfection."

She didn't budge.

Haval, however, did. He came to stand beside Finch, his hands clasped loosely behind his back. "If she has been your charge, ATerafin, she has been my responsibility. We do not have time to play these games."

"And yet, play them we must," Jarven replied. But he met Haval's gaze. "You are not dressed for tailoring."

"No. In the days to come, I fear that making will be beyond me."

"But not breaking, Haval?" He spoke the name with too much emphasis.

"As you say. Have you spoken with Duvari?"

"Duvari is not my concern."

"What did he say?"

Jarven rolled his eyes. "You are the death of fun."

"I believe I always was, in your estimation."

"The Kings are required in the ceremony of the god-born. He will not—and cannot—spare further effort to oversee, how did he put it? Terafin's petty problems at this time."

"I see you managed to offend him before he spoke."

"Duvari thrives on offense taken, as you well know. You chose him, after all."

"You did not disapprove."

"I did."

"Not in a substantive way." He glanced briefly at Finch. "Regent." He bowed. "We await your command."

* * *

She had no command to offer. The regency she had desired—the regency she had accepted—had nothing to do with forests and a wilderness that was sentient, alive, and dangerous even when at peace. The lessons she had learned over the decade by Jarven's side had accentuated things human, things mundane; greed, dishonesty, ambition—to be sure—but also their opposite. It was their opposite that had surprised her, but that was almost a given considering the way she had come to her den, the only family that now mattered to her.

Yet Haval waited, and clearly meant to wait, until she spoke. Jarven did the same, a malicious twinkle in his eyes. Jester moved, and she lifted one hand in swift den-sign, understanding that, ready or not, she *had* accepted the regency. Jay was not here. She was certain that Jay would return if she still lived, but she could not be certain when; Jay herself did not know.

Teller, however, she did not still with either word or gesture; he was right-kin, and his place was by the side of the ruler of Terafin. Finch.

Jay, she thought. *What would you do?*

No answer came to her: no instinct; no certainty.

No certainty but this: she had chosen to become the leader of Terafin, and she must lead. If she did not, it would likely be Haerrad who would; he was a man suited to, situated for, war.

And there was war here, waiting just below the surface of a tense and desperate peace: there were gleaming weapons, polished spears, and flames that had detached from the branches of the tree of fire as if they were simple leaves. Those leaves burned nothing, no matter where they fell. Ah, not nothing; Jarven attempted to pick one up. He did not make a second attempt.

She had no doubt in future he would, and the results would be different.

"Where," she asked, hardening her voice, "are the heralds?" It was not spoken as a plea; there was no fear in the words. She wanted the information, and wanted it now.

Jarven's expression lost light and joy instantly, his face becoming as expressionless as Haval's. She felt Teller shift; she was certain Jester was annoyed. Annoyed and alert. She smiled. "Please," she said, not even attempting to keep the amusement from the single word. "I've worked beside you for over half my life. I know when you're serious. And I know when you're wasting time."

"This is the part where you fold your arms and scold me about dignity?"

"I have never scolded you about your dignity or its possible lack. Dignity can, of course, be of use—but the lack has never harmed you. Unless you consider Lucille's disappointment or annoyance harmful."

And his smile, when it returned, was slower to come, slighter. It was paternal; she recognized that now. But inasmuch as he had ever had the inclination, he had chosen to be a father to her. A distant father, one who might let his child fall off a cliff should she be foolish enough to attempt to scale it without knowledge or equipment.

"Finch—"

"I am not wasted here."

"No. You are benightedly necessary here, but I feel that I have perhaps worked against my own best interests for over a decade. You cannot threaten me," he added.

"I would not even make the attempt. In the end, I do not hold your name. It is *possible* that your name could be revoked if that were the will of the House Council—but that would take time and would, no doubt, involve the shedding of blood, none of which would be your own."

"Of course not."

"But if I do not hold your name, and hold only the passing glance of your loyalty, the forest is not the same. The elders are not the same. You have accepted the gift—and perhaps the duties that gift might entail—of one of the forest elders. And he serves The Terafin completely. There is no game you might play—with words, with weapons—that will move him or cause him to swerve."

"Ah, Finch, you are wrong. Were he not at least partly akin to me in nature, I would not now be here."

She nodded, unmoved. "He is, I think, like you. Unfettered, unclaimed, you would be rivals, and in the end, enemies. But he is unlike you as well. He is *of the forest*, Jarven, and the forest is Jay's."

"Perhaps he is not pleased to be so," Jarven countered, aware of the significance of the use of that name. His voice was now smooth, harder, inflected in a way that suggested he had finally turned the whole of his formidable intellect upon a very tricky negotiation. Finch had seen this only a handful of times in all the years she had been at the Authority. She felt a brief chill; while she had been a witness to it, she had never, ever been the person across the table from him.

No, she had been serving tea and listening as if her life and future depended on it. She had been overlooked, but she had spent the majority of her life being overlooked. It had been safest.

There was no safety now.

She was no foundling now; she was no abandoned child. *Kalliaris* had smiled on Finch in her darkest hour, and she was here. She was Jay's. She was den. She was regent.

"Whether or not he is pleased to be so is irrelevant."

Haval lifted a hand in swift, almost invisible den-sign, but she was on alert now and caught it. *Be careful.*

If caution had hierarchy, Finch had been among its generals. She did not answer, did not acknowledge. Teller moved again; Jester came to stand beside her. Neither spoke.

"Irrelevant? That is harsh." And standing by her ankles, his fur sleek and golden, was the fox.

She bent to offer him the seat of her arms—it was hardly a cradle—and he accepted this as his due, allowing her to rise to her full height bearing his scant weight. It was not always scant.

"You have fostered an *interesting* mortal," the fox then told Jarven. If the den did not interrupt, and if Haval kept his distance, the fox felt no compunction. Then again, Jarven had said they were spiritual kin, and Jarven felt free to interrupt any event or conversation if the fancy struck him.

"I have hardly fostered her," Jarven replied. For the first time, he glanced away from Finch to meet the eyes of the creature that was, at the moment, his master.

"I did not notice her," the fox continued, as if Jarven had not spoken. Jarven's face was smooth, neutral; he had adopted a mask of respect. It was only a mask, but it was like dignity, really; it fooled no one who was part of the conversation. Not the fox, certainly, and not Finch. Jarven would not expect otherwise. "I assumed she was like the others."

"But you expected her to carry you."

"Oh, indeed. Respect—as you well know—is necessary in the wilderness. I knew her because the forest knows her. I accept her because the heart of the forest sings her name, even in its quiet sleep. But she is bold in a way that I am not and will never be: timidly."

"She does not seem timid at the moment, Eldest."

"Does she not?" The fox's nose tickled the underside of Finch's chin, and Finch looked down. His eyes, like his fur, were golden. They were, in fact, the same shade of gold, and for a moment he seemed to her to be all eyes or, perhaps, sightless; it was disturbing. "But I bit her once, and I was ill for a day afterward. What exactly did you feed her?"

"Cookies," Finch said. "And tea. The very occasional meal."

"I was not asking you."

"When it comes to trivial details, it is often me you must ask; they are inconsequential to the powerful." Her arms tightened almost instinctively.

"You bit her."

"Once."

"You *bit* her."

"I believe I have repeated myself twice. I have spoken the words three times." The last two syllables seemed to shake the forest, and the tree of fire shed leaves as if it were standing in a sudden gale. The fox's tail grew longer, wilder, the fur splitting and elongating as if the whole of the tail had been a complicated, invisible braid that had now become undone. Gold crept up Finch's arms and shoulders, twining around her neck, bypassing her mouth, her nose, and her eyes.

Jester cursed, which wasn't unusual.

Teller repeated the single word, which was.

Finch, however, said nothing. She did not even attempt to release the fox; the gesture, disturbing and oddly majestic, had made clear that he had no desire to be set down. Nor did she desire to do so. As if the table across which negotiations had started remained standing between them, she met Jarven's gaze—when he had pulled it, finally, free of the fox's eyes.

"My dear," he said, which was not promising. "Do you even begin to understand the game you intend to play? You have not yet set your piece upon the board, and I am willing to set this aside for another day, another time." He spoke the words as if they were a munificent offer—and from Jarven, they were. But such an offer spoke of power, and even condescension; he was willing to, as Lucille sometimes put it, "play nice," the implication being that she required it.

She *desired* it. She always had. When people played nice, life was gentler and the difficulties less catastrophic. She played nice as a rule *because* she desired that gentler life. Jarven was not, had not been, against such a life. He had lived it for decades. But on occasion he set it aside completely as a reminder that he could. As a reminder of what he might do, should he set his mind on it.

She understood what he offered now.

He was her superior. He was a man who had done things that she herself could not do and survive. The Terafin offices in the Merchant Authority were safe precisely because he was unpredictable, and the stories of his youth were almost legend. One did not cross Jarven ATerafin.

She had always known this. She had quietly pitied the pompous and overbearing men who assumed that Jarven was now in his dotage because he played a fool for his own amusement—and his own gain—as they would eventually discover. Also, to be fair, he liked to tweak Lucille.

But Lucille would never, ever, have stood as Finch was standing now. Had

Jarven always known that? Lucille had never been, never become, one in the long line of his protégés, some of who had not survived.

"I understand it no better than you," she replied. "But I understand it no less, either."

His brows rose. "Finch."

"Jarven."

"I haven't the time to truly engage you. Let this wait."

"I haven't the time to wait. I can, in theory, command you as regent. Your compliance would be as theoretical as my rulership." She adjusted her grip. "But I am not, in the end, the woman to whom you owe either obedience or allegiance. Not even Amarais was, although you did back her in her early bid for the Terafin seat. I require information. It is information you have. If you offer it freely, we might move on."

"And if I do not?" There was no warmth in the question, no amusement; there was a trace of his sharpest edge. It cut her in ways that the small, sharp teeth of the fox had not.

She chose her words with care, aware that at this moment it was absolutely necessary. "This matter involves the forest. It involves The Terafin's hidden lands."

He understood the quiet threat. She thought that her den-kin did not. But Jarven's expression made clear to her that he was not yet certain that Finch herself was not bluffing. She understood the value of a bluff. She understood the value of a lie. They were tools that she used very seldom because she was not good at either.

He should have known that. And perhaps he did. Or perhaps this was just his way of demanding a concession when the negotiations had demanded something that he could see no easy way of denying.

"So it does," he replied, after a pause. Giving her the space and the time to concede, to retreat.

"The forest," she said, because she could not retreat, "is The Terafin's. What I could not command from you, I might command of the forest itself." She spoke with a certainty she did not feel.

And the fox said, "He knows this to be true." Unlike Jarven's, his voice was warm, almost playful. He was amused.

Jarven's frown was meant for the fox; he had never enjoyed interruption on those rare occasions when he was entirely—and obviously—focused on his work.

"What this surprising child is saying," the fox began.

"If she is surprising, it has taken some work and nurture to create her,

Eldest," Jarven interrupted. The air grew chillier. Jarven bowed instantly—a full bow, a full obeisance, itself almost shocking to Finch given the charged atmosphere. "The lessons now are far fewer, the time between them greater. But the consequences are, therefore, more dire, and the choices made, more complex.

"She has been protected and cozened by those she considers kin—but in Jewel's absence, it is Finch who must shoulder the burdens of commander. Would you then protect her from even the slight sting of making those commands explicit?"

"Me? Of course not," the fox replied. "I do not foster the young and foolish. Nor do I feel it necessary to protect them."

Jarven nodded, as if the point had been conceded, but he was wary.

And right to be. "But she is not my foster. You are. And Jewel is the heart of this land."

"She was not always so."

"No."

"And you have no desire to be free?"

The fox chuckled. "It was Winter in these lands. Cold and endless. What freedom was there in ice? The roots of the forest did not grow or move; the leaves did not bud and blossom; the denizens of the land did not speak or sing or quarrel. Only the wily scavengers moved here, shadows of life. She woke the forest. While she is Lord, be the Winter eternal, the forest will remain awake."

"But Summer is coming."

"Ah. You misunderstand. It is our hope that Summer will at last grace the lands, and in Summer one chafes at rulership. But it is not Summer, Jarven. Tell me, do you consider all necessity restricting?"

Jarven did not consider the question rhetorical. He considered it with care. "If I accept the necessity, I do not resent it."

"Very well. You must breathe. Yes, even you, although lesser restrictions exist for you now. You must eat. And you must sleep."

Jarven nodded.

"These things are not required of us, except perhaps sleep—and our understanding of sleep is in no way similar to yours; were we not as we are, we might think of an entirely different word to convey the meaning under which we exist. However, Finch is getting impatient."

She did not deny this, although it was not entirely true. The fox was not Jarven. What Jarven would forgive, the fox might not. And, Finch thought, for the Terafin merchant—if that was what he remained—no matter the outcome of this discussion, a wall had been built, a gauntlet thrown. Her arms tightened.

The fox sneezed. He was so very like Jarven in many ways. But Jarven could not be held, could not be cradled, and could not enclose her in a golden cage. She understood that, no matter how soft, how warm, and how slight this might seem, it was a cage.

"It is not, foolish child," the fox said, as if she had somehow injured his dignity. "It is armor."

Jarven chuckled then. The edge in his expression was blunted almost instantly by the fox's explanation.

"I would let you play," the fox told his liege, "but Finch is the heart of the forest. Finch, Teller, that boy with fire for hair. If the entire city were to fall to demons and darkness, to gods and the firstborn, our Lord might be saved if these people survive. You care for your own survival—but only when you earn it. You are willing to risk death, to stare it in the face while you learn the rules and the meaning behind the encounter; you consider survival to be your responsibility and your reward.

"You therefore consider lack of survival to be a reward of its own—for lack of effort, for lack of intelligence, for lack of struggle. Your heart has always beat in time with the wilderness.

"But Jewel's has not. Therefore, you will accept it when I say—I who could kill you now without even blinking—that Finch may command *me*. What she commands of me, I will give. And if she commands me to surrender your services, I will do exactly that."

"It would be better for Finch were she to state that openly."

"Why?"

"Because had she, she would be signaling clearly that she understands—and accepts—what might follow from it."

"Ah. You will forgive me if I do not share this view. To me, she would be stating the obvious, and the obvious is often boring."

"A sword is a mortal weapon."

"Not merely mortal, but I shall concede the theoretical point."

"Should a sword hang upon a wall, it is considered decoration. It is there, it is clearly a weapon, it has an owner. But it does not have a wielder. A sword upon the wall is barely even a topic for idle conversation. If a mortal—ah, no, let me be specific. If Finch wishes to point to the sword on the wall, that signifies little. It remains on the wall. She might allude to it; it is the overture to threat. But it has no teeth.

"Should she, however, pull that sword from the wall and wield it, it becomes a weapon. A declaration."

"And you wish her to declare herself your opponent?"

"No, Eldest. I wish her to understand that she has clambered up a ladder and removed the sword from the wall. It remains in its scabbard. She has failed, through caution or justifiable fear, to draw it. But she will have to draw it if it is to have weight and meaning. And I wish to know how committed she is. She will require that knowledge as well."

The fox regarded Jarven as steadily, as intensely, as Jarven now regarded the fox. It was the first time that Finch had wondered who Jarven's mentors were—she had assumed, until this moment, that he had wanted, had needed, none. He was not a man given to need.

He was not a man given to actual weakness, although feigning weakness could amuse him, at the expense of those who were inclined to believe the lie.

"Teach her, if you must," the fox finally said, as if he were condescending to make a concession where none was earned or deserved. "But do so after Jewel's reign is secured. I myself might find it interesting to put Finch through her paces; she seems entirely predictable, but there is something about her . . ."

Finch cleared her throat, and both of them—fox and Jarven—looked to her, as if expecting the unexpected. She disagreed with both of them; she was not unpredictable. And even were she, she had no compunction at this moment about disappointing their capricious expectations.

"Although he is correct," the fox said. "You are not terribly playful."

"This is not the time for play."

"My dear," Jarven said, his tone reverting to the one with which she was most familiar, "there is always time for play. Make even the most dire of situations a game, as I do, and the outcome will be less crushing."

"If I survive."

His smile was sharp, unlike his tone. "Even so."

The fox cleared his throat. If he was unlike the cats—and he was—he shared one thing in common with them; he disliked being ignored or forgotten. He tickled the underside of Finch's chin with long, shining whiskers that seemed to move almost independently, which was more disturbing than Finch would have liked. But he spoke to Jarven. "When you fought the herald, you did not destroy him."

Silence.

Finch was not the first person to speak. None of the mortals were. Jarven's eyes narrowed, his lips compressed; there was a flash of genuine annoyance in his expression, although it was hooded almost instantly. Finch wondered if anyone else had noticed, then remembered almost ruefully that Haval was Councillor, some nebulous part of the forest. Even had he not been, he would have seen, have understood, and even accepted. Not for Haval uncertainty in his own observations.

He did not move, did not shift position; instead, he became utterly and completely still. In his dark clothing, with the lack of encumbering apron, he looked like a shadow.

"You found another herald."

"Clearly."

"And your injuries?"

"Irrelevant."

Haval nodded as if he agreed. "You did not destroy him. Did you retreat?"

"No. It was not necessary."

"Did he?"

Jarven's smile was sharp, almost predatory. "Yes."

"You believe that to be a feint?"

"The risk was high."

"His skills?"

"Weapon. Sword, shield. He had some rudimentary magical protections, but I believe those to be innate." He glanced at Finch, who merely listened. When Jarven's gaze rested on hers for long enough, she spoke.

"I am content to let Haval ask the questions. The information comes to me regardless."

"And you trust that he will ask the right questions?"

"I trust that he will ask the questions he considers relevant—but, Jarven, you only answer questions you feel are relevant. No, that isn't exact. Haval understands you in a way that I don't. And you understand Haval in a way that I don't. You don't say things that don't need to be said. Nor does he."

"You are content to allow his understanding—and mine—to guide you?"

"No. But Haval will answer questions without evasion when the situation is dire."

"And I will not."

"No situation is dire enough to you."

He laughed, then. There was actual warmth in his expression. Finch, however, could not respond in kind.

"The shield and the sword were blue," Jarven continued.

"Yes. I believe that to be the natural weaponry of the Wild Hunt. But it is not the only weaponry at their disposal."

"Ah."

"Did the herald fly?"

"No."

"And he did not attempt to wake earth?"

"He could not," the fox said, before Jarven could answer. "Not easily. When faced with mortals, perhaps. The wind and fire are quick to wake. The earth is not."

Finch wanted to correct him; Jarven was mortal. But the words would not leave her mouth. And Jarven knew. Of course he knew.

"The White Lady could speak to all elements with ease before the seasons came. She might bespeak the earth now—but seldom. It is costly. I do not believe the heralds will make that attempt."

"Fire and air."

"Indeed. However, in these lands, that will not aid them. Jewel has forbidden the elements freedom here without her express permission. If they come at all, it will be because they have been called by one of the firstborn princes."

It was Teller who said, "The Sleepers were all firstborn princes."

"Yes. You understand. They had the power to kill the gods," the fox continued. "And there is a god who now walks this plane."

"They will not negotiate with us," Finch said. Her voice was flat.

"They will not negotiate with you," the fox countered.

"Eldest."

The fox turned in the direction of the voice.

"The great tree says they will not negotiate with any of us while these lands remain in the hands of a mortal. They did not venture often into these lands."

"They would speak with me." There was no doubt in the fox's voice.

The speaker, a bark-skinned man of over six feet in height, who nonetheless resembled a rooted tree, nodded. "Yes, Eldest." He was carrying a spear; its haft was wooden. In the firelight, the pointed tip reflected nothing.

"The second herald?" the fox then asked.

Jarven nodded briefly in the creature's direction. "I did not choose to close directly."

"And?"

"I had some success in leading him astray."

"You were not lost yourself?" Haval asked.

"I found it rather more difficult to return than expected, but not impossible. The wilderness beyond our borders lies in winter; it is difficult to leave only the hint of tracks, the hint of a trail."

"But not difficult to leave none." It was not a question. Finch waited.

"As you surmise."

"Did you encounter the third and fourth?"

"No. I encountered a third, but the fourth does not seem to have traveled toward our lands."

"He would not be required to travel through the wilderness," Teller said, voice soft. That softness, marked with diffidence and respect, nonetheless served to catch the forbidding attention of the powerful. And it was attention, Finch thought, that Teller did not want.

They waited.

"If there is a fourth herald, it is not for the Sleepers that he comes," Teller continued, his voice steady, if quiet. Jester signed, but Teller shook his head slightly before he continued. "I do not understand why the heralds exist, nor can I claim to understand their purpose. But Sigurne herself came to my office; she would discuss the matter only there.

"The three heralds are to wake—and serve—the princes into whose service they have been commanded. But there were four princes, and therefore four heralds. Three of the princes rode with Moorelas, and in the end, three of the princes were condemned to sleep. Sigurne surmises that the heralds were also, in some fashion, sleeping—she cannot be certain. She said that the explanations given were scant, and they did not make mortal sense."

"I would like to speak with the guildmaster," Haval said quietly.

Teller nodded, as if he'd expected no less. Haval seldom treated either Teller or Finch with the same harshness he seemed to reserve for Jay.

Jester grimaced. He lifted hands and signed, *I'll go.* To Haval.

"The fourth Herald," Teller continued, "did not serve one of the condemned. He served . . ." He exhaled. "He served Meralonne APhaniel, before his fall."

Jester entered the Order of Knowledge wearing a seal that acknowledged him as part of the Terafin House Council. It was not entirely inaccurate, in that he had not only permission but the responsibility of attending Council meetings when Finch was present. He seldom made those meetings, and Finch overlooked his absence for the most part; she considered his presence to cause more acrimony.

The ring, however, was useful. Jester understood that speed was of the essence; he had commandeered a messenger carriage, had asked the driver to get him to the Order's front steps yesterday, if possible, and had leaped out of the carriage with alarming speed before the footman had had a chance to lower the stairs to allow for an exit consonant with the dignity of a House Council adjutant.

He was met as he entered the hall, its stately but opulent interior the public face of the Order. Jester, however, had seen enough of the magi to understand that there was a good reason why most of the halls did not have a public face; the mage-born were fractious, disorganized, and compulsive—on a good day.

This was, perhaps, not a good day.

He held out his hand, allowing the ring to be seen and very discreetly inspected. He was then ushered into a room that was meant for the use of the rich and the powerful while they waited. There was a cabinet with requisite amounts of alcohol, and a servant who appeared to exist solely for the purpose of dispensing it.

Jester did not sit. The chairs were too comfortable, and he could not afford to be comfortable here. Or possibly ever again. He did jump and pivot when the room itself shook, as if the whole of the floor had been struck by an angry god.

The servant, however, did not seem to be troubled by this. He offered Jester a deep bow. "Please accept the apologies of the Order for any discomfort the practices of its members may cause." As if something that felt almost like an earthquake was an everyday occurrence. Given his utter lack of panic—given, in fact, his pinched look of tired resignation—Jester suddenly believed that they were.

They had not been, once.

He accepted the drink he was offered but husbanded the glass rather than knocking it back. He was here as an official of Terafin and while allowances for inebriated behavior were made, they were made in larger social situations, not private meetings.

Jay had never navigated larger parties well; Jester could. He understood her disdain, but did not understand her clumsy lack of competence. She was stiff; she had the substance to be a power—she was The Terafin, and her rule was undisputed, inasmuch as the rule of the powerful could ever be undisputed. But she lacked the grace, the elegance, the certainty, that having power should have conveyed.

Of course she did.

Jester lacked the substance, but he understood the show. He could wear the clothing, eat the food, rub shoulders with those who would have been disgusted to know that he had come to Terafin from the poorest of the hundred holdings. From, in fact, an illegal brothel. He was largely unconcerned with their opinions—but never completely—because while he respected the possibility their power could be a threat to him, he felt no actual respect for them as people. He didn't require that respect in order to mime a semblance of it.

Jay, however, probably did.

And Jay had left Terafin to the den to guard while she tried to find some solution to waking princes that did not result in the destruction of most of this city. The problem with that was Jester did not feel up to that responsibility. He had no visceral fear for the loss of anything but his den. Did he desire it? No. But ultimately as long as those people were not bleeding out and dying in his lap, he didn't really care. They were strangers. They had no responsibility for him, either.

The only reason he cared—the only reason he could find—was Jay. Because Jay *did* care. She'd cared enough to come to the brothel for Duster, of all people. She cared enough when she arrived that she would not leave any of the rest of them to burn in the magical fires that had destroyed that building.

She proved, by her constant action, her loyalty, that there *were* people with no prior obligations who *would* help. And maybe, he told himself, as he gazed at the surface of his drink, he hadn't met them all yet—and if the Sleepers did wake, he never would. Maybe some other Jay, some other Jester, were growing up in the streets of the hundred holdings, and their lives would be cut short before they could ever meet.

He gave up and downed the small glass. No matter what he told himself, he didn't believe it enough that he could crawl out of the comfortable, irresponsible life he had inhabited.

He had come to the Order of Knowledge to deliver a message to the guildmaster—a message he believed she would heed. He expected that a page would open the door. He expected that he would be relieved of his empty glass, that he would be inspected for unusual weapons, that he would be asked basic, perfunctory questions—he bore the House ring, after all—and that he would be led up the stairs—a long, punishing, and somewhat unforgiving climb—to speak with Sigurne Mellifas.

He did not relish that. Nor did he relish the long, punishing descent, the return to flat ground, and the race back to the manse, where he would once again be surrounded by the prelude to, the echo of, war. He was not, in any sense, a soldier. He had taken the necessary task because it would take him, in the end, to the solid streets of the city itself. To reality, for however long it lasted.

And perhaps because he was not even close to the decent person he knew that others were capable of being, his disguised cowardice was rewarded.

The door did open, but it was not a page that stood in its frame.

It was not the guildmaster, either.

It was not, in fact, a man, although Jester recognized him. His hands fell to his sides, but he retained his grip on the glass. It was thick-cut crystal, or it might have splintered in his hand.

He did not bow. He did not nod. But for the moment, he did not speak; he knew better.

"Well met, ATerafin," said the chain-clad, silver-eyed man who had—until an hour ago—been the Terafin House Mage.

Chapter Seven

JESTER DID NOT LIFT his hand, did not wave his ring, did not lift his voice. The words of the forest folk, the words of Haval and Jarven, seemed to echo in a room that was suddenly too small, too ordinary, for them; it was far too ordinary now for Meralonne APhaniel.

He remembered the first time he had seen the magi fight—a battle that had destroyed the Terafin foyer. Jay had not been Terafin; Jester had not been ATerafin. That had come later. It had been easy to forget that mage in the intervening years; easy to be irritated by the omnipresent scent of pipe tobacco and oddly inappropriate clothing; easy to be amused by his apparent disregard for any authority save that of the guildmaster herself.

For a moment the audacity, the ignorance, of such assumptions was galling. Beyond that. Humiliating. And beneath that . . . insulting. On a visceral level he knew that it was the latter that would be his death. He did not imagine, as he stood before this man, that the death would be particularly pleasant; fast, painless deaths would probably be granted by accident, to those unlucky enough to be standing in the way.

Jester had been a bystander for much of his life; bystander was better, by far, than victim in his personal experience. But he had chosen to come here to avoid the detritus of preparations for a war he was in no way qualified to fight. And he had come to speak with Sigurne Mellifas.

He did not, therefore, bow—or kneel or grovel—which was not as hard as it should have been; his knees had locked. He forced them to move and headed toward the glass-fronted door of a cupboard that contained liquor. There he paused, as if choosing with care. Over his shoulder, when he trusted his voice to be steady enough, he said, "Can I get you anything?" almost as if they were in the West Wing and he was at home.

"I am here to inform you," Meralonne replied, "that Sigurne Mellifas is away from her tower, at the behest of the Twin Kings. It is highly unlikely that you will find her at home in the foreseeable future."

"She sent you?"

"She is unaware of your visit; I assume no appointment was made."

Jester refilled his glass. The attendant had vanished—hopefully on his own two legs. Had Jester the option, he would have joined the man. He did not; he was ATerafin. Being ATerafin had been better, by far, than the alternatives for well over a decade now. Almost two.

But nothing in life was free. He turned, full glass in hand, to face the man Teller had obliquely implied was the last of the firstborn princes—and the only one, in the end, who had not failed in his charge.

"The Terafin?" Meralonne asked, which was not the question Jester had been expecting—if he'd been expecting questions at all. The air seemed to move around the magi, lifting only the strands of his hair, which fell past his shoulders down his back, a second cloak.

"She has not returned."

"Can you hear them, ATerafin?"

"Hear what?"

"The dreams," he said, "of the Sleepers. The horns of the heralds." He trembled as the words left his lips, but not in fear.

"No," Jester replied. He did not look away. Could not. "But those dreams have been felt. They devoured one of my kin."

"Ah." For the first time since the door had opened, the magi moved; his feet did not seem to touch ground. "Do you understand what is happening?"

Jester shrugged before he could stop his shoulders from moving in the elegant gesture of nonchalance that had become second nature. He froze a second later, and once again forced himself to relax. It had never been wise to show fear where it was possible to hide it.

"Why did you wish to speak to Sigurne?"

As much as Jester disliked pipe smoke, he wished for it now. He met Meralonne's steady gaze. "Do you serve her still?"

At that, the mage smiled. "As much as I ever have. Mortals were oft a challenge in my youth; they were fragile and even if one could preserve their lives, those lives vanished so quickly. She is not what she was when we first met."

"Are you?"

"I am all that I was. All."

Jester did not like risk; but sometimes he was drawn to it, like gamblers compelled to place bets. He preferred games of chance that involved simple coin, simple gold, but understood that it was not the gold itself that was the draw. "Are you more? No, not more. Other?"

"Not yet, boy. Not yet, but soon. Why did you wish to speak with Sigurne?"

"Because we were told we could not speak with you."

"Your advisors were wise, but premature."

"Were they?" Jester drank. "We wished to speak to Sigurne because the fourth herald is not on the hidden roads, seeking a way into these lands."

Silence.

The air was charged; Meralonne APhaniel's hair rose across his back as if it were alive. His eyes flashed, the silver gleam so much like blade's edge they appeared to be weapons.

"If you seek to stop us—"

Us. "We seek to delay. We are aware that we are not, in any way, your equal."

This did not mollify the mage—but it did not further enrage him. Jester drank again.

After a long pause, Meralonne continued. "The heralds are not as you are. They are not as the men given to the Winter King's service. They are not as Lord Celleriant, the youngest of the princes of the Hidden Court. Without the Sleepers, the heralds would not exist at all."

Jester did not understand this.

"The heralds were created in the wake of the Lady's displeasure. She did not, for reasons no one of us understood, desire their death, their destruction. They had failed her, but—" He closed his eyes. "Perhaps she saw what must happen, in the end: the return of her enemy. The return of the god." Silence fell, its weight texturing the air. Jester found it hard to breathe.

"You do not understand what the Sleepers were, to their kin, to the White Lady, to her Court. We had lost much. To the earliest of her children she granted the power of herself, firstborn. You have seen Shianne," he continued, when Jester failed to speak, "but you have not seen—ah, no.

"Just as your Kings are loved and revered, be they as mortal as the most insignificant of your poor, they, too, were loved and revered. There were those among the White Lady's kin that could not bear to lose them. They spoke," his voice was quiet, the words so soft they should have been inaudible. "It was folly. But perhaps she knew mercy, of a kind—a Winter mercy. It is cold, ATerafin. She took four—four who dared to speak against the decision of gods and the White Lady herself, and she gave them what they professed to desire:

a chance to wake the Sleepers, should the possiblity of their redemption ever arise.

"She tied their existence to the Sleepers."

"She made them...for the Sleepers?"

"Yes, and no. They exist for one reason, and one alone: to wake the Sleepers. And should the Sleepers wake and finally walk this world again, the heralds themselves will vanish. They might have a glimpse of those for whom they surrendered their existence, but that was not the Lady's intent; she was angry, and her anger was cold.

"You do not understand, and I do not expect it. You and your kind have played by the side of a tepid brook and imagined you played in the ocean."

"You've played here as well."

"I have *waited*, ATerafin. I, too, have slept. My waking is not entirely in my hands, but I am not as my brethren. I failed; I did not disobey."

"And your herald?"

"His fate was not their fate. I did not betray the White Lady. I did not disobey her commands."

"He doesn't need to be here to wake you."

"I do not know what will happen, should he travel. I do not know that he has. I have not seen him, have not heard his voice, have not spoken to him. I know that he is alive." He bowed head, spoke a word that Jester did not understand, a crack of syllables that froze the air. Frost dusted the glass doors of the liquor cabinet in front of which he was standing. "He is alive.

"I slept. I *sleep*, even now. But I did not, and do not, dream. He is not, to me, what the heralds are to my brethren; he has not been sundered from the mortal realm. Unlike the three the forest has misguided and misled in the wilderness of The Terafin, he has roots here." The smile returned. "You wish me to tell you where he might be found? You wish me to tell you how to stop him?"

All in, Jester thought. "Actually, we were hoping Sigurne would."

Meralonne laughed. The sound was as close to normal as Jester feared his voice would ever become again. "And what makes you think she knows? Tell me, Jester, do you offer those who might become your enemies information about your weaknesses?"

"In general, immortals consider mortals incredibly ignorant; they don't have to be careful about hiding weaknesses that cannot, ever, be exploited."

"And you expect that I have so little regard for Sigurne Mellifas?"

A beat of silence. "No."

"No, indeed."

"Does she?"

"I would have once killed you for even asking; I find myself considering it now. But your Lord has embarked upon the only quest that now matters, and in respect—perhaps in envy—of that, I will hold my hand. No. She does not understand. But that is fair; I do not understand the whole of it myself. I understand only that the heralds will not die until the Sleepers do."

"But—"

"I have tried. Even in my weakened state, I am more than a match for all but a handful of my kin. Or I was."

"Wait. *You* tried to kill the heralds?"

"You seem surprised."

"Did Sigurne order you to—"

"No. But it is not the time, not yet, for my brothers to wake. If I understand what is now happening—to this world, to this city, to your Terafin—it is not yet time. There are only two ways to buy time; the first is forbidden me, by the dying magic of ancient gods and the will of the White Lady. But the second? No. The wilderness is waking, ATerafin.

"I faced and killed two of the three long before your Lord could hear the horns sounding. And they returned. And returned. And returned."

"And . . . your own?"

"Of course not. He is not, now, of the wilderness. I will not be what I am when he comes at last to wake me. I will not be part of your world, nor bound by it. But I find, to my surprise, that the tendrils of your benighted mortality are like the roots of the great trees. They are almost irrelevant when they first begin to seek purchase—but if they are few, they are surprisingly deep. I like your bards. I like your pipes. I like your odd food, your quaint and diverse customs. I even like your demonologists."

Jester stiffened.

"They are the only way, in the end, that we might commune with our dead. And the guildmaster? I am . . . fond of her. In the decades we have been together, she has aged, but she has not wavered. She understands beauty as I understand it; she yearns for it, although she has never truly *seen* it. If I speak of your Terafin and her mission, it is almost all of the truth. Almost.

"But I have safeguarded Sigurne from the moment she first decided to die in the distant Northern Wastes, and I am unwilling to consign her to the death that mortals will otherwise face. Did she mention the heralds?"

Jester nodded.

"It is odd," Meralonne finally said. He looked to the West although, at the moment, West was a wall with fine rails and baseboards but no windows. "I do not think he has yet begun to move."

"Then you—"

"No. The wilderness is waking, Jester, and I am *of* it. Even were he to remain in the West until the End of Days, I will not—I *cannot*—be what I have been. Mortals speak of choice; they have spoken of choice for as long as I have walked among them."

"Speaking as someone who lived for months with no real choice at all, choice *is* relevant."

"Choice is the prerogative of power, of the powerful. Even in your world, it has always been so. To you, then—and to Sigurne—my situation might be anathema. Were you to be what I am becoming, however, it would not be. It is as much a choice as breath is to you."

"The Chosen have disabled their beacons."

Meralonne nodded.

"But the Terafin's permissions are not in their control."

"No."

"Have you tried entering her forest recently?"

"No."

To his surprise, Jester said, "Try. If we can't have Sigurne, be Sigurne for now."

"She would not ask that of you."

"Who? Sigurne or The Terafin?"

"Either." He exhaled. "Shianne did not remain behind?"

"She went with The Terafin. As did the Wild Hunt."

He stared at Jester, his gaze so intent it seemed to sink, in the end, beneath skin, beneath all of the outward nuances Jester had so carefully developed over time. "Understand, ATerafin, that the Sleepers are my brothers. What your den is to you is the barest echo, the palest reflection, of what they once were to me. I would not see them harmed or destroyed, even were I capable of it. They are my kin, long-sundered, and I have survived in order to meet with them again. I have survived that we might ride out together, bearing arms in the service of the White Lady, and redeem ourselves. Even as I am—as I was—there was nothing I desired more."

"But you attacked the heralds."

"Yes. Strange, is it not?" He bowed his head, and it seemed to Jester, watching, that even that was somehow a struggle. "Very well. Sigurne attends the kings and the god-born priests. Let us test the boundaries of your leader's permissions."

Jester had expected that he would take the Terafin carriage back to the manse. In truth, he desired it; the cabin was enclosed, which kept the world at a temporary distance. He was in motion in the streets of the city but absolved of the minutiae of decisions: directions, roads, pedestrians. He headed out of the room to request that the carriage be brought round.

The servant, however, upon realizing that Meralonne intended to accompany Jester, shook his head. "I'll send the driver home. Is there a message you wish me to deliver to him?" Although he spoke to Jester, his gaze went immediately to Meralonne. Jester didn't even have it in him to resent this.

"Tell him that I will return to the manse with Meralonne APhaniel." He glanced at the magi, who still seemed a creature of silver and light, and said, "Unless you'd condescend to ride in the Terafin carriage?"

One brow rose in an echo of Meralonne's familiar arrogance. It was almost comforting. It was also a very distinct, if wordless, answer.

"I will not harm them," Meralonne said.

When Jester glanced at him, the magi added, "I will not harm my brothers. But they do not see what I see, in this long, long game. In the end, my resistance will not be enough. My compliance with the White Lady's commands were likewise insufficient; had it been enough, we would not have been trapped and lessened. It is coming, ATerafin. It is coming." As he spoke, he began to walk, not to the carriage yards but the public front of the Order of Knowledge.

Jester felt his stomach sink. He could accept magic—anyone who lived in the city did. It fueled streetlamps, protected buildings, dampened fires. But he did not consider those daily contrivances to *be* magic. They were like the cobbled streets; they simply were.

He felt the wind touch his face as he stepped into the empty drive, and he knew, just before he was swept off his feet, that Meralonne APhaniel no longer rode in carriages. He no longer moved through the city's many streets; they were beneath him, beneath his notice.

And he thought, as the streets became smaller and smaller beneath feet that no longer touched them, that that was for the best. He did not think that the magi would notice—or care to notice—just how much damage the wind he now summoned might do.

As they crossed the Isle—a remarkably short journey as the windswept bird flew—he did see not the Terafin manse, but the forest. The buildings that comprised the manse and its closest neighbors were no longer visible beneath the towering boughs of *Ellariannatte.* Those trees were taller than the trees that had always been the distinguishing feature of the more distant Common.

"This," Meralonne said, his words blown toward Jester by the cool air, "will be the test, ATerafin."

"If the forest rejects you, what will happen to me?" Jester's question was almost casual in sound. It was certainly not casual in feeling.

The magi's smile was sharp but genuine. "You will not land in the forest. I will ask the wind to set you down a safe distance away—but you will be deposited in the dim and dismal streets of your mortal city."

Jester did not believe that he was in no danger. He understood that the ocean had no personal desire to drown men whose ships capsized in storms; it had no *intent.* The air, if Jay was correct, did—but it was a capricious intent. While Meralonne commanded it, Jester was safe. He didn't feel safe; he merely understood that his fears, his abilities, his own intentions, were entirely irrelevant. Either he would fall, or he wouldn't. Begging for his life, exposing the uneasiness he refused to call fear, would bring him closer to death, not farther from it.

He was therefore determined to enjoy what he hoped would be a singular experience. He gave over dignity almost instantly, spreading his arms as if he were a gliding bird. Not a flapping one. He drew the line at that.

But the *Ellariannatte* drew closer, and closer again.

As Meralonne hovered just at the outer edge of what was far too large to be considered a grove, the trees moved. As if branches were limbs—or worse, rigid tentacles—they reached up to envelop both the magi and Jester, rushing in as if to trap them in a wooden, pliant cage.

Jester drew breath and exhaled it, unadorned by words. But he did look at Meralonne and was surprised into a different type of silence. The magi's eyes were no longer glittering, although his hair was a perfect spill of white, like living snow. His armor did not shift or change, but he drew no sword; he did not attempt to fight the will of the forest itself.

He glanced at Jester, his lips slightly thinned. "My apologies, ATerafin. The wild air informs me that it does not have permission to cross this boundary. I had thought—"

"What did you think?" Jester reached out and wrapped his arms around the thickest of the branches. Dignity be damned. He clung for his life.

"I had thought that were I to be acceptable still, the wind might carry us into the forest heart."

"Is *this* how you normally arrive?"

"Ah, no. What I summon, I summon within The Terafin's lands. The wind, however, will not cross over this boundary; I must call it again should I wish to fly. I must call it where the call can be witnessed, be heard, be examined. And it cannot be examined in that fashion from without."

It was a long, long way to fall.

Jester cursed.

Meralonne APhaniel laughed. The laugh was loud and far warmer than any other sound the mage had made in Jester's presence today, which really didn't make up for the sudden absence of buoyancy. But it was something, he thought. Whatever alchemical sorcery Meralonne expected would transform him, it was not done with its work, not yet.

Being sent to the ground hand over fist by giant trees left splinters and leaves in Jester's hair; it scraped skin that was pale enough to be unforgiving to blemishes. He held his breath more often than he cursed, and lost sight entirely of Meralonne, but did not close his eyes. The imperative to survive was strong enough that he watched, transferring his grip from branch to branch just as he himself was unceremoniously handled.

His clothing was much the worse for wear by the time his feet found purchase on ground he swore silently he would never leave again. And on that note, he turned to glare at Meralonne APhaniel. The mage, much like Jester himself, had been handed to ground by the trees that he would never quite see the same way again.

"Did you even *try* to call the wind?" Jester demanded.

"I did not see the point," the mage replied; he still looked enormously amused. "And there is, even for the immortal, some hint of the nostalgic in this particular enterprise. It has been long—so long—since the trees have been awake enough to condescend to play."

Given the tears in Jester's jacket, *play* did not strike him as the appropriate word; he was bruised, and no doubt would have bruises on the bruises by morning. He straightened out what remained of his clothing, thinking about Finch's resigned but grim certainty that Iain ATerafin would bring the entire treasury down on their heads if they incurred any more unnecessary expenses. Then he looked around.

"Well, we are certainly *in* The Terafin's forest," he told the mage. "Which, I gather, means you are either more powerful than the forest—" the ground rumbled, "or you are still considered at least something of an ally to the forest's Lord."

"It is not a mistake I would make, were I Lord of these lands."

"No, of course not. Were you Lord of these lands, it would be Winter and the trees would be asleep."

Meralonne's expression chilled.

Jester's survival instincts, however, did not step in to shut his mouth. "Do you possibly have any idea where we actually are?"

"Do you not?"

"It might have escaped your notice, but I am a normal mortal. I am not talent-born, and I avoid egregious displays of magic because I'm in control of none of them."

A pale brow rose, but the smile lingered. "I am surprised," he said softly. "And it is seldom that I am surprised. Yes, ATerafin. I believe I know where we are."

"Are we near the tree of fire?"

"Ah, no. But we are very near a significant tree. Be grateful," he added softly. "That fall would not injure me. It would, however—"

"Yes, I know. It wouldn't have done me any good at all."

"The Terafin values you highly; the forest understands this. It is not a trivial act for the forest to catch you thus, not even here. You have seen the trees move and speak—they are awake—and perhaps you believe that what occurred just now is some part of that. You would be wrong. Here, in this space, there is one central presence, and I believe he is now waiting for us."

"Us?" Jester asked. He was dubious.

Meralonne's shrug was familiar. "I believe you might find your way to the tree of fire. Why do you seek it?"

"The impromptu council of war is being held there."

"Ah. I am called. If you will accompany me, I will speak to your council in Sigurne's stead after I am done here."

Jester did not wander often in the forest. When he entered it, he searched for one of two people: Birgide or Haval. The tree of fire figured prominently in the success of that search, although Jester could not for the life of him understand why Birgide found any comfort in its existence.

This time, however, he followed Meralonne, and Meralonne's path did not lead to the burning orange yellow of that tree; it led into a dusk that was heading toward twilight. Although the trees that had broken their fall had been *Ellariannatte,* Jester could not tell from the trunks and the bark of the trees they now passed whether or not these trees were those ones. He had never developed Jay's love for the trees, and he had no particular sentimental attachment to them.

In his view, the trees of silver, gold, and diamond were of more interest, but even he knew better than to pilfer a few leaves for his own personal use. Not yet, at any rate.

And maybe not ever. If Meralonne was right—no, if Haval and Jarven were right—gold and silver might have far less value than food.

He did not ask the magi if he knew where he was going; he was content, for the moment, to be led. But the forest here seemed silent in comparison to the forest with which he was only passingly familiar, and he wondered as he walked just how far the forest stretched. He assumed these lands were still Jay's; there was no winter here.

But if there had been a spring or summer, it was hard to tell; the branches of these ancient trees were too high off the ground, and the simple illumination of sunlight seemed all but absent.

To his surprise, Meralonne chose to break their silence. "What do you desire from The Terafin?"

Jester hardly knew how to answer. The flippant answer he usually offered to this kind of intrusive question came to his lips but died before leaving them. He considered the question seriously instead.

In the absence of an immediate response, Meralonne glanced back at him. "You feel this is irrelevant."

Jester shook his head. "I'm afraid of the opposite."

"Oh?"

"It's relevant, but it's not a question I ask myself."

"You understand what she is?"

"Jay."

"That is only barely a name; in Weston it is a single letter. It describes none of her power, none of her potential."

He was wrong. "What do you want from her?" Jester asked, to buy himself time. But he regretted the words he'd let escape; he already knew the answer. Meralonne wanted what Shianne wanted. He wanted what Celleriant wanted. He wanted, in the end, what Jay needed: to find the Winter Queen and return Summer to these lands. Or rather, to the lands that bordered them.

Meralonne raised a brow but did not condescend to answer, and Jester knew he deserved this.

"I want her to be herself," Jester finally said. "Power changes people. It changes what they do. It changes what they want. It changes the battles they fight, and the way they fight them."

"You are not fond of the powerful."

"Not particularly, no. I've never been one of them." He hesitated, stumbled over a tree root, cursed almost genially, and righted himself. "I want what she wants. I want to be able to be what she wants me to be."

"And that is?"

Jester shrugged. *This* question, he had asked himself, usually in the dark of night when he wasn't quite drunk enough. He understood her attachment to Teller. He understood her attachment to Finch. He was attached to both of them himself. He understood what she valued in Arann, what she had valued in Carver—and even thinking the name, his entire body tightened, as if at an expected and anticipated blow. He even understood why Angel. If Arann was Chosen, Angel was hers. Had always been hers, from the first day she'd brought him home. He understood the sweetness she saw in Adam's youth, although he thought her overly sentimental.

He did not understand what she saw in him.

She had found Teller. Had found Finch. Had found Arann and Angel.

She had stumbled over Jester, locked in a room that still gave him nightmares half a lifetime later. No special insight, no special talent, had led her to Jester; she'd practically tripped over him. It had been an exceptionally lucky coincidence for Jester.

He had never entirely understood how it had been of any value to her.

He was not, and would never be, large. He couldn't fight—as Arann, Duster, and Carver could. His red hair and pale skin made him stand out in a crowd, no matter how costly visibility was, and although he had learned to disguise the color of his hair and darken his skin, that was too costly for the struggling den to be a permanent solution. He was not, therefore, the best of her thieves when thievery had been required.

He was not a peacemaker. He did not care to be close to people, or to have them too close to him. He disdained the patriciate. No, it was worse than that.

Although he had been unwanted, although her talent-born gift had not marked him as essential, as necessary, she had saved him. She had given him a home. She had taken him to Terafin in her desperate wake, sacrificing Duster to do so.

She had never questioned whether or not he belonged. Jester had. But he had never done it out loud. If he was to lose home and safety—as he had done before—it wasn't going to be because he'd argued for it. Or mentioned it.

"ATerafin?"

"I don't know. I do not know what she wants or expects me to be." There was no wind, no breeze, nothing to ruffle the leaves above them, nothing to add sound to their gloomy trek. "I suppose you always knew?"

Meralonne did not pretend to misunderstand him. "Yes, but not in the manner you think. It was not necessary to be told. Nor was it necessary to receive praise. We are the White Lady's."

"But . . ." He hesitated. His curiosity had been his one besetting sin, even when curiosity was far less than wise. "They didn't do what she wanted."

"We are not the White Lady; we merely belong to her. She is what we yearn for. Tell me, Jester—if you were to be sundered from your chosen kin, would you not desire to return to them?"

"Depends."

"On?"

"Was I sundered because I walked away? Was I sundered because they did? Am I hostage? Am I—"

Meralonne lifted a hand. "For us, it does not depend. She is the White Lady. Where she stands on the field of battle, be her enemy the god we do not name, it is her that we see, it is her that we yearn for."

"Even your dead?"

"Even our dead."

"Then *why*?"

"I told your Lord why; did she not speak of it?"

Jester kicked a tree root. He didn't expect to be told everything of relevance. But once—once, he had been. What the den knew, he knew. He exhaled. Had he ever expressed a desire *to* know? No. He had kept everyone, even Finch, at as much of a distance as he could. They were his chosen kin.

"She probably thought it irrelevant."

Meralonne stiffened. Jester knew that he was playing with a life—his own—but felt a brief, visceral joy. It was petty, yes. But didn't petty ultimately describe him? And maybe this conversation would be over.

"Or perhaps she thought you were not worthy enough to hear it."

Jester shrugged. Pettiness was a habit; once started, it was hard to stop. And, really, what did it matter? Knowing why changed none of the facts. They had betrayed the command of the White Lady they professed to venerate. And instead of dying for it, they'd been left beneath the streets of Jester's city, where their waking would kill thousands. Tens of thousands.

"Probably."

Silence again. It was shorter than Jester's had been. "We strove to be worthy of her. We strove to be the best reflection of her strengths. We killed for her. We would have died for her."

Jester wondered why Meralonne was telling him this.

"In some lesser fashion," his tone implied that he believed it was *much* lesser, "the Terafin regent has done the same. The right-kin. The one with the white hair."

"It's blonde."

"It is white."

Jester snorted. "And you want to know what I've done to prove myself?"

"I am not mortal. I will never be mortal. Perhaps you accomplish this in a fashion I cannot perceive. But I have spent centuries among your kind, and I confess that when I pause to look, I cannot discern it."

"If I had ever had to prove myself worthy of her—of any of them—I'd've been dead on the first day we met. And nothing's changed since then." The words that left his mouth were flippant in meaning, but he could not drive them out in a similar tone.

Why am I even talking about this?

As if Meralonne could hear the thought, he inclined his chin. "My apologies, ATerafin. I was curious."

"I thought you didn't care about mortals."

"In the general case? No. There is no point. But your Terafin is a mortal. And she is tasked with something that not even the strongest, the greatest, of my kin could achieve. I am forced to adopt some elements of concern. Tell me, do you think she will succeed?"

"Don't you?"

"No. I cannot see—and I have dwelled upon the question since I first became aware of what she carried—how she might achieve what we ourselves could not. Were she not Sen, I would not have left the matter in her hands." His smile was grim, bitter, careworn. "But I would have left it in no one's hands, even if I were certain of my own failure.

"Hope is a very bitter thing. The fact that she is Sen will avail her nothing in the wilderness. She cannot own it all; not even the gods at their zenith could. And she is wed to this place, tied to it, rooted in it. What she requires she will not find elsewhere."

"What exactly *is* a Sen?"

"I forget myself. Come. Can you not hear his voice?"

Jester shook his head.

"You make me doubt myself, on rare occasions."

"Oh?"

"If you cannot hear something so rich, so obvious, so deep, what hope that Sigurne, who is of your kind, will be able to do so? I might show her the wonders of this, or any other, land, and she might see it as you see it: akin to the lifeless, dull lands that birthed you."

* * *

"He hears me, Illaraphaniel."

Meralonne raised a brow before his silver eyes narrowed.

Jester shook his head again. "Oh, I heard that," he added.

The voice, unaccompanied by something as mundane as a speaker, said, "You are wrong."

It was not Jester's habit to argue with invisible immortals—if the trees qualified as that. "I have nothing against lying," he told the magi, "if that even needs to be stated."

"It does not. The problem with you and your kin is that you do not understand what truth is. In all practical ways, you are born lying, and you die lying."

"You are wrong, Jester ATerafin," the forest voice said again. "You have heard me since you touched the branches of my many trees."

Or since they'd touched him. He kept this to himself, however.

"But the use of the word 'hear' is limiting. When the forest speaks to one such as Illaraphaniel, words are not required; at times, they can be obstructions. Tell me, did you bring him here, or did he bring you?"

"The latter," Jester said, but felt compelled to add, "I asked him to enter The Terafin's forest. I assumed we'd do it the normal way."

The leaves seemed to chuckle, and the sun that had been absent nonetheless seemed to shed warmth in the still air. "And what, then, is normal to your kin?"

"Walking, for one." Jester did not recognize the voice; it was not the fox. Nor did it seem like the oddly playful voices of the tree spirits when they chose to step out of the bark that was their natural resting state.

"The forest is afraid of you, Illaraphaniel. It fears what you must become. What you are, in fact, in the process of becoming."

"And that is wise," the magi replied.

"The saplings were ever thus; they are vulnerable to many things, and any living being requires fear if it is to become cautious. But tell me, Jester, tell us: do you not fear him? Do you not see the changes that my own saplings see?"

"I see changes," Jester said quietly. "But to be fair, I've never particularly liked Meralonne."

The forest laughed. It was a gale of sound, the friction of tens of thousands of leaves. "You are bold, indeed. So, too, many of our young—but I must warn you, many do not survive it. If we cannot learn from such experiences—and death, indeed, is limiting—we might learn from the folly of those nearest to us. I try not to pity you," he added.

"Pity?" Jester was not offended, which was strange.

"You cannot see him as we see him; you cannot see him as we once saw him. To behold Illaraphaniel at his zenith was almost to walk at the side of gods."

"I've seen gods," Jester replied.

"No, child, you have not; you have seen their echoes, their spirits, the meager shadows that they could leave behind."

Meralonne had begun to walk more quickly, and with more obvious purpose.

"We owe a debt to the White Lady—all of us, whose roots must sink, at last, into the soil of the wilderness, high, low, or absent. And Illaraphaniel did not desert us. He did not fall prey to the presence of the gods, named or no. He heard us, always; we believe he was aware of even our sleeping voices.

"The Winter has been so long."

As the forest spoke, Meralonne finally surrendered; he summoned the air. Jester thought summon was the wrong word, though; there was deliberation, but conversely almost no intent that Jester could see. No; the wind came, in wide sweeping arcs; both the magi and Jester were caught up, and the roots over which Jester had been struggling to walk became irrelevant.

Whatever it was that Jewel had seen in Meralonne, whatever her talent had revealed, she had never quite put into words. The forest didn't need words.

Ah.

The forest didn't require speech. There were no patricians here, no political games; there were no artful contracts in which clauses attempted to undermine the superficial agreement itself. The forest understood what Jay wanted, had understood it better than Jester.

Or maybe not. Jester himself had never asked Jay for the words. He had never served her—inasmuch as he served anyone—because he had made oaths to her. Oh, he'd made oaths to Terafin; there was no other way to be adopted into the great house. But those words had meant nothing to him; they meant nothing now.

No.

No, it was best to be honest with himself; he didn't have to speak the words out loud, didn't have to convince anyone else who might be watching. If he required protection from even the thoughts he kept to himself, he was in serious trouble.

The words themselves had meant nothing; they were a means to an end, and the end was desirable. But the *end* itself meant something. To his younger self, half a lifetime ago, the end had been safety. Safety from the elements, from the dens that roamed the streets of the lower holdings, from the starvation that came with lack of money, from the thievery that came with the same lack. It meant an end to fear of freezing. It meant that he would never ever return to the place Jay'd plucked him from.

And all of that had been true. He had been safe from all those things.

But he had come face-to-face with gods, with demons, with creatures that existed on the periphery of his awareness in remembered snatches of children's tales—most told streetside by other kids. He had come to stand beneath the burning boughs of a tree of fire. He had endured the endless whining of winged cats—animals that would have terrified him had he met them in any other context.

And why?

Because this was where Jay was. This was where Finch was. He had accepted the House Name, had sworn the House oath, because he wanted to be where his den was. They would never leave him behind. He believed that now. And he had—for no smart reason—believed it, even then, in the twenty-fifth holding. He had believed it when the den had started to disappear—Fisher, Lefty, Lander; he had believed it, searching with increasing desperation in the under-city, in the dark, for people who would never return.

He had believed it when Duster had gone to fight—and die. He understood that Jay was sometimes naive. That it was hard to want what she wanted when men like Rymark or Haerrad existed. It was *easy* to believe that to fight those men, to win against them, she must become them, or very like them. It made sense that Jarven was the model of survival.

But Jay had never become them. Finch was more pragmatic—but Finch could not become them, either. Because she had Teller. She had Jay. Jester was no moral compass; there was nothing she could do that he would not forgive. There was nothing any of them could do—except possibly betray each other—that he wouldn't forgive.

What Jay needed, Jester understood.

She needed the den.

She needed the forest to have the same moral compass that she did.

And Jester had never had that. Oh, he was squeamish; he didn't really enjoy the thought of slitting someone's throat. But he had no opposition to it on principal. He looked up at Meralonne's back, which seemed to be retreating as night fell.

Jay would lose it, he thought, and knew it for truth. If what she'd built, if *who she was*, couldn't be preserved somehow, nothing would be preserved. She had been essential in Jester's life. Always. But Jester's life did not materially affect the entirety of Averalaan. Or it hadn't, until now.

And he realized, watching Meralonne, that he could not do it. Whatever he was required to be, it wasn't in him. He could care for Jay. No, damn it, he could love her—he hated that word, hated its use, hated the way it was a collection of trivial letters meant to be plastered over something that should never be touched or poked or described—but loving her didn't change his essential nature. He couldn't resent her for being what he wasn't. He'd never, ever done that.

But he couldn't live up to her. He couldn't be what she was, what she needed.

As he saw the back of the magi disappear, as he stopped all forward motion for one long moment, he heard, at last, the heart of the forest. Not the voice; that he'd heard when it chose to speak the first time.

Duster.

And he understood.

"She would have slapped me," Jester said.

"Yes. I am occupied with Illaraphaniel and, regardless, I cannot judge my own strength where mortals are concerned. We hear what she does not say. We hear what you do not hear. We do not understand why you do not hear it, it is so clear."

"I'm too loud most days," Jester replied. "It drowns out the quiet sounds."

"It is not a quiet sound." This time, there was a direction to the voice, and Jester followed it.

Remembering Duster. Remembering the truth of her. Remembering, as well, that they had needed her. That Jay had needed her.

"I can't give what she gave," Jester said quietly.

"Do you think she requires it? She has accepted what you give. She sees it, if you do not. And she is Lord. Her will is absolute to us. Her survival is our imperative. We are not concerned with you, except in that one regard. It would damage her, to lose you. It would damage her were you to lose yourself. Therefore, we cannot allow it."

"How can you prevent it?" he asked, more curious now than defiant.

"We admit that we are not entirely certain; mortals are fragile and complicated in ways that we are not. Your loyalties are muddy, your beliefs are often lies that you tell yourself, your talents are all but invisible. It is hard to hear you speak; we must listen, and we must extend the whole of our effort to do so."

"It's probably not worth your time."

Into the forest, through the trees, walked a man that Jester had never seen before, his skin the color of new wood, his hair a tangle of emerald and white that trailed down either side of his face. His eyes were green, white, blue, with pupils of stained ebony.

At his side walked Meralonne, but cloaked, darker and somehow smaller, as if the light that had shone so bright in his eyes had been extinguished.

"She would be angry to hear you speak so."

"Probably. But it's not like she hasn't heard it before."

The stranger smiled. "She has not," he said, lifting a hand to touch Jester's left shoulder. "It is not something you have offered her in your thin words. You have barely spoken of it in the silence of your thoughts, your own boundaries. But you must leave it behind now. We cannot afford to divert our attention. You cannot fight our battles.

"We cannot fight yours. What we give her, the wilderness could give, should she expend her will and her power. But no. It is not what she is. She is not aware of us, but we are aware of each other. We have been enemies in the past; we might be enemies in the future—but we work now toward one goal. You are part of that goal. Go back to the heart of her lands, and do not trouble us with your doubts or your fears."

"Here, fear is deadly."

"I'm not afraid," Jester said.

"You are. Your fear is an echo of hers, and it is the fear that is difficult for us—for all of us—to shoulder. Do not add to it. She needs what you give, even if we cannot see it ourselves." He turned to the magi.

"This is all that I can now do for you, Illaraphaniel. But I ask—no."

Meralonne's smile was weary. "I have lived too long among his kind," he said, indicating Jester. "And you have not. But I have never been ruled by mortals; what you hear, I have never heard."

"Nor had any desire to hear?"

Jester thought the question rhetorical.

Clearly, Meralonne did not. "I have heard," he finally said, after a deliberate pause, "the things I am capable of hearing. Even in the strange and unusual, we oft seek some reminder of our essential nature."

"And yet you have come to me."

"Not deliberately."

"Ah, Illaraphaniel. You have almost grown roots, who have the unfettered freedom of the great serpents. It is a wonder, to us, to see the shadows laid across your perfect brow. Almost, it moves us."

"It cannot last," was the soft reply.

"No. What you have given, I cannot hold for long—and should it cause harm in any fashion, I must release it. And no, Jester," he added, although Jester had not said a single word, "I cannot destroy it."

"Even if it would aid our Lord?"

"Even so." He turned to Meralonne. "I have given the gift that I could; I did not expect you might return. But I take pride, Illaraphaniel. When you find the Summer path, when you walk it, when you at last see the wild forge, you will return bearing some essential part of me, and I will fight at your side as your shield." He did not bow. The trees—the spirits—that Jester conversed with from time to time could.

"I have not returned to that forge or that maker," was Meralonne's soft reply, "but even now, you have become my shield. I cannot imagine that such a shield would break, even at the strongest blow the dead might strike."

At the mention of the dead, the man stiffened. "Do not speak of them here. The earth sleeps, but we still feel its ancient rage, and it is slow, very slow, to forgive."

"Not so slow as we," Meralonne replied. What the stranger could not do, he did: he bowed.

One hand reached out to touch his bent head; the other briefly squeezed Jester's shoulder. "Go, then. If the only other gift remaining is time, I will grant what I can of it."

"Eldest?"

"I do not wish to face you in battle. No—I do not wish to face you as enemy, as foe. Jewel understands in a way the others do not. If you ride through her lands, attempting to lay waste to those who dwell here, it will sadden her, but it will not sting or cut; she would not consider it betrayal."

"And that is why you can offer what you have offered?"

The stranger smiled. "That is beneath you, Illaraphaniel."

"Is it? I have come to believe that very little is beneath me, I have lived in her mortal lands for so long." He turned to Jester. "Come. They will be waiting, and they are not the most patient of men."

"They can be," Jester said.

"Be wary of the fox's get," the stranger said.

Jester glanced into the distance. "I always am."

They walked together toward the tree of fire, Meralonne following Jester's lead. This would have been humorous at any other time, because Jester had no idea where he was headed. The forest didn't immediately surrender a visible path, and the trees looked the same to him. But he understood, as he walked, that the magi was no longer certain he could find it on his own.

It was ironic. In the wilderness, the blind led the blind.

"How do you know him?"

"Him?"

Jester grimaced. "The tree. He *is* a tree, right?"

"He is a tree the way a tiny sand lizard is a dragon," was the almost scornful reply. No, it wasn't almost scornful; it was disgusted. And it sounded normal— or normal for Meralonne APhaniel, First Circle mage. Magi. Jester turned toward him to see that he was carrying an unlit pipe. One red brow rose.

"One does not summon fire in this forest unless one is its Lord," Meralonne said, voice curt.

Jester thought he would never hate pipe smoke again for as long as he lived. He said a silent benediction for the great elder tree of this forest, and the leaves above his head rustled and flew, as if in response.

The fox came to meet them before they had reached the tree of fire—but not before they had seen its colorful, miniature sunset in the distance. In the illumination of that odd, unnatural light, the fox's shadow loomed large; it seemed to imply something the size of a—Jester deliberately fumbled the word. Meralonne did not appear to notice—or perhaps he had always noticed. He treated the fox with a respect he seldom offered anyone else, not even Sigurne.

He offered the fox that respect now. The fox, head canted to the side, stared at him with unblinking eyes. He then walked into his own shadow, and it remained there, unmoving, as if it were a web he had laid across this part of Jay's lands. This was not a comfortable thought. Nor was Jester entirely comfortable when the fox came to stand at his feet, looking down his nose although his nose was pointed up, toward Jester's face.

He understood the command and knelt to lift the gold-furred, big-eared creature in his arms. Unlike the cats, the fox was easily carried; he weighed less than Teller's cats had when they were kittens.

"Isn't Jarven supposed to be doing this?" he asked.

"Jarven? He has other responsibilities. And he is far too wild to be reliable in this fashion."

"Didn't Finch have you?"

"She is in discussion with the Councillor and Jarven. I do not think Jarven is best-pleased with her." Jester's arms stiffened, and the fox chuckled in response. "He will do nothing to harm her while war approaches. Not while I live. And while I am tolerant enough to take Jarven as a . . . student, I am not so tolerant that I accept random, ill-thought demands." This seemed a non sequitor to Jester.

"In order to be what he is, he has accepted restraints. He has never ruled any but himself," the fox added, "and he believes that the bonds laid against him might be circumnavigated at a later date."

This did not surprise Jester.

"I did not believe he would be so foolish," Meralonne said quietly.

"You have some acquaintance with Jarven?"

"Some knowledge, very little acquaintance. Jarven's concerns were not my concerns."

"But they are now."

"No, Eldest."

"No? We had thought you would be forbidden the forest heart, you see."

"I had thought so, too. But the time is coming; can you not feel it?"

The fox nodded sagely. "It is almost a pity. I have not seen you revealed in your full glory for many a long year, and I would be witness to it when it happens."

"If not me, Eldest, my kin."

"Ah, yes. But they were not your equal, Illaraphaniel."

"You are mistaken."

"Am I? You walk, you speak, you have relative freedom; they sleep the sleep decreed by the gods and their Lord."

Meralonne did not answer, but the air seemed a little chillier where he walked.

"Really," the fox said to Jester, "you are more like Jarven than any of the rest of your kin."

"Do not make me put you down," Jester replied.

The fox chuckled. "Oh, very well. More like does not mean like. Finch understands Jarven; she accepts him."

"She accepts hurricanes as well."

"Yes, and he is very like that now: a force of nature. But it is *our* nature, not yours. Would you not agree?" This last was to Meralonne; the fox did not care one way or the other for Jester's opinion or approval.

"I consider your choice interesting; it is not one I would have made myself."

"No? But you could have chosen—"

"Do not speak her name here. She is not what Jarven is, and could I have altered her in such a fashion, I would not have."

"Even if she so chose?"

"Even so. To alter mortals in such a fashion is to change their essential nature. I have learned with bitter experience to appreciate what I see before me; I do not need to change it into something other."

"And you think him so changed?"

"Not yet, Eldest. Not yet."

"Ah. Would you care to make a wager?"

The disdain in the mage's expression was so clear Jester thought he'd recognize it from a mile away. Or more.

The fox laughed as Jester carried him at last to the tree of fire.

Chapter Eight

VENNAIRE'S HAND WAS COLD as he laid it against Adam's. The air itself was frigid with winter chill, although snow was absent across the roots of the great trees the Matriarch of Terafin had planted. The brush of palm against palm was delicate, hesitant; Vennaire was, inasmuch as the Wild Hunt could be, afraid.

Adam sensed it instantly as their skin touched—but even if he had not been what he was, he would have recognized it. Adam was not of the North; he understood just how costly it could be to acknowledge the fear of a man of power. Because any such attempt would be an almost public recognition, he did nothing to attempt to staunch the flow of that fear.

He knew, however, that Finch would have asked and smiled.

He had thought the Northerners so different from his own kin or the clansmen of the Dominion; they were loud and more prone to speak or act in ways that would be inconceivable to the clans. But they were not like the Voyani, either. House Terafin was an amalgamation of people who shared no blood ties. They shared an oath of allegiance—but blood was stronger and surer than simple oaths in the South.

Regardless, Vennaire was neither clansman nor Voyani. He was not human. He was unlike anything Adam had ever tried to heal. He had thought there was a chance—a small chance—that Vennaire might feel demonic in nature, because oblique references the Matriarch had made in recent times indicated that there was some strong connection between the two: Wild Hunt and demons.

For mortals like Adam, the results of encountering either would probably be the same; if there was a difference, it was not entirely relevant. Adam had faced the taint of demons before—in the previous Terafin's body.

He was, therefore, surprised. Touching the injured Arianni, he had thought that the Wild Hunt was very like the ancient, living earth. That the body of the now dead man was, like the earth, some part of the essential wilderness over which they now walked, and into which the roots of trees sank deep. But he now stood upon roots of trees that were not anchored in something as simple as soil.

No, he did not understand.

There was, in Vennaire, something else, something other. His was not a body in which all the elements essential to life were housed in some predictable order, but Adam could feel their existence as he examined Vennaire; it was as if they were shut behind a pane of Northern glass. There had been very little glass in Adam's life until he had come North.

Vennaire spoke; Adam heard the words at a great remove. And this, too, was unusual. He closed his eyes, or perhaps they were already closed, but the voice did not become clearer; as he focused, it became more diffuse, more distant.

So: the bodies of the Wild Hunt were not the bodies of their dying. He reached out again, in the way he had been taught by Levec. He could still touch nothing. The sensation of glass grew stronger, not weaker. He listened more intently, aware that Shadow's fear and dislike must be grounded in something, even if Adam had no idea what it was.

And then, for just a moment, he heard Shianne.

Her voice was clear as flute, clear as bell, clear as lute or the samisens of the clanswomen; she was singing. He had heard her song once and been moved to tears by it, especially when Kallandras had joined a harmony to the strength of her melody, but he had not listened like this.

His vision did not distract him. The beauty of her face, her form, the radiance of the light she seemed to contain, were now irrelevant. There was a purity to her voice, a purity to her song, that he thought he had never heard before. Not even the distant Serra Diora had come close.

He turned toward her, his hand still clasped loosely around Vennaire's.

Vennaire's hand tightened. It tightened enough that it was almost painful. Adam's eyes opened, and he blinked rapidly. He was standing in the same place, but Shianne was no longer singing.

Vennaire said, softly, "She never was." His eyes were dark, his brows drawn together in something that might have been a frown had it been less intent.

"I heard her."

"No," Vennaire said. His gaze moved from Adam's confused expression to the Matriarch's forbidding one, but he did not speak to her. Instead, he turned back to Adam, who was now trying to extract his fingers.

He bowed to Adam. He bowed low, and he held that bow; it was the most reverent gesture anyone had ever offered the young man. "You do not understand what you heard," he whispered, as Adam, hand still clutched in his, pulled him out of that bow. "But I heard it because you did. I heard it."

Jewel stepped in then.

In the time between the first hesitant contact of their two palms—healer-born and immortal—and now, the hesitance, the suspicion, had given way to something that was like respect. That had shifted into reverence. Worse. There was a desire in the gaze, a yearning, and a growing fanaticism that made Jewel far more uncomfortable than his distrust or his anger had.

"Adam," she said, "come away. We must leave this place."

Adam nodded and swallowed. It was immediately clear that he was trying to let go of a man who no longer feared the touch of a healer. She lifted her head, and this time—with no drawn swords in the clearing—Celleriant came.

His feet did not touch the ground, but the light his sword shed did, and the light of his shield encased his face in a glow that reminded Jewel of sun on winter ice. He spoke a name—the name Adam had spoken—but followed it with a volley of quiet words, his sword pointed in Vennaire's direction.

This was something Jewel did not want. But she wanted the Arianni to release Adam, and that desire increased in intensity the longer he failed to do so.

Vennaire did not draw sword; he couldn't, and retain his hold on Adam. He did, however, summon his shield, and he lifted it in Celleriant's direction.

Things might have gone from not good to very bad, but two things happened. Shadow growled, and Shianne spoke. The guttural animal sound should have clashed with the clarity of her voice, but they seemed to blend as they spoke the same words, or at least the same syllables.

Vennaire's shield slowly vanished, becoming almost porous as Jewel watched. In general, the Arianni armaments appeared and disappeared instantly; that was not the case here. She wondered what it meant but knew she could not ask. He released Adam's hand slowly, reluctantly, as if he had made the decision but could not force his body to obey it.

Shadow shouldered him out of the way before his hand could tighten again.

Adam grimaced; the Matriarch had prevented hostility between the gray cat and the Wild Hunt, and it seemed the cat wished to start it all over again. But he didn't insult Vennaire and didn't attempt to harm him; he did bare his fangs, but he did that to anyone if he was in a sulky enough mood.

He also stepped on their feet. In Adam's case, Shadow generally avoided him, which meant the Voyani boy's feet were safe. He was clearly annoyed enough today that he didn't bother. He did complain bitterly about the Matriarch's stupidity, but the Matriarch was immune to that, and she approached Adam as Shadow increased the distance between himself and Vennaire.

She lifted a hand in den-sign.

Adam shook his head. *I don't know.*

More?

Stillness which encompassed silence, and then Adam signed. *Yes. Not now.*

She nodded and turned to Shadow. His head was once again covered by the palm of her hand.

But as Adam turned to glance over his shoulder, he could see Vennaire, eyes focused and unblinking as they met Adam's. It was Adam who turned away.

When Shadow and Snow had been brought to heel, which meant Shadow was under Jewel's literal hand and Snow was flying ahead of the Arianni, Terrick returned from his scouting mission. He was not entirely comfortable with the ground as it was currently constituted, although the roots gave him no trouble; he wished to move across this unnatural bridge to the lands beyond the divide the trees had covered.

Avandar agreed, but not for the same reasons; he did not doubt the strength or the solidity of what Jewel had built. Neither did she, but she was far more reluctant to leave the *Ellariannatte*. Reluctance, however, did not stop her.

Throughout it, the Guildmaster of the Order of Knowledge remained silent, almost withdrawn. The only thing that caught his attention was the dress Shianne wore—but even Gilafas in his odd maker's trance was not foolish enough to approach her or touch her. Jewel took pity on him as he fidgeted, attempting to control the impulse.

"It is like the dress I wore to The Terafin's funeral," she told him softly.

"It is *nothing* like that dress."

"It doesn't look the same, no."

This finally pulled his attention from the dress; he was now staring at Jewel in open disbelief.

"It was made the same way."

He sputtered for one long minute. "The ring you wear," he finally said, when he had mastered what was almost outrage, "was made by me. The window in Fabril's reach was also made by me. It is the only thing they have in common."

She allowed the guildmaster to lecture her; she thought it safer than the alternative. Gilafas had no servants with him; no one to guide him when he lost track of reality. Jewel was the closest he was likely to come.

"Be wary," Calliastra said. Shianne walked beside Adam now. Calliastra often took to the skies, but returned, the arcs of her flight narrowing or widening, the perimeter starting and ending with Jewel. "The lands above and beneath your forest are safe for you, but they are not empty, and when you leave the cover of your trees, there may be resistance."

"Have you been seen?"

"Yes."

"But not attacked."

"Very, very few would be foolish enough to attack me when I fly."

Glancing at her, Jewel thought this was true. While the wings looked somehow right on the cats, they added a menace, a coldness, to Calliastra; at a distance, she might be a demon. And if Jewel were honest, not much of a distance was required.

"What might we face?"

"Winged predators. If you fear the great wyrms, be at peace; we are not yet near the territory they occupy. And even were we—" She stopped.

Jewel stopped as well, and the whole of the slender column gradually came to a halt behind her; only Terrick and Angel continued to move. "What?"

"I do not hear their rumbling cry."

"You said we're not close—"

"If you had truly heard them in my youth, you would understand why that has little relevance."

"You know where we are." The words were flat.

"No. But there is something about these lands that is familiar. I cannot tell if it is simple nostalgia or if it is fact; I must alight on the distant soil to be more certain."

The array of *Ellariannatte* roots seemed to stretch for much longer than the visible chasm had. While the roots themselves were not flat, Jewel thought the terrain didn't account for the difference she had expected in distance.

Shadow snorted. He had remembered, with a vengeance, just how ignorant she was, and in case anyone else took comfort in forgetting it, made certain to remind them. Loudly. Snow contented himself with distant snickers until Jewel called him down from the sky above the tree boughs. "Go home," she told him.

He protested—loudly—until he met her stony glare.

"You should never have left."

When he glared at her but failed to move, she added, "They're depending on you."

"Who *cares?*"

"I do. I want them to survive whatever is coming. I expect you to do everything in your power to see that that happens."

"*Everything?*"

"Everything, Snow."

"Did you *hear her?*" he demanded of his brother.

Shadow hissed.

Snow hissed back. Fur rose on either side, white and gray.

"You *know* what she *means.*"

"But she *said*—"

Shadow leaped.

So did Snow.

"You might have some consideration for the rest of us," Calliastra drawled. The godchild, however, appeared to be amused.

"*Snow.*"

Both cats froze.

"Listen to Finch."

"I don't *like* her."

"Then listen to Teller." She felt the curious, visceral compulsion take hold of her. "Go back to him, stay with him, and *keep him safe.*"

"Can I kill?"

She cursed in rapid Torra, which felt surprisingly good. "You can kill anything that is trying to kill my den."

"Quickly? Or slowly?"

"Enough, Snow. Go *now.*"

Shadow roared.

And Snow, looking resigned and resentful as only the cats could, pushed himself off the ground, leaving splinters in a rain in his wake.

It was another hour before they cleared the bridge of trees.

It was immediately obvious that, while there was forest, it was not Jewel's forest. The roots of the *Ellariannatte* gave way, at last, to earth; it made movement simpler. Here, the ground was flat, and the few roots that had grown above it were closest to the trunks of the trees that they sustained. But the bark was different, the leaves different, and the air itself was colder; breath hung in clouds whenever someone spoke. It was more subtle in the silence.

There was snow in the distance, a visible almost sparkling sheath of white that seemed to cover the landscape. But that snow had not extended to the edge of the cliff.

"It *did*," Shadow corrected her.

"There's no snow here," she pointed out.

"There *wasssssss*."

"Do you think your influence so shallow?" Shianne asked her. There was none of the cat's judgment in the question; she sounded genuinely curious.

"I don't generally have much control over the weather," Jewel offered. She found it hard to speak to Shianne the way she spoke to the rest of her companions.

"You have not wandered far in the wilderness if you believe that."

"Can you control the weather?"

"Now? No. Not without significant effort."

Effort which Jewel did not want her to make. Jewel transferred the question to Avandar with a simple glance.

"She is correct. I believe she could influence the wild lands, but it would be costly to her and the child she carries. She is not without power, Jewel. She will never, while she lives, be without power." And in silence, he added, *She is the equal of any of the magi; I would guess that she is superior. Do not think her helpless. She surrendered eternity; she did not surrender everything.*

Jewel exhaled. *What happened with Adam?*

I do not know. You must ask him if you wish the answer.

What do you think happened?

There was a beat of silence. *I believe he did as he desired: he touched the immortal. What he found was not, perhaps, what he expected—but Adam is unusual.*

Oh?

I do not believe he expected anything; he was willing to observe whatever it was that he touched. Were he to touch me, he would find a mortal. You, too, would be mortal—as Shianne herself is. But the Arianni are not what we are; the great cats are not what we are. And, Jewel, he has touched the sleeping earth, and he has wrested from it a path that would not otherwise have existed. You do not fear him. I will not even call you foolish, although I think it unwise. They, however, fear him for a reason.

Vennaire doesn't. Vennaire doesn't, anymore.

Avandar nodded.

Adam helped Terrick prepare food. The Arianni withdrew; they did not join the merely mortal for anything as mundane as a meal. They disappeared into this unknown, nighttime forest at an unspoken command; it was not Jewel's.

Shadow was bored. This was both good and bad, for obvious reasons.

He wandered around the fire without singeing fur or tail and eventually plunked himself down beside Jewel, knocking Angel onto his backside in order to make room for himself. Angel glared at the cat as he dusted himself off; he almost sat on Shadow's tail.

"I don't *want* to," the cat said, as he dropped his head into Jewel's lap.

"Don't want to what?"

Shadow growled. Jewel scratched behind his ears as she listened to him complain. She was warm when in contact with the gray cat; she was warm when in contact with the Winter King. But the Winter King, like the rest of the Arianni, was absent.

"I don't *like* him."

Oh. "You mean Adam?"

"Yessssssss. Him."

"Has he asked you to do anything?"

This touched off a loud, whiny round of *stupid girl*, comforting in its familiarity.

"You should have kept Snow. *Snow* should do it."

"I need Snow at home."

The gray cat continued to whine and mutter, his words shaking her body because he didn't bother to lift his head.

Calliastra approached Jewel from the opposite side and glared with disgust at the gray cat's head. Folding her arms, she looked down at him, her facial muscles twitching. Jewel was prepared for verbal spats, but Calliastra said nothing for one long breath. When she did open her mouth, she said, "I could do it."

Jewel did not understand the comment. She did not understand Shadow's complaints. Shadow lifted his head. "Are you *stupid?*"

"Not in comparison to you."

Jewel place a staying hand on the cat's head; he clipped the side of her face with a wing.

"You are not *hers*. You are *his*. What will he learn if he touches *you?* You will *eat* him!"

Jewel understood, then.

"You aren't hers, either," Calliastra snapped, arms tightening. "What will he get if he touches you? Fleas?"

Shadow roared in outrage, tossing his head in a snap that dislodged Jewel's palm. The Arianni returned to the clearing, drawn by the possibility of conflict. Even the Winter King appeared: silent, waiting.

Jewel rose. If, by chance, predators who existed in this forest had been sleeping, there was no way they could remain that way. Shadow had a dragon's voice.

She signed to Angel, who had also appeared from between trees. *Pack up. Leaving.* He nodded and went in search of Terrick.

To Jewel's surprise, Lord Celleriant also appeared; he came from the air, at the side of Kallandras of Senniel College. His expression was one of disgust as he glared at the gray cat; he spared some of that heat for Calliastra, but not much.

"You will endanger her if you continue your challenge. The forest has heard it, and not all its denizens are sleeping. Even were they, they could not fail to hear your voice. What were you thinking?" Unlike the rest of the Arianni, he was armed. But . . . he could be, without raising Shadow's ire. Or more of it.

Shadow snarled, tensing as if to leap.

"Lord," Celleriant said, "we must leave this place."

Jewel was already gathering the things that had to be returned to their packs. "Terrick has—"

"We must leave now if we wish to avoid battle."

Jewel turned suddenly as a glint of red in the forest caught her eye. Arianni swords appeared in that instant. Swords, shields, and the glimmering silver of narrowed eyes.

"Too late," Avandar said, lifting his hands.

It was no surprise to Jewel that Adam, half-drowsing by Shianne's side, woke immediately; no surprise that his first thought—and probably second, third, and fourth—was the pregnant woman he had come, in the end, to help. If the Arianni could be instantly armed and armored, the mortals could not; Terrick and Angel made more noise than the entirety of the Wild Hunt present. Then again, it was the mortals who required both the food and the shelter that could be confined to traveling packs; it was the mortals who could not afford to be without at least one of them.

Kallandras aided them; he was accustomed to travel and, at that, to travel in war-torn, hostile lands. But he was also accustomed to the winter of this particular world. He had traveled the Winter paths before, and they had not devoured him.

Jewel could not remember when she had learned this, or even how, but watching him, she thought he looked more at home here than in the glittering ballrooms of the patricians who were Senniel's patrons.

"Terafin," he said. "With your leave?"

She nodded. "Take Celleriant with you."

The breeze that touched the clearing was warm; it carried no leaves, but instead lifted bard and Arianni from the ground. In the distance, what had been a flash of moving red became brighter and far more constant, and Jewel understood that the fire, like the air, had been summoned.

Jewel.

The Winter King knelt by her side. She mounted, casting one backward glance at Shianne and Adam. If Adam's failed attempt to save the life of one of their kin had had no other effect, it had this: a handful of the Wild Hunt came to stand by his side. No, she thought, in front of him. He was safer now than he had been the first time they had encountered demons in the Winter lands.

She was certain that's what they would now face.

Terrick and Angel glanced at her while the Winter King rose, as if waiting on her command. She gestured to the packs, and Angel—sword drawn—grimaced. He understood, though; if the situation turned ugly—uglier—they had to be ready to move.

She wondered then if the box that carried the single sapling could carry everything else as well—she had never considered it until this moment. She could not take it out to test it—but she would if they survived.

Red blossomed against the white of snow; the snow became ice and water beneath the rushing bloom of color. At a distance, it was beautiful. Snow rose in a sheet, a wall; water fell on the fire. The air above Jewel's head whipped past frozen branches and ice crackled in splinters, tugged from the comfort of bark mooring.

At this distance, only the fire and the snow could be seen, but the red light did not entirely obliterate night's shadow. The fire rose sharply, gathering and climbing as if it were a vine of many tendrils climbing up a lattice of darkness.

Lightning replied—a flash of blue light that was incandescent and brief. *Celleriant.*

Avandar nodded. *He draws their attention.*

Jewel shook her head. The shadows cast by fire changed as the shape of the light changed—but there were now other shadows here, rimmed in a subtle red. Those did not move or waver.

The winter had nothing to do with the sudden chill in the air, and Jewel turned on the Winter King's back.

"Shianne—"

Shianne shook her head as another source of light joined the clearing: gold. She heard the Arianni speak, heard a whisper pass through their ranks, saw

Adam reach out to touch Shianne's shoulder, the tremble in his arm noticeable even at a distance.

Shianne did not speak; she shrugged off his arm with ease, lifting a hand. To it came a shield to join the golden blade, and only thus armed did she return The Terafin's stare.

"You can't fight—"

"Can I not?" the question was cool.

"You're pregnant!"

"Believe that I am aware of that," was the equally cool reply. "Do those who bear your living children cower behind the lines of those weaker than they? Do you not understand why they are here?"

Jewel opened her mouth to silence. In the distance, she heard the lowing of horns.

The Arianni responded in kind, their horns closer, the sound louder. But to Jewel's ear, the timbre of their horns was not as deep, not as low, not as consistent. They were angry, she thought.

But their anger was candle flame to Shianne's sudden bonfire.

"I leave Adam to you," she said, the words flying over her shoulder. The skirts of the dress she wore, for she did not wear winter clothing, flared in a sudden circle that spoke of the volume of fabric, their edges red as blood in the dim light. Snow's creation.

Jewel wished, for a brief minute, that she had not sent Snow away.

Shadow hissed. "He is *stupid*," the gray cat growled. He turned his head toward Calliastra. "Are you going to fight?"

Calliastra smiled, and her smile revealed literal fangs. "What do you think, you furry monstrosity? Do you *know* who is coming? Do you know who is waiting for us upon this road?"

"Who *cares*?"

"Oh, Eldest, *I do*." Her wings snapped open, snapped wide; they sheared the ice and bark off trees, although they did not seem to touch those trees. "Shandalliaran, he is not for you." She took a step, and beneath her feet, flickers of fire melted snow. Her fire.

Jewel had not seen her summon fire before, and when the godchild glanced back, Calliastra's eyes were the color of flame. Flame and ebony. Jewel thought Shianne would argue; her gaze—her mortal eyes—were hard and cold. She did not; she lowered her sword, lowered her shield.

"Who is it?" Adam asked of her—the only person in the clearing who would dare. Even Jewel could not find the words.

It was Jewel, however, who answered.

"Darranatos."

As if the name were a release, Calliastra leaped up, off the ground, her wings longer and larger than Jewel had ever seen them. Her skin was white, but glistening, her arms extended, her fingers curved and glittering. Gone was all semblance of, hint of, mortal woman—but she was not mortal, had never been. She had chosen—and Jewel understood this only now—to favor her mother, her mother's form, and even her mother's desire, but she had two parents.

It was to the latter that she now gave herself.

Shianne whispered a word, perhaps a name; it was lost to the sudden howl of wind.

Jewel found her voice. "Calliastra—the shadows—"

Shadow snarled. He did not call Jewel stupid, although that was clearly his intent. "*Watch.*"

The godchild did not remain airborne for long. She landed between the campsite—what remained of it—and the fire, and where she landed, the air screamed. Shadows that lay against the cold ground rose, rearing up as if in threat as Calliastra looked up at them. She laughed, and her laughter was a screech of sound; it should have been bestial. No, it was. But it was more, far more, than that.

The Arianni had weapons; Terrick and Angel had weapons. Calliastra did not condescend to arm herself. It wasn't required. She was the only weapon she needed. Her claws caught shadow's ethereal essence and tore it, shredded it, devoured it.

"*Darranatos!*" she shouted. "Have you come to *play?*" The last word echoed, rebounding off trees, off snow, off ice. The air caught the syllables, magnified them, and hurled them further.

Laughter returned; it was warm, almost velvet, in texture. "Do not stand between me and my prey, child, or you will perish. Your father may walk the world once again, but you are not in his domain now."

"I have no need of his protection," Calliastra countered, in a tone that made the word protection a vile insult. "Not against one who could not even defeat *one single mortal.*"

The laughter softened, but did not disperse. And disperse was the right word, Jewel thought; it seemed to linger like pleasant fog in the winter air.

Shadow growled, the sound low and resonant, and against the sound of the cat's fury, the sensation of amusement, of condescension, evaporated. In its wake, the air was very, very cold. The cat took a swipe at the Winter King's hind leg, but the Winter King was already in motion, and when he came to a stop, he was several feet above the ground.

Get Adam.

I do not think it wise.

Get Adam now.

Darranatos had not come alone. When he chose at last to appear, he cast off the raiment of fire, the disguise and the subtlety of simple flame discarded in the wake of Calliastra's challenge. She was taller, grander, and darker than she had ever been, and he? He was different as well.

He had wings of flame, and as he unfurled those wings, they were red light to her darkness, but Calliastra stood alone, and from the folds of his demonic wings came the forces that he commanded. What had Meralonne called him? A Duke of the Hells?

Jewel counted five demons, including Darranatos himself. Four stepped back, fell away, lost to fire as if it were fog. He barked orders in the tongue of his kind, a forbidden language that Jewel nonetheless wished she knew. Nothing he commanded was his equal, which was irrelevant. Angel, Terrick, and Jewel herself could be killed by demons that were otherwise considered inconsequential by the powerful.

By the powerful immortals.

Jewel had seen Darranatos only once, and she had fled to her forest, to the ground upon which she could face such a creature. She had survived. The cats had survived. Meralonne and Celleriant had survived.

But so had Darranatos. In the seat of her power, she had managed only to drive him away, and she was aware that she was very far from the seat of that power now. She pulled Adam up onto the Winter King's back; he was seated in front of her, and she wrapped one arm around his midriff.

"She shouldn't fight!" he shouted.

Jewel said nothing. She understood his outrage and understood as well that Shianne would tolerate it only from Adam. Given her expression now, perhaps not even Adam. Her eyes were golden, to the Arianni's silver, but they were glowing just as brightly.

Ah, of course. Shianne recognized Darranatos.

The horns of the hunt sounded again, but there was a difference to the notes, their extension, their depth. There was an urgency to them that implied an ending.

Calliastra moved first. She moved so swiftly she might have been the shadows cast by moving light. Her wings folded and spread, like whips in all the wrong shape; one of the four demons that had arrived with Darranatos did not move quickly enough.

But their Lord did; his fire parried her blow as if both fire and wing were made of steel.

The wind began to howl, and Jewel knew that Kallandras and Celleriant would soon join the fray.

The Arianni were not like Meralonne and, to a lesser extent, Celleriant. Where the mage exulted in combat, where the ferocity of the contest illuminated him from within as if it were the only source of joy he had ever known, the Wild Hunt was grim, silent, focused.

To Meralonne, all combat was a game. It was a game he might lose, but she suspected that was part of its appeal. Here, now, the Wild Hunt, Shianne at their center, felt the possibility of loss keenly. And perhaps, were Meralonne here, he would feel it, too. Perhaps this fight would be different than all the others.

He had not thought he could stand against Darranatos alone. She wondered, then, why he had not drawn shield, had not taken a stand against this demon; she knew that he recognized Darranatos.

No, he knew what Darranatos had been.

So, too, Shianne.

Meralonne had had centuries—more—to accept the loss of kin, the choice that had sundered the Arianni from each other. He understood the hatred that the White Lady bore for the Lord of the Hells. Shianne was too new to it; the loss was profound, sharp, the betrayal still inconceivable, the flames of rage unbanked by the slow diminishment of time.

Shianne's sword and shield were no longer imbued with the blue light of her kind, but the gold was the gold of sunlight at the height of the day, in a clear, almost merciless sky. She had lowered them, but she had not dismissed them, and as Calliastra lunged at a Duke of the Hells, Shianne began to walk. Behind the shield, the swell of pregnant belly could only barely be seen, and Jewel could imagine that she was not mortal, not with child; that she was one of the Arianni—a prince of a court that, at its height, had never been hidden.

As if they could see what Jewel herself could imagine, the Wild Hunt moved with her, her own betrayal—the choice of mortality and its slow and inevitable decay—the lesser betrayal. Shianne served the White Lady of their distant youth.

Darranatos served the White Lady's greatest enemy.

Adam strained against her restraining arm, and Jewel shook her head. He couldn't see this, and even if he could, she thought he would ignore it, the mute denial would make so little sense to him.

"No, Adam. I'm sorry. This fight . . . is not for us. It is not ours."

"She's—"

"I know. But even that, she undertook not for the creation of new life, but for the White Lady."

"The woman who imprisoned her!"

"Yes. She is as we are only physically. He could have been her brother."

"She will lose the child."

"No," Jewel said quietly. "She won't."

He stilled then. "You swear this, as Matriarch?"

"The Matriarchs don't swear oaths of that nature," Jewel replied. It was not an evasion. It was truth. She gentled her voice, leaning closer to his ear. "But I am not a Voyani Matriarch. Yes, Adam, I swear it. She will not lose the child to this."

"But why is she—"

"She's forgotten," Jewel whispered. "She's forgotten every choice she had that divides her now from her kin. She sees Darranatos; I don't think she's even aware of the other four."

Shadow growled.

"We're aware of them," Jewel said quietly. She looked up as fire flew from the bare ground toward the air; she saw it splash and fray as it hit shield—or perhaps sword. She could see the whirlwind, and in it, Lord Celleriant. Kallandras was invisible to her eye. He was mortal.

As Adam stilled, as he slumped slightly back, as if across a wall, she reached for the pouch that was strapped to her waist. In it were the things she had carried from Terafin, from home: leaves of silver, gold, and diamond. Leaves of fire. One dagger. One book.

She wanted none of them now.

But as she reached for the pendant she no longer wore, the ring that bound her finger flared to life in the encroaching night; the fire of demon, the wind of Arianni, harmonized with the gradual colors of sunset, the end of the day. And fluttering its way across a howling sky, apparently unperturbed by the wind's growing rage and the demon's explosive fire, came the butterfly.

It was pale, its luminescence gentle compared to the lights of war, but she recognized it immediately across a distance that should have been too great, given its size. She held her breath, watching its flight; butterflies in flight had always seemed almost drunk to her with their lack of straight lines, their elevated wobble suggesting hesitance.

Without thought, she lifted a hand as the butterfly finally closed the last of the distance; she turned her hand palm up, and it landed, its wings folding together until it was a slender sculpture of delicate glass.

And she remembered—how could she have forgotten?—that in the dreams of the Wardens, the trapped souls of sleepers who could not wake on their own had taken the form, the shape, of butterflies. She did not close her hand. Wind blew her hair into her eyes, but nothing disturbed the stately resting repose of her new passenger.

An Artisan had crafted this.

She wondered what materials had been used. She remembered the fate of the butterflies the Warden of Nightmare had crushed so deliberately: death, not wakefulness.

In her dream, she had thought the butterfly beautiful. She thought it beautiful now. But she thought the Arianni beautiful as well, and they were death. Adam sat up slightly; the butterfly was in her open hand, very close to his chest.

A roar broke the stillness; Jewel felt it as if it had come, much diminished, from her own chest, her own throat. Sunlight broke the falling night; fire edged it closer to darkness; swords clashed, and blue light struck the sky from the ground.

"Angel." He had moved. His sword was in his hand by his side. Terrick now carried his ax in both hands. They were encumbered by full packs; they did not intend to join the fight unless it came to them.

He turned to look back at her.

"Shadow."

The cat remained by the Winter King's side, his eyes as luminescent as Shianne's. If he heard her, he didn't acknowledge it; Jewel suspected that he had not. His eyes followed the Arianni, or perhaps, beyond them, Calliastra and Darranatos.

The first time she had seen this demon, she had seen only the monstrous. In this winter landscape, the only feature that remained identical was his burning wings; he could have been Arianni were it not for the color of his eyes.

As the Arianni were, he was beautiful; fire to their ice. Calliastra was darkness; velvet night.

Darranatos' fire struck her wings as if it were a spray of liquid; her wings shed it in the same way. Flames flickered and pooled beneath her feet, burning nothing, but the shadows that also moved in the light flames cast were not as ineffective. They rose up her legs, twisting and constricting as they did.

The butterfly sang.

As it did, Jewel realized that she had forgotten one person, and she turned to either side in a sudden rush of panic. *Gilafas.* She spoke his name, and when he failed to reply, repeated it.

She ordered the Winter King to search for him when the guildmaster suddenly appeared. "Apologies, Terafin," he said. He was once again behind his eyes; the vacancy that sometimes stole over him was gone. "I am not a crafter of weapons."

"Where were you?"

"Here," he replied softly. There was about him a dignity, a spareness, that underscored the sudden sense of desolation in his eyes. "For how long has the butterfly been singing?"

"Pardon?" She glanced at the butterfly. "You mean now? It only just started—but it sings frequently."

"Not that song," was his quiet reply. He lifted his hands, fingering the hem of the hood he wore; he slowly lowered it, his hands trembling. "Not that song."

She looked at the cloak; he noticed.

"It was a gift. One of Cessaly's many creations."

"She made it for you? Did she know that you'd need it?"

"No, not precisely. That is not the way making works."

Without another word, Jewel nudged the Winter King toward the guildmaster. When she was in reach of him, she bent, lowering her arm, and with it the hand that so carefully held the butterfly.

"Ah, no, Terafin. It is not for me."

"But it was made—"

"And remade, as some things are." He glanced up as fire once again changed the color of the sky. "We must away. In the mortal lands, it is almost Lattan, and I fear that it is only by the grace of the ancient covenants that we will find our way home in time."

She didn't argue. Instead, she righted herself, and after a moment's hesitation, gently placed the butterfly on her shoulder. Its song was soft, measured, but confident for all that. She could hear it above the clatter of blades, the roar of challenge; could hear it above cries of pain, cries of fury, words of triumph and exultation.

She could hear it the moment all those things died, could hear it when the echoes of those sounds had died as well.

She looked up then.

The Arianni and the demons had not been kind to the winter forest; trees had fallen in the wake of conflict, and trees had burned. Battle had made a makeshift clearing; fire had cleared away the accumulation of snow.

Shadow had not once joined battle; nor did it look as if he intended to do so now. He sat, his tail moving back and forth, his eyes turned toward that clearing and those it now contained.

Calliastra was a blur of shadow, of moving darkness; there was a power to her that implied her wings could cleave the deep stone of the hidden earth without effort. But the creature she faced was shining, radiant with a reddened light, as if by light alone he could burn away all darkness, all shadow. Tongues of flame left his hand, stretching, snapping, a many-tailed whip of fire.

To the sides, small lights flared: blue, red; his minions were fighting as well. The Wild Hunt had the strength of numbers, but Jewel had faced this demon before; she had no illusions. Here, Darranatos was a power.

"Shadow," she whispered. She knew, all sounds of battle aside, she had his attention. "Calliastra—"

"Yessssss?"

Even speaking the name, Jewel fell silent; the godchild's shadow grew, and grew again, enlarged by the fire Darranatos spread. She made some of it her own, and the windswept hair at her back glinted with its sparks, its bright, burning red.

Winter King.

It is folly, the Winter King snapped. *You will perish, there. Do not be foolish.*

But no, Jewel thought: Calliastra would perish.

She is the child of gods. This was what she was meant for; this fight, this battle.

She is not her father.

She is his vessel; his power is, in part, hers until her death. And her father is strong, Jewel. She will not perish here.

But she would. Jewel understood that she wouldn't die—not easily, and perhaps not at all—but the part of Calliastra that had come to her, first as Duster, and then as her own angry, isolated self, would be immolated in fire and shadow.

The Winter King's shock was greater than his outrage, but the outrage itself was growing. He did not understand, and Jewel thought it beyond his comprehension. What he saw in Calliastra now, he admired. Calliastra was strong. Her focus, her will, was undivided. She called power, and it came. It came, and she used it. There was no hesitance to mar her, no need for hesitance, no need for delicacy; everything here was raw, true, singular.

But Calliastra was *not* singular. Like any other person, she was conflicted, her hopes, her dreams, and her almost unbearable sorrow some intrinsic part of who she struggled to be. And what was she, absent that struggle?

We already have a Lord of the Hells. We don't need another one.

The Winter King struggled against the imperative of command she now laid upon him, but struggled in vain; she had been given his figurative reins by the only living being who could order him into servitude, and he had no choice but to obey.

It is not for my own survival that I am concerned, he snapped.

"Adam, get down. Stay with Angel. Or Shadow."

Shadow growled low; she could feel the sound as it traveled from ground to air, from air to the Winter King, who seemed to vibrate with it.

Adam dismounted; he did not approach the gray cat. He did, however, draw closer to Angel. The Winter King leaped up and up again until the ground was distant, and branches of trees brushed her hair. She tensed, but none of that tension was directed toward her height and the possibility of a fall; she would not fall while the Winter King carried her, no matter how reluctantly he did so.

No, she was watching Calliastra. Even Darranatos dimmed in her vision.

Jewel had accepted Calliastra, as she had once accepted Duster. And, as with Duster, Jewel needed to know, needed to believe, that Calliastra could rein herself in if that was what was required of her. No, if that was what Jewel required of her.

Duster had always been dangerous; the shoals of her anger, her pain, her rage, and especially the fear it would have killed her to acknowledge, were treacherous by turns. There was no current without an undertow; there was no place that was consistently safe to stand.

But, in her fashion, she had given everything she could. She had saved the rest of the den—the people who did not burn with her constant fury, the people who had not taken up a dagger, had not hardened heart and body, had not turned to face an unforgiving world to spit in its eye.

Beneath the Winter King's hooves, she could see what lay at the heart of flame and shadow: sundered Arianni and godchild. No snow reflected the light cast; it had been burned away, so much irrelevant detritus. Just as Jewel herself might be were she not cautious.

Were you cautious, you fool, you would not be here. It was the angriest she had ever heard the Winter King. No, she thought, it was the most disgusted.

And it didn't matter. Taking bitter winter air into her lungs, she exhaled a single word: "*Calliastra!*"

*   *   *

The cascade of syllables fled as sound will, lost to the clamor of the battle that had invaded this forest. Jewel opened her mouth to shout again and closed it before sound escaped; she *knew* Calliastra had heard. She seemed impervious to the name, to the woman who had called it, to the weight of the way the syllables had been shouted.

Darranatos, however, less so. He looked up—Jewel wasn't certain she would have taken the same risk—and fire crossed the night sky in an eye blink.

She was already evading—ducking into the Winter King's neck—but it was unnecessary; the great stag had moved, and was continuing to move, as fire chased his passenger across the open air, landing, at last, in a tangle of branches. She could almost hear the trees scream and remembered the danger in that: here, the earth was under no one's command.

The wind tore at that fire; the wind tore at all of the fire, spreading it thin or extinguishing it by dropping clods of dirt across its surface. In that wind, surrounded by moving debris, stood the bard and Lord Celleriant. They were not static; they were fighting—but they did not fight Darranatos.

One at least of his soldiers could take to air, and had. His blade, his shield, were luminescent red, a deep, bloodred that nonetheless seemed to shine with internal light. She could almost hear a name in the current of winds; could almost hear Celleriant's voice, raised in both challenge and recognition.

Celleriant is not Meralonne, the Winter King said, speaking as he moved through the streams of slender fire with almost contemptuous ease, *but he was born prince of the court—the youngest and last. He was born of the White Lady's power, of the White Lady's martial prowess, a hunter. It is here that he proves his worth.*

There's more to worth—

You do not understand the White Lady.

No, I really don't.

I pity you.

Don't bother. Your pity is irrelevant. What you want, I don't want. What you wanted, I never wanted. And what I want is in my hands. In our hands. Without thought, without something as concrete as words, she ordered him to descend and he did, the dance of hooves and fire and wind becoming intricate and constant. Inasmuch as it could be, that battle was his; hers was different.

It was impossible to approach Calliastra from behind; her wings were like moving blades. It was unwise to approach in any other way, but it was at least possible. And what did she mean to do if she approached?

She could not order—or ask—Calliastra to kill Darranatos cleanly, when it was possible she could not kill him at all. But she understood, as she had understood on that distant winter day in Averalaan, that if Calliastra could not bring herself under control, if she could not suborn her rage and her pain to her own will, to the deliberation of choice no matter how difficult that choice might be, Jewel *could not* take her home.

Calliastra did not have to be Teller or Arann or Finch to come home; Duster hadn't been any of them. But she had to be able to live in that home, where random things might rub a raw spot, where inexplicable things—like birthday presents—might send her into a towering rage. Where, even if she had just cause for fury, for rage, for killing intent, she had to be able to take a breath to register, to evaluate, the cost and consequence of that killing.

This was not the time to have this discussion. But it had not been the time to have it with Duster, either. Why had she, then? Why had she struggled her way back from pain and shock and fear to face that Duster? Why had it been so important?

Den.

She was den. She'd been den from the moment Jewel had decided to find her and save her. From the moment she'd saved Finch, really—and no, it didn't matter *why* she'd saved Finch. Only that she had.

Den was her family, her kin. They shared no blood except that spilled between then and now. There was nothing but will, intent, commitment, to bind them together, but it was a strong binding, and it was the one she had chosen as her personal fetters.

"Calliastra!"

She knew the moment she had Calliastra's attention, and even knew why. If the first cry had been crushed, aurally, by the din of combat, the second had risen above it just enough that it demanded attention. When Darranatos turned to look in her direction, Calliastra's attention was pulled by his.

On the back of the Winter King, who was constantly in motion, Jewel faced Darranatos and Calliastra. Only one of them appeared to be demonic. The other was beautiful, compelling, colorful; there was no malice in his expression, no bestiality in his movements. She was drawn to him the instant their eyes met.

Even memory was not a good enough shield. But, oddly enough, the Winter King's contempt was. It was not merely contempt for Jewel—that, she recognized, and it never completely left his interior voice; it was contempt for Darranatos, for the mockery of beauty. No, for the insufficiency of it. He was not

Ariane, not the White Lady, not the Lord of the Winter King's choice—the only Lord who would ever be worthy of service, of servitude.

Jewel had chosen to serve those beneath even the Winter King's notice.

It's not service, she told him, as she pulled her gaze from Darranatos'.

Is it not? I fail to see the difference.

I don't obey.

He snorted, tossing antlers that seemed, to Jewel, to be almost golden in hue, illuminated in the night sky by some interior light.

Darranatos turned from Calliastra as if she were now insignificant. He turned to Jewel, and he smiled. "So," he said, his soft voice nonetheless clear and audible over the clash of swords and the wild, angry voices of the elements, "it *is* you. Well met, little mortal. You are audacious indeed to leave the perimeters of your own small lands.

"Think you to reach Ariane? She is lost to you and all of your kind."

A roar rose then, swamping his words. Even the Winter King reared up in fury.

"But do not fear, little mortal. You will come under the aegis of *my* chosen Lord, and you will understand, in the end, that his is the greater power." And he gestured, his fingers dancing elegantly, limned by fire and shadow.

He was beyond her hatred, beyond her desire, beyond her rage; like earthquakes, like tidal waves, like hurricanes, he was a thing that existed outside of her, regardless of the terrible loss he might inflict. Some niggling thought intruded: she was not worthy of him. Would never be worthy of him, no matter how high she might climb, no matter what she might become.

It didn't matter. She had not been worthy of Amarais Handernesse ATerafin, either. But she had given her word to the departed Terafin, she had taken the House Seat, and she had struggled, in her fashion, to live up to it. To be worthy. It was the struggle, she thought, that defined her, not the success. Even thinking it, she lifted a hand, and with it, the ring that had been made of light and metal and strands of Ariane's hair.

Where fire and shadow touched it, they screamed.

The whole of the battlefield heard their cry, and silence descended: cold, Winter silence. Even the hooves of the Winter King were momentarily still.

Calliastra was first to recover, first to renew her attacks, first to return to the fire and heat of fury, of a history that was implied by that fury and of which Jewel was no part.

Darranatos glanced at her as if, for a moment, she existed in a separate world; as if her fury were no part of the place he now found himself; his eyes were riveted to the hand that Jewel had lifted and had not yet lowered. She saw how much of a game his combat with Calliastra was; he gestured, a movement that was almost a shrug, and the darknessborn woman flew into the trees that had not yet been leveled to the ground by their combat.

Calliastra understood, and the shadows rose, and rose again, as she herself did. She took to air, and Jewel moved, the Winter King almost part of her, as the godchild once again returned to air and Darranatos.

So much rage. So much pain. So much fury.

"Calliastra," Jewel said.

This time the wind carried her voice to the firstborn; her flight slowed, but her shadows did not diminish. No, Jewel thought; they grew, like shoots or tendrils, traveling to where Jewel herself now waited, as if seeking the light on her hand. As if seeking to destroy it.

She understood, as she waited, that the seeking was almost instinctive; that destruction itself was not the intent, not the desire; that a woman who had known the harsh shadows of hell and its many demons could not fathom what to do with warmth, with light: she might cage it, keep it, prove that she had the right of might to rule it. And ruling it was not, in the end, what she needed—it was just the only way she knew how to *want*.

"Calliastra."

Calliastra growled in response, a sound shorn of syllables, of anything but rage and pain. The temptress, the seductress, the vision of desire that had hunted in the streets of mortal cities was nowhere in evidence. No one, seeing this, could feel anything but fear or disgust.

"Is this what you want?" Jewel demanded. "In all the time I've known you, you've barely touched your father's power; now you have swallowed it. How many centuries, how many millennia, have you fought to be something other than his daughter?"

"And how many times have I *failed*?" Calliastra demanded, but she was arrested, mid-flight. "You *do not know* what he was like in the Court of Hells."

"Your father?"

"*Him.*" Shadow raced from her hands, her wings, streaking like unleashed vermin toward Darranatos.

"No. I don't. I've faced him only once."

"Impossible."

"Because I'm alive? I don't know what he was like. You do. But what he was, what he *is*, is not what you have to be. It's not what you are."

"This is the only way I can stand against him!"

"No. No it's not. I'm seer-born. You know this. There are other ways. You want him to suffer. You want him to suffer what you suffered, and I get that. But to make him suffer what you suffered, you would have to be as he is: pawn and slave to your father's every whim and desire. Is he powerful? Yes. But he was powerful before he made that choice, and none of that power is now his own."

Be wary, Jewel. He is listening.

Let him listen. She felt movement—Avandar's movement—saw orange and a hint of violet and blue as her domicis moved into position.

I can buy time, but given Darranatos, not much of it. If you must do this now—

It has to be now.

"You could have his power. You could have *more* than his power. You could make him pay for every humiliation, every terrible thing he has ever done to you. All you have to do is submit. Become what he is. Want what he wants."

"*Never!*" It was a shriek of rage, of fury and, beneath that, all of the twisted desire and the denial that had only barely held it in check for so long.

"Then come home. Come back to yourself. Come back to me." The hand with the ring remained steady; it did not tremble at all.

Terafin, be wary.

I am, she thought, recognizing the bard-born voice of Kallandras. She did not even glance in Darranatos' direction as she waited; no impulse, no seer-born instinct, forced her to move.

"So that *you* can own me instead?"

"I can't. I'm mortal. All of the ties that bind me to my den are ties of choice; they are not chains of command."

"But even you won't accept what I am."

"I will accept what you are; I will not accept all that you might do. You cannot eradicate the darkness because you were born to it. You will always feel it; you will always be subject to its whisper. But you *can* choose what you do with it. And yes, I could never accept the *Kialli* into my den."

"And if I feed?"

Jewel shook her head. "You won't have to."

"I will starve. I will wither."

Jewel shook her head. "You will, however, have to put up with the cats."

A low growl came from somewhere on the ground. It was followed by a volley of outraged words. "*She* will have to put up with *us*? *With us*? *We* will have to put up with *her*!"

The child of darkness and love seemed to shrink, to dwindle, to falter. She still had wings, and the wings still sliced air, but Jewel could see the feathers become something less ebon, less metallic. A choice was being made, or rather, Calliastra was struggling to make one; she stood on the boundary.

And she looked at Jewel, her eyes wide, a hint of brown, a hint of white implying that they were almost normal. There was hunger in the stare, a fierce, desperate hunger, and beneath it, around it, a self-loathing that seemed so deep it might be without end.

Jewel was not afraid. Later, she would be—that was the way it always went. Later, she would wonder what she'd been thinking. Later, she would wonder how she could have thought this was a good idea. She'd had whole days like that with Duster, and Duster had not been Calliastra's equal; she'd only had a short lifetime of pain and loss and rage to control.

Jewel's hands moved in den-sign. *Home.*

The darknessborn woman blinked, slowed, stopped. She then turned to glare at the ground. "I will deal with you later." And her voice was less full, less rumbling, less godlike; her expression was one of dislike, disgust, and . . . annoyance. It shifted, sharpening as she turned to face Darranatos once more.

But he was not looking at her.

Nor was he looking at Jewel.

Jewel bowed head.

Shianne had, at last, taken the field; she stood, sword golden, shield the same bright color, her light splitting the shadows across the ground as if it had been created only to burn them away.

Chapter Nine

J EWEL THOUGHT SHE COULD feel no sympathy for the *Kialli*. But she felt the strangest glimmering of pity, its distant cousin, as Darranatos stood, wings spread, before Shianne; he seemed frozen, almost paralyzed, by her presence.

He could not fail to note the color of her sword and her shield.

From his hand fell the whip; to his hand came the sword of the *Kialli*: long, red, shining. He raised his other arm, and to it came the shield. It was the first time he had drawn either on this field. Nor had he been pressed, forced, to wield them. Inasmuch as he was capable of it, Jewel thought this a gesture of respect; the only such gesture he was likely to offer.

He did not speak, did not strike, did not attack. Other combats, other fights, continued above or beyond him, but they were insignificant now. The only enemy of whom he was truly aware was Shianne.

Winter King.

The great stag drew closer to the ground, although his hooves did not touch it.

What would you now have me do? But he, too, was staring at Shianne; at the fall of her almost white hair, at the sword she wielded, the shield that hid the protuberant belly from immediate view.

She is not the White Lady.

No. No, she is not. But, Jewel? I see the echoes of the White Lady in her now, and I remember. How much worse must it be for him? I am the White Lady's. I serve you at her command, but she has not forsaken me.

Jewel did not agree.

Had she, she would have given no command. I am still hers. He is not. He will never return to her side. He will never, again, be hers.

But he was of her.

Once, perhaps. He is dead now. He is dead, and in Shianne's presence, he is aware of the enormity of the loss.

I don't understand why he—why they—left.

No. No more do I or any of the Arianni; it is inconceivable to us.

Jewel glanced at Calliastra; she was smiling. Nothing about the expression was warm, nothing about it, kind. She didn't notice Jewel at all. No, Jewel thought, she noticed only one thing: Darranatos' pain.

"Shandalliaran."

Shianne said nothing as she gazed at Darranatos, and the demon seemed to shrink, to dwindle, his wings of fire becoming raiment of the same bright, harsh color. The transformation was slow but steady, and when it was done, he faced her as if he were still, in truth, one of her kin. He did not set aside sword or shield; nor did she.

"Shandalliaran," he said again. "What has become of you?"

"Of me? How can you ask that, who stand as you stand? I see the shadows in you, and I see death—but not the death of our kind. What has become of *you?*" She was strong enough, Jewel thought, that she felt no need to hide her pain; it was in every syllable, mixed with confusion and a muted horror. He was not the first of the *Kialli* she had seen, nor the first with whom she had dared to speak.

But something about this *Kialli* lord was different. It wasn't his power, although he was by far the most powerful demon she had ever encountered—it was something other.

"We did not know," he said, after a cold, still pause, "what had become of you. Did you know that we searched? Did she tell you?"

"I have not spoken to her since the day she made clear her displeasure at what was done." Before he could speak again, she lifted a hand—the sword hand. "But what we did, we did *for her.* What has become of you, Darranatos? What have you done?"

Silence. In it, shadows gathered.

"Not for anything but the love of the White Lady would we have taken the measures that we thought necessary. Not for anything but her safety, her existence, would we have stepped off the path she decreed. In our long captivity, we listened for her song, and we sang it—those of us who were given that voice.

We lived and dreamed and yearned for the day we might once again prove ourselves worthy of her.

"We did not—we *never*—abandoned her."

"Shandalliaran—"

"*Why*? Why, brother? You were the first of the princes of the White Lady's court! You were the best, the brightest; we looked upon you, and we knew you to be second only to the White Lady. In you we could see—we could all see—the radiance of her glory, reflected perfectly. You were—" She stopped speaking for one long minute as if struggling, now, to find words.

And Jewel realized, listening, that she could understand their words.

Yes, the Winter King said.

Why?

You wear that ring, he replied. *And you have wakened it. Wish you to remain in ignorance, you must remove it, if that is even possible.*

"If I understand what I now see in you, I was not the first to leave her. And if you ask how, if you can ask why, you will never understand. Nor does it now matter. If you seek her, you will never find her. She made her choice, long ago, to stand against our Lord—and she alone, he would have taken and exalted above all others. She alone." The last two words were bitter, a grimace of sound, an echo of pain.

"Exalted as you are exalted?" The golden light grew brighter; shadows became dark streams of bitter smoke in its wake. "Valued as you are valued? We were none of us as worthy as you, *none*. I knew—I had heard—of the loss, the defection, the betrayal—but I had never imagined that you would be among them."

"I had never imagined that I would face you again while the world remained diminished, its glory hidden. And yet, here you are. And you, too, are diminished and much changed; more so even than I."

"Far, far less than you," was the soft reply. "Nothing I have seen—nothing—has grieved me more than this." She raised sword.

"You cannot think in your diminished state that you can harm me?" he asked. His own sword did not move, did not rise; nor did his shield. "Had we found you, I might never have been forsworn."

Even as he spoke, Jewel knew that forsworn was not the right word.

Shianne lifted sword, raising it as if it were a staff; sunlight illuminated the world, changing the color of the night sky. She did not bring the blade down; she was not close enough. But she lifted her chin and drew breath that sounded as if it were sucking in the sounds of the battlefield—those that still remained. Silence was all that was left; not even the voice of fire or air could be heard.

Into that stillness, she began to sing.

Jewel had heard her song before. This was a visceral reminder that memory could not contain the truth of the experience; what existed in memory after the fact was a phantom, a ghost, a haunting. One could yearn for it, as one might yearn for one's beloved dead, but could never return to it.

And to hear it again was a gift that demanded silence, awe.

Even from Darranatos. What her song demanded, he gave; he made no attempt to join her. Nor did Kallandras, this time; this song was Shianne's; it was of her.

It held them all; demons, Arianni, mortals; every note, every breath, every pause. As if they were all mere instruments, she drew the silence of awe, enlarged it, made of it a tribute, an offering.

Jewel did not weep.

The Arianni did.

And so, too, the demons. She heard the descant of their cries as they at last broke their silence—all but one. All but Darranatos.

Winter King—

No. No, Jewel. This battle is not yours, and the consequence no longer yours to bear. In this moment, Shianne has decided.

He'll kill her.

Perhaps. And perhaps that might be for the best.

The child will die!

She has given up eternity, she has surrendered her place by the White Lady's side. She is already doomed, already damned.

But she did it for *the child.*

No, Jewel. She did it for the White Lady. And if the child is lost, it changes nothing. She has chosen to take this risk, and you must allow it. You are not her Lord, not her master; you are a companion only, and if you walk by her side, the road you walk is not her road.

Darranatos lifted his sword, held it aloft; he alone, of all the *Kialli*, remained silent. Once again, his wings unfurled, spreading across the sky as if they were horizon. Jewel was not surprised when he brought his weapon down; was not surprised when Adam alone cried out.

But the song did not stop. She had understood the words that both Darranatos and Shianne had spoken, but the words of this song, relentless though they were, did not cohere or resolve themselves into something Jewel understood as language.

Darranatos was not so lucky.

He brought the sword down; it struck Shianne's raised sword, and the clashing light of the two—gold and red—burned the rest of the shadow away. But the gold sword held, and the voice of its wielder barely faltered.

Darranatos threw the shield he held away; it spun through the air and vanished before it struck anything as mundane as tree or earth. He brought the shield arm, now free, to the hilt of his sword and raised that sword again, this time in both hands.

The Wild Hunt did not move. The demons—if any remained standing, save Darranatos—were likewise frozen, immobile. Adam did—but someone caught him by the shoulder; she could see that, but no more. Whoever had caught him held him fast; he did not dart into the path of the red sword.

And the red sword came down again with far more force. Jewel opened her mouth on a wordless, silent cry.

The golden shield, raised against the blow, absorbed it; Jewel was certain it would shatter. It did not, but the ground split beyond Shianne; trees fell; debris rose.

He raised sword a third time.

He brought it down.

This time, Shianne lost her shield; she did not, however, lose her voice or her song, and it was the song that was her most potent weapon.

Darranatos did not lift sword a fourth time.

Jewel had seen the *Kialli* fight Meralonne before; had seen his delight and their recognition. But none of the *Kialli* had sheathed weapons and withdrawn unless forced to retreat; they had thrown themselves into the battle with everything they could bring to bear. Recognition was not enough to stay their hands. On either side.

It was not enough to stay Shianne's.

But Darranatos could not bring his sword to bear a fourth time. His wings folded, as did his knees, as if the wings themselves were the only thing now keeping him aloft. He did not kneel, not precisely; there was nothing of that grace or deliberation in the motion. But graceful or no, he was brought to his knees before her; Jewel could see that shards of Shianne's shield had lodged themselves in her arm, and knew, as she watched, that the arm itself was broken.

Adam knew it, too, but this time he did not struggle to reach her. No, he lifted a hand, as if in denial, as Shianne raised the sword she still held.

And this, Jewel thought, was the White Lady's mercy: she brought that sword down without hesitation, sundering head from body as it passed cleanly through Darranatos' neck.

The sword vanished; it had served the only purpose it had. The song, however, did not; she bent, she lifted the head from where it had rolled to a stop—eyes facing Shianne as if, even in death, she was the only thing worthy of regard on this field, beneath this sky.

She knelt at last, but even kneeling, continued to sing; as her shoulders curled inward, finally caught by gravity, her volume banked; she drew the song back, into herself, until Jewel could no longer hear it.

Only then did sound return to the field; only then did the elements continue their argument over the rightful ruler of the landscape; only then did the Arianni return, at last, to the combat that seemed to govern their life.

But Shianne did not. She did not stand, did not rise, did not lift her head; her arms, broken or not, cradled the head of the fallen *Kialli* lord until that head—like the body that no longer housed it—crumbled to ash and dust in her arms.

Then, only then, did she weep.

7th day of Lattan, 428 A.A.
Terafin Manse, Averalaan Aramarelas

Finch was surprised to see Meralonne and took no pains to conceal it. Teller, however, was not. She glanced at him; his color would have been terrible if not for the warmth lent it by the fire of the burning tree. She wondered again what he had seen on the day he had chosen to look into the Oracle's crystal ball. He would not speak of it, and even were he to be convinced to do so, it would not be here.

Meralonne offered her a very correct bow; she returned a nod, as might be expected of a ruler of one of The Ten. The forest denizens had been certain that he would be beyond them, that he would be one of the enemies they would face in the coming days.

Haval and Jarven were neutral; that was the whole of the caution they displayed. It was enough.

But the forest denizens, if they had been trained to bear very human arms, were not so cautious; after their initial, incredulous stares, they began to flock to Meralonne, to surround him. They chattered in voices that sounded to Finch like forest leaves in a gentle breeze; she caught words that were names, but little else.

He reached out as they spoke, his fingers brushing a burning leaf on a low-lying branch. It singed his fingertips and he withdrew his hand. They marked it, just as Finch did.

Jester was carrying the golden fox, and set him down upon the exposed roots of that fiery tree; he was not of a mind to be set down, but accepted that Jester's usefulness had come to a momentary end. It was to Finch he padded across the forest floor, and she thought, with surprise, that she missed the cats. If nothing else could be said about them, she could say this: they did not insist on being carried, and they did not bite her hard enough to draw blood.

"You are thinking loudly," the fox said, when he was safely ensconced in her arms.

"Why is Meralonne here?"

"You must ask your Jester. When I think mortals have no surprises left to offer one such as I, they nonetheless do."

As if she were speaking with Jarven, she said, "How is it that the elders have allowed Meralonne to return?"

"Ah, that." He raised his nose, his eyes meeting Finch's; they flashed a warning.

Jester, however, signed, *Not me.* She understood what it meant.

She then turned to Meralonne. "Are you, or are you not, here in the capacity of House Mage?"

A platinum brow rose.

"I speak as regent," Finch continued, when he did not answer. "And the forest recognizes that position." She could not fold her arms without dropping the fox, and forced her expression and tone to do the work instead.

He considered her for a long moment as the forest itself—save only the tree of fire—fell silent around them both. Even the fox gazed up at her with an arrested expression.

Jarven cleared his throat. Finch ignored him, which was never wise. But she wanted an answer, and she had, in as diplomatic a fashion as possible, made clear that an answer must be forthcoming. It was a test: of herself, of Meralonne, of the forest. And perhaps of Jarven, as well, although the results in that case were never fixed, never static.

"Then yes, ATerafin. While the forest is content to allow it, I will be House Mage."

"Very well. We had questions about the heralds and the sleepers which we hope you will be able to answer."

He inclined his head. "I will not, however, be responsible for what you choose to do with those answers, if indeed you have any choices remaining to you at all." His hair blew in the windless clearing; his eyes shone.

And Finch, at a distance, heard singing.

It was resonant, clear, the words themselves distinct and yet private enough they were unintelligible. She turned, as the magi had turned, her gaze following forest into darkness of night sky; she felt a sudden chill, and moved, fox in arms, to stand beneath the boughs of the burning tree. There was no warmth to be found there.

"Can you hear it?" he asked softly, so softly. His eyes closed as he lifted his chin, tilting into the wind that touched nothing else. After a long, long pause, he bowed his head.

"I hear a song," Finch replied, her voice as soft as his.

"The forest does, indeed, accept you."

"Where is it coming from?"

"Beyond the borders of Fabril's reach. But that song will be heard throughout the high wilderness, ere this eve gives way at last—to endless night, or dawn." He turned to her then, faced her fully, his eyes no longer shining. "Hear you the horns? They howl now. Come. You have not walked the forests, but you will need them soon." He held out one hand.

Jarven cleared his throat again.

This time, both the magi and the regent turned to face him. His expression was no longer neutral; it was grave, even haunted. He, too, had heard the singing, but what he made of it was not what Finch had made of it.

"You are young," he told her, looking down at her from a variety of removes. "Not the child you were when we first met, but not like the man that I have become. I once thought your origins showed promise—and in that, I was right. But what grew from the streets of those holdings was not what grew from the streets of mine.

"This is not your battle, Regent." He looked to Meralonne. "Leave her here, where she may plan. There is someplace that we now need to travel."

Meralonne however shook his head. "It is oft said The Terafin is young and naive; that she trusts too readily, believes too easily. But that is the lie you tell yourselves. Here, the forest does not accept those lies; nor will it, while The Terafin lives. And yes," he added softly, "she lives; she must live, for the forest is waiting." And he nodded to Jarven, an imperial nod that might pass between men of power, but it was to Andrei that he turned.

"Namann."

"Illaraphaniel." Andrei did not bow.

"This is the choice you have made, then? You would not be my chosen companion on this, of all nights—but I am reminded tonight that even those I might have chosen over all others could not, in the end, be fully trusted. It is not in my nature to trust you, but it is not in our nature to trust at all."

"You have spent long among the mortals," Andrei replied.

Meralonne laughed. "You say that to me?"

"Illaraphaniel—she is waiting."

Finch was confused. Meralonne, however, was not. The fox bit her hand—gently enough to draw the attention he craved without drawing blood; he was not displeased with her, at the moment. He indicated wordlessly that he wished to be taken to Jarven, and she did his bidding willingly, if only to be relieved of her burden. She complained about the cats—and the cost of them—but at base, they were almost kin to her. The fox was not and would never be. Like Jarven, he could be gentle; like Jarven, he could be playful; like Jarven, he could be indulgent. But more than Jarven, he could be capricious, and all affection was superficial.

Jarven would not kill Finch over a trifle; his injured dignity did not demand it. He might, she thought, be willing to see her dead—but her death would complicate his life in ways he would find, at best, inconvenient. And it would break something in Lucille.

Jarven gathered the fox with respect but held him as Finch had held him.

"It is not yet time for us," the fox told him. "Not yet, and perhaps not this eve. But come, let us follow where they lead; there is much to see."

Jarven said nothing.

"Do not spend your life needlessly."

Finch did not smile. Expression as grave as Jarven's, she said, "It is good advice."

"I am often entertained by good advice," Jarven conceded. To Haval, he asked, "Will you remain?"

"I will keep my own counsel in this."

"You are dour, as usual."

"And you are frivolous. But we are two old men who are set in our ways; it is folly to expect change now."

"You will seek the Kings."

"Will I? It has been many, many years since I considered the Kings my master."

"It was never mastery that was your concern; it was responsibility."

"You are being almost rude."

"It is, as you say, folly to expect change at this late date. Very well. I will, as advised, observe for the nonce."

Haval nodded. "You have always had an interesting take on advice. I have almost missed it."

Jarven laughed. He then walked away from the tree of fire. Finch watched him, concentrating on the dark shape of his back until she could see the exact point at which he faded from view.

Only when he was gone did Birgide Viranyi approach Haval. Her eyes were red; the pretense of normalcy was gone.

"Where is he?"

She closed those red eyes. Without opening them, she said, "He is gone to Moorelas' statue. They are gathered there."

"The god-born?"

"Yes. And the Kings." She paused and then added, "Duvari is with them. He is . . . ill-pleased. He does not feel it is either safe or wise for the Kings to be there."

"It is, no doubt, necessary," Haval replied, his voice dry and almost unconcerned.

"Will Jarven support the Kings?"

"If it becomes necessary, I believe he will make that attempt. Tell me, do you feel that he will be capable?"

"I have not seen him fight."

Haval nodded.

"Nor have I seen you do so."

"I am Councillor, if you recall. Will you go?"

Birgide tensed, and Finch understood that this was the heart of her hesitation. She was Warden and sworn to the forest. And she was *Astari* and sworn to the Kings. "If that is what you advise, I will."

Haval raised a brow, his expression as dire as the one he reserved for the hapless visitors who managed, regardless of effort and care, to step on his beads; since they were strewn all over the floor, Finch had never thought this reasonable.

"In theory, Warden, you have the freedom of the forest, and the forest extends across most of the hundred holdings. There is no reason that you cannot fulfill your duties while standing in the Common or any of the hundred, save only a handful. And I do not trust Jarven."

"No?"

"Ah, his intent at the moment does not work against ours, but he is in the most capricious of his moods."

"You do not approve."

"My approval, or disapproval, is irrelevant. At the moment, he needs to seek approval from only one living creature—and he has carried that creature with him."

"The elders do not yet find it trivial to walk through the streets of the actual city."

"No; I believe that is why the fox chose to accompany Jarven; Jarven does not suffer from any such restriction."

"Councillor," Meralonne said quietly.

"Apologies, APhaniel. Allow me to finish here." To Birgide he said, "Yes, that would be my advice. It is not an act of mercy; it is not an act of generosity. Understand that. I do not know what you will face, but there are demons skirting the forest's edge, even now."

"It is not the demons that you must fear," Meralonne added, voice soft.

"You are incorrect, APhaniel. It is not the demons *you* must fear."

Birgide lowered her chin as she faced Haval; she then lifted her left hand and placed it against her heart; a brief flutter of very deliberate motion.

Haval did not repeat it. He lifted his hand to shoo her away. And she went. "I am torn," he told Finch, "between a desire to have an end to these infernal horns, and a certainty that an ending spells doom for us all. I am not a young man, and the ringing in my ears causes my head to ache."

She smiled; she couldn't help it. In this dark clothing, with no visible sign of the apron he habitually wore when crafting, he had resembled Duvari; now, he was Haval Arwood again.

"You wish to take Finch with you when you leave for the city."

Meralonne nodded.

"And you will take Andrei as well. Andrei?" The Araven servant nodded.

Haval studied Finch in silence, his hands behind his back, his eyes half-hooded with narrow appraisal. "We cannot afford to lose you," he finally said. "Jester, you go instead."

Jester was not a happy man.

While he agreed with Haval in one particular—they could not afford to lose Finch—the implication that they *could* afford to lose Jester rankled. It rankled almost as much as the company he was now forced to keep: Andrei of Araven, and Meralonne APhaniel. It was not that he disliked the Araven servant; he disliked his obvious lack of anything remotely resembling a sense of humor. Meralonne was a discomfort for entirely practical reasons; if everything any of the forest denizens had said was accurate, he could become their worst nightmare without warning. What Jester did not understand was why the forest simply accepted this.

The only thing needed to make the day worse arrived before they had even found their way out of the forest.

"Where are *you* going?" The needling voice of bored cat filled the air.

Jester cursed, which caused Andrei to raise a brow. Silver gleamed to Jester's left, gold to his right. He could not see the trees of diamond, but wasn't looking. What he wanted, now, was the manicured grounds of the Terafin manse. And an absence of obnoxious cat.

"Aren't you supposed to be at home?"

"I'm *bored. Nothing* is happening. Where are *you* going?"

"We're going to the edge of the Common."

"Where?"

Jester had never tried to strangle the cats; he never imagined that he would get the better of the attempt. "If you *pay attention*, you'll probably be able to figure it out."

Night hissed. Hissed, and then yowled in outrage.

Two cats.

"Go *away*," the black cat shouted at the white one.

"No, *you* go."

Andrei looked almost as sour as Jester felt. "Eldest," he said, careful not to choose a particular one, "we would like to arrive in the city without attracting every danger that now inhabits the wilderness. You will wake them all, and we cannot afford that."

"I was here *first*."

"Sssso?" Snow avoided Night's claws. "Where are you *going*?" He came to land more or less beside Jester, but only because Jester was fast enough to move his foot out of harm's way.

"To the statue of Moorelas," Jester replied.

"Are *not*."

Jester surrendered. "Where are we going, then?"

Snow flicked Jester's chest with his wing. "The *wrong* way. You *could* try flying."

Fine. "We're trying to find our way out of the forest."

"Are *not*."

"We *think* we're trying to find our way out of the forest."

Snow hissed laughter. Above, so did Night.

Jester turned to glance at his two companions; Andrei's face was entirely expressionless. Meralonne appeared to be amused. Condescendingly amused.

"If we could avoid the game of stupid mortals," Jester began.

"They are not wrong," Meralonne said, at almost the same time. "But, ATerafin, you are not attempting to seek an exit now. The time has come where exits will be far harder for you to find."

"I've never had trouble before."

"You've never faced this night before. The forest encompasses the Common, and much of the hundred. It is in the Common that the land is strongest, that its power is closest to the surface. The *Ellariannatte* have always grown there, and the leaves have always bloomed. They are rooted in soil that is ancient and sleeping, but they are rooted, as well, in soil that mortals might dig or till. Think you that their presence was mere coincidence? There is a reason that the Sleepers lie here.

"The Common, *Avantari*, and Terafin are bound to the will of The Terafin and to the inhabitants of her land; they are waking, now. It is far faster and far safer for you to travel through the forest, not out of it."

"Do you see any convenient paths? Any signs?"

"Sarcasm is unnecessary," Andrei said. "Illaraphaniel is correct. But I believe that you will find the way regardless; had I not, I would have spoken."

"The eldest are correct, however," Meralonne said.

Jester blanched as the wind came at his call.

"It would, no doubt, be less complicated to fly."

"There's nothing to catch us if we fall!"

"We are no longer leaving the forest; there is nothing to silence the wind. If, however, you are concerned, you might ride one of The Terafin's cats."

The cacophony of outrage that erupted was predictable, annoying, and—simultaneously—oddly comforting.

Night and Snow argued about who should take Jester. Or, rather, who should be stuck with him. They didn't appear to notice the wind that swept across the forest floor, inserting itself between Jester's feet and the ground. When they did, they reversed the course of their complaints instantly, but arguing with the wind was not as simple as arguing with each other—or at least that's what Jester hoped.

Andrei, however, did not take to the air.

Jester glanced at the magi, raising a brow in question; the magi glanced at Andrei before replying. "The wind will not willingly carry him. It will carry him if that is my command—but that would be costly, and it is not a battle I choose to fight this eve. Unencumbered by you, Andrei will find his way to Moorelas' Sanctum."

"It is true, ATerafin," the Araven servant said. "You need have no fear for me; I am likely to arrive before you do. And," he added, glaring at the cats, "with far more subtlety."

Jester really did not enjoy flying. "Could you put me down? I'd rather walk there with Andrei."

"He will not walk as you would walk if he wishes speed," Meralonne replied, "and the forest heart would be alarmed. What he chooses to do on his own behalf, the elders will accept."

"What about Andrei ruffles so many feathers?" In the distance, Jester could see trees. And more trees. He could not, even at this height, see ocean. He couldn't see the spires of *Avantari* either, which was more disturbing. Meralonne had said that Jay's forest extended to the palace of the Twin Kings.

"He does not, as you so quaintly put it, ruffle mine."

"Which is why I feel it's safe to ask you."

A platinum brow rose.

Jester shook his head. Talking was easier than watching the landscape beneath his feet; there was nothing beneath those feet—nothing solid—to impede the view. It was a view he did not like.

"He is *ugly*," Night said.

"He is *stupid*," Snow added.

"You think we're all ugly and stupid," Jester countered.

"He is *very* ugly."

Meralonne glanced at Night without comment. Jester, however, frowned.

"Is it the wind?"

The brow rose again. "You are observant, for a lazy man."

"The more I observe, the faster I can get out of the way of real work."

"Given your current circumstance, I believe you need to move faster."

Jester shrugged. "It's Haval. The man's a demon."

Meralonne laughed. "An unfortunate—and entirely inaccurate—choice of words. He is Councillor, while The Terafin lives. He is not a man who relies on the regard of others, and he misses nothing he sees. I have often wondered what he was like in his youth."

"Not like you in yours."

"No. Come. They are already gathered."

The wind was not particularly gentle, and when Jester was finally set down on the edge of the seawall, he was a rumpled mess. Given the prior state of his clothing, it could be forgiven. He wore his House ring, not that that would buy him any mercy or consideration from Duvari. And Duvari was present, as were the kings.

They had once gathered here, half of Jester's lifetime ago, before he had become ATerafin. That had been the beginning of his life in Terafin; it had been the start of food, warmth, clothing that had been designed and constructed out of matching fabric, in his size.

But that had not been the first time the den had been in the place beneath the sanctum. In the streets of a fallen, buried city, they had scavenged through the detritus of the dead and the forgotten, slowly bringing historical artifacts— Rath's words—to light, where they could be furtively sold. This, too, he remembered.

He had never felt a desire to return to it. That hidden city had devoured his chosen kin: Fisher, Lefty, Lander. Although their findings had kept a roof over their head, food in their bellies, the cost, in the end, had been too high. They would have found a different way to survive all but the harshest winter had they understood the price they would pay.

And yet, that had brought them to Terafin. It had brought Jay to Terafin. She had become the woman who ruled the House. Impossible dream, that; Jester, not given to flights of pointless fancy, had never really thought of it.

No, that was untrue.

He hated the patriciate. He had hated the patriciate on the night he'd been confined to a room in a very illegal brothel; the hatred, like a seed planted violently and without his consent, had sunk roots that he had never, ever dislodged. This was not, given Kings and priests and Kings' Swords, the place to return to that hatred. But he had been set down apart from the main body, and was unlikely, without intervention, to be allowed to join them.

That suited him.

It did not, however, suit the cats. They understood, in theory, that they were not to intervene, not to interfere, but they used cat logic. If they were *here*, as Night pointed out, they weren't interfering. They were, however, loud; no whining was as loud or as grating, and they could keep at it for hours, in Jester's unfortunately unlimited experience.

"You might attempt to have them show your rulers some respect," Andrei said. He stepped up on the seawall, his clothing dry, his face pinched and starched, but it seemed to Jester that the sea had almost disgorged him.

"And lose my hand?"

Snow hissed laughter.

"They will not take your hand; they will not cause anything other than your dignity any harm."

"We *might*," Night said, as Snow said, "Says *who*?"

Jester straightened his torn jacket; he carried no comb or brush. He suspected Andrei did, but Andrei was Hectore's servant, not his own. "Do you know what they're doing?"

Andrei did not answer. He folded his arms, his expression remote, as he watched.

They weren't doing anything that seemed unusual or remarkable to Jester, if he didn't count the fact of the congregation itself. He could see golden eyes; they were the predominant color. Duvari's eyes were brown, which Jester knew; they were too narrowed for Jester to easily discern color otherwise. The Kings' Swords had separated the statue of Moorelas from the people who might otherwise have chosen to visit it—and for the most part, people gaped at a very safe distance, if at all.

He glanced at the windows of distant buildings before once again dropping his gaze to the carved reliefs that encircled the statue itself. And the statue was silent, grim, its expression determined.

"Did you meet him?" Jester asked.

Meralonne had landed so silently and moved so little, he might have been a statue himself. But he looked up to the height of the statue's graven face. "Yes, as you must know."

"It's a legend. A story. None of it has to be true." Jester shrugged. "Apparently, some of it is."

"Some, yes. He is considered a hero, to your kind. A great man. A giant." He smiled; the smile was weathered, the emotion behind it turned inward. "It is not the inclination of the Arianni to consider any mortal a great man. It was certainly not in the nature of the firstborn princes to do so. He was, or would have been, insignificant to us.

"But he had one quality that we lacked."

"He could wield the sword."

Meralonne transferred his gaze to Jester. After a long pause, he said, "He could wield the sword. Know you much of that weapon?"

"Just stories. Some say it was crafted by Fabril."

"It predates Fabril by centuries."

"Some say it was crafted by Myrddion."

"That is a better lie. Ah, no; it is a better belief."

"And it's not true, either?"

"No, ATerafin. No." He exhaled slowly. "It is painful to me, still, to be in this place." Jester understood that he referred to the statue the gods called a sanctum. "There are other stories of that sword that are closer to the truth, but it is irrelevant. We could not wield it. He could. He was one of a long line of people to make the attempt; he survived it."

"Did you try?"

"I am alive."

"Not an answer."

And even here, a glimmer of smile changed the shape of the magi's face. Or perhaps it was because he had acknowledged that the past pained him—he had been that truthful. "No, Jester, it is not. There was a time when it was assumed that only *namann* could wield it."

Andrei stiffened. Jester took this as a no. But he looked at Andrei again; he saw Hectore's servant, and only Hectore's servant. Hectore of Araven was a man that Jester had a grudging respect for; he was powerful, yes, and he was incredibly wealthy—but Jester's investigation had unearthed very little about the man that he did not readily publicly claim.

And Jay owed Andrei her life. She remembered her debts. She made certain that other people remembered them as well.

"He is not what *you* are," Night said.

"No." Exhaling, Jester added, "He's probably better."

Andrei's eyes widened slightly, but he did not speak.

"I've seen what Hectore's like; I would have strangled him decades ago, if I were in your position."

Andrei was clearly torn between stiff offense and amusement, and settled, to Jester's surprise, on the latter.

"And if I could have managed it somehow, I'd've buried Jarven. I can't understand why Hectore likes him; they're nothing alike."

"No," Andrei agreed, with quiet dignity. "They are not alike." He hesitated, rare in the Araven servant. "Do you understand what your Terafin is? What she must be?"

"I know *who* she is. And I know that if she has only one choice to make in order to save us, she'll make it."

"You trust her."

"I don't trust her more than you trust your master."

Andrei bowed. "Did she tell you," he said, watching the milling of the gathering begin to sort itself out into movements that were more deliberate, "that she offered me a home, in Terafin, serving her?"

Jester's *no* was drowned by yowling cat. Two yowling cats. Since everyone present was accustomed to hearing them berate The Terafin for her stupidity, their complaints raised no brows.

"I assume she meant in the absence of Hectore."

"You do understand her."

Jester smiled. "Finch would make that offer as well—but Finch wouldn't ask unless you were already homeless. She likes Hectore."

"You do not."

"I don't dislike him."

"Ah." The servant frowned. "Jarven is here."

Jester, however, had caught sight of Birgide. He turned to Meralonne and froze; the mage's eyes were shining like liquid silver—liquid that nonetheless burned brightly.

"No, Jester," Andrei surprised him by saying. "I could not wield it."

"Did you ever meet Moorelas?"

"I?" Andrei shrugged. "I was not, I was *never*, trusted. Not by the god we do not name, and not by the gods we do. I was not trusted by the firstborn; I was not trusted by their offspring—those that exist. The only home I could claim was inhospitable to guests, and I have—and will have—no offspring of my own.

"I served, in my time. I served gods. I served the firstborn." He lifted his head and seemed to Jester to gain inches of height as he spoke. The cats, to either side, fell silent, but their fur rose, as if they could hear words that he wasn't saying, and considered them all a threat. "But I was ever on the outside; necessary in some cases, but never trusted, never—" He shook his head, as if to clear it.

"Hectore trusts you."

Andrei glanced at Jester.

"He trusts you as much as we trust Jay. As much as we trust Ellerson. More, maybe. You have Avandar's competence. And possibly his lack of humor. Is that a servant thing?"

"Not specifically, to my knowledge. Do you understand what they do?"

Jester, watching the Kings, shook his head. He wondered, for the first time, why they were here. As the Exalted took their places around the sanctum, the Kings joined them. Duvari appeared to be arguing with the Wisdom-born King, to no avail.

Birgide Viranyi walked to Duvari's side only after the argument had finished; she joined him, her hands clasped loosely behind her back, her chin bowed. If the Lord of the Compact looked at her—at all—it was too subtle to be seen at this distance; nor did Birgide attempt to speak.

Were it not for the color of her eyes, she would have vanished into the crowd simply by standing still. But her eyes, like the eyes of the god-born, seemed to radiate light.

"What is she doing?" Meralonne said, his voice a whisper of sound, a whisper of Winter. To Jester's eye, she was standing as the *Astari* might stand, waiting upon Duvari's words—or gestures—before committing to action. He did not, however, doubt Meralonne.

It was Andrei who answered. "She is Warden." As answers went, it didn't offer much. But at the mention of the word, Jester raised his gaze from the men and women, god-born all, who congregated in a circle beneath the statue. Above the statue, above the permanent buildings around which merchants with carts and moving stalls plied their wares, he saw the trees in the Common. There had been no time in Jester's life when the trees had not grown, had not budded, no time at which the leaves had not eventually fallen; they were as much a part of the Common as the stones of the street.

He saw that they had multiplied, somehow; that they had grown, extending their dominance of the sky. The trees that had been lost to the concerted attack of demons had reappeared, as if the fires of demonic magic had never touched them at all.

"She is Warden," Andrei repeated, seeing what Jester saw.

"It will avail her nothing." Meralonne now sounded annoyed.

"You mistake my meaning, Illaraphaniel—and since it is you, I must assume you do so deliberately. She has not walked these streets as Warden before. She has walked them as mortal; she has walked them as one whose responsibilities have been entirely mortal—and entirely voluntary.

"She *is* Warden, here. And although the Terafin manse is situated upon the Isle, you know full well that it is the Common that is the seat of this land's power. Against you, at the moment, I think the Warden might prevail."

Had Andrei been anyone else, Jester would have stepped on his foot.

In a chillier tone, Meralonne replied. "It is not against me that she must prevail."

"No. Not yet, Illaraphaniel. But you will have need of her; you will have need of the roots the *Ellariannatte* plant. Can you not feel it? Can you not hear them?"

The magi did not reply.

"I hear them, but they are three, not four."

"Only three will come," Meralonne whispered. "The fourth cannot travel as the three can, and his journey has not yet begun. You must pardon me for a moment." He bowed—to Jester—and rose, as if the ground was no longer worthy enough to be walked on.

Jester watched as he drifted away, the motion too slow to be flight, but too graceful to be anything else.

"Are we expecting the Sleepers to wake?" he asked, when Meralonne was the same size as the god-born in the distance.

"We have been expecting it for some small time," Andrei replied, with the usual amount of disapproval.

"In the *future*, yes."

"It has not happened yet." He glanced at Jester.

"Why, exactly, did Haval send me?"

"I believe he felt that Finch was of more value to the House."

Jester snorted. Hands in pockets—one of which had been torn by his fall through the *Ellarianatte*—he said, "She is. But given who's already gathered here, what did he expect *me* to do?"

"Decide."

As answers went, it was unhelpful. Night and Snow hissed laughter, and Jester glared at them both.

Haval stood at the center of the people Finch privately thought of as trees. In the shallows of night, they were armed; they wore no armor.

"It is not yet your time, I think," Haval said quietly. "And Finch? Take no risks here. We will survive the evening."

The way he said it made her entire body tense; she lost words to a sharp, brief panic. Forcing herself to breathe through it, she found them again, but Teller signed. He had spoken very little, this eve, his expression drawn. *Morning.*

She signed back, but he had turned away, as if to avoid discussion.

"Will the rest of the city?"

Haval did not smile. "I do not know."

"Have you sent for Hannerle?" It was always risky, to mention Hannerle in the wrong setting.

Haval shook his head. "She is at home, where she wished to be. She will wait for me there."

"But—but your store is in the Common."

"Yes, Finch." His smile was weary; it aged his face. "Do not stiffen in that fashion. You are regent in The Terafin's absence. I do not dissemble. I am worried. It is difficult to allow others the freedom to make their own choices; it inevitably becomes the freedom to make their own mistakes. Mistakes are tools," he added, glancing briefly at her expression. "But they are not useful if they cannot be survived."

"You don't want to go home."

"I am practical. At home, as you call it, I am Haval Arwood, an old man who has not yet allowed all of his skills to atrophy. What I can do there is not, in any way, the equal of what I might achieve here; therefore, it is here I stay." His smile deepened. "And here, I am Councillor. But to my wife, I am Haval, always, and she is not—as you may have noticed—capable of curbing either her tongue or her temper. Every man and woman of power and note will be gathered in the Common; it is her best chance of survival."

Teller signed again, and Finch retreated.

"I'll go back to the house," Teller said, when Finch did not reply.

"Don't."

"Everyone else is there. Ellerson is there. If the forest overtakes the manse, someone needs to take charge."

"I'm regent. I'll do it."

But Teller shook his head. "I'm right-kin. I know the schedules of every active member of the council, past or present. Barston has ways of dealing with all of them, even the hostile ones."

"I'm regent," she said again.

"I know. But you let Haval send Jester to the Common; I'm only going to the manse. I don't understand why you have to be here; I understand that Haval wants you."

"Haval doesn't care—"

"Finch, he does. But right now he's almost like Duvari."

"Please," Haval said, pinching the bridge of his nose in familiar frustration.

"But you are, Haval," Teller replied, not budging. "You are now measuring everything—every possible death, every possible survivor—and you are making decisions based only on those calculations. It is a . . . cold math. Jay would not be capable of it."

"And you?"

Teller shook his head, his gaze growing distant. "No. I've proven, time and again, that I can't do that math when the math itself is largely irrelevant. I trust you," he continued, lifting a hand to forestall the obvious lecture. "But I do not trust you with my life. I do not trust you with theirs. I do not even trust you with the lives you hold dearest; you have set all of that aside.

"You will not kill us. You will not abandon us for your own advantage. But you would do the latter if it advantaged the greater number of people. You would leave us behind if the cost of protecting us was too dear."

Finch understood, suddenly, and she lifted her hands again; they moved furiously, even through their tremble.

Yes, you could. Jay wouldn't want it, Teller signed.

"She wouldn't want this of you, either."

"It doesn't matter. Someone has to go. If it makes you feel better, I'll wake Haerrad and leave him in charge."

Finch blanched. Teller's smile was wry, but genuine.

"I'd rather see the Master of the Household Staff in charge."

In a much more serious voice—and having had far more contact with the woman than Finch had—Teller said, "She will be. But she'll be in charge of the rest of the staff." He bowed to Haval and Finch, and when he turned to leave, Finch struggled with the visceral desire to grab him by the arm and detain him.

But he was right. She knew it; Haval knew it.

"His loss will hurt Jay more than anyone's," she said, when Teller was too far away to hear the words.

"The loss of any of her den will cut her—and I fear that she will face that before the end. But you are regent, Finch. None of your den but you could fill that position."

"Teller—"

"Teller could not *hold* it. By strict legality he could become regent; by custom, that role should already be his. You did not allow it, and your reasons for taking the regency upon your own shoulders are sound. Let him go; let him do what he must do. He is not a fool."

The first person Teller saw, upon his return to the manse, was Ellerson. The domicis was waiting with both tea and clothing. The tea was a boon; the clothing was unexpected. Looking at it, Teller raised his gaze from teacup to older man.

"You know."

Ellerson said nothing.

"Ellerson—"

"I am domicis, while I live. The future is always uncertain; it is the domicis who make calculated guesses and contingency plans. Barston is waiting for you in the right-kin's office." There was a subtle emphasis on the last two words.

Teller did not see the need for a change of clothing, but trusted Ellerson. He changed. He changed into a jacket that was decidedly conservative; it was more colorful than his usual attire, but the colors were mostly variants of the blue that denoted the House. Ellerson also brought out the House Council ring, and studiously ignored Teller's grimace of distaste. It was overly large, overly ornate; it got in the way of simple things, like writing. But he understood this, as well, and donned it. He might be required to write tonight, but writing would not be his primary activity.

"Jester has gone to the Common with Meralonne and Andrei." Teller glanced up to see the domicis' expression; it was wooden, stiff. "Finch remains in the forest with Haval. Is Arann with the Chosen?"

"With the captains, yes. Daine is in the healerie. Ariel is here."

"Can we take her to the forest?"

"I can make that attempt," Ellerson replied. Nothing in his voice implied that he felt this would be successful. "Snow was with her until perhaps a quarter of an hour ago."

Teller did not have the time. He had delayed too long in the forest, beneath the comforting blaze of the tree of fire. "Make the attempt," Teller said, voice gentle, apprehension clear in the lines of his face. "She's already survived an attack that left her an orphan." He thought she'd be safest in the castle that now stood where The Terafin's personal chambers had stood, but it was a longer, wetter walk, and Finch at least could speak Torra.

Ellerson nodded. "The Chosen are waiting."

Barston was in an office that was brightly lit; in the harsher glow of too many magelights, his eyes looked almost blackened. He did snap to attention when Teller entered the right-kin's office. Teller nodded crisply and indicated, with a motion of hand, that Barston was to accompany him to his internal office.

Once the door had closed, and the Chosen had taken up positions in the room, Teller sat on the desk. Barston was willing to accept this—barely—because there were no outsiders in the room, Barston's version of outsider being anyone except Teller and Barston himself.

"I will need to speak with the House Council."

"In aggregate?"

Teller did not wince, but he had worked in Barston's presence for half his life; Barston knew. "If possible, separately." "If possible" was a red flag for Barston, who merely nodded stiffly. "Jarven ATerafin, however, is not currently available. And no, that is not a challenge. The regent has deployed him elsewhere."

Barston waited, and Teller surrendered. "I also need to speak with the Master of the Household Staff."

It was not the usual hour for meetings of any kind; it was far too late, and meetings of import were arranged in advance between Barston and the aides to the Council members. Only in emergencies were such formalities dispensed with. And only dire emergencies could bring The Master of the Household Staff to Teller's office. Or rather, he thought, only things that that woman herself decided were emergencies. Teller was always polite and respectful in her presence, but she appeared to loathe his secretary, and the antagonism was mutual.

He had no doubt, however, that she would come.

She seemed to be possessed of no besetting sins. Jester admired her—at a safe distance—and there had been a kind of armistice between the den and the Household Staff since Carver's disappearance. This was hopeful; it implied that the woman, who terrified Teller more than any other member of the house, possibly including the demonic ones, had a heart.

If she did, it was a heart of stone. Or steel.

She arrived ten minutes after he had requested a meeting with her; she was, as appropriate for her station, unescorted. Nothing she did was ever inappropriate, as far as Teller knew. On the other hand, he didn't inquire; he considered her ferociously competent. She had a general disdain for patricians, or so it seemed; she had no desire to be one. Teller, however, thought she could have ruled Terafin with equanimity. He had never, ever suggested it.

She entered his office, her reaction implying that the Chosen were invisible, and offered Teller a stiff but socially correct bow. If her expression did not define hostility, it would have been a close second. It certainly defined suspicion.

She trusted Teller to be a loyal member of Terafin; she trusted him to put the interests of the House over his own. She did not, however, trust the den to understand the social demarcations that separated the serving staff from the rulers, and her frustration with this was well known. In their defense, the den had tried. But it was hard to treat a person who was better educated, better dressed, and better positioned as if they were somehow a social inferior.

They are not inferiors, Ellerson had said. *But their responsibilities are set, defined, and accepted. When you upset that balance, you upset the social status of those in the back halls, and the person who must deal with the waves that causes is the Master of the Household Staff. The Household Staff has a hierarchy; they are not slaves, and they are not ill-treated. They have both more and less freedom than the den.*

And less money.

Yes, far less than some of you. But far, far more than you had before you escaped the hundred.

The den served The Terafin. The Household Staff served this woman.

She did not demand to know why he had summoned her, but she waited with an expression that was just shy of demand—on the wrong side.

He exhaled. "The Exalted and the Kings are gathering at Moorelas' Sanctum."

He expected her to tell him that this was none of her business and was surprisingly uneasy when she did not. "Tonight?"

"Now."

"And The Terafin?"

"She works, even now, to preserve both the House and the city."

"Meaning she is absent." This, too, was almost shocking. Teller was grateful that Barston remained on the other side of the closed door.

"Yes. The regent is in The Terafin's forest, overseeing the gathered forces there."

She waited.

"I understand that this is unusual. We are not certain what to expect; nor are the magi. It is possible that nothing disastrous will happen, and life will continue as it has in The Terafin's prior absence."

"And if it does not?"

"There is a distinct possibility that we will lose the manse. Not the House—the House is far more than a simple building—but the manse itself. It is possible that we will lose much of the Isle, and the hundred holdings as well."

She stared at him.

Teller winced. After a brief pause he said, "When the Sleepers wake."

Her stare continued, her gaze unblinking. She was still waiting, and Teller gathered up the remnants of a courage he was afraid was deserting him entirely.

"We have only a notion of the possible difficulties our citizens will face. Earthquakes, tidal waves, storms called to rid the streets of . . . us. It has been implied that these would be almost ancillary; the beings who call them would consider them largely irrelevant."

". . . Irrelevant."

"They will, apparently, be angry, and their anger . . . is as potent as an ancient god's. The destruction would be casual—to them. Should they desire to be certain that we all perish, should they raise weapon against any one of us, there is nothing we can do to survive."

"Do you believe this?"

Teller really wished Finch could answer this question instead.

The Master of the Household Staff, however, took his silence as an answer. And it was. "What do you wish done?"

Teller smiled then; it was weary, careworn, but almost genuine. There was no panic in this woman, and he thought there never would be; he could almost feel the strength of her pragmatic resolve, the iron of her sense of duty. Both steadied him. "The forest at the back of the House—the forest that contains the *Ellariannatte*—will protect our people from natural disasters; the fires, the floods, the earthquakes will not reach or touch them there. There was some minor debate about whether they would be protected should the enemy attempt to ride them down, but in the end, the debate is irrelevant. We have a better chance in that forest than we have anywhere else in the city.

"If unnatural fires should start, move the Household Staff to the forest. If they are in the upper floors, enter The Terafin's personal chambers, instead. The doors will open should they be required to open for that purpose." He grimaced. "The cats may or may not be present; it will depend on the shape—and the scope—of the awakening."

"And The Terafin?"

"If she can be here, if she can thwart either the awakening or its consequences, she will be."

The Master of the Household Staff nodded. "I will take my leave; I will have to summon the Household Staff to arrange for safe exit should it be required."

Teller blinked. He had been afraid of this meeting, but could not now even remember why; fear had fled in her presence.

"The Household Staff is my responsibility. I will see them to safety in an orderly fashion. I would appreciate an actual warning, if time permits, but regardless, they are *my* responsibility. Do you understand?" She spoke to him as if he were an ignorant child. Barston would have been enraged.

Teller, however, found it comforting. Utterly comforting; he felt weight—and fear—drop away from his shoulders as if it could no longer find purchase.

As if she could see what he felt, the Master of the Household Staff frowned. "The rest of the House is yours."

Elonne came instantly; she arrived so quickly, she appeared to have been expecting a summons. What surprised Teller was that Marrick came with her. He had hoped to speak to them individually. They were the former Terafin's contemporaries, not his, but Elonne could make anyone feel inexperienced and clumsy.

Anyone, apparently, except Marrick. He glanced at the Chosen by the doors and smiled at Marave. She didn't appear to notice. Elonne frowned at Marrick but did not further acknowledge the breach of etiquette; she took one of the chairs in front of Teller's desk. Marrick, however, chose to stand, ignoring the empty chair.

"Have you heard from The Terafin?" he asked, without preamble.

Teller shook his head.

"You've called us with no notice; there's no meeting of the House Council scheduled."

Teller nodded, gathering his words. He was not, and had never been, chatty—but he understood the value of words. He understood them perhaps better than any other member of his den. He glanced at the open ledger on his desk, and carefully turned a page; it was not a casual gesture, and he made no effort to transform it into one. "The Kings and the Exalted, along with the High Priests of the temples not on the Isle, have gathered at Moorelas' Sanctum."

Marrick glanced at Elonne.

Elonne then said, "Is that of concern to us?" It was phrased as a question; Haerrad's response would not have been.

"Yes. It is of concern, however, to the entirety of the city, if not the Empire itself."

They waited.

"You are aware of The Terafin's forest."

"We are," Elonne said. "We are aware, as well, of the changes in The Terafin's personal chambers. The recent changes. Are they connected?"

"We are uncertain, but—and this is personal opinion only—I believe they are. I don't believe The Terafin made the changes deliberately. She has not returned."

It was Marrick who said, "And she'll return when the Sleepers wake?"

Elonne's brows rose very slightly; Marrick was smiling. It wasn't warm; it was a gallows smile.

Teller accepted both it and the words that he had apparently casually offered. They were often used dismissively; the statement simply meant *never*. It was a sentiment that Teller could hope and pray for now. "Yes. Or just before."

"What do the Kings intend?"

"I don't know. But I assume—the regent assumes—that they intend to delay the Sleepers waking for as long as they can." It was true; no discussion had been had. Teller was not Jay; no one was. But he felt that certainty as he waited.

"What do you need from us?" Marrick asked.

Teller bowed his head briefly, expressing gratitude at the question, because he knew, again, that Haerrad would not have asked. Demanded, perhaps. Commanded, certainly. But asked? No.

"In the event that the Kings and the Exalted fail or are forced to retreat, The Terafin's forest will be safe. Safer. The manse will not be. Nor will the holdings. Again, we are uncertain about the extent of the possible disaster. In theory, the wind, the air, and the fire will be restrained, as they were at the end of the first day rites for the previous Terafin."

"You don't expect that to hold."

"If The Terafin doesn't return?" Teller exhaled. "The forest elders don't expect it to hold. Not in the city itself. They believe it will in the forest. Therefore, a retreat to the forest must be organized, and it must be sounded when necessary."

"You wish to start this now?"

"I don't want panic to influence decisions. If we lose Terafin people to natural—or even unnaturally summoned—disaster, I accept that. But if we lose Terafin to panic—to *each other*—I can't. It would be a failure of leadership."

"Finch is regent."

"Yes. Finch is assembling the forest elders. They will be the bulk of our defense, if physical defense is needed. If you require her presence—"

Marrick lifted a hand. His expression was, however, serious; lines of intent, seldom used, changed the whole cast of his face. "Her presence is required, and she does what she can do. We are House Council, not frightened children; we will do what we can do." He smiled, but this smile was not the jovial facade behind which Marrick ATerafin had built his considerable strength. "It's not the way of people to trust youth; youth lacks experience. The mistakes that we've made, you have yet to make—and survive.

"But experience is our guidepost, right-kin. We have not faced the demons—literal and figurative—that The Terafin has. And she has faced them by your side. All of you, even Jester. It is her work, in the end, this saving of our city and our House; you do her work better than we could. But the work we can do? We do it better than you. Leave it to us."

"I am not certain Haerrad will agree."

Marrick grimaced at Elonne. "Even Haerrad has been less extreme in his criticism of The Terafin, of late. Do you understand why?" he added, to Teller.

"Demons. Assassination attempts. Obligation."

"Be wary of Haerrad's sense of obligation; it bites."

"All obligation bites," Elonne said. "And you well understand that by now. But this is Terafin. Haerrad will not fight us for advantage if what the Kings fear becomes reality." She rose and hesitated, standing in front of Teller's desk. She looked very much as if she meant to add more, but she shook her head, straightened her shoulders, and offered the right-kin a very respectful bow. It was not necessary and was, in fact, overly formal. Teller reddened, uncertain of how he might both accept and return it.

This, on the other hand, made her smile.

"We accepted Gabriel ATerafin because we knew him from the first succession conflict." She did not use the word war. "And Gabriel did not change. Until he retired, he did not change. You are right-kin, Teller; what we require of the right-kin is not what is required of The Terafin." Smiling a little more deeply, she added, "Do not think you have to change."

"Don't say that where Barston can hear it."

She laughed. Marrick laughed as well.

Chapter Ten

DARRANATOS WAS NOT THE only demon who died—if demons could even be killed—that day. Those he had taken under his literal wing, those who were less powerful, less awe-inspiring, perished as well. But not by Shianne's hands. Nor did she weep over their fallen bodies, for as long as those bodies remained; like Darranatos, they crumbled to ash and by wind were swept away, as if the fires they commanded had at last been freed to devour their physical forms.

Adam walked across the battlefield, the ground shorn of ice and snow, adorned by the warriors of the Wild Hunt who had both fought and fallen. The Arianni had begun to collect their living and their dead. The snow was dark with their blood, where blood had spilled. Jewel thought that even the demons' blood had withered to ash or smoke when the demons who had shed it had died.

Shadow, who disliked Adam, nonetheless chose to join the Voyani youth, which should have served as a warning to Jewel. But she could not speak—could barely move—in the wake of Darranatos' death; could not approach Shianne, who wept long after her arms held nothing but ash. There was something so large, so historical, and so personal to her pain, Jewel was certain her presence would be an intrusion, and she did not want to intrude, did not want to overstep the boundaries that existed there. That history was no part of her.

And yet that history had led to this moment.

The Winter King was likewise silent, but speaking to him did not involve breaking silence. *Did you know him?*

I? No. He was gone before I became Winter King; gone before there was a true

Winter. His name is not spoken, Jewel. In the presence of the White Lady, he has never existed, and he will not be mourned.

But Jewel, glancing at Shianne, did not believe this. Could not.

Shadow yowled, an annoyed screech that sounded nothing like a cat. He was, once again—and predictably—berating Adam for his stupidity. Adam, with the beleaguered patience that at times reminded Jewel of Teller in his youth, not only tolerated the remonstration but appeared to be apologizing.

Enough, Jewel thought, and began to march across the snow. Terrick had joined the Arianni in their search for and recovery of the injured and the dead; Angel joined Jewel. She dropped a hand on Shadow's head; he growled. The sound traveled up her arm and into her chest, where it seemed to reverberate as if trapped and desirous of escape.

Shadow ignored her as much as he could with her hand plastered over his head. It was Adam who had the full force of his attention, and Adam who weathered it.

"Do *not* apologize to him," she told the Voyani healer. "His behavior is appalling, and it will only encourage more of it."

Shadow shrieked.

Adam knelt at the side of one of the injured Arianni. To Jewel's eye, the injury was not likely to kill him. He gazed up at Adam with both fear and an odd type of hunger. And he held out his hand, indicating that Adam could take it. Adam, the healer.

She felt the cold then. Turning without thought, she said, "Master Gilafas."

He appeared to her right. "Terafin."

"Stay with me." She lifted her hands, gave Angel orders, and then bent her head as he left to carry them out. Here and there, across the field, she could hear something that sounded like music, like song. It was not Arianni song; nor was it bardic. Shianne was silent and drawn, her eyes like hollows that had been emptied of everything. She no longer carried a sword, and Jewel knew that she would never carry a shield again. But she rose, as if she, too, could hear song.

She met Jewel's gaze, held it, and looked away. Some light had gone out of her; she looked more mortal in this instant than she had ever looked. When Jewel beckoned, she nodded, and crossed the battlefield, unmindful of the injured or the corpses that were being gathered by the hunters as she walked.

Adam had taken one of the injured man's hands in both of his, and he clasped it loosely, as if afraid that pressure might break something. He threw a backward gaze at Jewel and mouthed the word, *Matriarch.*

Shadow hissed in outrage, sputtering on syllables that didn't quite seem to contain the necessary vehemence for his disgust.

Jewel hesitated. Angel returned. Celleriant and Kallandras came down from their invisible, wind-woven perch to stand near her; in ones and twos, the Wild Hunt did the same. The air was still; were it not for the injured and the dead, it might have been serene. No other evidence of the demons remained.

Vennaire came to stand beside Adam or, rather, behind him, as if he were a personal guard. Or as if he wanted whatever it was that Adam now touched for himself. Shianne noticed, but did not attempt to intervene. Whatever had passed between Adam and Vennaire had extinguished her suspicion of the latter.

Or perhaps all suspicion had become irrelevant. Jewel wanted to offer comfort, felt an almost painful need to do so. But there was no comfort to offer, nothing that she could say or do that would ease Shianne's pain, the obvious sense of her loss.

She surprised Jewel.

She reached out and placed a very gentle hand against the back of Adam's neck, which was exposed to air and moonlight. He did not react; did not appear to notice. He was still watching Jewel, awaiting her command.

She understood that and understood, as well, that this was somehow the moment. Out of the corner of an eye, she caught Angel's den-sign. Wordlessly, he told her what she already knew: he had her back. She remembered him on the day she first met him, remembered his hair, the agony of loss and rage blended perfectly in his expression.

He had stayed.

He had followed her to Terafin.

He had refused to accept the House Name—the only member of the den to do so. He had refused in spite of the fact that Jewel had wanted that name so badly for her den. To her, half a lifetime ago, demons and mage-born notwithstanding, the name had signified *safety*. Because it had signified power. She had wanted power because without power, she could not protect the people she loved.

Angel had taken the name when Jewel had taken the House.

He had taken a weapon from the armory of what was now a castle but had once been a war room.

And he had taken down the spire of his hair. All to say what she had known the first time she had seen him: that he was hers, that he served her, that he would fight for her and die for her, if that death could buy her life. She had thought it not for her own sake that she had brought Angel with her, on both this journey and the one previous to it; she had thought the decision an odd and dangerous kindness to Angel.

But she accepted, now, that this was a half-truth at best. With Angel at her side, she felt as much at home as she could in the wilderness; he was den. He was kin.

"Matriarch?"

"Shianne's arm," Jewel said quietly.

Adam nodded. When he looked at Shianne, his expression was younger, and far more uncertain; he was not asking for orders, but for permission—and even if her arm was broken, he was uncertain that he was not overstepping. Vennaire said nothing as Adam turned to the woman who had once been his kin. Healing an arm, no matter how unclean the break, was not the arduous work of calling a person back from the brink of death; it took power, but not enough to render Adam useless.

Shadow yowled in frustration, his head bobbing as he uttered imprecations and threatened Adam. "Shadow." The silence that followed the name was the essence of sulkiness. Jewel then lifted her hand, because she needed it. She needed both of her hands.

Her mouth was dry, her eyes closed. Was she afraid? No.

She was terrified.

Of what? The echo of her Oma demanded. *Of yourself?*

She was annoyed at this echo, this internal criticism. She felt that her Oma would be the first person to understand the profound fear. Her Oma, who had never been willing to voice any of her internal softness; who filtered love through criticism, through nagging, through reluctance, because obvious love—the kind Jewel's mother had shown her daughter when Jewel had been a child—was too weak. It would draw the predators, the jackals, the people who could see it well enough to manipulate it.

You aren't exposing weakness.

No? No. But she was exposing her heart, what remained of her heart, after her sojourn in the Oracle's cavern.

She plunged her hands into her chest, and flesh gave way beneath them, as if they were blades. Evayne had never winced, never grimaced, in Jewel's memory—but perhaps that was wrong. Perhaps Jewel had been so focused on what she pulled out of her own chest that she hadn't noticed the cost of the withdrawal.

She noticed it now. She noticed the pain, and the sensation of tearing; she noticed the sudden lack of breath, the growth of the insistent hammer of a heart made loud and wild by fear. She noticed the trembling of her own hands, and the way they had to reach, reach, and reach again, as if fumbling toward a center that both existed and could not be seen.

But her hands, as she pulled them out of her chest, remained dry; the blood that followed a normal wound was absent. Nothing she had done to this point in her life made her feel so other, so alien, as this: cupping the crystal in her hands, and understanding that it was, in a very real sense, her heart. She understood, for just a moment, why Avandar, Meralonne, and a host of other immortals—nonhuman, all—viewed her as not-quite mortal. What mortal could do this to themselves and survive?

She stood, and the light from the heart she now carried—she was almost afraid to claim it as her own—radiated outward, washing the field in a glow that almost changed its shape; the trees seemed unchanged, but the rest faded from her vision. She could see her companions, but they were stark in her vision, as if drawn in quick, mad dashes in charcoal by a perceptive artist intent on paring them down to visual essentials.

And yet, they moved, and they breathed.

Shadow remained stubbornly, essentially himself; his fur was gray, his coat a sheen of gently reflected light; his wings, each feather obvious and distinct, were folded. He had fallen silent—for Shadow—which meant only that he was forcing himself to acknowledge the fact that she wasn't always stupid.

But if Shadow remained himself, Adam did not.

Unlike the others, even Shianne, Adam was solid, full-drawn, full-realized. But he was taller now, and the shadow he cast far longer; his face was sharper, the planes hardened not by light or form, but by age—an age he had not yet arrived at but was stretching unconsciously toward. His eyes were wide as he looked at what she carried, but he did not look away. The boy who became flustered whenever he encountered the danger inherent in what he thought of as the business of Matriarchs might have; the man he had—no, that he *would*—become did not.

But she thought of Adam as she had first met him; Adam in the Sea of Sorrows. There, his gaze earnest, he had not looked away, either. He had seen the Serra Diora—a lone clanswoman among the Voyani, a stranger among people who had very, very little love for the clans—and he had understood some essential part of her isolation. The Voyani elders had laughed at his regard; they had assumed it was a puppy love, a childish fascination with things foreign and beautiful—for Diora was beautiful, even in her otherness.

Jewel herself had felt that, in some fashion—but she had never dismissed Adam's attention, his regard. Adam, too shy, too tongue-tied to speak with the

Serra often, had been the one to bring Diora the lute of Kallandras of Senniel, as if understanding somehow that music might strengthen her.

It was because of Adam's deep sense of duty, of obligation, that he had died.

She faced him now and accepted it: he had died. In any sense of the word as she understood it, he had drowned. It was only due to his hidden—no, his unknown until that moment—gift that he had survived the borrowing and the saving of that lute. She remembered Kallandras' serene expression as it rippled. She understood, too, that the lute, inanimate and voiceless, was a talisman of sorts, to the bard; it had become a friend.

Adam had understood that—or maybe he was akin to Jewel; the Voyani life did not allow for the gathering of possessions, and the few they were allowed to keep and carry with them—those not intended for show or sale—were precious in ways that had nothing to do with their essential physical nature.

And although he had understood, he had come to Kallandras to beg the favor of being allowed to borrow the lute—not for his own sake, not directly, but for the Serra's.

When the flash storm had hit the dry, parched sand of the desert, the ground did not absorb the falling water. The lute had been swept away in the flood. Adam had gone after it. Kallandras would have forgiven the boy its loss—but Adam would not have forgiven himself.

He was Evallen's son; the current Matriarch of the Arkosa Voyani was his older sister, the daughter, the one raised to rule. Ruling abraded the softer parts of the Voyani soul. No, Jewel thought, seeing the man in the boy and seeing him dispassionately, it was not just the Voyani. It abraded the softer parts of all souls. And that softness?

The Voyani wanted it. And so, in the end, did Jewel. If she could not preserve it in herself, if she could not sustain it in the face of the bitter choices she was offered—choices she, as ruler, *must* make, when others would pay the cost of her mistakes—she nonetheless wanted to protect it in others; to see it, to hold her figurative hands out to catch a hint of its warmth. Adam's sister wanted it, Adam's mother had wanted it.

Not all young men were warm in his fashion. Nor were they gentle. Adam had been given the care of children—the highest of the Voyani responsibilities—and the children had both troubled him, as children will, and loved him as only children could. She had noticed this at the time, and had watched it, but the knowledge had become stronger, deeper; she looked at the man who was not here yet, who would not be here for years, and saw in him the boy that he was.

That boy had faced demons, godspawn, and ancient, inexplicable magics; he had found the trapped souls of sleepers in the dominion of the Warden of Dreams, and he had sheltered them as if they were the Voyani children over which he had been given responsibility. He had—always—extended a hand, even before the power of the healer-born had asserted itself and saved his life.

She was not sure what he would make of either Arkosa or the Voyani who had finally come to their stopping place, their true home. Arkosa as city was a myth to them, a legend; it was no part of their lived history, and no part of almost all their customs. But she thought—she hoped—that behind the safety of its walls, feeding the children would still be considered the height of responsibility for those who had begun to cut their teeth on adulthood.

She did not know what Adam saw in the crystal. She had not taken it out to force him to look, to force him to retrieve some glimpse of a future she herself did not see.

But no, she thought, she *did* see.

She did not speak; he did not require it. The moment his eyes met hers, he nodded, and turned once again to the hand he had loosely clasped in his own, to the man who lay bleeding just in front of his bent knees.

She watched him. She understood as she did that this was the reason that she had drawn out this crystal; that *this* was the reason she had walked the Oracle's path and made the final, almost crushing trek across a tiny, barely lit room. This moment. She was meant to watch; she was meant to *see*, she was meant to witness.

Seer-born.

She did not know how healing worked. She had heard theories but, in the end, considered them almost pointless discussions, better suited to angry members of the Order of Knowledge than to rulers; she knew that healers *did* heal, and in any practical sense, that was the only thing that mattered. Or that had mattered.

But she had been wrong. Not that any of the knowledge of the healer-born would have helped her here; what Adam did was not what healers did. She knew she could ask—would one day ask, if she survived—Levec, and he would be as mystified, but far more grouchy.

And yet, part of her understood. She did not look in to the light at the center of the crystal, but she had no need to do so; what it saw, she saw, in some fashion. She *knew*. She *understood*. And she had chosen to know and understand in this place, beyond Fabril's reach, beyond the reach of mortals.

She was not surprised when Angel cried out; not surprised when Adam did—in shock, in fear—because she knew the moment when Vennaire would step forward and drive his sword through the chest of the injured man. She knew, as well, that the man was expecting the blow, that he even managed to offer a brief, wintry smile to Vennaire before the sword came down.

Adam tightened his grip; she could see the whiteness of his knuckles, could see the way the boy's hands became the man's; she could see the sudden color that changed the cast of his skin, darkening it, deepening it. She understood that he was trying, as healers will, to preserve the Arianni life, and knew that he would not be allowed to do so.

She knew what Vennaire knew.

This was their only way home.

And in the bitter cold, made brighter by her own observation, the glow of the things she carried, some solid and some intangible, in the cups of her palms, she waited, because she knew, *knew*, that Adam could find the path, but he could not walk it on his own. And even if he could, alone would avail them little.

It might kill him, but his death would solve nothing.

She stepped forward, shifting her grip on the crystal until she carried it in one hand; she reached out with her left hand and placed it, gently, on the top of Adam's head. He wore no hat, now, and heat rose from his tangled hair into the palm of her hand.

Shadow purred.

The irate repetition of what seemed to be his favorite word stopped. Jewel could see his golden eyes, unblinking in the light. "You could have spared her," he said, the perpetual whine she thought of as natural cat voice absent. "You both could have spared her. You could have done this the last time we stopped."

Jewel nodded; it was true. Had she known, she would have allowed Adam to do then what he did now; would have withdrawn the heart of her seer-born power from the chest in which it was sheltered.

But she hadn't known then. Hadn't understood what was required.

And she could not be unhappy about Darranatos' death. Yes, Shianne was in pain; that pain, that loss, dogged her every movement, her every expression. Regardless, Darranatos would not have died to any other sword, in any other moment. She wondered if some unconscious seer-born instinct had forced her to stay Adam's hand the first time, but she did not know.

Darranatos had been a danger, a threat to even the most powerful of the Hidden Court. Were it not for the sorrow of Shianne, Jewel was certain everyone present would be dead.

"Not *me*," Shadow said. "Or *her*." He meant Calliastra.

Jewel glanced at Calliastra; this was a mistake. Calliastra, born of two gods, was, like Shadow, solid, visible; nothing about her was shaky or obscured. And she was darkness; she absorbed light as if it were air, or sustenance, and the darkness in her eyes seemed to spread as she did. Her wings rose up, even folded as they were across her back; her skin was the color of ice or mortal death. This, Jewel could bear.

But even framed as she was by shadows that stole light and killed warmth, even pale as the death that she would inevitably bring to all those around her whose warmth she craved, her expression was an urchin's expression, a child's expression, torn by loss and fear and need; those desperate eyes were rounded, the line of her brow gathered in ridges of pain. No anger, there, to push someone away; no desire to appear strong. She was a cry in the wilderness, and her arms—her arms were outstretched.

Even knowing that they were death, this woman, this child, could not help but reach for those around her who might be able to grasp those hands in their own.

She almost stepped away from Adam, so strong was the need she saw, but Shadow stepped on both of her feet, nearly causing her to topple. She gasped, righting herself, and clutching tightly at the crystal; she knew that she must not be separated from it.

Her left hand was no longer upon Adam's bowed head; she had reached instinctively for Calliastra. And she would, she thought, determined. She would reach for Calliastra again, with these hands.

But not now, as Shadow reminded her. Not now. She turned back to Adam. Her hand did not tighten; he was not Shadow, who required habitual, constant reminders. She almost dropped her hand to Adam's shoulder but could not lift it; the impulse was wrong.

Adam's chin lowered further; she stood, she watched, the sound of her heart unnaturally loud, her breathing fading from her awareness. Adam's hands were glowing softly in this harsh, visual haze. His hands, knuckles weathered and lined by sun and sand; his hands, youthful and supple. She could not see his bent face, and yet she could sense the moment his eyes opened, as if they were shutters or windows thrown wide, and in haste.

He spoke a word that she could not hear; she could remember the sense of it, the tone of it, the texture of it, but the actual syllables escaped her, then and forever. Nor did it now matter. The Arianni were not mortal. They had no souls. They did not, upon death, shed their bodies and the pain of their life's end, and traverse the bridge to the beyond; nor did they come at last to the

Halls of Mandaros, where they relived the choices of their life, to be judged at last.

They were not *born* as mortals were born. She had been told that by an of-fended Shadow, and she had thought, at the time, that she understood what that meant. She was wrong, had been wrong. The word birth had connotations that Jewel could not escape, so she shed that word. They were created. They were created the way the first man, in some stories, some myths, some legends, had been created; they were offered, whole, to the world. Living, breathing, they were part of that world in a way that mortals were not. They were *of* it. They were of it, and they were of their parents, their creators.

And when they perished, their essence returned to those creators.

She thought of Darranatos then. She thought of the ash that was scattered by wind. She understood, in that brief flash of insight, that Darranatos, first among princes, would not die as the Arianni did; that the power that had been given him by the White Lady had been lost to her in the instant he had chosen to ally himself with the god she would not name.

Not for him, this slow unfolding of life and life's essence; not for him the return, at last, to Ariane. But for the man whose chest had been pierced by Vennaire's sword, it was different. They were gathered in the wilderness—high or low, Jewel was uncertain—and this single death was a sacrifice.

She did not know what Ariane would make of it; did not know if she would grieve. She could not imagine it—but until the moment Shianne had gathered the remnants of Darranatos in her arms, she could not have conceived of that grief among any who had been born to the White Lady.

What she knew was that Adam, healer-born, followed the fading life es-sence of the dying Arianni. What she knew was that Adam could see the path that it took; that he could—as he had done with the wild earth and Terafin forest—hold it somehow in place; that he could weave the here and the there together, forcing them to occupy the same space for a brief period of time.

It was not healing.

"It *is*," Shadow said, his voice soft. "It is what healing *is* to the wilderness. It is why he is to be feared and avoided. Those that were made can be unmade. They can be altered."

Adam did not hear Shadow; Jewel did. She continued to watch. What she had not seen on the day they had met demons in the Winter lands beyond the Oracle's cave, she saw clearly now: the strands of this place, the strands of these people, and the strands of the lands to which the Arianni dead must return. He followed the dead, caught some hint of the where, the how, and he held them.

This was where they must go. This was how.

Jewel lifted her hand from Adam's head and, kneeling, reached, instead, for his hands, placing the left palm down across them and raising the light. His eyes were closed, but she knew that he could see that light, somehow; that he could work with it, and by it, both.

She felt the minute he reached for it, and for her, and she stiffened; she heard Shadow's hiss by her ear, but the hiss was unnecessary. She *knew* that this is where she must be, and how. She was mortal. She was seer-born. She had visited the Oracle, had taken the Oracle's test.

Or had started it; she was no longer certain it was done.

She would not surrender Adam to the wilderness. She would not lose his future to his present, to this moment. She was Jewel Markess ATerafin. She had stood in the Stone Deepings, face-to-face with Ariane and the Wild Hunt. She had held that ground.

She had held that ground with far less visceral incentive. Adam stood before her, his literal future visible to the eyes, exposed by the crystal she clutched in a shaking, extended arm. And beside her, less solid but no less real, was Angel. If no others had been involved, it wouldn't have mattered at all. She understood that their lives were at stake—that, in the end, *all* their lives were at stake—but that was for later, if ever.

The now was enough.

She did not think of home. She did not think of Taverson's, or the hundred holdings in which she and her den had come together. She thought, instead, of Adam, of Angel, and of Amarais Handernesse ATerafin; of the promises made to the woman who had been both her ruler and her benefactor, surrendering in the process all hope of peace for herself.

And she thought of Finch, of Teller, of Arann; of Jester and Carver; of Ellerson. She thought of home, not as a physical place, but as an interior one: something she carried with her, something she was part of, no matter where she stood. She had never let go of it—and she never would. Never while she lived and, given Mandaros, possibly never, period.

She curved her hands and her fingers above Adam's, as if by so doing, she could pin him in place, could prevent him from following the path he sought, prevent him from being devoured by what she was now certain awaited: The White Lady.

Adam built his path. But he built it around Jewel, built it, in part, *of* her. She felt the cold of winter suddenly freeze the hand in which she gripped the singular proof of her encounter with the darkness in the Oracle's caverns: her own fear.

Her fear had made the room seem endless; the space of a few yards extending for miles in the dark. Every step she had taken had been an effort, and the weight of that fear had grown, and grown again, until she couldn't stand on two feet. She had crawled. She had—shaking, nauseous, unable to draw a full breath into her lungs—crawled the rest of the way.

If the fear had vanished when she had reached her destination, she might have forgotten it. Might have set it down, set it aside, and refused to resume its burden. But the worst fear remained, enclosing her so tightly she could barely move. And yet she had. Sweating, shaking, more terrified than she had ever been, she had moved. She had taken the knife.

She had cut into her own heart.

This, then, was what remained.

She closed her eyes. It made no difference. She had cursed and feared her talent for so much of her life, had hidden it whenever it was possible. But it was that talent that had brought her her den; that talent that had brought her to Terafin, and that talent that had given her a place on the House Council long before she understood the politics—of power, of necessity.

She would never consider it a curse again. A burden, yes—but responsibility was, because the cost of failure rose, and rose, and rose. Yet the chance of success was still there, no matter how faint, glimmering brightly; she could not let the darkness of her own fear eclipse it, or it would vanish from sight.

She felt the ground change; the air remained wintry and cool, the crystal in her palm a thing of ice that caused a pain that never quite gave way to welcome numbness.

She felt a hand on her shoulder; knew instantly it was Angel's and smiled; she felt the shift of paws across one of her feet—Shadow; she felt the wordless hum of something that might have been approval and the utter stunned silence that joined it. And she heard—

She heard the butterfly's song.

The butterfly's song changed the whole of the landscape that was, even as she watched, being knit together, being woven, by Adam. By the healer-born. She saw the wilderness from his eyes, felt it almost as he felt it: it was a living thing, a body entire, vast and almost unknowable to mortals such as they were. But the part that he could touch, he did. He understood the moment that the Arianni's life ended because he could see where what was not quite a soul began to move.

Beneath that movement, that figurative, intangible movement, he created a gate, a path. She saw, and she added to it, standing, both feet on the ground, her heart in her hand. She offered the wilderness that heart, or knowledge of that heart; she did not make demands of the land because she could not. She was not and would never be Lord here; she had not grown up in these forests and come of age in them; she had not wandered beneath the boughs of these trees, gathering fallen leaves as if they were the brightest and sweetest of flowers.

She heard a second song join the butterfly; she heard Kallandras' subtle harmony; she heard the sudden silence that swept across the Arianni—an absence of sound, of breath, a hush that was nonetheless full of life and awareness and yearning.

The moon came out in the skies above Adam's hands—skies which were cloudless now, and almost serene. And where they had been silent, as if sound might shatter the world, the Arianni began to sing. Their voices were quiet, whispers, their words almost unintelligible.

But she knew this song. Although she had never heard it before, it felt as familiar as cradle song—a cradle song for a cold, cruel people. She had thought that the powerful and the immortal were above—beyond—the need for something as trivial as love and affection, the things that she had valued all her life, and she realized, as the singing grew in volume, that she had been wrong.

But the definition of love to the Arianni was merciless and complete.

Jewel expected things from her friends. She expected some respect, some consideration, and some loyalty; she expected to both give and receive support. She expected those friends to share as much of a life with her as they could; she expected to join that effort with everything she had. She expected good days, bad days, and the days in between.

The Arianni expected nothing. They wanted—she heard it now—everything, but even were nothing to be offered, it would be enough to know that they were, somehow, in the presence of the Winter Queen.

The White Lady.

"Gilafas," she said, although she had not intended to speak.

He lowered his hood once again, appearing beside Angel so suddenly, Angel dropped instantly into a defensive stance.

"Yes," he said, as if she had—as if she *could*—command him. He did not touch Adam; instead, he drew leaves and branches from the folds of a robe that no longer seemed natural to Jewel's vision. Gilafas, however, was; he looked entirely himself. She could not see the changing shape of hands or face, as she did with Adam, but every line in the older guildmaster's face was so clear, so sharp, he looked too real, too solid.

The eyes that met hers were familiar.

The man she saw now was the man she had met in a dream—a dream from which she had awoken, wearing a ring. His smile acknowledged the recognition, but there was more to it than that; he seemed . . . younger, somehow. No, not younger; he seemed joyful, which robbed his face of years, of ages, of the patina of loss and regret.

She had watched him work in a dream, and it was in a dream, she felt, that she watched him now, for part of what he now worked with his maker's hands was what Adam was building.

And as he worked, she saw that the maker-born power was a power, like sight or healing, for the branches and leaves that he had gathered were put together in a form they could not have taken, and from their natural, irregular shapes, Gilafas built an arch; it stood, its wood grain revealed as if grain were inner light caught and caged by bark, and across those grains, the familiar and beloved leaves of the *Ellariannatte* were set, and they rustled, as if in a gentle breeze.

The arch was taller than the man; larger by far than the stained-glass window he had shown her, and she *knew* that the two were similar, although they had nothing visual in common. As he worked, the butterfly came to rest upon his shoulder, but its flight and its presence did not disturb him.

The Winter King came to stand by her side; he was silent, even in her thoughts, but she saw that he trembled; his hooves came, at last, to ground, but they left no mark, as if he were suddenly afraid to do so.

The singing grew louder until the voices were like storm—but a summer storm, not the ice and death of winter snow—and Gilafas continued to work, Adam to bind, and Jewel to witness.

Shadow's foot fell more heavily on hers; she glanced down at him and froze. He was cat, yes, and winged; he was gray, golden-eyed; but she saw in him now something reminiscent of her time in the Between, beneath the watchful eyes and changing faces of the gods.

Ssssstupid, he hissed, and the word thrummed through her, surrounding her. *You do not simply bear witnesssssss.*

She shook herself, because after he had made his opinion known, he, too, began to sing. There were no words she could understand, not even the sense of syllables, but his voice was not grating, not harsh; it wasn't the voice of the Wild Hunt, but it wasn't the voice of an animal, either.

His singing blended with theirs, and with the bard's, and with the butterfly's, and during it all, Gilafas worked, Adam struggled. Jewel's arm began to shake with cold and with the weight of what she carried. She did not lower it, though. Could not, until all work here was done.

As if the song itself sustained them, the Arianni continued to sing, their eyes upon Gilafas, upon Adam, upon Jewel herself. Voices rose, and rose again, as if to reach the distant heavens—the mythical place where the gods had gone to live.

And then, suddenly, the singing banked, the voices dropped. The Arianni were once again silent, but this was a different silence; it was the silence of something akin to prayer. And in the distance, so faint it might have been the product of that fervent yearning made real, a new voice took up that song: one voice.

Gilafas paused briefly; that single, quiet voice did what the raised voice of the host could not. It gave him pause, interrupting the flow of his labor, his making. Adam, however, did not raise his head; he did not respond to it at all.

Shadow growled. "He has listened to only that song this *entire* time."

The hand by which she kept contact with Adam tightened.

The song itself grew louder, the voice clearer, both deeper and higher; it made, of the earlier song, something pale and almost colorless, it was so clear. Jewel had heard Shianne's voice raised in song and it had all but immobilized her; she had believed that Shianne's voice was the voice of the White Lady. It was not and could not be.

The ring that Gilafas had made for Jewel almost burned her finger; she was suddenly afraid that it would be seen, its lie revealed to the one living being that Jewel would never, ever have exposed it to, for she recognized, at last, what the Arianni recognized, and she understood, as Master Gilafas stepped away from his rough and hurried making, that the Winter Queen would know.

The Winter Queen, whom she had stopped on the road in the Stone Deepings. The Winter Queen, who had so casually tossed both the Winter King and Celleriant aside for their failure to drive Jewel from that path.

The Winter Queen, whom Jewel Markess ATerafin had seen again, and to whom she had reached in silent, inexplicable yearning. Her hand had touched what it should not have touched, and in the wake of Ariane's passing, three strands of platinum hair remained, and those three had become Jewel's most highly prized treasure.

The moon grew clear, brighter, closer, its silver face shedding a light that might have caused the sun envy, and with it, oh with it at last, came the Winter Queen, framed by the arch that Gilafas had built.

She could not pass through the arch. Jewel understood that before any of her kin.

But Gilafas turned to Jewel and gently touched her extended wrist. "It is yours now," he said gently. "And I am weary." He glanced at Adam. "You must give the orders, Terafin, if you wish the others to pass through what I have built."

"But—"

"She cannot. She can see her kin; they can see—and hear—her. But she cannot cross over this way. Until the Summer trees are planted, there is no road that she might ride that would lead her, once again, into the world. She cannot be Winter Queen; the Winter has passed. But she cannot be Summer Queen either."

Jewel's nerveless hand fell slowly, and as it did, the light from the crystal dimmed. It made no difference now. Not to her, and not to the Arianni. She brought her hand to her chest and set the stone against it. This time, the pain that had accompanied its removal was absent, but it was nonetheless disturbing to have the very solid crystal sink through her coat, her shirt, her undershirt, and last, her flesh—as if flesh itself were simple adornment.

She dropped the now free hand to Adam's shoulder, which she squeezed. He lifted his head slowly and his gaze went straight to the arch, to the woman framed by it but held back by the rules of the ancient wilderness that Jewel did not understand.

Nor did Adam seem to be surprised; she thought, in that moment, that he understood it all, but he had, and would find, no words to describe that understanding. His eyes were darkly circled, his expression almost haunted. She reached out and caught the hand he raised in both of her own.

He did not appear to notice.

"Shadow," she said, because she would not let go of Adam, was afraid that she would lose him here.

Shadow understood what she wanted; it seemed to amuse him. Reaching up almost casually, he sank one long talon into her wrist, cutting her instantly to the bone.

Angel cried out; no one else seemed to notice.

Ah, no, not no one else. Adam did. Adam's gift did. The hand Jewel held in her own tightened around one of hers—the injured one. She gritted her teeth, glared at her cat, and closed her eyes. It was not a fatal injury, but the loss of blood would be disastrous if the bleeding were not stopped—and if Adam of Arkosa was lost in his yearning for, his desire for, the Winter Queen, he was healer-born nonetheless, and the whole of what remained of his power turned toward Jewel.

And she let him; she made no attempt to hide anything that she was, anything that she wanted, or anything that she feared; she wrapped his younger self in the force of her own personality, and held him fast; the healing would, and did, do the rest.

He did not even tell her, in the unique intimacy of the healer's trance, that her gesture had been unnecessary; it would have been a lie, and she was too close to him at the moment to accept it.

We need you, she thought. *Your sister, your family, your kin need you as well. Arkosa is waiting.* And just as she had done on the road in the Stone Deepings, she squared her shoulders; she raised her head to meet the eyes of the Winter Queen, and she stood her ground. She understood the yearning, the strange, inchoate desire that Ariane invoked simply by existing; she understood the reason that mortals and the Winter Queen did not, should never, meet.

As the wound closed, she glanced at her gray cat. He sat on his haunches, spine straight, tail twitching impatiently. He complained—about Jewel, about Adam, and about their spectacular lack of intelligence—but did so softly, as if afraid to disturb or distract the Arianni.

No, Jewel thought; nothing would disturb the Arianni now. Although their Lord could not join them—and did not even try—she was there; they were in her presence. She felt the awe and the hope and the desire; it was twin to the Winter King's.

And she would not surrender Adam to them.

It was, perhaps, selfish, but it didn't matter.

Shadow growled; Jewel looked down at her wrist. Adam had, midway through the healing, understood what the injury and the healing itself was meant to accomplish, and instead of withdrawing—as he had been taught to do, so severely, by Levec—he drew closer. Leaving her should not have been difficult; she was not dying. He did not need to find her, shelter her, and pull her back from the bridge; she knew.

She let Adam go, leaving some part of herself within him, as she had done when she had been called from the edge of death by a different healer. Adam was fourteen or fifteen now. He was no more wise or serene than she'd been at his age. No more wise or serene, she thought, than she was at more than twice his age. She rose, her arm sticky with blood, and made her way to the portal.

The Arianni watched her move; she was surprised that they had managed to pry their gaze from their Lord at all. But, of course, they had. Gilafas had just told them, indirectly, that Jewel was—once again—the roadblock. At her command, or by her request, they could travel to the White Lady's side; without it, they could not. This, then, was what Gilafas had built.

But Jewel had every reason to distrust Ariane.

Ariane had every reason to wish her dead. Jewel now lifted her hand, exposing the one thing she feared most. The ring did not so much catch light as shed it, and in the night sky, it was impossible to miss.

The singing of the White Lady stopped, and as it did, Jewel sensed movement among her host. She was tall; her hair fell down her shoulders into invisibility at her back. She did not wear the armor that Jewel had last seen; she wore a winter dress, but it seemed that winter, like distant gods, failed to reach her; the fabric seemed light, almost airy. But her breath came out in clouds, just as Jewel's did, warmth condensing in cold air.

To Jewel's surprise, she smiled when her gaze alighted on the lifted hand and the ring that adorned it, and Jewel's cheeks reddened. This was never going to be easy.

"So," the White Lady said softly. "You kept my gift." She recognized it, hidden as it was by metal and shape. There was no anger at Jewel's presumption; she seemed to believe—in a way Jewel could not, even now—that she had deliberately gifted her with those strands of hair for just this purpose.

Her eyes then moved past Jewel, and only when they closed did Jewel remember that it was not the ring, or its lie of a promise, that was her worst crime.

She whispered a name; Jewel heard it and understood it and could never repeat it. When the White Lady opened her eyes again, her gaze seemed frozen; she was the heart of winter. And it was as winter that she turned once again to Jewel.

Jewel did not bow, did not dissemble, and did not apologize. As she had done once before, she held her ground, aware that the single difference this time was that the Wild Hunt was behind her, their Lord in front. If they could not join their Lord, they could nonetheless obey her commands, and Jewel suffered under no illusion here: she would die.

As if he could hear the thought, Celleriant joined her, and seconds later, the bard did the same; Gilafas remained by her side, gazing into the portal, past Ariane, as if the Winter Queen were of no interest at all. It was shocking. It was also becoming crowded.

The presence of the Winter King did not help matters, but Jewel did not have the heart to send him away. Adam, however, she kept firmly behind her back.

And the Winter Queen knew. Of course she knew.

"Did you know," she said softly, "that Evayne and I share a parent?"

It was not what Jewel had expected to hear.

"You have come to me when none of my kin might, should they pass out through the gates of the Hidden Court."

Jewel nodded. She was seldom tongue-tied, but words evaded her in Ariane's presence.

"Will you not join me?"

More silence.

"I offer you the hospitality of the Hidden Court. You will be honored guest, not prisoner and not sacrifice."

Gilafas touched her sleeve. She did not shake him off; she could not look away. But Adam reached out; Adam touched the back of her neck; he left his palm against her skin, and she well understood why.

"No mortal who has not sworn themselves to me has been offered that freedom and that honor; will you decline it?" Although she rode no mount, led no host, and carried none of the weapons of her people, Ariane had never been more dangerous to Jewel than she was at this moment.

As if to underscore this, Jewel heard the sound of drawn sword at her back. Not Arianni blades; they could leave their hidden sheaths without even the slightest whisper of sound. Angel she thought, and she knew what he'd seen. The Arianni who had followed them, who had sacrificed one of their own without hesitation, had never served Jewel—and she now stood between them and their Lord.

"I haven't the luxury of time," Jewel replied, picking words and forcing them through trembling lips. "And time is not a pressing concern for the immortal."

"Oh?" And she looked past Jewel once again.

"But imprisonment is. Your ancient enemy once again walks the lands the gods abandoned. You have no responsibility to either me or my kin; your war with the god we do not name is older, by far, than ours."

The silence this time came from the White Lady.

Jewel, the Winter King said; Avandar was silent.

"But I have responsibility for them."

"Yes."

"There are no Summer trees," Jewel continued, and this time, she heard the whispers of the Wild Hunt behind her. And she knew, as she stood, facing the White Lady, that Celleriant had, at last, drawn both sword and shield.

Jewel, the Winter King said again.

"Without those trees, you will not be able to leave the Hidden Court."

"And without my presence upon the endless fields, you will not be able to win this war."

Jewel nodded. "The people who travel with me—mortal and immortal—are *mine,* saving only the Wild Hunt. They are my responsibility, my servants, my lieges; they bear arms in my name and with my knowledge."

"And you fear that I might harm them?"

"It is not fear, Lady," Jewel replied quietly. "You might honor them; you might elevate them; you might adorn them—and they might desire nothing more than that. But they are mine. If I accept your hospitality, they must be granted the full measure of that freedom."

"And if they choose to remain?"

Jewel shook her head. The fear, the paralysis, left her slowly, but it did leave.

"You demand, of me, a freedom that you will not yourself grant?" This seemed to amuse the Winter Queen, but it was a bitter, icy amusement.

"Apparently not." She felt Adam's hand tighten.

"No matter what agreement we reach, I cannot leave this place by the door you have opened. If that is what you seek to bargain with, it would be a poor bargain indeed to trade so much of my own personal inclination for the simple pleasure of your company." Her tone implied heavily that the pleasure would be one-sided—and Jewel accepted that.

She nodded again, *knowing* that this was true. She had to be careful. Years of merchant negotiations formed the ground on which she now stood; they were inadequate in every way. It was never a good idea to enter into negotiations in desperation; it was never good for one's desire, one's need, to be so clearly perceived.

And it was never good to stand, sandwiched between one's enemies. The greatest danger, however, was the negotiator. So she kept her gaze on Ariane when she heard the last of the weapons drawn: Terrick's ax, she thought.

"You have gone to my sisters," Ariane said quietly. "You have seen them both. And what you bring with you is death, of a kind. Tell me, mortal, why I should not have you killed for your effrontery."

The sky lit then, not with moon, but with blade; the Wild Hunt held its breath, waiting only the command of their Lord—the lift of brows, perhaps; the wave of hand.

Calliastra at last unfolded her wings, dimming the light of drawn Arianni blades because those wings seemed to cover all the sky. Her eyes were frozen, but they were pale and bright as she joined Jewel, towering over her, but mindful of Adam's position.

"Sister," she said.

The Winter Queen's brows rose. "You travel with my sister and claim to care for your mortals? You are not what I expected."

"No," Jewel replied. She kept her hands by her sides, her expression as neutral as she could make it. "They will not kill me," Jewel said quietly. "If they do, they have no way to reach you."

"And if they do, sister," Calliastra added, "they will return to you in death, and only in death; I will not leave one standing, save perhaps the herald of your ending."

"You claim this mortal, then?"

"While she lives, I claim her."

"She wears my ring."

Calliastra snorted. It was an inelegant sound, at odds with both her appearance and the gravity of her expression, and it was certainly not a sound Jewel would have dared to make in the face of the White Lady, where even the most carefully chosen words felt profane.

"I did not foresee your coming, sister," the White Lady said. She glanced once again at Shianne. "And perhaps I should have guessed."

"I had no hand in that."

"No? Very well. I see the shadow of the first, in her." She dispensed with the smile she had offered Calliastra; it was a shield. To Jewel, she said, "They are no good to me—or to you—if they return to me thus. But I know, little seer: I know what you carry. I have been waiting." And she turned, then, to look back over her shoulder; she lifted a hand.

Gilafas drew one sharp breath. No one else spoke.

Into the frame came a young woman. She was Jewel's height, perhaps a smidgen taller, and her eyes were far paler than Jewel's; she had no touch of the South to her skin, and little of the sun. Yet there must be sun, in the Hidden Court, for her cheeks were adorned with a dusting of what appeared to be freckles, even in the moonlight. Her expression scrunched those freckles as her cheeks widened, forced up by the breadth of her sudden, unfettered smile.

"Master!"

Jewel had understood, the moment that Gilafas began his making, why she had brought him—but she understood, as she glanced at the man, why he had come; the two were not the same.

"Cessaly." He stepped toward the portal, unmindful now of Jewel or the White Lady, and if the White Lady felt displeased, it did not show.

"You have my butterfly." The girl frowned. "What have you done to it?" Tilting her head to the side, she leaned in and around the Winter Queen, as if she knew no fear of that august lady.

"I have many of your butterflies. They came to me, but they could not return to you. I have kept them," he added softly, "in Fabril's reach. Have you need of them?"

She shook her head, but she twitched. "May I have that one?"

Throughout this discussion, the White Lady glanced down at the top of the stranger's very mortal head, for the girl was mortal. Nor was she young enough to be called girl, but there was something about her that was nonetheless youthful; perhaps the intensity of her focus.

Gilafas said, without looking back, "Give me permission to join her, Terafin."

Jewel said nothing.

"It is for this that I have waited and worked; only this."

She meant to ask him if he intended to abandon his responsibility to the guild, but the words would not leave her. She knew there was nothing she could say that would change his mind or alter his request. And she knew, too, that she must grant it.

The White Lady knew as well. She had not called the child to be hostage. She had called her only for this, and now she waited. It surprised Jewel almost as much as Gilafas' reaction to the Winter Queen; she might have been a particularly fine piece of architecture. He noticed her, but she did not command his attention; he did not have to struggle to speak in her presence; it did not cost him effort to look away.

Jewel turned to the Wild Hunt. They had never seemed so military as they did at this moment: swords and shields at the ready, eyes narrowed, all attention caught between their Lord and Jewel herself. She bowed to them. "If you will return to your Lord's side, do so freely."

They did not move as Gilafas had. Instead, they looked past Jewel to the only woman capable of ruling them. Only when Ariane inclined her head did their swords and shields disappear. They were not Cessaly, mortal and young; they did not bounce; everything about their movements was stately, deadly, graceful.

Shadow roared.

This time the Winter Queen's eyes did narrow, and as one, the host paused, turning toward the gray cat as their Lord did.

"You."

Shadow hissed. It was the laughter hiss; Jewel had never felt so mortified by it as she did at this moment. He was not standing as close to her as he usually did, and she realized that he had allowed himself to be variously shouldered or gently nudged out of the way—which never happened. She should have known, but thought was difficult when confronted with the White Lady, the

Winter Queen. She could not reach him without moving, could not drop a hand on his head.

The Wild Hunt had not yet passed through the arch that would reunite them with their Lord.

Jewel lifted a hand. "He is mine," she said. "They are all mine." She spoke of the three cats, and the Winter Queen seemed to understand this. Not even when Jewel had had the effrontery to attempt to negotiate with this woman, who was almost a walking god, had she looked so . . . annoyed. It was not an expression Jewel had ever thought to see on the Winter Queen's face. Rage, yes, or anger—but not something as petty as annoyance. It was almost human.

"That explains much," was the cool reply. "Too much. Were it not for the interference of these creatures, Winter would not have reigned in the world for so long."

"But the Winter King—"

"Do not imagine," Ariane continued, "that they are truly yours. Do not imagine that they serve; their very nature all but prohibits true service. They are willful, fractious, and sly."

Shadow appeared to consider these words accolades of greatness; his chest was practically a foot wider.

"I will not have him in my Court. I allowed it once, and to this day I rue that act of generosity. While I offer hospitality to the other members of your fellowship, I will not offer it to him."

"He is one of my companions."

"Indeed. And were I to accept his presence, you would bear the weight and responsibility for any of his actions while you sojourned in my court. I have been called cold. I have been called cruel. But even I would not entrap you thus."

"He will behave."

"You are mortal, Terafin. Even had he been a companion to you for all your life, it would be a mere handful of years in the tally of our long experience. He is wild; he cannot be tamed and cannot be owned."

Jewel said, "I cannot travel the wilderness without him."

After a pause, Ariane said, "You will not travel the wilderness; you will be at harbor here. There is nothing that he offers you that I cannot offer; no protection that he provides that I cannot provide."

"He protects me while I dream."

Silence, then. Shadow was practically preening.

"Do not think," Ariane said to the gray cat, "that you are invulnerable."

The cat's eyes glowed as the Wild Hunt once again drew swords.

"Shadow," Jewel said, in her most severe tone. Ariane said nothing at all, but the swords once again faded from sight. Shadow pouted. There was no other word to describe his reaction.

"The dreams of the Sen are dangerous," Ariane finally said. "The whole of the wilderness hears them. Do you believe he is necessary?"

"Yes."

"Do you understand that you will be responsible for any damage he chooses to do while he remains by your side in my lands?"

Jewel exhaled.

"Do not be foolish," Calliastra said, voice low. "There are things that the cats might do that you could not conceive of—and you would have no way to pay the price demanded in restitution. The closest you might come might be to serve—to fully serve—my sister, for eternity."

"I won't live that long."

Calliastra looked . . . frustrated. Or disgusted. Perhaps both. It was such a blessedly familiar expression, Jewel almost reached out for it with both hands. "You are entering the Hidden Court, the heart of my sister's domain. It is hers; there is no force alive—not even my father—that could wrest it from her, and it has been tried. It has been tried, it has failed, and it will *always* fail while she lives."

Jewel felt that she understood this, but it was clear Calliastra did not agree—and Calliastra, like Ariane, was of the gods, of things not mortal. She therefore waited.

"Time does not touch the Hidden Court, except at Ariane's whim. Were you to be trapped there, it would not touch you either, unless she desired it." She turned then to the woman she called sister. "She does not understand."

"Winter and Summer are seasons," Jewel said quietly. "Seasons exist in time; they require the passage of time."

"Your mortal seasons do, yes. But, Jewel, we have known Winter for centuries. Winter Queen or Summer, in the Hidden Court, there is only Ariane. Leave the cat; she is not wrong. While you are in the Hidden Court, you will have no need of him."

Shadow growled.

He did not care for Calliastra; nor did he care for Ariane. Yet he seemed to like Shianne, who had been some part of the White Lady from the moment of her creation. Jewel did not understand him, but then again, she'd never really understood cats. She said, "You are wrong." The words were spoken with conviction, and even as they left her, she knew that she would take Shadow with her, or she would not go at all.

Ariane seemed to understand this as well.

"You are careless, Eldest; you always were. If you choose to accompany the woman who foolishly believes herself to be your master—when none of the firstborn would dare to make that claim—you may well doom her, and if she does not escape this place, everything of value that she does not now carry with her will perish."

Shadow stretched a wing and flattened two of the Wild Hunt; they took no injury to anything but their dignity—but dignity was a currency that was valued far more highly than gold among the Arianni. He then sauntered over to Jewel, glaring at Calliastra as if she alone prevented him from returning to his place at the side of The Terafin.

Jewel. This time it was Avandar. *Decide, but understand one thing: the White Lady has not agreed to your conditions because she* cannot. *You have—and I suspect she is aware of it—the lone Summer Tree that still survives in the wilderness. But the change of seasons is not dependent only upon the sapling; were it, things would be much simpler.*

Jewel waited in silence; she felt, of a sudden, that she could not draw breath.

The Summer cannot come to the wilderness until she is crowned. And, Jewel, she cannot be crowned Summer Queen without a Summer King. You understand that the Winter Kings are drawn, always, from mortals; they are rulers, Terafin; they are pow-ers. That is the heart of Winter; it is cold, it is merciless.

But the Summer Kings are different; Summer is a different season. I would say— would have said—that we wish to face the god we do not name at the height of Winter—but in Winter, his power is also more prominent. The Summer is not his season, and he knows it. For that god, this situation we now face is the best situation: it is Winter, but she cannot fight him or face him upon any field of battle he chooses to take; she cannot leave the Hidden Court.

And he will know, Jewel. Darranatos is dead. Darranatos was his. He will know that Darranatos failed. He will not—yet—know how, or why. But no small power can exist that could topple Darranatos. Make a decision, but you must make it quickly; you do not now have the luxury of time.

Jewel shook her head, a motion that caught Ariane's eye. *I haven't had the luxury of time since we first set out to walk the Oracle's path.*

You must change the terms of your acceptance. One of our number must remain by her side as Summer King, or all effort will be for naught; if she crowns no Summer King, she cannot leave, she cannot be ally—or enemy to the god who dwells in the north—if someone does not remain.

Chapter Eleven

JEWEL CLOSED HER EYES.

This, Avandar said, his interior voice almost gentle, *is what Adam calls the burden of Matriarchs. It is the weight of choice when no comfortable choices remain. It is,* he added, *the cost of ruling, if one does not rule purely for power. Consider that,* he added. *If we are not born seeking power, we learn its byways and its avenues; we cannot seek power, otherwise, and remain sane.*

"He is *right*," Shadow said. "What will *you* do?"

No answer came to Jewel; no certainty. The gift had deserted her for the moment. She was left only with what she knew: that the White Lady must plant the Summer Tree, must change the seasons, must take, at last, to the wild roads. Hers was the balance of power against a walking god; she was of the gods but bound to the world—even if she had remained for centuries in the hidden wilderness.

That wilderness was waking now.

"Jewel," the White Lady said.

Jewel opened her eyes at the sound of her name.

"We are not friends. We cannot be. What you are is not what I am, and what you desire for your kin is not, in the end, something I am capable of desiring. But you are, in some fashion—all of you—the children of one of my parents. I did not wish your destruction in the twilight when the gods made their final choice; I do not wish it now.

"But the heralds are abroad; they begin to sound their horns for the final time. I cannot prevent it, even had I the desire to do so. Do you know where their masters sleep?"

Jewel swallowed. "They sleep at the heart of *my* domain."

For the first time, Ariane smiled. Jewel saw an echo of the Summer Queen on the features of the Winter Queen's face, and she thought for that one second that if this were the last thing she saw in life, it would be enough. She would hold this memory forever, even kneeling at the feet of Mandaros in the halls of judgment that awaited the dead.

He would judge her as she then deserved to be judged. She found words although it was difficult. "Can I not—"

"No. Even were it possible, you could not offer what is required. You are not Summer's and cannot be; even could you, your Empire will perish without you. All the people in it will be scattered—those few that survive. You will lose everything you have built. Those things are not of value to me save in one fashion: your lands will stand against my ancient enemy when all else falters."

Jewel wondered, then, if Ariane had spared her for this moment, this crossroad; if she had known, in the Stone Deepings, that this was the choice that Jewel would eventually have to make if she survived. And she wondered, as well, if this was the last of the Oracle's tests.

But even without her gift, she knew. The only hope her city had of surviving the Sleepers was the White Lady because the White Lady was the only Lord they would obey. She remembered, clearly, what Meralonne had said of the Sleepers in a carriage ride to *Avantari*. She did not doubt him. If they woke and emerged in the streets of the hundred holdings, they would lay waste to everything they could see.

Yes, she thought, this was why men and women of power seemed so heartless, so calculating, so lacking in compassion. Because the decisions had to be made regardless; no amount of pain or fear or guilt changed that fact. And if pain or guilt changed *nothing*, it was far better to dispense with them.

"One," she said, the word too quiet and too painful. "I will leave one member of my entourage in your court, should he choose to remain." And she bowed her head.

"Yes. I am Winter Queen, and I knew. I should deny you the hospitality you seek, but I understand all of what you bear, and in return for my freedom, I forgive your trespasses. I will accept the eldest as your guest; I will accept my sister on her own terms, should she choose to accompany you."

"I won't," Calliastra said, folding her arms.

Jewel turned to the daughter of darkness. To the daughter of love. She held out a hand. It was a mistake, of course, and she realized it too late to drop that hand; what Calliastra would accept in privacy, away from the eyes of the wilderness, she would find almost humiliating in public.

But there was no rage or humiliation in Calliastra's expression. "You have no time," she told Jewel. "You buy yourself time if you accept the offer of hospitality—but even that will not be enough.

"You have said your home will be my home. I will, therefore, return to our home; without the need to keep pace with mortals, I will be there in a handful of minutes. I will be waiting there if you survive." She pushed up off the ground, her wings snapping so close to Jewel's face that she could feel their tips across her left cheek.

Angel's expression made clear that she was bleeding, but he said nothing.

"Gilafas," Jewel turned to the guildmaster. "After you." He was gone through the arch before the last syllable had faded into stillness, but there was no silence; the young woman, Cessaly, who stood bouncing on her toes on the other side of the arch had thrown her arms wide, her expression the essence of joy. Of homecoming.

And this, too, Jewel would remember; it was very, very seldom that such unfettered joy was visible on the face of an adult. Gilafas, the stiff ruler of the Empire's most powerful guild almost knocked the White Lady over in his haste; some primal instinct of self-preservation must have prevented it. The Arianni were coldly, terribly silent watching this, unable to interfere.

The White Lady, however, laid a hand on both the girl's and the guildmaster's shoulders, and her expression was as gentle as Jewel had ever seen it. Calliastra had said that the maker-born were valued by the immortals and the gods, and Jewel now believed it.

In her secret heart, she wished—for just that moment—that the seer-born were valued in the same way. And then she shook herself and turned to the Wild Hunt.

"You have permission," she said, her voice quiet but steady, "to return to your home."

7th day of Lattan, 428 A.A.
Terafin Manse, Averalaan Aramarelas

In the night of Jay's forest, the wind felt bitterly cold; the nights beyond it had already started their turn toward summer, but here, it seemed that winter clung. Finch sought the warmth of the tree of fire as blindly, as naturally, as she sought the warmth of her chosen kin. And there was warmth, beneath the branches and the lowest of the hanging leaves, but at its heart, heat, the fire that burned and consumed. To her ears, the crackle of wood that nonetheless left the tree standing, was harsher, louder; the leap of white-yellow flames higher, as if the tree itself were reaching out to touch the unseen world beyond the forest's border.

Haval noticed; his expression was almost rigidly neutral. She glanced up once at the branches above her head.

"Finch."

Reaching up slowly, her fingers grazed a leaf; she snapped her hand back before it could burn.

"Yes," Haval said, as if divining her thoughts. "Without warmth, we perish, but it is dangerous to forget that what sustains us will also destroy us if we cannot approach with caution."

"I feel as if I *could* touch this tree safely."

Haval inclined his chin. "It is fire, Finch. If we understand its properties, we can create fires for our own use; we can control what burns, and where. But if we are careless, we lose control and, often, lives."

She nodded then, lowering her arm. "Is it time?"

He raised a brow.

"I ask for your counsel, Councillor."

His lips turned up in a smile that almost reached his eyes. "Yes, Regent, it is time." He lifted one black-clad arm, and around the tree of fire, the people she thought of as trees came out of the shadows. They were golden-skinned, all, but across their shoulders and backs were graven symbols that seemed to glow almost blue in the fire's light, and they carried spears and bows. They had always been lithe, tall, supple, but she had never before felt dwarfed by them.

"Birgide should be here," she said softly.

"Birgide is where she must be," Haval countered, "and Birgide is not, as you are, kin to the woman who has claimed and shaped these lands."

"I was trained to handle people like Jarven."

Haval nodded. "Inasmuch as Jarven can be handled, you have done well. And the wilderness, in the end, is not so very different. As Jarven, as the fire itself, it cannot be fully owned or claimed; it can be guided, it can be fenced in, but no more. Guide the forest, Finch. I will be here."

"Moorelas' Sanctum is—"

"I know. But I will be with you. Hannerle will understand."

"Haval—"

"She would not forgive me for decades if I abandoned the forest and its re-gent now. She knows what is coming, what might come; she has seen it far more clearly than even I." Finch remembered, then, that he had chosen Hannerle over any possible duty to Kings, to Empire. He had chosen to be what Hannerle needed.

"If the Exalted and the Kings cannot face the Sleepers, what can we hope to do?"

"Flee them," he replied. "But understand, Finch, that they were men of power. In a bygone age, they were significant. Do you think that they commanded no armies? Do you think that they ruled in isolation? You know that the heralds have been circling Averalaan for some small time; do you honestly believe that they are the only ones?"

7th day of Lattan, 428 A.A.
Moorelas' Sanctum, Averalaan

In the lee of the Common, at the edge of Moorelas' Sanctum, Jester perched on the seawall, resting both chin and arms around the one knee he'd raised. Andrei remained by his side but did not condescend to sit; Snow and Night had been attempting to occupy the same yard of the seawall, but even they kept their voices low—for squabbling cats who couldn't be called quiet by any but the most generous.

The Common held memories for him, not all of which were bad, but Moorelas' Sanctum, as the statue and environs had been called, was not among the better ones.

Half a lifetime ago, the Kings and the Exalted had gathered in exactly this place, and Jester wondered if what they had accomplished that evening had led indirectly to this one. They had made clear to the city that the statue was called a sanctum for a reason. Where possible, Jester had avoided crossing even the hint of its shadow since that day. The Kings had opened a way into the undercity that the den itself had not been aware of until Duster and Jay had managed to escape it.

Duster had escaped to land in Moorelas' shadow.

Duster was dead.

He understood that these were the thoughts of a frightened child, and kept them to himself, his arms tightening briefly around the one raised leg. It was night; there were no shadows here.

But lack of shadow did not mean safety. Absent the Kings, the Exalted, and their many guards and attendants, the Common was practically empty—but even that, Jester had expected. He had thought that the Kings' Swords—or worse, the *Astari*—would question him, tell him to move, but no one approached. Perhaps Birgide had spoken on his behalf; he did not believe he had simply been overlooked. Not when Duvari was present.

Or perhaps it was Meralonne, his feet once again touching earth, the bent form of Sigurne Mellifas at his side. They conversed. In the scant light of lanterns and torches, Meralonne's face could be seen clearly; Sigurne's could not. He did not trust either, but the lack of trust incurred no resentment. Their concerns were the whole of the Empire, against which one lazy ATerafin counted for nothing. In their position, he was certain he would do the same.

The Kings and the Exalted formed a circle, clasping hands as if they were orphans. They lifted their faces, and as incense was lit, they began to chant, their tones low and constant, the spoken syllables both clear and unintelligible.

For one hour, the Exalted and the Kings stood, ringed by those who had undertaken to serve and protect them, their faces turned toward the night sky as if beseeching the heavens. They seemed almost to sing.

Around them, braziers burned; incense rose from those tiny pyres, tended by robed priests, and guarded by the Kings' Swords. Those Swords faced outward. Although barricades had been put in place, the enterprising—and the homeless—could be seen in the shadows, their curiosity pulling them forward, the presence of the Kings' forces pushing them back.

Birgide remained close to those guards, her hands behind her back, her head tilted forward as if the effort of listening had physical weight.

The Kings' voices rose and fell, and it seemed to Jester, watching, that the trees of the Common grew as they spoke. Before the Common had been attacked by demons, Jester had known the location of each and every one of the *Ellariannatte* that had grown, until Jay's forest, nowhere else in the world. Almost all children did. And he knew that there were now trees in the streets where no trees had once grown.

His eyes found Birgide. He was surprised when she lifted her head and looked directly at him, her eyes slightly narrowed as if she had minor trouble focusing. He lowered his leg and pushed himself down from the seawall, intending to join her; she shook her head and bowed it again. He wondered if the Kings and the Exalted were aware of the *Ellariannatte* that were growing around them.

Wondered what people would think in the morning, because he was certain that these new trees were now a permanent part of the landscape.

Wondered if the merchants who were not wealthy enough to own permanent storefronts would now be out of a place to set up their stalls. It was a stray thought, but it was a stubborn one; something mundane in the midst of the threat of magic. And to those whose living depended on the open paths in the Common, it might be as certain an end as the Sleepers.

He bowed his head, understanding then that he was ATerafin, but the whole of his life and thought had roots in the simple struggle to survive in a peaceful, whole city.

If they were dead, those struggling merchants, those farmers, had no future. Jay had taught him that; had reached out and broken his chains, had dragged him along in her wake. Had never let him go. Survive, and there was hope.

Hope was painful in its own way. Hope meant you still believed you had something to lose. And tonight, in this growing forest, beneath the night sky and the stone eyes of Moorelas, there was too damn much to lose. Hope was fear. And, damn it, it shouldn't be.

Jester planted his feet more firmly on the ground and turned to Andrei. "Do you understand a word they're saying?" He nodded in the direction of the Kings and the Exalted.

"Yes."

Jester waited, but no explanation, no translation, was forthcoming. Andrei was at his most servantlike, here; stiff, humorless, watchful. Jester understood why, but that stiffness was not in him; it felt too much like fear, like conceding to fear. But this Andrei was, if familiar, not a man he could reach, except possibly by petty annoyance, and even Jester had limits.

The wind changed. It was subtle; subtle enough that it did not disturb the conversations of the powerful. Meralonne had left him to join those conversations, and he imagined that Jarven—in one form or another—was loitering close at hand, as well.

But if the wind was subtle, it was not the only change; he felt the sudden silence of the Kings as an almost physical blow. Although the Kings and the Exalted remained in their small circle, their hands joined, their faces lifted, they had ceased to speak.

No, Jester thought; their lips were moving. But he could no longer hear them. He could hear the silence as if it were the only form of communication allowed.

"Yes," Andrei said quietly. "They are coming, now. The horns have stopped." He glanced at Jester, his expression shifting into one of concern. "I am uncertain that the Councillor was correct," he finally said. "I do not believe this is the place for you."

"Haval, while annoying, is seldom mistaken. It is one of his least endearing traits." Although Jester could have spoken the words, he hadn't; Jarven had.

And Jarven, golden fox in his arms, appeared beside Andrei. His eyes were gleaming in the soft light, but his expression was absent his usual glee. "Eldest."

The fox nodded, the motion regal, if distracted. The almost obscene joy that Jarven habitually displayed seemed to have transferred itself in its entirety to the fox. The Terafin merchant knelt and set the fox upon the ground.

"You are certain?" he asked the fox.

The fox tilted his head to the side. "You are not?"

Jarven's response was a brief display of teeth that could barely be called a smile. "I am." He rose. He held one dagger in his left hand. "May I leave Jester with you?" he asked the Araven servant.

Andrei nodded. "For the moment. I cannot guarantee—"

"There are no guarantees. There have never been guarantees. It is what makes life interesting."

Before Andrei could reply—and his grimace implied that he meant to do so—the ground buckled beneath their feet.

Snow smacked Jester with the lift of a wing, and when Jester glared at him said, "*Stupid.* Climb on." His voice dropped into a low growl; his fangs seemed to grow. Jester grimaced and made his way onto the cat's back. The white head then turned, and Snow hissed at his brother.

"Not *yet,*" Night replied, although Snow hadn't spoken. "Not yet, but *sssooooon.*" He seemed to find this amusing.

Snow did not. It took a moment for Jester to realize that for Snow, the fun would be spoiled by having to carry Jester, and he almost climbed off the cat's back, but Andrei shook his head.

"They understand the way the wind is blowing, ATerafin. It pains me to admit this, but you will be safest where you are. I do not believe the eldest will drop you."

"I *can,*" Snow told the Araven servant.

"Yes, Eldest. But can and will have different meanings here."

The ground moved again; the ominous creak of stone under pressure overwhelmed Jester's awareness of the breeze and its movement. He watched the first of the stones laid out around Moorelas as it split.

A cry rose; the Exalted glanced once at the statue of Moorelas, lowering their heads in unison. Moorelas, the hero of wars so ancient Jester had never fully believed they existed, teetered precariously as it looked out to the seawall and beyond, to the Isle.

And then it righted itself, the angle of its head changing as it looked down at the people gathered beneath it. It had always been safe to wander at will around the statue's base at night—for those suspicious enough to believe in the omen of Moorelas' shadow—but there was no safety now; Jester finally understood, as he looked at the ground around the statue, that it was *all* shadow, and that shadow now covered the holdings and stretched, as Moorelas' stone eyes gazed across the water, to the Isle itself, as if searching for something.

There, to the east, to the north, meticulously and almost desperately, that stone face turned—but he did not turn south; he saw whatever he wanted or needed to see in the West. Only then did he turn his gaze to the people congregated around his feet, and, opening his mouth, he spoke. And he spoke in a voice that was many voices, all at once: old and young, male and female, grating and soothing, deep and high.

"We have done what we can, for as long as we can. Now, it is in your hands, children of a'Neamis." He lifted his great stone arms as the ground began to crumble beneath him. Beneath them all.

The High Wilderness

The quiet joy of the Arianni permeated everything on either side of the standing portal. They did not sing; they did not dance; they did not cheer. Nor did they fall all over the White Lady, hugging her or crying. If seen from a distance, the muted joy might not be noticed at all: they walked in an almost military formation, single file, toward the Lord Jewel had come to understand they yearned for constantly.

She lingered on the far side, unwilling to invade the privacy they had not asked for.

No, it was more than that. Yollana of the Havallan Voyani had been a figure of terror to Jewel; she was the single most intimidating person Jewel had ever met. She had surrendered—had *sacrificed*—her own kin in preparation for the *Kialli* infiltration of the Dominion of Annagar. Yollana had paid for that sacrifice; Jewel understood that now. But she had been horrified at the time, certain that with Yollana, there was no safety. Less safety, even, than being at a distance, because it was her way to use whatever was at hand.

Jewel had never wanted to rule. She had assumed, in a childhood so far beneath the seats of power, that the powerful had happy, carefree lives—and in some fashion, they did: they were free of the worries that drove the den. They would not starve. They would not freeze to death. They would not outgrow clothing they could not afford to replace; nor would they lose toes to lack of shoes.

Those fears, the powerful did not have.

But the fears the powerful *did* have occupied the whole of her thought now. One person must remain in the Hidden Court if Summer was to reign. One. Yollana could easily make that choice. She would have accepted without hesitation.

Jewel had never wanted to be Yollana.

The Winter King's interior voice was almost lacerating in its outrage. *Any one of these men would be* elevated. *They would be* exalted. *Do you not understand what they would become? They would be the Summer King—they would be the heart of the Hidden Court. Not for Summer the roads of war; not for Summer the last Winter hunt.*

She heard the yearning in his voice, and she remembered. This man—what remained of him—wanted nothing but Ariane. Winter or Summer. She thought that she could leave him as Summer King without guilt.

And she felt his pain.

Yes, he wanted this. Yes, she had promised that she would ask. But she *knew*, even thinking it, that it would be impossible. She could ask, but the answer would—and must—be no.

Think. I have thought you weak, but never foolish; ignorant, but never stupid. But this hesitance is folly. You think of your own loss; you do not think of what any of your companions have to gain.

But Avandar did not enjoin criticism to the Winter King's, if he was aware of it at all. He waited. The Arianni left them all, standing on this side of the arch while the minutes passed.

It was Kallandras who chose to break the unnatural stillness; Jewel had made a decision, and if, having made it, she could not fully commit to it, he could. He turned to her and offered her a bow that would have been appropriate only in the presence of the Kings or the Exalted. When he rose, he looked to Celleriant. And Jewel understood that the bard had not broken the stillness for her sake, but for Celleriant's; it was the first time that she had seen Celleriant look hesitant.

Kallandras did not attempt to offer Lord Celleriant comfort or assurances. The White Lady had granted harbor and safety to all of Jewel's companions. But the only one who was—who had been—part of that court was Celleriant, until his failure.

The failure alone did not count against him. But he had sworn an oath to serve Jewel as Lord and master—and that would. Yet he nodded to Kallandras, and when Kallandras entered the portal, Celleriant followed.

Angel waited. Terrick, however, did not. He glanced at Jewel, and when she met his gaze, he nodded. He picked up his heavy pack, shouldered it, and walked through the portal. Angel lifted his hands.

Jewel, catching the movement out of the corner of her eyes, hesitated. She understood that those who remained would not walk through that portal until she did and understood as well that she would lose one of them.

Shianne, however, placed a hand on her shoulder. Jewel turned to her instantly; the echo of Ariane in her features almost hurt to look upon. She realized that Shianne was almost as terrified as she was. They were not afraid of the same things; they couldn't be. But they were looking loss straight in the face, and even knowing it and accepting it was a constant struggle.

Or perhaps not. Jewel recognized fear, yet she could not with certainty say what caused it. She knew only that Shianne was not of the Arianni; she would enter the Hidden Court at Jewel's side or not at all. But Shianne had seen Ariane's brief expression when their eyes had met, and she could not even pretend that the White Lady would feel gratitude at the sacrifice she had chosen to make.

She was not surprised when the Winter King spoke. *She would kill you were she to think you would turn away before giving the White Lady what she requires; she would take what you carry through the portal without a backward glance.*

I know.

Must you then assume she is not what she is?

No. The fact that she'd kill me doesn't change the fact that she's afraid. Both things can be true.

One is irrelevant.

To you, yes.

Her fear will not harm you. It will not—

Fear is harmful. People are stupid when they're terrified. They make stupid mistakes, stupid decisions. You were once Tor Amanion. You ruled one of the Cities of Man. The city no longer exists. Her interior voice was as flat as it would have been had she spoken. *But powerful or no, Tor or no, were it not for the Sen, you would have been just as helpless as any other man.*

Fear is a tool.

Yes. Yes, it is. But to you and your kind, it is the only tool. You do not understand any of the others—and there are others, Winter King. There always have been.

Those tools did not save my city.

No—but neither did fear.

She had already made her decision; all that remained was guilt, and that was in the future. She had walked away from Carver for the sake of the entire city. If she did not do this now, the pain of that parting would be in vain; he would have been lost for *nothing*. Jewel lifted a hand, signed to Adam; she waited until his hand had fallen away. She left him with Shianne as she walked beneath the standing arch.

The moment she took a step, Shadow was beside her. He shouldered Avandar out of the way, growled at Angel, and took a swipe at the Winter King, his tail lashing from side to side as if everyone present was a threat. Everyone but Jewel, who grimaced and dropped a hand to the top of his head.

"Please do not make me regret this," she said, in the quiet tone that indicated she had run out of patience and was now dangling on the edge of its figurative cliff.

"Yes, yes, *yesssss*." The gray cat sniffed, stuck his nose in the air and accompanied her, head held high. But Jewel noted that his foot crossed the threshold of the Artisan-crafted arch at the same moment hers did; it touched ground on the opposite side in the same fashion.

Only when Jewel had cleared that arch and stood upon a path that seemed to have been built for just that purpose did he lower his head. No, not just his head. He stretched his paws out before him in Ariane's slender shadow.

The White Lady looked down upon the prone cat's head, as if from a great remove. She then lifted her gaze. "I bid you and your companions welcome to my home. We have had some time to prepare."

Jewel was accustomed by now to the speech of Kings; she did not, therefore, question the plural. Instead, she followed the White Lady's lead. Winter had reigned in the lands in which Darranatos had lain in wait, but in the Hidden Court, if the breeze was chill, no snow had fallen; all of Winter was in the heart of the woman who ruled it.

Shadow remained by Jewel's side. The uncharacteristic bow he had offered he shed as soon as he possibly could, but he walked silently; the only sound he made was the occasional growl. He did not otherwise speak, and he did not insult her; nor did he whine about boredom. Here, he looked like a great hunting cat, with the addition of wings whose feathers caught the sunlight in Ariane's land and seemed to encase it. It reminded Jewel of the butterfly's light.

Jewel had seen the Wild Hunt in the Stone Deepings. She had imagined that this court would reflect that experience, and indeed, the hunters that had come to her side from the side of the Winter King did. But there was a quiet, a hush, that implied a kind of throttled, hidden joy. They did not smile; they did not express it in any way Jewel could point to.

"No," Shadow said, his voice softer and far less whiny. "In the wilderness, it is unwise for the powerful to express anything that hints at love. Love is just another weapon."

If the Arianni heard the great, gray cat, they betrayed no awareness of his words.

"Shadow—"

No, Jewel, the Winter King said. *Enough.*

But the Arianni love the White Lady. It's impossible not to know it.

Think, but never *mention it here: the Allasiani exist.*

Shadow snorted but said nothing.

"Love," the White Lady said softly, "is also a gift, Eldest. Where the cost of the giving is not so high, it illuminates."

"And where it *is*," the cat countered, "it destroys. It is not *necessary*. Who *needs* it?"

"Need? Eldest, you need nothing. Nor did the gods when they walked. They might have existed without the wars that destroyed so much. I need nothing," she continued, voice soft. "I could exist for eternity in my Hidden Court and weather the passage of eras as they slipped away. Need has never defined our existences."

Shadow did not reply. His wings shivered.

Ariane then turned to Jewel, and to Jewel's lasting surprise, the gray cat gave way to the White Lady, who fell in beside her. Jewel looked at her feet as she walked. It was easier; to look at the White Lady was akin to staring at the sun. All beauty, all relevance, all power were contained in Ariane; in her presence, it seemed that life—and love—as mortals knew them were dim and gray and pointless.

And they weren't. Jewel knew it, but knew as well that the knowledge was shifting beneath her feet like loose sand.

She was, therefore, unaware when the path itself opened up; when trees gave way to architecture, when wildflowers gave way to more ordered white and green. But when the White Lady said, "I have another guest," Jewel looked up to see that she was no longer surrounded entirely by forest.

The Wild Hunt—the hunters—had dispersed; only Celleriant remained. He was silent and reserved, the joy of homecoming shattered by the circumstances. Kallandras remained by his side. Shianne, however, remained with Adam, and if Celleriant seemed joyless, she seemed lifeless in comparison. It was too much, Jewel thought with a pang: the loss of Darranatos, the consequences of her own choices.

She did not understand immortals; did not understand immortal love. She understood loss and the pain of it, but wondered if even that was a shadow of, an echo of, what Shianne felt.

And then she had no time to think. A table that reminded her of the table in her library—in all its incarnations—stood in the open, beneath a cloudless azure echo of a real sky, and seated at it—seated, but rising in haste to abandon her chair—was a young woman Jewel recognized.

"Yes," Ariane said, although Jewel had not spoken.

Seated at the table—but making haste to rise—was Evayne a'Nolan.

She was not the young woman that Jewel had first met in the ruined foyer of the Terafin manse, but she was not the older woman, either. She was younger than Jewel now was, but older than she had been on the night they had faced a bestial, wild god.

She wore her familiar robe. Her eyes were violet in a pale face; she wore a necklace openly that the robes usually concealed, a delicate silver lily. That the necklace had survived all her life experience and still adorned the neck of the powerful, older woman she would become was almost surprising. Her expression was gaunt, but even thinking that, Evayne's smile changed the cast of her features.

The smile was not meant for Jewel; it was certainly not meant for Ariane.

"Evayne!" Adam said, his voice rising slightly at the end. He took a step, and then glanced at Shianne and stopped. Shianne said nothing, but her expression was pure Winter; there was no welcome, no invitation. Perhaps, had Evayne been looking at Shianne, this might have given her pause. She wasn't. She had eyes for Adam, only Adam.

Her chair teetered as she left it.

Adam could not leave Shianne. But he took a step forward and opened his arms. It was surprising to see that he was taller than Evayne; it was surprising to watch her walk—run, really—into the circle of those arms. She threw her own around him and held on.

So, too, Adam; his cheek could rest across the top of her black hair, and did.

"I couldn't find you," he said. "I couldn't find you the next day. I looked. I'm sorry." He looked up to meet Jewel's eyes, his own moving in Shianne's direction, although they couldn't reach her.

Jewel, staring at the back of this young seer, nodded. She turned, approached Shianne, and offered her an arm. Shadow growled, but for once he did not attempt to position himself between Jewel and whoever she approached.

Kallandras, Celleriant by his side, approached Shianne as well. He offered her a bow—a perfect Weston obeisance. Evayne stiffened. She let Adam go and turned toward the Senniel bard, her shoulders curved inward, her head low.

Kallandras bowed. "I am here with The Terafin. We have come to deliver something of value to the White Lady. We crossed the winter wilderness, searching." His lips turned up in a smile; Jewel was surprised to see that it was both wry and gentle. "You sent me, Evayne."

And Jewel understood, then, in a flash of insight that had more to do with lived life than talent-born gift. Somewhere in their history together, Evayne had done something to the young Kallandras, had set him upon the path he now walked. He was decades away from it, now; this Evayne was not. She was too young not to feel the burden of guilt; it bowed her. Kallandras walked across the simple stones until he stood within arm's reach of her midnight robe. The cloth began to rustle, its hems undulating against the ground. The robe had not responded to Jewel that way.

"Do you remember the Winter paths we walked together?" he asked, voice soft.

She nodded.

"It has served me well. I am not the boy I was. My brothers are behind me, forsaken. You believe I hated you."

"You *did*. You still do."

"Yes. But I understand enough now. I see the shadow of gods across the lands; I see the walls that have contained the wilderness breaking, stone by stone. There are dragons in mortal skies now. There are forests that have over-grown merchant roads, and no caravans that pass through them ever emerge.

"And the Lord of the Hells no longer sits upon his distant throne. The world is stirring, Evayne, just as you said it would. Not one of the visions you showed me—"

"That I forced upon you."

"—That you showed me was a lie. And what you showed me was that I was destined to lose everyone I cared about, sooner or later. I did not understand then why you chose me; I better understand it now." He held out a hand, palm up, before her.

Evayne stared at it as if it were poison. And she stared at it as if she were drowning, and it might save her.

Jewel thought again: *I could not be you*, for she understood from even these words that what Evayne had shown Kallandras, she had forced him to see; she had not asked for his permission, his consent. Had there been no Evayne, there would have been no Kallandras at Senniel College.

"Evayne," he said softly. He did not reach out to touch her hand; he waited. He waited, as the seer herself had not done. How old had he been when they first met? How much had she forced him to witness? How much had he lost as a result?

How much, Jewel thought, did he have to forgive?

It was the question Evayne asked herself, if silently; she lifted a hand. It trembled. She could not lower it but could not place it in his.

He waited. He waited, and after a long moment, he lowered his empty hand. "For you, it has barely begun," he said softly. "But for me, it is almost over. There will come a time—if I survive—when I might, at last, feel gratitude for everything I have lost." He bowed. "I am no longer your enemy."

He turned away, and as he did, the paralysis that held Evayne dissolved. She ran the short distance, reaching for his shoulder, his arm, and he turned again and caught her. Jewel found herself holding her breath.

Shadow stepped on her foot. Hard.

"This is not for *us*," he told her, almost primly. He turned to Celleriant, whose averted gaze was fastened to the table at which Evayne had been sitting. He looked up, wary, as Jewel approached. It was awkward, and Jewel almost turned away, understanding what it had cost him to come here.

And yet this was what he had wanted. He might never return to this place; he might never know home again. But he was Arianni, one of the last of the White Lady's progeny; exiled or no, it was his desire to be of use to her. No pain or loss would change that.

She straightened her shoulders. Celleriant's loss, Celleriant's presence, provided the impetus that nothing else could. If she was mortal—and she was— she was *his Lord*. She was not his mother, not his reason for existence, not the person whose constant presence and approval he almost literally lived for, but she was his Lord. And in the Hidden Court, she could be that.

She turned to Ariane, who had remained silent throughout, and tendered her a perfect bow; a short bow, meant in the Empire as a gesture of respect among equals. Shadow hissed.

"We are weary and disheveled from both the road and the battle," she said when she rose, "and would much appreciate the chance to bathe."

Ariane's smile was slender and knowing. "Mortal customs are not our customs, but we have had mortals in the Hidden Court for all of their existence. We have facilities for your use. Cessaly?"

Jewel shook her head. She did not expect Cessaly to hear the White Lady, let alone answer, and was therefore surprised when the girl came racing toward Ariane, arms held wide, left hand carrying something in a clenched fist.

"Not yet," Ariane told her softly, "but soon. Will you show our guests to the baths you use?"

Cessaly nodded, turned to Jewel, and caught her hand.

*   *   *

Adam and Evayne did not immediately follow Cessaly, although everyone else did. Adam understood, from his first sight of Evayne, that Evayne was more than guest in this place. Evayne was kin—somehow—to the Winter Queen, and it was a kinship that the Winter Queen publicly claimed and acknowledged.

Ariane understood that this sister wished some time alone with Adam, and she said, "I will greet my lost kin."

Lost?

"They have been long from my side; they were lost in the tangle centuries ago. I did not expect them to return in this fashion." She did not bow but turned then, leaving Adam and Evayne alone in the clearing, with its table, its chairs, and the splash of gentle sunlight that came from no sun Adam could see.

Only when Ariane had left did Evayne touch Adam's shoulder. "You haven't changed," she said quietly.

He had but did not say this; he understood what she meant. She looked older to Adam; more adult. The obvious distress, the terrible realization of loss, was gone; it had sunk beneath the surface of her face. She had lost weight, he thought with an Oma's concern; he was far too polite to say so out loud.

She led him away from the table and the clearing, but not in the direction of what the terrifying Winter Queen had called baths; instead, she found a small lake, its shores a reminder of desert sand. There, she sat.

Adam sat with her. "Can you talk about what you've been doing since I last saw you?" But no, that wasn't the right question; he knew it before she tensed. "Sorry," he said quickly. "That is the business of Matriarchs. But . . . can you talk about how you've been feeling?"

She smiled then.

Although the baths were meant for mortals, Celleriant and Shianne accompanied Jewel, as did Terrick, Angel, and Avandar. Kallandras was slower to follow but did. No one, however, entered the water immediately, because the Ariane version of a bath was not a tub or basin. It was not even a pool, enclosed and protected from the elements.

It was a placid, still lake; the only thing that disturbed its surface was the water falling to the left in a spill of sound and light. To the right of Jewel's party were large, flat boulders, covered in moss; the shore of the lake was a white, white sand that suggested snow.

"It's warm," Cessaly told her, as if she could hear the thought. "They don't come here."

"They?" Kallandras asked.

She blinked, as if the sound of his voice was unexpected. Unexpected and fascinating. "The Winter people," she replied. And then, as if she wanted—or needed—to hear more of that voice, "Do you know them?"

"I have encountered them before on my travels. I did not expect to meet another mortal in this court, at this time. When did Evayne arrive?"

Cessaly made a face. "I was here when she arrived. It is hard to tell time here," she added apologetically.

"Time is not of import to the White Lady."

"Do you sing?"

He smiled. "Often."

"*Will* you sing?"

"I will not sing here without the White Lady's permission."

Cessaly looked crestfallen. "Just a little?"

The bard's smile deepened. "In the wilderness, my voice carries." As he spoke, Jewel noticed that butterflies had begun to gather around the boulders nearest the lake. Their wings caught light, reflecting it; they seemed like living jewelry, their wings spread as if to adorn the pale colors of the lake.

Kallandras noticed them as well—had probably noticed them first; there was so little that escaped his eyes. "Did you make these?"

Cessaly nodded. Her right hand was twitching; her left, still clenched in a fist, was now white-knuckled. Her expression was odd, and it took Jewel a moment to place it; she had seen something similar on the face of the guild-master when he had examined the dress she had worn at the first day of The Terafin's funeral rites.

"They sing," Kallandras said.

"Yes—but not properly. There was no voice—" She stopped. Her eyes were sharp, clear, the various elements of her face falling into lines that made focus her only expression.

"I will ask permission of the Lady," the bard said softly. "But in this place, all things that occur must occur with her permission. It is not for my own sake—"

But Cessaly had turned heel in that instant and all but disappeared in her haste.

After the bath, Jewel left her traveling clothing on the rocks. She had, with Avandar's help, removed the white dress which Snow had crafted for her, and with his help, had donned it. From her pouch, she had drawn both bracelet and tiara, gifts from Guildmaster Gilafas. They were not, she thought, for her; they had not been crafted for this moment.

But she wore them, regardless.

Avandar did not carry the various brushes and combs she would otherwise have at her disposal, but he made do with the pins that had mostly kept her hair in place during their journey, and when he was at last done, she stepped forward, shedding the self-consciousness that almost always accompanied this dress.

She had thought it fit for Ariane, when she had first seen it. She had thought herself unworthy of its almost unearthly beauty. Knowing now how it had been created did not make the wearing more comfortable—but it was not, now, something that she could simply give to the White Lady. Or anyone. Snow had made this for her, and she would not be parted from it while she lived.

Celleriant was first to bow, and his bow was low, almost reverent, as if the dress, rather than hiding her inadequacy, had somehow revealed her strength. Shadow came to her and sat, heavily, cleaning his paw and eyeing the butterflies that scattered the minute he approached. She placed a hand on the top of his head. But if he felt she was stupid—and he must, he was a cat after all—he said nothing.

It was Avandar's transformation that was the most astonishing, to Jewel—and possibly the most unwelcome. She had not seen what he himself packed to carry across the wilderness, and even had she, she was certain she would not have seen what he now wore. They were Southern robes in drape, in form, but they were heavily embroidered and dyed, and the wide sash that cut across his chest and waist caught the natural light and seemed to burn with it.

By his side, he now wore a sword. It was the sword that gave her pause, and she almost demanded that he set it aside, but the words would not come.

No, instead, the Winter King arrived.

He knelt instantly, with no command or indication from Jewel that he should, and she mounted in the same way.

Angel and Terrick had neither clothing nor uniform with which to play dress guards, and Jewel understood that was exactly what was happening now. But she would not leave them behind. If she was willing to be the Lord that Celleriant had sworn a blood oath to serve, she was nonetheless Jewel Markess ATerafin, and Angel was at the heart of the transformation from struggling den leader to House ruler.

Kallandras called the wind. As Angel and Terrick, he was not equipped to be a living adornment, but he did have other gifts at his disposal, and he used them now. Angel glanced up at him and said, "No." But Terrick nodded, and Terrick was lifted in the folds of the wild air.

Thus equipped, Jewel rode, once again, to meet the Winter Queen. In her lap was the small wooden box, a box so humble in appearance it looked immediately out of place.

I would release you from your oath, Jewel thought, glancing briefly at Celleriant. *If it were possible, and if it would make a difference to your White Lady, I would release you back to her service in an instant.*

Such was the gravitas of the situation that the Winter King did not immediately criticize her, although she could feel the weight of his momentary disapproval.

And you, she thought. *You swore no oath to me; you have done everything you have done in the White Lady's service.*

Yes.

Would you return to her?

That decision is not—and has never been—in your hands. This did not seem to sadden him. *She knew. She understood what you must carry.* He spoke with certainty. *She understood that you were mortal, and she understood some of the danger that you would face; she did not believe you would survive it on your own. And so, she sent us. She could not send her hunters because they could not return, and they could not walk the paths you have walked.*

There it was. Pride.

What we did, only we could do.

She did not argue; it was not an argument she wished to win. Instead, she lifted her chin, straightened her back, and allowed the Winter King to take her, with his stately, graceful steps, to the Queen of the Hidden Court.

Chapter Twelve

A THRONE SUCH AS JEWEL had never seen came into view. It dwarfed the woman who occupied it; its back grew in perfect, carved splendor, out of the trunk of a tree that was likewise without equal; that tree reached for the sky with such height, Jewel couldn't see the crowning leaves. But the leaves she did see were not all of a kind, and she recognized only a handful. She wondered what Birgide would make of this tree; she was certain it was the tree and the leaves that her Warden would see, not the woman who sat in repose beneath their shadows.

Arrayed around the tree were the Arianni, but they did not wear the armor that Jewel associated with them. They wore, instead, robes that caught light, even in the shadows; they reminded Jewel of the robes Evayne wore at any age. Their brows were adorned with slender tiaras, worked into such fine, interwoven tendrils they seemed fragile, delicate—too much so for warriors. But she understood, as she glanced across the gathered court, that they were here to support the White Lady in her chosen context; she was jewel, they, her setting.

She was not aware of the moment when Kallandras began to play; nor had she been aware that his lute was in his hands. She understood that gravitas, here, was as essential as breath, and did not turn to look.

Celleriant now walked to the left of the Winter King, Shadow to the right. Jewel *knew* the moment Shianne and Adam joined the procession but did not lift hand or turn head to acknowledge them as she pulled them along in her wake. Although she could clearly see Ariane and her living throne, she felt that this road was the longest she had ever walked, and the most difficult. It was fanciful; the practical side of her mind rebelled at the thought, but even her Oma's harsh voice had fallen silent, as if enspelled.

When she was a yard away from the foot of that throne, itself a mass of orderly roots that seemed to be embroidery made large, the Winter King knelt. Jewel alighted from his back; Celleriant was there to offer her a hand, something he had never done before. On the roads they had walked together, the practical ruled; here, it was different.

She remembered, as she gained her footing, the day she had first been summoned to *Avantari*. She had knelt, entirely abasing herself, in the Hall of Wise Counsel. On that day, she had given over all responsibility, for a brief period, to those exalted with crowns; she had not been a power and had had no desire to become one.

On this day, in the presence of someone far more exalted, she did not kneel, did not bow; she offered the White Lady the grace of a very structured nod, a lowering of chin, a straightening of shoulders. The eyes of the Lady's court were fixed to the dress that was now the best armor she could wear; what they saw in it, Gilafas had seen, although he had had no words for it.

No, she thought, they saw more. In some fashion, this dress and their Hidden Court were similar: they were of the wilderness.

Her hands were steady as she turned to Celleriant. Into his hands she placed the humble wooden box that she had carried from the Dominion of Annagar. It had contained a sword, a dagger, and in its history, perhaps many other weapons—but none, in the end, as potent as the one it now sheltered.

Celleriant's eyes widened almost imperceptibly as they met Jewel's, and she thought his hands trembled. But he did not betray himself in any other way. He did what he, as liege, could do: he approached the White Lady's throne and knelt there, bowing his head as he held the box out to her.

Jewel willed him to lift his face, to meet the White Lady's eyes, but even bearing what he now bore, he could not do it. Ariane did not motion a member of her own court to take what Celleriant now offered. Instead, she looked past him to the Lord he had chosen to serve.

"You have exceeded all expectations but not all hope," she said, to Jewel. "You know what you carry. You are, I believe, a mortal merchant; you have not bargained well. But I am the White Lady, and I understand its significance, regardless. You have done me a great service, made larger in all ways by the fact that I could not accomplish this task myself. Do you understand?"

Jewel inclined her head.

"I am in your debt."

"No, Lady," she replied. "We both, in the end, choose to fight the same war.

You are not my Lord; you are not my god; you are not my kin. You are comrade on the field we must take." Her voice surprised her; it was steady.

Ariane inclined her head to acknowledge the truth of the words—and there *was* truth in them. "You wear a ring. You feared the consequences of bearing it; you feared it was a lie."

Jewel inhaled, lifting her chin.

"I will make of it, instead, the truth. You are not mine, and cannot be, but in the lands that I rule, in the lands that I claim, you will be recognized. Only those bold enough to attack me—and they are not small in number in the high wilderness—will dare to raise arms against you, and should they succeed, they will pay." She turned to the left, and a man approached the throne. He bowed, much as Celleriant had done, rising when she commanded it. "But, in truth, I have crafted and offered such rings before, and no one of their bearers have ever done me so large a service as you have done. And so, I must ask, what boon would you have of me?"

"Save my city."

The White Lady smiled gently but shook her head. "I cannot grant that. Were the debt not so large, I would agree." As Jewel stiffened, she continued. "What I can save of your city, I will save—but I have been trapped here for too long, and the roads are not fully open, yet. I have reasons of my own to involve myself in your affairs, and I believe you understand some part of them.

"I will not be in your debt, Jewel Markess."

Jewel met the steady gaze of the White Lady, aware that all eyes were upon her. She found it difficult to speak and act as an equal to the ruler of this Hidden Court, and asking a boon of her felt like an impossible task. But she let her eyes fall to Celleriant's back. He remained kneeling, the wooden box outheld until the moment Ariane chose to accept it. He had chosen to swear an oath to serve Jewel—to truly serve her—but all that he wanted was here, in front of him.

"I am not firstborn," Jewel said, finding the strength to speak. "Service, among my kind, does not mean what it does among yours."

Ariane waited.

"The Winter King serves you. My Winter King."

"Yes."

"He serves me at your command. He serves me in spite of the fact that he wishes to be here, to be by your side."

Ariane nodded again.

"I wish to return him to you."

"Ah, but he is not yours. The command, and the service, was mine to offer, a penalty for his failure. Nor do I think it wasted or unnecessary." She lifted a hand as Jewel began to speak, her voice so soft Jewel was surprised that she could hear it so clearly. "You wish to ask me about the Summer King."

Jewel nodded.

"You understand Tor Amanion. You understand his service and his desire. You understand what he once was, when he was merely a man." She smiled as she gazed upon the stag by Jewel's side, and Jewel could feel his yearning as if it were a physical effect, a storm or an earthquake.

"He was a worthy Winter King, a worthy opponent upon the winter fields. Even as a mortal, he was a force to be reckoned with; his shadow fell long and dark. If you mean to ask me if he might remain here as Summer King, you fail to understand the needs of both Winter and Summer. He is not one born for Summer. Understand, Jewel: the Winter requires a strength that is borne in and of the desperate struggle to survive the cold and the hunters who revel in it; the Summer requires a different strength entirely.

"The strength of Winter resides, in part, in the Winter King; the strength of Summer, in the Summer King. There have been greater and lesser men to reign as kings in the Hidden Court, for mortals are never all of one thing or all of another—but if I understand what has transpired, and what will, this is the final Summer." Her words appeared to rob the Arianni of breath, of movement, of all semblance of life. She did not so much as glance at them; her eyes bore down on Jewel, and if her gaze was not unkind, it was far too intense to meet.

And yet, mindful of Celleriant, Jewel did just that.

"Against the foes we will face, we must choose a Summer King wisely. Summer Kings often fare poorly in the Winter. I understand your fear, and I understand your sacrifice. But Terrick is not of the Summer, and your Angel is not for me. The bard is likewise Winter's—Winter's and a different god's."

Jewel froze. "Adam could be Summer King."

"No."

"The choice, surely, would be his."

The Winter King was almost outraged; Adam, to his eye, was a boy in all ways unworthy of the White Lady. Jewel kept her hands by her sides; she did not look at the great stag. Nor did she look at the Voyani boy.

Jewel felt a glimmer of annoyance; she was certain, were the White Lady not present in person, it would flare to rage. "You understand, as well as I, why Adam cannot be your Summer King."

"Oh?"

"Your Summer King will not leave this court. Even when you ride to war, it is here he will remain."

The White Lady smiled. All of Winter was in that expression. "Yes. You do not understand; nor does your Adam. But you will. Come. Even in the timeless land, we cannot wait forever. But Adam is not as you are, Terafin. He does not desire this."

Jewel accepted the truth at the heart of the observation because part of her *did* desire this. Ariane was a power, akin to a god; she had knowledge and experience gained during the various wars of the ages that Jewel had hoped, still hoped, never to have. She could do what was necessary. She could make decisions without regret or fear.

Jewel was weary now, not of power itself, but of the responsibility that came relentlessly with it. To wish for a better world when she herself had been an orphan at the outer edges of society was a daydream; it came in the quiet of night, and often in stages of anger and resentment.

To wish for a better world now meant building that world, somehow. It meant carrying far more weight; she could not simply pick a pocket or snatch a purse and stave off death for a week or two. And it meant that her mistakes threatened people she did not know, could not see, and might never otherwise meet.

But so, too, Ariane. Ariane did not care. The lack of care was the reason she did not feel the weight of ruling in the same way Jewel herself did. And Jewel could not surrender the care of her Empire, her city, her *family*, to the Winter Queen.

"What, then, would you have of me?"

"When I am dead—and I am mortal, death is inevitable—I wish you to accept Celleriant, my liege, as your own. I wish you to accept his service once again."

"He is yours," the Winter Queen said. "By his own choice, he is yours."

"Yes. While I live, he is mine."

"And that was the whole of his oath?"

"While I live," Jewel repeated.

There was a murmur now, building to either side of the woman who ruled, who had always ruled, this court.

Celleriant himself said and did nothing; his arms remained outstretched, the weight of this hidden world carried in steady hands. He did not look up; did not meet the eyes of the Winter Queen. Nor did he enjoin his voice to his Lord's.

The murmur grew, and in its folds, Jewel teased out a single word: *forsworn.*

She understood, then, the magnitude of his crime; in the history of the Arianni, the forsworn had become—literally—demons. *Kialli.*

Ariane did nothing to stem the whispers, but the whispers did not become—as they might in a mortal crowd—the beginnings of a mob's anger. The decision was, in its entirety, Ariane's, and what she accepted, what she *offered*, they would accept. Jewel understood people, or at least people's anger and resentment. Had the Wild Hunt been mortal, they would accept their Lord's decision—but, conversely, they would accept it poorly. Celleriant, in their mind, would be a traitor; they would make of him an outsider, and keep him there, building social walls between those who had not committed the gravest of crimes, and he himself.

But she knew, watching, that what Ariane granted, they would grant; what Ariane accepted, they would, in the end, accept.

"And if I tell you, Terafin, that it is a gift that you offer me?"

Silence again, the ripples sudden with surprise.

"He is yours, as you have said—and as he himself has vowed. He was the youngest of the princes of my court, the last; there will be no others. He is not equal to the firstborn princes that you have called, for the entirety of your city's existence, the Sleepers." She smiled. It was cold. "But I am not what I was when the first of the princes of the court were born.

"If I grant what you ask, I am not granting a boon; I am accepting a gift— and it is, without doubt, a gift of value."

Celleriant's arms trembled then. He did not, however, raise his head.

"And Terafin, I understand your lack of comprehension, in this. If it will put you at ease—and you are odd enough, that I believe it will—I will accept this gift. But you have seen what I make of my kin in the Winter; you cannot believe it to be an unalloyed kindness on my part. He will be, and become, what he was when I first sent him from my side."

Jewel knew that this was all Lord Celleriant wanted.

But the Winter Queen rose, leaving the setting of her throne, and it seemed to Jewel that instead of being diminished, she was elevated. The throne on which no other monarch might comfortably sit had dwarfed her, and she was free of its confines. The air was chill; the stillness alleviated by a biting, bitter breeze, a sting of wind.

She approached Celleriant but did not touch what he proffered.

"Your boon, Terafin."

"Give me back Carver."

*   *   *

Ariane reached for the box that Celleriant held. In her hands it looked unfinished, far too rough, too common, too *ordinary*. The facts did not change or alter this impression. Nor did her smile.

When she held the box, Celleriant lowered his arms; he did not rise, and would not, Jewel thought, without her express command, her permission. "Lord Celleriant." And she gave it. It was odd. For Celleriant's sake, Jewel had become more regal in this wilderness than she had ever been. It was the only thing she could do for him; the only thing she could offer that might stem the tide of the humiliation he faced—and accepted—because he had chosen her as Lord.

He rose, then. He rose, lifting his chin, the fall of his hair straight and unmoved by something as simple as breeze. He offered Ariane the bow one would offer a foreign monarch; it was stiff with respect.

Ariane accepted it, although she met and held his gaze for a moment longer than necessary. He then returned to Jewel's side. She wondered if he would acknowledge, in any way, what she had asked for. And knew it didn't matter.

Her breath was short, slight; her throat almost closed. All the weight of her thought, all the weight of a bitter hope, returned to her; she carried it.

The Winter Queen had not refused the boon she had offered. Had not denied it, as she had denied the first, the most responsible, of her requests. And it *was* the first thing she had asked for, the salvation of the city itself—but it was not the thing that she *wanted*. Carver, however, was.

She wondered if there was kindness—Summer kindness—in the Winter Queen. She had refused the one thing that Jewel must put above all others; had claimed that it was not a certainty; had all but demanded that Jewel ask a different boon, a different favor.

And she had not rejected it. Had not spoken of impossibility. Had not even asked who Carver was, or where he might be.

"Be at peace, Terafin. No man can be Summer King—or Winter—who does not desire it with the whole of his mortal being. I can enspell; all my kin can. But our very presence was oft considered enspelling, with no intent on our part. Do you doubt it?"

Jewel shook her head.

Ariane turned to the Winter King. Softly, she said, "You have not disappointed me. You are mine; she cannot return you to me; I have not—and will not—surrender you. But serve her, at my pleasure, for a little while longer. You will know when you are done."

He did not answer, but Jewel knew, suddenly, he could. No other could hear his voice save the Winter Queen and the woman he had been ordered to serve. He bowed his great, tined head almost to the ground, and the shadow he cast in the odd light of this clearing was the shape and size of man.

Jewel expected the Winter Queen to open the lid of the Artisan-crafted box; she did not. She turned, instead, to Kallandras, the box held firmly in her hands. "I have been asked to allow you one liberty, Kallandras of Senniel."

The Arianni seemed neither surprised nor disapproving, and if Jewel had wondered how Cessaly was treated, how she was perceived, she had most of her answer in their reaction. They knew who had asked—or, given Cessaly—who had begged.

"You are wise enough not to truly sing in the wilderness without the knowledge and permission of the land's Lord; might you consider singing, instead, at her request?"

Kallandras swept a magnificent bow, a thing of supple grace. "At your command."

"Wait but a moment," she said although he had not begun. She lifted her head and spoke a single word.

A long word, at the heart of which was a name. She retraced the syllables a second time, and then, deliberately, a third.

And when the last of those utterances fell silent, Shianne moved past Jewel and the rest of her companions to walk into the presence, at last, of the Winter Queen.

None of the bitterness of regret adorned the Winter Queen's face, but none of the warmth of affection troubled it, either. She beckoned Shianne forward, as if the calling itself had not been, or was no longer, authority enough.

This close to the Winter Queen, Jewel could see the echo of Ariane's beauty; it was a fading thing, a thing which time would steal, as it had already begun to do. And even had that not been the case, Shianne was large with child; the slender waist of the Winter Queen was entirely absent.

She wore the dress that Snow had created for her at Jewel's request, and Jewel knew there was no shape or size she could be or become that the dress would not accommodate.

"I would have spared you this," Ariane said softly. "I did, as I could."

Shianne was silent.

"But that has been undone now." She bowed her head. "I will wake our sisters. They will ride with me into battle, because this will be the last great war."

Shianne remained silent, still.

"You do not understand the whole of what was done, and I am not what I was when you were first created; no more am I what I was when Darranatos was lost."

Now the court held breath, as if the very mention of that name had been forbidden them for eternity. But she was Queen, not subject; her will was absolute, her laws meant to be followed by those who were destined to obey.

And yet, Jewel thought, as her eyes were drawn to Shianne, her gaze held there by a compulsion that had nothing to do with gods, immortals, and eternity, they did not always obey. For no reason she understood, she thought of Andrei and bowed her head. No one, be they god or mortal, was a simple, cohesive whole. Even if they could cleave to one vision, one intention, their desires had to be managed, subverted, or denied.

"Remember," Ariane said, turning briefly to Jewel, "you have asked for the one boon it is in me to grant; I will cede no other." She turned to Shianne. "Will you not speak?"

Silence.

"Then sing, Shandalliaran. Sing for me. You alone are not forsworn, and yet you are lost to me, lost to us, just as certainly as if you were."

Shianne had been all but silent in the wake of Darranatos' passing; she had been pale, her eyes almost swollen with the tears she had shed. Her determination had given way, briefly, to sorrow, and the sorrow had not abated upon her entry into the Hidden Court. She stood across from Ariane, the White Lady of her dreams, her yearning, and Jewel understood that Shianne did not entirely know the woman with whom she was, after so much time, confronted.

Ariane spoke again, this time in a language whose meaning evaded Jewel's understanding, although she wore the ring that had allowed her to understand the Wild Hunt; Shianne lifted a hand and placed it, finally, in the hand that the White Lady extended. Had, Jewel thought, in some surprise, extended the moment she had called Shianne from the crowd to her side.

"You will never return to me," the White Lady said. "But I swear, while you live your brief life, you will never be far from me. I did not desire your captivity or your absence; I desired your existence. Will you sing for me? It has been long since I have heard your voice."

"I have heard yours," Shianne whispered. She hesitated, and as she did, the

White Lady turned toward the bard. She issued no commands, but instead inclined her head.

Kallandras nodded. The lute that he had played in a stately, quiet fashion, an aural carpet for Jewel to walk, he once again played, his fingers dancing across the strings in a quiet storm of sound. He did not sing, not immediately; the lute did that for him. Even without the accompaniment of his voice, the song he now coaxed from its rounded, wooden body demanded, commanded, attention.

But not nearly as much as his voice did, when he finally began to sing. Jewel had heard Kallandras sing before; she had always found it moving, regardless of the song. But she thought, hearing him now, that she had only heard an echo of the power of the bard-born; that perhaps he had been wise beyond belief to refuse to sing without the White Lady's permission.

Now she thought the air responded, as did the earth beneath his feet. Strands of the Winter Queen's hair moved, and above her head, above all their heads, the branches of the great tree swayed, gently shedding leaves in a carpet of colors: spring, summer, fall.

As he sang, Kallandras walked; the Senniel bards could do this in their sleep, or worse, without interrupting their performance. But this was beyond performance; he approached Shianne because the song he sang was not one he wished to carry alone.

Even Celleriant's gaze had moved from the White Lady to the bard, and it remained there for the duration of the song.

Jewel recognized the tenor of Kallandras' voice and felt her throat constrict at the painful, desperate yearning his song conveyed: he was a man who longed for home, but might never return, and he knew it. And yet, in that song, the desire for home, the love of it, made of home something very like the distant heavens—as real as safety or peace while one lived.

Shianne looked away from Ariane, toward the bard; her hand tightened on the White Lady's hand, and her arms trembled visibly. But she bowed her head as Kallandras sang, and Jewel was not surprised when Shianne joined him, her voice the equal of his, although she was now mortal. They had sung thus once before: as if the world had all but ended, and they were the survivors, bereft of any reason to continue.

She did not recognize the song; it was not the same song that Shianne had sung, newly born from stone, and free once again to move in the wilderness. Nor was it the song she had sung—as if only song could contain the intensity of emotion—for Darranatos' passing. Kallandras, at the request of the White Lady, had chosen.

But he was bard here; he understood that it was not, in the end, his voice or his song which Ariane desired. Jewel listened as he gave way, slowly, to Shianne; as he turned from melody to harmony, his voice blending with hers and supporting it; as his fingers shifted on the neck of his lute and the notes became a different kind of harmony.

She opened her eyes—when had she closed them?—only when Shianne's voice faltered. Although Kallandras adjusted his volume, his notes, it was impossible to cover for the sudden absence of hers.

But when Jewel's eyes were open, she understood why Shianne had momentarily lost her voice. Understood, as well, that the silence in this wild throne room was not the simple silence of an intent audience—it was far deeper and far more terrifying in its fashion.

The White Lady was crying.

She did not weep as Shianne had wept; she was Winter Queen. Her expression was remote, distant, controlled, as it had been since Jewel had approached her throne. But her silver eyes were closed, and tears caught light, trailing down her cheeks. Her hands held Shianne's, and it seemed to Jewel that those hands had tightened; that Shianne had attempted to pull away and was given no room at all to maneuver.

No one moved. It seemed to Jewel that no one breathed. Kallandras, however, continued the song he had offered the White Lady, reprising the melody of his opening; carrying, for the moment, the responsibility of the burden of sorrow, of pain, of loss.

And then there was movement, frenetic, harsh movement, a wild flapping of limbs that suggested frenzied wingbeats, although the arms and legs belonged to a mortal.

Cessaly ran to the White Lady, almost toppling two of the Arianni who had, as Jewel had, been almost spellbound with the enormity of what they had heard and what they had seen.

No one touched Cessaly. No one attempted to restrain her.

She did what no one there could otherwise dare to do: she approached the White Lady, her rough, sun-bronzed, callused hands reaching for Ariane's face. For her cheeks.

In those hands, she cupped the tears that Ariane now shed, as if they were precious stones, gems of higher quality than she had ever seen. And it seemed to Jewel, watching, that that was exactly what the tears had become: something cold and hard and bright; something that caught light, reflecting it and swallowing it simultaneously.

She remembered Gilafas then and cast about the audience; she could not see him. But Gilafas had done exactly this with the *Ellariannatte* and its branches. She understood that Cessaly meant to make with them; to use the talents of an Artisan to create. And Ariane was willing to allow her this freedom; the entire assembled court reacted as if she were a capricious, but beautiful, butterfly. No offense was taken. Indeed, there seemed to be relief and even surprised enlightenment.

Shianne's eyes widened as Cessaly retreated; she lowered her chin, but straightened her shoulders, and she once again took up the song that grief and surprise had caused her to abandon. This time, she continued; this time, she gave herself over to the emotion inherent in the song itself. She made no further attempt to retrieve her hands; instead, she tightened her grip, resolved in some fashion to sing what she would never be able to speak to the White Lady otherwise.

Jewel knew, before the song ended, what would happen.

It was visceral knowledge, not a conclusion drawn from observed fact, and as a result she was the second person to move. She was not Cessaly; she drew the eye and the disapproval of all in the audience who noticed, for all that she attempted to be more discreet. But the White Lady did not notice, and what the White Lady did not condescend to notice, her people could not.

No, she had eyes for Shianne, and only Shianne.

Jewel, however, had eyes now for Adam. She lifted her hands in den-sign and almost lifted her voice, but Angel's eyes caught the rough, deliberate motion of her hands; he turned instantly, lifting his hands as he did. She couldn't see what he signed; she could see his back.

And then she could see Adam. The expression of awe that informed his youthful features cracked as his eyes widened; he read her den-sign and turned instantly toward Shianne as the last notes of her song faded. He was, and had always been, very cautious when in the presence of women of power, and this should have been no exception; he had never been in the presence of so powerful a woman. But he was Adam, healer-born, and he understood Jewel's frenetic, silent gestures. He moved instantly toward Shianne and reached for her as the last of the song died into a stillness that would have been reverent had it not been for his presence.

Shianne did not appear to notice him; Ariane did.

"You," the White Lady said softly, meeting his gaze, "will never be mine." And speaking thus, she released Shianne's hand. Shianne stumbled, her hands reaching for the Winter Queen's almost of their own volition, but Adam caught them instead.

His eyes narrowed, and he turned, once, to look over his shoulder at the utterly silent White Lady.

Ariane said, "Yes." Just that, her voice soft and simultaneously implacable.

"Lord?" Celleriant's voice was soft in the same way.

"Shianne," Jewel said, "is about to have a baby."

Jewel had never personally witnessed a birthing before. As an only child—a state her Oma had alternately lamented and resented—she knew that midwives existed, but she had never seen one at work. She had seen pregnant women, of course, but had never desired to become one of them.

Had she, she would have lost all resolve.

Shianne was as white as a very expensive sheet; she gripped Adam's hands, hard, her eyes widening. She did not scream or cry.

Adam began to shout orders, but not in a panicked way; it was clear that although he was half Jewel's age, he *had* seen births.

He had seen children die.

He had seen mothers die, sometimes with them, sometimes on their own.

Jewel had arrived at the foot of Ariane's throne as Celleriant's Lord; she would leave, in the end, as Jewel Markess. She strode over to Adam, surprised when Terrick said, "I will acquire what you need. I would suggest we remove to the baths." Terrick, much older than any here save Kallandras, then departed.

Jewel placed a hand on Adam's shoulder. "If you mean to heal her, follow Terrick's advice. The moss is soft, and the water is warm."

He blinked, and she repeated the words in Torra. And then, continuing in Torra, she said, "You are healer-born, Adam. What you witnessed in the past—whatever it is—you can prevent. In your hands, both Shianne and the baby will be safe."

He hesitated. "Levec said—" He winced as Shianne's grip tightened. He tried to retrieve his hand, to no effect whatsoever; Shianne clung to him. Jewel had seen her look terrified only once before. This, however, was different.

"Kallandras."

The bard nodded, turning, once again, to Ariane, as if seeking permission to do as Jewel had wordlessly requested.

Commanded.

The White Lady nodded.

The air began to move with force and will, and it swept both Adam and Shianne off the ground; it was gentle, and this, more than anything, told Jewel that Kallandras had taken the wind's reins; he would have to placate it later.

Adam and Shianne, however, were carried to the side of what Cessaly had called a bath; Terrick had already taken blankets from the packs.

"Have you seen a birth before, Terafin?" he asked.

Jewel mutely shook her head.

"It gets a little bit messy. Sometimes," he added, "loud. This one has the Winter in her; she's birthed from the howling winds." It was, from the sounds of it, a compliment. Terrick, however, looked grim—as grim as when he hefted his ax and entered battle.

Jewel could not fail to know that women died in childbirth. Had she, she had only to look at the weathered face of the Rendish warrior to read that knowledge in the lines of his face. But she said, again, "Adam is healer-born."

She repeated this as the hours passed.

To herself, many times. To Adam when he seemed to flag. To Terrick, when the knuckles on involuntary fists grew too white. And to Shianne herself, but only once; Shianne would not be parted from Adam, and Adam appeared to have no desire to leave her side.

There was water. There was—much more disturbing—blood. There was obvious pain, fear, distress. Jewel repeated her own words to herself as she paced—and she did pace, like a great caged beast with little room in which to maneuver. She wanted to *do* something, yet there was nothing she could do.

Adam, half her age, was calm now, focused on Shianne. He did not enter a healing trance; he allowed himself to become her anchor, and he spoke to her, his voice low, his words encouraging. He spoke in Torra. Jewel wasn't certain that Shianne understood the words; she understood their intent, and she seemed to take comfort in between spasms of pain that caused her to stiffen and clench his hands.

It was Angel who tapped Jewel's shoulder, and Angel who drew her away.

"The Winter Queen wishes to speak with you."

But Jewel shook her head.

"You need to know she'll be all right?"

Jewel nodded.

Angel grimaced and said, "I don't."

"You've seen births before?"

He nodded. "In the Free Towns, not in Averalaan." In den-sign he added, *trust Adam.*

She did. But this was the first birth she had seen, and the most significant, and given that it had started in pain, had proceeded to blood, she needed to see the life that came from it; needed to know that there was a *reason* that it was so much of a struggle.

Angel did not try to move her again.

Later, she would remember that Avandar had not tried at all. Nor had the Winter King.

Jewel felt the time pass as slowly as if she were once again a child.

The very environs of the Hidden Court seemed to hold their breath; the quality of the light, the ambience of the atmosphere, did not change at all. Kallandras replaced Terrick as Adam's attendant and help; Terrick ate, but sparingly, with an eye to Adam and Shianne.

It was Adam who brought the infant into the world; Adam who declared it a boy; Adam who freed it from the umbilical cord which had been its sustenance, and who cleaned it, washed it, swaddled it; Adam who returned the infant to his mother's side. He looked relieved; he did not look exhausted in the way of the talent-born. As Jewel met his gaze, he smiled and shook his head.

"My people have given birth without healers for most of their history. And so, too, yours. The Houses of Healing exist for those with power, rank, and wealth—but that does not describe most of your citizenry. Or my people. She is strong," he added.

She was holding the child.

The child was looking out at the world with narrowed eyes, as if he understood everything his eyes saw. As if he *could* see.

And she understood then.

She understood, and wheeled, and the earth seemed to ripple as she strode across it in the sudden and unexpected depth of her fury.

Avandar joined her before she had cleared the lake area; he caught her arm, and she shook his hand free without breaking stride.

Jewel.

No.

Jewel.

She failed to respond for one long breath. *Did you know? Did you know at the outset that this is what she intended?* She could manage to keep the words contained, but only barely, and it was costly.

Did you not? Did you truly not understand?

Of course not! He's a child, *Avandar. A baby.*

Yes. A baby that the White Lady's kin chose to bear. Did you think she made that choice out of love for the infant—an infant that did not exist when she chose? Did you think that the pregnancy was inconsequential?

A baby. An infant. A newborn infant.

And what do you intend to do? Confront her? In the Hidden Court? Will you throw away your own life for the life of a stranger's child?

I won't buy *my own life with the life of a stranger's child!*

There is only so much effrontery the White Lady will tolerate. She will not tolerate this. The child is the mother's; the mother has already chosen. She chose long, long before you were born. She chose long before our *kind* was *born. Do you understand?*

Jewel had no response.

She became mortal—but she is not mortal as we are.

You're not mortal.

He may have flinched. She did not care.

And her child, Jewel, is not mortal as we are. It is the first—the first pregnancy of its kind. But the gods did not know then what they know now; not even Neamis. Ariane has said that she cannot crown a King who does not desire that crowning. Think. Did you not hear her words?

Shadows cast by looming branches flittered across her hands, her shoulders; she seemed, for a moment, to be walking into a net—a net meant for dragons, for things much larger than one mortal woman.

Jewel.

Jewel.

Her wrist suddenly burned with the force of the single word: her name. Avandar's mark was glowing.

You will die here. If you die, every one of your chosen kin will perish with you. Not just Angel, but all of your den. The forest you planted, the forest you rule *will be unbound in a moment. What do you think the forest denizens will do with the little that remains of your city then? You are angry. I confess it did not occur to me that you could not see this far.*

And her wrist bled. She could see the wound, but could not feel it, so potent was her fury.

Will you throw away everything you have done, every gain you have made, in a moment of fury? You cannot *change what will happen.* The tenor of his voice changed as she stilled. *What she said was true. She could not crown Adam. Adam will never be hers—not as the Winter King was. I could never have been Winter King, for the same reason.*

Babies are entirely dependent on the person who feeds them, cares for them, protects them. All babies.

You do not understand, he said again. *And even if you did, you would not be at peace. The babe is not the child of mortals. I had expected this from Adam. Not from you.*

Adam.

She froze, her wrist throbbing. She had heard the phrase "seeing red" for much of her life and understood it as metaphor—but her vision seemed filmed, unsteady, the air surrounding her thick with emotional fog.

This is why Ariane had asked her to name a boon when she had asked it.

Avandar nodded quietly.

She had. She had not intended to ask for what she had asked—and she felt, as she tried to inhale, that she had traded the life of an infant for Carver's life. Something he would have hated and would never, ever have asked.

To her lasting surprise, Kallandras joined her; she startled when he landed. What she had not allowed Avandar, she allowed the bard. He took both of her hands in either of his while she trembled with rage—and guilt.

"She did not agree to save your city," he said, his voice so soft she should have barely been able to make out the words. "Do you remember why?"

Did she? Her hands tightened; his remained loose. He did not intend to hold her here if she could not force herself to stay. "She couldn't be certain she could grant it."

Kallandras nodded. "I have spoken with Evayne. I asked her to come to you; she could not bring herself to do so. Not yet. In decades—her decades—she will do far worse than you feel you have done, here. But in decades, she will finally be strong enough to learn—truly—why she *must*. She is young, now, here. She was brought to the Hidden Court to learn the magics she must know in her own future. You have seen the results, in your past.

"Had you understood, when you walked through that arch, the fate of Shianne's child, had you asked that, in return for the Summer Tree, Ariane spare the infant, she would have made the same reply that she made when you asked that she save your city. If the infant is not born here, if he is not raised here, if he does not serve as Summer King, the sapling that you preserved and offered to her would have no meaning.

"Among us, there are those who would serve her as King; it is the whole of their desire. But among those, there are none who could serve as Summer King."

"She said Adam—"

"She was not kind, Terafin. But she said, also, that Adam would never be hers. Could he, he would be a Summer King beyond compare. But if he is moved, even to tears, by the White Lady, she is not, and will never be, the whole of his desire. Had you understood, had you asked for the infant's life, she could not grant that boon. And, Terafin, you are not bard-born. You are aware that the bard-born can command."

Jewel nodded, although it was not a question.

"They can make themselves heard across great distances, no matter what stands between them and their audience."

She nodded again.

"Are you aware that the bard-born also listen?"

Her nod was slower although she offered it to him.

"Then understand: that infant is not a child in the way of our kind. Perhaps he once was, but he has spent centuries—more—hearing the voice of his mother. He has learned to speak, to think. He understands the whole of his mother's desire; he understands the purpose of his existence. He has waited, and waited, and waited for this moment: to be born, at last, in the shadows of the White Lady, that he might love her as his mother loved her, and free her, as even his mother could not."

"He's an infant," Jewel countered. "And the very young *always* want to please their mothers. He doesn't know—"

"—What he wants? That is not true. You might argue that it is true of mortal children, that it was true of you; that consequences are things that are not clear to the very young."

"Kallandras, *he's an infant.*"

"He is an infant born as the instrument of the very gods, and that fate has never sat kindly upon the shoulders of the merely mortal. I understand the burden of guilt, and if you must shoulder it to remain true to yourself, I cannot relieve you of its weight. But, Terafin, in this, you, too, are such an instrument." He released her hands. "She will not grant what you ask because she cannot. This war has become the purpose of her existence, and she has humbled herself in order to fight it. But she *will* fight it. Should that war require the sacrifice of every citizen of our Empire, she would sacrifice them all without so much as blinking.

"You have not sacrificed an infant to save your kin. She would never have granted that request." He bowed then, and the wind took him, sweeping him gracefully into the air. He looked part of it, somehow, as if his feet had never truly touched the ground.

She was left standing in his wake.

The sun in a court that was timeless nonetheless turned; the shades of high noon ceded sky to dusk. Shadows slanted, and warmth dissipated; night fell. Jewel lingered near the lake Cessaly had called a bath. She had chosen to shed the white dress, to pack it—with care, although care was not required. She had also removed the fussy adornments with which she had girded herself, but she handled those more carefully.

The ring, however, she did not remove. This was not for lack of trying. Or perhaps lack of wanting to try, on some visceral level.

Angel did not hover. He understood her mood, understood her anger, understood her need to pace as if pacing were a foot race it was necessary to win. Even in the days when the den had been crammed into two rooms, her den-kin—with the exception of Duster—knew when to leave her alone. But he was never far.

Nor, to her surprise, was Terrick. Something had shifted in him when Shianne had gone into labor, and it had not yet righted itself.

Kallandras, for the most part, kept company with Lord Celleriant. But if the meeting in the vast, open-skied audience chamber had done nothing else for Celleriant, it had nevertheless made it clear that he *would*, one day, call this Court home again. The Winter Queen had made clear to all who observed that she considered Celleriant of value.

They did not doubt her.

Jewel wondered if they even could.

And her thoughts drifted, as she wondered, to the *Kialli*, and to Darranatos. From there, they moved to Shianne and her sisters. To Shianne herself. Darranatos had, in his fashion, loved the god they did not name. And he had, in his fashion, loved the White Lady. Even at the end, she had heard, in his rage and sorrow, the tremulous desire that the White Lady be *exalted*. If he had chosen to serve Allasakar—even thinking the name was an act of defiance—he had desired, for Ariane, a place, a singular place, of honor by that god's side.

She had never forgiven those who had chosen to desert her.

She would never forgive them.

And she would never forgive the Lord of the Hells. Jewel had not understood the depth of her enmity; she had assumed—and why?—that any living being must oppose Allasakar. The gods did. The gods had.

But for the Winter Queen, it was personal, and Jewel wondered then if the seasons—Winter and Summer—existed as they did solely because of that enmity; they had not existed in that fashion in Shianne's time.

That time, as so many others, had passed. She bowed her head. The whole of her focus was turned, had been turned, toward the newborn infant.

Perhaps, because it was, she did not immediately notice the presence of a visitor. She didn't notice, in fact, until that visitor cleared her throat.

Evayne a'Nolan stood, hands clasped behind her back, waiting for Jewel's attention. Jewel turned to fully face her. Some of the bitterness, some of the anger, deserted her as she studied the lines of the young woman's face, softened by dusk and the gentler lights that alleviated darkness. She had, she realized, never been older than Evayne. Even when Evayne had come to Terafin as a woman younger than the one who only barely met her gaze now, Jewel had been younger still.

What must it be like, to age naturally, while the people you knew jumped back and forth in time, in a constant and unpredictable way? How did you build a history with them, or with anyone? What must the future look like to one whose future was a simple march of entirely unconnected days? What home could you build? What family?

She shook herself as her thoughts returned to Shianne's child and turned away again.

"I saw you here," Evayne said, when Jewel's back was turned. "The first time I tried to look into the future—into the Winter Queen's future—I saw you."

"Did you tell her?"

"No. I've been told that I'll become better at understanding, at teasing out meaning from what I do see. It's—" She fell silent, and this time, when Jewel turned again, she continued. "It's harder. I have to make decisions when I'm uncertain—and I'm uncertain all the time." She exhaled. "This is the first time, since I made the choice to walk the Oracle's path, that I've stayed in one place. I—" She shook her head. "You know Meralonne."

Jewel nodded slowly.

"I saw him regularly. Day after day. He was almost normal."

"I cannot imagine the life that you would have to lead to consider Meralonne APhaniel almost normal."

Evayne's eyes widened, and then—to Jewel's surprise—she laughed. Jewel had never seen her laugh before.

"I understand that the Hidden Court is a dangerous place, that you would not be here were the situation not so desperate—but I think it might be the last home I will ever be allowed." This was said with no humor at all. "I have never seen the court in Summer. I have seen only the Winter face of the White Lady."

"You will see the Summer face," Jewel said, although the words left her mouth almost of their own accord.

Evayne heard the certainty and understood its source—she was perhaps the only living person who could understand it so completely. She bowed her head again. "What Cessaly makes now—and she cannot be diverted or interrupted, although the Arianni sometimes amuse themselves by making the attempt—she makes for you. She is not aware of it. She does not do it consciously. But it is for you, and you must take it and keep it with you." A shadow crossed her face.

Jewel could see herself in that shadow, in multiple ways. And she faced them all. "What have you seen of me?"

Evayne lowered her head, but not before Jewel saw the ripple of pain cross her features.

"Tell me, instead, about the child."

"Ariane will not leave when you depart. She cannot. The child is too young. But what she said was truth: time passes for mortals who remain in the Hidden Court. When you leave this court, you will leave almost in the moment you entered it, as far as the world without is concerned. If she leaves the court, she will leave the same way. But for the mortals within, time passes as it always passes. Even for people like me." The last was said with a trace of pain, of a bitterness that had not yet passed.

"When you are older," Jewel said, "all of this will make sense to you. Every choice you've made, every painful decision. You will look back on it, and you will understand it all."

"I understand it now," Evayne said.

Jewel exhaled. "Sorry." She ran hands through her hair although it was pointless; the hair was bound. "You'll accept it. You won't hate yourself, or hate the Oracle, or any of those things."

Silence for one long beat. "Is that how it worked for you?" There was no barb in the question; it was honest. Earnest.

"No."

This surprised a wry smile out of Evayne.

"I think that's how it works when you're older, though."

"How *much* older?"

"When you're older than I am now, you're a power. You're a power to be reckoned with. You don't look doubtful. You don't look conflicted. You move with purpose, walk with purpose."

"Maybe," Evayne replied, "I've just gotten better at hiding it. To me, you don't look filled with doubt."

Jewel stared at her. After a pause, in which she considered her words, she said, "Or maybe we've both gotten better at hiding it. I don't want to leave the baby here."

"If you take the child with you, she will never be free of this Court. She will not wither, she will not be damaged; I do not think the *Kialli* would accept it. They will kill the Arianni wherever they can—but I am not at all certain they would raise arms against the White Lady. And Jewel—I do not think we can win this war if the White Lady remains trapped in this court."

We.

"I don't understand all of what she did. But she is part of the wilderness. She always was. She was scion of gods, but not free to leave when they left.

Winter magic is the magic most used by the Lord of the Hells when he walks this plane. He will not be helpless in Summer—no god would be, could they walk as he walks now—but he will not be as strong. We have a hope of surviving his presence because the plane itself is not what it was, and it will not conform easily to his desires.

"But we need Summer. We *need* Summer." She hesitated, as if trying to decide how much more she could safely say. Then she lowered her head. Head lowered, she continued to speak. "I envied you. I *had* friends. I had a family. My mother—my adoptive mother—is still alive, but from the day I turned sixteen, I haven't set eyes on her. I might never see her again. I wanted—I *so* wanted—to ask my mother's advice. I wanted to visit my friends.

"I never wanted to leave them."

Jewel waited.

"I left them because it was the *only* way I had any hope of saving their lives. But their lives are lost to me, anyway. You *have* a home. You have a family, even if your parents left you orphaned in the streets of an unfriendly city. If you make this decision—if you choose to leave the baby to Ariane—you'll still return to them. You'll return to a home. You'll see that home when the sun rises, see it when it sets. You'll hear the voices you know and love in something other than memory. Your kin, chosen or otherwise, will see you, and they'll know you.

"I envied you."

Jewel was silent.

"I envy you still." Her smile, however, had a glimmer of something else in it. "But I begin to understand why I live the life I live. There are things I know I must do that you could not do, because you have so much to lose."

"I don't—"

"You do. Your sense of who you are is necessary. It's not what I have. It's not what I'm *allowed* to have. But it's necessary." As she spoke, Jewel saw a hint of the woman she would become in the lines of her face, the set of her jaw. "This is necessary. I am sorry. If you try to interfere here, I will stop you. I have no choice. If every action I am to take—if every action I have *already* taken—is not to be wasted, not to be pointless, I have no choice."

Jewel exhaled until there was no air in her lungs, until she felt the lack as an emptiness, a hollowness that must be filled. Her hands were fists; she felt she might never unclench them.

"Will he be happy?"

And Evayne said, "Does it matter?" The voice of her anger, her envy, at last finding some escape.

Chapter Thirteen

7th day of Lattan, 428 A.A.
Terafin Manse, Averalaan Aramarelas

FINCH STIFFENED BEFORE HAVAL did. She turned, almost blindly, toward the tree of fire, reaching for its trunk. Haval, who had been silent, frowned, the line etching itself into the corners of his mouth, his eyes. He did not ask her why she had startled, which was good—she asked herself that question and could come up with no answer, no explanation. Haval was a man who relied on instinct—but he could turn instinct into pointed, acute observation should words be required to explain it.

They were not required now.

Haval raised his voice. No, Finch thought, as his words cut through the fog of sudden fear, that was wrong. He honed it. But he was Councillor in this forest, and his voice—cold, sudden, sharp—was the only voice the forest heard. Until the moment he spoke, Finch had not realized that she was *part of* the forest. But she would not forget.

"They are coming. Prepare."

She did not ask who. As the ground shook beneath her feet, she thought she understood. She had never desired the presence of demons—she considered herself far too rational, far too sane, to ever desire that. But in the wake of Haval's grim expression, she thought demons would be the safer threat.

When Barston threw open the door to Teller's office, Teller jumped. Barston was stiff, officious; many members of the House thought he was possessed of only one or two expressions. They might have preferred that to the open expression of panic on his face. It chilled Teller, because Barston *did not* panic. Ever.

But as Teller opened the book on his desk, Barston entered his office, and Teller saw immediately the reason for his secretary's expression. Behind Barston, armed and armored, were two warriors who did not appear to be even remotely human.

He was accustomed to Celleriant, who was not mortal. His skin was pale, his eyes, silver and his hair a perfect platinum. But if Lord Celleriant was other, he was an ideal that existed at the far range of mortal daydreams.

Not so, these two.

They were golden-skinned, green-eyed; their eyes were a single color. Instead of hair, they had trailing leaves, and their fingers were long and gnarled, resembling roots far more than they did human hands. But they wore armor now, and they carried long spears. They did not blink as Teller met their gaze.

He swallowed.

Barston was silent. The etiquette of the right-kin's office was largely political, and Barston could deal with even the most enraged of patricians without so much as raising his voice. This, however, was beyond him. Sadly, it was also beyond Teller.

The Chosen—Marave and Gordon—did not enter the office, which was unusual. They were tense, but they had not yet drawn weapons. Teller closed the book on his desk and then lifted it, tucking it under his right arm.

To Barston he said, "Send a message immediately to the Master of the Household Staff."

Such was Barston's dislike for that august woman that he almost immediately sank beneath the patina of his normal self. "Do you wish me to have her summoned?"

"Yes. Make clear," he added softly, "that it is an emergency; this is not a council of war, but the beginnings of the battle." To the *arborii*, he said, "Will you wait here?"

"We are to accompany you," the one on the left said. "If you remain here, we will remain here. If you are to leave, we will be your escort."

The Chosen didn't even bridle.

"What has happened?" he asked.

As one, they turned to look at a wall. It was, Teller thought, the wall that faced the heart of the city itself.

The Master of the Household Staff might have had her own mage-born talent, given the speed with which she responded to Barston's summons. She did not seem to find the presence of the trees worthy of more than the briefest of glances. Teller had always admired her—from the safest distance possible—and that admiration now grew. He hoped, however, it didn't show on his face; she would not approve. He never quite understood her position in the hierarchy of the House; he knew only that she was the person Jay found most intimidating. Or terrifying.

"It's time," he told her. "Gather the Household Staff and lead them to the forest."

One of the two trees said, "It is best to approach from above. The path between your dwelling and the forest itself is becoming less stable."

"Above?" the Master of the Household Staff said. "Do you mean from The Terafin's personal chambers?"

The question confused the trees; it did not, however, confuse Teller. "Yes."

"That door—"

"I will make certain the door is open." He headed toward the smaller door of his own office. "My duty now is to rouse the *rest* of the Household and see them safely out as well."

"Perhaps you could forget to inform a Council Member or two," she replied. It was the only indication that she was highly unsettled; under normal circumstances she would never, ever have forgotten herself so much.

Barston had regained his composure. "I will send word to the Council members currently in residence."

But Teller shook his head. "We won't have the pages to deliver them; they are Household Staff." And not a single one of them would be left behind; not when they received their orders. "I will go, in person. You," he added, "will close up the office and evacuate."

It was a comfort to Teller to see Barston's mutinous expression. It was a hint of normalcy in a day in which normal would be otherwise painfully absent. And he was taking advantage of the presence of the Master of the Household Staff; if Barston was willing to argue with Teller, he would not condescend to do so while "that woman" was present.

7th day of Lattan, 428 A.A.
The Common, Averalaan

For one long, breathless moment, Jester thought the ground across the city had broken; that the whole of Averalaan's hundred holdings would now fall and shatter, just as the city-beneath-the-city once had. All its citizens, many of whom were just waking in the darkness before the dawn, would fall with it, and time would make skeletons of them, just as it had made skeletons of the citizens of that darkened, ancient city through which the den had scavenged.

He did not fall, although the stone carvings beneath his feet gave way; Snow's wings snapped to the side, and he hovered, as if the existence of stone itself were a trifling convenience, easily dismissed. The Kings, their *Astari*, the Exalted, and the priests that attended them had not clambered onto the back of a large, winged cat—but they did not fall as the stone fell. And from the vantage of Snow's back, rescued from the grim pull of gravity, Jester could see that the stone that had crumbled had been the carvings, laid out in a very large circle, around the base of the statue of Moorelas.

That statue, unlike the stone, did not immediately crumble or fall; Jester could not see what was supporting it. But perhaps that was because his eyes could not penetrate the darkness beneath the statue's feet, not immediately.

Moorelas raised stone sword and looked down. Stone did not generally offer much in the way of expression, but it seemed to Jester that he could see sorrow in the graven face. Sorrow and loss. It was a brief glimpse, no more, because Jester could now see what Moorelas saw.

Beneath the statue's feet—beneath what had once been stone that had purported to tell his legend, his story, something was, at last, rising from its temporary grave. It was not a figure, not a form, not a person or even persons, although Jester had expected three. He wasn't even certain what he was looking at as it rose, slowly, from that darkened, hidden place.

But it did rise. Snow growled, the fur on his immediately visible body rising almost in time to the sound of his voice.

And Jester fell utterly silent, became completely still, all movement dependent on Snow, as his mind resolved what his eyes were seeing: A spire.

A spire was rising from beneath what had once been, and would never again be, a sanctum.

The High Wilderness

Cessaly came to Jewel at dawn, and the dawn in the Hidden Court was glorious. Jewel saw the brilliant hue of sky, the welcome return of sun and light, and felt it from a great remove. Sleep had been slow to come, and much interrupted.

Cessaly, however, did not rush in; she waited, almost as hesitant as Evayne had been. This woman, Jewel could believe was almost her age; her expression was careworn and almost adult. "It's time," she said quietly. There was a gravity to the words, and to the line of her shoulders, her chin.

"I made something."

Jewel nodded.

"I think it's for you."

"You're not certain?" she asked, before she could bite back the words.

Cessaly's smile was almost weary. "I'm never entirely certain. Sometimes I'm moved to Make, and I can't see anything else. I can see what I envision, but that's the whole of my focus, my will." She exhaled. "But sometimes the making is arduous, and it takes everything I have. Every talent-born speck of power. Sometimes, then, I can open my eyes and see the world clearly.

"And, today, I can." She lifted her hands, her palms cupped. Her fingernails were chipped, her hands rough and reddened. Jewel's eyes narrowed. The hands had been bleeding. Although Cessaly had taken some care to clean up, she didn't have, or perhaps couldn't tolerate, attendants.

Jewel's hands remained at her sides. "Did Evayne send you?" she asked, refusing to raise them.

"Evayne?" Cessaly frowned in confusion.

Evayne had said she had lived in the Hidden Court, but Jewel had not thought, would not have thought, to ask for how long. Cessaly had been in the wilderness for longer. But Cessaly's confusion did not clear.

She wondered, then, what the Guild of Makers might look like with Cessaly as its titular head and shied away from that thought; the brief amusement it afforded her was both bitter and unkind, and neither would do her any good.

It was, in any case, neither bitterness nor unkindness that kept her hands at her sides; she knew the flavor of this emotion. She was afraid.

She did not hear her Oma's voice, but could feel that aged woman's disgust; words weren't necessary. Jewel had faced *demons*. Gods. Immortals. She had walked in halls so ancient she could almost taste the dawn of the world in their fall. Was she, then, to be afraid of the gift of the maker-born?

Artisan, she thought, correcting herself. But, regardless, her Oma's disgust would not be moved. "What—what is it?"

"It is, I think, a ring," Cessaly replied, her brow creased.

"You think?"

"You will understand, Terafin."

"Did Gilafas tell you that it was for me?"

She looked almost shocked at the question, which probably meant no. But her face creased in a soft smile. "Thank you. Thank you for bringing him to me. He has been searching for too long."

"Will you come back with him?"

"He will remain by my side until we at last return to Fabril's reach," she replied, which was evasive.

"But the Order—"

"I do not think it is safe for him to travel where you now travel. I have begged the White Lady this one boon, and she has granted it. If you are worried for Gilafas—and I see that you are—be at peace. He will be safer here than he would be in your own city."

Your own city, Jewel thought. Not ours.

"I have spoken with your cat. He is difficult, but warm, and I would trust him with your life. But not with Gilafas'. Trust me, instead."

"It is not you, Cessaly, who will keep him safe or fail to keep him safe. It is the Winter Queen."

Cessaly smiled; her hands remained extended, her fingers curved gently to form a cup of her palm.

"What will it do?"

"What is needed," Cessaly replied. "Only that. It is a work, but it is not a work of war; it is not a scepter, not a sword, not a crown. It will not be a bulwark behind which to stand; it will not be armor in which to wage war. And it cannot protect you from the consequences of the choices you must make."

Jewel listened to the list of everything that Cessaly had not made, and she felt her shoulders unclenching. There was something in that solemn list that seemed apologetic, as if, somehow, all Making must be an act of war, or in service to it. But the Guild of Makers was not the wealthiest of guilds because they made weapons and armor—although they did that, as well. No: they were wealthy because what they made, they made well, and often, they created and captured the essence of beauty—not a seen thing alone, but a thing felt.

And maybe it was to deny that apology, that implication that the creation itself, because it was not part of this long war, was less valuable, less important, that Jewel lifted her hand, opened her palm.

Cessaly closed her eyes. Jewel could now see that her arms were trembling, as if unaccustomed to the physical effort of keeping them still, of keeping them half-raised. Or as if she had borne a great weight she could now set down.

Jewel felt warmth. Only warmth, as if there was nothing at all between Cessaly's callused palms and her own. She could not ascertain shape, size; could not see what Cessaly had Made at all. And yet she *knew* that Cessaly had passed something into her hands—something whose weight she was obviously relieved to shed.

"I don't understand," Jewel whispered.

Cessaly said softly, "I don't understand, either. People ask me *how* I Make. They ask me *why*. But, Terafin, how do you *see*? Why do you see? To describe it at all is not in me. I understand that I do Make. And when driven, I understand why. But they are felt compulsions, things that seem to move me, more than to be driven or commanded. I can tell you how to work gold or silver or platinum. I can tell you how to carve wood. I can explain all these things, and in detail—I couldn't always," she added, with a trace of rare self-consciousness. "But none of these things answer the question that people are actually asking of me. Of us.

"If you ask, I will tell you what went into the making. But what went into it is not what it is."

"I don't understand what it is. You said you thought it might be a ring—but I can't see or feel a ring."

"What do you see or feel?"

Jewel was afraid to answer truthfully, but that fear, at least, was normal. "Nothing."

Cessaly did not look concerned. "It was difficult to work with the materials. And I do not think Gilafas understood. But you will," she added softly. "Can I come and visit you after this is over?"

Jewel blinked as Cessaly retrieved her hands. She looked at her own cupped palms; they remained, to her eyes, empty. But she knew that what Cessaly had given her remained with her; knew as well that she could lower her hands, and she would not drop it. "If we all survive, yes. Come visit me. You can bring Gilafas. Or he can bring you."

Cessaly lowered her gaze and shook her head, side to side, as if exaggerated motion were breath. "He must go home."

"But—"

"And I must stay here." Lifting that gaze again, she added, "I promised. But—the ways are open, and *she* promised that if the ways opened again, and if we had somehow helped achieve this, I *could* visit."

"She will keep her word," Jewel heard herself say. And then, in almost the same tone, added, "And I will keep mine. You will be welcome in my home at any time you care to visit."

The maker-born girl's eyes became suddenly more sly. "And can I Make with the things I find there?"

"Not without permission."

This seemed to satisfy Cessaly.

"Eat. Eat and sleep."

Cessaly nodded. "I wanted to see you before you left, and you'll be leaving soon."

Jewel nodded again.

Packing to leave was not an exalted event. Although legends made much of leave-takings and Jewel could be forgiven the feeling that she was walking in legend itself, there was no ceremony. The Winter Queen did not summon her court, did not preside upon her unearthly throne, and did not bless them with gifts. Or words.

The Winter King—Jewel's Winter King—joined them as they packed.

You don't want to stay?

He did.

And if I order you to remain?

In the end, it is the White Lady's commands I obey, and she has made clear what she desires of me. Jewel had thought he might radiate despair and was surprised he did not.

Did you not hear her? What I have given her no one else could have given her—her freedom. She will ride, Jewel. She will ride—not to hunt, but to war. She will summon the whole of the host.

But you'll be stuck with me.

She felt his instant disapproval, and for some strange reason, that buoyed spirits that were almost as low as they could become. How much more would she have to surrender? How much of herself could she abandon—as she was abandoning this baby—and still *be* herself?

Celleriant was likewise subdued, but Jewel had expected that; nor did she order him to remain. She understood, on a bone-deep level, that he was *hers*. He was hers, not in the way the den was, but perhaps in a way that was as close as the Arianni themselves could come: he had chosen. And while she lived, he would fight for her; if it became necessary, he would die for her.

And if he died, she thought, he would never truly come home. Would never again see the Summer Court, see the wilderness at the height of its wakefulness. She had never liked him; he was too cold, too austere, and too casually bloodthirsty for that. But she had not, on the day she had ridden up the side of a great tree, wanted him to suffer. And the only time she had seen him weep— She shook her head.

As if he could hear that thought, he turned toward her. And, to her great surprise, he smiled. If the smile was not precisely warm, it was as close to warmth as she had ever seen him come.

Terrick and Angel shouldered packs, and if Jewel thought that the White

Lady had left them nothing of significance, Terrick demurred. "She spoke with Angel while you were speaking with the young woman. We offered to call you, but she seemed to think the young woman's meeting was too important to interrupt. She's lightened the bags we carry a great deal." Something in his tone made this sound less appealing than it should have.

"Is there something wrong?"

"No." He could have said yes, could have *shouted* yes, in the same tone.

Jewel signed to Angel, and her den-kin grimaced behind his Rendish companion's broad back. "Her attendants emptied our packs for us. They didn't openly criticize their contents, but they made clear that we were to leave them behind. I imagine, given their disposition, to be burned."

And well they should be, the Winter King said. *They are not fit for your use.*

We used them well enough on the road here. On all the roads.

And what she has condescended to share will be far, far more valuable; it will not wear, it will not fray, it will not tarnish. Dirt will not cling to it, nor water, where water is undesired. She has gifted *you with things ancient that were highly coveted in* my *reign.*

Do you even know what she gave them?

I know that it will be of far more use, far more value, than what they had.

Which meant no.

She didn't ask Angel if he trusted the gift; doubting Ariane in a fashion that could not be ignored was never going to be wise. Jewel herself trusted the Winter Queen in this regard but understood why Terrick was disgruntled. Kallandras joined them shortly thereafter. He asked, in the way of the bard-born, after Master Gilafas, but Jewel shook her head. "He'll join us when he's able." Lifting her voice, she called for Shadow; he came instantly, as if he had been directly underfoot all this time, unseen and unheard.

His voice was not the Winter King's; he said nothing. But he paced restlessly, and Jewel was certain she would hear a volley of his favorite words—*stupid* and *boring*—the minute he was no longer a guest in the White Lady's court. And that, too, was comforting.

What was not comforting was the prospect of what she might face upon her return. But she understood that Ariane would come, at the head of her host; that she would, as she could, preserve what was left of Averalaan in the face of the enraged princes whose slumber had finally broken. It was Jewel's job—if it could be called that—to hold out until that moment.

The last Summer.

The last Summer, the last Summer King.

She felt the shadow of doubt as she fastened buttons. Shianne had found

Ariane markedly changed; might the Sleepers not, in the end, feel the same? And, if so, would they obey her? Would they heed her at all? She had no answers. No insight, no certainty, came to alleviate her doubts.

Regardless, she had her duties. She could not remain here, waiting. *But these lands are timeless.*

No, Terafin. When you are told that you will emerge at the same moment you left, this is not accurate. In the eyes of the immortal, it is truth. One day, two days, are of little relevance; they might notice the passing of hours more keenly because the sun has set or risen. But time does pass. It is why the White Lady did not bid you wait here, in safety, until she is ready.

No, it's not. This, Jewel spoke with certainty. *She's afraid that if I remain, I will do everything in my power to influence the child as he grows.*

He did not directly disagree, but instead said, *Nonetheless, the point remains. To the Wild Hunt, no time will have passed. But to you and yours, a day might pass, or even a few hours, before the White Lady might at last take command of all roads that lead into—and out of—her lands. Can you risk those hours? Can you risk that day? You, too, will age, as the child ages.*

I'm not worried about aging.

No, Terafin. Worry, instead, about the lost hours, the lost day.

She bowed her head. Lifted it and turned, almost blindly, toward Angel. Angel who could not hear her discussion with the Winter King and had not spoken a word about the infant. Nor had he spoken with Adam; no one had. Adam had remained with Shianne and the child, as if the whole of the world and the threat of gods and demons was less relevant, by far, than the immediate needs of a new mother and her babe.

But it was time, now, for Adam to leave. Had they been in a more neutral court, a more neutral land, she would have been almost relieved to leave him here; she had no doubt that Ariane would protect him. But here, the line between protection and ownership was far too thin, and Jewel understood that this was not the place that Adam must at last call home. She did not know why, but she did not question it; perhaps later, she would.

Adam could be Summer King.

Almost gently, the Winter King said, *She said he will never be hers.*

Yes, by his own choice. But if he remains here—

No, Terafin. He might offer to take the child's place—and indeed, I think it likely if he remains—but it is not enough to offer. What she requires, I do not believe it is in your Adam to give.

He's not— She stopped. Squared shoulders. What she had been about to say was not, on some fundamental level, true.

He is not yours?

She did not agree. Could not agree. *He's* one of *mine*, she finally said. *He's den.*

You did not choose him.

He didn't need a family when I first met him. He doesn't need one now. He has a family to return to, and they're waiting. But she exhaled. *Finch found him in the Houses of Healing. Finch brought him home. And he's made a second home for himself here, with the den. He* is *one of mine. And I will not leave him here to her.*

He would be safer.

Jewel did not reply.

And if he wishes to stay?

She lifted a hand, signed a single word. *Adam.*

Angel moved. She could hear his retreat but did not turn to witness it. When he returned, Adam was by his side. But so, too, Shianne. Shianne wore the dress Snow had created for her at Jewel's request. Her hair was pulled back, bound in a very patrician style that implied power, certainty. Her eyes were gray—gray and clear. To Jewel's great discomfort, Shianne bowed. To her. It was not a perfunctory gesture; it was a sweeping, graceful physical expression of utter obeisance.

Shadow hissed and stepped on Jewel's foot before Jewel could tell Shianne to rise, and to stop. His foot was not light.

Shianne lifted her face, to meet Jewel's embarrassed gaze, and an odd smile touched her face, shaped by curve of lip and corners of eyes and something other that Jewel couldn't immediately name.

"I have asked one boon of the White Lady," she said, rising.

Celleriant was instantly alert, but Shianne had turned, briefly, toward Adam.

"And that boon?"

"I wish to travel with you now. She will come to your city when she is capable of leaving, and I . . . do not wish to stay."

"But—but—the baby—"

"No child will be cared for as this child is cared for, and no child born to mortal parents will *ever* be so exalted as he will become. It is not his death that will free the White Lady, do you not understand that? It is his life. It is his commitment to Summer and the White Lady herself."

"Adam says that the child desires this."

Jewel turned immediately toward the Voyani youth. She even opened her mouth. But the words would not leave her.

"He is not like other infants," Adam said, voice unusually hesitant. "From the first, Matriarch, he *had* voice, he had thoughts, he had a will of his own."

"He had *his mother's* will."

"Ah, no. He had mother love—and in some fashion, no matter how broken it might become, we all have that. But in time, we grow away from it, apart from it." He frowned. "No. It is not that. When born, we are new; what we have is that. We do not name it, we do not understand enough *to* name it. We change because we find the words and the thoughts to name it—but by that time, we name other things as well. It is not that our love lessens, but it is no longer the center of our world, no longer the whole of it; our world becomes larger, and larger still.

"His world is not the world an infant sees."

Jewel could not believe that these words had come from Adam. She had expected something different; had expected that, of all people present, he would be the most upset, that he would shoulder the most guilt. That he would judge her.

And he wouldn't; she saw that now. To Adam, no matter what he might call her, she *was* Matriarch. Matriarch of Terafin, a clan that disavowed blood ties, but nonetheless was kin. Had Adam been Havallan, he would not have flinched when Yollana had sacrificed—literally—three Havallans against future need.

What would the Voyani do, should their Matriarchs be monsters? What *had* they done?

And Shadow said, "They killed."

She startled.

"But you will be different. You are Sen."

"I don't want to *be* a monster."

"No. But that is a word, and it is a word that others choose. You will be what you are. At last." And lifting his head, he roared. Jewel could feel the ground beneath her feet tremble. The wind rose, tugging at her hair, at Angel's. It pulled at clothing, at scarves; the only thing it did not touch was Shianne's dress. Even her hair, however, flew in its folds.

So, too, the Arianni, the Wild Hunt. They had been entirely absent until Shadow roared; they were not absent now. In the light of early dawn, they brought a harsh, blue light, carried in hands and across arms.

Jewel immediately dropped her hand to the cat's head; because he hadn't bothered to remove his foot, he was practically standing on top of her.

They were ready for combat.

Shadow, however, sniffed. He sniffed *loudly*, as if the presence of mere Arianni swords was almost an insult to his dignity.

"Shadow—"

"I did *nothing*," he said, before she could follow his name with more words. "I said *good-bye*."

The Arianni did not look nearly as skeptical as Jewel herself felt.

"I said it so it would be *heard*."

One of the Arianni turned to Jewel. His sword was lowered, but it did not vanish, although the blades of most of the others did. Jewel did not recognize him, but she'd always had difficulty telling the Arianni apart. "You ask too much," he said to Jewel.

It was Shianne who replied, her voice chilling instantly into something appropriate for a very bitter winter. "She did not ask it of the Lady. I asked. The boon granted was granted *to me*."

Silence.

"Do you have so little faith in the White Lady? So little trust? She did not argue, did not refuse."

"It is not the White Lady we do not trust."

"Ah. So your lack of faith is in me?"

"You are not one of our people."

"No. And you believe, somehow, that I am now helpless? I, who was born when the Lady was young, who was gifted and graced with the heart of her power? Do you believe that I am incapable of surviving what mortals, born without these gifts, can survive?" A flicker of fire entered the ice; it was a striking combination.

To Jewel's surprise, it was the Arianni man who took an instinctive step back. In some fashion, it surprised her; the Arianni she knew—albeit only two—seemed to revel in combat, regardless of the possible outcomes. And she had no doubt—at all—that that was exactly what Shianne was now offering.

You think of her as mortal, Avandar said.

She is.

So, too, am I, Jewel. There was the slender edge of a smile in the words—the kind the unwary could cut themselves on. *She is not what your den is. She is not what your Angel is. She will age, yes. She will die. But should she desire it? She might destroy the entirety of the Council of the Magi before that death. You cannot sense her power. You see her only through the lens of her sacrifice. You think of her as lesser than she was. So, too, does she. But you have never fully understood what she is.*

Do you think she could win?

Oh, yes. But that is an unfair question. If she challenged this man, and he won, he would pay. Ariane has made clear that in the limited length of time remaining to Shianne, she is to be valued. While she lives, she is Ariane's, and only Ariane's.

Does he envy her?

No. Envy of Ariane is not in them. She is their heart. They will want what she wants.

But—

The Allasiani?

Jewel nodded.

They will want, he repeated, his internal voice softer, *what she wants. We want and need different things, and there will often be conflicts between those desires. Did you expect that she would be different? The difference is one of scale. She made her choice, Jewel, but that desire remained. It was reflected in some fashion in those who were part of her. None of that now remains. She will destroy her ancient enemy, or she will see him destroyed. And she will not care if she must destroy the rest of the mortal world to do so. Remember that.*

He then turned to Shianne, who stood, unarmed but no longer helpless. "Lady."

Shianne inclined her head, her bearing military, her demeanor cold.

"Come. The gate."

She turned. She did not speak to the man again; he might have been invisible for all the relevance she now granted him. But she did turn to Adam, and her smile, if hardened by the expression in which it sat, was warmer. "It is almost time," she told him gently. "To go home."

He flushed.

Jewel almost said that Adam's home was in the distant South, but she could not force the words from her lips, and realized, only then, that Shianne did not refer to Averalaan.

Only let him *make his way* home. Let him return alive and whole.

Shadow removed his paw.

Together, in a silence made tense by Shianne's august displeasure, they made their way to the frame that Gilafas ADelios had built. The guildmaster and Cessaly did not come to make their farewells, and Jewel wondered how old Gilafas ADelios would be when he did, at last, return to mortal lands.

Shadow, however, hissed. "Do you not *understand?*" He uttered the sibilant word *stupid* three times, as if it were a charm. Celleriant was instantly offended, instantly angry. Of course, he was; they remained in the lands of the White Lady, where dignity and respect were the necessary adornments of the powerful.

Jewel placed a hand on the cat's head, a gesture as natural, by this point, as breathing.

"There *are* no mortal *landsssss.* There *never* were. You were *stupid.* You thought what *you* saw was all there was *to* see. The world is *waking.*"

"Shadow, could you tell me this after we've left?"

He hissed.

She did not particularly care what the cat said or how he said it—not for her own sake. But she could see that Celleriant did, and she wanted Shadow to be more mindful for his. Which, she accepted, would never happen for long; it was almost miraculous that Shadow had been so well-behaved, so silent, for the time that had already passed here.

There was no hesitation, as she approached the standing arch of vine and branch and leaves, *Ellariannatte,* all. She did not pause, did not turn back, did not speak. Almost as if she were fleeing, she stepped firmly through that arch. As she did, she noted that Shadow's steps matched hers; that he lifted forepaw and set it down as she lifted leg and set down foot. He had passed through the arch the first time in exactly the same way.

His feet did not remain long on the snow-covered earth; he pushed up, off it, spreading wings in a snap of restless motion. The sky could contain the force of the great cat's restlessness, and Jewel was grateful for it.

Her breath hung in mist the moment it left her lips; the air was mercifully still. She watched her companions emerge, counting them one by one, as she had done only during the final days of foraging in the undercity. The realization caused her to stop.

The Winter King was last to leave the lands of his beloved White Lady and, unlike any other member of their company, he did turn once to look back, but he did not linger.

Only when they were assembled did Angel say, "You do know how to get back to Fabril's reach, right?"

Jewel had considered this before departing. "Yes," she replied, but her hands signed *maybe.*

7th day of Lattan, 428 A.A.
Terafin Manse, Averalaan Aramarelas

Teller was right-kin, although he was a relatively junior member of the House Council. Jay, however, had been a member of the House and its Council since their early years in Terafin; Teller could not, therefore, be unaware of the political machinations that threatened the rule of The Terafin. He had come to understand that hierarchical position—at the top of the House—was no guarantee of either power or authority, unless one saw it from outside of the House.

He wondered, as he accompanied the Master of the Household Staff, what

The Terafin—past or present—might have achieved had her authority been unquestioned and absolute. The Master of the Household Staff had far, far more practical power than The Terafin herself. She gave orders without raising more than a brow, and those orders were instantly obeyed. As she swept through the halls, those halls emptied; the Household Staff fled.

Teller was uncertain if they fled because they were terrified of her or because they were terrified of what her orders, accompanied as they were by both the right-kin and the two living trees, might signify. He suspected, however, that it was the former, and if he had ever doubted the use of fear, he repented.

His own task was more difficult, and he therefore started with Marrick. He understood that Marrick was powerful, and that Marrick's web of connections were diffuse and not entirely predictable, but of the most senior members of the Council, it was Marrick with whom he was most comfortable.

Marrick, given the hour, was not immediately available; given the right-kin, however, he became available as quickly as a patrician who was accustomed to setting his own schedule could. He was surprised at the presence of the Master of the Household Staff, but he was not a servant; the greater part of his well-contained surprise was caused by the *arborii*. They extended him the courtesy of twin nods, each precisely timed and identical.

He did not waste words. "It is time?"

Teller nodded. "Take your people—and any of the people you have influence over—to The Terafin's personal chambers."

Marrick nodded, grim now. He had questions—Teller could practically see the way he restrained them—and turned toward the interior of his private rooms. "It would be best," he said, without looking back, "if the House Council could discuss this when we have removed to safer quarters."

The closest suite to Marrick's was currently occupied by Iain ATerafin, and Teller went there next, because he suspected that the Master of the Household Staff's presence—even if she failed to speak, as it was not her place, would sway that member of the House Council almost as quickly and certainly as the presence of the trees had moved Marrick. Nor was he wrong, but he found it interesting to watch Iain's response. Unlike Marrick, Iain's contacts were not founded upon social interaction, or at least not the type that turned a working day into Jester's version of normal hours. He was attired for work, and he looked as if he had been doing just that; his fingers were slightly ink-stained.

His eyes alighted first on the tree spirits, and then upon Teller, but his gaze came to rest upon the Master of the Household Staff. She would not, of course, flout rules in the presence of the right-kin, but she did give a brief, very stiff, nod.

"Right-kin," Iain said, offering a passable bow. "How may I be of service?"

"It is time," Teller replied, "to gather the entirety of the House and lead them to safety. Word," he added, "has been sent to allied Houses, and, with luck, they will be doing something similar." He had not said this to Marrick, although it was truth. But Iain was the type of man who would actually care.

"Gather your people and lead them to The Terafin's personal chambers. The Chosen understand the difficulty we face; they will allow anyone into those chambers that the chamber itself does not reject."

Iain's glance was brief, appraising. He nodded. Like Marrick, he asked no questions, but perhaps for different reasons.

By the time Teller reached Elonne's chambers, Elonne was waiting. There were no servants attending her, no pages ready to carry her messages or greet possible guests. She did not offer Teller a seat and did not take one herself; she abandoned the protocols of polite greeting, although she did offer Teller a deliberate nod, the acknowledgment of a peer.

She did not appear to notice the Master of the Household Staff; nor did she appear to notice the tree spirits who now served as Teller's guards. "You have had word."

"From the denizens of the wild forest," Teller replied. "It is time—"

"It is past time," one of those guards said.

"—That we move our people. We are, however, to take those that we can gather to The Terafin's personal chambers."

"And will our people be there to lead and guide them?"

"The Chosen are already marshaling the House Guard," Teller replied.

"What has happened?"

Teller understood that power did not admit readily to ignorance. He understood that the right-kin was, in theory, The Terafin's voice in The Terafin's absence; that it was at the right-kin's discretion that people were allowed to make appointments to meet with The Terafin at all. But he also understood that political caution now might be too costly in the very near future.

"I don't know. The forest elders sent the trees to me. The Terafin desired the safety of Terafin, and she understands that Terafin is its people. If the buildings are lost, they can be repaired." With a brief, wry grin, he added, "It isn't the first time a god has destroyed significant parts of the manse."

This surprised Elonne enough that she offered him a smile in return. "Very well. Have you spoken with Haerrad?"

"I will speak with him after I leave you. The pages that serve the right-kin's office were among the first sent out. Haerrad, however, will not accept the word of a page."

"No," Elonne replied gravely. "At this juncture, I believe your presence is necessary. I will speak to my own people on your behalf."

"Approach the forest," Teller said again, "from The Terafin's personal chambers."

Elonne nodded. To Teller's knowledge, Jay had not received Elonne in the later version of her personal chambers, but some word had clearly filtered down. Or up, he thought, glancing at the Master of the Household Staff.

He nodded and left her rooms. The Master of the Household Staff then excused herself. She was aware of Haerrad's disdain—or perhaps resentment—for her authority, and where she was the perfect aid in dealing with men and women like Iain, she would not be of aid in regard to Haerrad, the man Teller thought of privately as the most difficult member of the House Council.

He had become less openly hostile in the very recent past. But the past stretched out beyond that, and Teller had had personal experience with the lengths to which Haerrad was willing to go to get what he wanted.

Fortunately for the House, none of those involved alliance with demons.

Teller was not surprised to see that Haerrad, as Elonne, was waiting. Nor was he particularly surprised to see that Haerrad had retained the use of personal House Guards, although the House Guard was, in theory, subordinate to the Chosen in a state of emergency. He had no doubt—or very little—that the Chosen had called up the House Guard, and was certain that they had not deployed these to Haerrad's command.

This, however, was not a matter for the right-kin; it was a matter for the Chosen and the captains of the House Guard. He was not apprised of all the subtleties that such command involved and did not feel the need; he trusted Arrendas and Torvan, daily, with his life. The captains of the House Guard were far less of a known quantity, but, again, they were not his immediate concern.

No. Haerrad was. Haerrad was not, as every other member of the House Council was, attired in a manner suitable for the daily life of a patrician of notable power. He was attired for war. And the war itself was not to be a thing of pomp and circumstance; he wore armor that had clearly seen use in a context with which Teller was unfamiliar. He carried a sword, and if the sheath and pommel were ostentatiously fine, Teller was suddenly certain the sword, too, had seen practical use. He did not look like a House Council member, standing in the very finely appointed room in which he greeted guests.

His smile was grim; he understood what Teller saw and understood, as well, the whole of his thought.

"We're evacuating Terafin?"

Teller nodded, momentarily at a loss for words. Haerrad had that effect on him even in day-to-day circumstances. The House Council member looked up at the *arborii*, assessing, as he did, their arms, their armaments. Haerrad did not unsettle them. They met and held his gaze, assessing him just as carefully, which should not have surprised Teller, although it did.

"We've been advised to evacuate through The Terafin's chambers," Teller began.

He did not finish.

Beneath their feet, the ground trembled; it was not subtle, and it was not short.

"They are coming," the tree spirits said, almost in unison. They lifted heads the same way, and looked to the south, as if the walls of the Terafin manse—the most powerful of The Ten—were now so insubstantial they could barely be seen at all. They stood taller; the rumbling tremors of a shaking building did not seem to concern them. Nor did it seem to move them.

It did concern Teller. The Terafin's personal chambers were not on the first floor; if the building collapsed, he wasn't certain what would become of them. Or rather, of the door that led there. He was absolutely certain that those who made it past that door would be safe—for a time.

But the air grew colder, as if every window in the manse, all of them glassed, had shattered and the whole of winter was now free to enter the interior, even if winter had, in theory, passed, and the air itself had become seasonally warmer. He thought nothing, now, would surprise him.

Haerrad, however, tried.

"Right-kin, with your permission, my men and I will take the exit to the grounds." It seemed, to Teller's momentary shock, that he was actually asking permission.

"It is The Terafin's desire," the tree spirit said, "that *all* members of her House retreat to the forest."

"You are creatures of theory," Haerrad replied, as if he conversed every day with trees that were taller than he, and armed as he was. "Your roots are deep, and you seldom walk among us as you now walk. But we are men. We put down subtle roots, and they do not bind or hold us when action is required.

"What The Terafin—what *my Lord*—desires, I, too, desire. But few, indeed, of the people who shelter here are capable of self-defense. The Chosen and the House Guard will remain to secure the premises."

Teller opened his mouth to say that Haerrad was not, in fact, a member of the House Guard, and certainly not one of the Chosen. But he was uncertain to whom he would have been speaking, and therefore kept the words to himself.

As if Haerrad could hear the thought, he looked—down, as his was the greater height—at Teller. "You are lambs," he said with a grin. "And lambs—with cause—fear wolves. But right-kin, even The Terafin understands the *need* for wolves. Her predecessor understood it better—it is why she never removed Jarven." Something in Teller's expression spoke to Haerrad. "Jarven is here?"

Teller exhaled. "Jarven," he said quietly, "is where the Kings are."

"You never knew him in his prime."

"No," the *arborii* who had done most of the speaking said, "but he will. Teller, we must away."

"We're not finished yet."

"Then hurry. This is not our place of power, not where we must stand if we are to protect what is important to Jewel."

Teller then turned to Haerrad. "Yes," he said. "You are right. We are not what you are, and what you are is necessary. Go and defend the House and its people as only you can; I will find the rest of the lambs and see them to safety."

Haerrad nodded. He turned to the House Guard, who clearly took their orders from Haerrad, and only Haerrad, and they exited his rooms in a din of noise and motion, certain of their destination *because* Haerrad was certain.

On the first day Teller had come to House Terafin—in the shadow of demons and death—the Terafin manse had been a blur, but a rich one; he had wandered its halls observing the almost obscene proof of great wealth on every wall, every floor. The ceilings were so high, the halls so long, that he had thought the space an endless maze of treasure; surely gods must live this way in their distant abodes.

He was quiet, one of the quietest members of his den, and he had observed servants and their positions with some care, hoping that he might steal something—anything—that the den could sell to stave off starvation in the grim future that surely awaited them. But he knew, as well, that the rich and the powerful didn't trust him—or them—and even with some cause. They had never lived with the desperation, the struggle to simply *survive*, that the den had faced, day in and day out.

Half a lifetime had shrunk those halls; familiarity had shrunk the manse. Only today, as he hurried through it, did some ghost of that first long trek haunt him; he felt desperate, afraid. The reasons were entirely different. Here, without the threat of starvation, the threat of freezing to death in the winter, of being shoeless or of wearing the rags that were like flags to the magisterians that protected the Common as they could from random thieves, he had room for an entirely different kind of terror. The lives of the people in the manse had been left in the den's hands. In his hands. Jay had trusted them with this.

The ground shook again, and he began to jog, and then to sprint; he found his voice and raised it.

8th day of Lattan, 428 A.A.
The Common, Averalaan

The wind swept across the Common, howling but wordless. Words, however, could be heard in a rising descant, a song of distant terror, as buildings that had stood for centuries listed to the side; the roads cracked, fissures growing wider and deeper.

From beneath the ground, from beneath those streets which had housed the rich, the poor, the landed and the homeless, the peak of a dark spire gained height, widening.

The Kings did not fall; the stone fell away beneath their feet, but the air held them, the wind protected them. Jester was safe with Snow, and Snow, being all cat, began to circle the spire as it rose, and rose again, as if flight were an act of smug defiance. Jester, on his back, felt none of that. His eyes went to the ground, to the building that, even now, continued to break it. Chunks of stone fell, to vanish into darkness, and he thought of those fallen buildings, those fallen blocks of much larger stone, that the den had navigated with rope, magestone, and luck.

He was half a lifetime from that navigation; it was in the distant past, and he seldom thought of it. But for the moment, he might have been sixteen again, desperate and afraid of life, because in the main it held pain and death.

The peak of that spire widened, and beneath it, all of a single piece of stone to the naked eye in the light of a dawn that had only begun to encroach night sky, came the rest of a tower; in width, it was equal to the space that Moorelas' Sanctum had occupied moments before. The statue itself was gone, just as the bits of stones were gone, into the darkness below; Jester did not know how long the fall had been and how much of that statue remained.

Nor did it now matter. The tower itself was not the only element of the emerging building, and more of the Common was destroyed—or would have been destroyed—by the width of the rest of it.

But the *Ellariannatte* that had accompanied Birgide were there, and as Jester watched, their roots, exposed, began to twine together, to form some kind of a bridge, a landless land upon which a man could stand. Many did—the Kings' Swords were deposited across those roots by a wind that had swept them, armed, armored, toward uncertain safety.

"ATerafin."

Jester was not surprised to see Andrei. He was slightly surprised to see that he kept pace with Snow, and Snow seemed to find this mildly offensive. But the cat did not speak of boredom now; beneath Jester, his body was tense, readied.

Andrei had sprouted wings. He did not wear armor, and that was a pity; wings on the back of the Araven servant looked wrong in every particular.

"What—what is that building?"

"I do not believe you have seen it before," he replied.

"Is it from the—the ruins of the city that used to be here?"

"No, ATerafin. It is new. It is entirely new. But the stone in that ancient city was not quarried as the stone in Averalaan is; it is older by far. You have heard of the changes The Terafin made—at a distance—in *Avantari*."

Jester nodded, and then, because Snow continued to move, said, "Yes."

"This stone is akin to that. The city that fell to ruin, the city the gods destroyed, was worked of that stone."

". . . The entire city."

"Yes. And it was a city that has not even been conceived of by your makers, your Artisans, your artists—except perhaps in fevered dream." He spoke with a hint of hush, a hint of reverence, but when Snow's flight brought him closer to Andrei, Jester saw none of that reverence in his expression.

"Ask your companion," Andrei said, "to retreat to the forest."

"We're—"

"The forest is here," Andrei added, lifting an arm.

Jester looked toward the Common. The *Ellariannatte* had proliferated, spreading.

"The Kings' Swords have been tasked with saving those who are unfortunate enough to live above the shops in the Common; the merchants who otherwise travel here will be turned away—if they survive to reach us." He glanced at Jester again. "Do not think about the deaths you cannot prevent, ATerafin. Think about the lives you will save. Understand that, without your Terafin, the survivors would be counted in the dozens, and not all of them would thank you for it."

"And Hectore?"

"He will survive. Hectore, his wife, his grandchildren, most of his children. While I survive, he will survive."

"Shouldn't you be—"

"No. The danger, the worst of the danger, will be here, and it is here we will face it."

Jester was mute for one long moment.

"You are thinking that there is little you can do to be of aid." It was not a question.

Jester watched as the base of the building itself rose. To his surprise, where it encountered the floor of tree roots, it was the stone that cracked, the stone that crumbled; he could see that *Ellariannatte* were attempting to root themselves, in part, in the rising *walls*.

"Snow," he said, suddenly. "Take me to Birgide."

"*Who?*"

Jester cursed. "Take me to The Warden."

"Why *me?*"

"Because I'm on *your* back, and I can't get there on my own."

"I could *drop you.*"

Jester cursed again. "Then drop me in front of the damn Warden!"

Snow hissed. "She won't *like* it."

"Birgide is used to me by now."

"Not *her, stupid* boy."

Ah. "She won't dislike it."

"*She* wants *you* to be *safe.*"

"Yes," said Jester, thinking inexplicably of Duster, of Lefty, Lander, Fisher— all their lost, whose shadows in their absence were longer and darker than the shadows cast by the living. "But she wants to save what she can of this city, and there's no way to do that without risk."

"What can *you* do?" Snow demanded.

"I'm Jay's," he replied. "And I think that here and now, in the forest this place is becoming, that actually counts for something."

Snow hissed again—laughter in it—and did as Jester had all but demanded.

As they flew, his wings clipped the crenelations of a building, that, broken in places by trees, continued to emerge from the ancient darkness below.

Chapter Fourteen

THE MASTER BARDS OF Senniel College moved through the hundred holdings; they had abandoned Senniel at the behest of their bardmaster. She sent them, she said, into danger; there was, for the unwary, death. She did not offer them the choice, even though they were not young men. The greatest member of their order was absent.

But when they saw the spire break the ground of the Common beneath the feet of a statue that could no longer be seen, they understood why. One man among their number was no longer of Senniel College; he had come to the general meeting the bardmaster had called. And he had traveled with them across the bridge from the Isle, into the holdings themselves, although he was of The Ten, and not subordinate in any way to Solran Marten, the woman who commanded them now.

He wore bardic tunic, bardic colors, the blue and purple that implied Royal association. But he wore, as well, the signet ring of his House: Wayelyn.

"Come," he said, with a joviality that did not sound forced to those without the gift to hear it. But the Master Bards did have that gift, for the most part; they were talent-born, bard-born, and it was said with some truth that one could not lie to the bard-born. "It is Lattan; without the current crisis, we would still be expected in the Common tonight for the festival of lights."

No man said what all thought: that if it was a celebration of life, there might be little indeed that remained to celebrate. He was aware of the fear, regardless, and the joviality fell away from his voice as he turned to look to the South.

"Kallandras will come."

"And what can he do?"

But The Wayelyn moved on. As he did, he began to strum the strings of the lute he carried; it was not, strictly speaking, a necessity. Nor was it a command. But the Master Bards likewise armed themselves; they understood what he did not put into words. Here, in these streets, with a building that loomed larger and higher as the moments passed, their biggest enemy would be fear.

That they were wrong did not make their presence less essential.

As he sang, The Wayelyn turned his attention to the West. What he was waiting for, no one knew for certain—but every member of the college had heard the song that had so embarrassed the Kings; every member of the college now understood that at its heart there was some grain of truth. And perhaps, The Wayelyn thought, every man and woman present hoped that it contained more than a grain.

Because if it did not, in the end, they were doomed.

Birgide's eyes rounded as Jester slid off Snow's back. "What are you *doing?*"

He reached out, almost casually, and placed his palm against the bark of the nearest tree. This was not difficult; he might have reached in almost any direction and touched a tree. There was no silver here, no gold, no diamond—the detritus of mortal dreams of wealth. But there were *Ellariannatte*, the Kings' trees, and he understood, now, that they had only grown here because the Sleepers were here.

The Sleepers had always been here.

"I'm gallantly coming to your aid," he replied.

"This is not the time for humor," she snapped. Her eyes were bloodred, almost glowing with a fevered light, and the veins beneath her pale skin looked almost—almost—like the grain of wood. He understood that Birgide was not den, not truly; that she did not know den-sign, that she served another master. But here, in the heart of the forest that she had suffered so much simply to be given permission to steward, he could not see the difference.

He would teach her, he thought. He would teach her den-sign. He doubted she'd be all that interested in learning but was confident that she would.

One hand on the trunk of a tree, he reached out for Birgide Viranyi with the other; it was not the first time that he had held her hand. She stared at his hand as if she didn't quite recognize what it was.

But he shook his head. "Take my hand, Birgide."

She blinked again, this woman who had always loved the isolation of the forest. But Jester understood that it was not the isolation, exactly, that she had loved. She loved the fact that forest was alive, that the trees were alive, and that they did not hurt her. Had not hurt her.

She loved that she could learn them, know them, that she could plant them, and they would *grow*. She did not need to fear them, only fear *for* them. They did not accuse her, did not judge her.

But she was not a tree.

And he thought, were he not here, she would try to become one; that she was, in some fashion, doing that even now. Jester was not of the wilderness. Of the den, he was most tightly wed to the patriciate that he secretly loathed. He was their peacock, their irreverence, their distance, their disdain. He went to the powerful, drank with them, listened to their drunken murmurs as if they were weathervanes; he saw which way the wind was blowing.

That had been his value to Jay, to the den; he understood that now. But he understood Birgide Viranyi in a different way. She was *Astari*, yes. But she was like the den: she was alone. She was what Jester might have been, had he lived her life and not his own. Oh, she hadn't been sold into slavery and probable death by her own kin—but she had suffered at the hands of kin until she had grown strong enough to leave them, just the same.

Why did people want family? Why did people want kin?

He understood it, at a remove, because he himself had the same yearning. Had he despised himself for it? Maybe. But there wasn't a lot, if he were truthful, that he didn't despise about himself. And he had found his family, his chosen kin. They were his den. They were, in the end, what he was willing to give his life to. And for.

Did Birgide understand that *that* was the choice she herself had made when she had chosen to become Warden? No, he thought.

But he hadn't understood it, either, the first time he'd encountered Jay. Jay had simply been a way out. A way out of the brothel. A way to survive. Everything else had come later because Jester could not fail, in the end, to trust Jay. Not even Duster had been able to do that, and Birgide was no Duster.

She stared at his hand. Stared at the hand that he had placed against the trunk of the tree that she had willed into growth, into being. He understood that the forest heard her voice, that until Jay returned, it was the clearest voice the forest *would* hear. Haval thought that the den had influence.

And Haval, that bastard, was never wrong. Cold-blooded, yes. But not wrong.

Jester understood only now why Haval had so cavalierly sent him. Jester, not Finch. It was not because Finch was too important—although Finch was, in Jester's estimation, of far more objective value to the den than he himself would ever be.

It was because Jester was the person who'd been set to dog Birgide's every step. Jester was the person who had carried Haval's messages, who had asked Haval's questions, and who, in the shadow of that duty, had asked questions of his own. Jester had shouted at the wilderness on the day Birgide became Warden, because Jester understood, personally, viscerally, what Jay herself wanted.

Birgide reached out slowly and placed her palm over Jester's. He closed his hand around hers, interlacing their fingers as she frowned.

"What I'm doing," he said, his voice genial, even casual, and calculated to annoy, "is reminding you."

"I'm *busy*, Jester."

"Yes. You're doing what I'm too lazy to do. Nice trees, by the way."

Her brows rose. Her eyes, however, did not get any redder; it might have been a trick of the light, but the glow seemed to recede, although the color remained.

"You're Warden," he added, his tone just as light, just as irreverent. "But to be Jay's Warden, you have to be human. You have to put your pants on one leg at a time."

He almost laughed at her expression; he could not prevent himself from grinning. "I could really use a drink. Or ten."

After a shocked pause, Birgide said, "When we first met, it was a small wonder to me that The Terafin hadn't strangled you."

"And now?"

"It's a *large* wonder."

He laughed.

"Duvari is here," she added, her own lips resisting the tug that would have transformed her expression into a smile.

"Definitely ten drinks." Jester's grimace, on the other hand, did what his humor could not.

"He is entirely focused on the protection of the Kings."

"Yes. But if it were up to Duvari, the rest of the Empire would be composed of toddlers, none of whom had any brains or money. The man doesn't understand danger; he invents it."

"You're wrong. I understand that the patriciate fear—and dislike—Duvari. But he has to succeed in his duty every single time. His enemies only have to succeed once."

"He makes enemies," Jester countered. "And increases his own workload in the doing."

"And would you have him be you?"

"No. But he probably has people like me."

She did not answer.

Jester shrugged. "You've met Haval, right?"

She nodded, the gesture instantly more reserved.

"I'd rather Duvari was—and please *never* quote me on this—like Haval. Haval is a ruthless son of a bitch, but he doesn't rub people the wrong way. Duvari does it so often, it's like that's his intent."

"Duvari does not dissemble, no."

"You mean lie?"

"He makes his position—and his duties—clear. There is no question of his loyalty. He cannot be bought, cannot be bribed, cannot be blackmailed. There is nothing he wants, nothing that can be used as a lever, nothing he loves."

"Love is not a lever."

Her hand shifted; Jester's tightened.

"It *is* a lever," Birgide said, her voice tighter but at the same time somehow less contained. "It is something that can be used as a threat. Where people love, they are vulnerable. Surely you must understand this. Were it not for her den, The Terafin could make decisions that were materially better for the entirety of her House and the House's position. It is *why* the heads of The Ten very seldom marry, very seldom have children. Historically, that has not been wise."

"It's not been wise," Jester countered, "because *historically* they were in danger *from* their spouses. You might call that love—but I think not even you would be so cynical."

Beneath their feet, the roots of the *Ellariannatte* tightened, shifting as if to entrench themselves.

"But let me give you that: that *fear* for our safety—that fear for the safety of anyone, or anything, one loves—is a vulnerability." His tone made clear he was not yet done. "What Jay is—sorry, what The Terafin is—is defined by what she loves. It's defined by how she values love; it's defined by how she fulfills responsibility."

"Love and responsibility are not the same."

"Why not?" Jester was accustomed to playing devil's advocate; it was an amusing pastime. This was an argument he had had before, while men and women were deep into their cups and more likely to complain honestly.

But it was different this time, and he knew it. He could play games with anything; could turn the most hallowed things into sport for words, for scoring conversational points, for debates that had, at their heart, a sense of intellectual hierarchy. There was no ego in this; the stakes were high enough that he could not quite make a game of it. Might never make a game of it again.

Jarven could have.

Jester was not Jarven. If he had some of Jarven's external characteristics, he did not have Jarven's drive, Jarven's ambitions, Jarven's desire to win. What he wanted, what he thought he had always wanted, was a world in which *win* did not also require someone else to *lose*. He had accepted that winners and losers was just the way the world worked, that the desire to have a different way was naive, foolish; that it made a mark of those who believed it. It disappointed them, embittered them, forced them at last to become the thing they despised.

He did not think he had descended to that level, but he understood why: he had Jay. He could consider Jay a *winner*, could consider himself a winner by association. But Jay herself did not, had never, broken it down in that fashion. No. If she was, at heart, simple, she broke it down in an entirely different way. She loved what, and whom, she loved. That love defined her, and in some fashion, it defined them, as well.

What she had offered, perhaps because her own family had not been theirs—Jester's, Finch's, Birgide's—was love. And even if one could never, ever admit that that love existed, all the den, even Duster, perhaps especially Duster, had in the end reached for it. Had risen above themselves, and their belief in their own lack of worth, to continue to reach for it.

"It's love that defines Jay," he said, ditching the title that defined her to outsiders, to strangers. "And it's love, therefore, that defines this forest, this small patch of wilderness that she claimed.

"You can say it's a weakness. You can say it's a vulnerability—but, Birgide, it takes *strength* to be vulnerable, in the end. It takes strength to take risks. You're in this forest; you're Warden here because she's what she is." He hesitated. Drew breath. Started again. "You want to say I'm wrong. I'm not. The reason you wanted to be Warden was to protect *the forest*. But you didn't see— maybe because none of us really thought about it that way—that the forest is what it is *because* it's Jay's. You wondered why she let you in when she avoided all the magi—who still resent her for it, in case you were wondering. You wondered why she trusted you when she *knew* you were *Astari*.

"But I don't."

Birgide's hand was rigid; she would have withdrawn it, if Jester hadn't held onto it so tightly. And she could still fairly easily retrieve it; he knew that as well. She was *Astari*. Her unarmed combat skill was vastly superior to his own.

"She may have said she wanted to spite Duvari; she certainly thought he disapproved of your request. And that might even be part of it—if I were in her position, it would have been *all* of the reason.

"But if you really believe that—no." He shook his head as he studied her neutral expression. "You don't believe it. You didn't understand. You still don't."

"And you do?" The words were almost a whisper.

"I do. But I understand it only because she found me. In an entirely illegal brothel, with a handful of other kids. She'd come to rescue one person. She didn't know us. She took a risk—a big risk, given demons and mages—to take us with her. I didn't care *why*. None of us did. What we cared about was our own skins.

"If she'd rescued us and turned us out in the streets . . ." He shook his head. "She didn't. Do you know why I think she let you into her forest?"

Birgide was mute, watching him.

"Because she knew how much you wanted to be there. You didn't want it the way the magi wanted it; the forest wasn't a thing to be dissected, to be studied. You were ready to love that forest, those trees, the awe and wonder of them. You didn't *need* to name things first, to be first to present the knowledge; you didn't need them to advance your own position in some other hierarchy.

"Birgide—she knew you would love the forest in a way that even she couldn't."

It was not silent in the absence of Birgide Viranyi's words. In the distance, beyond the odd shelter of *Ellariannatte*, Jester could hear shouting. It had not yet devolved into screams, but he had no doubt it would. He could hear roaring—but he thought that was Night or Snow, and at this very second, it didn't matter.

"And," he said quietly, "you do. I didn't know it. I didn't understand it. I'm the cynical bastard, in case that wasn't clear. I didn't think you should be there, but I'm willing to trust Jay."

"And you understand it now?"

"Yes. Better than anyone, actually."

Her hand was trembling.

"I saw what the forest demanded of you. I saw what you were willing to sacrifice. I understood that there was a very good chance you wouldn't survive the test the wilderness demanded you pass. And I saw that you understood it as well. You faced it, you were *willing* to face it, because what you wanted more than anything else was a home that you had the strength and will to protect.

"I don't know what you call that. I call it—when I am being disgustingly earnest, as I am forced to be now—love. And Birgide, people who *can* love that way aren't all that common, in my experience. People choose fear, instead.

"You didn't take the position of Warden—if something as mundane as 'position' can describe it—because you loved us. We're all aware of that. But I think it's because, on some level, you want what we want, that you could. To me, then, you're den."

He waited for her response; waited for her denial. He understood that there were some people who could never, would never, admit openly a truth that others could see regardless. He was surprised at the tension he felt as he waited; it wasn't like him, and he certainly didn't enjoy it.

But what she said, in a low, low voice, was: "It's not up to you."

And he wondered as he met and held her gaze, if this was how Haval always felt: this mixture of triumph as suspicion became certainty. He hoped not.

"Yes," he told her. "It is. Finch brought Adam home. Jay wasn't here."

"I am not Adam."

"No, you're not. But, frankly, neither am I." He shrugged; he couldn't choose a different gesture, because both of his hands were occupied. "I've seen what the rest of us haven't seen, and oddly enough, they'll trust me. Jay will trust me. She confirmed the House Name I didn't theoretically have the right to offer, either."

But Birgide knew, in the eyes of The Terafin, that the House Name did not have the weight, the import, of den. He could see that and understood that it was not just perception on his part; she allowed it. She had decided to take that risk, here, at the edge of the end of the world. "Carver," she said, aware of what the name now meant to the den.

Jester waited, anyway.

"Carver. Merry."

"You really did do research."

"It wasn't research; it's not even a secret in the back halls. And Merry's made no secret of—" She shook her head. "But she was never den."

"No," Jester agreed. "She didn't want that, though."

"And that makes a difference?"

"Yes. The only person she cares about is Carver. She doesn't mind the rest of us—I think she actually likes Finch and Teller—but we're her *job*. Carver is different."

"And the rest of you?"

"Well, we don't want her the way Carver does." Jester shrugged again. "And because she's part of Carver's life, we keep an eye out for her. But she's ATerafin Household Staff, and she's proud of that—and being den would destroy the life she's built."

Her eyes were red, would remain red, but her skin no longer resembled a living tree when seen in cross-section. And her hand, for all that her eyes were, and would remain, unnatural, was callused. Hells, it was probably dirty—but it was, conversely, a clean dirt, and Jester could live with that.

"Welcome home," he said, grinning. "It's not much, and it'll probably make you even more shocked that I've survived it all these years."

She said nothing. But he understood this nothing, as well; she had no words for it. He wasn't debriefing; she didn't *have* to come up with words for it. But she turned as Snow landed, snorting impatiently.

"They are *coming*," he snarled, his anger—and the height of his fur—meant for neither of the people he addressed. "Are you *ready*?"

Birgide closed her eyes, inhaled, and nodded, her face losing its tension. "Yes," she said, when she opened her eyes. "Yes, Snow. I am finally ready."

8th day of Lattan, 428 A.A.
Scavonne Manse, Averalaan

Muriel A'Scavonne almost regretted following Colm Sanders' advice. Stacia had been in a truly terrible mood throughout dinner, and it had descended into near-tantrum when she realized her mother would not be moved. If Muriel often felt abandoned to her fear and despair by her husband, he was at least a pillar of support when it came to her decisions regarding the discipline of her daughter. If Muriel said her daughter was not allowed to traverse the Common for the festival of lights, he acquiesced.

Stacia, however, did not. When it became clear that pleas would not avail her of the necessary permission, she turned to shouting and demands. They went *every* year. Why were they not allowed to go *now*?

Colm Sanders had not been forthcoming; he had made clear that the near-disaster with the riding lessons would pale in comparison should Stacia and her parents make their customary trek to watch the magi at play among the heights of the *Ellariannatte*. Muriel had not revealed to her husband that it was Colm Sanders who had been behind her decision. Had she, they would already be in the Common. Her husband did not take the advice of a low-born soldier, and he would be offended and suspicious if he discovered that his wife had done exactly that.

Stacia, however, understood this game. While she was bitterly resentful of Mr. Sanders, she nonetheless failed to mention his existence where her father could hear it. The appearance of an extra servant was not his problem. Nor was the oversight of that servant.

He did not *enjoy* the ruckus that Stacia caused and retreated to his smoking room with a pipe. Only when he was well away from the table and the shouting itself did Stacia wheel in rage, and storm from the main rooms, which were appropriate for a young lady of her station, to the back rooms, which were not.

Normally, Muriel sent Barryl to watch over her. Tonight, however, she did not. Stacia was disappointed, heartbroken and enraged; Muriel was worried. Deeply worried.

"Open the door!" Stacia shouted.

The door to Mr. Sanders' room remained closed.

Muriel, however, did not scream, rage, or lift her voice. She knocked.

She was surprised when he opened the door to her wearing armor and his swords. His expression was grim, that grimness emphasized by the scars he bore. But he offered Muriel an awkward bow and stepped out of the doorframe to allow her to enter.

Stacia stormed in on her mother's heels, her hands fists, her eyes bright with both tears and emotion.

Colm Sanders looked down his nose, his eyes narrowed. Stacia kicked him.

"That's enough of that," he said.

"Why did you tell her that we can't go?"

"Because, Stacy, we can't. You and I will probably survive, even if we're in the Common. But neither of us will be awake. If *you* go, your mother at least will accompany you. Who will watch her? Who will protect her when we sleep?"

This was the heart of Muriel's fear. Colm Sanders expected that both he and Stacia would, once again, be drawn into the world of the dreamers. He had not said as much to her. He was willing, however, to say this to her daughter. It was why, in the end, she had followed.

"She has *guards*!"

"And how long would those guards last when faced with Darranatos? How long did they last during the victory parade?"

Stacia opened her mouth, but words had, for the moment, deserted her.

They deserted Muriel now for entirely different reasons, and he knew. "Go upstairs," he told Stacia. "Go to bed."

"But—"

"Can you not hear her?"

"You don't *let me listen*!"

"I thought we might have longer. We don't. Go upstairs."

Stacia trembled in front of this old soldier. "If we're going to be sleeping anyway, why are you wearing that armor?"

"Habit."

"Liar."

"Stacia!"

They both turned to look at Muriel. She could see that her daughter was determined. She could see, as well, that her daughter was afraid. But Stacia's eyes widened; Mr. Sanders caught her as her knees buckled. He grimaced. "Can you have her carried to her room? I would take her—but I won't make it, either."

"If you can wake yourself—"

"I will not be able to wake myself now. Even if Stacy was capable of it, she wouldn't be able to, either. This is why we are here. This is why we sleep."

She started to speak; she was not certain what she might have said. There was shouting, now, in the back halls; voices were now raised in something approaching panic. She opened the door and stepped into the halls, and long years of training brought that noise to a close—but not the panic. That, Muriel could clearly see.

"What," she said, grabbing one of the pages, "has happened? Look at me. Look at me and tell me what you've heard."

"It's—the Common. In the Common—Moorelas' statue is gone—and something else is growing up beneath it. The streets are breaking. People are—"

"Who told you this?"

"Marie—she was there, and she's run back. It's—" He stopped. Muriel let her hands fall away. She turned to the half-open door.

"What is this?" she asked of Colm Sanders.

"We don't know for certain."

"What do you *think* it is?"

He closed his eyes, Stacy in his arms. "The Sleepers," he finally said, "are waking."

She was frozen; she could not find humor or derision or doubt. There was nothing, now, to stand on. She bowed her head for one long moment, trying to order her thoughts, her fears. ". . . I will go to my husband," she finally said.

"Stacy—"

"Keep her here. Keep her here, and wherever it is your dreams take you—guard her, protect her. Bring her back to me."

The High Wilderness

Jewel felt the cold envelop her the moment both of her feet were on the other side of the portal that Adam and Gilafas had built. Although she'd taken care to find her heavy mittens, she did not don them; instead, she dropped a hand to Shadow's head. It was, as the cat always was, warm, and the contact protected her from the bite of chill wind. She leaned into the great, gray cat.

Adam felt the cold instantly; she could see a tremble set up shop in his body. She looked at Shadow and at the Winter King.

Shadow said, "*He* can carry Adam." As if he could read her mind. But . . . he had always been able to do that.

The Winter King was not, to Jewel's surprise, annoyed. As if Shadow's snippy words conveyed Jewel's actual command—although she hadn't spoken a word—he knelt by Adam's feet, positioning his head with care so that he did not knock the Voyani youth into the flattened snow.

Adam clambered onto his back instantly; where the Winter King was, there was warmth. Jewel believed privately that the Winter King could follow a path through the deepest of water, and those he carried wouldn't drown.

Of course not.

But to Jewel's surprise, the Winter King did not rise when Adam was fully seated; he remained kneeling. He was not waiting for Jewel.

No, he was waiting for . . . Shianne.

Breath hung in the air like personal clouds, but Jewel's drifted because she almost forgot to breathe. The Winter King had refused, any time she asked, to carry Shianne. She had given up asking.

Shianne looked, not to the Winter King, but to Jewel herself. Of course, she did. Jewel's first instinct was to offer a helpless shrug, but she bit that back as unprofitable, and instead said, "Accept what he offers."

"It is offered?"

Jewel nodded. "If it were up to me, he would have carried you every step of the way from the moment you first joined us."

"You do not understand why he would not." This seemed to amuse Shianne, and Jewel was content to see some glimmer of an expression other than despair upon her face.

"No."

"And you do not understand what has changed?" Shianne had turned her attention to the great stag, considering him as if she, in turn had some share of his former reluctance.

"You had a baby."

"Yes, Matriarch. I delivered the child who was with me for so long, I almost feel empty. I lived for, I existed for, the moment in which all of my choices, all of my sacrifices, would redeem me in the eyes of the White Lady." She bowed her head for one long moment. Lifted it again. "And redemption also . . . leaves one empty."

"You could go back—"

"She has said she will wake my sisters. You will see them, if we survive. You will see what we once were when the world was new, and the gods were our companions."

Shianne would not be, would never again be, one of them.

But it was not pity that moved the Winter King; pity, like its better cousin, compassion, was so foreign to him he could not speak the language, could only barely understand it, and always from a condescending distance. Pity, Jewel thought, was likewise not a language that Shianne understood. These two, Winter King and Shianne herself, were of a kind; what they loved, what they devoted themselves to, was the same.

And yet, they were with her. They would be with her until Ariane came to claim them. Or until she herself died.

Shianne mounted the Winter King, settling in behind Adam. She draped one arm around the young man's waist. Even now, the baby delivered safely, her quest at last completed, she was gentle with Adam, and Jewel was certain that she would defend him in the face of the most dangerous of attackers.

Perhaps it was not for Jewel's sake she had chosen to leave the White Lady, but for Adam's. And perhaps Jewel would never know. She did not understand the Winter King, did not understand Shianne, did not understand the White Lady. At the moment, that understanding was irrelevant.

Across a field covered in red, red snow, she turned, almost unerring, in the direction they had come. Time was no longer held in abeyance, and time had never been on her side.

It did not occur to Jewel that the absence of the guildmaster would cause difficulty. She had been so preoccupied with the fate of the infant that she had not considered the situation pragmatically. Nor had Avandar offered his usual advice.

One did not, even in the time when the Cities of Man were at the height of their power, command an Artisan. It startled Jewel to realize that Avandar considered Gilafas an Artisan of old. Given that he had, in the end, created the door through which she had entered the Hidden Court, the change in attitude made sense. It was a bitter sense.

Angel signed; she grimaced in response. He understood what she didn't even lift hands to say and winced. There was, however, no doubt in him.

Had there ever been?

Winter King.

Jewel.

Can you retrace our steps?

Yes. I am not certain that is wise, however.

Why not?

It is the wilderness, Jewel, and blood has been shed here. Lives have been lost, and lives offered. The wilderness is not all of one thing, and it does not remain all of one thing. The shape of the unclaimed wilderness bows to the whims and demands of those who traverse it. Where that will is strong enough, the impression lingers, and it can linger for a long, long time.

Jewel nodded. She turned to Terrick, lifted a hand, and lowered it again, chagrined. "The Winter King informs me that the lands beyond this battlefield may not resemble the lands we passed through to arrive at it."

Angel signed; Jewel signed back. She then climbed up on Shadow's back far less gracefully than Shianne had on the Winter King's. Shadow complained but adjusted his wings enough that mounting wasn't difficult. "I'm not *him*," the cat growled. "I might *drop* you."

Terrick and Shianne stiffened; Angel and Adam did not. Jewel thumped the gray cat between the ears as she adjusted her seat.

To Terrick, Angel said, "He won't hurt her."

"Why are you so certain? If I understand what has happened in the past, he *has*."

"He was being controlled."

"By *what?*"

"Something as powerful as the White Lady. He won't admit it," Angel added quietly. "All three cats have a ferocious sense of the importance of their own dignity."

"You wouldn't know it."

Angel chuckled. "We should ask the Winter King to take these." He indicated the packs that they now carried. Terrick had been hesitant about accepting the provisions of the White Lady, but they hadn't exactly been offered. Angel, however, appreciated the sharp decrease in weight. It would be far easier to travel significant distances.

"You don't arm yourself," Terrick observed.

"Neither do you."

Terrick nodded. "When we entered the forest the first time, it felt watchful. Hostile. It was silent like a predator."

"And now?"

"It is silent like a grave. Even the wind is too quiet." He exhaled, his breath wreathing his face. "If we have enemies here, they are in hiding. I do not understand the winter of this wilderness."

"It is the winter of all of the wilderness," Celleriant said. "It is these lands themselves that confound you."

"And I would find other wild lands less incomprehensible?"

"No. But this road was once walked by Fabril, and the hint of his name remains."

"He claimed these lands?" Jewel asked.

Celleriant was silent for a beat. "Yes, Lord. The time I have passed among your kind has given me some insight. You did not intend to claim the lands you claimed. You fought no battle of dominance; you did not unseat a different Lord; you did not understand the nature of the lands themselves. And yet, Lord, you did. The lands in which your home and court are situated are now— and while you live—yours. But even when you have passed away, those lands will remember your name. They will remember until they bow to the will of another Lord."

Kallandras glanced at him, the gesture subtle but pointed. It was unnecessary. Jewel heard Celleriant's words as if they were the shell that covered an enormous egg; while they were true, there was something beneath them, something substantial.

"Do you hear my name here?"

Silence, as if Celleriant were struggling to find an answer, as if the answer that came to him was not, somehow, in a language Jewel understood. And yet, the Arianni—all the Arianni—appeared to be able to speak any mortal tongue at will. His answer, when he finally offered it, did not seem to justify the hesitance.

"Yes."

"Is it the trees?"

"Perhaps." He was, once again, not lying. But something else had caught his ear, something else had disturbed him. He turned to Kallandras. "Can you not hear it?"

The bard frowned. "My hearing is not the hearing of your kin," he finally said. "I do not even hear the echoes of Fabril's name in this place."

"It is not the echo that is of concern to me. Fabril was an Artisan, and even in the high wilderness, the lands knew his name; they would not take it as their own, would not shelter behind it—but it was known. It is not unexpected to hear it here, so close to his home."

Shadow, however, hissed. The irritated hiss. "We will die of *boredom* here." He clawed the ground, flicked his wings out, clipped Angel's shoulder. Jewel pressed the palm of her hand down on the top of his head.

"This is important," she told the gray cat. "I'm sorry."

"Are *not*!" He hissed. "We will be *late, sssstupid stupid girl.*"

Angel threw the cat a look that could best be described as disgusted. "If you're worried that Snow and Night are having 'all the fun,' stop."

"They *are!*"

"I doubt it. They have to watch the rest of the den." *And they're probably complaining about it just as loudly*, his expression added.

"*Why* do we have to *wait?*" He pawed the ground again. And then, lifting his head, Jewel's hand notwithstanding, he *roared*.

The trees that comprised this winter forest shook. The earth beneath the gray cat's feet trembled. Ice cracked, lines radiating out from where Jewel sat, for as far as the eye could see, as if she were a heavy object dropped onto the surface of a frozen pond.

No, she thought, it was not she herself that was that object, it was Shadow. Shadow, the giant, frequently annoying, winged cat. Shadow, whom the immortals called eldest. She knew, *knew*, that he was not simply a cat writ large; that he could follow her into her dreams, could stand guard while she slept. But some part of her failed to hold on to this thought; it slipped away, as dreams did. What he was, what he had been, was a very mouthy, very sulky, very demanding . . . cat.

But reality intruded, shattering—quite literally—that perception, that visceral belief.

Shadow growled: *It can* all *be true. Stupid, stupid,* stupid *girl.*

The cracks expanded; the ice shattered.

As it did, the landscape changed. The patina of winter—and blood—broke, dissipating; the forest itself remained. The skies were no longer dusk skies or night skies, not as Jewel recognized them. But she did recognize these skies; they were a deep, clear amethyst. It wasn't the skies that drew—and held—her attention, though. It wasn't the sudden lack of snow; the air was biting in its chill, even in snow's absence.

It was the man who stood down the footpath that traveled in a narrow line that jogged around trees in the distance. She knew instinctively that that way was home, but the forest behind that man was darker and far more intimidating beneath these sudden skies.

It didn't matter.

She leaped off Shadow's back—or tried; he growled and pushed himself off the ground, as if forbidding it. But he did not roar again; his impatience was now banked. "It is *him*," he said. "He is *calling* you."

"Take me to him. Shadow—take me to him *right now.*"

The cat sniffed. "You don't *need* him," he said. "You have *us.*"

"If I'd never met him, I wouldn't. *Shadow.*"

Beneath her feet, she could see Angel begin to move. In the taut line of his shoulders, his arms, in the purposeful length of his stride, she saw a recognition that was twin to hers. But he drew sword, as well.

She signed, but of course he couldn't see her hands, couldn't therefore take comfort from the message she instinctively sought to impart. And if Shadow did not take her down, he would reach the newcomer first.

The cat, however, understood. He was put out, but not in a way that implied great danger—which was good. Jewel herself felt none.

No, what she felt was wordless because there were too many words jostling for position, for prominence. She let only one escape.

"Rath!"

He looked up at the sound of her voice. Although he was at a distance—a distance Shadow closed in a lazy, defiant spiral—she could nonetheless see his expression. And she had no words for that, either, almost as if finding words to describe it was crossing the high walls he had always placed between them. She had loved Rath. He had been family to her, while he lived.

He had never said this out loud, never put it into words. He was, had been, cynical, suspicious; the reluctance he had felt when he had first found her, homeless and beneath a bridge in the poorer holdings, had not been feigned. He needed and wanted that separation. He needed, and wanted, to think of Jewel as temporary.

Even when things changed.

She knew. She knew and understood. How could she not? She'd been raised by her Oma, a woman who believed that joy and love offended the gods enough that they would destroy a person who did not hide them carefully. Gods were envious, spiteful creatures in her Oma's experience. In Jewel's, they were not so simple; she understood only that she would never truly understand them.

And none of that mattered. Rath was *here.* She had thought—had believed—that he was dead; he had disappeared, and he had never returned.

But even as Shadow came to land, she realized that that knowledge had been deeper and more certain than belief. She had *known.*

"Yesssssss," Shadow said.

Rath was dead.

And Rath was here. Here was *not* where he should be. How long had he been here? How long had he been waiting? It had been years since his death.

This was *not* the bridge that separated the living from the Halls of Mandaros. She had seen that bridge. She had almost crossed it herself, shedding the fear and the terror and the weight of responsibility. She understood that it was *peace* and *freedom* that awaited him there.

And this wilderness, these lands, did not contain them.

She was angry, and it was an unfocused anger, but none of it was on Rath. Angel had not reached him; he had slowed, and as she gestured, she heard the sword return to its sheath. She reached out for Rath, and then let her arm fall away.

He looked the same as he looked in her very foggy memory. He had not aged. She had. The hand she lifted did not bear the Terafin signet, as it should have.

"Rath," she said again. Doubts developed gravity, weight—but they were not doubts about his existence, about the truth of what she now saw; she *knew* that this man was Ararath Handernesse. And the Handernesse ring, she did carry.

His smile was the same smile that she had seen so seldom, a splash of warmth on an otherwise weathered, closed face. "Jewel. You've grown up."

She did not feel the truth of that as she faced him. She did not feel that the half a lifetime she'd lived since she had fled the Hundred Holdings at his written command had changed her—or strengthened her—at all. What she wanted, for a brief, visceral moment, was to go home with Rath. To go back to the apartment he had found for them. To go back to the time when Rath knew everything, and she herself knew almost nothing.

And that time was gone.

The fact that it had existed, however, had changed everything. If the past was a country that could never be truly revisited, it was nonetheless a forge in which things were made, tempered, honed. And things that were forged in such a place must eventually leave it in order to act in the world.

"Why are you here?" she managed to ask.

He saw the fear and the shadow of guilt in her expression.

"It is not because of you," he told her. His voice was neutral, but for Rath, neutrality had always been gentle. "It was a choice I made. A choice I was given. I did not understand, at the time, that this is where that choice would lead—but I have learned some things since then."

"But the bridge—"

"Yes, Jewel."

"Your sister—"

"Yes. I know. But I believe she will wait for me, and perhaps it is a mercy that I have been trapped here; I am not certain that I am ready—ever—to face her."

"She'd be so happy to see you."

Rath said nothing.

"She's the person I talked to. About you. About our life in the holdings. When I felt grief, it was to The Terafin that it was safe to express it. She didn't know you as I did; I didn't know you as she did. But . . . we shared the experience of being part of your life."

This seemed to embarrass him. Embarrassment, clearly, was not the province of the living alone.

"Have you been trapped in this forest for the entire time?"

He didn't answer.

"Can you leave it?"

Again, he met the question with silence.

Shadow, however, growled. "You are *wasting time*."

Jewel ignored his words, but said to Rath, "Shadow came to the den only recently."

"You still have your den?"

"Every one of them that survived. Not all of us did."

"I see Angel behind you. I did not recognize him."

"It's his hair."

"Yes. There is a story in that, no doubt."

She lifted a hand again; held it out, palm up, in invitation, not command. "Come with us," she said. "Come home." Her voice shook. She let it.

He lifted his arm and placed his hand gingerly across hers, as if testing the contact. But his hand did not pass through hers. It was solid. It wasn't warm; it wasn't the hand of a living man—and it wasn't, in the end, the hand of a corpse, for which she was profoundly grateful. It was tangible. It was real.

He seemed almost surprised by this.

"Can you climb?"

Shadow hissed. "Why do *I* have to carry *him*?"

"Because," Jewel replied, "You're the only one who can." She spoke with absolute certainty because she was.

Shadow hissed. "Why don't *you* carry him?"

"I will. But I'm riding you, and if he's coming with me, you're carrying him as well."

Shadow had never been fond of practical, logical replies when they didn't suit him, although to be fair, he wasn't fond of them when they did, either. Rath, looking dubious, climbed up on Shadow's back.

"Are we *done* now?" the cat demanded, stalking across the forest floor to where the rest of Jewel's companions waited.

"Yes. Now we're done. Let's go home."

She discovered the slight flaw in that plan an hour later. Although the Winter King had said he could retrace the path they had taken—and Jewel believed him—the path seemed to have lengthened. Traversing it did not seem to bring them any closer to the home that she now desired.

8th day of Lattan, 428 A.A.
Terafin Manse, Averalaan Aramarelas

The first time Teller approached the wrong door, the tree spirit grabbed his wrist before he could touch it. He froze instantly. His fear of failing the House—be it staff or junior members who had managed to crawl up the hierarchy enough that they had the right to be quartered in the manse—had all but driven the other fears out of his mind.

There was, however, a *reason* they had lost Carver, and the bruising grip of his forest guards reminded him, instantly, of that loss.

"The manor is not stable," the tree said softly. "And the doors are becoming less and less safe. It is why," he added, "the inhabitants are to go to The Terafin's personal chambers. That door will open, only and ever, into lands that she rules."

"And the rest?"

"They will open into lands ruled by others. We have almost no time, Teller. The ways are opening, and these halls *will not* be safe. Can you not hear it? Can you not hear the awakening?"

Teller could feel the earth shake, as if in response to the question. But he could only hear his heart and the creak of wooden joists. "We're almost done," he said. "There's only one or two places left to check."

He could not tell them, did not even try, that he was worried about his cat.

8th day of Lattan, 428 A.A.
Terafin Forest, Averalaan Aramarelas

Finch stood on the interlocking path that bridged the manicured gardens designed and labored over by the gardening staff, and the forest that had grown in the wake of Jay's leaves. The sky was brilliant with the colors of dawn; she could see that sky clearly because she faced the manse, not the forest. The colors were not the most striking thing she noticed.

It was the spire, the *tower*, that had risen, was still rising, in the hundred holdings. It seemed a thing of jet or ebony, but it reflected the light of day as it rose; there was a majesty to its sudden presence that almost drove fear away, the sense of awe was so profound.

Jay had told them about the Sleepers. Finch would have sworn she understood; was she not standing here? Had they not made preparations? But words alone, dread alone, could not convey the truth of the experience. As the spire rose, as it reached a height equal to *Avantari's* and still continued its climb, she understood in a visceral way why the Sleepers were so terrifying, even to the distant gods.

She was regent to *one House*. She was not King, nor Queen. She was not magi, had been born with no talent, no hint of magic, to help her navigate the world. What she knew, she knew well—but the Merchant Authority was not the training ground for this kind of emergency.

She missed Jarven. Jarven would have been at home here.

But Jarven was not regent. Jarven was not the de facto ruler of Terafin; Finch had taken that mantle. She wore the clothing that Haval had made for her in the wake of an assassination attempt, and she wore the House ring. She was dressed for the type of battle she understood well: political.

Her role here was not to fight Sleepers or immortals or the beings the wilderness birthed. If the city depended on her ability in that regard, it was doomed. No, she thought, squaring her shoulders. She could not *fight* as the guards fought. But she was here to save lives. If this were a battlefield, Finch was now the Terafin standard. And she understood the importance of a standard on a field of battle.

Arrayed behind her were guards; not House Guards, but the denizens of the wilderness that Haval had both armed and instructed. She found their presence comforting, yet knew that most of House Terafin would not. She had, therefore, asked the Chosen to stand beside her and to stand among the forest guards, and the Chosen had instantly understood why and agreed.

Torvan was with Finch; Arrendas was not. Most of the guards who wore Terafin colors were House Guards, though. Because Finch was regent, and Finch was here, they accepted the orders she gave with alacrity. They accepted the golden-skinned, much taller forest guards the moment they understood those guards took orders from their regent. They were ready; they were watchful.

When the earth began to tremble beneath their feet, the forest guards did not seem to notice; the House Guard did. So, too, Torvan. He had asked—not commanded—that she retreat to a safer position; she had refused. Nor did he press the issue; she understood both why he must ask and why she could not accede.

She glanced, once, over her shoulder. Haval had remained in the forest; he had sent Finch out. She was surprised at how much she missed his presence; he was not a comforting man. But she had Torvan.

Torvan had been their first friend in the House. It was because of Torvan's intervention that Arann had survived. He was not, and could not be, den—but he understood the den, and inasmuch as it was possible to do so, supported it. Jay was now The Terafin the Chosen served.

In her absence, the Chosen supported the regent, and if historically they had had to hold their noses to do so, there was nothing perfunctory about that service now.

"They're coming," she told him, eyes narrowed.

He nodded. The first of the evacuees were making their way toward where Finch now stood.

8th day of Lattan, 428 A.A.
The Araven Manse, Averalaan

There were perhaps a handful of exhausted servants that remained asleep while the world was transformed; Hectore, not being a servant, was not one of them. Nor was his wife. Even his grandchildren, all of whom he had gathered beneath his large, expensive roof, were awake. They were not precisely *quiet*, but they were awake.

They had arrived the day before; it was his grandson's birthday. His entire family was with him. It had been Andrei's suggestion that they celebrate it in grand style—thus forcing his children and their children to come to the manse; his suggestion that it be an evening party, with the attendant exhaustion which would prevent that family from leaving for their own scattered homes, meant they would be confined to the one space Andrei felt would guarantee their safety. The seventh of Lattan had passed into the very early hours of the eighth.

Nadianne was dressed and likewise awake. She watched him patiently while he spent some time with the more fractious grandchildren, but only with half an eye; most of her attention was given—as was the older children's and their increasingly frightened parents—to the windows. From the safety of the manse, they watched the rise of a dark spire; they watched the tower rise beneath it. The bulk of what Hectore assumed was the rest of the building was obscured by the more densely packed architecture of the city itself.

His wife turned toward him as he joined her. "Are you certain," she asked, voice as soft as she could make it, "that this is where you must be?"

"No," was his frank reply.

"Andrei is out there?"

He nodded.

"Hectore—"

"He cheated," Hectore replied, before she could ask the question that obviously hovered behind her slightly parted lips. "He asked."

"Asked?"

"He said he had never truly asked a boon or favor from me, in all of the years he has otherwise tolerated my company. And he begged one boon of tonight."

"That you remain in Araven."

"That I remain in Araven."

"I confess surprise that you granted it."

"I said no," was Hectore's genial response.

His wife waited patiently for the explanation that was certain to follow, and he did not even consider keeping her in suspense. "He then informed me that our survival was essential to his own. He considered the gravest threat to his safety—to his existence—to be our deaths."

"Your death," she countered.

"No, Nadianne, our deaths. Our home is his home. It has been his home for the entirety of our marriage; it was his home before that. But home, to me, is part of life; what, then, does home mean if the lives of my family are lost?"

She was not given to being demonstrative in public, but nonetheless now leaned into his side, beneath the weight of the arm he slid around her shoulders. She was cold; he could feel her tremble.

"What will happen?" she asked.

"The Sleepers," he said, "will wake."

8th day of Lattan, 428 A.A.
The Common

Around the base of a building that seemed all of one piece of stone, the *Ellariannatte* grew. If Jester had thought Birgide's work done, he repented; he even felt a hint of guilt. The trees continued their magnificent, sudden growth at Birgide's unspoken command. He lost sight of the Common as it became a forest of trees in full growth, leaves in full bloom. The wind's rustle was loud above his head—above all their heads—and Jester thought he could almost make out words in the sound.

He glanced at Birgide; her chin was tilted up, her throat exposed, as if the words he could almost hear were the voices of a crowd, to her. This did not surprise him; he had come to understand, on some level, what Warden meant. But the tears were almost a shock.

"They'll die," she whispered. "They'll be destroyed. And they'll be destroyed in defense of people I don't know. I . . . do not like people. I don't trust them. But the forest has always been like salvation to me."

He understood then.

"It's what *she* wants," Birgide continued. "It's what she wants *of* the forest. That it be harbor and shelter."

And it wasn't, precisely, what Birgide wanted.

"You're not betraying them," Jester said quietly, speaking to the heart of her pain.

She did not answer.

"They aren't children. They have their own thoughts, their own desires. You aren't deluding them or lying to them—you are commanding them. It's what Duvari does. It's what I think Haval used to do. It's what the Kings do every time they declare war."

"It's different with people."

"How? You think every member of the army is there freely and happily because of their spotless loyalty?"

"It's different with the *Astari*."

He didn't argue that. He knew he shouldn't be arguing at all. Not now, and not so close to the building. To Jester's eye what was a grand, large cathedral of a building had stopped its upward climb. He could see fully exposed—but closed—doors; could see the wide, gleaming stairs that led to them. He could see the width of the building itself, and the complicated carvings that adorned the pillars between which the doors were nestled. Above them the tower stood.

There were no visible bells, no obvious windows; it was a pillar of perfect stone, untouched by the roots of the *Ellariannatte*, unblemished, undamaged. It suggested gods and their glory, suggested myths, legends; everyday street stories did not have the gravitas to do likewise.

And yet, it was the street stories to which Jester's thoughts turned.

When the Sleepers wake.

He could not now remember the old rhyme, although he remembered the jumping game to which it was set. But he thought that it presaged the end of the world.

"It won't be enough," she whispered. "I should have come sooner. I should have started earlier. It won't be enough."

"You sound a lot like Jay," he replied. "Stupid." This didn't even annoy her, and he changed his approach. "Some lives," he told her, "are better than none. Whatever we *can* save, we must save."

"You don't like people, either."

"I don't like patricians. It's not the same. And Duvari," he added, as she opened her mouth. "I don't like him, either. But people? I *am* one. Not a great one, as it happens. Not impressive. Not particularly talented. Not much of anything. So, absent money and House Name, the people we're rescuing here? More like me than the patricians. That's enough, for me.

"Birgide—*one life* is better than none. And you are going to save a lot more lives than that tonight." He did not say, did not add, that she could plant more trees; although this was true, one did not tell a grieving parent that they could have more children.

"It's not enough."

The neutrality of her voice caught him before he loosed more words. This time, there was no guilt in it.

"We need to transform enough of this city; we need to spread the lines of Jewel's active dominion. We'll catch people who were unfortunate enough to live too close to the Common—but I need more time."

Cursing, Jester looked up. Cupping both of his hands to bracket his mouth, he shouted, "Snow!"

The cathedral doors began to roll open.

Chapter Fifteen

The High Wilderness

JEWEL CALLED A HALT to the trek through darkened forest. The air was winter air, although there was very little evidence of snow. The light that filtered through to the forest floor was not sun's light; she could not tell how long they had been traveling. The Winter King said he was not lost, and she believed him—but time had passed, was passing. She wondered, then, if waiting in the Hidden Court would have been the better choice, in the end; if she gained a handful of hours leaving before Ariane could and did, what use were they if she was trapped here, meandering across a landscape that had literally lengthened in the time she'd been gone?

But . . . she would not have found Rath. She understood this: she would not have found Rath. She asked Rath, while she rode, about his death. He knew he was not alive, and the spare facts of death did not seem to disturb him; he accepted what he could not change.

He told her of his meeting with Evayne; told her of the ring that he had accepted from Kallandras; told her of the choice he had made. Angel walked by the Winter King's side. Of the den, Angel was the only one who had come to her after she had left Rath's place, but he'd heard the old stories. He knew how the rest of the den had come together. And he'd met Rath because Rath continued to train the den; he just hadn't wanted to live with them.

"I did not want you to die. And I had come to understand that we did, indeed, face demons; that the actions I took—was taking—at the behest of Sigurne Mellifas, would inevitably be discovered. I am not a man who is fond of large amounts of company, and your den had become quite a . . . crowd. But that is not why I asked you to leave. I thought—" he broke off.

Angel signed briefly, and Jewel did not then twist in her seat in an attempt to see Rath's expression. He surprised her. He continued.

"I thought that you would be safe if you were quit of me. You are Terafin now?"

"I am The Terafin."

"That was not my intent when I sent you to my sister."

"No. It wasn't her intent when she adopted me, either. But the people she'd groomed to succeed her were assassinated. I survived. And I think—I think she understood, viscerally, that I would always survive. She understood what I wanted, what the den wanted. In the end, she wanted me to take the House."

"And you?"

Silence. Breath. "I wanted her to be at peace. I did not want the House."

"You are The Terafin."

"Yes. Because I promised her that I would take the House and rule it. I don't think she would have asked it," she continued, her voice softening, "if not for the demons. The demons I could see. The magics I could detect. It was because I was seer-born."

"And the war for the House?"

"There was no war. We were prepared for the infighting," she added. "But . . ." she shrugged. "Demons. Magic. Gods. In the end, the House Council agreed with Amarais: they believed I would survive an apocalypse—and that the best chance that Terafin would survive rested with me."

"Jewel—"

"I don't want it," she whispered. "I'm—I don't want it."

"What do you see?"

She shook her head. She felt his arms tighten around her; felt his chin as he rested it atop her head. "I'll take you. I'll take you back to—to where you should be."

"Yes," he said softly "You will. But not yet, Jewel."

"Not exactly yet. I'm not sure how, from here."

"And you will be sure when you are home?"

Silence.

He chuckled. "I'm unwilling to face my sister—I told you, I'm a coward. But let me carry, instead, the news of your triumph, and I will have the courage to approach her: I will have at least something she wants."

"She might not be there."

"She will."

"And I might not triumph."

"Jewel, you already have. You have done more than she herself could have done. Should you die in the face of the Sleepers, you will still have done more. One failure does not destroy past success."

"It does," she told him. "It renders success meaningless. Where are we going now?" She frowned. She had, unconsciously, directed Shadow, and Shadow, without complaint, had followed the unspoken, unintentional orders she had given. He did not fly, did not run, did not appear to notice something as trifling as scenery. But he did not call Rath stupid and did not complain about his presence.

"No," the cat growled. "*He* is not *stupid.*"

Of course not. She was. She exhaled. "Let me get down for a minute."

Shadow hissed. It was petulant.

Jewel dismounted slowly, planted both feet as firmly on the ground as she could, and grimaced. She lifted her hands, but they were shaking.

Angel was by her side—not so close as to crowd, but close enough to leave no doubt that he was right here, if needed. And she did need that. She understood that she could ask nothing of him—there was no burden he could relieve her of. But that almost didn't matter. What she needed now was the reminder of what home *meant.* Angel signed.

Jewel folded her arms at the elbow and reached into her own chest.

8th day of Lattan, 428 A.A.
The Order of Knowledge, Averalaan Aramarelas

The wind swept across the silent men and women who stood ready at the heights of the tallest tower the Order of Knowledge boasted. They had been told to gather and wait. Their orders had come from Meralonne APhaniel; permission to stand at these heights had come from the guildmaster. Both Sigurne and Meralonne were absent, but the wind told them that one, at least, was now returning.

Gyrrick stepped forward before Meralonne could be seen, conveyed by the turbulent air. From this height, they could see the Common; they could no longer see the statue of Moorelas. It had been toppled or destroyed—they could not tell which—by the rise of a building that rivaled *Avantari* in size. Around that building, *Ellariannatte* grew, and in numbers. The magi were familiar with the position and the number of those trees; they were the perch from which they created displays of colored light and illusion on the eighth day of Lattan, the longest day of the year.

Today, although day had not yet dawned, and no welcome light had crested the horizon.

Planning and preparation for such a celebration had, of course, been done— but the hours between now and then stretched out into infinity. The warrior-magi that Meralonne had trained had seen battle, a battlefield, in the Dominion of Annagar. And before that, they had seen battle rage across the Common. In both cases, they had been pointed, like weapons, toward the *Kialli* and the demonic kin who served them.

Meralonne appeared in a gust of wind that threatened to rip the flags off their masts. His eyes were silver, not steel, but steel ran through them as he looked down upon the warrior-magi he had risked the guildmaster's wrath to train.

They bowed to him in perfect unison and rose at his command in the same fashion; they could feel his words as if words themselves had a physical component; as if he were bard-born.

He waited. The wind that supported him midair began to reach for their armor, their hair; they felt its chill fingers across their upturned faces, their exposed cheeks. But it was warm when compared to his eyes, and Gyrrick wondered, distantly, if he had ever truly known the man he had chosen to follow.

"You were trained for this day," Meralonne told them, without preamble. "You were honed in the lands of the South, but it is *this* fight that you were meant for."

They did not understand, but did not ask.

"You have seen the dark spire rise; you have seen Moorelas' Sanctum breached, and the statue itself finally fail. Do you understand what comes?"

Gyrrick found his voice first. "The Sleepers."

"Yes. The Three who slept are waking now. They will step into the streets of this city—your city—from the depths of that cathedral. It was the place at which they failed in their charge. Do you understand?"

Gyrrick nodded. There was no person present who had not heard the story of Moorelas, offered in song, in legend, in children's game.

"The god we do not name has returned. He gathers his forces in the distant North. If the Sleepers have any hope of redemption, it lies, in the end, with the enemy they failed to destroy. They were not gods," he added, his voice softer. "But they were kin to gods."

"Could they have destroyed him?"

"With Moorelas' help, yes." He shook his head, his lips curving in a way that implied pain. "It is the past. You cannot walk it. But they have woken, and it is into these streets that they will first walk. As the gods did, they alter the land their feet touch, until that land is more pleasing to them.

"And this land, this small, mortal city, will not please them."

"If they could stand against a god and survive, what do you expect of us?"

"I expect you to stand—for a short time—against them."

Silence.

"And, Gyrrick, against me."

The silence grew weighty.

It was, again, Gyrrick who broke it, carrying the weight of every member of this force that Meralonne had taught. "You? Why you?"

"You have long understood that I am not like the other magi," Meralonne replied, turning to look toward the heart of the Common. "When the gods were bound by the covenant to which they agreed, they left these lands and the wilderness slept without the divine to invoke it, to warp it, to create with it.

"So, too, the firstborn—who could not leave, as the gods had chosen to leave. But they could be sequestered in small pockets, in hidden courts. They were. In some fashion, they were sleeping, just as the Sleepers were."

His smile, when he turned it upon them again, could not be described; Gyrrick did not think he could even make the attempt. There was Winter in that smile, ice, steel; there was power in it, but sorrow and weariness as well, as if the one must come inevitably from the other.

"I have been sleeping," Meralonne continued. "But not in a fashion that is possible for you and your kin; I was not trapped, as my brethren were trapped. I could—and did—wander these mortal lands. I could watch your kind as they crawled out of the wreckage caused by mine; I could watch your attempts to build, and build again, when what was built first inevitably failed.

"I thought, at first, that my survival was a great wrong—but it was a fate decreed by the Lord I had failed, and I accepted it." He was restless, and the wind reflected it; Gyrrick would not have been surprised had he simply turned and vanished.

He did not. That was the thing Gyrrick would remember most clearly about this conversation.

"I learned to hear your tiny voices. I learned to live your tiny lives. I learned to find beauty in small things I would not have noticed when I had true freedom. But I likewise found beauty in things that I would have noticed, even at the height of my power."

Gyrrick was silent, but he met, and held Meralonne's gaze.

"Yes," the magi replied. "Sigurne. It is to Sigurne you must look for your orders; it is Sigurne you must protect if my name is not protection enough. And in this place, at this time, it may not be. I have seen what my brethren have not seen; I have lived in a fashion no one of my kin has willingly lived. But I have come to understand, as the wilderness slowly wakes, that what I once was was not destroyed; I, too, was sleeping.

"And, Gyrrick, I have attempted not to wake. When the wind calls my name, I hear it, but it is contained; that much, I have learned. I do not know what will wake in me when I am at last reunited with the firstborn princes." His voice trembled, but it was not with fear.

"When?" Gyrrick asked. Just that.

Nor did Meralonne pretend not to understand. "I do not know, for certain—but soon, Gyrrick. Soon, I think."

"And we will know?"

"You will know. It is to the guildmaster that you owe—and have always owed—your loyalty; it was for the guildmaster that I chose to teach you at all. But you will be needed, should this city survive—and if it does survive, it will be in large part due to your efforts—yours, and the mortals who have made it their home. The Terafin's forest grows, and it grows quickly. I do not desire your deaths, but when the time comes, I am not certain to remember that. Desire mine, at that point. Prove to me that you are the last, the strongest, of my students."

As he spoke, the wind at last reached for the magi; they leaped into its folds, and Meralonne carried them to the edge of the Common. He saluted them once, from the air, as he left them.

8th day of Lattan, 428 A.A.
The Common, Averalaan

The doors were taller than the most forbidding doors that graced *Avantari*, the palace of Kings. They were wider, thicker, and their hinges were utterly silent, as if such noises were an insult to the dignity of those who resided within.

Jester had hands on a dagger that he had no illusions would be of use; it was a comfort to him, a sign that he was willing to struggle, even if that struggle availed him little but personal dignity, in the end. And that was not like him.

"Steady," a familiar voice said, somewhere to his right. That he took comfort in the voice said a lot about his state of mind, because it was Jarven's.

"She needs more time," Jester said, voice flat.

"And you know this how?"

"Because she *said so*. Or were you not eavesdropping, then?"

"Interesting. Eldest, may I set you down?"

A golden fox appeared at Jester's feet. In form and shape, he was both beautiful and harmless; his fur was sleek, its patina warm. He looked up a perfectly formed nose, the demand—it would injure his self-respect to make a request—completely obvious in the gesture.

Jester knelt and offered to carry him by the simple expedient of opening his arms. He was not terribly surprised to find the fox heavy. Nor did he need Jarven's quiet reminder that respect was of tantamount import when dealing with the forest elders. He understood that he carried a predator, and that that predator was of far greater danger than Jarven.

But, philosophically, he also accepted that death was death, and he could only die once. It didn't matter if the fox was vastly more dangerous than Jarven; didn't matter if Jarven was vastly more dangerous than a violent gang of roving youths in the poorest of the holdings. Death was death.

Death was coming.

"How much more time?" the fox asked, the words slow and patient, as if Jester's ability to understand them were in grave doubt.

"She didn't say."

"Can you ask her now?"

"You can't?"

The fox chuckled. "You are not nearly as unintelligent as Jarven assumes."

This did rankle, but only slightly.

Jester forgot about time, forgot about Jarven, forgot about everything except the fox in his arms and the men who were emerging from the building that had devoured so much of the Common.

They were three.

They bore the blue shields of their kind, but there was a difference to the color, to the texture, of that luminosity: in the hands of the three, the shields seemed more like captured lightning than simple light. They had not drawn swords, not yet, and Jester felt a faint and ridiculous hope.

"Birgide," he whispered, mouth dry. But he did not ask the question the fox had asked. There was no measure of *time* that she could give him that would make sense. Not now.

He felt the ground beneath his feet shift, and since that ground was now the twined roots of towering trees, he understood the answer: *not yet*.

"Soon," he told the fox.

"Tell me, what do you see when you look at them?" The fox might have been talking about flowers in the Terafin gardens for all the urgency contained in his voice.

Jester had no words. And that was also not like him. He had seen gods in the Between—as seldom as humanly possible—and they had not had the effect upon him that these three men had. Gods were not Sleepers. He understood that, now. They existed in the Between, and it was only there, in the half-shaped, mist strewn world that they might be perceived at all. They were not part of the world in which humanity lived and worked and struggled; they were other, they were at a distance.

These men were not.

Jester remembered that the gods had once walked the world. He understood it in some fashion, because one such god had been responsible for death and destruction in the Terafin manse, hard on the heels of the den's first arrival. And he knew that the threat that shadowed the Empire—the world itself— was a god enthroned, for the moment, in the Northern Wastes, ruling his Shining Court.

But the bestial god and the distant shadow did not have the power, the grace, the *immediacy* of the three who came fully out from under the line of the magnificent arch.

They had the long, pale hair of the Wild Hunt, yes; they were of a height, if he attempted to view them objectively, with Celleriant.

But Celleriant was an echo, a shadow, a hastily drawn charcoal sketch in comparison; what they were, Celleriant was not, and would never be. Jester considered Celleriant beautiful, but he distrusted patrician beauty. Beauty in a physical sense was, for Jester, a warning, a caution. He kept his distance from it, and in general, it kept its distance from him.

But these men?

They were far more compelling. Far more exalted. He felt, mouth dry, that he should not even dare to cross their paths or meet their gazes; that he should not dare to call these lands his home, that had been their prison. That *none* should call them home, given the profanity of the act of caging them.

The fox bit his hand.

He didn't make a sound, viscerally aware that any sound from him would attract attention he did not want. But the pain had returned him to himself, for the moment.

"You see them," the fox said. "You understand."

He did.

And he hated the understanding and hated himself for falling under that spell, for considering himself worthless in comparison. He understood fear of power. He understood the need for invisibility. He understood that he didn't measure up to most threats—he'd grown up that way. He didn't worry about what was *fair* or *just*; those were arguments for people who had enough power to care. Demanding fairness or justice had always been games played by people with the certainty of power. For Jester, orphaned, sold, and only barely rescued? He stayed out of the way of the powerful. He didn't care about *fair*. He cared about survival. Being right was of no value if it was his corpse in the street.

But that was fear. There was *no* objective worth that defined his life. He was not immortal. He was not a god. But he had as much right to walk the streets of this city as they did. More, even. It was his home.

"Sorry," he said quietly to the fox in his arms.

"You are mortal," the fox replied. "As is our Lord. It is not a besetting sin, but you are coming to understand that there are no besetting sins in the wilderness. There is power, and there is survival. You will be fine, for the moment. I am not certain our Warden is up to the task set her—but time will tell. Set me down, Jester. I will return to you, if you remain."

"And Jarven?"

"Is Jarven; his business is not my business." The fox leaped delicately, gracefully, to the ground. He then made his way over the gnarl of entwined roots, his feet leaving no trace as he passed through the barrier of trees that Birgide was, even now, attempting to thicken.

And as he walked, he seemed to grow, to shift in size—and in shape—to become something other, something larger, and something infinitely closer to the divine. Jester had understood, intellectually, that there was a reason the fox was called elder and treated with respect by the forest denizens—but they treated the damn cats the same way.

Here and now, Jester wondered if the cats, like the fox, could adopt other forms. On the night they had almost—almost—killed Adam and Jay, they had returned to Jay's side enlarged in size; it was only their voices and their behavior that had established them, firmly, as the winged petulances the entire manse knew.

But they had never taken on a form that was almost—but not quite— human before. The fox did. And as one man, the three who now stood at the crest of the grand, wide stairs, looked toward him. He did not, however, leave the shade of the *Ellariannatte*.

He bowed. It was an oddly graceful bow, not Imperial, and not Southern; it almost seemed like the overture to a complicated, complex dance. The branches above the fox seemed to weave and bow in a similar fashion.

The three who stood before the open doors did not return that bow. But one among them stepped forward, as if by silent assent. He spoke a long word that Jester did not understand; he assumed it was a name. Or a song; it seemed to be a verse.

The fox replied in kind. And then, in a language Jester could understand, he continued. "It is not our wish to detain you, nor is it our wish to show any disrespect; it is not the desire of this most ancient of places to dishonor you or your kin."

The stranger looked up, at the crown of trees; his gaze then fell to their roots. "And will you speak on behalf of your Lord? Does your Lord know so little of respect or reverence that she does not venture forth to greet us?"

"She is gone to the court of the White Lady, on an errand for that august person," the fox replied, his voice far more neutral. A thread of defiance ran through these offered words, a hint of a dare that Jester—could he find voice—would never have expressed.

Silence. Jester understood the texture of that dare, understood the implication in all the words the fox had chosen. They were truth, but, like Jarven, the fox did not prize honesty; like anything else at hand, it was a tool to be used only when it engendered the desired reaction.

"We do not recognize your Lord's name," the first man said. "We hear it, but it is so slight it contains no weight, no meaning. It is almost ephemeral."

The fox said nothing.

The trees, however, seemed to shake at a wind that touched nothing else—and there was wind now, but the branches did not move as if conversing with its currents. Jester glanced back at Birgide and froze.

She was pale, trembling as if she were kin to those branches, these trees. She did not have the elegance of the Arianni, did not compel as the immortals did, but what he saw in her now felt like the heart of rage. Or fear. Or loss. He had released her hand to become conveyance for a creature that could have easily walked the short distance he all but demanded to be carried, and he regretted it.

He turned his back on gods and knew it. He turned away from the sense of awe, of dread, of something that was too raw and too deep to be called worship. Why?

Because he had meant every word he had said about Birgide. The others might not know it yet, but Birgide was den. She was kin.

He reached her side and, once again, grabbed her hand, as if his own hand was an anchor. She did not try to pull away; did not seem to even notice that

Jester was there, at her side. But her hand tightened, returning his grip, and as it did, she closed her red, red eyes.

The High Wilderness

There was pain. Jewel understood, in that moment, that there would always be pain. It was not, however, strictly physical. Although her hands appeared to all watching—and in some fashion to her, herself—to be piercing her chest, they cut nothing, tore nothing physical; there was no blood, no gaping hole, nothing that threatened to end her life.

She closed hands around her heart. She felt it, not as crystal; it was not hard, it had no sharp edges; it was warm, its softness belying its visual shape. And she understood, as she looked at it, that it was not pain she felt; it was fear. Fear had always been her enemy.

Shadow did not step on her foot, did not call her *stupid*, did not tell her to put it away. Nor did he tell her that this was suicide, that it was folly, that it was unsafe. The latter, she did not need to be told. She had walked the Oracle's path, and she understood that there was no safety in this act—that there would never be safety in it. There was fear. And what she saw would confirm that fear, if fear was allowed to be the only measure by which she judged.

There was *so much* to fear.

But all of the things she feared—the death of her den-kin, the destruction of her city, the loss of her home—were layers wrapped around a single core. She was afraid that she could not prevent those things. She was afraid that she could not save anything. She knew who she was. She knew that she was not— had never truly—been up to the task.

Shadow did not speak.

No one did. She thought she caught a flicker of movement, thought Angel might have signed, but no one said a word. She was looking at her closed hands; hints of light, of something that might be light, leaked from between her fingers. She pried her hands open, almost as if they belonged to someone else. Her hands were in her way.

As was she.

She was not up to the task.

She had sent Duster to lead the den out of their home. She had sent Duster *to die*. She had given orders that the undercity be abandoned, but she had lost Lander anyway. She had failed to lead The Terafin—and Meralonne—to that

undercity, had failed to warn people in time, and she had been utterly powerless to save the people who had been spirited into the darkness and the torture
and death that awaited them in that terrible, terrible Henden.

She had failed to save Amarais.

In all the futures she had been haphazardly shown, there had never been
enough information for certainty, and when she had, in the grip of talent, been
certain, it was immediate, visceral—a thing more felt than thought. Thought
had come later.

She was seer-born, but she was only one person—and in spite of that, people
pinned their hopes on her. Those hopes continued to accrete; she was bowed
by them, bent with their weight, because she could not live up to them.

She could not walk away from them; could never walk away. But here, in
this place, she felt so immobilized by the weight, the breadth, of those hopes
that she could not walk at all.

She closed her eyes, bowed her head. One thing at a time. One thing.

She had to go home. She had to *get* home. And she had to do it now.

Her mouth was dry as she forced her eyes open; her arms shook. She discarded the what-ifs and the should-haves because, in the end, they would not
help her here. Perhaps later she might—as she so often did, and so bitterly—
learn from her mistakes. But even if they had lessons to teach her, she could
not change the past. Had never been able to change it.

She had managed to change what had not yet become the future.

One step. One step at a time. What she needed to do now was go home.
What she needed to find, not by the querulous instinct of a wild talent, but
with deliberation, was the path that would take her there. And this was why
she had followed the Oracle. So that she had that choice.

Choice itself was terrifying, because if one *had* the choice, the responsibility
that came with making the right one was much, much larger. Helplessness was
not what she wanted, but when she had had no choice, her mistakes had not
doomed other people.

But her choices wouldn't have saved them, either.

"Jewel," Rath said, startling her.

She did not look at him but clung to the familiar and long-absent sound of
his voice.

"I am here because I wore a ring that was crafted by, made by, the Winter
Queen. I was, while alive, one tool in her long and bitter war. But she does not
surrender what she owns."

"If I'd known—if I'd known—"

"I would have been the boon you asked for."

She swallowed. Swallowed and frowned. "How do you know? How do you know what I asked for?"

This time she turned, her heart in her hands—and in her expression, her voice.

"I was there. I have been there since I invoked what the ring offered."

"I didn't—"

"See me? No. But you were not meant to see me. I told you: the Winter Queen does not easily or willingly surrender what she owns. She did not go to great lengths to hide my presence; it was not necessary."

"Could she have made you visible?"

His smile was gentle. "I do not know. I did not ask."

"But—"

"There are none who can easily interfere with the Winter Queen in her court; they are *of* her in a fashion that mortals cannot be. Were she not born to this world, were she not of it herself, she could not have contained me, could not have held on to me. There is a place the mortal dead go, and it, too, is beyond her.

"It is where Shianne will go. She suspects this, but does not know. Could she, the White Lady would do what was done—to me—to hold Shianne forever." He glanced, then, at Shianne, who was utterly still.

"How are you here?" the mortal child of Ariane whispered. "How came you to leave her side?"

"There exists, at court, one who flouts—without intent—the intention of a woman she does not understand, and she is coveted, celebrated, and indulged."

Jewel whispered, "Cessaly."

"The young Evayne brought your Artisan materials with which to craft. I am uncertain that Evayne herself knew what their purpose must be, and to ask Cessaly is to hazard an answer that will merely add layers to confusion. But it is because of Evayne that I believe I am meant, and was meant, to be here."

"If you were meant to be here, Ariane could have . . ."

"You understand the difficulty. She is what she is. Had you asked it, yes. But you did not ask. And yet, I believe that this is, in some fashion, her intent as well. Come. You have something to do, and I have something to do, as well."

"And that?"

"I failed you once," he said softly.

She bridled instantly.

"No, it is not your accusation. Were it, I might refute it, and with ease. It is the accusation I turned—and have turned—on myself for half your life. I cannot change the past, but it haunts me."

"What can you do if you're dead?" It was Angel who asked.

"Remain," he replied. "Where Jewel goes, I will follow. What she faces, I will face."

"You won't be able to do anything."

"We shall see. Mandaros is . . . ill-pleased with the Winter Queen." He placed one hand on her shoulder, and she felt its warmth, as if that warmth had been dredged from memory and made, once again, real.

Angel was right. Rath was dead. He could not do what they could do. How foolish, then, to feel his presence as if it were comfort or shield.

"Will Mandaros be angry at me?"

"Oh, undoubtedly," was his airy reply. She heard an echo of Jester in it, which surprised her. "But I won't, and I consider that of more import."

She didn't mean to laugh, but she did, and if it was brief, it was genuine.

Angel's surprise made clear to her that she hadn't laughed much—at all—recently. And the word recent stretched out for days and months. He signed a single word, and she shook her head.

"You will have to tell me," Rath said, "what I've missed. But now," he added, "look. If I understand everything that's been said—in my presence—this is the reason you walked the Oracle's path."

Shadow, sulking, said, "Is *not*." He sniffed. "You only like *him* because he is *stupid*. Like *you*."

Jewel grimaced. "Shadow, please."

"What? What? *What*?"

She hoped Night and Snow didn't have the same reaction to Rath that Shadow did. "You're just saying that because you can't step on him, knock him out of the way, or destroy his things."

"And believe," Angel said to Rath, "that you're going to appreciate that." He dodged the wing Shadow flicked in his direction, as if to make his point.

"We can only be grateful," Celleriant said, "that your cat did not disgrace you in the White Lady's presence."

"Surely the cat would only disgrace himself," Avandar said.

Shadow snarled and hissed.

And Jewel felt, as they squabbled, that she *could* do this. She turned her gaze into the thing that she had once called a seer's heart, and she looked.

Angel watched. Of the people present, he was the most tense, the most worried. He had always found inactivity stressful. She was the Lord he had chosen, but she was kin as well. He had admired her, but admiration had given way to something else, because admiration was something that was distant.

He wanted to help her. He wanted to be of use. And he knew, watching her now, that there was nothing he could do, no part of this burden he could shoulder. He could be here, for all the good that might do. Shadow stepped on his foot.

Angel frowned at the cat, and his expression froze.

Shadow's eyes were glowing. It was not the subtle silver patina that sometimes enveloped Arianni eyes; it was not the subtle gold that sometimes—especially in darkness—seem to light the cats' eyes from within. It was a brilliant gold, an intense gold; it reminded Angel of the sun.

His mother's distant warning not to stare at the sun almost made him avert his own gaze, but the cat's foot grew instantly heavier, as if Shadow did not understand mortal anatomy, and meant to fix Angel's attention in place.

"You *are* useless," Shadow said, his voice, unlike his eyes, completely normal. "And *stupid*. But *stupid* is what *she* needs." A growl chased the words. "She needs you to *be* stupid. She needs you *here*."

"To do what?" Angel hadn't meant to speak. He knew that Jay, eyes fixed on the crystal, body rigid, did not hear him.

"You will know." He lifted his foot as Jay bit her lip hard enough to draw blood. She tore her gaze away from the crystal; Angel was suddenly afraid she would drop it. But Rath, seated behind her, put both of his arms out, one to either side of her, to steady her. Dead or not, he seemed solid enough—to Jay—to brace her in a way that Angel could not.

"This is not where we need to be," she said, and if her color was terrible, her voice was not. Angel heard the absolute certainty in it. The den had lived and died by it, when they had made their home in the hundred holdings; it was a voice that demanded instant action, removing all need for thought.

Shadow turned; he was not pointing the way they had come.

The Winter King turned as well.

"Kallandras?" Jay said.

He nodded.

Jay put her crystal away. Angel understood that she thought of it, on some primal level, as her heart; he couldn't. It was a deliberate choice.

Jay then reached for the small pouch she had kept by her side for their journey; it was crafted of leather that time had diminished, something that would be considered very much beneath the station she occupied in *Averalaan*. Here, however, all mortal stations seemed irrelevant, and things as worn as the pouch implied familiarity and prior use.

She took the single leaf that she had given to Carver, and that Carver had chosen—at great cost—to return. It was slender, blue, metallic; it was not a thing of her forests, and yet it had come indirectly from the lands she claimed. Nestled among leaves of silver, gold, and diamond, it nonetheless stood out, and it came instantly to the hand that trembled in search of it, as if it were alive.

No one asked what she intended. Shianne had been birthed to the wilderness the gods once ruled; everyone else understood exactly how the Terafin forest had come into being. They trusted her to do what was necessary.

The certainty that sometimes came with vision offered no comfort at all, because certainty had never offered absolution. Angel understood the burden of the guilt she carried. Had it been in his power, he would have relieved her of it—but he also understood that it was an essential part of who she was, and he did not want that to change any more than it already had.

Her skin paled, her eyes closed, as if the lids themselves were too heavy to keep open. He moved instantly to stand beside her, ignoring Shadow's glare. No cat words chased after it.

She did not dig. Did not orient the leaf, did not do anything that might visibly be construed as planting it. But she hadn't done that in the Terafin forest, either; the wind had carried the leaves, as if at her command, and the earth had accepted them. Here, she simply laid the leaf across the ground and rose.

Angel had enough warning to brace himself as the ground beneath his feet shifted.

8th day of Lattan, 428 A.A.
Terafin Manse, Averalaan Aramarelas

Teller understood the danger of doors. He entered none of them, but he did throw them open, raising his voice to shout. As he worked his way through the manor, his voice grew hoarse; he husbanded it between the opening and closing of doors. But he had opened three that were no longer connected to the manse that had been, had become, his home; they made of that home something instantly strange and dangerous, threw into doubt the stability he and the den had worked all of their adult lives to build.

The fourth such door he opened, he could not close.

The door became insubstantial, its brass knob losing solidity, its wooden frame buckling as if under great and sudden weight. Teller heard the crack of hard wood and had just enough time to get out of the way as something leaped through the open frame.

The guards that the forest had sent to him leaped into action, then, but it was a subtle, strange action; it seemed, for a moment, that they were frozen in place, rooted as their distant bodies were rooted; their skin developed the rings, the circles, the grain, that defined wood—when that wood had been cut from a toppled tree.

"Teller," one of the two said, voice creaking, "You must *leave* this place. It is no longer safe."

"But—"

"There is a reason that we were to evacuate the manse. If you cannot escape it, and soon, you will not survive."

"I don't understand what's happening—"

"No," was the grave reply. "You do not. But we are not Illaraphaniel. What he might face, we cannot face. We can root the fabric of this place in the forest, but it is a momentary shield, not a wall."

He realized that was what they were doing. But even so, the shape of the hall had changed, and the texture of the floor: it was no longer carpet-covered wood, but stone, and the air was cold enough he might have been outside, in winter, and not in the Lattan warmth.

He was afraid of snow. He was afraid of the loss that came with it. On a visceral level, he remembered the horror of running through it. He remembered the loss that came at the end of that desperate run, and his own failure to acknowledge the truth of his mother's death. He was no longer that boy, but that boy was at the heart of the man he had struggled to become.

Laid bare, he felt the fear grow, felt the certainty of failure loom larger and larger. The air was cold. It was so cold.

8th day of Lattan, 428 A.A.
The Terafin Forest

The largest body of Terafin evacuees arrived twenty minutes later. Finch spoke to them; she made herself instantly visible. Today, for perhaps the first time, she understood viscerally that she *had* power. And, of course, she did: her power in the Merchant Authority was commensurate with Jarven's. She had grown from a child who had desired invisibility because being unnoticed was the best hope of safety she had, to a woman who understood the steps, the dance, of the powerful. She had grown into the role and had learned to fight by the rules of engagement that the powerful understood and used.

She had never considered herself a power. There had been too much fear, too much struggle, in her life. She had constantly felt—and still felt—that she teetered on the edge of destruction, and one push, one successful gambit on the part of her many enemies, would cause her to topple into the abyss. She had reached for the tools at hand, had learned to wield them, just as she had learned to use lock picks under Rath's tutelage.

With those tools at hand, she had become more of a target, not less. She had stepped into Jarven's office, had orchestrated her way around Jarven's plans. People had tried to kill her. People would, she knew, continue unless she could find them first.

There was no power in being the victim. No matter how high she rose, there were always those who stood higher, whose reach was longer, whose word carried more weight because it was heard so clearly. No matter how high she rose, there were always those intent upon transforming her into that: victim.

She understood that to remove those people, she would need to plan with care. She desired to remove them because it would make her own survival more certain. But she could not do what she was certain Jarven would do, or would have done, in his own lean, early years—because Jarven had not, in the end, had her den. Had not thought to build it.

For Jarven, the den was Finch's liability. It demanded loyalty, and the return on that loyalty was something he failed to discern, failed to value. Jarven had rivals. Where respect for their abilities allowed, he had a kind of affection, but his own interests were his only guide. He assumed that all men, all women, behaved this way. Assumed that they wanted, in the end, what he wanted—and that they were merely too stupid or too incompetent to achieve it.

He had focused on only that; nothing else was relevant. She knew Jarven considered her remarkably naive, that he regretted that naïveté because it prevented her natural rise to power. She would never become a worthy rival.

He did not understand—and would never understand—that it was not an act of naïveté. It was a choice. He could not see the strength she derived from it. Could not understand that when she had people she loved—yes, loved, a word that caused Jarven to wince if uttered with any earnestness at all—they *became* the reason to learn to wield the tools that the powerful had at hand.

The responsibilities that she shouldered were shared. She could not do what Arann could do; was not Teller; did not have Carver's easy access to the back halls—she could think that now, if not without pain—and could not be Jay. Could never be Jay.

She didn't have to be Jay. She accepted it, fully and completely, *because* Jay loved her. Loved them. Jay turned, in the end, toward things she loved, not things she hated. Finch had chosen to become regent to help Jay, to protect what they'd all built.

But she understood, watching the Terafin Household Staff and the Terafin junior members as they arrived at the edge of a forest Jay had only barely intentionally planted, that she *did* have power. It was a power that was granted *to her* by the people who came to her. It was a power that they accepted and believed in even when she couldn't.

She accepted now. She understood that it was their acknowledgment of her title and position in the house that allowed her to extend a hand that could calm their fear. It was perhaps the first time that she truly understood that the powerful simultaneously did not feel powerful, yet also were.

She was so relieved to see Daine and his various trainees, she could have wept. None of that, however, showed on her face; none of that was offered because it implied fear, and it was a fear she could not afford to share.

Daine, however, signed to her. *We're fine.*

Yes, Finch thought, he was, and his assistants were also fine; apprehensive, but as they stood in front of her, she could see that fear abate. She noted that Vareena, the little *Astari* girl whose existence had almost become a political disaster, was at his side. To Finch's deep surprise, Vareena lifted her hands—in den-sign. *I'll protect Daine.*

Daine reddened; he could read what she'd signed. He said distinctly, "I'm in charge, Vareena."

The younger girl rolled her eyes.

Finch had been busy with the affairs of the Merchant Authority in the wake of the attack that had destroyed the governing council's office—and, after that disaster, the whole of the Merchant Guildhall. She had not, therefore, had much chance to watch Vareena. She knew that the girl had once felt it her duty to kill Daine, to keep the knowledge of the *Astari* within the *Astari*. She knew Daine knew it as well.

But Vareena had clearly reached some sort of peace with herself, and with Daine's continued existence. And Finch did not question it. Maybe, later—but now, no.

She signed to Daine, automatically delegating some of the duties she'd undertaken; Daine was, now, the healerie. It was his role within the House to care for the injured; the healerie was a neutral, safe space. He was younger than Finch, yes. But the talent to which he'd been born elevated him in the eyes of the House and all its myriad members.

Marrick ATerafin offered her assistance as well, although he did not ask permission. He bowed—visibly, obviously, and respectfully. "You are certain these forests are safe?"

She answered in the same fashion. "Yes. The people who stand beside the House Guard are the forest's guard, and they will protect Terafin and all who seek shelter here. The manor is no longer safe."

Marrick had seen what Finch herself had seen: the distant, new spire across the bridge. Marrick had the authority, not of regent, but of Councillor; he had the easy, genial charisma that implied familiarity, kinship. She had seen him put these to use in pursuit of the House Seat, and understood that they, as any other weapon, could be used in a different fashion.

As more of the House Council appeared before her, she surrendered more of the act of guidance to them. She even offered the Master of the Household Staff a distant and superior nod—that august woman disdained, instantly, those whose understanding of household hierarchy was so poor they attempted to treat her like a peer.

Where Marrick was genial and comfortable, the Master of the Household Staff was not. But her starched, intimidating disapproval did not so much calm fear as redirect it into familiar channels. There wasn't enough fear of unknown disaster to displace fear of the known Master.

Her glare made clear that even if this was an emergency, there were rules that were to be followed. Her glance grazed the growing number of House Council members, landing, significantly, on the regent. Her unspoken message to the Household Staff was utterly clear: they had better not embarrass the Staff in public. Period.

Frightened whispers became nonexistent almost instantly. Although there were no back halls in this forest, the proper behavior expected of Household Staff was necessary, regardless.

Finch had never been comfortable with the divide between the Household Staff and the rest of the House. She had, in her first month within the West Wing, found the stiff distance very difficult. She had assumed that the Household Staff were people, just as she was, and their job—their work—was at least work she herself would have been qualified to do. Treating them as if they were invisible had seemed wrong. Pretentious. Judgmental, somehow. She had therefore tried to make clear that she didn't consider them in any way lesser or inferior.

But the Master of the Household Staff had chosen the servants who tended to the West Wing personally. Merry had been one of them. And she had explained, hesitantly, that attempting to befriend the servants was the worst possible way of approaching them. It made them feel uncomfortable, for one.

It was Merry who had attempted to teach them the etiquette that separated the staff from the rest of the House. Did some of the staff resent the den? Yes, probably. But if they did, they kept it to themselves; they had no choice. Expressing it in any way that might reach the Master of the Household Staff was as good as simply walking away from the job, and the Master of the Household Staff had ears in every wall.

"We see your mess. We see what you leave behind when you're in the privacy of your rooms. We hear your arguments. We know what you're eating, when you're not eating enough, when you've bloodied a shirt or two. We know you put your pants on one leg at a time, same as the rest of us. It's just—your job is *different*. And if it weren't for your den-leader," and she used that word with a grimace of distaste that Finch could almost see, at the remove of half a lifetime, "The Terafin would have died. Servants are mostly lucky. When a House goes to war with itself, when a leader is determined over the bodies of the dead, the invisibility of our positions mostly save us.

"But not all of us. You think we should dream of being more," Merry had said, the words tilting up at the end, as if there was some question in the statement.

Finch was quiet.

"Why?"

Because, Finch had said, you clean up after everyone, and you could be the person that everyone else has to clean up after. Because you could make all the decisions, instead of just suffering through the results. Because then it would be *you* who would be important.

Merry, however, had shaken her head. "No. Then other people will think I'm important."

"That's what being important *is*."

"Is it? I have my work to do. The House Council has theirs. But, Finch? More Council members have died of poison or violence than any of the Household Staff. Our work stays the same, no matter who rules, and no matter how vicious the infighting becomes. We keep the House going."

Funny, to think of that now. But Finch did. Because Finch was important in just the fashion she had barely dared to dream of on the day Merry had spoken to them. What she had not understood, on that long-ago day—or all the days that had come before it—was the cost, the weight, of those decisions. She had power, yes. And she had the responsibility of that power.

What she wanted now was to support someone she could believe would only make the *right* decisions. She wanted to be the one who created a space called home for them. She did not want to rule Terafin.

She had not understood Merry's thoughts at that time, hadn't understood what Merry had understood. Merry had considered the Household Staff essential. But they worked in The Terafin's service, trusting that the decisions that The Terafin made would preserve their house and, by implication, their place in it.

She inhaled. Exhaled. Stepped out of the way of the Master of the Household Staff, but only very figuratively. She allowed her eyes to glance off the serving staff, both the people she recognized and the people she didn't.

Only when the evacuees had slowed to a trickle did the worry that had been nameless shift, deepening and widening. The fear that replaced it had a name.

Teller.

The High Wilderness

The tree took root, and it grew, just as the *Ellariannatte* had grown. Where it grew, the air was still—still and cold. It did not reach the height of the *Ellariannatte*; nor did it possess the solidity, the density, of the other metal trees; it was slender, as young trees are, and ringed in varying shades of something that might have been blue bark.

Jewel watched it rise from the ground; watched its branches spread; watched it bud and watched those buds unfurl as new leaves. Those leaves then fell, and this time, wind carried them, and Jewel knew, the moment the wind did, that this was the only road she must follow to its end.

Shadow knew it as well. He shouldered her, and she nodded; she did not move until he spoke. "Get on." The words were almost a growl. She felt, as they penetrated her awareness, that she was dreaming, had always been dreaming; that reality asserted itself in unexpected ways because she had never truly been awake.

She climbed up on the gray cat's back and waited for Rath to join her.

Shadow hissed impatiently, but she could not tell whether the sound was meant for the scion of Handernesse or her. He joined her, sitting once again behind, and Shadow pushed himself off the ground.

The cat was not a bird, and she considered his flight for the first time. Gravity did not appear to be the deciding factor in aerial buoyancy, at least where the cats were concerned; they could skim ground and return to the heights without flapping their wings to gain speed, to gain momentum. They seemed, to Jewel, to be momentum personified when they flew.

At the moment, Shadow's flight path followed the drift of leaves. They were caught in winds that touched nothing else—Jewel could hear the whispered breeze; sometimes they spun as if caught in storm, their edges clinking against one another. But they moved and fell, returning to the earth, and where they touched that earth, they took root and grew. She counted the trees as Shadow passed them. She understood that they would be three dozen in number, and not more.

The blue leaf had been given as a gift to her by the people the Warden of Dreams had almost killed; they had each passed a leaf into her open palms. The leaves themselves should have been of insignificant weight; they had not been. But she had understood, mutely, that it was the price of their passage, and she had accepted them. Perhaps because she had thought it a dream, for it was in dream that they had all, young and old, been ensnared. She did not know if they understood what they had given, because she wasn't certain she understood it herself. But she was afraid that she did.

And even the fear had a name. No, it had several names.

She began to recite them: they were mortal names, human names, all. They were invocations, they were pleas, they were apologies and, threaded through them, gratitude. She did not know what would happen to their waking selves, and she was afraid to examine the answer, because the answer would change nothing.

She had to be Adam's Matriarch, she had to be The Terafin. She was far, far closer to understanding Evayne than she had ever wanted to be. This path of trees, this path made of *people*, was her only way home.

She had to get home. She had to get home *now*. She did not speak of what she had seen in the crystal; to speak of it was to speak of fear, of terror, and she did not wish to burden the others with either.

But that was not all of her reason, and the other, more immediate, was the desire to give no voice, even indirectly, to fear and terror of her own, as if the words had power; as if speaking them would cause the futures she had seen to harden, to become the only possible futures.

She had once shared every wyrd, every prophetic dream, with her den. In the twenty-fifth, she had gathered them around a table so small it could barely be called a kitchen table; she had gathered them in the kitchen of the West Wing. She had spoken of her nightmares, and Teller—always Teller—had inscribed them before the den attempted to drag some sensible meaning out of them.

Only Angel was here, but even to Angel, she did not choose to speak, because she understood the vision her heart exposed. It was not subtle. It was not rife with symbolism that made no sense to her. She could arrive home in time, or she could fail, utterly. She could find—or make—a path that would take her to the manse, or she could lose her city, her House, and everyone she cared about that she had not taken with her. The Winter King had been right. Of course, he had. She had wasted time in the Hidden Court, secure in the belief that she would return to the world having not lost a single minute.

She begrudged the minutes now. She begrudged everything.

If she did not arrive *in time*, she would lose her den, and it would start with—

Teller.

And Shadow growled: *Yes.*

Chapter Sixteen

8th day of Lattan, 428 A.A.
Terafin Manse, Averalaan Aramarelas

TELLER DID NOT KNOW every member of the Household Staff, nor did he know every member of the House Guard. Many of the people who worked within the manse lived outside of its walls. He assumed that the Master of the Household Staff had given orders that the manse was to be evacuated by all the people who wished to *remain* on the Household Staff, and assumed, as well, that fear of that Master would override all other fears.

He assumed that the Chosen would have the House Guard in hand; he knew that Finch and Jester were in the forest. He assumed that Haval was with them, and he trusted all three. Daine had the healerie under control; Ariel was in the forest.

He knew that his cat was likely not with them.

He knew that the cat was only a cat. That no one would understand *why* he was now racing through the kitchen quarters in a mad, desperate rush, while his breath hung in clouds, and frost dusted every still surface in sight.

Had he not been certain that the rest of the manor residents would be ordered or shepherded out—and there were at least two Council members he thought would be fractious, not including Haerrad—he would not have searched. Could not have searched. He personally valued his cat more highly than he valued many of the House Members, but his personal valuation did not absolve him of the responsibility of his office.

He had fulfilled the responsibility of that office.

He cursed his cat in three different languages, because there was no one to hear him; no one but the forest guard who would not abandon him while he searched. Teller's cat might very well be outside by now. He might be risking his life—and it was a risk, the forest guard had made this very, *very* clear—for no reason whatsoever.

But this was the last place he could look. It had taken him too much time to even get to the kitchens, a place that was normally forbidden to all but a select handful, Teller not being one of them. Too may doors had opened into territory that had nothing to do with the manor itself, and the last three of those doors could not be closed at all. The halls that he knew—and the halls with which he was only passingly familiar—were becoming all of one thing, none of which was the home in which he had spent his adult life. Doors had become almost irrelevant; he had not had to touch them himself. Pages did that.

Today, he would not have allowed them to take that risk.

He was grateful that the doors that led to the public halls were almost decorative; they were always open. But now that those halls were empty of all save Teller and his unusual guards, they felt empty; his steps echoed.

He was not surprised to see snow.

He was not even surprised to be running, in increasing desperation, through it.

He had done this before, on the day his mother had failed to come home, and snow reminded him, always, of that loss. It reminded him now of what he had found at the end of that long, desperate trek.

8th day of Lattan, 428 A.A.
Scavonne Manse, Averalaan

"You can stop pretending," Colm Sanders said. "She's gone to speak with your father."

Stacy's eyes opened. She did not, however, demand to be put down. "I hear Winter," she said, her voice quiet. "I hear Jewel."

He nodded. So did he.

"She's afraid."

He nodded again.

"We won't be sleeping, will we?"

"What do you think?"

"I think we won't. Or maybe we will, but we'll never be awake again." She looked at her hand, lifting it. Her eyes widened. "She's—she just said my name!"

"Aye, lass. She did. I heard it."

"And Lillian's. She said Lillian's name."

"I think she's saying them all."

"She hasn't said *yours* yet."

"She won't forget it." He smiled. "I'm not as much fun to be with as you or Lillian. She'll probably say mine last."

Stacy nodded, completely in agreement with his assessment. "My mother will be sad."

"She will."

Colm was a man who believed in the gods. Or rather, believed in their existence. He was also a man who believed that the gods didn't give a damn about men like him. Or girls like Stacy, for all that her life seemed blessed in comparison to the life he'd led. He didn't have it in him to resent her; might as well resent the ocean or the sun. She was from a different world.

She was in a different world now.

Colm hadn't been entirely honest with Muriel A'Scavonne. Stacy had tried, but Stacy's explanations were incomprehensible to her mother. Even Colm Sanders—who had experienced the same things as Stacy—could only make heads or tails of her words because he'd known exactly what she was trying to say.

Who'd've thought a man who faced death on the battlefield at the hands of demons would be such a coward? But he was, and he knew it. He could not handle her mother's tears.

"Look! Look at my hands!"

He did. But he was looking at her face, at her expression, and after a brief glance at the hands she'd lifted, his gaze returned to that face. Her eyes, widening in wonder, lost fear and apprehension. She was glowing. Light could be seen shining through her skin. That light grew brighter, and brighter still, as the skin itself grew transparent, as if to let that light out into the world.

He watched as Stacy began to dissolve. She had done it, he thought. Jewel. The Terafin. She had planted the leaf. Had planted the leaves given her by the dreamers.

He was impatient now. His hands were only barely beginning to shine, and Stacy had already gone to wherever it was he—and the rest of the dreamers—must go. But if he could not endure Muriel A'Scavonne's tears, he nonetheless meant to keep his word to her. As he could, and if he could, he would protect her daughter.

8th day of Lattan, 428 A.A.
The Common, Averalaan

Gyrrick and the warrior-magi fell the last few feet toward a ground that was becoming, as the seconds passed, increasingly unfamiliar. The wind howled past them all; Meralonne had not chosen to land. He had, however, dropped them at the feet of the guildmaster and her attendants.

One of those attendants was Gavin Ossus.

Gyrrick did not understand—and further, did not like—Gavin. Although they had come from similar places, and evinced similar abilities, Gavin treated everyone like a rival. No, like an enemy, a foe; someone to guard against. But Gavin had respect for Meralonne, and Meralonne's teaching, and Gyrrick had come, with time, to understand that men like Gavin were necessary. Liking him, not liking him, was irrelevant. Especially tonight.

He therefore extended a nod to Gavin before he offered Sigurne a full bow. To his surprise, Gavin offered him the same nod; he could see the same acknowledgment in Gavin's expression. Today, all differences of opinion were, and would be, irrelevant.

The guildmaster had never looked as frail as she did now. And never, Gyrrick thought, as determined; the contrast, resting as it did on one face, was striking. "I cannot leave the Kings," she told them. She did not offer explanations, and none were asked; there was no time to listen, even had she been willing to offer them.

"In my absence, you must do—both of you—what you were trained, in the end, to do. We have received Royal permission to use the whole of our magical arsenal in the open streets."

"And our task?" It was Gyrrick who asked.

"You are to protect the citizens of Averalaan, and you are to survive doing so."

"The Kings—"

Sigurne's smile was almost gentle. "I will retain Gavin; Matteos will remain by my side. Olivia will arrive shortly. But, Gyrrick, none of us can do what your cadre can do. In the main, it has never been necessary. You have *all* practiced; you have all learned what to do if the magic you call upon becomes suddenly greater than you expected. Those lessons will save you tonight, because tonight the talent-born will be stronger than they have *ever* been. The trees that you see here, and the trees that will grow elsewhere in the city are necessary; they are not to be harmed, where you can prevent it. It is by the grace of those trees that the majority of the population who can be saved will be saved. Shepherd the civilians to the cover of the trees."

"What enemies do you expect we will fight?"

"Not," she replied, "the Sleepers. You will know the Sleepers on sight. You will flee them. Do you understand?"

He nodded.

"But like Kings of old, they ruled, and they ruled over others less powerful. It is those that you are meant to counter, where you can. It is against those that you have some hope of survival."

"Not demons, then."

"Think of them as demons," Sigurne replied. "They will be as dangerous in the end; the practical differences—tonight—count for little, if anything."

"Meralonne—" He stopped himself.

"You are no longer under his command. Avoid him at all costs if you encounter him. Do not attempt to reason with him; do not attempt to engage. It is . . . likely that he will not remember who you are."

And he understood the frailty then. This was the first major encounter of its kind that Sigurne had faced without Meralonne, and he thought that the whole of her fear was not his absence, but what his presence might mean in the end.

He turned to the warrior-magi; he gestured. To their hands came the weapons that Meralonne had taught them, at great cost, to summon. They summoned them now.

Gyrrick had no intention of closing with his enemies, for his was a bow. He was mage, not archer, but these arrows did not require that he be one; in some fashion, they were of him; they flew true because he was mage-born.

Sigurne turned as Gyrrick and his warriors departed, remembering the bitter council argument that had produced them. Remembering as well that she had been on the losing side. Inhaling, she turned; she lifted a hand. On it, a ring rested, and in the growing light of dawn, it glowed faintly.

The High Wilderness

Follow the trees, Jay had shouted, as Shadow leaped into action. *Don't step off the path they make.* She was gone, the great, gray cat sprinting ahead of the rest of her companions.

Angel watched her retreating back. He lifted his hands in den-sign and lowered them again; she wouldn't see any of the words he might have signed.

Terrick assessed the situation with a brief grunt and began to jog, not sprint, in her wake. The Winter King turned to Celleriant and the bard before he, too, leaped into action. Adam and Shianne, upon his back, would remain close to Jay. Angel would be too far behind.

He felt the urgency of that, the emergency inherent in it, but understood why Terrick had not chosen to sprint: they didn't know what waited them at the end of this line of metallic, faintly glowing, trees.

"What are you doing, boy?" Terrick barked, slowing as Angel slowed.

He didn't answer. The leaves, like the metallic leaves that adorned the trees in Jay's forest, did not fall; they were not *Ellariannatte*, not living and growing in a fashion akin to normal trees. Silver, gold, and diamond were not, after all, living things—not in the world that the den inhabited.

These trees, like those, were unnatural. They were not the product of nature; they were, as the other three, the product of dream, desire. And in Jay's forest, when a leaf fell from one of those trees, it fell for a reason.

He did not understand how, or why, but what Jay planted was hers. Even here, in the middle of the unclaimed, winter wilderness. He understood why they were not to stray from the path made of roots and covered by crowning branches; more than that, she did not explain, and Angel—as any member of her den—did not require immediate explanation. That would come later, if it came at all.

He could not ask her what she wanted done; she had already told him. They were to follow these trees. They were not to step out from under their odd shade; they were not to find flatter, more comfortable ground to traverse. But leaves had fallen, and they had fallen by Angel's feet.

He turned to glance back; he had not come far from the first of the trees she had, by leaf, planted.

"What are you doing?" Terrick demanded.

Since the answer was self-evident, Angel didn't reply. He retraced his hasty steps to retrieve the leaves that had fallen, and realized, as he did, that each tree seemed to shed one. Only one. The leaves were cold, but not icy.

Terrick, however, said nothing else. His impatience was almost a physical force, but he understood that the imperatives of the wilderness did not conform to the imperatives of the oathsworn; that what Angel now did might be necessary in some fashion to the Lord he had sworn to serve.

As they resumed their pursuit of The Terafin, each tree shed a single leaf; Angel gathered them all.

8th day of Lattan, 428 A.A.
The Common, Averalaan

Jester did not trust the fox, but that wasn't surprising; Jester trusted no one outside of the den. He accepted the cats because Jay accepted them, but understood that beneath the veneer of selfish, squalling, spoiled brat lurked death. The fox was cunning in an entirely different way. Cunning, ancient, and not without power of his own.

He rose from the bow he had offered the three men, the motion graceful and yet, at the same time, artless.

"My Lord will grant you free passage out of her lands." There was a subtle shift in tone, the softness of obvious, proffered respect being shed. "But the denizens of these lands are hers; she has claimed them all."

"All?" Even at this distance, Jester could clearly see the speaker. He could hear the scorn offered in that single word.

"Even so."

"The mortals do not recognize your Lord," the man replied.

"It is not required. They are hers."

"How long have we slept, that you have forgotten us? Slept we so long that the worlds have forgotten even the echo of our names?"

"We have not forgotten," the fox replied. This time, there was no grace, no elegance, in the words; there was the edge of anger, the warmth of it. Jester didn't understand why, and that was not his concern. "But mortals exist a handful of years, no more, as they habitually did. They remember, deeply, the things that touched them, the things that scarred them, but even as we, their memories last the length of their lives, no more.

"They have stories, of course; so, too, the firstborn. But those stories are not experience, and the echoes they hear, they attach to their personal experience."

"And how much has this world changed," the second Sleeper said, "that the mortals *dare* to gather here, at the heart of our domain?"

Birgide stiffened.

"How much has it changed that they dare to hinder us? How much has it changed that they *offer* us *safe passage* through lands that they barely grasp?" As he spoke, he lifted a hand.

A sword came to it. As it did, the shield that he carried—that they all carried—caught fire, but it was a blue fire that scarred vision, burning itself into Jester's eyes. Had the shield itself boasted heraldry, or even the shape of words, he might have remembered it forever, might have spoken what he saw aloud, just to attempt to eject it.

There was nothing there. Just the shape of a shield, and beside it, fire caught in the shape of a blade.

The fox, however, did not step back; he did not appear to notice the blade at all. "Barely grasp? How long have you slept, little hunter, that you have forgotten *me?*" As he spoke, he grew; the ground beneath his feet almost buckled. He gained not only height, but fur; his shoulders broadened, his hair spread to cover the whole of his golden form. In the light of the armaments the Sleepers carried, Jester could see that his hands had sprouted long, curved claws.

The Sleeper did not move. But the other two now drew their swords as well.

"Think you that *I* would serve a paltry, *insignificant* lord? Think you that such a lord could rule *me?*"

"What is he doing?" a familiar voice asked from behind Jester. Jester did not turn, although he recognized the voice. Or perhaps because he did. Meralonne APhaniel had landed.

Jester understood that Jay believed he was one of the Sleepers; that he alone had not been condemned to the captivity of sleep by the gods in the distant, almost unknowable past. But he had seen Meralonne, had known him, known of him, for half of his life, and not even when the magi gave himself over to the fierce exultation that drove him when he fought for his life had he been the equal of these men.

"Warden."

Birgide's eyes were closed and remained so. Her jaw was clenched and her arms, stiff and trembling; Jester's hand, where it grasped hers, was almost numb, the knuckles white.

"Where are the heralds?"

Jester did turn, then. Meralonne's sword hadn't come to hand yet, but he wore the armor of the Arianni, and his eyes were flashing silver. He seemed, to Jester's eye, to have gained inches of height, and his hair, as it sometimes was, was caught in a wind that touched nothing else—although the wind's howl could be heard, clearly, from the ground beneath the overlapping branches of the Kings' trees.

"Warden," Meralonne said again, "where are the heralds?"

"We haven't seen—" Jester began.

Meralonne lifted one imperious hand, cutting Jester off without actually looking at him. His gaze was fixed upon Birgide, as if by gaze alone he could force her to divulge the information.

Birgide's mouth moved, lips trembling. "They are . . . not here."

"Where are they, Warden? Where? It is urgent."

Birgide shook her head, and Jester, reaching out with his free hand, caught Meralonne's arm. And almost lost his own, the sword came to the mage's hand so quickly in response. Meralonne's eyes were liquid silver now, and whatever guise he had adopted to live within the Order's halls was so frayed and fragile, light could be seen almost beneath his skin.

He was, Jester realized, as much of a danger—to them all—as the Sleepers, nameless, on the stairs of their giant cathedral. He released Meralonne, his hand numb and tingling.

"You are brave, ATerafin. Brave and foolish beyond belief. So, too, your Lord. This is *why* a mortal was never meant to be Warden; Birgide is not even talent-born; she has no touch of the wild in her that the forest did not lend to her itself. A Warden sees *the land*, boy. A Warden *knows* when those lands have been breached.

"And if the heralds are not by the sides of the men they were *created* to serve, they are elsewhere, within *these* lands, and they now have power they did not have when they blindly searched, and searched, and searched. Do you understand?"

He could feel each word hit the silent Birgide like a blow.

And Jester said, in the quiet way of a man who has made his choice and will accept any price that choice demands, "She is Warden because Jay wanted her to *be* Warden."

"And now, she will pay for that desire, that choice. If she values this city and the mortals who crawl across its pathetic surface, she will pay."

In the distance, Jester heard the shouting change tenor. Voices that had been raised in fear were now raised in panic through the human alchemy of terror. He turned and turned again as he heard the crack of wood. He was ATerafin, but he was not a leader, not a ruler. Here, now, the only person in sight who mattered was Birgide.

Blood trickled from the corner of her mouth.

The Sleeper who had first spoken raised his voice again, and this time, Jester heard that voice deliver the essence of, the very heart of, command. His body vibrated with the syllables; he could not translate them, but he understood them regardless. The man was speaking to the wilderness.

And the wilderness, in the form of the fox who was no longer small enough to be carried in anyone's arms, replied. This word, he did understand.

Jewel.

The Sleeper laughed, his voice a rumble of warmth and surprise. Smiling, he spoke again. The earth moved beneath Jester's feet, beneath Birgide's—but no, it was not the earth; it was the overlapping roots of the *Ellariannatte*.

He heard the leaves above his head rustle, as if in a gale.

And the fox, once again, spoke a single word. The same word. The same name.

A third time, the Sleeper spoke, and a third time the wilderness replied. The fox then said, "She is mortal, our Lord, and her reach is subtle, but roots grow deep, as you yourself must remember; we are an old, old land. Not even for the sound of your beloved and absent voices will we be swayed. She is our Lord."

Meralonne did not sheath his sword. He gestured, his lips twisting in a brief grimace, and Jester thought he had attempted to summon his shield—for he had no doubt that a shield had once existed. None came.

Birgide almost buckled, as if at a physical blow, but Jester could now see why: the Sleepers had shifted position; the third of their number, who had remained silent, gestured almost casually at the wall of *Ellariannatte* that Birgide had constructed in an attempt to somehow contain them.

It had been a wasted effort; trees broke, and trees fell at the simple motion.

He spoke and spoke again, and the trees continued to crack; Birgide's hand clutched Jester's as if that grip was the only thing that now kept her on her feet.

The fox did not turn, nor did he take a step forward. He stood, as if he were one of the trees.

But when the first man raised voice again, the fox said, "The wind hears you, but you are not Lord of these lands, and the wind understands the will of the Lord in this place. The earth will not waken at your command; the water will not rise. Not without her permission, and she has not given it.

"I say again that my Lord offers—with all due respect—safe passage through her lands. She will not contain you, will not cage you, will not demand recompense for the damages done should those damages be minimal."

And the prince of the ancient wilderness raised sword and said, "These lands are not *hers*."

He brought the sword down, driving it through the stone beneath his feet.

The stone rose up around him, carrying him, and Jester remembered the two rooms in *Avantari* that Jay had transformed without will, without intent.

Meralonne said, "Warden," his voice soft, his gaze almost transfixed upon the Sleepers. "Hold the ways shut for as long as you can."

Birgide bowed her head but did not lift it. In a trembling voice, she said, "I cannot hold the trees and the ways, both."

Meralonne did not tell her to abandon the trees. "ATerafin," he said to Jester, "I leave the Warden in your care." He glanced once at his shieldless arm and shook his head.

"It is time."

Jester expected him to leave as he'd arrived: in the folds of the wind. Meralonne had been given permission to summon the wind. Or perhaps the wind had been given leave to respond. Regardless, he chose to walk.

Jester had seldom seen Meralonne engage an enemy.

But as Meralonne walked toward the back of the fox, as he walked toward the Sleepers, Jester wondered if he had any intention of engaging this enemy at all.

People streamed into streets that were, even now, edged in trees that had not existed the evening before. They were bewildered, but these trees were the Kings' trees, and they had grown up in a city in which the Kings' trees were, if not common, familiar. Children in the holdings had gathered those leaves as if they were flowers. Children from the Isle had done the same, as The Wayelyn knew; he had gathered them himself, surrounded by frowning guards and an extremely disapproving mother.

He shifted his hold on his instrument as he surveyed the streets. There wasn't so much a crowd as a congested stream; people were wide-eyed, confused; he was certain that some of them were not entirely certain they had yet escaped sleep.

And he could understand that; the shadows of a new tower—one that stood in place of Moorelas' statue, fell across that portion of cobbled road that was not shadowed by the high branches of new trees, with no risen sun to cast them. None of the buildings in the Common, none close to it, approached those trees in height, although several might boast similar age.

Even as he watched, those trees continued to grow; their roots broke cobbled stone, dislodged the earth beneath it, and began to intertwine, forming a rough and uneven road, a path that no longer had anything to do with what had once been familiar terrain.

Tallos called his name. **Wayelyn.**

He did not turn. He greeted the sleepy and the terrified, smiled at the children who were old enough not to fear strangers, but young enough not to resent condescension. **Yes.**

You are certain?

Through the trees. They form a path.

Not, Tallos replied almost primly, **an easily traversed one. You are certain?**

The Wayelyn bit back a sigh. **Yes, Tallos. I am certain. You were, perhaps, not attending Solran?**

I heard her, was the testy reply. The full force of Tallos' bard-born voice expressed the heart of his irritation—and the heart of his irritation was fear.

There was, about the city, a hint of shadow, a cold wind that spoke of death. But the voices raised here were not the voices raised in the Henden of 410 A.A; the people who wandered these reformed streets were not, yet, doomed. There was *something* that could be done to save them, or as many of them as they could reach; death was not the only kindness the bards could offer.

Today they did not sing sleep. Did not sing death.

The Wayelyn, in that Henden, had not been among those bards. He had been with his House, with Wayelyn, a symbol of the rule of order, a symbol of strength.

He was here tonight.

To the chagrin of his House Council, he had armed himself not with title, not with obvious wealth—although he was wed to both—but with lute. He felt a small pang of guilt; had felt it the moment the great cathedral—if that had even been its function—had risen from the ground. There would be panic, on the Isle.

But the Isle was not yet under siege.

Through the trees, he repeated to Tallos. His tone conveyed the barest hint of disapproval; Tallos was not a young man; had not been young in that Henden that had scarred them all. Solran, however, had not asked him to stay within the confines of Senniel. In The Wayelyn's opinion, a request would have met with the stone wall of Tallos' resolution.

A command would have carried the day, but it was not in Solran to command him; not tonight. The Wayelyn did not know what the Order of Knowledge had discussed with the Kings; nor did he know what the Exalted had discussed with their parents—the gods who existed just within reach of their living children. But he understood that tonight, all bards were necessary, and every Master Bard within the confines of Averalaan was out in these streets. Solran had emptied the college of every able-bodied person within arm's reach. And she had done so as bardmaster to the Kings.

Nor were the bards solely from Senniel; many of the bards from other colleges throughout the Empire regularly made their way to Averalaan for the celebration of lights. They, too, were in the streets, on the ground in which legend had stepped, firmly, into reality.

Songs would be written, of this dawn. Songs would be sung.

But only by those who survived.

The Wayelyn raised voice again, lending it the urgency of command. He was considered something of an outlier, among The Ten; he did not dress or comport himself in the typical manner of patricians. But he was The Wayelyn, and accustomed, in the end, to both command and obedience, where it was not his own; Tallos approached the largest group of people he could find and began to give them instructions.

In the end, Tallos was forced to lead them—and Tallos, bard-born, had a voice that might soothe the most terrified of people. They wanted the comfort, now, of leadership; they wanted the assurance of safety. And he gave it to them, inasmuch as it was possible.

Jester knew that Haval and Finch were on the move—in a manner of speaking—when the shadows across his feet began to ripple. He looked up, looked away from Birgide, who seemed for the moment as rooted in place as the trees she loved, and saw the *arborii*. They were tall; silver-barked, golden-barked, brown-barked; some had eyes of ebony, and some of pale wheat. He watched them pass between the rows of the *Ellariannatte*, their weapons raised, their shields taller than he stood.

The roots creaked beneath their feet—their bare feet—as they approached Birgide. She did not lift her head, did not open her eyes, but even so, she spoke.

"Protect the people of this city. They will retreat into The Terafin's forests; see them to safety, where it is possible to do so."

"At what cost?" one said.

"Any." Her voice was low. "They are coming."

"Yes." They did not salute; nor did they bow or raise arms in an obvious gesture of respect. But the single grave word was all that was required. "And, Jester?"

"I'm staying," Jester said, before Birgide could answer.

"We cannot afford to lose you," Birgide whispered.

"According to Haval," Jester replied, "Finch is the valuable person. I'm staying, Birgide. Don't waste their time. If they drag me off, I'll come back."

Birgide was silent.

"And I'll come back alone, isolated, without so much as a guard. Unless you put me in a cage." He glanced at the tall, broad trunks of the *Ellariannatte*, aware that she could do just that.

"Leave him," Birgide whispered. "Unless the Councillor commanded otherwise, leave him."

They walked past her then, single file where the trees were most tightly placed, but three abreast where they were not. Their hair was a tangle of leaves, of vines, of moss; some bore buds and some bark. They wore no helms, no armor except their shields. Jester had seen them train and did not understand why Haval felt they were up to the task of fighting—not with the weapons they now carried.

Those weapons seemed symbolic, to Jester—as symbolic as their presence here, in the Common, as the forest that Jay had planted spread to cover the streets.

It was not.

"Warden," the fox, almost forgotten although he had not moved, called. "They are coming. Stand your ground."

It was Jester who asked—who demanded, "For how long?"

The Sleeper looked past the being who had been—who still was—fox. Jester did not look away in time; their eyes met.

"It will be an interesting evening," the fox then said as he glanced at Meralonne. "Illaraphaniel, is it time?"

To Jester's surprise, the mage shook his head. "Not yet. Not yet, Eldest, but soon. I know who you are. I know who you were. Not even I would be foolish enough to attack you from behind."

This seemed to please the fox, or rather, the creature that had once been fox, and had never been fox at all. "They hear you," the fox said.

"Yes."

"Be careful, then; they look certain, now, to speak your name."

Meralonne nodded.

Birgide whispered a word in a language Jester did not recognize; he looked up then. Above them all, the colors of dawn had begun to spread; to leak into the darkness that was, by sun's rise, almost obliterated. What had once been midnight, what had once stretched naturally toward the vivid blue of clear, Averalaan skies, shifted color, becoming, at last, a deep, clear amethyst.

Jester almost closed his eyes. But if he was here for Birgide, he was here as witness. He watched as the amethyst skies opened, disgorging, at last, the creatures that had once flown above the library. Jester had seen Celleriant and Meralonne engage them; he had seen the cats hunt them.

They had always done so at a distance, at a remove.

Now, the dark wings of dozens of flying creatures grew larger and larger, as if they might, fully extended, blot out the sky. Jester had no names for them; some seemed bestial, in form and shape similar to the cats; some seemed vaguely human but winged. And the last, the last shape had wings that he thought might cover the newly risen cathedral if they were spread, tip to tip.

And this one, he did know, from childhood stories.

Dragon.

The Sleepers lifted voices, almost in unison, and the almost incoherent mass of aerial creatures shifted in an instant, as if they had drifted lazily in the sky waiting only for a command.

Birgide was aware of the shift in the skies above them both; aware of the creatures that accompanied that sudden, sharp drift of color. She was aware, as well, that they were not the only soldiers in the army of the Sleepers, but they were the only ones who were an immediate threat. She raised her face, opened her eyes, and saw nothing.

She opened her eyes again, as if she had failed to give her lids even the rudimentary command the first time; either they would not obey, or she was blind. She did not give in to panic because she had no room for more of it. Instead, she tried to speak.

Jester's voice accompanied the attempt. She was aware of him as a pressure on her hand; aware of him as a warmth. There was no other warmth in this place; there was the heat of fire and the debilitating chill of the worst winter frost; he remained between them.

She could feel the fall of every tree that that her enemies destroyed; where she could, she tried to fortify the trees, to inure them to the magic the Sleepers commanded so casually. And she was aware that it *was* casual. The trees were like insects to them.

They were so much more than that to Birgide.

"The gates," she whispered. "The demi-wall."

Jester cursed.

"We're not going to make the gates," he said, his voice unusually grim.

She smiled; tasted blood in it. Her own. "The others can't land. Not yet."

"Birgide . . . there's a dragon."

"Not yet," she whispered again.

The Wayelyn heard the tenor of screams shift before they banked. He understood that the silence that followed was not a cessation of terror, but a deepening of it. It was the long breath drawn before the true scream.

Into that silence, he laid the whole of his voice, strengthening the power he now exerted. He labored under no illusions; people would die tonight. There was a very good chance, if the enemies were at all strategic, that he would be among them. The best work of the bards did not guarantee the city's safety.

But fewer people would die with his intervention.

He did not lead the citizens he could gather to the forest; he ordered other bards to do so. If the bards were fractious—and they were, given their vanity and the healthy certainties of their own egos—they were responsible; not for something as petty as momentary prominence would they rebel against his commands.

He did not count the citizens that passed from the range of his voice into the hands of others born to the same talent; he did not count at all. The shadows that struck ground were as chilling as demons themselves might be; he was certain that the people whose lives he now struggled to preserve couldn't tell the difference.

Gyrrick noted the shift in the color of sky; he noticed the change in the play of shadows, although the shadows cast by the looming crowns of the Kings' trees were dense enough across the ground.

He noticed the chaos in the streets; saw people—of all ages—join the crowds in the streets themselves. They were like shadows themselves, to his eye, and they became almost insubstantial as he marked them; they were not the threat. Had they not been watching the skies around the spire of this new and unwelcome building—and how the magi would argue and fight over what its existence meant, if they survived—they might not have noticed the winged creatures that now approached from above.

But even those who paid little attention to anything but the new trees froze when the dragon roared.

Gyrrick felt that the sound of its voice was a blow, a physical sensation. He was mage-born, not bard-born, but he understood that the dragon possessed some thread of the bardic talent. Its voice could not be ignored; no shout, no scream, no other growl could equal it.

"Gyrrick," Darniel said. "Yours."

He grimaced. The bow he held in shaking hands flared to life as he gazed up, and up again, to see the dragon. The harpies had not yet landed; nor the gryphons; they seemed to avoid one another as they claimed dominance of the skies. The trees seemed to shift their crowns to prevent descent. Here and there, Gyrrick could hear the enraged cries of the predators; once or twice, he heard screams of pain.

He highly doubted that his bow—his arrows—would count for much against the dragon, the only creature in the sky who seemed likely to land, regardless of the trees' attempts to hinder it.

The forest guard stepped out of the forest itself and into the streets of the city; they took care to remain beneath the shadows cast by the *Ellariannatte.* They flinched as the trees of their expanded forest were attacked, but did not appear to be injured by the destruction.

Finch watched them. Although Haval had taken command, in a fashion, he had given orders to the trees with regard to Finch. Finch had half expected to be left behind in the safety of Jay's wild domain. Haval, however, had chosen to allow her to accompany his small army.

She wore the clothing of the Terafin regent, in itself impressive only to those with no experience of the wealthy patriciate. But she walked beneath the standard of Terafin, the House colors visible even in the shadows, the banner magicked in some fashion so that it might be seen. And she understood why.

The forest guards were not human. Although their forms were similar, there was nothing about them, even at a distance, that looked like people. Haval did not stand out in any significant fashion, but Finch did. So, too, the Chosen who accompanied her. She had not wanted to take them.

Haval, however, had insisted, and, as usual, he was right.

"We cannot leave all of our forces in one place," the tailor told her quietly. "And I fear that they will not be enough." They had both seen the dragon, but when Finch's glance went, immediately, to the partially obscured skies, he shook his head. "Not there. The Sleepers were not, according to legends, beings of air or wind. No, Finch; these are not the only dangers the citizens of Averalaan face." He raised his head and looked to the south. "There are others, and they will approach on the ground."

She didn't ask how he knew, nor did she ask what he could see; she could see the crowded streets of the Common, made new—and difficult to navigate—by the encroaching forest. She had walked those streets as a child; had come with Jay, avoiding the magisterial guards. She would *never* have dared to approach the Terafin Chosen, or the Terafin House Guards, circling the streets to avoid them as they passed.

"It is the festival of lights. On that day, the banners of The Ten are not terrifying and even the children you were did not go out of your way to avoid them."

"We did." Ironic, then, that she was here as one of the voices of authority; that she required people who were living as she had once lived to do what she had not dared to do then: approach. Trust. But no, she thought, there was one occasion on which even the den might approach the standards of The Ten. Advent. The gathering of The Ten, ten days in which each of the great Houses took turns, one House per each day, offering food and drink to any who approached the platforms set up for just that purpose, was ceremonial.

And it was now to the ceremonial that Finch's thoughts turned. She had not, of course, come prepared as The Ten would be prepared; she had no food, no wine, no water with which to tempt the hungry. But her own experience of those blessed days of celebration guided her demeanor. She could not project as the bards did; could not awe as the magi did. But the people of this city—the people in these streets—had grown up, as she had, celebrating that one day of each year in which Terafin offered its bounty to the citizens of the hundred holdings.

To her, they had seemed magical, the scions of The Ten, the people special enough, talented enough, impressive enough to be offered a *House Name*. They had seemed so far above her she couldn't resent them, couldn't resent what they had. The House Guard, of course, wore dress armor, dress uniform; she had assumed—they had all assumed—that somehow House Guards were, like the people they served, perfect.

She had never dreamed that she would be on the other side, never dreamed that she would be *regent* to the most powerful of The Ten. It was to that foolish, naive child that she now turned, and from those early, almost daydream impressions that she now drew.

She understood why Haval had all but commanded the House banner that she, as regent, could request. Because Haval missed nothing. It was the exact banner, in size, in shape, that Finch herself had approached, once a year. It was the banner that offered—for one day—the safety of approach for people like the den.

She glanced at Torvan. He was not wearing the perfect, polished armor that he was required to wear on that day; she knew, now, how very little he respected armor meant entirely for display. She also understood why—on a day when his actual combat skills might be required—she wished he had.

"Captain," she said.

He glanced at her, although his gaze flitted away, constantly in motion.

"You are to serve me now as if it were Advent."

"Finch—"

"We need these people to trust us. We need that trust to be personal and instant."

His lips thinned, but he considered her words, and she watched his expression until she was certain that he understood why. Torvan was not a fool, but the whole of his focus, from the moment he had approached her in the back of the Terafin manse, had been turned toward her protection.

He nodded, grim now. He did not tell her that he would not be able to protect her properly; he understood why she required this of him. So, too, Marave. Finch then gestured at four of the forest guard. "Hold the banner," she said softly. "We will make our stand there." And she pointed toward a copse of trees shadowed by the dark spire in the amethyst skies.

Farther from the dark cathedral, the winged forces finally found space to land. The *Ellariannatte* had spread throughout the hundred holdings, but not with the speed that the trees in the Common had multiplied; people had stopped, for a moment, to gaze up at the crowns of these new—and inconvenient— trees, in wonder and awe.

Whatever the Kings had been expecting, it was not this; precious few of the Swords had taken to the streets beyond the Common, where the Kings now stood.

Awe did not disappear immediately; it shattered only when the winged creatures began to kill—and feed.

The first of the Master Bards to die was Alleron, veteran of many wars, a man who had walked through torture and torment—if not his own—during the Henden of 410. He was older, wearier, and although in his youth he had been sent across the continent at the behest of Kings, he had spent the past few years in Senniel College, teaching.

The Wayelyn himself had sat by Alleron's feet, listening to his humorless, stern lectures—lectures that could not and did not hide his love of music, of composition, and, in the end, of audience. Siobhan had admired him, in her tenure as bardmaster; Solran, her successor, did the same.

He could quiet a panicking crowd. The stern lack of humor he brought to a rambunctious class of the talent-born could be brought to bear instantly, it had become so instinctive. Every person present had a disappointed parent or two in their background. Every person, anywhere.

And when the screaming started, it was Alleron who spoke first, who *sang* first; Alleron who approached through a street becoming something unwieldy and other with the proliferation of trees. It was Alleron's voice they heard, and it was to Alleron that they turned, because in his sternness was the hint of a distant authority. Authority that promised, in some measure, safety.

It was, therefore, to Alleron that the enemy also looked.

His weapon was his voice; it could be used to comfort. It could be used for other things, as well—but as any man, he could not speak two things simul- taneously. He spoke to the people whose panic he had broken, his voice sharper, the words shorter. And then he spoke to the creatures who had found purchase, at last, in the cobbled stone of the main streets.

His voice had power, this bitter morn. It was a power that had grown steadily with the passage of time. In the last few weeks he had achieved a peak that had never been his, even in his distant youth. He felt the truth of it now; the grounded forces of their ancient enemy froze for a moment in the act of hunting, of killing, of feeding.

But when they moved again, they moved toward the bard.

People streamed past Alleron, toward where the *Ellariannatte* grew thickest, and he held his ground as they, at least, escaped. He poured power into his voice, into his commands; it hit the winged predators in a wave, as if it were a strong wind and they were a field of wheat.

He knew it would not last. But while he spoke, people continued to flee— both toward him, in his bardic colors, and past, where they vanished beneath the shadows of branches, stumbling over the rounded curve of great roots. He knew what awaited him when his voice gave out.

And he knew it would give out soon.

In service to the Kings, he had walked the edges of battlefields before, raising his voice to pass the messages of Commanders to their soldiers. That work was fine, precise; it required practice and knowledge. It did not require strength in the same fashion; he had never once been ordered to bring an entire enemy army to its knees.

He could not have done it, on any of the occasions he had served at the Kings' pleasure. Not then. He could do it now, but understood, as he did, the cost he would pay. But there was cost, and then there was cost.

The largest scar on the heart of the man Senniel students would have sworn had no heart was the Henden of 410. He had, of course, survived to bear that scar, but his nightmares always returned him to the streets and the screams that had grown in volume, hour by hour, to all but break the will of a city.

He had been all but powerless then. He had forced himself to sing *sleep* to the terrified, the tormented—the tortured were beyond the reach of even his voice. Sleep was all he could offer them. He had had power, yes. He had had prestige. He had had enough money that he might never fear starvation or cold. He had been accepted by patricians across the breadth of the Empire as guest.

And all of that—everything he had built for himself, of himself, in his adult life—had counted for *nothing*. Those lives, those citizens whose voices he could hear so clearly, were beyond him. Beyond them all.

And *these* citizens were not. Yes, dozens had died—and more would join them—but here, at last, Alleron could save them. His power and his knowledge could make the difference between painful, terrible death and the possibility of life.

He would willingly have died on that Henden's darkest day, if his death had somehow been able to buy freedom and life for those to whom he had been reduced to singing lullabyes. On that day, the coin of his own life had been worthless. On this day, beneath these strange and terrible skies, it was not.

And he spent it freely.

The power of his commands diminished; his voice grew hoarse. He did not stop. He heard The Wayelyn's sharp concern but could not reply. Every time he forced the enemy to stop, people ran past them, ducking out of the range of their exposed and bloodied claws; every time he demanded they freeze, the injured who could move struggled free.

And this was everything he had wanted, on that long-ago, terrible day. This was what he had daydreamed of, in the wake of the terrible nightmares that had been that Henden's only gift to him.

He knew the moment his power began to falter; knew the moment when the last command he could utter left him. He felt the tremble and shudder of mage fevers, and he forced himself to give more. Because every second bought life, even if it was not his own, and every second bought peace.

And as the creatures he did not name broke free from the moorings of that shattered voice, he heard horns; saw the gleam of metal, of armor, in the distance behind them. A banner flew—and although his eyes were not so good as they had been in his youth, he recognized it.

Even as the winged creatures leaped, claws extended toward him, he smiled.

Siodonay the Fair was in the streets of the city over which she presided as Queen, and at her side, the Princess Royale, Mirialyn ACormaris, and their swords were as bright as their armor.

Chapter Seventeen

THE WAYELYN HEARD ALLERON'S voice more clearly than he heard his own, and he understood, instantly, what Alleron was attempting. He knew the cost; they all did. But he was the only bard to speak to Alleron as the bard-born do. Alleron's lack of response was response enough. As he could, he commanded the bard-born, ordering them to stand their ground or leave the streets depending on the ebb and flow of the crowd that now fled in all directions, as if they were ripples on the surface of a pond into which someone had thrown a heavy stone.

He did not have the experience that the Master Bards did; he had not seen the battlefield in the same way, had not delivered—and accepted—messages that might otherwise be lost in the battle's din.

He utilized the experience he did have, and knew, bitterly, that it would not be enough. When Alleron fell silent, he understood that the Master Bard's voice would never be raised again. He felt it as a blow but could not allow it to stop him. There would be time for grief later, if the city survived.

Averalaan was the heart of the Empire, its crowning city. It had existed in one form or another before it was newly named; this would not be the first time in its history that the demonic preyed upon the citizens who worked in its most common streets. This was the first time that he contemplated its end; the Sleepers were not concerned with either the citizens—even as slaves—or the structures in which those citizens both worked and lived.

He saw a flash of fire—golden fire—streak past him; heard the shriek of pain that followed in its wake and turned. Ten yards away from where he stood, a flock had landed, *Ellariannatte* leaves protruding from their raised wings.

One had been pierced by a golden arrow that even at this distance seemed to burn.

The magi had arrived.

Gyrrick did not carry a quiver; he knew nothing about fletching. What he knew could be summed up in two words: magic and intent. He had devoted his life to the study of magic, to the understanding of the talent to which he was born; more than that, he could not say about himself. If asked what he loved, his answer was magic; if asked who he loved, his answer was vague. Magic had been his toy, his entertainment, his devotion.

When asked to learn the arts of magical warfare under Meralonne's tutelage, he had not hesitated. He had first drawn bow on a day when most of his compatriots had failed to grasp the lessons Meralonne had attempted to teach them, and he had held on to that bow while his companions had been pared away, one by one. Two had died in the attempt to create what Meralonne considered their only true weapon. Their deaths had angered the guildmaster, and Gyrrick had understood, when that anger had been seen, categorized, absorbed, that the only member of the Order of Knowledge that Meralonne considered, in some fashion, an equal was Sigurne.

But when she had attempted to put a stop to these deadly lessons, Gyrrick had defied her. He was not the only one; he was simply the only one to have already succeeded. Because he understood, the moment he had first drawn the bow from the core of himself, that Meralonne was right. This was his only true weapon.

He had drawn it—for real—on the day the Common had been attacked by demons in the past year. Where simple swords and man-made arrows had failed to pierce their targets, Gyrrick's arrows flew true. Struck true.

He had been taught to summon fire; he had been taught to chill the very air; he had been taught to see, and to defend against, magical attacks. He knew that in a different part of the city, those lessons were being put to use by the mage-born. Had he been deprived of his weapon, he would be scattered among them. But those spells were not these arrows, and there was very little the winged predators could do to stem their flight or divert them.

He shouted orders to the bards, shouted different orders to the people under his command, and began to move. The guildmaster had given orders, and Meralonne had made clear that it was Sigurne's orders Gyrrick was to obey.

Throughout the hundred holdings, horns began to sound.

Those who understood the call of horns knew what they presaged, and those who did not nonetheless took comfort in the sound: the army had arrived.

The banners of Queen Siodonay the Fair and Mirialyn ACormaris were carried at the head of a host of the *centrii*. So, too, the banners of Kalakar, for the Kalakar House Guard had left their house all but undefended; they rode at the command of The Kalakar. Mixed among them were the Kings' soldiers, those men and women who had come victorious from the South. They had not thought to fight a war when their feet at last touched the soil of Essalieyan; they certainly had not thought to battle in the streets of the city itself. Most of the Kalakar forces were therefore unhorsed.

The Berrilya's forces were likewise on foot, all save a handful—and The Berrilya abandoned his horse when he saw what awaited: chaos, civilians mixed in with the enemy, the dead already numerous in the streets.

He turned to the man by his side. "Orders?"

"The Kings command you to defend the citizens, where possible, against the aerial threat." Almost without thought, the young bard looked up as the vast, almost silver underbelly of a creature out of legend blotted out the sky.

The Berrilya nodded. "We go," he said, "to the North. Follow the tree line." Lifting an arm, he signaled two units. "Lead the citizens into the trees."

A decarus saluted.

"Our concern," The Berrilya continued, answering the question no one asked openly, "are the winged creatures. Attempt to fend them off with bows; keep the combat at range for as long as possible." He glanced up. He did not mention the dragon. They waited for the signal of the bard before he set his men in motion.

Jarven studiously avoided fleeing, screaming people. He stepped fastidiously to the left or right of bodies, pausing only to examine those that were not human. So, he thought, observing the wings, the claws, the flattened tail, of the creature that had died to the magi, the whispered reports had been true. The creatures that occupied the skies above The Terafin's library were in no way natural.

Ah, no. They were not native to Essalieyan, not native to any lands that mortals had called home. The hides of these creatures were tough, more animal than human; the claws were claws. He detected no hint of magic about them. Magic, however, was not necessary. Very few of the citizens found in the holdings would survive such a creature's attack.

He heard the raised voices of the magi, nodded, and rose.

The sky above the city was a shade of amethyst, a clear, deep purple that contained, at the moment, no clouds; no clouds save one. Above him, above them all, was a great, winged creature he presumed was a dragon, given its size and its voice. In the sunlight—where was the sun?—it almost glittered, and childhood fancy called that glitter scales; when it opened its jaws to roar, he could feel the sound in the earth beneath his feet. It was the dragon's voice; at this remove, that was troubling.

Its roar was like the howl of the bitter winds in the Northern Wastes; people froze in terror every time they heard it. Nor was their fear simple panic; Jarven had far better control of visceral impulse than they, and he could feel the chill pierce skin, as if cold, as if freezing, were pure emotion, and not physical at all.

He was armed but chose not to be seen; he did not engage. As if he were standing upon a cliff that overlooked a battle, rather than on the field itself, he surveyed, he calculated.

He knew that he was not—or had not been—the equal of the Chosen on their own fields of battle and had never desired to be so; they served another. He served, as he had always served, himself. He was ATerafin because it suited him; it had been a goal because it was a fine weapon indeed with which to do battle among the patriciate.

That battle was now irrelevant. What he had learned in his years in the Merchant Authority, what he had learned before he had proven himself worthy enough to be offered the House Name, would do him little good today. He shook his head. He understood that he was mortal and understood, as well, that his mortality had been elongated, stretched; that he had the vigor and the strength he had once possessed, in the streets of the poorer holdings.

He had left those streets behind, but the cunning, the survivability, he had brought with him. And one part of that was his understanding of people.

He had only rarely engaged in the politics of the House; he knew the ways in which the House and its constituent members could turn upon itself, and he knew that surviving obvious entanglement might prove difficult. He had considered it, briefly, on the day The Terafin had died—not Amarais, but her predecessor. But if he was a man who valued the weight of position, he was also pragmatic. With weight came the yoke of responsibility. Could he advance the House? Yes, in theory. But Terafin was not the underdog in the Council of The Ten; it was, only arguably, the premier House.

And babysitting the fretful egos of the House Council might have caused him to murder them all and replace them with people less likely to be demanding.

But no. Murder was not, as he had believed as a youth, a simple affair when one lived among people. For one, the magisterial guards existed to discourage it. And when discouragement as a broad principle failed, they existed to investigate. Jarven was confident that he could slip under the net of that investigation—but that game would have to be played, and he could not afford to lose it.

Had never lost it, in fact.

But violence and murder were not something he enjoyed. If forced to descend to them, he had misplayed his hand. He did not, in the eyes of society, *lose* the game, but the eyes of society were frequently averted or turned inward in such a way that they did not see what was in front of their faces. Therefore, what they saw was irrelevant. To Jarven, it felt like a loss.

Someone had once asked him—ah, no, *Haval* had once asked him—in that peculiar, flatly neutral fashion, if Jarven valued people at all. Given their duties at the time, Jarven considered the question both impertinent and intriguing. He had always considered Haval intriguing; they were men possessed of the same raw ability, but Haval's use of that ability had never been completely predictable.

Is that a personal question? he had replied, after genuine thought. Haval did not respond to the slightly pointed teasing. *Yes.* Nor did Haval offer sarcastic rejoinder. He simply waited, aware that Jarven had not finished.

As a reward for that patience, which Jarven was not above testing with a much longer pause, he said, *Yes. Where there is only one man—even be he as impressive a man as I—there is no contest. There are no games. There is no hierarchy. No winner, no loser. There is a wasteland, Haval.*

And the Kings? They are, in your scenario, the absolute winners?

Jarven had laughed. Jarven chuckled now. *That was clumsy, but I will allow it. The perception of winning that others have is irrelevant to me. Do you believe that the Kings are, in any way, free? They rule, yes. They can, with some finesse, condemn a man to death. But they are not free to simply kill him themselves. They are not free to react as people; they carry the weight of the crown, the dignity of the crown, the responsibilities of it. They were born to it, and they come into their own only upon the death of their parents; they cannot retire, cannot leave the palace without a flock of humorless men and women to stand between them and any meaningful interaction.*

But I believe them to be necessary. I believe they hold the fabric of society stable, inasmuch as such a thing is possible. It is in part because they exist that I am free to do as I desire. I consider their existence of value to me.

Haval had simply nodded.

Jarven sighed. He had not yet been seen, but invisibility, such as it was, was annoyingly wearying. He turned, then, toward the heart of the Common. Toward the Kings.

*   *   *

In the South of the city, The Kalakar stood in a loose knot of her people. Her Verrus stood beside her, surveying both land and sky. Neither liked the fact that they would be fighting in the city streets; that they would, in the din and clatter of a battle that would bring down AKalakar, be surrounded by screaming, terrified civilians. Very few of her people were trained for combat in cities. The only unit she had once commanded that could fight anywhere were the Black Ospreys, and they were gone, their colors laid to rest, the people who had sworn by them in the Dominion, serving as guards to the newly established Tyr'agar.

The Ospreys, on the other hand, had never been particularly careful about civilians. She looked at the tree line. It was a literal line, which wound out from the Common, roots snaking through the hundred holdings as if they were long, long fingers in which to grasp and hold Averalaan itself. They were called the Kings' trees by the citizenry.

They were called something else by her experts. The Kalakar, however, chose to refer to them as The Terafin's trees. And although The Terafin was fully adult, the difference in their ages made her uneasy. The Terafin was, in some fashion, naive. Naïveté would correct itself, given both time and experience, but mixed with that naïveté was a dangerous, unpredictable power. More proof of that than these full-growth trees was not necessary.

But if more proof were required, she had it in *Avantari*.

She did not distrust The Terafin. She had seen the girl in her youth, had understood the value of her talent to her House, and had watched, where possible, as that girl had matured. She trusted The Terafin's intent.

It was not her intent that was in question. It was the power itself, and her ability to consciously control it.

"Kalakar?" Korama's tone was grave.

"Sorry. I was thinking I could use a drink."

His expression pinched, but only slightly; someone who did not know him might miss it entirely. She knew him well.

"Tell Vernon to take his people to the edge of the tree line. We've been told that we're to guide our citizens to the trees themselves, or through them."

He did not ask who ordered it; there were only two people present who could command The Kalakar, and the Kings were on the field, albeit hidden behind the trees themselves. He nodded as The Kalakar dismounted. She glanced, once, at her standard bearers, understanding the need for the standard.

"What are we to do with those?" Korama added.

"They're not attacking us," she replied. "And they're accompanied by Terafin House Guards." She glanced, once, at the tall creatures that stood a head—easily—above the tallest of her men.

"Does this mean The Terafin is in the city?"

Ellora shook her head. "We've received no such word from *Avantari*."

"The Kings and their court are much occupied."

"True—but my instincts tell me that if she were present, we would know." She glanced, once, toward the demi-wall in the distance, remembering The Wayelyn's song. What he hoped for, Ellora couldn't guess, but that damnable song of his had been heard in every tavern in the city—possibly every inn across the Empire by this point—carried by bards who should have known better.

"Get ready," she said, lifting her voice as the winged creatures grouped to land.

Jester felt Birgide tense, which should have been impossible; her body was shaking, her hand clutching his so tightly his fingers were almost purple and he could only barely feel them. She didn't speak; her lips moved, but no sound escaped them. Blood did.

He hated everything about this war.

Meralonne gestured. The wind came at his call, lifting his hair, his cape, and eventually, the whole of his body, as if it desired to separate the magi from the earth.

"Illaraphaniel," the fox said softly.

"Retreat," Meralonne replied, passing to the left and over the fox's form. "The Warden requires your aid."

"She does not. She is Warden. It is not a position I would take, nor one I have ever been offered."

"She does," the mage replied. "You serve the Lord you serve; can you not hear the trees?"

"I am not certain I should allow you to pass."

"Eldest." He did not put into words what Jester thought obvious: he was windborn, airborn; the fox could not impede him.

"Oh, very well. But if I was not looking forward to engaging the three, I think it unlikely that your presence would make the possible outcomes better for me."

"My apologies, Eldest." His voice was soft, so soft it might have been a whisper. It was as clear to Jester's ears as a shout or a scream. He looked up to see the wind curling strands of platinum hair—hair that caught light as if it were threads to be spun, raiment that someone like Jester could never wear.

And as one man, the three froze.

If Jester had expected Meralonne to defend the city, he gave up all hope in that moment, for he could see the three as clearly as he could Meralonne; the distance between them made no difference to the clarity of his perception. He could see grim and frosty condescension melt instantly, could see the widening of shining, silver eyes, could see the lowering of weapons, of shields, forgotten in the moment. He could see their joy, and he would remember it for the rest of his life: it was incandescent. Had he thought them beautiful before?

Yes. Beautiful and distant, harsh as the storms through which ships did not sail had they any other choice. When they saw Meralonne, that impression shattered. Here, now, in the moment of discovery and return, he could find no words for what he saw—and he felt a painful yearning to somehow be part of it, to be worthy of what they offered, without caution, to Meralonne.

He hated himself for it but could not banish the response.

He had not understood why Meralonne assumed he would become the fourth of the four, why he would lose all desire to protect the city he had defended against the magical and arcane for so long. He understood now. He could not imagine anyone who could stand against what was so completely and artlessly offered. He was bitterly certain he couldn't. And certain as well that it would never *be* offered to anyone who was not Meralonne.

Not even the White Lady. She was their Lord, their ruler; she was their god, if gods could be said to have any need of them. But Meralonne was kin.

The air carried him to the stairs that the Sleepers had partly descended; he himself did not land. But he lifted his arms, held them open, as if he could gather the sight of them to himself, and hold it as closely as the air, as breath.

"Foolish child," the fox snapped.

Jester nodded in agreement; he could not look away.

"Do not make me bite you again; your blood is bitter and thin."

Jester forced himself to look at the forest elder; he was once again a golden fox. ". . . Eldest."

"Yes, yes." He looked up, expectant.

Jester knelt—awkwardly—to offer the fox a cradle composed of one arm. Birgide's grip was too tight to easily disentangle, if that was Jester's desire. It wasn't.

"I did not think it wise," the fox continued, as Jester once again unfolded his legs, "to ask a mortal to serve as Warden. I wish you to bear witness to that."

Jester asked the only relevant question. "Why?"

"Mortals are poor vessels. They are inflexible, delicate, and ephemeral. What was done when the forest accepted her as Warden was what *could* be done. Mortality is not of the wilderness; no more are animals."

It was unwise to bridle. Therefore, Jester did not. He even welcomed his growing resentment because it displaced the Sleepers and Meralonne APhaniel, although they shadowed his thoughts.

"Wardens are not like your mortal soldiers," the fox continued, pointing with his nose. Jester was not free to move much, but the fox wished to approach Birgide. "They are not many; they are *one*. Illaraphaniel's presence will buy us time, although I do not believe that is now his intent. I require physical contact," he added, as if this was not obvious.

"What are you going to do?"

"I am going to aid the Warden."

The reason for the fox's prior words became suddenly, sharply clear. "What will it do to her?"

"I do not know. It has perhaps escaped your notice that the winged frostwyrm has taken to air above us?"

It hadn't, and the fox knew it. Jester used irritation to brace himself because he had nothing else.

"What the harpies and the gryphons cannot do, the frostwyrm can. Its breath is winter breath, and the trees freeze at its touch. They will either die or sleep, and if the forest sleeps, you are all doomed."

"And what can you do?" The question was perilously close to the dangerous type of impertinence.

"Were you not beloved of our Lord, I might rip out your throat," the fox said, confirming just how close. "I chose to sleep in the winter. And I woke, Jester, when our Lord first stepped foot in our lands. I did not wake because she did; I woke because I heard her name and her voice, and it interested me. I do not require summer in order to simply *be*. I am older, *by far*, than the cursed seasons of the high wilderness, and I am not subject to them."

Jester apologized the moment he could slide a word in edgewise. The fox was bristling. "Apologies, Eldest. My choice of words was poor. I did not mean to question you or your abilities; I meant only to ask what it would do to the Warden."

"That," the fox replied, in a far less rumbling voice, "is the heart of the matter. I do not know. But there is only one warmth that might help your mortal kin to stand against the frostwyrm's voice and breath in the whole of the forest."

The tree of fire.

Although Jester did not speak the words aloud, the fox knew. "The burning tree. The tree that is part fire and part anger and part death. It is now those trees she must grow."

"She can't."

"Not at the moment, no. And perhaps you are correct—but what she does with the *Ellariannatte*, she might do with any tree, any plant, that grows in our Lord's lands. And it is that tree, with its bitter, burning roots, that she must bring to your gray, pathetic city."

Jester almost said no. He opened his mouth to tell the fox to go to whatever variant of the Hells immortals occupied. But Birgide spoke. For the first time in what felt hours, she forced breath to accompany the movement of her lips. "How, Eldest? How can I contain the fire without harming the rest of my trees?"

The irritation bled from his tone as he turned toward her. "You must wake The Terafin's trees," he replied. Since the trees were obviously awake—and armed—this made no sense to Jester.

But it clearly made some sense to Birgide. She whispered, "They're not real trees."

To Jester's surprise, the fox chuckled. "Is that what stopped you? Warden, Warden," he said, shaking his head, "they *are*. They are not the trees with which you are familiar; they are not the trees to which you devoted the passion of your life, if not the whole of it. But they are real now. And they will wake properly, wake fully, only at the command of two people: the Lord of this land, and you.

"Wake them. They are merely sleeping."

Jester had seen flashes and hints of silver and gold among the forest guard, and he had assumed, on some level, that those who bore them were the spirits of Jay's almost mercantile trees.

"What can I do to help her?" he demanded of the fox. He could not keep anger out of his voice and didn't try—but the anger only revealed the truth of what lay beneath it: Jester was afraid. For her. A woman who didn't drink, didn't smoke, and preferred the company of clean dirt to people.

"Oh, hush, sapling. Hush."

"She can't do this on her own."

"No. But I am willing to offer her aid if she will accept it."

"I'd rather do it myself."

"And what will you do? Will you shake the trees? Shout at them with your thin, reedy voice? Kick their trunks?"

Jester's arm tightened, which was stupid. He forced himself to relax, inasmuch as it was possible. He wasn't Jay. He didn't have her *knowing*. But even absent that gift, he was certain that this would destroy Birgide, and he felt that he had only just found her.

He was certain it wouldn't destroy the fox.

The fox snorted. "You are not a very smart mortal."

"No. But you consider Jarven smart."

"Ah, no. I consider him daring. Ambitious. He is a small flame in a gray land. You are not his equal." This didn't bother Jester at all. "He would never do this."

"You're wrong."

"Am I? How so?"

"He would do it if it preserved him. He would do it if, by doing so, he could win his game. Everything is a game to Jarven."

"And that is not true of you?"

Jester didn't answer.

"Very well. But I will remove your hand if you so much as whimper, do you understand? It will make things more complicated for me, because you are Jewel's, and she is not pragmatic where her den is concerned."

"What—what am I supposed to do?"

Birgide, however, whispered, "No."

"I won't take anything from you," Jester said, voice low. "I won't be Warden. I don't want to be caged in a crop of trees that I can't even name for the rest of my life."

He had to practically press his ear into her moving lips to hear her answer. ". . . Idiot."

He almost laughed.

The fox, annoyed, leaned across Jester's chest, opened his pointed mouth, and bit Jester. Bit them both, where their hands were joined.

8th day of Lattan, 428 A.A.
The Terafin Manse, Averalaan Aramarelas

Teller finally found his cat. He was grimly aware that he would have allowed no one else the luxury of the foolish attempt; a cat's life was not worth the risk to their own. Certainly the Master of the Household Staff would have forbidden it.

Telsey was not best pleased to be manhandled—she had never truly liked being cuddled or held. She let him know. When her obvious vocal displeasure failed to produce the correct results, she scratched his hand, drawing blood, but not enough of it to cause a mess. She didn't like the cold winter frost that now covered the floors of the manse; didn't like the cold stone that had replaced a warmer wood.

He knew how Carver had been lost, but the forest people remained by his side; they seemed as relieved to see the cat as Teller himself.

"We must leave, Teller."

Teller, exhaling a mist of breath that lingered in the still air, nodded.

He had responsibilities as right-kin, and he was failing those. But this cat had come to him in the winter, as lost and patchy as Teller himself had once been, and although Jay had never really liked cats, she'd allowed him to keep Telsey. The manse was home to other cats, which meant home to far fewer mice, but Telsey was his.

Given the amount of damage the three winged monsters regularly did, the damage this one small pet could do amounted to almost nothing. Of course, repairing the damage amounted to more than he had ever earned in the twenty-fifth holding, which was a stupid thought to have now.

But stupid thoughts were better than incoherent fear, and he understood the difference viscerally when he heard the loud, sharp crack of what might have been a wall nearby.

Here, he trusted the forest spirits; one led, and one followed, Teller sandwiched between them, the cat finally settled in his arms. There was no sunlight in the winter world the Terafin manse was fast becoming. The halls seemed wider, although that might have been an artifact of how empty they had become.

Twice during the jog that led—in theory—to either Jay's rooms or the terrace, the forest people called a halt; once, they picked Teller up, forbidding his feet to touch the ground beneath them. There was no visible difference to Teller's eyes, but he did not argue. Telsey did.

Teller could almost see sunlight when the forest people stopped him again, one hand on his left shoulder.

"Do not move, Teller."

Teller nodded. He had none of Jester's natural sarcasm when worried, and none of Jay's anger. About now, the heat of that anger would be a blessing. As if words were movement, he remained silent, and because the sound of his labored breathing calmed with the lack of movement, he heard, once again, the sound of something cracking. He looked across the hall; this should have been one of the public galleries. No sign of Terafin's patrician grandeur remained, although he could see the frames of paintings beneath a dust of frost or snow.

The forest people now conferred, their voices muted and hushed; he heard the sway of laden branches, the bustle of moving leaves, in their syllables, and without intent, huddled into them. If they noticed at all, they did not object.

Finally, the guard whose hand kept Teller from advancing at all shook his head. "We are too late," he told Teller softly. "And now, must do as we can. We cannot reach our Lord's lands with you. Ah, no, that is imprecise. You cannot reach our Lord's land from this place."

Teller did not tell them that they were in the Terafin manse, because he understood instantly that they were not. If wardrobes could open into lands that could swallow Carver and Ellerson, it made bitter sense: every door was now a path into unknown lands.

"Can I move?"

"No. If you move from this place, you will no longer be in our Lord's domain. This patch of ground is safe, for the moment. We will anchor it. When our Lord returns, she will close all of the open doors, deny all of the paths that lead from elsewhere to here; this is the heart of her domain."

"The Warden?"

But the forest guard who spoke now shook his head. "The Warden cannot save you, now. The princes are awake, and their voices can be heard by all who once served at their command. This place," he added softly, "belongs to them now."

"But you don't?"

"We are rooted in Jewel's domain; we cannot be uprooted here."

"Could you go home?"

"Yes."

"Can you be killed here?"

They did not answer the question; it was drowned, now, in the calling of horns. Teller had heard horns like this before, in the foyer of the Terafin manse, and on that day, death had come.

"You must be still. You must remain silent. When the host rides past us, you must still all but breath—and if you can, breath as well for a short time. They will not notice us; to them we will be trees, no more. They ride in winter; they do not expect to hear our voices. If you are still, if you are quiet, they will take you for an animal, no more. They are called to war; they will not hunt or kill until that battle is joined, if you give them no cause.

"The walls between our lands and yours are very, very thin today—and tomorrow, they will not exist at all." He did not lift his hand. "Your kind is not good at silence or stillness," he observed. "But for now, you must not take a step in any direction."

Teller asked the only relevant question, then. "What if their call to war *is* to ride down, to hunt down, my kind?"

"Then you will perish here. Against those who ride now, we cannot stand for long. But, Teller, it is the desire of our Lord that we make that attempt."

And he thought, no, it's not. Jay would never ask the servants to pick up a sword and fight to protect the House Council. She'd ask them to flee, to hide, to send word if it was safe to send word—but maybe not even that much.

8th day of Lattan, 428 A.A.
The Common, Averalaan

When the dragon roared, the whole of the Terafin guard froze. Even the House banner seemed to stiffen, the small movements of weighted cloth vanishing until the dragon's voice could no longer be heard. At that point, movement resumed, and speech; tears and shouts of anger or fear.

Finch motioned people toward the trees, adjudicated the quarrels that occurred when panicking people saw something other than fear for their immediate survival. Some people wanted to go back to their homes, to retrieve whatever possessions they prized. Finch could not order them not to do so, and she did not try. There were too many people to deal with; she could not prevent what might well be suicide.

Only where there were small children did she attempt to intervene, but even then, it was costly. She could hear the clatter of weapons in the distance, and that distance was diminishing.

Arrendas came to report. He was armored as a member of the Terafin Chosen, but the weapon he carried was not a sword; it was a pole-arm of some type. Finch had never been martial; she didn't have a name for it, and at the moment, it was not relevant.

"Torvan and Marave will remain with you." It was not a question.

"Where are you going?"

"To test a weapon," he replied, with a half-grin. "Can you hear the horns?"

She nodded. Horn calls reverberated throughout what she could see of this forest-transformed city.

"The last two mean there are now non-aerial enemies approaching."

She started to answer and stopped as a blaze of fire streaked up from the ground, illuminating a purple day that was already bright.

Arrendas nodded. "We're out of time, Finch. When Torvan tells you to leave, heed him."

*   *   *

The Kings were situated beneath a grove of *Ellariannatte*. The central tree was natural; it had existed as part of the Common for the entirety of Sigurne's life. The rest of the trees, however, were not. She now watched what remained of the Common with care and deliberation. The *Astari* could defend the Kings against simple physical attack far more effectively than she; her role, her responsibility, was protection against foreign magic.

Queen Marieyan had remained within the confines of *Avantari*; so, too, the princes. The Kings' Swords considered that wise, and Sigurne had not the heart to tell them that wisdom would avail them nothing, in the end. She understood that what Jewel ATerafin had, unconsciously, made of large parts of the palace itself, *any* demi-god might make with equal alacrity. But the Kings were not fools; they knew what she knew.

They knew that there was no safety anywhere on the Isle, anywhere in the city. But against such creatures that had filled this sky, *Avantari* had defenses, and some of those defenses were ancient. Had the Kings not been required for the ceremony itself, they, too, would have been ensconced behind the walls of their home. They were not worried about the princes. The princes understood that if the palace came under attack, they were to call upon the aid of the gods that had parented them. They would enter the Between, the land where gods and mortals might meet without danger to either one.

But they could not enter the Between if they did not have both time and the ability to prepare. Regardless, they were ready now, for attack. The palace was as safe as any mortal place could be; the preparations—the braziers, at least—were in place. They remained in their home.

Queen Siodonay would not. Nor would the Princess Royale. They had girded themselves in the armor that was meant for royal parade. As they had done at need in the darkest of hours Averalaan had ever faced, they did now: they rode. Theirs was not a mission of mercy, but of war; they meant to fight. They meant the people of this city, attacked by intruders who had appeared at its very heart, to know they had not been deserted by their rulers.

Something tugged at her protections, her permissions, and she turned to look in the direction of the Kings; because she was too quick, she was almost blinded by what she now saw.

In the place of King Reymalyn, there was a golden glow, fringed with the colors of every magic known to the Order, and tinted with colors she did not. She blinked, blinked again as Matteos Corvel was startled into a curse. Gavin Ossus was younger and more inherently suspicious; he squinted, uttered two words, and continued to look. Sigurne did not. Those two words dampened the visual sensitivity toward magic, and she could not be without it. But she did narrow her eyes until they were almost completely shut as she shifted her gaze to King Cormalyn.

He, too, was a brilliant slash of multihued gold, and the gold, she realized, was the color of his eyes. Of their eyes. She understood what she now saw, and once again shifted her attention.

The Kings were armed with Fabril's gifts: the sword and the rod. She had never once seen them wielded. It was believed, even understood, by the Order that the princes were taught, each generation, how to call upon the power of those Artisan-created symbols of the highest office in Weston lands—but they were not taught within the city itself; they were taught in the Between, by the parents of their blood, the gods of Justice and Wisdom.

The Exalted were not likewise armed. They were not without power, however.

If the Sleepers were not *Kialli* lords, the powers the Exalted could bring to bear were not absolute in their effect. But the Sleepers used Winter and Summer magic, both, and if what Sigurne had inferred from years spent at the side of Meralonne APhaniel was true, it was Winter magic that the Sleepers would use most freely, for it was the Winter of the hidden world.

A new light caught the corner of her eye, and she turned, and turned again; she could not find its source.

"Matteos, can you see it?"

Matteos Corvel was silent. His gaze, however, was riveted upon Sigurne herself. And as she lifted hands to reinforce the weave of defensive spell, she saw it: the ring upon her hand. She had never desired to wear it, never desired to discover, in the end, its purpose.

But she was guildmaster to the Order of Knowledge; she had come of age in the Northern Wastes. Her first teacher had been a demonologist; her second, a demon himself. What she desired had never made much of a difference to her circumstances, or she might have remained at home with a family that needed her and grieved at her absence as if it were death.

And to them, it had been.

What she had become—apprentice to the Ice Mage—was worse, by far, for her family and clan than a simple death would have been. And when the mage had at last died, at the hands of no less a mage than Meralonne APhaniel, she could not return to life in their eyes; she was tainted.

Yes, what she wanted had made no difference then. It had made no difference to the Ice Mage. It had made no difference to anyone except Meralonne. Because on that day when she had made her extraordinary act of defiance, on the day that she had earned her freedom, what she had expected—what she had desired—was death. And because both of these were true, Meralonne had not killed her.

Instead, he had brought her to the Order of Knowledge. He had taken her under his figurative wing. He had been one of her many teachers, for the Order was not small, and with time, had become the greatest of those who had informed her life with his lessons.

But she had understood on that distant day, without the need for verification, that Meralonne was neither human nor mortal. It was understood in the Order, but it was never spoken of except by the callow, the young. And tonight, as the ring she had so reluctantly donned flared to life, enveloping her in something that seemed like a fine, silver mist, she had all the confirmation she might have required, had she not witnessed him first in the glory of combat.

Meralonne was gone. What remained of him, she did not yet know, could not yet say. But this ring, he had offered her as a bridge, a tenuous, slender thread that might still, regardless, bind them together while she lived.

Across the city, the dragon roared as he circled. He was not yet looking for a place to land, in Haval's opinion. The other creatures, however, did. There seemed to be no end to them. Different in form and appearance from the vultures that circled mortal skies in the wake of a battle, they nonetheless reminded Haval of those carrion birds.

Vultures, however, did not create the corpses upon which they would feed.

He was aware of the presence of the forest guard, as Finch had taken to calling them.

"Councillor."

"How many?" Haval asked.

"Some few thousand," the tree replied, divining the question's context and meaning with a rapidity that only those who served under Haval directly ever had.

"That is not what you wish to report."

"No. What do you wish us to do with those who break the . . . laws?"

"Cage them," Haval replied. "Where it can be done with subtlety, kill them."

"We do not understand why some break those laws in the face of war."

"People are capable of great acts of heroism. They are also capable of egregious stupidity. In general, in an emergency, the best that a person can be comes to light. Sadly, the worst also comes to light." He turned his attention, once again, to the skies. But the forest guard did not leave him.

Instead, he said, "We have lost Teller."

Haval stiffened. "He is dead?"

"He was not yet dead."

"He did not evacuate the manse with the rest of the Terafin occupants?"

"No. We are with him, but he cannot move now, and we cannot reach him, who were not in his company when the fracture occurred."

"Fracture."

"The Sleepers have summoned their hosts. They have opened the ways to their own lands, and those lands are spreading across the manse. What would you have us do?"

"Continue as you have been."

"But Teller—"

"The Terafin, your Lord, would not sacrifice the many for the one, no matter how beloved that one is. She is lord, not mother, not child. You understand the heart of her desire, of her love. But I understand the heart of her duty, and in the end, duty is enough a part of her that she would not countenance the risk."

"We think it will break her," the forest guard said at last, although this took some minutes to emerge. "The eldest says—"

"It may," Haval replied. "But what you have failed to understand because you are not mortal, is that the loss of hundreds, or thousands, of lives would also break her. I am not lord; I am Councillor only. What I have offered must be measured against what the eldest—far older, far wiser—offers. But whatever the decision of the forest, it must be made soon."

When the forest guard failed to move, Haval said, "She is Lord. She understands that when she sends soldiers into battle, some will die. No matter how beloved they are, no matter how talented, no matter how worthy, some will always die."

"She did not send Teller to war."

"Yes," was Haval's soft reply, "she did. He will not be the first person she loses to war, and she has survived."

This time, the forest guard once again vanished into the shadows of the *Ellariannatte*.

Arrendas had not lied to the regent because lies were not necessary. He had not been entirely truthful. He considered Finch ATerafin a different caliber of ruler than The Terafin; Finch, in his opinion, might one day rise to become as Amarais. He had offered his oath of allegiance to Jewel Markess ATerafin. He had not offered it to Finch.

But if Finch did not hold the oaths of the Chosen, she had their loyalty regardless. If she could not ask for or take the oaths of those who might join their number, it was not required. While they lived, while they breathed, and in the absence of The Terafin, she was their commander. Only when her commands were nonsensical did the Chosen invoke The Terafin's specter. She accepted it, of course.

But were she two decades older, she might have the sense to command them to do as they were now doing: watch the dragon's very slow descent. They meant to meet it on the ground when it did finally land. They were, of course, a proud force of men and women; Arrendas did not consider this simple vanity.

But The Terafin had opened up the armory that had come to her when her personal quarters had first been transformed, and the Chosen had accepted her offer. They understood that the weapons they bore into this battle were Artisan weapons, all; they were meant for wars such as this.

Some spoke. Arrendas' weapon did not, or if it did, he could not hear it. It made no difference. The weapons that could speak spoke of this fight, this battle, and that dragon, to the exclusion of almost all else.

8th day of Lattan, 428 A.A.
The Terafin Manse, Averalaan Aramarelas

Teller had listened to Lord Celleriant speak of the Arianni. He had even asked the occasional question, which was met with frosty disapproval, as if the questions of the merely mortal were so far beneath the subject of which the question had been asked it deserved death, not answers.

Answers had been given, regardless.

He knew that the Arianni served Ariane, the woman they called the Winter Queen. Sometimes they called her the White Lady, and Teller had assumed, at first, that Winter and White were interchangeable. She was the heart and the head of the Wild Hunt; she was their reason for existence. They were not Chosen; they did not take oaths. They were hers.

But they, like the Chosen, had will and choice, and that had consequences. Thus the Sleepers existed. He understood this as well. What he didn't understand was the host that, at last, came riding through the widened halls of winter stone, their horns a cacophony, an unadorned concert of death.

In seeming, in bearing, they were indistinguishable from Celleriant; they wore the same armor, and their perfect platinum hair was a stream of snow down their backs; they had no need of capes or cloaks with hair such as theirs.

Not for the Arianni the braids of the far north; not for the Arianni the cut-close crop of the Empire.

They did not ride horses. They rode what looked, to Teller's entirely inexperienced eye, to be stags, but stags unlike the Winter King; their coats suggested the patina of well-polished and aged silver; one or two were golden, as the fox the trees called eldest was golden.

But their antlers were smaller than the Winter King's crown, and their hooves heavier against the stone. Yet even though they made this much noise, there was something unreal about them; they seemed to move at the speed of dream, or nightmare. Lord Celleriant had never felt unreal in quite this fashion. If he was condescending and arrogant—and he was—the shift of his mood could be easily read, and the things that might cause it, both observed and learned. These riders were all of one thing.

He did not ask his companions their opinion, although he had no doubt they could answer the question he couldn't quite formulate; the riders were closer now, and Teller had the sense that they would hear both his voice and his words. As the forest guards had commanded, he was still, silent, his only movement the very slight rise of his chest. Even his cat had stilled at the sound of the approaching host, as if understanding instinctively that this was the time to be quiet.

It was a small mercy.

The forest guard said nothing, did nothing, until the horns sounded once again, shattering stillness and more. The ground beneath Teller's feet shook, and beyond his toes, it fractured, all but falling away to expose what lay beneath it. There were no joists, no darkness that hinted at basement storage; instead, there was the darkness of ancient earth.

And that earth now rose, its surface pebbled literally by shards of stone and broken roots. No more proof that these weren't Jay's lands was required; Teller knew that the earth would not lift itself at any command but hers without her permission, and Jay would never give permission to these fell, grim riders. He wondered who had commanded the earth; wondered what that command entailed, even as he watched.

But the ground beneath his feet did not break or shatter; the rising of the earth did not dislodge the fine polished, wooden planking. The forest guard whose hand remained upon Teller's shoulder now drew close enough that the whole of his torso was flush with Teller's back and head, and his legs braced Teller's as well, all of this in silence. The tree spirits did not otherwise move, not even to breathe; breath, if trees required it, could be had in the forest in which they were rooted.

And that forest bordered these winter halls in some fashion.

The horns sounded again, and this time there was a subtle difference in the notes, one of beat, of timing.

The second of the forest guard, the one who did not speak, now stepped in front of Teller, his larger feet touching what remained of the broken stone in the wake of the earth's rising. He did not speak, but speech was not required, for the last of the riders slowed, turning to look back at the earth itself.

That earth had formed columns, rounded and taller than the previous hall this Winter landscape had supplanted, as if a different building was emerging, whole, behind the host. And between those columns stood the lone forest guard.

"What is this?" the hunter said, and as he spoke, the host slowed, turning back as the Arianni shifted the direction his mount faced.

Teller could see him, but only barely; the forest guard stood before him like a living shield. His long arms bent as he leveled the weapon he had only just learned how to use.

"Do not move," the guard who held Teller said softly. "No matter what is said or done, do not move. The land upon which you stand is not theirs."

"If they attempt to cut me down, can they?"

"Yes."

Teller did not ask the obvious question. He did not understand what the tree spirits now hoped for; did not understand how they expected to survive, or rather, how they expected that he might. Given the expression on the faces of these hunters, he did not think he would survive for long.

Chapter Eighteen

JESTER CURSED THE FOX. As the elder growled at the obvious lack of respect, Jester said, "I wasn't whining." The fox did not remove his teeth. They had pierced skin, and any rejoinder save growl was functionally impossible.

It is not.

Great.

I simply chose not to dignify your pathetic attempt at justification with comment.

He's lying.

The fox's voice had not jarred Jester for reasons he could not explain, but this voice did. It was Birgide's. He opened his eyes and saw her, eyes closed, head bowed. She hadn't made a sound.

I do not understand why mortals have such a dim view of lying, the fox added. *Lies are merely a patina one places over words, a type of dance, a verbal performance. They do not change what is. They merely change what is believed, and one can change the beliefs of fools with ease. Folly persists. Were it not my lie, it would be another's; they cannot see the world as it is.*

It is dangerous, indeed, to walk the wilderness when one cannot observe it, cannot understand it. My lies, such as they are, are not the words of a god; they do not change what you label truth. Do you understand?

I understand, Jester said, *that this hurts a lot.*

Were you not beloved of the Lord I serve, I would sever your hand and eat it. Doing so now, however, would damage the Warden, and it is to succor her that I have come.

Jester wondered if Birgide felt pain.

Of course, Birgide replied. *I am accustomed to hiding it better. Far better.*

Why, exactly?

Because there are circumstances in which expression of pain is viewed as an invitation to receive more of it.

Do you understand what the eldest wants us to do?

Yes.

Can you do it?

She did not answer. But he wondered at the nature of lies. Words. Silence. He could hear, in the absence of the former, doubt. Fair enough. He had doubts of his own. He wanted to help her. He wanted to be of aid. But what she needed now was not lock picks, not sleight of hand, not loud, flamboyant distraction. She needed something solid. She needed someone competent.

Gods knew that wasn't Jester.

He was surprised on some level that any of them were still standing, and this included a fox that would no doubt take that surprise as a personal insult.

I will not, the fox replied. *The four are gathered, and we are closest now to where they stand. Do you not hear them? They have called their ancient hosts, and soon they will be mounted. When they ride out into your streets, they will cut a swathe of death through anything that stands in their way, or in their reach.*

If people were smart—and demonstrably, most weren't—they'd flee.

Their reach is very, very long. Warden. You see what your impertinent colleague cannot, and you were born as he was born. He cannot now see what you see, cannot hear what you hear, but nonetheless he wishes to plague you with his ignorance.

Birgide laughed.

It was not a sound. It was felt, a small well-spring of mirth where none should have existed. He had been surprised by her earlier laughter; this was stunning in comparison. He felt, for a moment, that he did not know her at all; that he had never known her at all. He had assessed her—at Haval's unfortunate command—but understood now that that assessment was entirely based on her competencies; he understood the ways in which she might harm or kill.

He did not understand anything else about her. Ah, no. He understood that she loved the *Ellariannatte*; that she had spent her adult life attempting to root them in foreign soil; that she had come to Jay because of the rumor of those very trees. And he understood as well that Jay had allowed her into a forest that she had forbidden angry, drooling mages, because Jay had perceived in an instant what it would mean to Birgide.

Birgide had not thought about it in that fashion. She had assumed that Jay's offer, that Jay's acceptance of her, was tied to Duvari, in a bad way. Jester had made clear, or so he thought, that Jay's decision was more than that—but in the tangle of the Birgide he was now aware of, he understood.

She was Warden because, in the end, Jay—shoveled into The Terafin's title, The Terafin's schedule, The Terafin's clothing and seat—nonetheless understood the hope for, the desire for, joy. For home. And she had, Jester thought, understood that home for Birgide Viranyi could be found only in the silent confines of the forest itself.

But it was a home of Jay's making.

Just as the den was and had been.

Jester and Birgide had much in common in the early years of their life, and almost nothing in the latter half. But Jester had learned all the shades of home in the years he'd spent with the den. He understood the way Jay picked things up—he'd been picked up the same way—and found something of value in even the deadliest of them.

Duster, he thought.

The leaves of silver, gold, and diamond.

The tree of fire.

Birgide herself.

Birgide could hear him. And he could hear her, although she did not speak, did not try to put her chaotic thoughts into palatable words. The fox was almost, and would have liked to be entirely, absent. But he did not intrude—not the way either Jester or Birgide did. He was a bridge. No, Jester thought, he was *the* bridge.

Jester wished Finch were here. Or Teller. Or Arann. Anyone but Jester, who was not the most welcoming member of their family. Birgide didn't trust any of them, of course. But here, the pain of fox teeth binding them together in ways nothing else could, she would have. And, instead, she got Jester.

You can do this, he told her. *You can do this because you're* like *the tree of fire. You're like the trees you couldn't study because they didn't exist in your world. What you're doing now, in Jay's name, they'll do as well. You only have to call them.*

How do I do that? There was anger in the words. Anger and fear.

Jester smiled. *I have no idea at all.*

His amusement annoyed her. Had possibly always annoyed her. But annoyance was not rage, and it certainly wasn't fear.

You know I don't want this?

Jester said quietly, *Yes. And before Jay, I never wanted anything, either. It was safest. What we wanted, what we valued, could be used against us or broken or taken away. The pain wasn't worth the risk. But, Birgide, this is. You were willing to die if you failed the forest's test. You've already taken that chance.*

I wanted the forest.

Yes. But the thing neither of us understood is that the forest is Jay. You can't have one without the other.

The Ellariannatte *existed before her.*

Yes, Jester agreed. *But now they will grow anywhere in the city. They will grow anywhere that she walks.* He stopped.

How do you know that? Did she tell you?

And the truth was, Jester *didn't* know that. He looked down at the fox, who had, he assumed, been silent throughout. His arms tightened, but only slightly.

Oh, very well. It is true, the fox said. Jester could feel Birgide stiffen. *The forest is its Lord. The wilderness is waking. A change of seasons is in the air we breathe. And yet we are awake, who lived in winter until Jewel woke us. She offered us three gifts,* the fox continued, his voice recognizably his own, but altered by the absence of sound. *Three gifts, and those gifts were accepted. But the rest was unforeseen. Understand that the Lord of the land is the land. If you wander the wilderness, if you wander the many demesnes, you will come to understand.*

You will never, the fox added, *understand it so well as we, for we are of it; it is our home.* Before Jester could reply, the fox added, *But what you understand of our Lord is mortal, and that, too, is part of what she is. Perhaps a mortal Warden was inevitable, and perhaps a mortal Warden is the best, the most, our Lord could do. You understand war, Warden. You understand death. You understand the preservation of lives, for your deaths were in service to that cause. You understand that those that rule require service, protection.*

In the wilderness, they do not. If they are so easily killed, they do not rule. They cannot. But it is not our Lord you protect now. It is what she values. It is what she holds dear—too dear, too close. It has been a long, long time since I loved as she loved— it is an act of youth, an act of defiance, an act of hope. And hope is dangerous. Where it is lost, it destroys.

But she is young. As you are. Therefore hope and love are inevitable. Hope, then. Love, then. And in service to the truth of that, the strength of that, wake your forest. It is waiting, Warden.

It is waiting.

The Wayelyn had heard and sung songs of the ancient Wild Hunt; he had penned a fair few in a youth of yearning and broken dreams. The horns of the hunters were not mortal horns, the notes not mortal notes. In his talent-born hearing, they resonated as if they were words or more than words; he could hear the whole of their intent. They did not sound a simple retreat, did not throw a simple direction into the din of clashing arms.

Mortal service was imperfect, incomplete; mortals required rest. Sleep. They were subject to the dictates of time, and a simple change in the weather could kill them. Not so the hunters; they were not so weak that they fell prey to something as negligible as time or a simple shift in the temperature of the air.

And they had been born to the forest, they had wakened the trees. This was their natural environment. In it, mortals foundered, mortals fell. In it, they screamed, they shouted, they wept.

But the hunters did not. They had come to reclaim this forest in the name of their lords.

All of this, The Wayelyn heard. But the one thing he could not hear, did not hear, were the names of those lords. He raised voice, commanded the bards to gather those they could reach; it was time, now, to retreat. The trees were the only safety offered, and he was not at all certain they would be enough. Solran had prepared them for this: she had made clear that in the worst case, all of the city would perish when the Sleepers woke. And in the best?

In the best case, they could save thousands. But they could not stand and fight. There were others who might do that for some small time, but they were few.

"Wayelyn."

The Master Bard turned.

"It is time, now, to do as you have commanded. I am impressed."

In the brightness of this purple dawn, The Wayelyn turned in the direction of that voice. He did not recognize it; was not even certain that it was a single voice. And he could not clearly see the speaker, although there were no shadows in which that speaker might hide. Here, even the shadows cast by the Kings' trees were thin, sparse. It was to drive panicking people to the thicker shadows that The Wayelyn now worked.

"Impressed?" the bard asked. He had husbanded the power of his voice, understanding that the tools to which he had not been born were of similar value: he wore Senniel's colors, and he had both the age and the gravitas of a man of power; he knew, as they all did, how to work a room. That the room was the size of a city made the endeavor far more of a challenge, and it made the bardic voice a very helpful tool, but the voice alone was not the only necessary tool.

"Impressed. You must, however, vacate this road. It is down this road that the hunt will ride. And Wayelyn, this hunt is *not* the hunt of the Winter

Queen. It is an echo, a memory, something trapped and preserved. Only the wilderness gives it form, and it cannot be moved by mere weapons. I will stand my ground here; if you are standing even in the edge of my shadow, you will be devoured."

"Who are you?" the bard all but demanded.

Silence, and then, softly, "I am Andrei. For the moment, and while this city stands, I am Andrei."

The Wayelyn did not recognize the name but heard no lie in the words. No lie in the blurred overlap of voices. He was moved to bow, but it was a gesture of respect, not a political maneuver, and he once again lifted voice, demanding what this Andrei had demanded. If the Master Bards did not heed his call to flee, he was certain they would at least heed the demand to empty this one street. Bards were very good at avoiding danger while simultaneously breaking the rules.

"Sigurne."

Sigurne glanced at Matteos. He had served her for years; she understood the question inherent in the lift of the second syllable of her name, and shook her head. "They will come here," she told him. "The Kings stand here."

"They should retreat to the Isle."

"The time for that is passed. It was gone the moment Moorelas fell and the spire rose to take his place."

"Can't Duvari intercede?"

"If you have not noticed, he is as grim and fell as death. Were it in his hands, they would be well away—possibly in a summer retreat, well quit of the city. It is not, however, in his hands. They are Kings; they are our Kings. And it is to the Kings, now, that the four will ride."

"Four?"

"Four," she said softly. "They will not fall here, not easily."

Matteos looked out across the city, or the parts of the city he could now see through the trees. "How long?" he asked, his voice soft, his hands shaking. "How long do we have?"

"As long as we have ever had," Sigurne replied. "Until our lives are spent."

"That is not what I was asking."

"No?" She exhaled. "Look at them, Matteos. Look. Fabril crafted weapons for their use against such a day as this." She did not tell him that this would be the only day, for she believed that Fabril's gifts were meant for a different battle, if they but survived this one.

But she could see the Kings clearly in this place. She could now see the

Kings, even when the trunks of these towering trees should have obscured them. She could hear their voices when those voices were raised, although they were not raised now.

She did not know what the sword was meant to cut, to pierce; did not know what the rod was meant, in the end, to rule or command. Nor was it necessary; the comfort of one old woman in the bitter haze of this new sky was irrelevant. The ring on her hand burned a bright sigil into the air, and when she opened her mouth again, she whispered a single word, and it was like a prayer.

And beneath the purple sky, above the wreckage of trees made brittle and cold by its breath, the dragon finally descended.

None of the training the House Guard received had involved an opponent of this size. Seen from the sky, its size obscured by distance, it had seemed enormous, but as that distance diminished, the truth grew, and grew again. Buildings gave way—far more easily than the trees had—and Arrendas hoped that those buildings were as empty as the street had become. He spared no other thought for the possible victims; if rescue was to come to them, it would not be at the hands of the Terafin Chosen.

But the Chosen stopped a moment ten yards from the closest part of the dragon: its tail. The tail was forked, and it moved, rising and falling. As it landed, stones shattered, trunks splintered. Its hind claws could be seen, raking runnels through broken shards. Had the dragon spoken, Arrendas would not have been surprised; it did not. It roared.

A plume of frost distorted the heat of the air, as if the creature had swallowed the whole of winter and now disgorged it at its own convenience. The dragons in Arrendas' childhood stories—and there had been many—were creatures whose breath melted gold and armor; fire was their weapon. This dragon did not breathe fire.

But he thought that the frost it did breathe would be just as deadly.

"Gordon."

The Chosen stepped forward. Of the Chosen, he was the only one who had taken a shield from the walls of The Terafin's war room. Gordon's choice had been a kite shield.

"Flank?"

Arrendas was captain. Grimacing, he said, "We don't know how to kill a dragon."

"Kill it? Are we sure we know how to survive one?"

Arrendas chuckled. "We're about to find out." He backed away, taking advantage of the natural alleys that formed between buildings. He did not, however, retreat. Given the destruction of other buildings, being caught between them meant that falling stone or timber might do the dragon's work for it.

"Corrin, stay with Gordon. The rest of us will try to attack from the flank." Corrin's weapon of choice had been a bladed pole-arm. It had the reach a sword did not, and it had come from the walls of the same war room. He had practiced with it from the moment he had taken it down, but in theory his skill with a sword was greater.

"I want a raise." Before Arrendas could answer, he added, "You know Gordon's almost impossible to partner."

"Says the man who almost lopped my arm off."

"I was testing the shield."

The Chosen spread out, leaving Gorden and Corrin in the alley's mouth. They moved quickly, but not silently; their movement was partly obscured as Gordon raised his shield and bellowed for the dragon's attention.

"Finch. It's time."

Finch shook her head. She could see the line of stragglers, thinner now but no less desperate. She could almost see an end to them but knew that there would be no end; not while there were still survivors. "We need to move."

"Yes."

"I mean, we need to move down the tree line."

"No."

She glanced at Torvan; he had folded his arms.

"He is your Chosen," Haval said. Finch, accustomed to Jarven, didn't even startle at the unexpected voice. "It is time to retreat. Can you not hear the horns?"

She could; they all could. "We're not done yet."

"Finch, you are done. You feel that greed is emblematic of the patricians who see both financial gain and their own pleasure. This is true; I will not deny it. But you define desire as *greed* when you do not approve of that desire."

"Haval—"

"You are, now, being greedy. You have saved many, but they gather in the forest in which they are lost. Unmoored, they will seek order, seek hierarchy, seek petty power."

"They're alive," was her flat response.

"Yes. And I say again, you are being greedy. You want just one more. Just two more. Just that handful. Value what you have already gained. What you have done here is more than Jewel could have asked; more than she would have dreamed of, in her terror." Haval could see that he had failed to make his case, but he was Haval; he regrouped.

"You have value to Jewel. You are, therefore, of value—incalculable value—to the forest and its denizens. If you now take the risk that you intend to take, the whole of their power will be focused, not on those who have none, but on *you*. I will remain," he continued, when she finally stiffened.

"You're important, too."

"Not in the fashion that you are, and I will not play word games with you. I will remain with the forest guard; you will retreat. I will continue to oversee the evacuation. If I die here, Jewel might grieve—but she has long expected that my death at least will not come at the hands of time."

Torvan could see the moment her resolve shifted.

"Will you go with Haval?" she asked him.

He shook his head. "You have a detail of two. It is a number meant, in its entirety, for trusted friends and allies. Marave and I will remain with you."

She turned then and gave the House Guards orders. "Take the banner and follow Haval Arwood."

Haval grimaced. "I am not of Terafin."

"You have never had ethical issues with lies. If you would like, I will give you my House ring; you may use it to its best advantage."

Torvan did not blanch. Marave, however, had more difficulty containing her outrage; it could be seen in the stiffening lines of her hands. Her face, however, was blank.

Haval smiled.

Finch removed the House ring from her cold fingers and held it out. The man who had been her tailor had never been her advisor; he had considered her, in some fashion, too close to Jarven. He did not lift his hand; instead, he shuffled his until they were clasped behind his back. "You waste time."

"I am regent," Finch replied. "This decision is within my power to make."

"I will not require the ring. If necessary, I will, no doubt, have the aid of one who wears the ring legitimately. I had hoped to avoid it, but he is a plague that returns at moments of weakness." Haval then bowed to her and turned, as if she had nothing of relevance to add.

Into the streets of a city transformed rode the ghosts of the Wild Hunt. They could be seen through the trees; could be heard across the whole of the city, their horns raised, the notes eerily omnipresent. They did not come from a single direction, but many, as if each of the three Sleepers commanded a separate force. They came from the north, from the south, and across the bay.

The one small mercy was that if they did cross the water, the hooves of their mounts skimming the surface of gentle waves, they did not stop to wreak their destruction across the Isle itself, where the Ten and the Kings made their homes. Perhaps it was because they were drawn by the lords they served; perhaps it was because they aimed for the dark cathedral that even now cast shadows that seemed to grow longer, grow darker, in the winter light.

It was not winter in Averalaan; Lattan was the height of its summer. But on this day, beneath these skies, it felt as if winter had never ended, might never end. The cold was sudden, bitter; the frost touched buildings, touched trees, reddened faces already bright with exertion. The skies were not clear, but the largest of the creatures that had held dominion in them had landed. Its breath was not the flame of children's stories, but the frost of the far, far North.

And the predators, winged all, continued to land. Where they could, they angled themselves toward the citizens who bore no arms and had no martial training, picking off the slowest of the runners, or those who were in the most open of spaces. Many fell attempting to reach the cover of trees, for the dragon had destroyed dozens in its bid to create a space from which it might rule land as it had ruled sky.

The bards had ranged far in their quest to catch the attention of the citizens of their capital, but distance was not the impediment to the bard-born that it might have been to any other such searchers. The trees, however, thinned markedly as the bards and the Kings' Swords rode out from the Common, and reaching the safety of trees was no longer a given; where the trees were thinner the creatures from above found it far easier to hunt.

Nor did the bards have weapons other than voice or instruments by which they might defend the helpless. They had walked before, each and every man and woman, upon fields of battle, and those fields had left scars in memory. Those scars would be deepened by today's work, if they survived. So many had not.

The Kalakar and The Berrilya had commanded much larger armies in service to the Twin Kings than the forces they now commanded, but they had not gathered those forces in haste, had not taken the reins of command without plan. Their plans, however, had not included the winged; nor had they included a dragon. What they had expected to face were the hunters, and those hunters came, beneath the cover of hostile skies.

To the south, The Kalakar's men were readied; to the north, The Berrilya's.

And toward the bay, where the last of the forces drew closer, stood the Kings themselves, in the lee of the cathedral. In Averalaan, by royal decree, no buildings save cathedrals were to have spires taller than the spires of *Avantari*, the palace of Kings. This building therefore defied royal law; the height of its tallest spire was greater by far than the tallest of *Avantari's*, taller than the height of the cathedrals that were home to the Exalted and the god-born of the Triumvirate.

The magi stood with the Kings; the Exalted stood with the Kings. Solran Marten, Bardmaster of Senniel College, stood with the Kings, passing royal commands through her bard-born aide to the bards who had passed through the Common, heading into the wilderness of the city streets in a bid to save those they could. Solran reported every lost Master Bard in a dry, neutral voice, the names a way of marking both time and loss, as if loss would be the only marker of time in this long, terrible day.

She could not count the number of lives saved in the exchange of Master Bards for citizenry, nor did she try. The cold had become bitter, as if brought by the amethyst skies and the dragon who had ruled them; although the magi could, to some extent, protect those enclosed in their magics from the worst of the winter bite, no one had come to the Sanctum prepared for cold.

Nor could the power itself be casually spent; the magi husbanded their gifts against future need. And that future was fast becoming present as the horns continued to sound.

Finch, escorted by Torvan and Marave, returned to the heart of Jay's forest. The din and clangor of battle faded with every step she took, and she longed, now, to turn back. But Torvan had reminded her of her duties: she was regent, and the Terafin forests were, in Jay's absence, her responsibility. Ah, no. They were the Warden's responsibility, but the people who had entered the forest because of some vague promise of safety were not.

She was cold; her hands ached with it, and her skin was numb. She sought the tree of fire. No footpath showed her the way, but one had never been required before, and indeed, it was not required now; she could see the red-orange glow of that tree's many leaves and branches as she walked past the standing trees of metal, of diamond.

She was not prepared for what this tree had become. Its fire had always been warm, but the growth of its trunk and its many branches had never reached the height of the *Ellariannatte*; it had only barely been equal to the trees of silver, gold, and diamond. She saw, now, that it had, in the space of time she'd spent in the streets of the Common, become far larger, far grander; it burned more brightly.

Leaves fluttered in a gale of wind that touched only its height; she almost forgot to breathe as those leaves were torn free. If such a tree knew seasons, this tree had finally come into them: the leaves were carried by a wind that otherwise touched nothing, and she watched their graceful flight, light tracing arcs that remained in her vision as the leaves floated past.

She would have been afraid to touch them; would not have lifted a palm to catch them if they fell. Or so she thought. But when a leaf plunged suddenly to land a yard from her feet, she bent. Her hand was shaking as she reached for the leaf; she had come to understand that no leaves fell in this forest without intent. Not yet.

But before her fingers touched its white-gold stem, another hand interceded; another hand lifted the leaf.

"This is not for you, little mortal—not yet. Perhaps not ever."

Finch exhaled and glanced to the side, to meet the eyes of Calliastra. Her pulse quickened, whether due to excitement or fear, she was never certain. "Is Jay—Is Jay back?"

"Not yet. Don't look so disappointed. She paused a while in the gardens of my sister, but I do not believe my sister will either detain or destroy her; there is too much that depends upon your Lord."

Calliastra felt, to Finch, like the absent Kiriel. There was something about her that made it very hard to turn one's back—and Finch had lived with raging, furious Duster. She was not, however, the child she had been when Duster had been alive; she could, and did, expose her back to Calliastra.

Calliastra had come with Jay. And Calliastra wished, somehow, to stay with her. Calliastra was in the forest; Calliastra's shadow—longer and darker than height dictated—was acceptable to the forest. There was only one way that could happen.

"Is it for you?" Finch asked softly, finding her voice quickly and without apparent struggle.

"It is . . . hot. Almost too hot for my fingers. I think yours would be charred to bone—but the forest is Jewel's, and Jewel is . . . unlike any other Lord I have met in the wilderness. The forest accepts me."

Finch nodded.

"Perhaps the Warden is unaware of my presence."

"No. Jay meant for you to be den, and all of the den is welcome here. Not all of the den is beloved, but it doesn't matter. What Jay accepts, the forest accepts, warts and all."

Calliastra laughed. Her voice was winter and darkness and velvet and . . . light. Finch felt her mouth dry, her lips open; she had lifted her hand slowly toward Calliastra's face before she realized it was in motion. Calliastra brushed that hand away. "It is true that Jewel accepts me, but I do not think she would forgive—ever—the loss of you. It is hard, to be in the forest; I feel the lives of the hundreds that gather beneath and between the trees; I hear the voices of those trees raised in warning. They . . . are not friendly."

"They will not hurt you," Finch said quietly.

"No. But not, perhaps, for lack of trying." She lifted the leaf. "I will take this, I think, but I will not remain. There is work, now, for me to do." She turned, and Finch watched wings unfurl from between her shoulder blades, stretching like thunderous clouds across a clear sky. They were almost as wide, tip to tip, as the dragon's wings. Calliastra looked up, to the cover of trees, as if they were a simple veil her gaze could easily pierce. But she said, before she leaped into the skies, "I spent much of my life among your kind, your mortal kind. It is the only place, in the end, that I could find sustenance."

Finch understood exactly what that meant, but Calliastra meant for it to *be* understood.

"People thought to use me, confusing one desire for another; I was weapon, to some, assassin to some, dream to some. I have been desired all of my existence. Desired and dreaded, desired and feared. I have been loved," she added, not lowering her gaze. "And that was worst of all. But, Finch, I have been the echo of your Duster, in my time; it was how I first approached your Jewel. I understand that Duster needed some duty, some sense of her position within your den, that belonged to her alone. And perhaps I am no different.

"What I do now, you *cannot* do. Not any of one of you."

Finch said, "The Sleepers."

"Yes."

Finch struggled for words and found none.

"They cannot easily kill me. One to one, I would say it would be impossible, but they are the greatest part of my sister's power—the greatest part remaining her. She is coming," Calliastra added.

"Jay?"

"Yes. And my sister. It is only to hold them in check for long enough that I have arrived here—and I have arrived late, I see. Go, now, and see to your terrified flock; they will let fear drive their actions soon, and fear is a genuinely ugly driver." She pushed herself off the ground, then, and leaves fell in the wake of her great wings.

King Cormalyn gestured, rod in hand, and the trees surrounding the royal gathering parted, roots pulling back as if they were the toes of misbehaving children. Beneath the roots that had formed a path in the absence of the cobbled streets of the Common lay a smooth road of stone. It unfolded as the trees moved, stretching the new gap in what had been the seawall.

Duvari glanced, once, at Sigurne, which surprised the guildmaster; she nodded in answer to his wordless question. The road would hold. The road might extend from the ruins of this Common to the Isle itself, and it would not falter; not while the King wielded Fabril's rod.

The Kings' Swords made to move into defensive position around the monarchs, but King Reymalyn bid them stand their ground, and they froze almost to a man, although the Verrus looked to Duvari, and not the Kings themselves. Sigurne could not see Duvari's expression, and it did not concern her. While he would take advice from the guildmaster on magical matters, this matter of safety was not magical in nature. As Cormalyn had done, Reymalyn wielded Fabril's gift; it was like lightning in his hand; the edge of the blade seemed to extend far beyond the reach of the sword itself.

Matteos focused his gaze not upon the approaching host, but behind, to where the cathedral stood. She understood this, as well. Let the Kings now face the enemies that rode across the waves in the bay; the magi were meant to defend against the dangers that might come unbidden upon them.

No, she thought, not unbidden. For if the Sleepers had demanded the very skies shift, if they had commanded the cathedral rise, if they had called forces from the air and through the city streets, they had not yet themselves made a move.

She thought of Gyrrick and his warrior-magi, now; thought of the trees of Terafin, still growing and spreading their roots across the streets of the hundred holdings, and thought, last, of the ring that encircled her finger. Meralonne had never made explicit the ring's purpose; she had assumed, presumed, that it was meant to preserve her life in the face of the wrath of those who had been laid to sleep by the very gods, when the gods had last walked this world.

She did not know if that would be boon or bane to her.

If she alone survived in the wreckage of the city that had consumed her waking hours for the whole of her adult life, what purpose had her life served?

And yet, even so, she remembered the first flight of the man who had come to kill one rogue mage and the demons he had enslaved, and some small part of her remained that young, desperate woman, resigned to death in the winter world of her distant youth.

Resigned to death, she had shown no fear, and in truth, had felt none. She had made her choice, had understood the price to be paid for it. Meralonne had been a singular gift at the end of that life, a brief glimpse of something that could not be swayed by mage or *Kialli*, that could not be destroyed. He was not heroic; no more were storms that swept the wastelands. She had labored under no hopeful illusions. Meralonne was a predator. Just as the mage and his demons were. He hunted different things.

Ah, no. No, she thought, he dabbled. He fought. He was at his brightest, at his best, when presented with the possibility of death; he threw himself into combat with a ferocity he reserved for nothing else.

He had obeyed her commands, when she chose to give them, and he obeyed them precisely because she seldom chose to do so. His had been, in many ways, the power behind the figurative throne. He had been the foundation upon which she stood.

And that age was ending.

A light illuminated the cathedral that had grown in place of Moorelas' Sanctum. It traveled up the side of a black, bleak tower, changing in one flash the whole of its appearance as it drove the shadows away. She was not a master of architecture, but she did understand the basis for its structural stability; thus it was, with those who could summon magics capable of destroying that stability.

As light traveled across the visible surfaces of the building—those viewed through the towering boughs of *Ellariannatte*—she remembered: the Sleepers had been imprisoned; jailed in slumber and in physical space. This, then, was reclamation of sorts, and a hush descended upon the whole of the gathering as they watched what the Sleepers made of that prison, that place.

Meralonne had desired that she witness beauty as he perceived it, and she did, and she thought it a deadly gift but also a real one, because it both expended power and bought time.

But she understood, watching, that the cathedral itself was no longer a part of the city; where it spread, no *Ellariannatte* grew, and in the confines of that patch of land, the Sleepers had invoked the earth, and the earth had obeyed. She glanced, once, at the *Ellariannatte*, and thought: *they will not hold*.

Finch, with the aid of the House Council, moved among the refugees. Terafin had prepared for its own evacuation, and more besides; there was food. It could not feed the entire city for any length of time, but the water in the forest was clear and cool, and water would become an issue before food did, if they were careful.

The House Guard had the effect of the magisterial guard, and people huddled at a respectful distance. Finch had once been one of those people, and today, she remembered it clearly. But she understood that she was not one of the Mother's Daughters, here. The comfort she could afford to offer was scant. She was, until and unless the Kings took to the forest, authority made manifest. Fear of that authority was only one tool, but she understood people well; for some, it was the only tool to which they would respond.

Thus, rulership.

She understood, better than Jay, why people sought power. She understood that power came in many forms, and today, she wore as many of them as she could bear. She, who had been part of the West Wing for her entire life in Terafin, had hated the social walls erected between the Household Staff and the den, but understood that it was her word that would carry the weight here, not the word of a servant, be they ATerafin or no.

She deputized, among the refugees; she counted, and counted again, breaking the new arrivals into manageable group sizes. She looked for Farmer Hanson and his forbidding, intimidating daughter, his "useless" sons; they were not here. Nor was Helen, and that gave her pause; Helen was older, and not very mobile.

But absent, as well, was Haval's wife, Hannerle.

Helen and the farmer might not have arrived to open their stalls for the day's business. But Hannerle lived in the Common. She froze for one long breath and then continued to move. Each person present, no matter how old or how young, was as valuable to someone as the three were to the den. The people present were alive; they were more real than fear. She could not let fear guide her actions, or she would have lost before she had started.

And she believed that, clung to it, reinforced it, until she returned to the House Council.

Jester was in the Common. Haval was in the Common. Arann was with the Chosen. These, she expected. Daine was present, and tucked into his side was Ariel, her eyes windows into a past that she never spoke about. Finch did not count her den. She knew that Jay and Angel were somewhere in the wilderness. They were beyond her, beyond them all.

Turning to Barston, she said, "Where is the right-kin?"

He met her gaze for a beat longer than necessary, and then said, "I do not know, Regent."

Her voice sharpened; she managed to control its volume. "Where is Teller?"

Jester heard the question.

Surrounded by trees, his hand bleeding, the fox's tiny teeth enlarging the wounds they had caused, he *heard*. He lifted head, opened eyes, and froze. Standing in the grove of *Ellariannatte* at its thickest were the people he thought of as trees, but they were not the trees Haval had trained. They were not adorned in the gold and silver of their leaves; they wore armor in plates that gleamed beneath what could be seen of amethyst sky. They carried swords, shields; they looked like suits of armor, like weapons come to life.

They stood around Birgide and Jester, facing outward; Jester was under no illusion as to who they protected, here.

Movement caught his eye; for a moment he thought of pitchforks and torches, but that was a mundane fancy that had no place in this changed universe. There was fire, yes, but it was not carried by men; it was not carried by anything. It approached, bobbing and weaving, and he saw the leaves of fire.

Only the leaves.

But those leaves moved on a current of air that Jester could neither feel nor see, fluttering toward the newly wakened soldiers of gold and silver, coming to land on their shoulders and helms as if they were butterflies. They did not melt the metal, but Jester noted that they did not seek purchase on any living bark. Nor did they land on the Warden.

The fox opened his mouth. Since manners in the wilderness were meant entirely for interacting with the powerful, he then turned and spit. Loudly.

"I hope," he finally said when he had stopped, "that you appreciate this." He glanced at the soldiers and nodded with approval. "They are not the trees that once grew in the wake of the gods. They are not, in any real sense, trees at all. The Warden understands this now."

Jester looked down at his hand; it was still clenched tight around Birgide's. Her fingers eased their death grip. Jester's, however, did not.

She opened her eyes; opened her cracked lips. No words emerged, but they weren't necessary. Jester grinned, and her eyes narrowed with customary annoyance.

"What? This is the safest place to stand, and I don't intend to leave it."

Birgide shook her head. Just that. But the butterflies of flame launched themselves off their armored perches, and the soldiers—he could not think of them as trees—began to march. He blinked and blinked again; he had not attempted to count them when he'd first set eyes on them, but he would have put their number at a dozen.

He would have been wrong. They marched out of the copse of trees, and also simultaneously remained. Jester closed his eyes and listened to the fall of their feet across a path made of roots.

They walked in all directions; Jester caught Birgide as she sagged.

"Remain here," the fox told him. He seemed to be smiling. "It is, indeed, the safest place for one such as you to stand."

"You're leaving?"

"I am considering my many options," the fox replied, a hint of buoyant excitement in his voice. "But perhaps you cannot hear what I hear."

Jester waited.

"It appears that one of the firstborn has taken to the skies around the citadel."

"The Sleepers?"

The fox threw a very familiar look of disgust over his golden shoulder. "They are of the White Lady. But she is not. Can you guess who I speak of?"

Jester said, "Calliastra."

"She will not be able to take them all, but they will find her a challenge."

"You're going to join her?"

"I think I might," the fox replied. "I found their courtesy . . . lacking." He hopped lightly across the roots, maintaining the form that he usually wore.

Haval saw the soldiers of gold and silver as they joined the ranks of the *Ellariannatte*. They did not require arms; nor did they require armor. He suspected they might require more firm ground than the roots of trees, given the density of at least one of the base metals. But this gold and this silver were not mortal and inert.

Haval gave instructions to the spirits of the *Ellariannatte*. "Take those who will follow you into Jewel's lands. Return when they are safe."

They spread out in packs—half a dozen trees accompanied, where numbers permitted, by at least one Terafin House Guard. He added metallic warriors to those numbers; their instructions were different. They were to intervene—and destroy—anything that attacked either the *Ellariannatte* or the civilians they shepherded. Anything. They accepted his orders in silence. Haval did not ask them if they knew how to use the weapons they carried.

He followed the tree line, taking care to remain beneath the boughs of the trees that had once grown only in the Common, and he moved toward the heart of the Common. Toward his home.

There was, however, a problem, if one did not include the ground-based forces that appeared, from the sound of horns, to be converging toward the newly risen building.

A dragon.

Haval noted the break in the line of the trees; he could see the remnants of trunks, some taller than Arann.

The den, individually, understood the importance of the den as a whole;

they failed to understand their significance as disparate parts. He closed his eyes briefly. If Jewel did not return soon, the safety of the den might be irrelevant.

"Sleeping on the job?"

"I am attempting to think without the distraction of visual noise," Haval replied, without opening his eyes. "Can the dragon be injured by regular weapons?"

"If the last five minutes are any indication, no. I think it likely that ballistae might have a salutary effect, but they were not considered wise within the city."

Haval turned to his troops, gazing across the sheen of their armor, their weapons. He had watched the Chosen in utter silence, part of the shadows cast by trees; he had seen enough.

The shield that had been taken from Jewel's armory was proof against the breath of the frostwyrm; it was not, however, adequate to damage the creature, and the man who wielded it was wearing armor that was not proof against incidental damage.

The breath of the creature appeared to freeze anything it touched, even the walls of the buildings themselves; when it lashed out with tail or lunged with sizable jaws, debris flew in all directions. Brick, stone, and timber did not seem to even attract the dragon's notice. All three caused the Chosen difficulty. One man was downed by it—Haval thought a bone had snapped though he could not be certain.

The Chosen had attempted to flank the creature, but the dragon's wings were problematic. Where they could, the Chosen pressed close to the bulk of its body to avoid the dragon's breath and tail; they could not avoid the wings. Those wings had also sheared through the sides of buildings; the Common was crowded.

It would be less crowded soon.

"Councillor."

Haval nodded his permission to speak but did not take his eyes off the combat.

"They are ready."

He turned then. Drifting with care among the spirits of living trees were moths of flame, sparks of a fire that, uncontained, would do what the dragon had not yet managed.

"Interesting."

"If you are not inclined to aid us," Haval said, "Your silence would be appreciated."

Jarven chuckled.

"Go to the Kings."

"It has been many years since either of us have undertaken such service."

"You have stated that you feel younger than you have in decades." Haval lifted a hand, and the moths came to it. He had, twice, lifted a hand to touch the low-hanging branches of Jewel's tree of fire. In neither case had the obvious occurred; he had not been burned.

But these small flames were no longer attached to that tree, and he felt their heat as a warning. He was aware, as they circled his open palm, that he was not lord here, not commander, not Warden. The Lord, however, was absent, and the Warden appeared to be inclined to give weight to his commands.

He did not know what effect the fire would have against the frost; there was only one way to determine that. He sent the fire to where the dragon rampaged.

Arann flattened as the dragon's wings passed over his head. Kauran was not as lucky; the wing's arc clipped him. The clatter of steel against steel was the sound of blade against armor; Kauran staggered back at the force of the blow. He toppled, managing to crawl out of reach of the wing as it returned to a heightened position above the dragon's back.

Arann was one of a handful of Chosen who had taken a sword from the war room's wall. He had discovered that the weapons arrayed there shifted; although they appeared to be solid and almost mundane, not all of the Chosen could see all of the weapons. Some of the Chosen had said they felt compelled to choose specific weapons—or, in Gordon's case, the shield—but Arann had not; nothing had, in subtle or unsubtle fashion, called his name or attracted his attention.

Left to his own devices, he had taken a sword, one of a pair. It was the least ostentatious of the weapons arrayed there; there was one gem in its hilt, but it was a small gem. It had seemed, to his eye, to be the most used, the least pristine; only the blade was perfect. Use had not chipped its edge, and there were no obvious pits or hints of rust.

He had not been raised to arms; had not been raised, in fact, to violence. Given his size and his strength, violence had come to him anyway. He had been given rudimentary training in the handling of a sword; old Rath had been disappointed in his general competence. Compared to Angel or Carver, the sword did not come easily to Arann, although he handled its weight with ease.

But when he had chosen to join the House Guard, he had forced himself to set aside his dislike of, distrust of, physical violence. He had learned. He was not the best, though not the worst, of the House Guard. He was, he was certain, the least competent of the Chosen. And he was certain that he could not become proficient in any other weapon with any speed.

He had therefore looked only for swords; he had touched nothing else.

The sword he now carried was a hand and a half sword; too large for a smaller man to wield comfortably, it fit Arann's hand like a glove. He had drawn it before they chose to engage the dragon. Nothing special had happened; it was a sword, its blade flat and perfect and heavy.

But when he drove it into the dragon's exposed wing, its edge separated flaps of glittering ice. Blood ran down the blade and that blood caught fire—a golden glow of warmth that did not blind the eye. He felt the warmth of hearth fire, the warmth of spring; the winter chill that had permeated the Common with the fall of Moorelas evaporated.

The dragon roared and turned toward Arann; it roared again as someone on the opposite side of its bulk struck. Gordon's shield was somewhere nearest where the head of the beast had been before they had grouped to attack. Arann raised his sword as the dragon's massive jaws opened two yards from where he stood, poised to throw himself to the right or left of the conic breath.

He saw wings snap up and out; could not tell from the sound that followed whether they had struck man, building, or both. He bent into his knees, shifting his hold on the sword; it was hard to dodge and roll while carrying a weapon. Hard to do it while wearing armor.

Screams joined dragon roar, and Arann stiffened. They were not familiar voices. They were too high, too hysterical, too fragile. One stopped, banked suddenly—by dragon tail or claw or falling wall—and the others redoubled in volume. Once, half a lifetime ago, he would have told the hysterical, terrified people that screaming was the worst possible choice: it made position and location completely obvious; it alerted predators who might not otherwise be alert.

He had never been loud, and he had taught the peculiar silence of heightened caution to anyone in reach who would listen. He could not teach these unseen strangers that lesson, now.

High above the dragon's chosen ground, flew what Arann thought of as vultures, waiting, waiting; they circled lower at the sound of terror. Fear made people stupid if they couldn't control it. And he understood why they couldn't.

This was the Common.

Dragons did not exist. That lesson was drummed into children, had been drummed into them for centuries, each passing out of that childhood belief and into the solidity of adulthood. Dragons could not exist. No more could swords that shed warmth and light, or knights that wielded those swords in pursuit of justice. Stories, all.

But the dragon was here. The winged vultures circled. And Arann stood in a broken street, newly made ruins gaping where walls and windows had shattered, listening to the terrified screams of people he could not see, and understanding, as he did, that this sword existed. He was not a hero. Not a knight. Not the final charge of the Kings' Swords. But he remembered his stories, now: remembered the tales of the Blood Barons, and the first of the Twin Kings, Cormalyn and Reymalyn, and he remembered that the final battle had taken place in the city itself, where cavalry was almost useless.

Then, there had been demons and magi; now, there was dragon and vulture and the horns of a distant, new foe.

Stories, he thought. Stories were what history became. History was reality; it was blood and death and loss; the grief and rage of the moment made real because people were living it, breathing it. Glory, gallantry, heroism, all existed after the fact as bards spread the tales, made newer and prettier, to those who were safe enough they could pause to listen, to daydream, to become, for a moment, one of the valiant warriors who fought on the side of right.

He understood, now, as the screams tilted into a silence of exhaustion and terror, that those soldiers had not thought of themselves as heroes; they might not have thought of themselves as right, either. What they'd desired, on that long-ago day, was survival. Of themselves. Of their comrades. Of the way of life they had chosen, and the Kings to whom they had committed the whole of their service, even if that service ended their lives.

But, he thought, even struggling for survival, it *was* the way of life they'd chosen, and they would live or die for it. The stories might be fodder for the young, the hopeful, the painfully naive—but the kernel at the heart of those stories was truth. Was he afraid?

Yes. Only an idiot would be without fear.

The dragon's jaws opened. Arann's knees unbent. He held the sword in both hands, discarding his shield. He could see flame and fire—some early morning candle or stove knocked over by the devastation—and he could almost feel their bracing warmth, although such fires were death.

Sparks of fire flew, as they did when the fires were not doused; they found fuel in exposed timber, dry wood, and they spread, leaping as they did. Above his head, the air swirled, and embers caught fire, growing in size as they passed overhead. He did not watch; could not, without diverting his gaze from the largest threat to life: the dragon's jaws.

This close to the dragon's breath, he could hear the howl of Northern winds, could feel the chill of blizzard, the certainty that weather was as deadly as any predator. But even in the North, men built, men made; shelters existed in which survival from weather was almost guaranteed.

Fires burned, for warmth.

Fires burned here.

The dragon exhaled, and Arann lifted the sword; held it before him in two steady hands, as if breath were tangible, solid, as if it could be cut. He felt nothing as the dragon exhaled; saw no frost, no ice. But he felt resistance as he brought the sword down; felt something pushing back against the edge of the golden blade.

He had the whole of the dragon's attention now, but he was not the only member of the Terafin Chosen to stand his ground in this place, and if his weapon was, truly, a thing of legend, of story, so, too, were the weapons of his comrades.

Arrendas shouted a command to Gordon. Take the shield. Protect the civilians. Get them to cover.

The captain had seen what Arann's sword could do. And the captain, like Arann, understood that at this moment, in this small section of the city, the Chosen, like the earliest of the Kings' Swords, followed their Lord and the way of life she had chosen.

Chapter Nineteen

HECTORE OF ARAVEN WAS one of the wealthiest men in the Empire; he had elected to remain—for sentimental reasons—in residence on the mainland. The Isle was home to the wealthy and the powerful; the address itself an indication of status. Hectore, however, felt a disregard for status conferred by something as simple as an address. The land on the Isle was expensive, and much of it leaseheld by the Crowns; he could not have the grand and enclosed estate he had come to value for both its privacy and its size were he to live on the Isle.

Nor could he occupy the manor he now did, a building that had seen many architectural changes over the years. While he understood the advantage of the Isle, the disadvantages that accrued by such a move were far greater.

Today, for perhaps the first time, he wondered if he had made the right choice. He was not a man given to introspection, or at least that form of introspection that was commonly called regret.

One of his grandchildren, the youngest, shoved the door to his personal offices open, flying across the threshold without so much as a by-your-leave. "Grandma says more people have come and you have to meet them."

As he was not seated, he engulfed said grandchild in his arms, lifting her, shrieking, from the carpeted floor. "Well, then. It's good that you came to get me. It wouldn't do to upset Grandma."

"She won't be *upset*, she'll be angry."

"Fair enough. It's sometimes hard to tell the difference."

"It's not hard at all," his granddaughter replied. She then obligingly cataloged the differences while he went in search of these so-called new people, her voice dropping in volume as he walked. She was not dressed for company but was now dressed for morning; when the first of the people had arrived on their grounds, she had not been. Hectore had half-hoped that she would see the evening out in pleasant dreams; that she would wake to a morning not much different than the mornings with which she had, until now, been blessed.

He had ordered the gates open to allow people entry, but he was not so foolish as to leave the gates wide once they had been granted it; the Araven guards had therefore been called up, to a man. Hectore's manor was not in the poorer holdings.

But when he surrendered his grandchild and exited the foyer, he saw the color of the skies, hidden from view by heavy curtains and a desire for a moment of privacy and peace in which to gather his strength. He had seen skies this color only in one other place, and he felt a brief, visceral hope: that she had somehow returned with those skies. That The Terafin was home.

The things that gathered in the skies, however, could not be hers. Nor, he thought, could the new building that dominated the mainland's skyline. He had watched it rise. He had watched it rise, reliving, perhaps, his ancestors' dread beneath the rule of the Blood Barons.

Andrei was not in residence.

Nadianne had asked, three times, when he might be expected, and Hectore, usually so good with words, had had none to offer her, not even for her own comfort. He had learned, in his first marriage, that lying to one's wife was never as wise as it seemed. It was easy in the short term, but the returns could be ruinous.

But Andrei had told him two things: that the manse Araven and its grounds would be safe and inviolable until Andrei returned, and that Hectore was to keep every member of his family that he valued—which would, to a greater or lesser extent, be all of them—upon the grounds. He did not care what excuse Hectore made to achieve this and winced only once when Hectore turned a pleasant invitation into a patrician's demand.

Accordingly, Hectore went to greet his new guests. Was he safe? Yes. He was safe, and his family as well. But his neighbors were not and, beyond that, the people upon whom his fortune had been built. They sought entry into his domain because the streets without were chaos and battle; the din of raised swords, raised voices, and conflicting horns could be heard almost constantly anywhere else.

But not here. And here, the skies, although amethyst, were clear; the creatures in the sky did not cross the boundary his fences marked.

And so he let them in. And clearly, given the clothing and deportment of the newest arrivals, word of safety, of sanctuary, had traveled. His beleaguered House Guard were almost overwhelmed. Almost.

But they understood why Hectore had commanded them to open the gates; understood why the grounds that bordered the manor were slowly filling, and understood that, until this battle ceased, they would continue to fill.

The differences between the two Commanders who had waged successful war in the Dominion of Annagar were almost legend among the troops who followed them, and the depiction of these differences, a matter of oft heated retort and rejoinder.

Today, however, they were the two Commanders of the Kings' armies. The difference in style was lost to the greater press of humanity, trapped in a city that was being transformed, instant by instant, breath by breath. They were Kings' soldiers first. The rest of the divisions didn't matter.

To the north and the south, they met the host of the Arianni, the servants of the Sleeping princes whose waking seemed to usher in the End of Days. And they fought. Their training was experience: the experience of wars in the South and the introduction of the demons and the ancient earth that had literally sundered the battlefield and its combatants from each other.

That experience did not include homes—their own—and civilians of all ages and hierarchies; it did not include screeching, panicked chickens, dogs, horses, pigeons; nor did it include the elderly, confused by the din, who were—in at least two places—attempting to direct their families to build *barricades*. One had to admire their determination in the face of otherwise nameless panic; most of the people who the army encountered had one destination in mind: away. That the definition was nebulous did not dim the strength of their imperative.

The Kalakar, however, was a known entity—by standard, by insignia—and her presence did much to persuade the would-be builders that their best chance of survival now lay in a different endeavor. Where the armies were present, the barricades would be irrelevant. This was not, of course, the truth, but Ellora only needed to be believed for a few minutes, and that, she could easily manage.

But the streets were not empty, and some of the living that occupied them were not human. Their pursuit of panicked civilians ended at the human wall of the armed forces, whose first job was to pin them to ground in some fashion.

The mounted ground forces that had come at the Sleepers' call did not seem to acknowledge the winged predators as allies; they cut down those who did not move or instantly surrender the road to their progress. The winged creatures did not appear to accept the Arianni host as allies, either—but they obviously considered them far more of a danger than the humans. Even the armed and armored divisions of the Kings' armies did not appear to be a threat to them, although the armies made sure they regretted that.

But the aerial advantage was not small, and the forces were split across the terrain of a city. They could be certain that no enemies waited in ambush in the opened windows above the street, but that was all. They could not be certain that the earth would not break beneath their feet; could not be certain that fires would not erupt in the wake of panicked abandonment; could not be certain that the water would remain relatively calm in the harbor.

They could be certain of one thing: that the time they bought containing and engaging the enemy forces could be translated directly into lives: the lives of the civilians who were normally left far behind on the eve of war and battle. They were literally fighting a staying action, not for the safety of their homes, but for the safety of *some* of the people who lived within them.

The Kalakar used the emotions, the desperation, to create a single, focused goal, a driving force behind which she could rally her *centrii*. The Berrilya used the very strict adherence to protocol, hierarchy, military rules to keep his men in line. They achieved the same ends aware of all the differences between this battle and the last one in which the army had engaged as an army.

And above them, Andrei watched. It had been his intent to distract one of the hosts; he knew of The Kalakar, knew of The Berrilya, and could feel the power of the Kings from his position at the height of a building that had not yet been structurally damaged; it was too far from the dragon.

For reasons of his own, he had no desire to engage that beast, and would do so only if the men who now stood in its way faltered. But . . . they did not falter. And he recognized the weapons they bore—all the weapons. He could name them. He could have—had he so chosen—instructed the mortals in their use.

But that instruction did not forge the bonds that this battle would, if they survived it; such was the way of weapons like these.

He had expected a fourth host, a fourth army. He had seen Illaraphaniel join his brethren; had felt—at a distance—the radiance of their mutual joy, the exuberance of homecoming. In all his long life, he had yearned for such a joy, and only in this semblance of a servant had he found something approximating it. His envy was bitter, profound, expected, but it had been centuries—more— since that envy had turned to rage and destruction. He did not hate the Sleepers because they had what he had desperately lacked; did not hate them because they were born to it, where he had been born to division, distrust, disgust—both his own for himself, and others for him.

Yet Illaraphaniel had not called his herald, and his host had not come at his command. Perhaps neither now existed? He had not passed through the long, mortal age as his brothers had, sleeping at the command and judgment of both gods and the White Lady who had created them; he had lingered, diminished in almost all ways, bitter memories the only proof of his prior existence.

And perhaps that diminishment had robbed him, in the end, of the regalia of his station. It had robbed him of his shield—but the wrath of the White Lady had likewise scarred his brothers, for their shields proclaimed none of their names, none of the truth of who they had been before they had ridden out against Allasakar at the side of Moorelas.

The lack of name, however, did not diminish the three who had slept. The mortal buildings that stood between Andrei and the princes did not diminish them; he could see them as if stone and wood were the flimsiest of veils. Only the trees blocked his vision, but he could see, through narrowed eyes, that they would not do so for long; they were becoming as insubstantial to those eyes as the dead wood and stone in which mortals made their homes.

And would not make their homes for long.

He rose, taking to air, as the light of the four grew; the canopy of sky paled directly above them as the building on whose steps they still stood became a thing of beauty, of splendor: a Winter building, created at the dawn of their ancient power. What the earth had swallowed at the command of the departed gods, it had released; the princes, all, had transformed it into a challenge and a declaration. *This* was their palace, in this gray, drab land. This was the place where they had fallen, and this was the place that would mark their long return.

Nothing lived in their lands without their express permission. Nothing. And the mortals had not received that permission, had not asked it, did not even know *how* to ask it. Andrei heard their names. He heard it in the hooves of their summoned hosts. He heard it in the roar of the dragon. He heard it in the screeching cry of the harptalons. And he heard it in the distant air.

But the leaves of the *Ellariannatte* rustled; the leaves of the trees of silver and gold chiming in, and they spoke a different name with the full force of their remaining life.

He was not given to cursing, and would have abstained even had he been, but he felt the stirring of resentment for Jewel ATerafin. Had she not been so desperate to cling to her mortality, her name would be the *only* name that Andrei could hear, for these lands were some part of her domain and she had failed, in every way that counted, to make them her own. She had accepted only the forest—and only because it was separate from the rest of the city.

And the city was paying the price for that.

But as he angled his flight toward that palace, those spires, he shook his head. What she wanted was not so different, in the end, from what Andrei himself wanted: that this home that she loved, this place that she had chosen and built for herself, remain inviolate, remain itself as it had been.

And had she accepted the power and its truth without reservation, it would not have.

Hectore.

Finch could not force an answer from the tree of fire. Nor could she make sense of the answer the forest guard—stopped in haste—had to offer.

Where is Teller?

Haval was not present within the heart of the forest, and had he been, there was no guarantee she would receive an answer to the question—but even the lack of answer, or more specifically, how he avoided answering—would tell her much.

In the end, she left the House Council in charge of the growing number of people; left the forest itself in charge of making room for them if not the dwellings to which they were otherwise accustomed, and she left the tree of fire. She had noted that the fox was willing to approach it, but he did not touch it; nor did the other trees.

And the fox was not here. She wasn't even certain he *was* a tree; she was only certain that he was, like the other trees, wed to this land, and that this land was Jay's. He was not, however, the only elder. And she did manage to catch one of the forest guard and ask to be led to the great tree that Haval had once said was the true heart of these lands.

Finch had glanced at the tree of fire.

"It is the flag that she planted," Haval said, although she had not asked. "It is a statement that the forest understands. But it is the heart of her intent; it is not the heart of this place."

Because Haval was far stingier with information than even Jarven, she had not asked him more. Teasing meaning out of Jarven's words, lack of words, or misdirections had become second nature to Finch, but Haval still confounded her. Jarven was warm, and humor was one of his many tools—and the one which Finch saw most frequently when they were alone. Haval seemed entirely absent that humor and that warmth.

Were it not for Hannerle, Finch would have found it impossible to trust him, and the instincts that Jarven had honed made trust difficult. But Jarven had come into her life after Jay, and Jay trusted Haval. She wished she had badgered Haval. The forest guard did not speak of the elders—or to them—unless they were addressed. They spoke with Finch and answered her questions, but they answered them almost as if either they—or she—were confused children. Her questions made no sense to them. Their answers made little more sense to her.

But she knew immediately when she reached the ancient tree which she hoped to ask for more information. One glance made it clear that this tree was not like any of the others that grew in this wilderness. It was thick, wider across the trunk than even the tallest of the *Ellariannatte*. But its boughs were not all so high above the ground; indeed, it seemed short in comparison to the growth of the Kings' trees. Short and wide; wider still as she approached it, shorn at last of the forest spirits who had led her down the path to this clearing.

When the lowest of the branches had become the whole of her visual horizon, she stopped. She could feel age here, an echo of things so ancient they might have woken at the dawn of time. She felt slight, insignificant, the weight of a lifetime of learning and experience no more relevant than the passing glance of a stranger on a crowded street.

She wondered, briefly, what it would take to become relevant in her own right, for she understood that she was important to the forest because she was important to Jay. In and of herself, there was no difference between her and the refugees who now sheltered here, growing in number. She was regent of House Terafin, and in the human empire, that was significant; there was no higher power she could achieve or, rather, none that she was willing to achieve. It meant nothing here. It had never meant anything.

She understood now why Jarven had made the decisions he had: Jarven believed that this was to be the future, and Jarven was unwilling to become irrelevant in any game he was forced to play simply by existing. But she thought that the power of the wilderness was the power of the talent-born; one could not simply, by work and dint of intellect and learning, gain it. It must sting, to have a lifetime of achievements rendered all but useless.

"Does it sting you?" the forest asked. And she felt the question as an earthquake, although the ground beneath her feet did not move. "Do not kneel, Finch. It is not necessary."

"Is it offensive?" she found voice to ask.

The air rumbled. ". . . No. But you understand that we each seek gestures of respect we can both understand and replicate."

She swallowed. "Eldest—"

"If you had time, mortal child, I would teach you my name—but it is long and difficult for one such as yourself, and time has never been your gift, either to give or to receive. It is not in your nature. Come, approach without fear."

Finch approached. Fear was an essential part of the reason she had come; she could not simply shed it. This was the heart of the wilderness, a place to which, and of which, she was not born. She was aware of its otherness, aware of the fact that she did not belong to it.

"Child," the tree said—she could see no face, no mouth, no spirit such as the *Ellariannatte* possessed, "You must learn. You must learn to belong to it; it is what your world will—and must, now, if I understand the reason for your presence—become. But come, ask your question."

She didn't ask the tree how it knew what that question was, because for a moment she understood: she had asked it in the forest. She had asked it *of* the forest.

"What do you want from Jay?"

"That is not the question you came to ask."

"I know."

"Ask that question, then."

But Finch hesitated. The air trembled; she could not, for a moment, discern why: anger? Amusement?

"The latter. You have come to this forest, you have heard its voice, you have given commands in the Lord's stead—and only now do you think to ask the cost? This is why we think of you—of all of you—as young."

Finch nodded. "But, Eldest, that isn't an answer. It's a criticism I absolutely deserve, but it's not an answer."

"Do you now think that you deserve an answer?"

Finch shook her head.

"And if I told you that I will answer only one question, is that the question you would allow to stand?"

And this, Finch thought, was the burden that was placed, always, on those who ruled, those who lead. She understood in that moment that Jarven was, had always been, wrong. She was *not* a ruler. She was never going to become what she believed a ruler *should* be. "No."

"No, indeed. Ask your question, Finch ATerafin. Ask, but understand: I cannot change the answer. There is no guarantee that you will like the answer you receive."

She opened her mouth, wordless, as if the gentle warning was an answer in and of itself. She found her voice with difficulty, speaking above the fear, or through it. And when she spoke, her voice was not quiet; there was a surprisingly lack of hesitation in the words themselves.

"Where is Teller?"

Jester heard the question.

Arann heard it.

Haval heard it.

Daine heard it.

In the skies above the remade cathedral, Calliastra heard it. Only Calliastra smiled, because only Calliastra understood the why of it, the truth to which such hearing spoke. The answer, she did not hear, and in some fashion it was irrelevant. She bowed her head a moment as she unfurled her wings, revealing the darkness of their full majesty. Below her, trapped for the moment upon the ground nearest the grand stairs that served as inanimate herald, three men looked up.

Angel did not hear the question.

But Jewel did. Had she not been on Shadow's back, she would have frozen or stumbled; Shadow, however, did neither.

Where is Teller?

Her heart was not in her hands; it was, figuratively, in her throat, blocking all words, all momentary breath.

She had walked away from Carver. She had chosen to leave him. And she wondered, while she struggled to breathe, struggled to tighten her knees to retain her grip upon the back of the great, gray cat, if she had done that—*could* do that—because on some level she had known what must come: that choices she made in a future that had not yet unfolded would return Carver to her.

Where is Teller?

As if the question was asked of her, she once again reached into her chest—but she did it without thought and without fear. No—that was wrong. She was afraid. She was terrified. But she was not terrified of what her hands would touch, would contain, would cup; it was the lack of an answer that would doom her. Doom them all.

She recognized the voice, heard the shallows of Finch's anger inform the question, and beneath those shallows, the echo of her own fear, made visceral, made suddenly real. That fear spoke of things that were not fear, but history, and a history that was good, perhaps even necessary to the people that Jewel and Finch had become.

"Shadow—"

"We are *close*," the cat growled, voice low, more of a sensation than a sound. He did not tell her not to do what she was, even now, doing. Nor did Rath, seated behind her, the arms that braced her drawing her more closely to him, as if he could prevent what Shadow could not: her fall, at speed.

The cat was not a cat; the man who now offered her protection and stability was already dead. Nothing in Jewel's world had fully made sense since before she had come to Terafin, and she accepted that because she had no time to worry at it, to interrogate it. Even the pain she felt as she pulled out what was a physical representation of a metaphorical heart was insignificant now.

The one thing that *did* make sense, the one thing that had *always* made sense, was her family: the den. They had her back. They'd had her back when the world had started to twist and warp, becoming an echo of itself, seen through nightmares. Or dreams. They'd had it when she had promised Amarais the only thing Amarais had desired so that she might go to the Halls of Judgment in peace.

They were the foundation on which she stood. They were the foundation from which she could govern.

Where is Teller?

The question echoed; it had pierced the whole of her thought, cutting through all other fears as if it were a blade. She did not know of whom Finch asked the question. She could not hear an answer, if an answer was offered at all. But something had set Finch off—and it wasn't small or trivial; that wasn't the way Finch worked.

It no longer mattered.

She did not pause to wonder *how* she could hear Finch. She hadn't paused to wonder how she could tell the wild elements to knock it off, clean up after themselves, and go to their rooms, either. Not when she'd done it, and she'd only wondered later, when all the consequences began to spill into her lap, one after another.

She had, between her palms, the heart she had traveled to the Oracle to be able to control. It lay there, the clouds beneath a crystalline surface rolling slowly into themselves, white becoming gray, gray becoming darker before once again giving way to white. She had left her den, left her House, and walked the Oracle's path so that she could have *control* over the visions that had been boon and bane to her since her childhood.

Well, she had control now. She could ask the question. She could see every single answer that might possibly exist for it, and as she narrowed her eyes, she steeled herself for all of them.

"Where is Teller?"

"You don't need to *asssssssssk* out *loud*. If you do, *everyone* will know what you're *thinking*."

"She *doesn't* think," another voice said. It was Snow.

"Is your brother also here?"

"Why do you need *him*?"

Which was yes. She relaxed very slightly, although her arms were tense and shaking. The cats, in all their chaotic, self-indulgent, childish glory, were part of home to her. Maybe they always had been.

They almost killed you.

And that, Jewel thought, was as real as anything else in this wilderness; it was both true and distant, known and yet not viscerally felt. What was real, now, was the question to which she had demanded an answer.

And it was a question of now, a question of not-yet, and a question with roots in things that had already happened. She could not change anything but the not-yet. It was to the future that she therefore looked. But that future made no immediate sense to her, and because it didn't, the past and the present poured in while she watched.

She saw the forest guard, armed with House weapons; tall, lithe, yet somehow rooted. She saw the golden fox, saw Jester, saw Birgide—and saw, as well, the flight of leaves of fire, drifting through the city with intent, as if each were independently alive. She saw the deep amethyst of familiar skies; saw the winged harptalons and, worse, the dragon; she saw the rise of a dark cathedral, and also its miraculous transformation. She saw the dead: men, women, children; saw the dying who had failed to somehow reach the line of trees before they were felled. She saw the host of the Arianni riding across the surface of the bay; saw them riding through the streets, and felt her throat constrict. But she saw the banners of The Kalakar and The Berrilya, and thought of another battlefield, another war, and she felt *hope*.

She saw the *Ellariannatte*; heard the bardsong, saw the magi with their golden weapons. She did not see Teller.

She saw the Sleepers; saw the three become four, felt the onset of sudden dread take her lungs, stilling them. But the sky above the newly formed building darkened suddenly, not into the deeper hues of purple that might herald the fall of a night she had never once seen in her personal chambers, but a shade of midnight; great wings unfurled, trapping and shunting sunlight aside. Which sun, she did not know. She had not seen sun in the skies of her personal chambers, either; just the light that implied that sun existed, somewhere.

Feathers long and sharp as scythes extended from that midnight, and at the heart of the darkness was a woman she recognized. Calliastra in flight. Calliastra in the mortal lands which now also contained her father. Her eyes were a shade of violet, ringed with gold, and seemed far, far larger than her face; they called the attention, compelled it, until they were the only thing that Jewel could see; all else was momentarily forgotten.

But the eyes widened before narrowing into obviously angry slits, and although Calliastra in fury remained compelling, the visceral urge to look away and seek safety allowed Jewel to once again regain some modicum of control. She pulled back, pulled away, and froze.

Calliastra was far closer to the ground than she had been; she had pulled her wings in, but Jewel suspected they were not necessary to her flight. The light was harsh and bright in comparison, and it fell in spokes through the tears in a darkness that was more shadow than feather.

In that light, she truly saw the Sleepers.

Had she not been mounted on Shadow, she might have frozen completely; might have forgotten the crystal through which this vision had been granted. Not even when approaching Ariane upon her growing throne had she felt so overwhelmed, so awed. These men were the heart of Winter, devoid of even the promise of warmth that was early spring. But winter, seen from a remove, could be beautiful, and in the dead heat of summer, one might yearn for it. Yearn for the pristine fall of white, the clarity of sky, beneath which the world might be hidden or transformed. Only when the cold set in and the lack of warmth and shelter made itself felt did one remember that the winter was death.

But before then, it was an expanse of pure, pale, untouched white; it was a stillness that held everything it touched; it was too large to command, too large to understand, too large to question—and where there were questions, there were no answers. They were an act of nature, like earthquakes, like tidal waves, like storms that destroyed, unseeing, the ships that were unfortunate enough to be caught out at sea when they hit.

Jewel had seen gods in the Between. She had heard their voices, a chorus of perfectly overlapping sound. She had been aware of what she was not, but she had not felt the visceral desire to bow, to give her life over instantly to beings who were older, wiser, vastly more experienced. Nor had she felt ashamed of her mortality, of her singular vision, her tiny voice.

These men were everything the gods had not been, and she understood, in a rare flash of an intuition that was not subconscious, that this was because they now walked in the mortal world.

And she thought of the god they did not name, and of these men, and thought that maybe, just maybe, that god might encounter more than just feeble resistance if he faced the Sleepers. But another thought occurred to her as she looked at their cold, piercingly beautiful faces: He *had* faced the Sleepers, once.

At the end of that encounter, he had assumed the mantle Lord of the Hells, and the Sleepers had slept. And now, eyes blazing a kind of silver light that did not blind, they had woken, and they surveyed the ruins of a city that they did not—yet—rule.

Shadow fell across their upturned faces, and to her surprise, the three moved as something hit the stairs on which they had been standing, shattering what she assumed was stone. And, in a fashion, it was; it was living stone. She could, from Shadow's back, feel both the shattering and the way the resultant pieces pulled back together, remaking the stairs that were no longer directly beneath the Sleepers' feet.

And she could see that one of the Sleepers—only one—rose in the folds of wind, taking to skies that were filled with streaks of shadow lightning and beating, dark wings. She should not have recognized him because he was almost of a piece with the other three; his hair was fluid, long, each strand catching and holding light as if it were glass or diamond; his sword was blue fire, blue lightning, something that scarred simple, mortal vision.

But she did, regardless: he was Meralonne, he was Illaraphaniel, he was her House Mage. She opened her mouth to shout orders, but snapped her teeth shut again at the enormity of even the thought. Who was she to give orders to *him*?

Who was she to give orders to Calliastra, with whom he closed? She saw the clatter of his blade's edge—which could be heard more than truly seen—against long, dark claws, and heard, of all things, the wild exuberance of Calliastra's laughter.

"And will your brethren skulk like cowardly mortals upon the ground?" Her words could be heard across the whole of the city, Jewel was certain. They could be heard across worlds, after all.

She could not likewise hear Meralonne's reply. Perhaps he had not made one.

A second winged creature joined the fray. Both of the combatants turned to look at him, and both, to Jewel's eyes, wore similar expressions, their rounding eyes and their silence betraying surprise. Or shock.

She had seen this creature once before, in the dim recess of a room that had been carved, overnight, in the basements of *Avantari*. His form flickered as his wings extended. They were not Calliastra's wings; they were not all of one thing, and to Jewel's admittedly inexpert eye, there was no way they should have allowed the body to which they were attached any aerial buoyancy. At all.

But even so, changed utterly in every conceivable way, she knew that this creature was Andrei. He had come to face the Sleepers. He had come to Calliastra's aid. That would be tricky, because Calliastra was prickly in the same way Duster had been, and you didn't *have* her back unless she'd agreed to a plan that required it before she started to fight. Or unless she might actually go down.

"I will not let you harm them." It was Meralonne who spoke.

"And I will not let them destroy this city."

"It is not yours, Namann."

"It is as much mine as it is yours, Illaraphaniel. And they are coming, soon, your brethren, the lost princes. Can you not see what is happening beneath our feet?"

Meralonne did not look.

Calliastra, however, did. Her eyes lit from within, her lips rising at the corners in what appeared to be genuine—if dangerous—delight. Beneath their feet, the Sleepers had spread out on the lowest edge of their grand staircase. They bore their shields and their swords as if, finally, prepared for battle, and through the trees she could see three men struggle to join them.

No, not men: they had the platinum hair that was characteristic of the Arianni, and also the silver eyes. But their armor and their tabards—strangely fuzzy even in the searing vision granted by the crystal—were torn, dented, tattered, and the weapons they carried dim with . . . blood. They did not, however, carry shields; they carried instead poles to which flags had been attached. No, not flags; they carried standards. Ah. These, then, were the heralds.

Without warning, Andrei swooped down, and Calliastra did something other, but before either could reach the heralds, the trees seemed to . . . close. As if they had been a door and were now reasserting their existence as living wall. Those trees were *Ellariannatte*, all; they were her trees. And she could see them stretch out, and out again, into the city, the trunks like a map, a code, something that could not be missed.

The Sleepers, however, moved toward that living wall.

Jewel heard two things as they raised swords and brought them down, angled as if to slice: The cracking, sudden and unmistakable, of living timber, and the screams of Birgide Viranyi.

The swords did not stop with that first blow, but the edges of those blades seemed to extend far beyond their visible reach; more trees shattered, and at the far side of what she could only call a palace, the trees began to *wither*.

She understood, then, why the Sleepers had not yet taken to air. Understood as she watched that somehow the *Ellariannatte* were rooted in a world, in a wilderness, that did not yet belong to the Sleepers. And those roots were being poisoned, being destroyed; what remained would be theirs; they could make of it what they desired, because they could then command every part of the wilderness their voices could reach, and the wilderness *would* obey.

It was happening, now. All of the fighting she had seen, all of the dead, all of the civilians who had managed, against increasingly dire odds, to make their escape, became all but irrelevant. The trees died, and as they did, the heralds stepped forward, at last, to stand in the shadows cast by the lords they served.

Before, she had thought the Sleepers beautiful. She had thought them powerful. She understood, at the moment they stood before their heralds, that they had merely been waiting. The harptalons, the dragon—they weren't even an attack; they were a diversion, a way of *passing time*.

She saw the Sleepers share a glance, as if they were of one mind; the three on the ground then began, very slowly, to rise. The air now carried them, and they turned their attention to Calliastra. To Andrei. And to the whole of the city, where the trees trembled beneath them.

Those trees would wither. They would die. Or they would shatter.

There would be no escape left to the people who still fought, or fled, on the ground. The Sleepers would make the lands upon which the city itself stood theirs, and nothing would escape.

The question she had asked, the question she had torn out her heart *to* ask was gone, forgotten; it tumbled into names and places and history and events—the whole weave and weft of Jewel's life. Everything that had ever mattered to her. Everything she had both hated and loved. There was *no place* for any of it in the wilderness the Sleepers had once ruled and would now rule when the trees at last failed.

And they were failing, she thought. Failing, and falling, because the Sleepers were almost gods, and no actual gods were present. Just the daughter of the god they did not name, and against the three—or the four, for one herald was still absent—she would not stand for long. Not here, and not now, because Calliastra did not build home or rulership in the way the ancient Arianni did and could.

She didn't question how she knew this; had no *need* to question. Neither

Calliastra nor Andrei could do what must be done—must be done *now*—if Jewel and all the mortals in Averalaan were to ever have a home again.

She thought of Taverson's as she rode.

She thought of Terafin. Of the thirty-fifth, of the twenty-fifth. Of the hidden city, whose ancient fate hinted at the fate of Averalaan itself. She could not see the trees that lined the path Shadow now flew down, but she felt them regardless. They were *not* her trees; this was *not* her land. But they, too, were echoes of that home, and they spoke of it, sharpening resolve and fear simultaneously. They began to glow; she saw that. It was a faint, pale light, easily lost in the light of the magics that were, cupped in the palm of her hands, being summoned.

It was also a familiar light. Perhaps, had she not held her figurative heart in her hands, it would have taken longer for her to recognize it, but she did hold it, and the recognition was instant. It was the light of butterfly wings, first seen in a dream that had almost killed her, absent the forms of the butterflies themselves.

She knew that she was not sleeping now. Was not dreaming. The Wardens were no longer captors, no longer jailers. And yet, she thought, the entirety of the world she had lived in since she'd wakened the first time had been very like a dream, a conscious exertion of waking thought over a landscape that was no longer quite reality.

She could not, for a moment, remember how she'd woken that first time. Could remember only that when she had, the world—the physical world—in which she'd been sleeping had changed utterly and irrevocably. The Terafin's personal chambers had become different, other—they could be *reached* from the manse, but were no longer a part of it. The library still contained books, but it had no longer been the library in which The Terafin had done the most personal, the most private, of her work.

And the skies above those books had been the same amethyst that now overhung her city. She had not deliberately made those changes; that had never been her intent. She therefore understood the risk inherent in what she now did:

She took the dreaming in both of her hands, understood that in some fashion it was *part of* the wilderness, and chose—intentionally, willfully, deliberately—to *wake*. To wake into the world that she knew. To open eyes in her own home.

Her home was the city of Averalaan. It was the city beneath the amethyst skies. It was the city in which trees were, even now, being felled by those who were *no part of it*. The skies were littered with predators, and the streets as well, and she could see the host of the Arianni clashing with the Kings at the edge of the line of land that defined the bay. Those Kings were armed with weapons that, like the light of the metallic trees, suggested the living that they ruled; more than that she did not see. It wasn't necessary. What the Kings held, they would hold until the moment the city itself fell.

That moment was coming, was almost upon them all as the Sleepers commanded the air, and the air answered; she could see the earth rise up beneath them, like pillars to the gods of the sky, and she remembered the pillars in the ancient, deserted halls that had once housed the White Lady and . . . her sisters.

That land, the land upon which the palace stood, was theirs; had been theirs since the moment of their waking; it was not the land in which the *Ellarian-natte* grew. But the land into which they now walked was not theirs, not yet.

It was *hers*. It was hers by birth. It was home.

Shadow flew clear of the trees, the blue, metallic trees that had made a path she could follow, into the clear, deep skies of amethyst, and beneath her feet she could at last see what had been made of that city, and what would be made of it. She held the crystal in her hands, all but forgotten, and if she gazed into its depths, she was not aware of it. She didn't require the seer's heart to see what was happening, and what needed to happen in response.

She didn't need it to feel the intensity of rage, of belonging, of ownership; didn't need it to feel the visceral urge to protect.

"Easy, easy Jewel," Rath shouted in her ear. He had to shout; she might not have heard him, otherwise. "You don't use an army where a magisterian will do."

His words made a jumble of sense, which is to say, very little at all; the words had meaning individually but would not resolve into something she could use. But they wound their way through the chaos of anger and fear and made themselves heard and felt.

Shadow said, "There are only armies here." There was no whine in his voice. "What she does, she cannot do timidly, or she cannot do it *at all*."

And Rath said, "She must, Eldest. She must, or what she is left with will not be what she desires. What we protect is fragile, in the end; it is worthy of protection, but it breaks far more easily than what we must protect it from." His arms tightened around Jewel. "But she has prepared for this in ways that she does not fully understand.

"She can do what must be done."

*   *   *

Birgide collapsed forward, as if the invisible chains by which she had willingly been bound had been cut or smashed to pieces. Jester, who still held her hand, caught her awkwardly, teetering as he tried to balance her weight, and his own, with one free arm and one entangled one. She was surprisingly heavy when completely unconscious, which made retreat from this particular grove cumbersome in the extreme. He had expected to find himself within Jay's forest— which is absolutely where he intended to flee. He did not, however. Yards—perhaps less—from the shattered trunks of *Ellariannatte*, he could see the now unimpeded view of a building that he hated on sight. It had risen from the depths of the undercity, the hidden city, and had been transformed in its ascension; it was the very pinnacle of wealth, of untouchable power.

Jester had hated the patriciate, even when he had become one of their unofficial number. There was no compromise in this; he hadn't much liked himself, either before or after. Hadn't, in truth, trusted himself with anything at all but the den. He could not hate this building; could not hate the Sleepers. It was like hating mountains. Like hating life. Come to think of it, he'd managed that before.

He did not hate it now.

"Birgide," he said, lips pressed to her ear. "Birgide. We have to move."

She did not respond at all. He heard the crack of timber, near now; saw the tree closest to him tilt. He felt the ground beneath his feet—roots all— shudder. He did not, could not, feel fear. This tree might fall, but Birgide was beyond the pain of its loss for now, and he was certain—as he had only ever been in Jay's presence—that it would not fall on them.

"Birgide, she's back," he told the unconscious Warden.

As the tree line peeled away, the full majesty of the building that had replaced a third of the Common was revealed. And Jester looked at it, looked up at it, and felt . . . nothing. No awe. No surprise. It was . . . a building. In the sky he could see six figures; the dragon was no longer above them, its breath freezing—and shattering—the same trees that stood as living shields.

But they hung for a moment, suspended, as if they were a painting and not reality. He could feel the breeze become wind, but the wind did not howl. It seemed, to Jester, to sing.

He turned although it was awkward. Turned to see that he had been wrong; the sky was much wider than his field of view. Above the palace, there were six. But in the skies to the west, he could see new figures approaching. And he could hear, in case his vision was not good enough, the roaring of very annoyed cats.

He could almost hear their words. They had *missed* something. People were having fun *without them*. He had never liked the cats, but he had never hated them, and his lips moved in a grin that was instinctive.

Now he understood why Birgide had collapsed. If she was Warden, the forest was her responsibility—but it was not *hers*.

It was Jay's.

And Jay was home. He stopped struggling with Birgide's weight then. Stopped struggling at all. Jay was home and the city itself, while damaged, had not been destroyed, and he believed, viscerally, that it *would not* be destroyed.

Haval felt the wind change. The forest force that accompanied him—and that obeyed him—stiffened simultaneously, although admittedly in the case of the silver-and-gold guards, it was more subtle. They did not cry out, did not shout her name, did not abandon him as they waited for her orders, but he felt the change in them.

He was grateful for it. He called the fire—the small leaves that burned upon command, and only then; they had flocked to him as if they were birds, and he had made use of the flame against the wings of the aerial attackers, until they had no choice but to close on the ground.

He was not a romantic man; he did not see, in their enemies, grandeur or myth. Nor did he feel elevated or empowered by the weapons at hand. They were not the weapons of his distant youth; not the weapons of his prime. But weapons were weapons; one had to understand them before they could be put to use, and one could not hesitate to use them when necessary.

He was slightly sentimental, however. He knew his wife would be within her home, and he knew that she would leave it only when it was safe to do so. He had taken basic precautions, but Hannerle was not the den; he could only do so much. And he could not afford to visit yet; could not afford to see the results of those precautions. He was not Jewel, not Finch, not any of the den. He could wait.

Jewel commanded the air, and it came at her call, catching Avandar, Terrick, and Angel. Celleriant was with Kallandras, and Jewel knew that the bard could summon—had already summoned—wind of his own. She had given him permission to do just that, in any land that she ruled, and could not imagine a time when she might withdraw that permission.

The Winter King kept Shianne and Adam safe. Safe and close.

Night and Snow were sulking—loudly—as if this was simple play. And it might have been, had she not been able to clearly see the huge swathes of wreckage in the hundred holdings. The Isle had come under desultory attack, but that was not her concern, although the seat of her power was *on* the Isle.

She saw small fires gather in one or two locations; saw the dragon, slowed by that fire, that now stood and fought in a clearing that had not existed in the streets before its arrival; she saw the distant gleam of weapons that should have been invisible at this distance and *knew* that it was her Chosen who faced the creature. She trusted them. She had trusted them since the day she had arrived at the front gates with Arann. She had trusted them *even though* they served Amarais, not her; that they were sworn to that service; that they would die in it, even if that service required them to turn on the den.

And now they were *hers*. As much hers as the den. As much hers as Terafin. They fought with the weapons she had granted them. They fought with the ferocity, the dedication, of the Terafin Chosen. They had chosen to take on the dragon because of who they were, and Jewel believed in them utterly.

She heard the dragon roar; saw its breath.

Without thought, she spoke to the wind, and the wind replied in kind, and Terrick flew—uncomfortably—toward that dragon. But Angel, she kept by her side.

The trees in the city were new, yes. Some had been broken and some destroyed. She said to Shadow, "The spire!"

"It is *not yours*," Shadow hissed.

Jewel repeated the command.

On the ground, the Chosen saw her pass overhead. They saw the shadow of her cat, and they heard her voice as if it were thunder. Except for one; he heard it as if it were *home*. He did not look up; instead, he said, "The Terafin has returned to the city!" His voice was a shout. No, it was a roar, as loud in all ways as the dragon's.

Arrendas did look up as she passed; he did not salute. Could not offer her more respect than this: he struck out at the dragon's side, and his blade pierced the scales that had given them so much trouble.

The sky's deep amethyst faded into a color that might, at dawn or dusk, be almost natural. The shadows above their heads deepened and lengthened as the whole of the clearing made by destruction and gilded by death became ringed with *Ellariannatte*, their branches long and high.

Chapter Twenty

ANGEL REMAINED BY JAY'S side.

He did not move of his own accord; he had no control over the wind. He did not look down, he looked across.

She shouted a name, and the wind carried it across a battlefield made of sky and wings and distant swords.

"Why *me?*" came the disgruntled reply, as a winged predator the color of new snow flew toward Angel. "Why not *him?*"

The cats could preen, fly, and fight at the same time, and Night did. Angel, however, was deposited onto Snow's back.

"Where is *your* sword?" Snow demanded. "Why aren't *you* carrying it?"

Because he was carrying leaves. He did not say this; instead, he tucked the leaves in his cold hands away because the cat was probably right. "I didn't train in mounted combat," he said, in his own defense. It was not a defense that stood up to the cats, or perhaps, not one they noticed. Snow was perfectly willing to share his opinion of Angel as he headed toward the largest wings in the sky at present.

Calliastra's.

Every instinct Angel had ever developed told him that the sky was not the place to be. But he was on Snow's back, and Snow was already annoyed. Apparently, everyone else was having fun, and they'd started without him.

Angel did not draw blade as the cat accelerated. He hadn't lied. He understood that the sword was magical, but he did not trust himself to handle it well while moving in directions, and at speed, over which he had no control.

He could almost hear his father's harsh bark, used specifically for training the sons and daughters of the Free Towners.

He was grateful that he had not drawn the sword when the lightning struck.

It flew from the heights, but not the sky, as the Sleepers finally tore free of the ground. Their upward movements had been slow, stately. When they reached the heart of the sky, they unfolded. Their shields and swords seemed almost trivial—statements, not weapons or armor; it was hard to imagine, from this vantage, that armor or weapons would be of use.

Meralonne APhaniel was the only one of the four who did not bear a shield; he had lost it on a long-ago Henden, the year Angel had followed Jay to House Terafin. That had been a dark, dark Henden; not even the events which had produced the grim and ceremonial privation of the six dark days had come close.

Angel did not, could not, recognize, the fussy, arrogant mage in the man he nonetheless knew he must be: he was almost of a piece with the Sleepers, his sword a spread of angry light that seemed to dim the sky in comparison.

That light stretched now, like four elemental hands, spread flat against the ground below their feet, below their spire, and what it touched it burned; the flames were blue; blue and white. Buildings flared and crumbled, but the buildings were collateral; it was the trees that shuddered, consumed in what was barely a wave of the hand.

Nor did that light cover only the ground; it spread in waves, as if they were the heart of all light and all fire; it caught those who had not gained ground in midair. He heard the screams, cut short, of distant creatures; the wind carried the smell of charred flesh. Charred flesh and ocean air and the odd, cloying sweetness of something he did not know to name, blending and twisting together in a way that spoke not of home but of the wilderness at war.

From the cobbled ground below, corpses vanished, blown off the streets by the force of the Sleepers' power, and through those streets, as the crowns of the *Ellariannatte* caught fire, buildings rose; buildings and four great pillars. No architects were needed to plan them, to carve them, to raise them with their teams of men or horses; nor did they look unstable, for all their height.

But Angel had seen pillars that rested easily in the heights of silent, still air. These were not things of man, and not meant for them. He had wondered, once, who had lived in the buried, hidden city beneath the streets of this one. And he knew it didn't matter. What lived here—what would live here—would be these Sleepers, these four.

Snow roared; Angel drew the sword he had considered unwise. Sheets of pale blue air—like waves, like tidal forces—traveled toward the cats, toward Calliastra. Fire singed Snow's fur, and the roar became a snarl of fury; the white cat was trembling with it and had apparently lost the ability to form something as petty as words.

Angel didn't like his chances of remaining mounted, but he trusted Jay.

"Don't," the cat snapped. "This air is *not* her air; this wind is *not* hers. She *cannot* command what *they* command. If you fall, you will die. They are *awake* now. They are awake, and they are *angry*." The fire sputtered, as if it had consumed the white cat's rage, but Angel could see that, like waves, the blue light in the sky continued as if it would never end.

He glanced down, and down again, and he saw the city—his city by adoption, not by birth—give way, slowly but inexorably, to the city desired by these Sleeping princes, these scions of the court of the White Lady. There was no room for Angel in it. There was no room for *people* in it. And soon, there would be no people in its streets and, even if they somehow survived, no place for them to live. They were being hunted, even now, by the small armies of the Sleepers. He could not hear their voices; could not hear their shouts or screams.

Only the voices of the Sleepers were audible. He could hear their words; they were thunder. They could not be unheard. And he understood them, just as he understood the Winter Queen when she chose to speak to the merely mortal. Adam heard her speak Torra; Angel heard Weston. Terrick heard Rendish. The language itself didn't matter.

The only place in the city that he could not see buildings in the process of being devoured by sudden gaps in the earth was almost *on* the water, and there, from the relative safety of Snow's back, he could see the Kings. They were not as fine, not as glittering as the cold, cold beauty of the White Lady's princes, but they were just as solid. They faced the gathered host of the Wild Hunt, but Angel thought they would persevere for some time yet.

And it wouldn't matter in the end. If the Kings survived, and there was no one over whom they could rule, what purpose did they have? But even thinking it, he saw that where they stood, people did not fall, and perhaps that was purpose enough when lives—all lives—were in peril.

He raised his sword as the next wave was almost upon them; it was warm in his hand, and it seemed to vibrate enough that it should have been hard to hold steady. It was not. As the wave reached them, he told Snow to pivot, and Snow did—with complaint. But Angel's sword sliced cleanly through the blue, viscous air, and it passed harmlessly to the left and the right.

Snow acknowledged that Angel had *some* use, but only a really, tiny bit.

Angel accepted this because—and he would never acknowledge this where the cats had even the slightest chance of hearing it—a complaining cat was far more comfortable than a grim, silent predator. It made him feel that he was at home, and that home was still relevant.

Above the complaints, he told Snow where to fly, where to hover, when to change altitude, and the cat continued to both grumble and obey, but made very clear how boring Angel was. And how bored Snow was.

Angel was not, however, the only person present in the air who could hear Snow; Calliastra snarled in outrage. Snow responded in kind, while Angel deftly used the blade upon which he had sworn his oath to The Terafin as a very precise shield. He remained in the air nearest Shadow and Jay.

But Shianne and the Winter King did not.

Angel was not surprised to see them go, but he knew that Adam was with them. Jay trusted both the Winter King and Shianne. She was certain they would survive. But Adam, no. He half expected the wind to pluck Adam off the Winter King's back and drop him on Night—and it seemed to him, in the glance he could spare, that the wind tried.

But he remembered that the Winter King did not lose a rider that he had accepted and understood the full force of those words now. Shianne, adorned with golden blade, drove the Winter King through his paces as she headed directly for the Sleepers, those lost brethren that had not been asleep when she had last walked the world, before time and circumstance had forever altered her very nature.

She was not of them now. She would age and she would die, just as Angel and all of his kin. But some essential part of who she had been was still who she was. The *Kialli* recognized her. Meralonne recognized her. The Sleepers would recognize her as well; she was certain of that.

Angel wasn't sure this was wise. She was angry, if that word was not too small to contain the whole of her rage and her bitter sense of betrayal.

Lord Celleriant was not. If Celleriant felt a similar anger at the demons, he had never expressed it, and in combat against them he had been almost savagely joyful, not furious. But against the Sleepers? No. There was something akin to sorrow, to grief, but not rage.

Then again, Celleriant served Jay. He served her truly, not as the Winter King did, but by his own oath, his own blood, something that none of the Arianni would do. Serve a god? Maybe. Serve a mortal? Never.

Angel could not watch her progress while he darted between these odd, aerial attacks, but he knew the moment the Sleepers became aware of Shianne, because those attacks were suspended. The changes upon the ground, however, were not.

As one man, three of the four turned to her; Meralonne did not, but he was already aware of her existence, of her presence, at Jay's side.

The breath of the world seemed held as they stared at her on the Winter King's back, Adam in front of her. Her sword was reflected for a moment in the width of their eyes; they seemed transfixed, silent, unable to find words.

Shianne, however, was not.

And she spoke three names.

Narianatalle.

Fanniallarant.

Taressarian.

Angel could hear the syllables; he could hear Shianne as clearly as if she, too, were a prince of the ancient court. But her voice had always held power, and never more than when she met her distant and sundered kin. These men were of the White Lady; they had not abandoned her for a different god, a different lord. But they had not obeyed her orders, either; it was a lesser betrayal than that of the *Kialli*, which did not change its essential nature. But it was a betrayal that had occurred because of their love of, their regard for, their loyalty *to,* the White Lady.

The White Lady acknowledged their existence, in a fashion. But she had surrendered them to the gods for their failure, and the gods had decreed that they sleep. The gods, however, were no longer here, no longer anywhere in this world, and that sleep, once broken, could never be assured again.

None of this mattered to Shianne. She had heard the story, had listened, had, in a fashion, grieved—but it was not at their fall; it was at their folly. If she failed entirely to understand the *why* of the *Kialli*, she could sympathize with the why of the Sleepers' refusal, in the end, to obey their Lord's command.

Had she not done the same?

But she, too, felt the visceral, eternal hatred that the White Lady now felt for the god they did not name; it was both a burning heat and a rage that was also bitter and chill. They had been tasked with his destruction, and in the name of love, of loyalty, they had *failed*.

All of her anger, all of her sorrow, were contained in the enormity of three names, and they were names that Angel had never heard spoken.

"No, *stupid* boy—*no one has*. No one can *speak* those names, not even the *other* one."

"She did."

Snow did not reply. He veered toward Night, clipped his side, and veered away, as if the whole of the destruction and transformation that continued beneath their feet was irrelevant, a game. But if it was, it was a deadly game; Snow did not approach the Sleepers. Calliastra engaged only one: Meralonne. And the other winged figure seemed, for a moment, to bow in Shianne's direction, and then it was gone.

They did not move toward her, but waited, their silence watchful, measured, and just as turbulent as the silence that had fallen after the names had left her lips. They saw the Winter King, saw the mortal boy, and saw the color of her armaments; they understood what that color must mean, but simultaneously failed to understand.

The Winter King slowed as he reached them; Shianne did not dismount. Nor did she divest herself of her sword—no more did they. The silence was terrible, and it was Shianne who broke it first.

She was mortal, but the bard-born were mortal as well, and she had some measure of their power. Her voice was heard; even the pillars that rose out of the earth seemed to freeze, to hesitate, at the sound of her voice.

But Angel did not understand her words; they were not meant for him. Nor were they meant for Jay or those who fought or crawled upon the surface of the changed and changing city.

Kallandras came to float, freely, by Angel's side. Celleriant, however, remained with his Lord, watching. The brief glimpses of his expression afforded by Snow's careening flight implied Winter; a lack of motion, a lack of color. And Angel thought: they are all, in some fashion, forsworn. And they would change that in a heartbeat if they now could.

Angel urged Snow toward Jay, lifting the hand that did not carry the sword. He gestured in broad den-sign, and at a distance, he could see Jay blink, frown, struggle. She still held the seer's crystal cupped—or clutched—in her palms, and the light it emanated changed the cast of her skin, lightening the untouched strands of flyaway hair, emphasizing her expression.

He signed anyway.

She saw it.

She saw it but could not acknowledge it; she did not dare lift either of her hands. The seer's crystal, the seer's heart, was not a fragile thing—it could not be and survive—but it was not invulnerable; it was a metaphor made real. It was the heart of her power, and she could not use that power if she could not hold it thus; the power, instead, used her.

Information streamed in, images blinking in and out in rapid succession.

She could see the sky and what it contained; could see the streets, made unfamiliar by the growth of trees and the newly rising buildings; could see the bodies—not all of them human—that lined the street, giving way as the shape of the streets did to the things that were growing from the earth beneath them.

And she understood that the ancient earth was awake now, and that it built as the Sleepers commanded. So, too, had true stone remade parts of *Avantari*, at her angry and hasty command. But the streets of this city were not the wooded, shadowed darkness of her forest, and in these lands—

No.

Avantari was not, had never been, Terafin. But the earth as far as the Kings' home had heard her and obeyed. She had been afraid, on some level, ever since; the Kings had justifiably been alarmed by what she had—without intent—achieved. She had understood, when she had finally seen what the stone from the Deepings had wrought, *why* the Kings were alarmed. Why Duvari's hatred of her had increased so sharply.

Avantari was not Terafin.

But *Avantari* and its environs had been shaped by her word, her voice, her commands, regardless.

So, too, the apartment in the twenty-fifth holding—and she had not even *been* in the city at the time of that shaping. And she had—

No.

But she held her heart in her hands, and No was not permissible, not acceptable; it was even harmful. She could almost *feel* the city slip away from her, as if it were a single, living entity whose attention had been captured—and held—by invaders with more power, more gravitas, than she had ever, and would ever, display. She could see them clearly and understood that they were kin to gods in a way that she and her kin, near and far, could never be, and never hope to be. Not even the Warlord, her domicis, who was immortal.

She had caused an entire family to *disappear* because she had dreamed. Because she had desired a place of safety—and safety was the den before everything in the undercity had gone bad. Safety was Lefty, Fisher, Lander, Duster—all alive, all bickering. She remembered the dream.

And she *knew* that the people who had lived in that apartment on the day, in the minute, of that dream's start were gone. She did not know if they were dead; knew only that they no longer existed in the hundred holdings. That apartment, those rooms, were now empty, and would remain so. And why?

She understood the need for shelter, understood the imperatives of poverty, understood the plight of orphans, with no family, no matter how poor, to champion them. And all that understanding *had not mattered*. What she wanted—from the distant safety of the Oracle's abode—she had created, somehow, and that creation had eclipsed the real. It had eclipsed the truth.

The changes she had wrought in *Avantari* were as nothing in comparison, although the anger of the Kings was the greater threat. No one had died. No one had simply disappeared. There was nothing in *Avantari* that Jewel wanted—not on the first day she had set foot on its steps, not on the day the two large rooms had been created, and not today. Everything of value was now in the streets below her.

But no, that was not true. Had never been true; there were servants and their complicated hierarchies who had, no doubt, remained in the palace proper, and they *had* value. But they did not have the responsibilities that the god-born Twin Kings had. Their loved ones would notice their absence, their loss—but the entire Empire would feel the loss of the Kings.

It was not up to Jewel—it must never be up to Jewel—to define worth.

All of these people—both the dead, in their growing number beneath her, and the living, had value. Even the people she hated. Even the people she had, indirectly but deliberately, killed. She could not, at this remove, decide who deserved to live, and who to die. That wasn't her responsibility. It was the responsibility of the two men who now fought—successfully—beneath her feet, beneath Shadow's wings.

She felt something that might be love and might be awe and might be envy as she extended the brief glimpse of those two men almost unconsciously. In the crystal, in her heart, she could see them as clearly as she would have if she were standing beside them. She could see the lines of their faces, worn by time and wind and sun and the heavy toll of the responsibility Jewel was grateful was not hers.

In their hands they carried the weapons—and they were weapons, no matter their shape—crafted long ago by Fabril, and those weapons provided the foundation for the resistance of the forces that fought alongside them: *Astari*, magi, Kings' Swords.

She could see Hectore, walking and standing among people from disparate social strata; could see Andrei—and recognize him in spite of his constantly shifting shape—swooping down across the malformed streets, claws colliding with the claws of the surviving predators who still sought to gain dominance among the terrified and the helpless; she could see Arann, his size, his strength, turned toward the task she had set him. Had set all of her den.

And she could hear the earth's slow voice, a frenzy of whisper, of words made manifestly real, as buildings continued to take shape. She had forbidden the earth any action that she had not countenanced, or commanded, herself.

And she had not countenanced *this*. But these buildings, in shape, in architecture so similar to the undercity's ruins, did not shudder or shiver or *move* as the earth moved; the buildings constructed by the citizens of Averalaan did. People did not live in what the Sleepers commanded be built—not Jewel's people, at any time of her life—but they *could*.

And they would have roofs that did not sag or disintegrate; walls that did not tilt, did not lean, were not troubled by something as inconsequential as weather. Her crystal shifted images, rolling past the buildings that were, even now, continuing their slow rise.

She saw Jester, saw him struggle with Birgide's weight, and drew breath, a hiss of sound that mingled fear and anger; she did not know what had happened to Birgide. And the crystal answered, as if she had asked, had demanded, an answer to that question; images flickered by. Voices. Words. The sense of time passing in each. She saw blood, Birgide's blood, and heard her voice, although the Warden chosen by her forest did not speak them aloud.

She lifted her voice for the first time since she had arrived above her city.

"*Birgide.*"

Birgide Viranyi stirred.

Jester knew why. He had heard Jay's voice, the single name heavy with multiple meanings. He would bet that anyone who still lived had. He lifted a hand in den-sign, although no one would theoretically see it. He might have lifted his voice, but he had no desire to shout into Birgide's ear.

She's fine. This was more hope than truth.

"Birgide!"

He gestured again. He could not use den-sign to encapsulate the whole of his thought: that the trees were, even now, falling at the command of the Sleepers, and that he wanted Birgide to be unconscious for all of it; she had suffered enough, and her suffering wouldn't change reality. She felt the loss of those trees as personally, as profoundly, as Jester had felt the loss of his den.

But if Jay could see Birgide, she couldn't see Jester's den-sign. And perhaps she could see neither. Birgide was a part of the forest in a way the den wasn't.

He was there, bracing Birgide, as she lifted her head. He felt the tremor of musculature, the shifting of stance—into *a* stance—as she struggled to gain her feet. The Terafin was home, and Birgide had her duties. Jester, who had avoided duty as if it were just another word for enslavement, felt shame. It was brief; he couldn't afford it, either. But he wondered what she had been like when she served Duvari.

"I still serve Duvari," Birgide whispered.

He looked down at their hands, still joined.

"Nothing Duvari has commanded of me has been like this," the Warden continued, briefly closing her eyes. "But . . . nothing Duvari has commanded of me has been so important to me personally, either. I accept it, Jester. I accepted it on the first day, by the tree of fire." Her smile was crooked, but genuine; her eyes were no longer a burning, bloodred. "I wanted this," she whispered. "I still want it. I will always want it. I didn't realize," she added, "that you were part of the bargain. I might have been more cautious, if I had."

He surprised himself. He laughed. It hurt. He tried to extricate his hand, which was numb from lack of circulation, but Birgide shook her head. Inhaling, she gained inches of height, relieving Jester of her weight. She raised her chin, raised her head, but did not speak.

Words made no difference. But she was smiling grimly.

The glitter of trees of diamond could be seen among these half-formed buildings. Jewel then turned, briefly, to Night. She didn't speak, but Night hissed in displeasure anyway. He flew off.

"Celleriant."

"Lord."

"Be prepared."

"They will not harm her."

"They will not harm her," she said softly, "if you are prepared." She lifted her voice once again. "Calliastra!"

And the goddess—for she was that, here, said, *I cannot save them both.* It was a cool, definitive statement.

Jewel, however, shook her head. She did not argue.

"Haval." No. "Councillor."

Haval did not smile. His expression did not change at all; it gave nothing away. He was certain that Jewel could now see him, but did not look for her. He could hear her voice, and that was enough. He was not a man given to fear, not a man given to acting on that fear; he absorbed it instead, examined it, dissected it. Even here, in the lee of the Common, which might never be the Common again.

Not thirty yards away was what remained of *Elemental Fashion*. He had given the scant years remaining of his youth to it; had given the years laughingly referred to as his prime. And he had given the whole of the rest of his life to Hannerle. Yet at the moment, he felt no fear for her. No fear for the life that had absorbed him—with her permission—since Jewel had become Terafin.

He did not know, now, what life held in store for them. Did not know what "normal," if such a thing existed, would become. He was aware of Jewel in a way that he had never been aware of her before. He nodded as if it answered a question, and it did, but not perhaps a question he had asked.

The streets here had changed in both shape and texture, and where the trees had been toppled, there were gaps that spoke of earthquake. These, he circumnavigated. The forest guards did not; gravity did not compel them to fall. Haval, however, was mortal, human. And he listened as he moved, scanning the streets and the skies above them.

He was surprised when the last of the forest guards joined him: they were crystalline. Nothing that hit them seemed to be worthy of notice, and they, as the spirits of more natural trees—if such a thing could be said of the *Ellarian-natte* which had sprouted full-grown in the streets—did not seem compelled to fall when they stepped across gaps in the earth. But falling stone, falling timber, did not slow them, and as Haval watched, he realized they were now going where he had not: to what remained of the store he had built with his wife.

He could see bolts of fabric unraveling in the streets; the dirt and the debris would damage them beyond repair, and they had been costly. He could see shards of glass and the twisted metal that had once held them in their wooden frames; those frames, listing, were now empty. The door was gone, and one wall had been reduced in size, tumbled in by the fall of a tree.

The diamond soldiers, in shape and form similar to those of silver and gold, proceeded directly through the absent door. They did not knock down walls that Haval was certain had very little structural integrity remaining. He turned to the spirit guard and briefly sent them to the north, where his eye had caught a flicker of movement.

He was almost *Astari*, he thought. He understood the fear that hovered beneath the surface of words though he shelved it because it was too costly. The responsibility, the duty, was the greater weight, the larger necessity. He was not a man who lied to himself. He was not a man who lied to his wife, except by omission, and all other lies were simple tools, offered to create a desired effect, a useful response.

But he watched the soldiers enter the building; caught glimpses of them as they passed the gaps in windows, the gaps in what were once solid walls. He had not approached this building because he could not afford—the city could not afford—the slow paralysis that now made itself felt.

The forest guard moved at his quiet command; they did not pause as he paused, did not cease to breathe, because they did not require breath in this form; they did not lay down arms. In ones and twos he had lost these guards, sometimes without warning, but they had come from the trees that were the heart of Jewel's domain, not the trees that had grown at the command of her Warden. Some of the spirits had been destroyed by the aerial attackers, but they returned because those attackers could not—yet—reach their roots.

They had retrieved the fallen, the injured, and those who had managed to survive their hiding places, and they had returned to Finch in that fashion.

The diamond soldiers, however, would not. They were not as lithe, as limber, as the spirits of the *Ellariannatte*, which was only to be expected. Nor would they dissipate in the same fashion.

"Councillor?"

Haval did not respond. Hands loosely clasped behind his back, he waited. They did return; he was aware of the passage of time yet did not mark it precisely. Above and around him, lightning flashed sporadically from the clear skies above. He did not hold his breath. Did not otherwise acknowledge what he now, in some small compartment of his mind, feared. There was no fear he had not faced, and would not, in the end face.

The soldiers returned from the ruins of his store, carrying Hannerle. She was either unconscious or dead. They did not, however, deliver her to Haval; they delivered her, instead, to the more mobile *Ellariannatte*, and without so much as a pause to receive his orders, they carried her away, on the pathways into the forest that were, even now, being eradicated by the Sleepers.

The diamond soldiers then turned to Haval. They were not so numerous as the rest of his soldiers; there were four.

In silence, they waited his orders.

"The pillars," he said. "Destroy them."

"Daine."

Daine rose quickly, turning in the direction of the voice. Because Verena was almost preternaturally aware of her surroundings, he failed to knock her over. Even the water she carried in a too-full bucket failed to slosh over its rim. Although he had made clear to her that the forest itself was safe, she did not believe him. And wouldn't, either; he knew that much.

He knew more. But he had been taught, time and again, that some division between healer and healed must be maintained for the sanity of both.

One of the forest guards looked across the very impromptu healerie that Daine had established. "Daine?"

"Tell Healer Levec that the healerie is under his supervision." The younger healer almost laughed at the expression that flitted, like a passing breeze, over the spirit's face. It reminded Daine, perversely, of his own years as one of Levec's students. No one wanted to be the bearer of bad news when it came to Levec. To be fair, no one wanted to be the bearer of *any* news, because Levec's temper could make any news bad.

He dried his hands as Verena set the pail down.

"Where are we going?" she asked him.

"You are staying here."

She snorted.

"*Daine.*"

He surrendered. He didn't tell the theoretical nurse trainee to follow him; short of incarcerating her—and the forest guard had offered—she would. "Just—no weapons."

"Why not? We're leaving the healerie."

"If we need your weapons, we're already dead."

Verena bridled. She was not like Birgide, not like Duvari; she was not like any of the known *Astari* Daine had observed. But she was twelve. Maybe equanimity would come with time. Jay didn't give him instructions. He wasn't certain she was even aware of what he was doing; he understood instinctively what she wanted of him. He probably always would. He had healed The Terafin. He had called her back from the brink of death.

Just as Alowan had saved the previous Terafin.

And that had saved Daine. He could acknowledge that now. Having The Terafin, having Jay, as part of his thoughts had offered him a brief glimpse of a world that was not ugly, political, self-serving, and he had clung to it until he could widen that glimpse.

The leaves overhead rustled; he heard the wind whip through them. He wasn't surprised to see leaves fall, torn from their branches as if by a gale. Verena looked up without pause, scanning the forest for the minute changes of shadow that implied possible assailants.

Daine did not. He was certain that, for the moment, the forest was safe. But the howl of the wind was unsettling, regardless. It implied storm, and if the entirety of the forest was now Averalaan's shelter, it had no walls, no roof. Some tenting existed, but not nearly enough to cover the growing number of people who had taken shelter here.

And one more was now arriving.

Unlike the others, she came alone, carried by one of the forest guardians as if she weighed no more than a young child. He looked up, met the eyes of that spirit, and then looked down, understanding that she would be carried until the exact moment Daine himself told the tree to set her down.

He understood why The Terafin had called him; understood what The Terafin wanted of him now. And he thought it was too late. But he had not waited in the mess of a massive—and growing—healerie; Jay had, indirectly, told him that there would be no time. No time.

He said, as he lifted his hands, "I'm sorry, Verena."

She tensed; he knew this, although he didn't look back. But she didn't ask him what he was going to do. She knew. She hesitated. Daine was standing too close to the forest's edge. And the woman whose face he now framed with both open palms, was dead.

No, not dead. Not more dead than Verena herself had been on the day Daine had found her. It would weaken Daine immensely, to do this thing. The injured were arriving by the dozens. The numbers had slowed, yes—but not by enough. He thought of Levec and grimaced.

She could not tell Daine not to do this, although she did try. Her mouth opened on the words, but no words escaped. In the end, she accepted what she could not change. To the tree that stood, woman in his arms, she said, "You'd better kneel, if you can. He's going to fall over."

Eldest.

The fox looked up. "Lord."

Defend my forest.

He glanced up, to the Sleepers. "Your forest is not yet under attack, Lord. And the Sleepers—"

I'm here. *Defend my forest. Defend my people.*

There was no doubt in the command, no doubt in the words, no hesitation at all. There was a force of fury, of certainty, that caused the golden fox to smile, as if at some remembered event in a distant past.

"Lord." He glanced, once more, at the princes of the first age of the world, and then shook himself, frowning.

The trees grew. They had achieved their full height on the day Jewel ATerafin had first entered the wilderness, or so Birgide Viranyi had believed. But now they grew as Verena watched. The wind above their crowns was a torrent, a scream of rage and fury, but no more leaves fell at the sound of its voice.

A small creature that might have been a fox if not for its color peered out from between the trees at the young woman; it appeared to raise a brow at the daggers she carried in either hand. She did not consider it a threat, but knew, conversely, that it could be, if it were of a mind.

It wandered over to where Daine now knelt against the forest floor. "I see," it said. "You will watch over them?"

It took Verena a moment to realize he was not speaking to the tree, but to her.

"I'll watch over him," she replied. "Nothing will get past me."

"Ah." He met her eyes, tilted his head, and huffed. "I see you are already bound. Mortals are surprising. He cannot be moved yet, but when he can, you must direct him to the tree of fire."

"And his patient?"

"Patient? Ah, you mean the woman? She must, of course, accompany you. It is the Lord's desire."

Jewel grimaced. It was an expression she had worked—hard—to remove from her repertoire of expressions as it was considered inappropriate for The Terafin. No one who would now be offended could see it. Her hands tightened, but only briefly, as the crystal's vision moved, the Kings overlapping a familiar face.

"Jarven."

Jarven looked up. "Terafin." He did not raise his voice. If she was aware of his presence, he did not feel the added volume he could muster would be relevant. He was, unexpectedly, surprised. He could see Jewel ATerafin clearly. The buildings that stood in the way—admittedly many of them new and not yet fully formed—did not impede his vision of her at all.

He could see the winged cat beneath her. Could see the shadows cast by the cat's wings as they lay against the ground; they were larger—by far—than the physical form of the cat suggested. He was ATerafin, his home was the manse; there was no way he could be unaware of the existence of The Terafin's three cats. But he had not spent time in their presence since he had concluded his various negotiations with the forest elder.

Did she know?

No, he thought. Not consciously. No more had her den, not even Finch, the one person in it he felt should have. When they spoke of the cats at all, it was with tolerant affection or amused disgust.

He could see the tendrils of The Terafin's hair whip free of whatever normally confined them; could see unruly curls become slightly straighter in the colder, drier air. He could see her expression, and in it, the heat of determination, the movement of thought. She was not what Jarven was. Had never been what Jarven hoped to become.

He thought she might be more, and that did not even annoy him. It was almost with pity that he spoke, when he chose to speak again. "What would you have of me, Terafin?"

"Go to Sigurne. No matter what happens, protect Sigurne."

Again, she had surprised him.

"And not the Kings?" he asked, as he began to move. He did not expect an answer. Nor was he now far from where the magi who served the Twin Kings directly had chosen to make their stand. What he had not expected—and this was to be a day of small surprises—was Sigurne's position. Although he could see the clear signature of her power in the barriers erected at the Kings' backs, she was not behind them.

"You might," he said, through slightly clenched teeth, "set me a task I am not certain to fail." He looked up, and up again. Sigurne Mellifas, the guildmaster who had resolutely refused a patrician style of name, was climbing the air. She did not fly, and her progress was slow; she appeared to be walking up the steps of her tower, absent actual stairs or walls or visible destination.

Jarven could not see what she climbed, could not see how. He understood the base functionality of the air when it was summoned, but the air itself chose both the path and the locomotion; she was mortal. She could not have roused the wind.

But no, he thought—those were rules, and rules were meant to be understood and absorbed completely only because there was no other way to figure out how to break them.

Ah, no, that was inexact. One could break rules one did not understand; fools tried it frequently, which occasioned the necessity of the magisterial guard. But fools seldom profited from such breakage. Jarven had learned that lesson early. He had been a boy discontent with his lot in life, and determined to improve it, but he had not suffered from the need to appear to be in control. He was content to let others do so. He learned from their mistakes. He then made mistakes of his own, but they were more subtle if no less ambitious; he stumbled but did not fall.

He would not fall now.

He could not, however, circumnavigate the barrier erected by the magi; although he had passed unseen through the carnage of the rest of the city streets, dodging even the notice of the dragon, he would not be able to do so here. He knew the protections placed down by the magi but was certain that decades had shifted that understanding as the enterprising among the mage-born fortified and tweaked the base spells.

No. Best to avoid them. Avoid, however, did not mean a wider than necessary circumnavigation. It might, were the guildmaster's progress not so slow.

But he knew what—or who—her goal was. In this fight, she had been stripped of the power behind her figurative throne. She had accepted the loss on the face of things, which had not surprised him.

This, however, did. She was old now. Too old for the office she had held for decades. The Guildmaster of the Order of Knowledge could not afford to be sentimental. Could not afford to be foolish.

He did not hesitate.

They did not speak Shianne's name.

Jewel watched, listened; she could hear even the tremor of their breathing at this distance, as if it were the breath of the world. She saw them through the filter of the crystal now; she saw *everything* through that filter. Distance—the distance between the Sleepers and her actual eyes—no longer mattered. Beneath her feet, tottering unevenly, one of the four pillars began to vibrate. It did not, however, fall; it shivered, it wobbled, and it settled back into the earth.

The earth had built it; the earth had not, clearly, finished with it.

It began to teeter again as the old earth ran up against the diamond trees.

Jewel told the earth to stop.

The earth, however, did not.

And in the distance, one of the Sleepers raised his head. Hair spilled down his back, down his shoulders, as if it were liquid, and as Jewel looked into the crystal she held in her hands, he met her gaze. She should have felt a tiny moment of satisfaction when his eyes rounded. She didn't.

Beneath her feet, beneath the feet of anyone who had managed, thus far, to survive, the earth reared up, and up again, as if it were an enormous serpent. It was not the only serpent. The wind rose as well. Shadow snarled in annoyance.

"Do *something*!" he told his rider, as the air attempted to grab them both and dash them against the nearest waiting surface.

Shianne did not speak the names again, but they lingered, syllables carried by a wind that had grown increasingly agitated everywhere but around the princes themselves. Had Shianne not been mounted upon the Winter King, she might have fallen. She allowed the great stag to navigate, although her sword was a brilliant gold, a Summer gold. Here, the wind did not hear her voice as it heard the voice of the three who had once been brethren. She could cut it, could drive it back; she had that power. But of the elements, the wind was the quickest to anger.

The power of her brothers had not diminished with the passage of time and the changing of the world. They were, in her eyes, all that they had once been, and she ached at the memories because she knew she was not. She would never again be what she had once been; she would never ride out at the White Lady's side, into a world that was a constant sea of changes, of surprises, half-willing to transform itself to meet the desire and command of the firstborn.

That world was waking, but it would never again hear her voice.

Not as her brothers now heard it. Their shields were unadorned, a sheen of blue with no distinguishing marks, nothing to remind those who could see them of the glory of their achievements. To mortals, they were legends, stories. Ah, no. To mortals, now, they were gods.

They had not changed.

But the White Lady had. The world had shifted beneath their figurative feet. And they had known that it would.

So, too, Shianne. Her blade the wrong color, her voice the wrong texture, her life riven—forever—from the White Lady for whom she had sacrificed everything, she could do what had been forbidden every other living member of that Hidden Court. She could speak their names. Their lost names.

Not even the gods could now do that.

They had turned to her, their eyes glowing bright, the shock of those names—those felt and familiar and *lost* names—a compulsion. And they recognized her, even in her fallen state. They knew who she had once been. They could not know what she had done, could not know why she had traveled to the city that had, unbeknownst to her, been their jail and their cage, but she came bearing sword, shield; she came upon the back of a Winter King. That a mortal youth sat before her signified little; he was irrelevant.

As one man, the three spoke a single word.

Shandalliaran.

She reverberated with the sound; it was a force almost as strong as the wind's gale in the heights. But it was only a sound, now. It evoked memory, and memory in this place was pain, but she had expected pain. There was a hollowness where once there might have been communion, an echo in all ways of returning at last to the White Lady's side.

She said, her voice as solid as the firmament far below, "You walk the skies of the Lord of these lands, and the Lord has traveled here at the behest of the White Lady. Stand down, if you will not face her wrath."

* * *

Jewel heard each spoken syllable as if it were a spell; the air shook with it, and the stone that now rose from the depths of the earth seemed to shudder. Had the syllables been words, they might have been an anguished cry, a plea, an accusation; they might have listed innumerable crimes as a testament to things broken, things betrayed, things destroyed.

She could almost see them, they were so solid, so tangible. Had her hands not been occupied, she might have reached out to grasp them, to hold them, to draw them into herself—or to push them away. She could not, did not try, but as each syllable faded, she thought of the spells of the magi, for their spoken words were similar in some fashion. She could not, however, repeat either Shianne's name or those spells; being witness to either gave her none of the power and none of the control the original words had.

She was seer-born, but the first of the Sleepers moved toward Shianne so quickly it seemed that the sky had stuttered; one moment he stood beside his brothers, and the next he was away; his sword traced an arc of light in the sky that seemed to leech all color from it. Around him, beneath his feet, above his head, the sky was now gray and pale—but the wind whipped his hair into a stream that seemed to rise and fall as a liquid around his shoulders, his back.

His blade struck Shianne's; the result was a lightning that traveled in all directions. Shadow cursed and moved; light singed his right wing and raised gray fur into bristles. The same light reached for Jewel on her perch atop his back; although the gray cat dodged, he could not evade it.

It was Rath whose hands damped the flames that had spread in a slow, blue crawl up her shoulders; his pale hands were limned in that fire for one long second before the fire went out. The Winter King moved and moved again; the fall of the blade a second time hit the tines of his antlers.

Winter King.

Understand, Lord, that I am not—and was never—their equal. I could not face even one and hope to survive for long.

Then don't face them. She can't fight without you.

Jewel, she can. *I do not know what you see in her, but you must understand. Her mortality is not the whole of what she is; I, too, was mortal. If I choose to leave her here, it is here she will stand. She will not back down in the face of the three. She cannot.*

Then take her away.

To where?

To the White Lady.

The ways are not open yet.

Blades rose, blades met; the clash of strike and parry once again caused lightning that streaked in all directions. Where it hit the ground below, it burned. The fire was blue; blue and gold.

Jewel had never before seen stone burn. She had never heard it scream.

There is a danger, Avandar said.

Can you put the fires out?

Yes. But not without cost. They will know I am here.

She did not ask him if he had faced the Sleepers before the judgment of the gods and the White Lady had rendered them irrelevant. She knew the answer. Nor did she now command him, because she *knew* what he would do. She did not tell him not to draw sword; the danger to Avandar that she had always feared was irrelevant now. She understood that he could not die. If the Sleepers destroyed him here, he would cling to life in some fashion; the world itself would build a cage that would contain him, and it was that cage from which he longed to escape.

War would not, and had not, freed him.

She knew the moment he unsheathed the sword, and she understood in that instant that the weapon never left him; it was as much a part of him as breath, as power, as the history that he could not escape.

And she saw the two Sleepers turn, instantly, toward him; only the nameless man who now attacked Shianne in earnest failed to look, even once, in his direction. But to look, Jewel thought, might be death.

Shianne parried the third blow from the wakened prince.

The fourth such strike was hers. Her eyes glittered—with power, with tears, even the view from the seer's heart could not easily divine the difference— becoming hard, cold; her jaw set as those eyes narrowed.

And Jewel understood that the Sleeper had attacked her in earnest, affording her the respect she had once been due, in a bygone age, when gods still roamed the world, creating and destroying in equal measure.

Adam was in front of her, behind her shield.

Winter King.

The Winter King did not respond verbally to the unspoken command, but Adam fell, toppling from the stag's back.

Kallandras caught him in the folds of the same wind that now held the bard aloft. Adam, wide-eyed, flailed a moment before he realized that he would not fall.

"Kallandras—take him home!" The bard, like the stag, did not answer. He did not carry his lute; he carried, instead, the dual weapons that she seldom saw him use.

Shadow growled. Without a word, he headed toward Adam; Adam, flailing again, met him halfway.

Jewel started to tell the cat that there was no room and stopped as Rath gently disengaged.

"I am dead," he said, voice gentle. "My weight is entirely a matter of history and regret. And the boy is healer-born. You may need his talent." He stepped to the side of the cat; Shadow's wings passed through him.

Adam sat behind Jewel; there was no room in front. Her hands still cupped the crystal, its light and shadow revealing the battlefield of Averalaan, on earth or in sky. Shadow hissed; it wasn't silent, but was wordless. He did not like Adam, and Jewel was surprised that he consented—however grudgingly—to bear him.

Adam reached into the pouch he bore, his hands shaking so much it was difficult to open the simple, mortal flap. He did not touch Jewel as a healer; had he not been upon Shadow's stiff back, he would not have dared to touch her at all.

The Oracle had given him a ring to bear; he was meant to return it to its owner. The Oracle had said he would know when. Now seemed like the right time, but both of her hands were occupied with the crystal she had taken from her chest.

"Yessssssssss," Shadow hissed.

Adam found the ring. Found it. Held it, his right hand a fist. His left, he laid against the back of the Matriarch's neck.

Shianne and the Winter King now began their attack in earnest. Avandar, sword unsheathed, turned to the two and said, "Shianne's Lord is not my Lord. *My* Lord has claimed these lands."

"And who is this lord who can command the service of the Warlord?"

"Jewel Markess ATerafin," Avandar replied.

"We know of no such person."

"Your failure and its punishment have left you, of necessity, in ignorance."

The air chilled instantly; the sky darkened. Only where the blades of Shianne and the Sleeper clashed did they brighten—but each time they did it seemed to Jewel that the sky itself would shatter.

"Do you not hear her name? The trees speak it, and the quiet earth murmurs it constantly. The air did not leap to your command when you first stepped foot on these lands, and it will not carry you for much longer; she has returned."

"I hear no such name, and the earth has wakened—as it once did—to our voices."

Avandar's smile was thin, cold, and very proud. "Not your voices alone."

Beneath their feet, the first of the pillars finally fell, and no other rose in its place. But it fell across buildings, the weight of rock crushing the stone walls that had not yet fully formed. Shards and dust rose, and the wind caught them, and Jewel remembered how unsafe it was for the elements to mingle.

The Sleepers who had not moved to attack Shianne moved in concert toward Avandar, but it was Calliastra who drew first blood: her wing clipped the face of the one on the right, and he wheeled in something too cold and proud to be called rage, although at its heart, that's what it was. The wide, wide arc of sword slashed air and shadow and the stone or metal that composed the second spire of the new palace. It cut an arc through trees and buildings hundreds of feet below.

Jewel's hands froze, her grip tightening.

Avandar continued, unperturbed. "We will offer you free passage from these lands; we will demand no recompense for the changes made, the damages done. But you *will* leave."

"Your Lord is no longer Lord of these lands."

"Is she not?"

"She is mortal."

"Yes. None but the mortal may be Sen."

The silence that greeted the words was broken only by Shadow's sharp inhalation.

"This is not the city of a Sen," the Sleeper finally said. His casual gesture said *behold*, and Jewel did, although Avandar seemed both surprised and unmoved.

A mountain rose from the bay.

Ships in port were upended as if they were paper boats made by children. The air became a battleground of magics such as the magi themselves had never seen. Sigurne, however, continued her climb. She did not trust the wind; it was part of the wilderness. The ring up on her hand glowed, and although the runes were unfamiliar, she understood what they said, what they were purported to say. It was a slender shield, and perhaps a useless one. She had no magic of her own to spare beyond this halting climb; the barrier on the ground absorbed the force of the Sleeper's strike—a strike that had not been aimed at the Kings or their forces.

Those Kings were beneath notice, beneath all but contempt.

As the mountain shed its water and the contents of the bay rolled down its peaked sides, she understood that. But the mountain created a valley and it was the shape and size of those forces; the Wild Hunt rose in the wake of stone and dirt, and some at least would never rise again.

This was how gods fought, she thought. But no, no. This was how gods must have *conversed*.

"Guildmaster," a familiar voice said.

"ATerafin."

"This is not perhaps the wisest or safest of places to stand."

"Your concern is noted."

His dry chuckle was broken by the sound of blades and the screech of a bird of prey. "Do you think to engage the fourth?"

"In a manner of speaking, yes."

"You are not his equal."

"No. I never was. But I am not you, ATerafin. I accept, and have always accepted, the difference. I have no ambition to become more than I am; I merely desired to become all that I could be."

"I believe he said he would not recognize you."

Jarven ATerafin was not the company Sigurne wished to keep on her lonely climb, and had she power to spare, she might have attempted to enforce some privacy. But the shields below still held, and Matteos was there. Jewel was here; Sigurne could see her, suspended upon the back of the gray, winged cat. What the gods had expected of that young woman, Sigurne could not say, although she had had some sense of it.

Meralonne had expected at least as much. But the mountain grew, the harbor was gone, the buildings in a quarter of the hundred holdings had been crushed or supplanted. The trees—they had been a whisper of hope as they spread; were they not called the Kings' trees? So, too, the warriors of gold and silver, and the butterflies of flame. The weapons The Terafin had granted her Chosen had been used to great effect upon the frostwyrm and the harptalons, and the Chosen had fought their way to The Kalakar's men, to join them in the defense of the street.

But no new trees grew to sustain the hope of flight, of escape, and the trees that stood in the city were no more proof against the transformation demanded by the Sleepers than the man-made buildings had been. The mountain's rise in what had once been bay was the first real threat to the Isle. She could not see the Isle's fate at all and could only pray that its fate was not that of the harbor.

"Sigurne, this is not the place for you."

The guildmaster said nothing.

"I have been tasked with your safety. With your protection. And given the battlefield you attempt to enter, I am all but certain to fail at that task. I would prefer not to drag you from your perch . . ."

"I would almost welcome the attempt," was her brittle reply.

He fell silent.

"Do you believe he would come to your rescue? Have you failed to understand his essential nature?"

She did not answer.

"I would not have thought you capable of such risible sentiment."

The disdain of the powerful had never bothered Sigurne. The ambition frequently had, because those with ambition were those most likely to become kin to the man who had enslaved her in her youth. Her own family had performed funeral rites for her so many years ago the memory no longer caused pain. She had given her life over to the task of ensuring that it did not happen again—not in the distant North, and not here.

She understood, however, what the *Kialli* were.

She understood what Meralonne was. She could see, in the wakened Sleepers, what he must have been in his youth—if youth was a word that had meaning to the immortal at all. He had no shield, but had he, it would have been the only one of four to bear his heraldry.

But Meralonne's herald had *not* arrived in the city. She did not understand why the arrival of the heralds had changed everything, but demonstrably it had. She understood only one thing. Meralonne had closed with the darkwinged, dangerous creature who responded to Jewel's voice, and he had closed from the air. The Sleepers themselves had not taken to air until the advent of the heralds.

Could not, she thought. She understood the significance of their sudden, physical rise; she could not be certain that this climb served any true purpose. But she climbed the stairs of her own tower, and in the past few years the ascent had grown longer. After today, tonight, she might never ascend the tower again.

She lifted one hand, and Jarven's irritant of a voice failed to mar the moment.

Across the sky, Meralonne APhaniel turned to look at her. She met his gaze, held it, her eyes narrowing in a squint necessitated by distance, by age. Beneath her, more of the city fell, more—and different—rose, the Kings fought, the warrior-magi trained by Meralonne himself by their sides. She saw the mountain, saw the sudden shift in the water, the river itself widening, the banks changing color into something that was emerald green and pale white. The movement of people—and there *were* people in the shifting streets—seemed inconsequential, the movement of dust or grit thrown by wind to no ill effect.

She saw the Sleepers, engaged in their combats; saw the domicis of whom the *Astari* had always felt such bitter suspicion unmasked at last; saw the white cat beneath Angel ATerafin as he circled The Terafin he served.

And she thought of Meralonne the first time she had seen him in flight, in combat; that image had been burned into memory. He was cold, yes, and deadly, he was savage and joyful and proud, he seemed at home in the Northern Wastes, and at home among the demon-kin to whom he then laid waste. He had not, then, been the equal of what he now was.

She had waited for death at his hands, and because she waited, it had never arrived. But she had expected death, had felt entitled to no more. She was a repository of all knowledge forbidden by the Kings, by the laws of decency and sanity by which they attempted to govern the ungovernable: curiosity, experimentation, discovery.

In some fashion, her life had always been in his hands; he had opened those hands and returned it to her, teaching her, in all ways but one, how to fly. The hand she lifted trembled in the gale; she did not fall.

Illaraphaniel, the gods called him; the gods, the immortals. His silver eyes narrowed, his perfect brow creased. He had shed—as he habitually did when he forgot himself—all semblance of age, and even wisdom. What wisdom was required by the storm, the earthquake, the tidal wave?

Mortals gathered, finding strength in numbers. Sometimes they found companionship; sometimes friendship; sometimes they built family. The whole of the city was defined—had been defined—by moments too small to attract the attention of the immortal. Even the untold deaths beneath them seemed inconsequential, an oversight, a side effect.

But it was for these mortals, in the end, that Sigurne had toiled.

And it was on the shoulders of a mortal far more given to sentiment than she that the fate of what remained of this city—and perhaps the Empire beyond it—rested. Sigurne did not know how and could not ask. Her part in the whole tapestry was almost finished because the tapestry that had defined that life was done. The world was waking, a god walked the plane, and the immortals now returned to lands they had been forbidden by the covenant of gods long vanished.

It was time.

"Guildmaster," Jarven said, his voice sharper. He had been a dangerously perceptive man, aware always of weakness, of folly. He took risks. He played games. Where the coin the game demanded was his life, he laid that upon the table—but deliberately, not recklessly. This would not be a risk he would take; this would not be a game he would join. He would not, she knew, see the possible gain in it, even should the risk be rewarded.

Sigurne lowered her hand; the ring, of course, came with it.

She then stepped deliberately off the last of the magical stairs she had expended the power to build.

Chapter Twenty-One

SIGURNE FELL. SHE DID not close her eyes; nor did she attempt to protect herself from the impact of the ground that now rushed up to meet her. The wind was gravity's wind, the fine debris in the air the result of wyrm's breath or the breaking—in too many places—of the merchant roads. The flash of light, the extension of lightning and fire, changed the color of the world; the shadow of the spire that had grown first darkened it. She thought the sky blue, now, leeched of its deeper amethyst.

Jewel had returned.

"That was a very foolish gamble."

Her descent had slowed, but not by a cradle of air; a hand gripped her left arm with enough force she was certain it would bruise on the morrow, should there be one. She found voice, if not heart. "You are an interesting man, ATerafin. I am absolutely certain that the magic you now use is not covered by writs of exemption."

"You are?"

"I sign them all."

"And you *read* them first?" He chuckled at her expression. "It has been my curse in life to encounter, always, those completely absent any sense of humor. I apologize for the harshness of the landing, but I am new to this."

"You have not, yourself, leaped off any great heights as a test of this trick?"

"Of course not. I do not take risks for the sheer joy of the risk itself; there must be some goal, and in the case of this particular party trick, some reward that is worth the possible failure. I," he added, "am likely to survive in any case."

Jarven's face was pale, insubstantial, above hers; he was transparent, now, the field of his invisibility dampened, perhaps by the strain of this half-flight, half-controlled fall. Because it was, she could see what occurred beyond him; her face was turned, now, toward the sky.

Her eyes widened, rounding; she found her voice in a desperate rush, gilding it, for the first time since she stepped into the sky, with power.

"Meralonne! *No!*"

"Ah. I see I have become dangerously superfluous," Jarven ATerafin said. He released her arm instantly, throwing himself across the gap of air toward the height of a new stone building. It was Sigurne's weight he braced himself against; Sigurne's momentum he used to fuel his own.

Blood touched her arm and face, regardless.

The air caught her before the earth did, and she rose in its folds.

Meralonne glanced in the direction Jarven had leaped; he did not pursue, although his flashing eyes were narrowed edges. He looked down at Sigurne's hand and then up, to her face. With one hand, he brushed away the spattered blood. "That was foolish."

She said nothing.

"And all but fatal." He turned to the skies but did not rise again. "Why did you take such a risk?"

"The Terafin gave the air permission to heed your commands until such a point that the forest itself no longer recognized you. And you never truly landed."

"I cannot fight them," he said, voice soft, gaze raised. "I had thought that I might stand against them for some small time, but it is not in me, Sigurne. Not for any reason, save one. I engaged Calliastra only because my brothers had not yet been freed of their final moorings. Do you see them?"

She nodded.

"They are not yet what they were, but they are becoming. You will not recognize an inch of this city when this battle is done—and it is almost at the precipice."

"The Terafin has returned."

"Yes. But she is merely Jewel ATerafin. She has the seeds of the absolute power required to defend these lands, but they have not blossomed—and I am uncertain, now, that they will."

"She has visited the Hidden Court," Sigurne said.

For the first time, Meralonne wheeled to face her.

"Evayne a'Nolan came to us with this news: Jewel has visited the Hidden Court, she has carried the sapling to the Winter Queen, and the Winter Queen has agreed—for reasons of her own—to come. The Terafin does not need to defend this city against your brothers indefinitely. She only has to hold out until the White Lady arrives."

"She cannot. As she is, she cannot."

"Not all of our people have perished. They shelter in safety in The Terafin's forest."

"She cannot hold even that," was Meralonne's soft reply.

"Can you not bespeak them?"

"They will take only one thing of import from any attempt to stay their hand: that the White Lady is coming. You do not understand. It will not stay their hands. If the White Lady is to come, they will create a city worthy of her visit. Think you the change in the landscape extreme? It is nothing to what it will become."

The city rose and rose. The buildings that had lain in ruins beneath the mortal city streets seemed to rebuild themselves as they struggled skyward for dominance of the landscape. Jewel could not bespeak the earth, here. No, she thought, she could not *command* it. Avandar could, and did, but even his will did not halt what occurred beneath their feet; it altered the buildings created, it altered the earth's becoming.

But the sky, now, was a deep azure, and the winged creatures that had harried the troops on the ground were dead. No more joined their number. It didn't matter. The Kalakar and The Berrilya became increasingly isolated on the flats of the roads they had chosen—the only surface in the changing city that seemed to hold its original form.

"It is no accident," Rath said.

Jewel nodded; she understood. She glanced, once, over her shoulder and saw that walls had risen, unimpeded, around the city. They were not walls that could be manned; they were not walls that could be guarded. They were all of a piece, a gift from the earth or the stone of the Deepings, and they shone orange and violet and gold, in her vision. "Shadow."

Silent, the cat flew to the height of the wall, and for the first time since entering her own city, Jewel stepped off his back. Nor did he remonstrate with her.

He would not, however, allow Adam to climb off his back, although he cursed and threatened the young man as he refused. He hovered, however, his paws skirting the height of the curtain wall.

Adam tightened his knees, flailing, but Shadow remained almost still, suspended before Jewel. The Voyani youth held out one arm, one fist. "The Oracle," he said. "The Oracle asked me to return this to you."

Her eyes widened. She held out an arm, opening her palm into a cup beneath his shaking fist. He managed to pry his fingers open, and she felt the heavy weight of the Terafin ring—the ring worn by the House ruler. She had surrendered it to the Oracle as the price for her passage through the wilderness, and it had not been returned.

Until now.

She didn't know why the Oracle had chosen to give that ring to Adam, rather than return it to her in person; she didn't have time to care. Although it had been the easiest thing to surrender, it had *not* been easy. And here, above the whole of the city in which she'd been born, she placed that ring upon her finger.

She was The Terafin.

She lifted her head to thank Adam, but Shadow had moved.

Jewel had not created the walls on which she stood—she was certain of that. But they were solid beneath her feet, and from their height, she could see everything that occurred in the city. She could, she thought, see everything that occurred in the city through the lens of the seer's crystal, as well, but it was . . . not the same.

Ararath Handernesse joined her. She glanced at him—at him, not into the crystal—and frowned a moment. "You have a shadow."

He said nothing, turning instead to look out upon the city. "The Handernesse estates," he said, "are gone. Can you see them? I think only my godfather's remain untouched, but they are, even now, overshadowed by what is emerging to replace them."

Araven would stand, she thought, because Andrei would stand. She would not worry about Hectore. She did not worry about the Kings. Her Chosen, yes. But she had given them the weapons that she could, and she believed in them without reservation. It was, now, that belief that was definitive, and she knew to think too deeply was to rock it, shake it, possibly break the full force of that spell. No—not a spell. Not that.

She heard, thinking of her Chosen, a loud, Rendish cry: a war cry. It was clearer in that moment than it should have been; she should not have heard it over the breaking of earth and the thunder of magic and the arms of those who had chosen to stand, to fight.

She knew where Terrick had gone.

She lifted one hand, and in the howl of wind, in the clash of dark lightning and bright, butterflies flocked to her hand. No, not butterflies: leaves. Leaves of fire. They did not burn her; they warmed her. Angel, hovering on Snow's back, looked down from the height, but Snow, in spite of his urging, would not land on the wall. More leaves flew to her, and more, until she had not one leaf, but a wreath, a crown of fire. She set it upon her head, without thought. This crown existed, this fire existed, because she had been attacked upon her own ground, her own land.

And now, she thought, it was time to stand her ground. Again.

At last.

Leaves from the forest that could no longer be seen flew, just as the leaves of fire had flown; leaves now of gold, of silver, of diamond, leaves of *Ellariannatte*, the trees that she had loved in her childhood in the Common that was only a memory now. The streets she had played in were gone; so, too, Moorelas' statue. Moorelas was lost. She *knew*. But the trees would grow again, and the people would return.

These leaves she gathered; they graced the palm she freed, shifting her grip on the seer's crystal, but did not remain there as the fire had done; almost, they seemed to seek the contact as if they were living children in need of comfort. As she had done the first time, she opened her hand and she let them go, and they flew of their own accord toward the earth beneath these walls. This time, however, she knew what they would do. They flew, as if they were tiny birds of prey, and they landed, and where they landed, they took root.

They grew in an instant, and as she watched them spread, she felt the breeze against her upturned cheeks, and she felt the ground beneath her feet, although she stood on the height of stone walls. She felt the currents of rivers; she did not look into the crystal itself. As she had done on the first day of The Terafin's funeral rites, she did now, deliberately lifting her voice to bespeak the elements.

Now it was her roots in the earth, and the earth—stirred by fire and gold and living *Ellariannatte*—seemed to lift its figurative face, turning toward her. So, too, the breeze at the heights, playfully rearranging the stray curls of hair that usually managed to fall into her eyes, and removing, as it did, any hint of the dust and dirt accumulated by travel.

And she heard—oh, she heard—the voices of the bard-born, raised in a song that had terrified her in the rapidity of its spread, the ridiculousness of its depiction, and she did not even grimace, because the song itself was part of this wilderness, part of this forest, part of this dream. It was The Wayelyn's song.

The earth continued to create its buildings, but those buildings were hers. Ah, no, not all of them. To The Kalakar and The Berrilya, she spoke, and her voice was the earth's voice, deep and endless, but it was Jewel's voice as well.

"To the Kings."

As one, they looked up; the soldiers under their command did not. Jewel could meet their gaze at this great remove; could see the shift of lines, the acknowledgment.

She saw them begin their retreat, although the retreat was complicated by the presence of the host that served the princes. Walls of fire grew, and branches from it, between the body of the host and the body of the two units of the army, and she saw—clearly—that Ellora had accepted the strategic command. The Berrilya was slower to do so; Jewel was Terafin, not King, and he did not owe her obedience.

She gave her Chosen the same orders, and they were quicker to obey, for the dragon was bleeding out the last of its life in the streets it had cleared. It lifted its head and roared a final time, its broken wings fluttering as if it might still escape. And she caught its breath before it could freeze or shatter her newborn trees; caught it as she had once caught fire, compressing it in her free hand, as if she stood before the dragon. And this, too, she planted.

As the tree of fire, it was singular. There was one tree, and only one, and it grew, or seemed to grow, from the failing body of the dragon. The Chosen retreated, making their way to the Kings as if they knew where the Kings must stand; there was no clear path, but she noted that it was Arann who now led the way, and smiled before she turned once again to look at the single tree.

It was all white, a tree of frost, of ice, its bark the color of snow, its leaves the color of frost; no two leaves were alike; they budded and blossomed and even the earth stilled for one long breath.

But not only the earth. She saw that clearly as the crystal pulsed in her hand. The Sleepers turned as one man. They had been entangled in combat in the sky: Shianne, Calliastra, and Avandar remained in that sky, as did Celleriant and Kallandras—but the storm that swept the sky threw them toward the mountain that had risen from the bay, and perhaps beyond.

The princes had control of the air; they had control of the skies above their palace. She had taken the earth because it was in the earth that the trees were planted, and into the earth that their roots sank deepest, and the Sleepers knew. Of course they knew.

They did not fly toward her; she was certain that the wind above these walls would fail to heed their commands. But she saw, rising from their forces, three great stags—golden, not white, as the Winter King was white—and she knew that the permission of the air was not required. They conferred, briefly, as one, and then they separated: one rode toward the combatants that had been swept, momentarily, from their chosen field of battle; one rode toward the Kings, and the third, the last, to Jewel.

Not all the people of the city had escaped it; those that survived were few. She could see their faces in the crystal she held; they passed by in flickers, like a stream of possible loss. She could not contain them, could not reach them all; like the water of a stream, they evaded her grasp, slipping past her ability to memorize, to *act*.

And she could not. She could stand and face the prince of that ancient court, that other Queen, or she could die. She chose, as she had always subconsciously chosen, to survive.

The air obeyed Meralonne. He did not attempt to bespeak the earth; had not once made the attempt since he had returned to the side of his absent, sleeping brothers. Sigurne watched him in silence. She knew that he desired her survival, which meant, here and now, she would survive. She bore witness.

"Is this," she asked softly, "beautiful to you?"

"Is it not beautiful to you?" was his equally soft reply; the words were laced with awe and loss and a growing sorrow; the latter weighted his words.

"No, APhaniel. It is . . . worthy of awe, of terror, of admiration. It is not beautiful."

"Can you not see them?"

"I see them. I see what they have built, what they are building."

"Did you not think me beautiful when first we met?"

Sigurne said, after a long pause, "When I first saw you, yes. And every battle you fought after that first one was an echo of that day, a reminder. You were . . . perfect, to my eye. You were everything that I had dreamed of being, on the nights when I nursed injuries and hatred and helplessness. You were the avatar of my younger self and her pain."

"And now?" he asked; he had not looked away.

"You do what I cannot. Even had I the power, I could not do as you do. You taught me to do what I could—and I have faced demons since then—but I could not be you. Yet I feel at peace now," she added. "They are as you were—but more so; what they do now, you did not do. And it does not compel me in the same way because they do not speak to my ancient anger, my pain, or my helplessness. Mortals are, as you said, frail.

"They will destroy—have destroyed—what I have built. Not because there are mortal laws which they might follow, as you did, but because to them, the whole of what we have built is so much dust, detritus. I cannot do what they can do. But I could not do what Darranatos could do, either. I have seen the mountains rise," she continued. "The harbor destroyed. Moorelas' fall. Things I could not have conceived of except, perhaps, in the nightmares that linger moments only after waking. I understand what the gods must have done when they walked these lands. I understand why *we* could not have survived."

"And yet," he replied, "you did."

She nodded.

"She makes her stand."

"Yes. And Meralonne, she is not what you were to me—but if I am powerless, and I am, I am no longer that young, captive girl barely out of childhood. She is mortal, she is not the scion of gods or their children; she is too short, and her hair is always unruly, and her clothing is dirty and road-worn. I am certain her boots are the same. Her skin is freckled or cracked and reddened by cold; she now has lines in the corner of her eyes, and her eyes are not silver or gold.

"And to me, now, she is truly beautiful."

"Because she will do what you cannot?"

"No. Because she will *try*. You do not believe she will succeed."

"No, Sigurne. We wake slowly, who do not sleep naturally. And as she is now, she might stand for some small time against one of my brothers, but she will not stand against three. She lends power to those in whom she has faith, belief—but it is mortal faith, mortal belief."

"The Sen once created cities that could stand against the gods."

He nodded.

"And you said she is Sen."

"Ah, yes. There is, however, a difference. She is not as they were. She could be, Sigurne—but she is not. And I do not know if she will wake in time."

Jewel moved without thought, her hand tightening around the core of the crystal she was now forced to hold in one hand. Even dodging, she did not lift both feet; she *knew* that the wall would shatter if she did not remain in contact with it. The attack itself was a thing of sharp fire and ice; the Sleeper did not raise or lower his blade. But her cheek bled; she felt the sting of the cut in the cool air of the height.

"Be careful, Jewel," Rath said.

Jewel. Two voices. She swept them to the side.

The Sleeper meant merely to dislodge her; she could feel his power seep into and around the stone of the walls. The walls were of far less significance than the mountain that had risen in the bay; altering their shape and their purpose should have been trivial. And it would have been, had Jewel not been standing on the heights. She had no weapon that was equal to the weapons the Arianni carried; no weapon that was equivalent to Avandar's. She had fire, and she had frost, and she had the leaves she had taken from the dreaming forest of the Winter King—the Winter King who had evaded his own death for so long death had become the only thing he yearned for.

In death, or near it, he would see the Winter Queen again.

She thought, as she dodged again, that the Sleepers were akin to that Winter King, whose existence had thrown the seasons of the hidden world off-balance for so long. He had built his palace of ice, his forest of gold and silver and diamond; he had captured—and held—the cats, encased in stone, but nonetheless living, and he had waited.

And waited.

Perhaps he had refined his palace. Perhaps he had labored to grow the trees in his forest. Perhaps he had spent centuries in search of the proper skin for the cats.

Shadow growled.

But he had built them *all*, in the end, for Ariane. She understood that now. He had built them all in preparation for the Winter Queen's arrival, for her attack. He had hoped—and she saw this, too—that Ariane would gaze upon his creation with wonder, with delight, with whatever passed for affection or even love in the heart of the Winter Queen.

She did not know what had become of that Winter King—the greatest and the last. She did not know if he became, like her own Winter King, a mount, a creature of service to her, who might live for as long as Ariane herself would live. But she was certain that he would not be forgotten; even the Wild Hunt must remember him, and when they used the title he had graced for the span of his life, he would be their first recollection.

Three times she dodged; the fourth time, she could not. Shadow's growl became a roar and a flurry of furred storm struck the Sleeper. His eyes were round with surprise, and then narrowed in fury—but it was a tactical fury. He roared a reply, but it had words in it, syllables that carried enough power to wake the dead.

She was not surprised when the remnants of the divided host began to charge in formation *up* the side of the wall. They met a wall of fire long before they reached the heights, and their mounts could not pass through that fire; nor could they find purchase up its side, as they had with the stone itself.

The wall of fire did not gutter at the command of the Sleeper; nor could he summon air to tear it away or earth to smother it. He broke it instead, and the fury as he landed upon it and rent a great gap in the flames was unmistakable. Lifting his voice, he shouted, and she saw that one of his brothers began to ride toward him; in the air she could smell the faint tang of burnt flesh.

Two, then. She was surprised that fire could rip or tear; no mortal fires did. They required sustenance, but she gave them that: leaves from her crown flew down to that wall. The wall did not impede the Sleeper. It would not impede his brother; it simply stopped the host from joining the fray. She could not dodge the whole of that gathered force as she now dodged the attacks of their master.

Or masters, for the second group had gathered. But the wall of fire was a ring that circumscribed the whole of the walls that now stood around this emerging, faltering vision of a city. And she understood what that city might become.

Anything.

Anything at all.

This was a battle that gods might have engaged in, but on a smaller scale. What the Sleepers wanted of a city, Jewel did not want—and would never want. She had marveled at the palace of ice, of glass, but she had had no desire to live in it; she did not believe that it could be made a home. Home for Jewel was the Common. Home was the Terafin manse. The difference between the two, when she had lived in the hundred holdings, had been the difference, in the mind of a poor child, between mortals and gods.

That difference did not exist in this moment. Home was, and had always been, about the people in it. In the city the Sleepers would create, there would be no people. No patricians, no Kings, no servants, no farmers, no little old ladies with useless sons. There would be no Taverson, no unexpected help, no families. There would be nothing of the life she had stitched together over the past two decades, and she *did not want that.*

They would throw away the complexity and beauty and frustration of life in this mixed and complicated city to do what? Impress a Queen who would never, in the end, appreciate what they built?

No.

Above the ring of fire, untouched by its heat, there now grew a ring of ice, and it expanded, thinning, until it was a dome. Beneath its height, the two Sleepers now closed. Shadow roared again. A third time. Night came. Night came, and Snow came with him and, on Snow's back, Angel. Snow paused for just long enough to eject her den-kin, and Angel came to a skidding stop to Jewel's right.

He wielded a sword openly, understanding that it was not meant to cut flesh or, rather, not only flesh, and his hair flew in the chill breeze at the height of the walls. Jewel could see the ghost of the spire that he had worn as both crown and promise until the moment he had—finally—accepted the House Name. He had always had her back. He wanted nothing more from her than that right of position: at her back, at her side. This road that she had walked he had asked to walk with her, and she had said yes because she hadn't the heart to say no.

She even smiled, the expression a flicker, lost easily to the sudden flare of light and heat and cold, to the charge of electricity that spoke of storm cloud and lightning, to the gale of wind that could not displace them. There was no curtain wall here, but Angel did not fall, and Jewel would not.

She *would not*.

And so, at the last, across the heights, grew trees of stone: obsidian and alabaster and jade-green marble. They became her walls; they became her roofs; they became her shelter. Where they were shattered—and they were—they served as shield; they took the blows meant in their entirety for Jewel Markess ATerafin. For The Terafin. For the Lord of this contested land.

She responded with fire. She responded with ice. She responded, at the last, with blood, because she could not dodge everything, no matter how keen or intuitive her reflexes. She remembered her first meeting with Isladar, in an alley in the Common. And she remembered that, bleeding, she had slowed, and in slowing, bled more, until the body's need to survive could not compensate for the speed of the demon's attempt to kill her. Being seer-born in that moment had counted for little.

Being den had counted for everything.

She glanced at Angel as she bowed her head, trying to minimize her movements, trying to hoard stamina, and she flashed a brief sign. He wielded his sword in two hands; he could not respond in kind. But he nodded, eyes narrowed, knees bent, weapon once again rising to the ready.

She did not doubt that she could continue to stand—on this wall, beneath these trees and above them—for as long as it took for Ariane to arrive. Nor did she doubt that the Winter Queen—the Summer Queen—would honor her word. She very much doubted that the city would ever again be what it had been, but she knew—she *knew*—that her own people were within the heart of the forest that she had first discovered, first planted. If she could hold now, she could build later, and what she built would be better. Those who survived could return to dwellings that they had conceived of only in dream—if at all—and by presence make a home of them.

She gestured once, and a barrier of ice rose over one dwelling like a dome, and she *knew* Hectore had looked up, had seen it; she did not know if he understood, but she whispered his name, even if the sound, too slight for her own ears couldn't possibly reach him.

Hectore lifted his chin as he stood on the balcony that overlooked his estates. The grass was ruined, and he very much doubted the flowerbeds would survive what had become an occupation. Nor would the cellars and the food supplies, but those he begrudged far less.

He turned to Andrei, remembered that Andrei was not present, and grimaced. But he lifted his merchant's voice—a voice he seldom had recourse to use in the splendor of his manse—and informed those gathered in fright beneath him that the barrier above their heads would protect them from . . . everything. Rescue was coming, and the Kings were on the field.

If it was a field that could no longer be seen, could no longer be recognized, those alterations existed entirely beyond the fence line, and Hectore of Aravan was grateful that he had never given in to demands that a man of his import should be possessed of a manor upon the Isle. There, the grounds—and the safety they now presented to those who had sought refuge here—would have been much, much smaller.

As it was, although he had instructed his guards to turn no one away, it was very tightly packed, and the calming of the crowd was an emergency in its own right; he could see the waves of fear pass through them at every sight, every sound. He missed Andrei and felt a touch of fear himself—but he was no stranger to fear, and it did not ride him or command him.

Jester heard her voice. One arm around Birgide, he had pulled the Warden through the ruins of her forest, following a path that she indicated by the heavy movement of her awkward steps. He lifted one hand and signed, although he could not see Jay. He could see the light in the sky, a type of nightmare rendition of the festival of lights orchestrated by the Order of Knowledge every year on this day.

Birgide shuddered, but her eyes had cleared, and when she turned to look over her shoulder, she froze. He felt her stiffen, felt her straighten; he removed the arm that had carried half—or more—of her weight. She turned her gaze toward his, and he was surprised to see her smile. In this place, at this time, he had none to offer in return.

"Can you hear them?" she asked.

Jester, lifting his voice, said, "What?" Before she could repeat the question, he added, "We're to go to the tree of fire. When she can, she'll meet us there."

Birgide shook her head.

Jester put his figurative foot down. "It wasn't a request. Those are her orders, and I don't really think that *now* is a good time to quibble with them."

Birgide's eyes were wide, but they narrowed as her forehead creased. To Jester's surprise, she then broke into a run. At least, he thought, as he started to follow, she was sprinting in the right direction.

Avandar.

He did not answer with words, but images—not unlike the crystal's—flashed by. Calliastra was bleeding black mist into the skies around the one Sleeper that had not yet come to attack Jewel directly. She was not the only one injured; she was the only one enraged by that injury.

The injury was costly on both sides. Silence, and then: *You are bleeding.*

She was.

Something had struck her right arm, just above the bend at her elbow; her right hand was numb. But numb or no, her grip on the crystal, its images moving past her so quickly it was a stream of constant color, did not falter. She didn't tell him it was nothing; it wasn't. Small cuts like these slowed her down, and she could not afford to be slow. Not here.

She was not surprised when Shadow dumped Adam off his back. Not surprised when the Voyani youth raced the few yards to her side. She did not order the gray cat to take the healer back. Nor did she order Adam to retreat. She understood, *knew*, that this was why she had brought him here. This was why he had not traced a path through the wilderness to the home—and kin—that waited.

She barely felt his hand touch the back of her neck as she slowed her frenetic dance. This was not the first time he had stood thus; not the first time that he had closed wounds that might otherwise be her death. Shadow did not even tell her she was stupid. He did not speak at all.

None of the cats did.

They roared—but they roared in unison; she could discern which level of bestial power belonged to which of the three. Adam, eyes closed, did not see the three cats. Jewel thought she would have seen them regardless, although her eyes were not closed.

She remembered clearly the metamorphosis that occurred after the conflict with the Warden of Dream and Nightmare; remembered, less clearly, the size and shape they had first donned when she had met them, in the flesh, in the forest of metal and diamond. And she remembered the instant growth in size and stature, the deepening of their voices made far less threatening by the continued pettiness of their constant whining.

But to the immortal, there had been no difference. They recognized the cats in any form and shape. What they saw, Jewel and her kin did not see.

Until now.

They were cats the way dragons were cats, but without the scales. Their edges were blurred, smudged—it wasn't the drift of raised fur, but something indistinct, something even her seer-born eyes failed to grasp. She had seen, in Meralonne, a precursor to what he had, or was, becoming; she had seen the truth of demons in the eyes of the men whose forms—or literal corpses—they chose to inhabit. But she had not seen this in the cats.

They were like living nightmares: larger in all ways than they could possibly physically be, indefinite in shape; they seemed to her half-finished or unfinished, and even the colors by which she'd offhandedly chosen their names began to bleed into each other—and into sky and blood and light. They were called "eldest" by any immortal who felt tolerant enough to interact with them—but they had passed through the tangle and back without apparent harm.

Corallonne had not been concerned for them. Nor had Calliastra.

And yet . . . even in their sudden transformation, the center of their forms retained the colors for which she had named them: white, black, and gray. They had shed wings as if wings were superfluous and, given the movement of their enlarged mass, they were. She could see the glitter of teeth, even at this distance, and the teeth were also the color of their names, polished and hard and long.

Jewel! Two voices now. The Winter King—hers—and Avandar's, raised in consternation or even fear. She was almost confused.

There is danger, Avandar said, as the Winter King said, *Beware your former cats!*

Certainly the cats seemed more of a threat to the Sleepers than Jewel herself did in comparison.

They won't hurt me.

You do not understand what you have unleashed—

They won't hurt me. Can't you hear them?

As if they had heard the Winter King and Avandar—and given Shadow, they might have—the cats started to add layers of syllables to their roars. They weren't drawing room words; there was nothing polite, nothing measured about them. But she understood them in all the languages she knew, because she could *hear* them in all the languages she knew.

MINE.

Adam closed the newest lacerations; healed the fractured shin. He glanced once at Angel, but Angel, teeth clamped in a thin line that was now partly red, shook his head emphatically. Adam accepted what Angel did not say. And he did not say what he felt as he healed The Terafin; it wasn't necessary. If the Matriarch survived, in some fashion, the city would survive.

Adam had not seen Arkosa rise from the sands of the Sea of Sorrows.

But he watched now as this city—whatever its ancient name must be—struggled to rise from something that was not a desert. He thought of Arkosa, of home, of Matriarchs and the bitter history that had driven his people from their cities, and he wondered if the other Voyani clans had made the trek to their homes, as Arkosa had.

He understood the need for cities now, although he had never truly seen a living city until he had come to Averalaan. He understood the why of their ancient defenses. Had he not seen a mountain rise from the waters of the bay? If she survived, the Matriarch would drive these enemies beyond the walls upon which she had taken her stand.

And she *would* survive.

Jewel sent a whisper to the bards and a whisper to the Kings as Arann reached them. The host of the Arianni did not breach her wall of frost, those few that had ridden through the gap torn in walls of flame. She did not understand why they could not travel as the Sleepers did but did not question it further.

Instead she turned her thoughts, at last, to her forest, the heart of her domain.

To Finch.

And Finch was not in the lee of the tree of fire.

The eldest, rooted, did not reply, not immediately. Finch felt minutes stretch, testing her patience, heightening the growing fear that had driven her away from the tree of fire. That fire had not existed in this forest until Jay; the eldest, however, had existed for as long as the forest itself.

She did not have the power of the Warden. She could not compel obedience; could not force him to offer the answer that now consumed most of her thought. Will was not power, not for someone like Finch.

"Where is Teller?" she asked.

The tree said, "I have answered, Finch."

Drawing upon the facial neutrality she had learned at Jarven's side, she said, "My apologies, Eldest; I did not hear your answer."

The branches shook, and leaves fell. Three leaves.

"It is difficult," the tree then said, "to speak with mortals; it is taxing because there is so much you do not hear, so much you cannot see." The earth beneath Finch's feet rumbled; she traversed the ground quickly, and knelt to pick up the leaves, because kneeling provided stability. She could not tell if her hands were shaking because of the fear she could not quite contain, or because the whole of her body shook in response to the tremors.

"My apologies, Eldest." She forced her voice to be steady. "I did not realize that this was meant to be an answer. You are, of course, right: I cannot understand it."

The rumbling continued until Finch had retrieved the third fallen leaf. "You will need these, Finch," the tree said, "if you survive."

She said nothing, but bowed to him, the leaves in her hands immeasurably heavier in the wake of his words. "Can you tell me—in words, so I can understand—where Teller is?"

"He is not, precisely, here," the eldest said. Before she could repeat the question, the eldest continued. "I can see him, Finch. But even I cannot reach him. He cannot hear my voice, just as you cannot hear it; he cannot perceive the roots of our Lord's lands, just as you cannot. But he is injured, and the trees that are rooted beside him are withering. He will be lost to the wilderness and the dreamscapes of the Sleepers."

Silence.

"Show me."

The words were not Finch's words, the voice was not hers. She recognized both instantly, and felt, for a moment, a giddy relief: the strings of tension and fear had been suddenly cut.

Jay was home.

Jay was *back*.

"*Show me.*"

Meralonne APhaniel stiffened. A brief smile transformed the cast of his expression; there was sorrow in it, and resignation, and a touch of surprise. "It is gratifying, on occasion, to be wrong."

Sigurne did not ask what had transpired, but he turned to her fully, the fury of light and blood above them apparently irrelevant. When he held out a hand, she took it.

"Come," he said. "I do not believe it will be safe to stand here." She rose as he did.

Shadow roared. His voice contained words, but there were too many, and they were too complicated; to understand them required thought, concentration, deliberation. She had no time for them. She could not hear the eldest's answer, but she could feel it in the chill in the air, in the tremor of the stone beneath her feet, and in the beating of her own heart.

Had Adam not been with her, she would have died, because she locked her legs, locked her arms, refused to obey the physical imperative of instinct that had kept her alive. She held the heart. Whatever she had carried in her right hand—leaves, she thought—she dropped; she cupped the seer's crystal in both of her palms.

Shadow came in from the left, a cloud in the shape of a giant winged cat; only his eyes seemed solid. Solid and endless. She thought he meant to knock her off the wall, but even so, she could not move or speak or look away.

She had found Teller.

It was cold. It was so cold his body shuddered in an attempt to generate *some* heat. He was bleeding, but, ironically, the injury had been caused by his cat, and not the men who were mounted upon stags similar to the Winter King Jay rode. Only a handful of these mounted men had remained; the rest had followed the road that had disappeared behind them.

The forest beings, set to guard and protect him, had done their best. Teller was certain that they had done better than Haval had ever expected—but in the end, it was not the mortal weapons to which they had been trained that were their power. They had not abandoned those armaments, but had set them aside, near Teller, where he might—if he let go of his cat—retrieve them. They were meant for the failure the spirits now saw as inevitable.

Teller was aware that trees were felled by men with axes or saws. He was aware that the wood was then dried and became timber; those parts that could not be salvaged—the knots, the gaps and evidence of insects—could be burned for warmth. The host of the Wild Hunt did not carry axes; they carried swords. But those swords did not seem to dull or notch; they did not lose their edge no matter how often they bit into flesh made of wood. All of wood, sap serving as blood. The forest guardians had conferred very little as they had interposed themselves between the Arianni and Teller.

The Wild Hunt had asked the *arborii* to step aside, and they had refused. They had refused extremely respectfully; they obviously held the Wild Hunt in high regard.

"He is our Lord's Teller."

"You are not, now, in your Lord's lands."

Again, they bowed heads respectfully and apologetically. "We are. As you are in your Lord's lands. We will not trespass; we understand the power of, the strength of, your Lord, and we owe his kin the greatest of debts, for they woke us fully."

Almost, the Arianni seemed confused, as if the words that Teller had heard spoken were in a language with which he was entirely unfamiliar. That confusion cleared, however, pushed aside by something far colder and far more imperious.

"You will either step aside or be destroyed."

"That is not, yet, within your capability," the tree replied, in a sorrowful, deep voice.

"It will be. Our Lords have woken. The punishment decreed by the gods themselves has frayed and ended; nor are there gods to invoke its fetters again. If you will not stand aside, you will perish. Think you that any might hold these lands against *our* lords?"

And the tree's single word reply was enough to unleash the force of the Wild Hunt's fury. "Yes."

Avandar's voice, the Winter King's voice, became inconsequential as she stood her ground. Standing her ground was much, much harder than it had ever been.

Not so hard as it will, Jewel Markess. The memory of a dead ruler's words; the Terafin spirit, who had come to her as Torvan ATerafin in the Terafin shrine. *The years have given you wisdom, of a type, but they have not changed your nature. You are ATerafin in times of peace.*

What is The Terafin's name?

Amarais, born Handernesse.

No, Jewel, born Markess, that is not her name. She is The Terafin.

And I'm Markess.

Yes. You are standing on the edge of the field of battle. The time is our distant past, during the baronial wars. Two sides are readying for a battle that has been long coming, and upon this battle, the fate of the Empire rests.

She could hear his voice so clearly, she might be standing once again beneath the Terafin shrine erected, in the end, for its rulers. She had not understood that, the first time she had approached it. The shrine had been shelter of a kind; a quiet space in which to confront her own fears, her own failures, her own bitter regrets.

You stand upon the edge of the field in that battle; you have seen skirmish, you have seen war; you have both ridden and marched as a soldier. But you are not a soldier now; you have a rank, and a responsibility. Into your keeping the standard has fallen.

She had come to understand the nature of both the shrine and the responsibility that it had guarded, and guided, for centuries. The spirit was gone, finally, to the Halls of Mandaros. There was no further advice to be gained . . . and no peace.

You know that if the standard falls, the hope of the regiments fall with it. That you are, while keeping this piece of pretty cloth, and its bearer, safe, succoring those men who cannot see you, those thousands who will never even know your name.

With you, in this war, is your young adjutant. Teller ATerafin.

And she remembered. The memory was a living thing, a vicious thing; it cut her in ways that even the Sleepers had not. She had almost left the shrine that day. She had not liked the direction the conversation had taken; had not wanted to follow its turn to its end. And had she left? She might not now be plagued by these endless, echoing words. But she had not left. She had not lifted hands from the altar of Terafin, upon which men and women offered House Terafin everything.

A small group of men, with a mage and the use of two demons, is about to spring its trap upon your standard. You have the vision, Jewel, and because of this, you see clearly. You also see, clearly, that you have two choices: You can go now to warn the mage—in which case, the flag will not fall to this attack—or you can ride, in haste, to that stop thirty yards away, in which your adjutant is pacing out his nervous attention so as not to disturb you; he has always been considerate.

You cannot do both.

Jewel Markess would ride to the aid of young Teller.

Jewel ATerafin would summon the mage.

You do not have the luxury, now, of being both, and for this, I apologize. Amarais would know her way to the only choice available, and she would accept it. But it is not her war, Jewel; it is yours.

The first of the spirits had fallen, his limbs pared from him by the impact of a sword's edge, over and over again. He did not surrender; he fought—but his weapon had been the roots he had planted, the roots he had grown, in what had once been a Terafin hall. Teller could not immediately recall which hall because it was a Winter landscape now. Only a small patch of wall and floor remained; the snow and the cold had eaten everything else.

Teller crouched on that small patch; he had been forbidden movement, but the warning had not been necessary. He understood in some fashion that the reason the Arianni swords were having such a difficult time *was* the patch of wall and floor. This was still the Terafin manse. It was still Jay's.

The second spirit fared no better than the first; splinters flew, clinging to Teller's hair and his clothing. He could not prevent the Wild Hunt from entering this tiny patch of sanity and sanctuary, and when they did, he would die. He imagined what Jay would say when she realized he had come all this way for a cat. He *knew* what Barston would say, and maybe, just maybe, death would be a mercy, because he would hear neither.

The snow reminded him of the first day he'd met Jay, in the hundred holdings. He had been running through its endless white, looking for his mother. And she had come running through that same white, leaving different footprints, looking for him. His entire world had come to an end when he had found what he sought in increasing desperation.

And it had started again when Jay found what *she* sought.

She had given him his life back, albeit in a different form. She had not left him for starvation and death. It was, he thought, as the spirit finally lost its arm, her life. Hers to use. If he died here—when he died here—he wanted to tell her that. It wasn't his death that defined him, it was the decades she had given him. He regretted nothing. Anywhere she had been, any home she had offered, had been home *because* she was in it.

He bowed his head then, protecting a cat that wanted to escape into the wilderness. And he knew that if they removed his head or his arm, the cat would run. But it had a better chance of survival without Teller than with him.

The sharp crack of timber was loud, almost final.

She had left Carver.

She had gifted him with the blue leaf and *she had left him*. She had understood, in that moment, that she could not choose Carver, because to do so was to doom everyone else. She had paid that price. Had thought that *was* the price. Of power. Of the Oracle's test. Of rulership. It had not destroyed her. It had not broken her.

But Carver was not Teller.

Carver's death *had not* been certain. She understood that only now. She had abandoned Carver for the sake of the rest of Terafin, which included the rest of her den. In just such a fashion had she abandoned Duster, but the difference between the two decisions had obscured the similarities.

Duster had not been Teller, either.

But she had expected that both Duster and Carver had had *some* chance to survive. The fact that Duster had died did not change that fact. Some chance was not certainty.

There was no chance, now, that Teller would survive. She could not command the Arianni, and she could not command her own forces—any of them—to ride to Teller's aid. They could not reach him now. They could not reach him in time.

She shouted for Night, shouted at Shadow, and they understood but did not move, did not leave the combat into which they had thrown the whole of their weight and power.

We can't. You do it. Shadow's voice.

Shadow who had walked through her dreams and her nightmares.

Shadow who had almost killed her, the only one of the three who had the strategic sensibility.

Shadow, who was never, ever wrong.

Teller. *Teller.*

I can't leave!

You don't have to, *stupid stupid girl.*

Shadow—

Think. Be less *stupid, or he will* die, *and you will—*

Silence. The only thing Jewel could hear, now, was the beating of the heart she had pulled from her chest.

She was seer-born. The talent had been part of her life for as long as she could remember. It had saved her life—*her* life—dozens of times. Possibly more. She had gone to the Oracle, had taken the Oracle's opaque, confusing, and terrifying test, in order to find the White Lady and save her city from the beings that were now destroying it.

And that had been true, on the surface of things. It had been true on a deeper level as well. But it had not been the whole of the truth.

Her talent, her power, had saved her life, yes. But it had not saved the lives of her den. Yes, she had found Finch, found Teller, because of the power. But she had had no control over it. She had had no warning when Ellerson and Carver disappeared into a closet. And if she passed the Oracle's test, she *would* have that power. She would have the control to direct her vision. She would be able to see the things that threatened her den, her kin, at her own command.

It wasn't about empires. It wasn't about gods. It wasn't about the firstborn or the Sleepers or the White Lady, except indirectly. It was about *family*. Her family. Her chosen kin. She had not wanted to fail them again.

But because she was seer-born, she had a singular moment of clarity, a moment of perfect understanding. Shadow was right.

She could do this.

But she could not do it and remain The Terafin. She could not do it and remain Jewel Markess. She could not live as she had lived. She had recreated the entirety of her personal rooms, dragging them into some part of the hidden wilderness that would, after today, no longer *be* hidden.

She had made *one mistake* in a dream, and an entire family had disappeared from a run-down apartment in the twenty-fifth holding. One mistake—while asleep. She had not made those mistakes while waking, while wakeful. She would never make those mistakes while awake. And *if* she did this, if she made this choice, she might *never be awake again.*

"No," Rath said, as if he could hear it all, his voice the only intrusion in the terrible, gathering silence. "Not as you are now. There was a reason—I was told—that the Sen were not rulers of the cities they had created—cities that could stand against the very gods. Jewel, I will be here. Where you cannot wake yourself, I will wake you. It is the reason, in the end, that I was bound. It was the reason I was offered the ring. I chose the moment of my death, and the demons who were the cause of it did not retrieve the information they might have retrieved—but the ring was a ring of binding, an oath ring.

"You will not be awake again—not while the wilderness is the whole of our world. But I will guard your sleep, and I will wake you when it is necessary."

"You don't understand what's necessary. You don't care about the nameless people no one remembers. You don't care about the strangers, the—"

"You do. You always have. And it will be your city, you who were trained, and raised, by my sister. I will remain here, Jewel. When you leave, I will accompany you across the bridge, to the Halls of Judgment where Mandaros waits. But choose, or you will have no choice."

Jewel bit her lip.

Nodded.

She had not taken the Oracle's test, in the end, for any of the reasons she believed she had—but conversely, had taken it for all of those reasons as well. Because it was only in this fashion that she could be, as Avandar and Meralonne had called her, Sen.

She had always been afraid of the fragility of the crystal, because she had always assumed that it was the fragility of her own heart: the pain of loss, the fear of it, the shadows of death and war reaching, always reaching. But no. No.

It was not fragile. Even as she began to apply pressure from both hands, both palms, even as she chose to crush it, to break it, she understood that.

It was simply the expression of everything she could possibly become or be, all at once. It was, in its entirety, Jewel Markess ATerafin. All of them. All of the possible pasts that could lead to this moment, and all of the possible futures that led from it. They were contained, entrapped, folded into a space that she could conceive of and hold in two hands.

And in breaking the crystal, she freed them all.

Chapter Twenty-Two

TELLER HUDDLED PROTECTIVELY AROUND his cat as the last of his two defenders fell. He could see the swords that had slowly carved their way through those guardians—a familiar blue glow, edged and perfect. He was not brave, had never been brave. But he had tried very hard to be kind. To be polite. To observe and to understand the people around him—and to accept them. All of them.

He had learned wisdom, over the years, but it was at heart the wisdom of the powerless. And he had not, in the past year, been powerless by any definition of the word his younger self could understand.

All that he had built for himself over the past decade had become, in the short space of one night, irrelevant. Although he did not huddle over the corpse of his mother, attempting against all reason to make her *wake up*, he felt that that moment and this one had a bitter continuity.

It was the snow and the cold that would have killed him on the day Jay had come running across the holdings, the rest of the den in pursuit, to save him. In the wilderness, it was winter, as it had been on that day. And this winter would kill him. His eyes were shut as he waited, and the waiting extended the seconds, the minutes, of fear; it was not the cold alone that caused him to shiver.

But he looked up as he felt the wind change. The breeze was warm, and there had been no warmth in the manse for some time. To his great surprise, the forest guardians—both of them—stood before him once again; he could see the knots and the patterns of grain that composed their flesh. The clothing they had worn had been destroyed by sword and magic, but they looked untouched, unmarked.

His legs were tingling as he forced himself to his feet. The cat came with him, but movement had become much simpler, because there was no snow. In a widening circle that seemed to have started at the point of his feet, the snow vanished. It didn't melt; it simply ceased to exist. The halls that he had known for the duration of his life in the Terafin manse did not precisely return, although he could see the slate floors beneath his feet, shorn of the roots that forest spirits had planted. There was carpet as well, in Terafin colors, and the walls had begun to adopt their former adornments. As if in a dream, he watched paintings materialize between the supporting beams that held the roof above his head. The roof and a second story.

But the supporting beams were not wood or stone or whatever they had once been; they were trees. And the arches that formed doorways were trees as well. *Ellariannatte.*

"Jay," he whispered.

One of the forest guards said, "Yes."

The Arianni had frozen, as if they had swallowed the winter; they were too pale, too colorless, for the world that now enveloped them. For one long moment, they stared at the forest guard, and then their swords vanished.

"Don't hurt them," Teller whispered.

"Our Lord is not pleased," the tree spirit replied. "They attempted to kill you."

"I am aware of that." He bent and set the cat down, and the cat took another spiteful swipe at his already abraded hands before flouncing off. "But they will not try again."

The Wild Hunt stared between the two guards, and Teller met their silvered eyes and saw confusion. As if, he thought, they were waking.

"These lands," Teller continued, "are the domain of The Terafin. Have you business with her?" As if they were simple political visitors, and his duty was to determine whether or not they were to be granted The Terafin's time. And that had been his duty, as right-kin.

"Teller," Jay said. She stood between two trees that formed an arch at the end of the hall. "They are *not* guests."

Teller winced. The forest guards were right—she was angry. He lifted his hands in den-sign, saw her expression at the cuts that had changed their color significantly, and grimaced. *Not them. Cat.*

This did not improve her mood. He thought very little would, but didn't care because her presence had significantly improved *his*. The forest guard did not part to allow him to go to her side, or he would have been there already. Sadly, the unarmed Arianni remained between the guard and Jay.

Something was wrong; it took him a moment to understand what it was.

Neither the tree spirits nor the Wild Hunt had reacted to Jay's presence at all.

Don't kill them, he signed.

Her lips compressed into a thin line, and he winced. He had not seen her this angry since the time—since the time that Haerrad had arranged to have his limbs broken. To the Arianni, he said, "Are you here on behalf of your Lord?" Before they could answer, he added, "We expect the White Lady's arrival shortly, and as you must imagine, we are woefully unprepared. If you will, you might find respite in the forest. I have been informed that you will be aware of the moment of her arrival."

If the rest of his words had been almost incomprehensible to them, these last words were not. A murmur of sound rose, a different breeze. They did not forget Teller, not precisely, but turned to one another. He could not understand their words; they were soft. But soft or no, they carried something that seemed—to Teller—to be a strange mixture of fear and elation.

"You know they don't deserve this, right?" Jay said.

"If we got what we deserved half the time, we would never have made it this far." His lips quirked in a smile, he added, "I'm not sure I did anything good enough in this life to deserve you. Thank you."

She had never been comfortable with gratitude.

He shook his head. "This is the second time you've run through the winter to find me."

"I'd really appreciate it if you never make me do it again. After this is all over, you and I are going to have a discussion about the importance of household pets in an emergency."

He winced but didn't argue.

"Now, go find Finch. I think she's hysterical."

Teller looked openly skeptical, and the forest guard did not move.

"She thinks you're dead."

That would probably do it. He stepped forward, into the rigid backs of the *arborii*. "We have been asked to escort our *guests* to the forest proper," he told the trees. "And I've been tasked with finding Finch."

"She is with the eldest," one of the trees said, except *eldest* wasn't the word he used. It was longer and deeper, and Teller heard it at the same time as he heard the familiar, spoken word.

"The fox?"

This silence was different. ". . . No," was the hesitant answer.

To the Arianni, Teller offered a Weston bow. It would have been flawless had his clothing not been covered in splinters. "You are not required to accept the offered hospitality," he told them.

But they had turned, again, to the forest guard, and when they spoke, they spoke something that echoed the word that was not quite *eldest*, surprise in their tone. Surprise and something else.

"Yes, even so."

They then bowed to Teller, the gesture almost reverent. "We will accept whatever hospitality you now offer, and we will attempt no further harm of any living being in your Lord's forest that does not attempt to kill us."

This seemed reasonable to Teller, but it clearly surprised the forest guard. As they began to move, Teller asked them why.

"There are many, *many* ways in which the powerful might be offended," one finally said. "And attempts to kill or destroy are only one, and not, in the end, the most significant when it comes to war in the wilderness."

When Jay walked into the clearing around the forest elder, Finch rose. Her skirts were damp at the knees, but the skirts didn't matter. For a moment, nothing else did. She ran across the short distance—three yards, no more—and enfolded Jewel in a hug that demanded that hug be returned.

"I'm sorry," Jay said. "I'm sorry."

Finch shook her head. "You're back."

"I'm back."

"For good?"

"For good. Teller is on his way here," she added. Finch pulled back. Jay was wearing the traveling clothes she'd worn on her pilgrimage to the Oracle. That clothing, however, was so clean it might never have been worn. "I kept my promise," she whispered.

Finch, attuned to Jay, said, "Yes. You became Terafin."

"I want you to take the House."

Finch stilled, understanding at last the reason for the apology. "If you're back—"

"I'm back, but there's too much of me. There's too much. I am having a hundred conversations right now, while I talk to you. I am talking to Teller. I am talking to Angel. I'm talking to Arann, and to a little girl who somehow managed to survive the collapse of half her house. I'm talking to Farmer Hanson. Helen didn't make it." She exhaled. "Taverson was happy to see me. I'm sure Duvari has very, *very* mixed feelings. Jester wants Birgide to stay with the den."

"I can't take the House," Finch said quietly.

"You can—"

"I can't. You're not dead. And no one—*no one*—will contest your rule of the House now."

Jay shook her head. "No one but me. I can't rule the House. I can't attend the Council of the Ten. I will not be welcome in *Avantari*."

Finch's eyes narrowed. "You've *saved* this city."

"Yes. But it isn't the city it once was. It's changed—and Finch, it will *keep changing* if I walk its streets. What happened in the basement in *Avantari* is nothing compared to what *will* happen if I—" She shook her head. "I want you to take the House."

"Haval."

"Terafin." Haval glanced in the direction of the woman he had chosen to advise, his hands loosely clasped behind his back. She was, to his eye, younger, and her eyes were bright. Too bright, for all that they remained brown. There was a warmth to them that implied tears.

"Councillor."

He closed his eyes, feeling his age. No, he thought, not his age. His experience, the difference between the life he had led and the life Jewel had led. He frowned as he looked past The Terafin.

Her smile deepened. "You can see him."

He offered her no answering smile; his face had frozen for one long second, and it was not a mask.

But Jewel's smile did not falter. "It's not me. I didn't bind him." As if she understood the whole of his reaction.

"Ararath."

"Yes, old friend. We have come full circle. I left her, in the end, in your hands for a time. I absolve you of that responsibility."

Haval shook his head.

"You cannot advise her now. And Hannerle is waiting."

Haval closed his eyes; his hands tightened briefly.

"She's not," Jewel added, "very *happy*, but she's waiting. I think she's terrifying the *arborii*."

"Terafin—"

Jewel lifted a hand as if to ward off that word, that title. But she did not say this, did not disavow it. Instead, she said, "I do not release you, no matter what Rath says. He didn't ask for my opinion."

"And what need have you of a Councillor now?"

"Not me," she replied. Some of the brightness faded from her eyes, her expression. "Haval—"

He lifted a hand. "No, Jewel. There are no more tests. Ah, perhaps that is inaccurate. There will be no further tests from me." Throughout the city, the stone buildings that the Sleepers had commanded from the earth continued their rise—but they were different buildings now, in shape, in appearance. Among those buildings, the trees had also shifted, spreading across the city between these new houses of stone. The mountain in the bay had vanished.

But the citadel that had heralded the waking of those Sleepers had not.

He turned from his brief consideration of the city that she was building and looked toward the height of those towering walls. There Jewel stood, arms half lifted, palms empty and turned toward the city as if to gather the whole of it—every detail, every nuance—into herself. He then turned back to the girl who stood before him.

"I . . . can't be Terafin," Jewel told him.

He nodded.

"Did you know, Haval? Did you know that this was what I must become?"

"No. Not precisely. But I understood what the cats—your cats—feared, and I understood what you yourself were so afraid of that you could not even examine it." He exhaled. "You will have me safeguard and advise your regent."

"If it's not you," she replied, "It'll be Jarven."

"Young Finch is not that foolish. Nor is she that sentimental."

Jewel nodded. "She was always a better choice than I was."

"Perhaps. But you were seer-born, and she was not. In return for this service, what am I offered?"

"Some protection from Jarven," Jewel replied, with unexpected seriousness.

"You believe I will require it."

"Haval—you *are* Councillor. You accepted that role in the wilderness."

Silence.

"Did you think, truly, that you would remain unchanged? Birgide accepted the role of Warden, and she is not what she was."

"I accepted the authority of the title because it seemed of value to the forest to grant one."

But Jewel shook her head, her hair flying into her eyes. She shoved the strands out of those eyes, and Haval thought it had been quite some time since he had seen that gesture. It was almost endearing. "You cannot lie to me here. You will never be able to lie to me again."

"I will never be able to *successfully* lie, no. And that was not a lie, except perhaps by omission."

Jewel nodded. "What you have accepted, you cannot now discard. There is no honorable retirement. You are Councillor, and the forest hears you. I hear you," she added softly. "And I am aware that offering protection from Jarven is perilously close to insulting. It will, however, be of great comfort to your wife."

He stilled, then. "She does not dislike him."

"She adores Lucille. She does not trust, will never trust, Jarven. I have been speaking with Hannerle," Jewel added, with a wry smile. "She will not decry the responsibility you have undertaken, and she wants her home to be more or less what it was. I have *tried*, but—" She closed her eyes. "It is hard to remake a city when so many versions of that city overlap. It won't be the same," Jewel added, "and I apologize for that.

"I will keep Hannerle safe. No harm will come to her unless the walls fall. No assassin will touch her, and no threat against her will be safe, because no threat—while I live—will remain hidden. She understands what I need from you."

"You require—"

"I need you to watch over Finch. I need you to guide the regency."

"If you can preserve my wife—"

Jewel's expression grew strained. Ararath placed one hand on her left shoulder, and this seemed to steady her.

"The Kings will rule. The Ten will be the Ten. Finch will be Terafin—" She exhaled. "Finch won't be Terafin. She will be regent. And don't argue with me—argue with her. I've *tried*, Haval. She will not listen. Unless I'm—" Jewel swallowed. "Unless I'm *dead*, she will be regent, and she will not allow the regency to end."

Haval bowed his head. "I am not anticipating an angry wife with any great joy, and Hannerle *is* fond of Finch. She persists in thinking of Finch—and Teller—as children."

"But not me."

"No, Jewel. You are seer-born. My wife understood from the first that you could take care of yourself; she understood that you would probably have no choice in the matter." He paused. "Thank you for seeing to Hannerle."

She could have pretended to misunderstand him but did not.

He watched her as she gazed up at herself as she stood atop the walls, a tremulous smile adding to the impression of her youth. The woman on the wall did not seem slender and youthful to Haval's objective gaze. She did not seem human at all. The young woman at his side, however, he knew—had known—for half of her life. And he wondered, then, if the Sen were truly mortal. He did not know enough, not yet. But he was certain that if he paid attention, he would learn.

Later, it would be said that The Terafin was, literally, everywhere. Every living person in the city, every living person in the forest, could see her standing upon the city walls, no matter where they were. Those walls, so high and so unnatural, were a song, a story in the making, and that song was raised by every bard who had survived. But every living person could also see her standing beside them or in front of them; each person could hear her speak. She did not linger long at the side of those who had never met her, but they heard, in her words, the promise of safety, of survival. Those who had remained in the city and its ruins, those who had managed to survive the breaking of earth, the rising of stone, the falling of trees and the detritus of what had once been their homes, she led to the forest itself. Nothing that fell—and things continued to rise and fall in loud and terrible waves—caused any further harm, and in some cases, The Terafin *lifted* the injured and bore them to the harbor of trees.

There, they met the tree people, and the tree people were so obviously The Terafin's servants that they felt no fear. The panic caused by sudden, catastrophic change—and death, and loss—receded across the survivors of Averalaan in a single wave, and they turned their attention to the Lady on the Wall and the battle she fought for their sake, and in their name.

The forest grew in a more orderly fashion throughout the city, and the *Ellariannatte* that had been felled in the Common were replaced; renewed as if they had never been destroyed or harmed.

The dead, however, did not return to life.

The Sleepers could not gain purchase. They could cause damage—and did— but the city over which they had claimed dominion was no longer a mortal city; it fought their commands, fought their intentions; all harm done to buildings or trees reverted, as if time itself had become a thread that the woman who was Lord of these lands had pulled. She wove with it. She gestured, and the earth quieted and would not respond to the Sleepers again within the confines of the city. So, too, the wind and the water, and the harbor had been rebuilt around the absence of the mountain.

The sky was a clear azure, the sun high; a glimpse of the moons could be seen in the height of the daylight sky.

Adam of Arkosa's palm retained contact with the back of the Matriarch's neck, but not because by doing so he could preserve her life; he knew that she would take no further injury from the Sleepers. Not yet. She might stand thus for hours, for days, for a week, and their attacks would no longer reach her. He thought nothing would.

In his days in Averalaan, this strange, crowded city, he had healed many people. Levec had taught him everything he could; had lectured him—almost endlessly, like any angry Ono—about the things he could not. Nothing Adam had learned in the Houses of Healing, nothing he had learned in House Terafin, had prepared him for this. He knew the Matriarch. He knew her well; he had called her back from the brink of death, and some part of her remained within him. And he could feel that, feel the familiarity of it—but it was one small echo, and it was almost overwhelmed by the constant, shifting, subtle differences.

This is what he might have felt had he attempted to heal a countless number of people simultaneously, something that was—according to Levec—impossible. And dangerous. Adam, young and foolish, had asked how something could be both impossible *and* dangerous, and Levec's icy response had made clear that this subject was closed. It was *impossible*. Adam should not even attempt it.

When Adam had nodded and ducked his head, Levec's growl could be heard anywhere in the very large room.

"Use your head for something other than toughening the palm of my hand, boy."

Some of the students found this intimidating. It made Adam feel almost nostalgic.

"The body knows its healthy state. But it can't *achieve* that state without the healer's intervention. We move the body toward health. We remind it of its natural state."

"But—time—"

"*No.*" One growl of an exhalation followed. ". . . And yes. The young always remember the wrong words at inconvenient times. I would not waste breath, but you are dangerously powerful. Dangerous to yourself, for the most part.

"There is a reason we do not attempt to heal two people at the same time. It is not only a matter of time, but a matter of . . . state. It is far too easy to get those states confused."

Adam had considered this in the lee of Levec's ferocious glare. "We might . . . mix them up?"

"It is possible to confuse the best state for each, yes. It is possible to cause an overlap which is *not* good for the patient. Each person obeys the laws of their natural bodies, when no harm is done. They will age in certain ways, their hair and eyes will be certain colors, their skin certain tones. Consider those natural laws. No single person can be two people at once, and no single body can bear the weight of two different laws. It is possible to force them to make the attempt.

"It will not turn out well."

But the Matriarch was more than one physical law. More than two. The whole of her body was now a blur beneath his hand. It was a familiar blur, but the edges, the limits that a body naturally set upon Adam's talent, were so rough he thought that healing her would possibly break something in her. But she was not like the earth; was not like the Arianni. She was mortal, but . . . a multitude of mortality, standing in one place.

The dead man shook his head. "Let her go," he said, in rough Torra. "She is safe now."

Adam understood the ways in which the dead could drive the living; this was new, and were it not for the obvious comfort the Matriarch derived from this dead man's presence, he might have been afraid. He was not. He had learned, however, that it was unwise to let the dead rule the living, and he turned to look at Angel.

Angel's expression robbed him, briefly, of breath. He was of an age with the Matriarch, but seemed much younger, his eyes shadowed, his hair hanging in a loose and unruly frame around his gaunt face. He had lowered his sword.

Adam lifted one hand in slow, deliberate den-sign. The movement was enough to draw Angel's attention. Angel did not speak but signed instead; his hand was trembling. Of course, it was. He was injured, and those injuries had not been miraculously healed as the city itself was being healed.

Adam let his hand fall away from the Matriarch. He walked beneath the lines of trees at the wall's height, covering the two yards that separated Angel from his Lord. Angel's eyes narrowed, and he shook his head. Adam, however, ignored this. Angel, he knew, would never hurt him. When the healer, half Angel's age, held out a hand, it was steady.

Angel's grimace deepened as he shed the haunted look that had stolen all other familiar expressions. "This is nothing."

"Do not make me summon Levec."

At that, while the Sleepers drove themselves into and around the Matriarch, Angel laughed.

And the Matriarch turned instantly toward the sound of laughter.

Every singular instance of The Terafin turned toward that sound, and for a moment, it could be heard by all of Averalaan, just as she herself heard it. It was warm, that laugh; it implied a history that was not all pain, and it implied—by its very existence—a future that would likewise not be all pain, no matter how grim the present.

And the words of one man, she lofted above the din of every other voice, even her own. Levec's words. "If you summon me, he's not the one who will be in trouble." Other voices joined in Angel's laughter, even Adam's: the voices of Levec's healer-born students. His colleagues. Anyone who had history with the healer not known for the sweetness of his temperament or patience.

On the height of the walls, Angel ATerafin placed his palm firmly across Adam's, and Adam did what he could to staunch the flow of Angel's blood, his lips folding in a frown that was familiar to anyone in the den who had seen him heal.

Angel did not speak. He did not ask Adam if The Terafin had somehow changed. The answer was obvious to both of them. Nor did he ask Adam how. Even had he, Adam would have had no way of answering, because words could not convey what his gift had revealed. Nor did he think it necessary. Angel would not leave her service while she lived.

Or while he lived.

Adam, however, said, "She must stand only for a handful of hours now. And she—"

He stopped speaking.

In the heart of the city—in what would *become* the heart of the city—the white tree that she had planted from the captive breath of a dying frostwyrm began to grow. It had been as tall as the tree of fire when it had first pulled itself from the dragon's corpse; Angel had thought it twin in some fashion to that tree, whose full growth had been modest in comparison to the rest of the trees in Jay's forest until the very end.

It was not; he saw that now. White bark, white branches, and delicate, translucent leaves reached toward the wall's heights until, at last, it stopped. It was now taller than the tallest of the Kings' trees, and it caught light, absorbed it, and reflected it as if it were the heart of winter—the heart of what made winter beautiful.

He had not expected that, but as he watched, the leaves that had formed a burning crown across Jay's brow at last unraveled, and those leaves now flew to that same clearing. They did not bind the tree, did not attempt to melt it or destroy it; instead, they sought purchase in the same ground, some little distance away from the most obvious of the ice tree's roots.

The earth did not devour them; it made room for them, as if they were seeds. Angel watched as those seeds—like all the seeds of Jay's various trees—blossomed. He recognized the tree of fire as it emerged, leaves of flame—white, orange, gold, red—budding and unfurling as branches thickened and spread. And this tree also stretched for the sky, gaining a height it had never achieved in the heart of Jay's forest.

It grew until it was the height of, the width of, the tree of ice, and its flames were reflected in leaves that had been almost without color. But these trees now looked oddly unbalanced to Angel, as if they were two points of a triangle and the third had not yet been decided. He glanced at Adam, who still held his hand; Adam's eyes were closed, his brows drawn together.

One of the Sleepers flew down to the trees. He was bleeding, but everyone on the walls, with the exception of Adam, had been.

"Shadow."

The amorphous cat hissed.

"Snow. Night."

Angel did not understand what Jay intended. The cats were not pleased to be drawn away from their battle; the Sleepers were worthy foes. But he watched as the cats rippled, briefly, their colors and fur solidifying, their shapes almost retracting into themselves. Night roared in rage when an Arianni blade swept through his left flank. It was not a deep wound, but in Night's opinion, it should never have happened at all.

He'd blame Jay.

She didn't seem to notice.

Something flew from each of the cats; they looked almost like leaves to Angel's narrowed eyes, although they might have been feathers. At this distance, they had no color. But they, like the leaves of fire, were accepted by the earth, and from those leaves or feathers, the third tree grew. It was—no surprise—taller than either the tree of fire or the tree of ice, although not by much, and while its branches spread and grew, the buds across them remained closed.

Meralonne watched the trees grow in almost silent wonder. He seemed young, even youthful, to Sigurne's eye, and his own eyes were bright with excitement. He, who had lived millennia, had not yet grown jaded enough that excitement was beyond him. Sigurne, however, offered a wary awe.

"How long?" she asked.

He did not answer until the third tree outstripped the first and second in height, and even then, his answer was a chuckle. After a pause, in which it became clear that the existence of buds must remain a promise for the future, he turned to Sigurne. "How long?"

"How long can she stand?"

"Against my brethren?" His smile was a mix of both joy and sorrow. "Had you asked me in my youth, my answer would be different. But even against Darranatos as he was, she could stand thus indefinitely. The cities of man were proof against even gods—as long as those gods remained beyond the walls."

"And we are—we were—powers in the ancient world, but we were not the equal of gods."

"You were sent to kill a god."

"Ah. Yes. But we were four, then, and the fifth was Moorelas. It was not our hand that could slay that god. Even had we abandoned Moorelas, even had we taken to the field of that god's stronghold with our full power, our own armies, I do not believe we would have been enough."

"Moorelas was mortal."

"Yes, Sigurne. But the weapon he carried was a weapon made by gods and the maker-born when magic was freely available, and the wilderness was all of the world. That blade was lost—lost to us all—when we failed in our charge. The mortal world could not contain it, and I believe it slept as we slept."

Sigurne was silent for a brief moment. "That was informative in a fashion, but it was not an answer."

"Against us? She could stand until exhaustion drove her from her feet—and even then, Sigurne, when she slept, I believe she could defend what she is, even now, building. Do you not understand what the trees signify?" When Sigurne did not reply, he said, "This is the heart of her domain now. This city *is* her forest. She will take the weapons that are wielded against her, and she will forge from them weapons of her own; she will make them a part of her lands.

"It is not how other cities were built," he added.

"The cats, then? Surely they were not wielded against her?"

"I believe she intends that they never be wielded against her again. I admit I am surprised that they offered what she asked of them—but it is done." He closed his eyes; he was almost trembling. "But she will not have to stand until exhaustion drives her to sleep. Do you not know the date?"

Sigurne's eyes narrowed as she considered the question and widened slightly as she answered. "Lattan."

"On the longest day the roads are open, and those who have been constrained by the fraying rules of an ancient covenant are free to travel."

Sigurne did not ask him what was to happen. Instead, she turned, once again, to the trees. "Will you take me to them?" she asked.

The air was all of his reply; it lifted her gently off her feet. "We will wait there," he told her. "For it is most assuredly there . . ." He did not finish.

Nor did Sigurne press him.

The golden fox found Finch by the side of the great tree. Finch noted that he took care not to approach that tree, although he offered no disrespect. He did not display the same respect for Finch. "Come," he said. "It is almost time, and we are wanted."

"I highly doubt we are wanted," Finch replied. She glanced, once, at the ancient tree, and heard the rustle of what might have been a chuckle in the leaves overhead.

"Very well. You will, of course, be insignificant—but *I* will be wanted."

"And where is Jarven?"

"He is not here. You are." There was an edge in the fox's voice now, and Finch remembered his teeth. He looked at Teller, sniffed, and waited with a growing aura of petty impatience.

Teller raised a hand in den-sign, and Finch, schooling her face, refused to grimace. Instead, she dusted leaves off her skirt and made her way to the fox's side. But she did not leave Teller behind.

Teller straightened his own clothing; it was clothing meant for the right-kin's office, but not perhaps in its current state. He then offered the fox a respectful bow, bending in time with Finch as she opened her arms and lifted the golden elder.

"Come, come. Do not linger, or we will be late."

"Late for what?"

The fox sighed heavily, theatrically, and refused to answer. But Finch could feel a tremble in the whole of his slight body. For a moment she thought he was afraid.

"Anyone wise would know some fear," the fox said, although she had been far too wise to put that thought into words. "But anyone alive would be . . . excited. Yes, I believe that is the word. It is a pity that the eldest does not choose to uproot himself or fashion a more mobile form that he might occupy. I have never completely understood why, but it is irrelevant; he may miss the event on his own."

* * *

It was day above the city that had once been Averalaan. As the accumulation of minutes inevitably became hours, sunlight recolored the edge of the sky, shifting the azure that it had become upon The Terafin's ascension into a blend of brilliant colors. It was an astonishing sunrise, a thing of beauty; it was almost impossible for anyone watching to consider it an omen.

Sunrise.

Dawn. True dawn.

Although the sun had not fully risen, people began to gather beneath the boughs of the three trees, as if those trees were the Kings' trees, and the place they grew, the Common. Some of those people were mortal; many were not. There was, for the moment, uneasiness but no fear as they stood almost side by side; they were all there by The Terafin's grace. As if the combat above their heads were the displays of lights and magical fire offered by the magi every year, they watched. Nothing disturbed them.

No enterprising merchants were there to take advantage of the crowds, but the bards returned from the safety of the forest, armed only with their chosen traveling instruments, and they moved among the crowd, their voices raised. They sang the song The Wayelyn had written.

So, too, The Wayelyn himself. He sang as history unfolded; sang while the darkness of the sky receded and dawn heralded the beginning of a new day. His performance encouraged participation; timid voices—some with a questionable sense of tune—joined in. But when Kallandras began to sing, people fell silent—even the Master Bards of Senniel. They had a talent in common, but the power of Kallandras' singing was not the product of talent alone; his experience was not their experience, and his power had always been the greater power.

Thus did the dawn of Lattan begin. It was the beginning of a new age.

At the height of the walls, The Terafin looked down upon her city; she gestured and the gates—for there were gates, now, such as had never existed in the city in any of its historical iterations—rolled open. Just beyond the shadow of the walls themselves stood a small army, and at their head, on the back of a white, white stag, rode a woman in robes of gold and green and azure; her hair was a platinum sheen, more like silk than hair, and it fell past her shoulders, down her back. Almost, it seemed to blend with the coat of her mount.

All voices stilled except Kallandras of Senniel's, and it was to the accompaniment of his song that the Summer Queen at last entered the city.

But from the moment the gates rolled open, the aerial combat ceased. All motion above the ground, and almost all motion upon it, ceased as well. This exalted visitor gazed at the city, at its new buildings, and at the inhabitants gathered around the three great trees, with eyes a luminous silver-green. She nudged her mount forward. Behind her came the rest of her entourage, an entourage fit in all ways for a Queen that had walked out of legend, out of myth, or, more intimately, out of children's story.

Two of these, were it not for her commanding presence, might have been familiar to some of the watchers: the Guildmaster of the Order of Makers and his apprentice, missing for over a decade. But they were arrayed in strange clothing, and they were mortal, and the onlookers might be forgiven if their eyes passed over them as they walked.

All eyes, however, fell upon the mortal man who sat astride the Summer Queen's mount. He was, unlike the maker-born, wearing ratty clothing that had seen better years, and his feet were bare; his hair was dark, and covered half his face, and his hands were sun-bronzed but dirty, as if he had been plucked from the gardens of the Queen in mid-task, and ordered to accompany her in a singular position of honor.

They felt curiosity and a sharp sense of envy—for if such as he could ride with such a Queen, might not that Queen then look with kindness upon them?

Angel and Adam, on the walls above the procession, stiffened. Angel signed; Adam signed. Neither were foolish enough to disturb the arrival of the Summer Queen with something as profane as spoken words.

But the cats—complaining—came to them at an unspoken command; Shadow gathered Jay, Snow took Adam, and Night grudgingly accepted Angel's weight. Very grudgingly. Nothing would silence these cats.

And they *were* cats again. They were solid enough to ride, solid enough to touch. They circled, their passengers on their backs, as if they couldn't quite see the point in landing; they certainly let it be known that they couldn't see a reason for all the *fussing*.

Their voices broke the Summer Queen's spell, and people who could see nothing but Ariane at the head of her procession now frowned and looked up at the sky in disapproval.

Angel was tempted to point out that the only fussing at the moment came from the cats themselves, but decided against it; the cats would argue. Vociferously.

As it was, they flew loudly, roaring to indicate that whoever happened to be under the spot they intended to land on had better move. There was nearly a pileup as the cats predictably chose the same spot on which to land. Angel, however, was off Night's back practically before his paws touched stone; he was running toward the Summer Queen as if he couldn't see her at all.

He was joined in his headlong rush by Arann, in the newly dented armor the Chosen of Terafin wore. Jester, Finch, and Teller were more circumspect; they walked. They walked quickly.

Nor did the Summer Queen mistake their approach for aggression, and understanding that the Summer Queen was guest here, not monarch, her escort did not leap in front of her, bristling with wrath and weapons. She glanced at the mortal she had deigned to carry this far and spoke a single word. He did not dismount; instead, the air lifted him, buoyed him, carrying him silently until the flats of his bare feet touched the city streets. He stumbled, righted himself, and turned to look at the den. His den.

Angel reached him first; he was not burdened by the weight of armor that slowed Arann—although not, truthfully, by much. He didn't stop short, but opened his arms and nearly knocked Carver over.

Arann's added weight accomplished what Angel's charge had not, and the three of them teetered before falling unceremoniously at the feet of the Summer Queen. Jester, Finch, and Teller arrived before the three had managed to sort out the tangle of arms and legs and emotion, but didn't join them on the ground. They were aware of the woman who watched, a small, quirked smile lessening the austerity of her regal expression.

Last to come was Jay, and she made her way to the side of her den slowly, her hesitance clear, as if she knew viscerally that she no longer belonged with them. She lifted her hands and dropped them perhaps a half dozen times. She had no words, and den-sign required at least some of them.

Angel noticed. Had he been less encumbered, he would have caught those shifting hands and dragged her into the center of the den, Ariane and the gathered host be damned. He couldn't, but he did try.

Jay then collected herself and turned toward the Summer Queen; she froze again. This time, Shadow's growl caught her attention. She flushed and dropped her chin in the Weston nod offered between equals.

Ariane waited.

"Welcome," Jay said, "to Averalaan."

"That is not the name I hear the trees speak," Ariane replied, her voice gentle and amused.

"No? No, then. But it is the name its people speak. I am one of them. I was born in the hundred holdings. I've spent my life in Averalaan. The city . . . is mine to protect, mine to defend, mine to keep safe. It is *not* something I own, and it is not . . . something I rule."

She turned, then, and waited.

The Twin Kings' procession was far more ragged, far less impressive, than the Summer Queen's had been. Once people had caught sight of that Queen, it was almost impossible to voluntarily look away; she had cast no spell, but no spell, no enchantment, was required. Her presence alone commanded attention, and held it.

But . . . Jay waited. She waited in a silence that was broken only by the movement of the Twin Kings, and the Twin Kings—armed now with the rod and the sword that Fabril had crafted for their use—made their way to stand by her side. They each offered Jay the nod that was offered to equals, and she replied in kind.

They offered Ariane bows, instead.

Ariane inclined her head, but the amusement faded as she regarded Jay from eyes of silver, of green.

"The Terafin has greeted you in our stead," King Cormalyn said, his golden eyes shining. "She is the heart of our defenses, and the city hears her voice."

"And I serve the Twin Kings," Jay said quietly. "They are my monarchs. I am their liege." She glanced at King Cormalyn.

The King nodded. "The Terafin is, of course, ruler of her own lands, and it is our understanding that she walked those lands to reach you. But we have enemies in common. You are welcome in the city. You are welcome in the Empire, should you choose to travel it."

Ariane's mount knelt. She dismounted with the ease of long practice; the flow of her skirts did not impede her at all. "I accept your hospitality, and I offer you—should you desire it—the hospitality of my own court, for that court and the many roads that might be traveled to reach it, is open now.

"But I must speak a moment with your liege, for promises were made between us, and not on your behalf." She bowed, then, so gracefully, so perfectly, it robbed witnesses of breath. When she rose, there was silence, even from the god-born.

Jay waited on the nod of the Kings before she spoke. And when she spoke, her voice was . . . a tangle of voices. She was pale, and it seemed to Angel that she trembled enough that she could not quite be seen clearly. "You are welcome in my forest. There are those among my own followers who are eager to see you again, and they cannot easily leave my lands. There are those," she added, "who can, and they are here. But they understand why you have come, and they will not interfere."

"I find your choice of buildings interesting."

"They are what I know best."

"I do not think you have seen many buildings such as that one." Ariane turned toward the cathedral.

"Only as ruins."

"Very well. I have returned to you your kin; I have paid the earth's price in his stead. And now, I believe your city contains some of my kin."

Jay nodded.

The Summer Queen walked, and the crowd parted in an instant to allow her free passage. They backed into the people behind them; stepped on the feet of strangers, in a rush to avoid her. To avoid impeding her. And she accepted this as her due; of course, she did.

It was Teller who reached Jay's side first; Teller who touched her sleeve; his grip on her elbow tightened, and Angel could see his knuckles whiten. Jay did not appear to notice. But she didn't appear to notice Ariane, either. She was trembling in place.

Finch joined Teller, grabbing Jay's other arm. Shadow hissed but did not intervene; he muttered the word *stupid* loudly enough that Ariane turned to glance over her shoulder. Satisfied that the word was not meant for her, she then proceeded to ignore the great, gray cat.

Jay had not, Angel realized, dismounted.

"Shadow," she whispered.

"Yes, yes, *yessssss*." He pushed off the ground.

"Home."

The white cat and the black cat joined their brother.

But Teller did not let go of Jay's arms, and this proved awkward; Jay didn't seem to realize they were there. Shadow however, did. He growled. It was a warning growl, but it had no teeth in it.

Teller, however, shook his head. "Jay."

"I have to go," Jay whispered.

"I'm not telling you not to. But—take us. Take us with you."

Finch frowned at Teller, signing with her free hand. Teller signed back. And Angel once again climbed up on Night's back. Night shrieked in outrage but made no attempt to unseat him. To Finch, Angel signed, *I'll go.* He made the same gesture in Teller's direction though he knew Teller wouldn't see it. Teller was a shade of gray-green that made no sense. They'd *won.* They hadn't saved everyone, no—but they hadn't lost everyone, either. Jay was home.

Carver was home.

And Teller was terrified. Teller, who had looked into the Oracle's crystal.

"Teller." Teller nodded without turning. "Get on Snow's back. We'll go to-gether."

"You don't—"

"We won't let her out of our sight. We'll go *together*, but—we have to go. Look at Jay."

Teller swallowed. He had to force his hand to unclench, and even then, seemed to be fighting every screaming instinct to do it—he might have held on to the edge of a cliff with just such determination, when the alternative was a fall that would kill him.

Turning on Night, Angel smiled at Finch. "Get him home to Merry—but maybe have him changed and bathed first." The black cat pushed off the ground as Shadow did; Snow was not far behind, Teller clinging to his back.

The cats did not fly to the Isle. They did not return to the Terafin manse. Their flight was short indeed; it led them to the steps of the cathedral—a cathedral reformed by the Sleepers into a thing of spires and light and windows. It was a palace that had no equal, and it was solid, it was real. Angel understood Teller's reluctance then. But he understood, as Shadow landed, that *this* was home now.

Home for Jay. And home for Angel.

He dismounted as Jay did, reaching out to offer Teller a hand, which Teller accepted, unseeing. They followed Jay through doors that were already open, into a hall that was taller, by far, than any hall Angel had ever seen. They were dwarfed by it, insignificant. But Jay . . . was not. She walked as if in a dream, and Teller rushed to catch up with her. He grabbed her sleeve again. Angel didn't think it necessary but walked with care to one side of her shadow.

The gray cat was content for the moment to allow Angel the privilege of his spot, and that should have been a clue. Night and Snow took instantly to the air, and Angel thought he understood why the halls were so large, so tall. The cats would live here.

"Yes," Shadow said, although Angel had not spoken. "This is where *we* will live. But it is where *you* will live, as well."

"Are we supposed to move the entire Terafin manse here?"

"She *could*."

But Jay said, "No."

And Teller said, "That's not up to you. It would be up to the regent."

"It's up to me. I'm The Terafin."

Teller's smile was slender, but it was genuine. "The Chosen serve you," he pointed out. "They're not going to agree to live across the bridge if you're liv-ing here."

"The Chosen serve *me*," Jewel snapped, "and they'll follow my orders."

"They're not House Guard. They're *Chosen*."

She wheeled, beneath that vaulted, light filled ceiling. "You have *no idea* what could happen to *anyone* who shares a roof with me. You have no idea how dangerous it could be. The foundations of this building were created to jail the Sleepers. To keep them—and their dreams—from destroying the city that was built above them, do you understand?"

Teller did not answer.

Angel, however, understood. And he understood that, as she gave vent to worry and frustration, her voice lost the echoes that made it seem . . . too much like the voice of a god.

"I can't go back to the Terafin manse," she said, her voice dropping. "I can't. I'll survive anything I—I dream of. I'll survive anything I do in—in my sleep. You saw what happened to Ellerson and Carver."

"That wasn't you—"

"It wasn't me, no. But what I do would be much worse, now. The Sleepers weren't awake. The Warden of Dreams interfered."

"They were here, though—and they still affected the manse—"

"They were in the ruins of a building. But it was made of the same stone as the basements in *Avantari*. And it is whole now. It will remain whole."

"Jay—"

Shadow growled. To Angel's surprise, he was growling *at* Jay, not Teller. He did step on Angel's foot, however. "You are *stupid*. He is *right*."

"But I can't—"

"*We* can. We can, *stupid* girl."

"But we don't *want* to," Night added, from the heights.

Shadow's roar should have shattered glass. For miles. Snow hissed laughter.

"We can't move everything all at once," Teller continued. "But the Chosen, at least. And the rest of the den."

"There's no place—"

Shadow hissed.

Jay bowed her head and surrendered. She looked up at Teller, and her eyes threatened tears—a storm of tears—but she would not allow them to fall where anyone could see them. "Fine," she said, voice gruff and momentarily completely singular. "But you work out the details with Finch. You can let go of my arm," she added. "I'm not going anywhere."

He signed: *promise?*

And she signed: *promise.*

Teller looked to Angel, and Angel said, "Go talk to Finch. I'm staying put."

And that offered Teller whatever comfort he could take; he did leave then. He tried not to look back, but failed several times. Jay did not move again until he was out the doors.

She then turned to Shadow. Shadow growled—at Angel—and stalked ahead. "It's too hard," she whispered. "To be just one thought, just one thing, to see just one reality."

Angel shrugged. "There's no reality that contains you that scares me. Except the ones that I'm not in."

"And they exist," a familiar voice said quietly. Old Rath. He had not aged, but then again, the dead didn't. "Go, Jewel. Let me speak a moment with Angel."

Angel didn't like it. Shadow, however, sniffed dismissively and growled when he made to follow Jay.

"Her fears are not unfounded; they are not foolish. I spent some time as a captive in the Hidden Court, and I learned. About the Cities of Man. About the Sen. It is not something I would *ever* have chosen for Jewel—but in the end, it is not something I chose. She chose. I think you are beginning to understand what she is and what she fears.

"She will create a space for herself; she will live in it. Think of that space as The Terafin's personal chambers. Within that space, nothing will be stable."

"Nothing but you?"

"I am dead," Rath agreed. "She will—ah, she *should*—be able to speak with you. With all of you. But . . . she will not be able to do it often. It will be important," he added. "To the shape of the city, to its continuity. It will be important to the Kings and the rule of law. And it will be important to her. But she will be trapped here until—and unless—she decides that she no longer cares what happens to the city and the people in it.

"You think she would never decide that. But that future does exist. She is, at heart, mortal. And she never could stand to live alone, in a silent home."

Thinking of the apartment in the twenty-fifth holding, Angel said, "She won't have to."

"That was not real."

"Does it matter?"

"Yes, oddly enough. The wilderness understands reality; it merely changes it with ease. It can create dreams and phantasms, but those who appear to live in those dreams are not actually alive; they are . . . part of the landscape. They conform as nightmares or dreams conform. The only place in which that would not be true is the heart of chaos, and that is nowhere near here."

Angel thought of the tangle but did not disagree. "What do we have to do?"

"What you have done," Rath said quietly. "Survive. And love her."

"How—how often can we speak with her?"

"One hour a day? Perhaps up to three. You would have to ask Cessaly."

Angel's eyes widened.

"It is Cessaly's maker-born gift. It was created by the greatest maker the world has ever known. She . . . was not the one who explained it," he added, his grin wry. "And I do not understand the whole of it. There is some risk, because in order to create the materials, something of great value to one of the firstborn was destroyed. Not that this made much of a difference to Cessaly," he added. "She is a miracle."

"Are you telling me that if she hadn't made something for Jay, we could never talk to her?"

"Not and be guaranteed to survive, no. Or at least that was my understanding." He smiled. "I will be here—and the Sen of the ancient cities did not have that. I am . . . part of Cessaly's making; the Winter Queen—or Summer—no longer binds me. Jewel does. It is a binding I would have chosen for myself, and it is a binding that will be of aid to her. What she wants, Angel, is what she always wanted. Her family and her home. She will have the power to keep that safe now."

"But we won't have her."

"How often did you see her when she was acting Terafin?"

Angel said nothing.

"The difference, now, is that you will have to see her. She will require that. Because in some fashion, she understands the difference between reality and dreaming—it is just very, very slender at the moment."

"Will she—can she leave?"

"For one hour a day—but . . . I don't recommend it."

"Then this is just a cage for her—"

"Yes. And it is a cage of her choosing because she could not see any other way of preserving the things that matter most to her. She would have willingly died to do so. And she is not dead." He seemed to exhale. "The Kings need her now. There is a god walking this world. She can secure this city against him."

"Is she . . . is she still mortal?"

"What do you think, Angel?"

Angel bowed his head. "I think we'll be here. Is there a specific time?"

"No. But in the wilderness, it is the change of light that marks the day, and she is *of* the wilderness now. Go to your den. Tell them. Angel—I will stay. Until she leaves to cross the bridge to Mandaros and his Halls of Judgment, I will not leave her. She is kin to me; I failed her once, but I will never fail her again."

Epilogue

THE MORTALS GATHERED IN the clearing that would, in time, become the Common, came from all walks of mortal life known to the city, for there were Kings, Queens, and the Princess Royale, and there were beggars in their threadbare, splinter-dusted rags. They had lost the city that had been home to them for all their lives, but a city was, as they stood bearing witness, being rebuilt, and if that city was marked—forever—by the losses of a single day, it held the faint promise of hope.

Hope was its own burden, its own pain. But better to carry it than to set it aside forever, no matter how sharp its edges when it shattered yet again.

The Summer Queen, as she was called and as she came to be remembered, walked across the stones that radiated outward into the city, a web of streets that held no interest for her, and the crowd gave her room. Even the Kings themselves. But her followers seemed to melt into the trees at the edge of that clearing, until only she remained.

If her isolation was a signal, it was a signal that the crowd did not understand. They did not approach her; they did not speak, did not dare to tread even upon her shadow, so powerful was her presence. They followed with gaze alone until she passed by. Where she walked, flowers grew in her passage— even through the stone; the sun seemed to follow her, and it seemed to the witnesses that that sun would never set if she stood beneath it.

But she came, at last, to a stop.

Kneeling, heads bent, were three men. No, three of the Winter people. They wielded no weapons, and they wore no armor; their brows were unadorned. They did not speak, nor would they until she had given them leave.

She did not do so.

Turning to look over her shoulder, she frowned into a crowd that had diminished. One young woman bowed her head and separated from that crowd, as if at silent command. She was shorter than the Summer Queen, and younger; her hair was a ruddy brown, too light be remarkable. Her skin was sun-dark, her hands sun-dark; she wore sandals on her feet.

To this stranger, the Summer Queen said, "There are only three. Was there, then, no fourth?"

And the stranger approached until she reached the Summer Queen's side. She did not answer the question immediately but considered it as if the answer to the simple question—three or four—was both momentous and difficult. At length, she shrugged.

The Summer Queen's eyes narrowed, their green losing warmth. "It is not a question that is beyond your ability to answer."

"It is not a question," the woman countered, "that is *mine* to answer." She smiled. "I have never chosen to live in your Court, sister, and even had I, you are not the lord I serve."

"And you claim to serve now?" She eyed the woman's clothing with obvious disdain. "The appearance of servitude does not become you."

"No? Ah. No." And speaking thus, the woman shook her head. What had been mousy hair became ebon; she gained height, lost the traces of wrinkles, of age, that she had adopted. She then turned to the kneeling men. "Whether or not they were three or four, they are three now. Will you not bid them rise?"

Ariane did not answer.

"They were—they are—worthy foes. And you will not see their like again, I fear. Not in your Court. Were I as you, I would forgive."

"No, sister, you would not. But it is Summer, not Winter, and in the dawn of Summer, there is warmth."

"And at the end of Summer, deserts," Calliastra replied, but softly, softly.

"Narianatalle."

The prince in the middle of this kneeling formation slowly lifted his face; his cheeks were glistening. He opened his mouth, but no words emerged; his eyes were shadowed, dark.

None who could see him could doubt the strength of his feeling for this Summer Queen; none could fail to see his yearning. He made no attempt to hide his tears. Nor did he rise or otherwise move.

"Am I now so lessened?"

He tried to answer. He failed.

"Am I not the White Lady?"

Silence.

"Sister—"

She lifted a perfect hand, and Calliastra fell silent. "Of the princes of my Court, of the princes left me, you were my best. I did not doubt you; when the Lord of Shadows called your brothers, you did not hear his voice. I chose you."

He bowed his head, seeing, in the end, no forgiveness and no mercy, and accepting—as all the Arianni must now accept—that he deserved none.

"My enemy once again walks the mortal world—as, now, do I. The Sen of this new city is my ally, and it is on her behalf that I have traveled."

He did not lift his head.

"I did not destroy you when your disobedience resulted in failure. But the effects of that failure abound. I paid the price demanded of me in order to weaken my enemy—but my enemy remains." She lifted a hand. "You have slept. It was my hope—for even I had hope—that you would have some chance to redeem that failure." Her tone made clear, then, that no such hope remained.

"Tell me, Narianatalle, am I lessened by my choices?"

"Lady."

"I cannot trust you, in the end, to do what must be done." She raised a second hand. "But you were mine, and dear to me; you were birthed in an age of joy, of beginnings. I offer you a choice. Live as you have lived, in exile but awake." She did not give voice to the alternative.

Narianatalle, however, understood it. He rose. Met her gaze, held it, read something in the unblinking green of a Summer that all his kin had yearned for during the passage of centuries. He did not smile; his expression was grave, stricken. But he did not argue. Instead, he approached the Summer Queen, understanding that the warmth of even Summer would be denied him while he lived.

"I will return to my Lady," he whispered. "And when you ride out, at last, against your enemy, I will be some part of your power."

"Yes." She held out a hand, and he placed both of his across her palm.

He began to fade. His eyes widened, and his mouth; there was no pain in his expression.

To the other two, she now offered the same choice, and as their brother had chosen, so, too, did they. It was Taressarian who said, "Life without you is a hell not of our choosing, Lady. Winter, Summer, the endless seasons of the world, are bitter indeed. If you preserved us, if you preserved your making, for the moment when you might, at last, ride against our ancient enemy, know that we are grateful to be of use, of service."

Only when they were gone did she turn. Lifting her face, she spoke a fourth name.

"Illaraphaniel."

"Do not," Meralonne told Sigurne softly, "interfere. Do not speak. Do not attempt to touch her with your magics."

Sigurne reached out to him; the ring on her hand was a band of white light. He was weeping, but silently; tears traveled the pale expanse of his face without pause.

"Understand that she created us. That the power that was lost to her at our birth returns to her now. She offered them a choice, and they chose."

"And if she offers you that same choice?"

He shook his head. "She will not. She will not, Sigurne. Remain here."

The wind carried Illaraphaniel to the White Lady; he folded instantly into an obeisance that even the Kings did not command of the least of their subjects.

"Rise," she said softly.

He obeyed, unfolding instantly. His expression, however, was shuttered when he at last met her gaze, as if to shield her from the knowledge of his pain.

"Of the four, Illaraphaniel, you were the only one who obeyed the commands given you. You failed, but that failure was not, in the end, of your making."

He was silent.

"Would you now return to me as completely as your brothers have chosen to do?" Before he could answer, she said, "It is an idle question. The god the mortals do not name now walks the world again. He is not what he once was—but neither am I. What your brothers returned to me will strengthen me, but I am one, not many. I will not offer you the same choice.

"The princes of my Court are few. The dreams of the ancient world elude me. But I will wake those who have slumbered in some fashion for the entirety of an age. You have seen Shandalliaran."

He said nothing.

"She will not return to me now. She cannot. But it is by her sacrifice that this final Summer has arrived." The Summer Queen turned, then, to stare into the distance, as if her gaze could pass through trees and buildings to catch a glimpse of the woman she had named. "And I will wake her sisters. I will wake my sisters.

"We have lost much, and much has changed. But here," she added softly, "I feel almost as if the world is new. Such is the power of the Sen." Her smile was gentle. "Will you return to my Court?"

"It is all I have ever desired."

"You failed me in the Winter," the Summer Queen said. "But it is the birth of Summer, and I accept that that failure was not on your head. If you are desirous of return, there will be a seat for you at my many tables, and a mount for you at my side."

"But not yet," a new voice said.

Jewel ATerafin stood by the side of the White Lady; she cast no shadow.

Meralonne's gaze narrowed; he offered no argument, drew no weapon. Sigurne thought it a close thing, and she moved to stand between Jewel and the mage upon whom she had relied for the entirety of her tenure in the Order of Knowledge. She was aware, as she did, that she was no match for either of these two powers—but the stay of hand would not be, in the end, because she could overpower either.

"Sen," the Summer Queen said.

"Summer Queen," Jewel said, bowing her head for a moment longer than necessary. Sigurne could hear the echoes that attended her first words, as if they were being repeated almost, but not quite, synchronously.

"Has he served you well?" the Queen asked The Terafin.

"He has. But his service was never mine to command; it was merely mine to request."

"To mortals, surely, there is little difference. But—ah. He is coming."

"The Oathbinder?"

"The Oathbinder," she replied. "And then, if he so desires, mortals will understand the weight and the cost of service."

Jewel frowned. "We understand it now."

"Not as you will. Not as Illaraphaniel and his brethren did. But you have interrupted our reunion for a purpose." She did not seem to resent this interruption.

Meralonne did.

"He has a role to play," Jewel said softly. "And if I understand what occurred yesterday, the Sleepers waited upon their heralds before they could unleash the full force of their waking power."

The Summer Queen inclined her head.

"His herald has yet to arrive."

The Summer Queen turned to Meralonne. Meralonne said nothing.

"And I am bidden to tell you that the sword has been found."

Winter existed for a moment in the eyes of the Summer Queen, a reminder—if one were necessary—that the Summer Queen was not mortal, would never be mortal; she was elemental, a power in a shape that seemed almost human, but that nonetheless drove tidal waves, earthquakes, avalanches.

"And who, within your own lands, would dare to give commands that you must heed?"

"My Kings," Jewel replied softly, "but it is not at their bidding I have come."

"My sister?"

"The Oracle?" Jewel grimaced. "No. She has yet to visit. But you know Evayne, and you will understand the significance of her words."

To Sigurne's surprise, the Summer Queen bowed her head; her eyes closed, becoming a fan of ivory lashes. She was silent, and that silence continued. No one broke it. Sigurne would not have dared; there was something now in that silence that spoke of pain, and the pain of the powerful oft turned to anger without warning.

In the end, she might have remained silent, but Meralonne moved. Meralonne knelt, once again, his head bowed almost to knee; his hands were trembling. Sigurne would remember that for as long as she lived, for she had never seen those hands tremble before. Almost, she turned to Jewel, to snap or bark, for although she understood what Jewel *was*, the history of all that she had been, from the moment Ararath of Handernesse, estranged from his house, had come to her tower stood between them.

But the Summer Queen's eyes opened in that moment, and she regarded the top of Meralonne's bent head. "And will you now turn away from your sole desire?" she asked, voice soft.

And, oh, his hands. He clenched them, making fists of them as if to hide the tremors. And it came to Sigurne that it was not merely the loss of the opportunity to once again serve by the side of this woman, but the pain of the loss of those he would never see again: the Sleepers. His brothers.

He did not resent the Summer Queen. Could not, Sigurne perceived. She had suspected it, had been *told* the truth of it, but had never understood the truth of it as she did now. There was nothing the Summer Queen could do to him, nothing she could demand of him, that would shake what he felt for her. Nothing.

"Lady," he whispered, as if he could not raise the volume at which he now spoke, "My herald has not arrived. As I, he has weathered your absence among the mortals. He is traveling as we speak, but there are difficulties; I do not believe he will arrive before you take your leave."

She waited in silence.

"And when he does arrive, I fear he will not be what my brothers' heralds were; he is not as I am, and the centuries—" he shook his head. "I—"

"Speak. I will not censure you."

"I failed. I failed you. I am not what I was then. But if the Sen is correct, if the word she carries is truth—"

"It is truth," the Summer Queen said. And her word, Meralonne could not doubt. Could never doubt.

"I would not return to you as failure if there is any other option." He lifted his face and met her gaze; his eyes were flashing silver. "And there is, Lady. What I failed to do—what *we* failed to do—I will do. I will redeem myself."

"You have no brothers now. What reason have you to believe that you alone can succeed now, when you could not succeed then?"

"He will not," Jewel said, "be alone." She avoided looking at Meralonne; avoided meeting his gaze. Her expression was not the serene expression of the Summer Queen; her sense of guilt was writ large across the lines of her face, the tighter line of her mouth.

"Will he not?" the Summer Queen asked softly.

"I *will* return, Lady. But I will not return to you as a failure, a failed prince, unless you command it."

"The choice is yours, Illaraphaniel." She smiled; her eyes, as Meralonne's, were shining, but hers were green now, the color of emeralds. Without turning or looking away, she said, "Sen, did my half-sister tell you where this sword might be found?"

"No."

"Then perhaps, Illaraphaniel, that will be your first task. Without it, we cannot hope to accomplish what must be accomplished; the Lord of the Hells is not Breodanir and did not prepare for his return; there are no ceremonies of release, no rites. No weapons, save one." She bent then; she did not bid Meralonne rise.

Bending thus, she brushed his forehead with her lips, her hand resting briefly upon his cheek. "Rise," she then said. "Rise and walk with me in these strange lands, for you have experience of them that I lack."

And he did as she bid. Sigurne did not move. They passed into the space that existed between the three great trees and were lost to sight almost instantly.

Sigurne then turned to Jewel.

"I cannot stay," Jewel told her. "I am not truly here. And I am sorry, Sigurne. I am sorry for Meralonne. I am sorry to have extended his exile. But . . ." she shook her head. As she searched for words, she began to fade, transparency becoming invisibility.

"And I thought you had been lost," the golden fox said. He sounded vaguely irritated, which for Finch should have been a warning that could not be ignored. She did her best to ignore it, however; the fox was once again lodged in her arms, as if she were a palanquin bearer and he were a temperamental patrician.

"Well," said the much rounder and darker talking animal that walked by their side, "You were obviously mistaken. I was, perhaps, dallying overlong. I returned," he added. "But I am, at the moment unrooted."

This soured the fox's mood further. Finch wanted to put him down and step away.

"I am unlikely," he said, voice tart, "to bite *you*. Anakton, however, is a different story."

"Come, come, let us not hold grudges. I did not want to sleep. But the world is waking. Can you not feel it? The air speaks. The earth speaks. The trees— ah. Did you hear what the Sen said?"

"I heard. It is not necessary to repeat it."

"We exist now in interesting times," the creature the fox had called Anakton said. "And I, for one, anticipate them. I may," he added, glancing up at Finch, "shadow Illaraphaniel. He will probably want company."

The fox stared, speechless, at the waddling fur-ball on the ground. "You have not changed *at all.*"

"Well, perhaps not—but that is our nature. Come, show me your Lord's lands."

"I cannot show you much while I am being carried by a mortal."

"Then walk on your *own* feet."

The fox sighed. Loudly. Finch might have called it a roar had a mortal creature made that noise. "Fine. Fine. But I feel that you will owe me a boon after this."

"You may add it to the many I already owe," Anakton replied.

Finch set the fox down. "Go back to the Terafin manse," the fox told her.

That was not, however, her intended destination. She walked through streets that were familiar; they had been much changed, but the basic shape and length remained the same. She made her way, unguarded, to what she was almost certain was the Merchant Authority, making her way up the equally unguarded front steps. They were wide, stone stairs, all of a single piece.

She entered the building, and saw that the main floor, with its wickets, had changed: it was much larger. Or perhaps it only appeared large because it was so empty; she was not certain she had ever seen it so shorn of activity as it was today. It was not, however, her destination. She slid into the halls, and from there, to the stairs that led to the Terafin offices. They had become her second home, in some fashion, and if Averalaan had been transformed so drastically, the rest of the Empire had not. The wheels of commerce, of trade, would—and must—continue to spin.

But not today. Not today.

She reached the doors of the outer office, and they rolled open; she had not touched them and wondered if she would ever have to touch them again. She wondered, as well, what the carpenters and stonemasons would do if every building in the city had been repaired or replaced as this one had. It might become a problem, but . . . later.

Lucille's desk still sat opposite the open doors, although Lucille did not occupy it. And Finch's office sat behind that desk. The doors were closed. In theory, they would be locked—or would have been locked—but she did not approach them immediately; she paused, instead, at the desk the junior clerks normally occupied. These were of wood, not stone; they were flawless, their surfaces missing the dents and dings and ink stains of the desks that had stood here before. So, too, the empty chairs tucked beneath them.

Terafin colors adorned the walls. Finch glanced at the ring she wore and dredged up something that resembled a smile before she headed, at last, toward the office she had shared with Jarven. She was not surprised when the doors rolled open before she reached them and was practical enough to think it useful for those days when she carried the tea service into the room. Those days, of course, were almost entirely behind her; Lucille now found it an offense to the dignity of House Terafin when Finch insisted on doing so. And Lucille was never wrong.

A half-smile touched her face as she entered the room. Lucille had survived. Lucille would—just as Finch now did—return to the offices that were her dominion.

She was not surprised to see Jarven.

Nor did he look particularly surprised to see her, although he did frown when their eyes met. His eyes were brown, as they had always been, but flecked with gold or light in a way that lent them an unnatural sheen.

"You meant to be unseen?" she asked, correctly judging his expression.

"Not for any nefarious reason, I assure you. I only attempt to sneak into my office when I am avoiding the interminable meetings foisted upon me by Lucille."

"True enough. I would have assumed you more likely to sneak out."

"It is practice, no more," Jarven replied. "Lucille's appointment book is refreshingly empty."

Finch cringed, which caused Jarven to chuckle. "Your Jewel certainly made changes in her reconstitution of this city; I do not think all of them will be welcome."

Some clearly weren't to Jarven. Finch glanced at the shelf on the wall to the right of the doors. There were books on it, but they were not immediately familiar to her. She winced. "Your protections?"

"She clearly does not appreciate the value—or the cost—of those books."

"You believe that monetary value will have meaning."

"Unless she is Sen of the Empire, of course it will." His eyes narrowed. "I perceive that you are attempting to be annoying; you have clearly come to the same conclusion."

She laughed. Laughed, crossed the room to Jarven, and hugged him tightly.

"Finch, please."

She did not release him.

"I am certain I have taught you far, far better than this. You are being practically maudlin. In public."

"No, just in front of you." She did not lift her face; her words were muffled.

"Finch." His voice gentled; he returned the hug, but stiffly. "Do you think I am leaving?"

"You are."

"I have been a set a task by the eldest. I cannot—yet—find a way to accomplish it, which is vexing. Regardless, you are no longer a child." He exhaled. "You were not a child when you first crossed the threshold of this office at The Terafin's command. You are not Lucille; you know who I am, and you accept it; you have no hope of changing it or altering it."

"I know who you were."

"That is fair. I am only beginning to learn the limits of who I now am. And the bindings; the laws are different, but they are frequently as much of a nuisance in an entirely different way."

"I don't want to be your enemy."

"Ah. No, and you never have. But what you are and what I am are not, now, the same. I had thought perhaps you would become the only protégé I might leave standing. But you do not have the ambition; you lack the necessary drive." He pulled back, gently releasing himself from her arms. "You will not be able to remain in this office if you take the House."

"I won't take the House."

"Ah." He shook his head. "You will take the House in all but name; you will, I think, have no choice."

"The name is important."

"Perhaps. But if you will not be The Terafin, I will not be yours to command."

She snorted. It was a very Lucille-like sound. "You weren't The Terafin's to command, either."

"I was, when it suited me. But it will not suit me in the same fashion. There is a much larger game, and The Terafin has knocked all the pieces off the closest board I might study. I am annoyed," he added. "There were demons in the city, but they are gone; I believe they were reduced to ash in the moment of her ascendance. She can defend this city, and these Kings—but that defense is required, Finch. And she cannot command the whole of the Empire in a like fashion."

"Why are you so certain?"

"I spoke with gods in the Between. They were *not* pleased to see me," he added, with an almost delighted smile. "And they had warnings of their own to offer. But if you are afraid of what I will do, be at peace. The game I wish to play—the game I wish to win—has moved. It has not ended."

"I will leave my office in your hands. I will retire."

"Will you leave the House Name?"

He looked almost offended. "You want to divest me of my *name*?"

"No. No, Jarven." She exhaled, let her arms drop to her sides, and straightened her shoulders. "I don't suppose you've taken a look at the files?"

"What files?"

She flinched. "They're gone as well?"

"Yes. Apparently, The Terafin did not consider the legal proof of our various negotiations any more valuable than she did my protections. I will, however, be present when Lucille does return to the office; I would not miss her reaction for the world."

Hectore's manor was the only manor in the more expensive holdings that had persisted through disaster, destruction and transformation unchanged. The people who had sought refuge on his grounds—where grass had been destroyed and flowerbeds depopulated beneath the growing press of far too many feet—were likewise unchanged; they had survived where others had not.

They were grateful to Araven, but they would return to homes that had been materially altered. Hectore was profoundly grateful that the Araven manse had sheltered and protected so many, but he resented the lack of improvements to his own manor. The gates, however, had been opened, and people had begun their exodus to their own homes. He imagined, gazing across the city, that there might be some conflict about those homes, but for the moment, that was not his problem.

He fidgeted, and his wife frowned. Her frown, however, was minor; he was among family, and if his family could not accept the minor gesture of irritation—or nerves—they could move out. It would, he thought, be safe now for them to do so. On the other hand, Nadianne seemed the most irritated—and the most tired—and he eventually retreated to the outdoors, to examine the damage done to his grounds.

It was there that he found Andrei.

Or, rather, there that Andrei found him.

"You have managed to survive," Hectore said, when he saw the shadow of Andrei's wings cut across the ruined grass.

Andrei landed and those wings—awkward wings, really, given their shifting composition—folded, disappearing as the Araven servant struggled for control of his physical form.

Sighing, Hectore turned to glare at him, folding his hands behind his back as he waited for Andrei to, as he put it, get ahold of himself.

"I *have* been busy," Andrei said, speaking through slightly clenched teeth.

"As have I," Hectore replied. "And under the watchful glare of my wife, who for some strange reason believes the personal dignity of Hectore comes second to the dignity of Araven. We have no food in the pantry," he added.

"None?"

"You missed the excitement. Apparently, half of the hundred decided that Araven was a safe haven during the upheaval. Look at this grass. And the flowerbeds!" Hectore shook his head. "My roses."

Andrei was, once again, himself.

No, Hectore thought, he was once again the self he had chosen to be decades ago. "Nadianne was worried for you."

"Apologies, Hectore. Things were somewhat . . . hectic."

"You were not injured?"

"Not appreciably."

"And The Terafin?"

Andrei was silent. Hectore, who had continued to examine damage—and calculate the cost of repairs—turned to look at his servant sharply. Andrei remained silent for a beat. Two. Three. Hectore's glare did not subside. "You must have seen her," he finally said. "It is said that everyone did."

"Everyone," Hectore said sharply, "who was not *in* Araven. What exactly did you do?"

"I protected your family," Andrei replied. "And now, I must alter those protections. She is Sen; her protections will now be the greater of the two." Andrei exhaled. "She will live in the cathedral that heralded the start of this . . . incident. Hectore—"

"She will not be the same."

"No. But I believe that she would be grateful for your company, should you choose to offer it. And it is certain that Finch will require some guidance if the city is to once again resume its place as the heart of the Empire."

Hectore would discover one advantage over the next few days: Araven's records had remained exactly as he had placed them after he had signed them.

Avandar Gallais had been injured in the aerial battle; Calliastra had called him reckless—but with a low, delighted laughter that still traversed his spine. No sign of injury remained; nor had he availed himself of the Terafin healerie, such as it was.

Then again, the Terafin healerie was not yet occupied. Nor were its many offices, or its many halls. That, however, was to be expected. He was not, after all, in the Terafin manse, but in the cathedral that would supplant it, if Jewel did not have her way.

The fact that the healerie existed at all made clear to the domicis that Jewel knew she would not, in the end, be able to keep her people out. Or perhaps her emotional desire was not in line with her intellectual decision. It mattered little.

He was not surprised to see Haval Arwood. The neat and fussy tailor appeared to be waiting for him. When Avandar approached, Haval bowed; it was a shallow bow, meant to indicate more respect than a simple nod of acknowledgment. Avandar returned that bow, measure for measure. When he rose, he moved, and Haval fell into step beside him.

"I have a favor to ask of you," the Terafin Councillor said.

Avandar indicated, by nod, that he could continue.

"I am aware of your condition. The Terafin made it clear some time in the past. My educated guess about your willing servitude concerns that condition. You came to serve her because you felt—or more likely, were told—that she could cure you."

"Yes."

"You could not know, at the time, what she would become."

"No."

"Did you suspect it?"

"Not until the first day of her predecessor's funeral rites."

"And you have come to ask her to alleviate you, at long last, of your burden."

Avandar was silent. He did not entirely understand Haval Arwood; the man was far, far too cunning not to be a threat. But Jewel had always trusted him; she trusted him still.

"Yes. Has she spoken of it to you?"

"No."

"Then this is a favor to you and not a request from my Lord."

"Indeed."

"Ask it, then."

"You are Warlord."

Silence.

"I have had some time to discuss it with those who would know you by that name. You are not invulnerable, but your injuries do not kill you, no matter how severe. Decapitation does not kill you. Nor does fire or lava, although I believe you are not immune to pain."

"Not at all."

"You have never served a Sen."

"No."

"And you served but one god."

Avandar nodded.

"Jewel can grant you what you now desire."

Avandar stopped walking. "And you wish me to decline what she offers."

Haval nodded.

"You wish me to decline the only reason that I came to her, the only reason that I agreed to serve her."

"Yes." Haval held up one hand before Avandar could speak again. "But on the condition that you will not outlast her. She has never feared for you. Because you came to her as domicis, she has never truly feared you, either. And no, I did not consider that wise. Now I do not consider it relevant.

"But she is concerned about the effect of her presence on her den, on her Household Staff—saving perhaps only their master—and on the citizens of her city. She will not, therefore, live among them in any prior sense of the word. And that presents difficulties for us."

"She will not harm you."

"She will not intentionally harm us, no. But she is aware that the intentions of a deity are irrelevant. We might crush a single ant without any awareness of its existence at all. She cannot, therefore, live entirely among us.

"The decision is yours, of course. She has not come to me for advice. She will not consult me in this matter. Any agreement she has made with you—if one exists at all—exists between the two of you. But she is Jewel. She will offer."

"If you understand, if you have been informed of, my history, you understand the weight of the favor you ask."

"I did not say it was a small one."

Avandar glanced at Haval.

"You are not, now, tired of life."

"I am not *now* tired of living. Not at this precise moment. I—as the Wild Hunt—feel almost young again. But I was mortal, Haval. And I have lost everyone and everything I have ever cared for, not once but times beyond number. If this opportunity slips away from me, I might never have it again. What, then, is the incentive you offer?"

"None, of course. Should you acquiesce, you will remain by her side as domicis until the end of her life—and I am not at all certain that the end of her life will be the normal span of years. Are you?"

"The Sen did not die of old age," Avandar replied.

"Surely they did not die at the hands of their enemies?"

"No. They cannot be killed in the heart of their strongholds—and this is the heart of Jewel's."

"But they died."

"Indeed. The cities, however, had time to build and maintain other defenses. Those defenses differed between the cities, but the cities themselves were not uniform. What the Sen built could not be toppled easily from without. There is nothing now from which she cannot protect herself."

"Nothing except herself." Haval did not smile as he met Avandar's glare. "She has never been able to live comfortably on her own. She will have the cats, and they are company of a kind. But there is only one mortal to whom she has an attachment for whom she has never felt fear."

"And you disapprove."

"Ah, you mistake me. I disapproved of her trust. But her lack of fear where you were concerned, no. If you could not be killed, you would not abandon her. Death could not deprive her of your presence. She will offer you what you desire; it is in her nature to do so. And today, tomorrow, next month, she will not regret it, because it *is* what you desire."

"And you are so certain that her death will be my death?"

"I am."

"You will pardon me if I do not trust your opinion."

"Of course. There is always risk, and our goals are almost diametrically opposed in this. What I want is the safety of our city in this new age. And the safety of this city now rests on the shoulders of one young woman. Were she what she was, I would have no concern. But she is not, as you are well aware. Her emotional state is now almost a physical force—as much a law of nature as storms, as earthquakes, for those of us who now live within these walls. Were I in your position, I know what I would decide—but we are different men. Were I you, I am far less certain.

"But she, at least, will never abandon you. Death will not claim her. Your enemies cannot assassinate her. You will, however, have to tolerate the cats."

"And I am to serve her until she at last surrenders to madness?"

"Yes."

"Very, very few men have had the courage—or the gall—to call so large a request a favor."

Haval nodded. "I have other matters to see to now. I believe you know where you will find The Terafin."

The interior of the Terafin manse was more faithfully recreated here than it had been on the Isle, although it existed beyond the very large doors at one end of the forbidding halls. Avandar walked until he reached stairs, mounted those stairs, and proceeded to the doors that had, in a different building, led to The Terafin's personal chambers. He was not attired as domicis; he was attired— still—as warrior, as Warlord, although he did not wield a sword.

To his surprise, these doors did have guards: the Chosen. Torvan and, he thought, Marave. They did not stop him, although their eyes flickered past his face in acknowledgment of his station: domicis to The Terafin.

To his surprise, the doors opened into a library. Not the library into which the wilderness had encroached; there were no tree-shelves here. But he heard the trickle of water that implied the fountain remained. He could not, however, see it. He recognized the table. Only one book remained upon it—the book that Jewel had taken with her on their journey to take the Oracle's test.

She had passed it.

"Yes. She passed, Viandaran."

Avandar stiffened. From between the rows of shelves behind the table came a familiar figure. "Oracle."

"Well met. You have survived not one age, but two. This is the third, Viandaran. If you desire it, I will offer you a glimpse of the future."

"I do not desire it," he replied. "I have nothing with which to pay your price."

The Oracle's face could barely be seen, recessed as it was within the frame of her hood. But her lips folded in a smile. "Think you that you are the only person burdened as you are burdened?"

He did not answer.

"Very well. The future has not concerned you for centuries, and I imagine it will not be of great interest to you now." She reached through the folds of her robe and removed the heart from her chest; it beat now with blue-gray light. "But the future is, of course, of interest to me. It is what I am."

"Firstborn—"

"Hush. Keep your voice down, or you will disturb them." She held the orb in her hands, lifting it. "I will tell you what you might have seen, had you the courage to look."

Avandar's anger was a flash, a tremor.

She smiled. "Or perhaps I will answer the only question of relevance today. When Jewel dies, you will die."

Silence.

"It is, in part, a death of your own making, although that was not your intent. You marked her; it was meant to save her life, although in my opinion the mark was irrelevant in the end. But that mark, that binding, was made in the Deepings, where hints of wild magic slumbered. And she has built on that since her ascension. Unless you remove it—and there is some possibility that you can—her death *is* your death.

"But she will grant you death now, and it will be a clean, instant death. Certainly, the cats have counseled her to do so." Her smile deepened at his expression. It then faded. "They are not, as you must understand, cats; they are held in that shape by the visceral will, the need, of the Sen. All caution has been taken—by my sister, by her Artisan—to succor Jewel on the road that lies ahead.

"But the attachment between such elemental forces can never be one way— and Jewel was born mortal. You have avoided attachments, inasmuch as possible, for centuries now. This last one is yours to avoid, if you desire it. I must leave. But, Viandaran, I owe your Lord a great boon."

She replaced the heart she held. "Mortals have often been surprising." She bowed then, holding that bow, as if she knew what his answer to Haval's request must be.

He passed through the library, noting the absence of the extra door that led to the rooms she had occupied before she had joined the House. The hall was short, and at the far end was the conference room. There would be a small dining room as well. He was surprised at the fidelity; she had not spent much of her tenure as Terafin in these ordinary rooms, but they were almost exact.

As domicis, there was no room into which he could not enter; the Chosen forbid him nothing. Nor did the cats, although they complained. So he entered her bedchamber, assuming, given the Oracle's words, that he would find her asleep. To his surprise, she was not.

Her bed was occupied, but not by Jewel; she had pulled up a chair and sat by the bedside, as if the occupant were ill and she meant to nurse them. Jewel looked up only as he approached the opposite side of that bed, and she held a finger to her lips.

Calliastra lay between the covers.

"I had to send the cats away," Jewel whispered. "Or they would have destroyed things. More things."

Avandar did not tell her it was irrelevant. What they destroyed, she could remake—and probably would, in her sleep.

She is dangerous.

Not to me.

Were you a ruler of old, that would be true. You are not. She is dangerous to your kin. She is dangerous to your kind. You forbid her to feed, and she has not—but she must. She spent far, far too much power in the fight against the Sleepers, and it is not power she can easily replenish if she does not want the attention of her father.

Jewel said nothing.

Jewel. You do not understand. Calliastra is firstborn. She is the daughter of both of her parents; it is why she is . . . as she is. She can stop herself from feeding. She has, before. But the hunger grows. If mortals cease to eat—at all—they will eventually perish. They will starve to death. That is not what happens to the firstborn. Calliastra will not starve; she will not die. But she will, in the end, break. She will feed in a frenzy—and she will not stop until that hunger is satiated enough that she can, once again, control herself.

Avandar, am I Sen?

Yes. But you cannot change what she is. She is not . . . as I am. She cannot be altered as I was altered, at the whim of a powerful deity. She is a deity in her own right. You cannot remake her. No more could you decide that Cormaris become a god of butterflies and daisies. To make the attempt is to destroy her. That is all you will achieve.

And if that's what she wants?

Is it?

How could it not be? Jewel inhaled. *It's what you want. And you are not Calliastra. If you lost your family over and over again, it's not because you killed them. I understand half of what she wants. Half of what she wants is all of what I want. It's what I need. She needs it no less than I do.*

He did not reply; it was true. That was the tragedy of Calliastra.

And I would not have survived had I eaten *my den. Any one of my den. I think I can change her.*

You cannot. He did not lie. It was impossible to lie to one seer-born. He examined this woman; she was no longer the child she had been when he had first come from the domicis hall to serve her. Her eyes were brown; flecked—as his own sometimes were—with gold, with light.

Can she kill me? she finally asked.

Here? Now? If you desired it. He paused. *And perhaps if you did not. She is conflicted, always; it is her nature. Ariane could. Namann could. But not without will, without effort, and they would not, in my opinion, be guaranteed to succeed. If the god you do not name was present within the city walls, you would die. But no. There are very, very few who could now end your life.*

I am going to keep her, she said, fierce now. She looked up at him, glaring, and he saw the shadows beneath her eyes; understood that she was physically exhausted.

Have you eaten?

She blinked; he might have asked the question in a dead language and received the same lack of comprehension.

You will require food. And sleep.

I don't want to sleep.

No. I understand. Regardless, you must. He looked at Calliastra, and a slow understanding dawned. He was, momentarily, too stunned to find words, and even had they come readily, he was not sure which he would have chosen. He settled, as was his wont, on outrage and anger. *You have let her feed on you.*

Jewel said nothing. It was an angry, obstinate nothing.

Does your lack of caution know no *bounds?*

She folded her arms, her lips thinning, her jaw tightening. *It's my life. I can't— I cannot just abandon her. I promised.*

So, too, young children with no understanding of the consequences of their given word! I understand!

And if you are wrong? If you cannot control what is taken? If you cannot give her what she needs without destroying yourself? The entirety *of the Empire depends on the Kings. Your den. Your foolish, stupid cats—*

Shadow growled.

If you die, they will die. The Empire will fall. Be more aware of the risks you take!

"She is aware," Shadow said, without the whine that distinguished most of his speech. "And *we* are aware."

"You guard her sleep," Avandar said, voice low. "You have never been attentive enough, otherwise."

"So? She will not be *eaten* in her *sleep.*" The cat materialized in the room, as if his body were an afterthought. "She is *stupid,*" he added, in a much more normal voice. "What did you *expect?*"

And he understood, as he stood shaking with something that was perilously close to rage, that it was too late. It was too late for him. He almost demanded his own death, then—the death she had not thought to offer because she did not wish to wake Calliastra—because his death would absolve him of all responsibility for hers. Because if he were dead, he would not have to watch— again—as she died. And she was certain *to* die; she was a babe in the wilderness. She was a *fool*—

Shadow was hissing laughter. It was not entirely kind laughter, but he was a cat.

Avandar understood Haval's "favor." He understood the Oracle's presence. He even, he thought, understood the debt she thought she owed. Calliastra continued to sleep. She looked young. She looked vulnerable. And the fact that she was willing to be either meant that she had, for the moment, found a home that she was willing to take the risk of trusting.

She was at peace.

It was foolish. It was more than foolish. All prior experience demonstrated that there was no such thing for Calliastra. But . . . that was also her nature.

"And yours?" Shadow asked, voice sly.

Avandar glanced at the great, gray cat with his usual frosty disdain. *And mine.*

9th day of Lattan, 428 A.A.
Terafin Manse

The back halls were in an uproar. They had never been the quietest of places; even during the busiest parts of the working day, servants rushed headlong from one room to the next, carrying buckets, mops, cleaning rags, and other necessities of their duties in what amounted to a headlong rush.

This was, of course, acceptable. What was not acceptable was that same headlong rush in any visible, public part of the manse. Today, however, the rushing was far more frenetic, far more intense. The servants who now crowded the halls were far more numerous, and conversely, far less focused than was usual.

And, of course, they were. They were to travel across the bridge—en masse—to the new Terafin manse. Were it not for the location of that new manse, the halls might have been shrouded in gloom; the manse was in the hundred holdings, but not upon the Isle, where all the rulers of The Ten had lived . . . until now.

The Master of the Household Staff had, of course, scouted that new building. She had pronounced herself satisfied with both its condition and its architecture, and word had trickled down—like pebbles becoming an avalanche—that the building that had all but destroyed the Common upon its first rise through the streets of the city was more the Terafin manse than the building in which the servants had worked for the past year.

This building was not. It retained much of the general shape of the former manse, but whole sections had been transformed dramatically, and it was difficult, in many places, to close the doors to various rooms, because those doors no longer existed. The back halls, the sprawling network by which servants could become effectively invisible when not actually performing their duties, had likewise suffered some alterations.

Carver wished that one of those alterations had been to make them *wider.*

"You are certain," Finch had said, to the august and terrifying Master of the Household Staff, "that you wish to facilitate a transfer of the staff immediately?" Carver had been surprised at her tone, because it implied that there was only one acceptable answer to the question.

If Carver had been surprised, the Master of the Household Staff had been glacial. "I am." She did not look down her nose at Finch, not precisely, but the gesture itself was evident in her expression and her tone of voice.

"Very well. The Chosen have indicated that the building is ready for occupancy." She hesitated and then added, "It is, in their estimation—and I am aware that our estimation is not, where it concerns the Household Staff, of great use to you—safe."

Finch had, of course, been correct. Their estimation was of little value to the Master of the Household Staff. Her own, however, was above reproach.

Finch's hand had fluttered briefly, and Carver, accustomed to the Master of the Household Staff, did not react in any way, although it had been a trial.

But even the dour, grim Master, whose given name Carver had never, in his years in the back halls, learned, returned to the manse with a kind of purposeful excitement that was palpable if one had any experience with her. Yes, the quarters were ready for occupancy, and yes, the Household Staff would occupy those quarters *immediately*. That, after all, was where The Terafin was now situated, and she had none of her own servants with her, save her domicis.

Carver assumed that the ruckus in the back halls was mirrored in the manse proper, but the frenetic preparations of the House Council and its various attaches took place in a much larger environment.

It had not, he thought, been even a day.

But much had happened in the course of that day, and the sun was only barely cresting the horizon.

Not all the servants could leave immediately. They were to move over the course of the next three days, but it was *expected* that they would not let the public halls go to humiliating ruin in the meantime.

But the one mercy—and it was as questionable a mercy as any offered by the Master of the Household Staff—was that the servants who tended to the West Wing were to be in the first wave of evacuees. This caused predictable squabbles in all levels of the House hierarchy, but no one, save perhaps Haerrad, was foolish enough to let their displeasure be known.

Haerrad, however, was in the care of the healerie. Carver wasn't certain how he felt about that; his dislike of Haerrad since Teller's injury had not abated. But Finch seemed to have made her peace with him, and it was Finch, not Carver, who would deal with the consequences.

The healerie was to move last. The right-kin's office was a terrible mess, but the entire den, with the unfortunate exception of Teller, could avoid it; apparently the transformation of the manse during the height of the Sleepers' attack had swallowed the paperwork. It had also swallowed some of the art. Barston's stiff upper lip had almost shattered at the blow, but he had managed—barely—to hold himself together.

Finch's assurance that there would be no further loss going forward had only barely mollified him. Carver, however, doubted that she could make that claim with authority.

He had come home. He had changed his clothing, offering what remained of the clothing in which he had left the manse to the fireplace. He had found shoes, and he had put them on while around him the den bustled, the West Wing a miniature version of the back halls, but far less crowded.

Last, he had watched the den leave. They were the first to go; only Finch remained behind.

She watched him now, her arms folded, her lips pursed. "If you wait much longer," she finally said, "you'll miss her entirely." Before Carver could answer, she held up a hand. "If you miss her entirely, she's going to wonder whether or not you've changed your mind."

"She won't."

"She might. Many things have changed today. We haven't discovered all of them. And you were presumed . . ." She shook her head. Not even she could finish the words. "She knows you've come back."

"You told her?" Before Finch could answer, Carver smacked himself on the forehead. Of course, she hadn't. But nothing remained hidden from the servants for long.

"Go. Barston is not the only person to have lost valuable House records. I am about to meet with Iain. Our treasurer."

"He's coming here?"

"He is. And you know how hard you find tears."

Carver slid into the back halls. They were narrow and poorly lit, but that made them feel like home. He had the right to live in the West Wing as an occupant, but it was in the back halls that he had made himself useful to Jay, and in the back halls that he had found Merry.

He was surprised to see Berald, close to the doors that were used for the West Wing; Berald, being a senior member of the Household Staff, had the duty of overseeing those under his purview. Apparently, Carver had become one of them.

"I have run as much interference as I can survive," the older man now said, as he unfolded his arms. "It is . . . good to have you back."

"I'm not sure the Master of the Household Staff agrees," Carver replied, an easy smile transforming his expression.

"No one has been foolish enough to ask." Berald's careworn smile was a blessing. "In your absence, however, she was forced to make do with Jester."

Carver laughed. He could not imagine Jester and the Master of the Household Staff comfortably occupying the same room for more than two minutes. He wanted to know more—and on any other day, he might have taken the time to find out. But now that he was in the back halls, he felt a sudden excitement, a sudden anxiety.

He was home. His second home.

Or perhaps—and this caused him some guilt—his first home. The den was his family. It had been his family, with all of the squabbles and conflict that implied, since the day he had first run across Jay, hiding in an alley near Taverson's. But Merry?

Merry was family as well. Not the den, and not the den's family. Carver's. No home, he thought, was complete without her in it. He wasn't certain if this had always been true. He had been drawn to her from the start, and she had been against any possible entanglement, because the den were important House people, and she was a servant.

But there was, in the service, something of the den *in* her. She was not hard, not polished, not patrician—and she had never evinced any desire to be so. She did not despise the patriciate, as Jester did; she just considered them irrelevant, except in one way. They kept the House going. They served to make the House more powerful. And Merry was ATerafin.

He made his way, flattening himself against the wall more than once to avoid collision, to the room Merry shared. And he froze, once again, outside her door. He could not understand what was wrong with him. He hadn't been this clumsy or this nervous since the first night.

As if the thought were words—and at that, shouted words—the door opened. Viv had swung it wide. She looked up at Carver, blinked, and then shook her head. "You know we're *really busy*, right?"

He nodded.

Viv snorted. "Fine. *Try* not to get us all dismissed, hmm?" And she stepped out of the room, pushed Carver into it, and shut the door firmly behind him before he could find the words he was usually so glib with.

And . . . there she was: Merry, hair pulled tightly back and off her face, her skin glowing with the sweat of her endeavor to pack up the things she would need to take with her to her new home. Her arms fell to her sides, but even so, she did not drop the brush she was carrying.

She stared at him, her mouth hanging half open. Her eyes rounded, her mouth opened; she tossed the brush onto the bare mattress so that she could raise both of her hands to her mouth.

He was almost embarrassed. That was the truth. He had thought of hundreds of words, had thought of what he could, or would, say to her. He had known he was home when Angel had practically knocked him off his feet; had felt the reality of kin when Arann had achieved, in his armor, what Angel had not quite managed. He had thought he would never see his den again.

And he had accepted that, just as Duster had, and probably less angrily, in the end.

Coming home at the side of the Summer Queen had not been part of any of his wildest—or darkest—dreams. She had found him, and she had offered him his freedom because that was Jay's one request of her. Carver would never have dared to ask anything. He would never have dared to approach her at all. She made beauty intimidating, terrifying, belittling, simply by existing.

And seeing her that first time, he had been robbed of words, of breath, of sound, for even the earth had fallen utterly silent as she stood upon its surface. She was like staring at the sun. A long-ago voice, robbed of face and identity by time and inadequate memory, told him *don't stare at the sun. You'll go blind.*

Even so, he could not close his eyes. He could not deprive himself of the sight of her. He thought that, had she offered him a place in her court, he would have accepted. In any position. Just to continue to be in her presence.

She had not offered.

And he had come home. To his den, waiting in the streets of the city as if they'd expected him, their shock, their joy, their surprise and even their tears proof that they hadn't. They were not beautiful in the way the Summer Queen was. But they were warm, they were *real*, in a way she was not. All his history, from the thirty-fifth holding, to the twenty-fifth, to the most powerful of the Ten Houses, was reflected in their eyes, their expressions, and their joy.

It was their joy that he had reached for; it was their joy he had made his own; he had swallowed the echoes of it until he, too, resonated with the joy of homecoming.

He would not forget the Summer Queen; she was a force of nature that did not—at the moment—threaten his life. Like the ocean and its storms. Like the most brilliant of sunsets. Like the stars and the moons on a particularly clear night.

She was not kin. She was not *den*.

And, more significant, she was not Merry. He swallowed, his throat thick as he met Merry's eyes. "I'm sorry." It was a whisper of sound, but it was what he could manage. She stood frozen in the room's center, her hands still covering her mouth.

Carver lifted his arms, held them open, offered her a half-smile.

She almost knocked him over as she leaped into those arms. Chin resting on her head, her hair, he said again, "I'm sorry."

She said nothing, not even his name; he was almost certain she was crying—and the Master of the Household Staff did not hold with tears; they were a sign of weakness, and she expected better from the ATerafin under her command.

But he knew, as he held her, that he was fully, finally, home.

The magi came out on the evening that the Summer Queen had ended the threat of the Sleepers. Every year, when the sun had finally set—and this was the longest day of the year—they made their way to the Common, and this year was no exception. Sigurne had, of course, already received the permits required by the Kings; apparently, the paperwork of the magi, in all its many forms, still existed. Although the hundred holdings had been substantially transformed, the Isle had seen far fewer changes; Sigurne's writs of exemption, unlike the merchant contracts in the Merchant Authority—or the Port Authority for that matter—remained where she had placed them.

It was not her custom to join the magi in their display of celebratory illusions, but she made an exception this year. She thought, if age was kind, she would make an exception for every year that remained her.

The Common was less crowded, and that gave her brief pause. But it was not empty. Parents, grandparents, brought children of varying ages, as they had done every year on this night. There was an intensity to their gratitude, and an intensity to their grief, that would lessen with time. But this night was the first night of a new city; it was history in the making.

The bards came, as they often did; the merchants, however, did not. The Ten were present, but their own supplies had been compromised; they therefore came as citizens of Averalaan, not as rulers. And on this eve, the Kings and their Queens also joined the crowds.

Jewel was present. She was surrounded by her den and her Chosen, and she had come to the Common to watch the magi's show of lights. This had been one of her favorite times of year; she could almost hear her Oma admonishing her to avoid strangers because strangers were dangerous.

The three cats had taken to the night sky under firm instructions to leave the magi—and their illusions—alone, and Calliastra watched them fly almost wistfully.

"You can join them," Jewel said quietly.

Calliastra shook her head and looked at her feet. She was young, tonight; Jewel had come to understand that her appearance, her physical form, was not a simple thing. It reflected her mood and her desire.

"You need to be here," the godchild said. "Nothing you do can hurt me, but hurting these people will hurt you. I can remind you that *this* is where you are."

Jewel swallowed and nodded. Her eyes were tired, now; things were blurry, ill-defined. The trees, she could see clearly. And Calliastra. The people were less distinct, their outlines slightly blurred. That blur would increase with the passage of time.

This was her city, and if she wanted it to remain that way, she could not remain long in its streets. But she wanted to see the lights. She wanted to be part of this festival; it was a continuous link to her childhood, and she had watched it every year, sometimes at a remove. She could exist more easily in the forests that had been brief harbor to those citizens of Averalaan who had survived but did not wish to spend the time in the company of the Summer Queen.

No, that was a lie; she did. But not if it meant missing this display.

The magi that worked above the trees were fewer in number than they had been. But they, too, understood the import of the festival.

Still, she turned from the skies when she felt the presence of her den. Two of her den, Carver and Angel. Carver was now wearing shoes and appropriate clothing, and the two were conversing. Carver grinned. Whatever his experience of the wilderness had been, it hadn't broken him. She was grateful for that—but broken or no, she wanted him here.

Jewel walked toward them.

Angel slid a hand into the satchel slung over his shoulder; he withdrew a single leaf.

Jewel stared at it for one long beat.

"He gathered them," Carver said, when Angel failed to speak. "Every tree on which your path home was built dropped a single leaf. He picked them all up."

"There are thirty-six," Jewel said. "Thirty-six leaves."

Angel nodded.

Carver didn't seem surprised at the number. "You know what they are."

She hesitated, and Angel signed.

"I know who they were."

"Can you—can you somehow release them?" Carver's hesitation was marked because he didn't usually bother to hesitate. "I spoke with two of them."

"When?" But even asking the question, she *knew* the answer. She wondered if it would always be this way. She lifted a hand, brushing her own question aside. "I can't."

"Can't release them?"

And this answer, too, came instantly, although the knowledge was new. And bitter. Over the heads of her two den-kin, she could see the buildings that would form the new horizon of Averalaan. She could see the people in the streets of the city itself. She understood that they were here because of thirty-six people who had become the heart of Averalaan the moment she had planted the single blue leaf that remained in her hands when she walked out of the dreaming.

"I can't release them," she said. "I can't change what they've become."

"But if you made them—" Angel stepped, hard, on his foot. Carver swallowed the words.

"Who did you talk to?" she asked.

"Stacy. I don't know her family name."

"A'Scavonne," Jewel replied, without thought, without effort.

Carver caught her by the arms. "She wanted to save her mother. Is her mother still alive?" As if he expected Jewel to know the answer.

And she did. "Yes."

"Then she did what she wanted."

Angel carefully handed the satchel to Jewel. She knew what it now contained. Knew, as well, that he wanted her to plant these individual leaves.

She did. But she did not release them to the wind, as she so often did. Instead, she walked away from the heart of this new Common, until she reached the boundary of it. No, that wasn't exact. She reached what would *become* the boundary in the years to follow. She was, even now, marking that boundary.

She knelt, taking the first leaf from her satchel; she set it down against the stone of street and the stone absorbed it, drawing it into the earth itself. What emerged was a tree of blue: blue bark, blue branches, blue buds. She spoke a name.

"Lillian Vess."

A woman stepped out of the trunk of the tree. Older than Jewel, but not by much, her hair was the same frazzled mess that Jewel's often was by the end of the day. She bowed to The Terafin; Jewel's bow was lower, held longer. If it surprised Lillian, none of the surprise showed on her face; she waited until The Terafin rose.

"May I go?" she asked.

Jewel nodded. "You will not be able to leave this city."

"Why would I want to leave it? My life is here." Lillian's frown was more felt than seen. She straightened her skirts, glanced once at the brief flare of light high above, and walked with purpose away from the Common.

Calliastra said nothing. She shadowed Jewel almost as closely as Angel did when there was danger. Thirty-four times, including the first, Jewel set a leaf down, and the leaf became a tree. But the trees did not reflect the people who then stepped out from them; they were all of a height and of an apparent age. In the night, they seemed to reflect light.

They didn't.

Carver and Angel followed as the magi slowly retreated, leaving the moons and stars for illumination. Magelights, which had existed in the streets before the city had been rebuilt—in an instant—would have to be added to the land-scape. The Terafin's office was already besieged by the bewildered and the angry among the various bookkeepers of the capital of the Empire, but Jewel had no idea how to return what they'd lost.

No, that wasn't true. She had some idea, but she was afraid to make changes to what now existed, because other changes—unintended—might follow. Per-haps later. Later, when she better understood her own limits and the damage she might do.

"You understand, already, the damage you might do," the thirty-fifth man said. He stepped out of the trunk of his tree—she would forever think of these trees as people, a mortal variant, made strange and wild by the scion of gods and the ancient wilderness—said. He was taller than Jewel; taller, but less immediately obviously, than Carver or Angel.

Something about his expression reminded Jewel of her Oma. For a moment, the memory of that terrifying, paradoxically comforting woman stood beside the man, her lips folded in a familiar frown. Ah, it was the arms. The arms were crossed in the exact same way.

"You've made your choice," her Oma said, her voice as clear as any living person's. "You've made it, and you'll live with it. I won't hear whining, do you understand?"

Yes, Oma.

The man was standing, silent, as if waiting orders.

"Colm Sanders," she said.

He nodded. He didn't seem surprised that she knew his name. Then again, he wouldn't; her Oma wouldn't have been, either.

His eyes narrowed. "You shouldn't be here," he finally said.

"I have to plant the last of the leaves," she replied.

He nodded. "But before you do, I have questions."

"I don't have a lot of time left to answer them."

"Then answer quickly." His voice was a snap of sound, a sergeant's voice. An Oma's voice, for all that he was a man, a soldier, and a Northerner.

Jewel nodded. She could swear she could hear Calliastra grinding her teeth, and she lifted a hand in brief den-sign before she remembered that Calliastra couldn't yet read this truncated language.

"We're clearly alive in some fashion. I don't feel any different. I don't, judging by your reaction, look different, either. What will happen to us?"

"You can't be a soldier in the Kings' army anymore, unless war comes to us—as it did yesterday. You can't, as you suspect, leave the city; you are part of it, now."

"Can we die?"

Jewel swallowed. "No. Not yet."

"Will we die when you die?"

She lowered her head, because it was hard to meet his steady gaze. And then she forced herself to do it anyway, to lift chin, to raise face. "No. You are part of this city. Only when the city fails will you fail. Your lives will be lived within the boundaries of Averalaan—although those boundaries include the wilderness that hears my name. You are necessary, and will be necessary, when I am gone, if the city is to survive.

"A god walks the mortal world. While I live, the city will stand; when I die, it will stand *only* if you stand. You. The thirty-six. I won't insult you. And I won't apologize. Everyone that now lives in the boundaries of Averalaan owes their lives to you. Everyone.

"On the morrow, in the heart of the Common, in the center of the three trees that will define it, your story will be writ in stone, and for those who cannot read, it will be spoken by that stone. This city will know and understand what you have sacrificed—and what you will sacrifice in future.

"You will not starve. You will never grow hungry. You will not age. Until the city itself is gone or the wilderness is destroyed, you will be here. I don't imagine," she added, voice soft but steady, "that you care all that much about monuments and the honor of strangers—but you are only one of thirty-five." She lifted the last leaf. "Others will care."

She knelt once again, a final time, and she placed the last of the leaves upon the stone of these new streets. Colm Sanders, unlike the others, did not leave. He waited.

She knew why.

And so she planted the final leaf, holding it for just a moment longer than she had any of the others. She waited, rising, while Carver held breath and Angel said nothing. Even Calliastra was uncharacteristically silent.

The cats, above, were not.

Shadow came to land on Carver's foot. Snow and Night circled above them, above the tree, insulting each other and their brother. Hissing laughter. Hissing annoyance. Threatening the last of the magi, for the magi, while done with magics, were not done with the usual cleanup required after their audience had gone home for the year.

Shadow glanced at Colm Sanders; Colm Sanders looked down at the cat.

Jewel, however, focused on the tree, waiting for it to disgorge the last of the thirty-six dreamers.

Stacy A'Scavonne exited the tree in an excited rush. She bypassed the dour Sanders and headed straight for Carver, who bent and opened his arms, sweeping her off her feet in a way he wouldn't have dared had her parents—and her guards, for of course she would have them if she visited the Common—been present.

Only when he set her down did Stacy's jumble of excited greetings fade. "She's still sad," she told him.

"Not all sadness is bad," he replied.

"But you're here, and you're not dead."

"Yes. She isn't sad about me now."

"About me?"

"A little, yeah." He set her on her feet. "Stacy, this is Jay."

"I think you're supposed to call her The Terafin."

"Well, your mother's not here."

She nodded and turned to Jewel. "I'm not sad," she said. "I'm going to live *forever*. My mother's alive. And my father. And our servants."

Jewel nodded.

"And I can go home and tell her that I'm *never* going to die!"

Colm Sanders said nothing, and he said it so forbiddingly that Jewel could only nod. "Yes." She turned to Shadow.

"He's living with us, right now," Stacy then said, pointing at Colm Sanders.

"He is."

"We have to go home." She was looking at Colm Sanders but failing to meet his gaze. Jewel realized, then, that she was afraid. Not terrified, but afraid. As if she understood that not all of her mother's reaction would be happy. "You're coming, right?" she asked him.

"I'm coming. I probably won't stay in your mother's house."

"Why not?"

"Because you won't need guards now, and it will only remind your mother that you slept and couldn't be woken."

"But you'll come back with me now?"

"I will come back with you now. We should leave," he added. "It's late, and she'll be worried sick because both of us are gone."

"Shadow."

The gray cat hissed, but it was a soft hiss, and he didn't accompany it with the usual torrent of disgust. He stepped forward toward Stacy, whose eyes lit up.

Jewel didn't even need to tell them that Shadow would fly them home. Colm Sanders understood, and so did Stacy. She was going to go home on the *flying cat*.

"Can I visit you?" Stacy asked, as Colm Sanders lifted her and placed her firmly on the back of the great winged cat. "I mean, when you're not busy?"

"Yes. You can visit me any time you like. You won't need to make an appointment, and you won't—it will be safe for you to visit me."

"But it won't be safe for everyone."

"No. If you wish your parents to meet me, they will have to make an appointment."

"Because they're normal?"

"Because they're normal."

Colm Sanders seated himself behind Stacy, looking grim, where she looked excited. Shadow pushed up, off the ground, but Jewel could hear Stacy's last words clearly.

"Can we circle around the top of the new trees before we have to go home?"

"Why did you pick up the leaves?" Jay asked, as she began the climb up the steps of the new Terafin manse. The front of the building had been altered in the passage of hours; it looked far more like the manse on the Isle than it had when she'd claimed it as her residence.

Angel was silent for three steps. "I thought it had to be done," he finally said. "I thought you would do it, if you had the time."

"You knew?"

"You said their names. I heard you speak their names. I recognized one or two of them, because we were in the city when the sleeping sickness started, and Adam was shuffling between the Houses of Healing and home. I thought—" He shook his head.

"If you could do everything yourself, you would. But you can't. None of us can. What you wanted, we wanted. Even Duster." He did not glance at Calliastra as he spoke Duster's name. "I don't know. I just knew I had to pick them up.

"I have your back."

"You always have." Her smile was shadowed, her eyes wide. She'd been out in the streets too long. "But this—this was more important than demons, to me."

He signed, *I know.*

She signed back. *Thank you. Angel.*